"You can get off me now," she ordered, mimicking Autumn's haughtiest tone.

He didn't move. Instead, he locked his gaze on hers and, with slow deliberation, laid his left wrist flat against her right.

Summer sucked in a breath and went rigid beneath him as a fresh surge of energy shot through her. Only this time, instead of an electric thunderclap that stunned the senses, this surge fired up every sensual cell in her body. If Dilys hadn't been straddling her, she would have wrapped her legs around his waist and dragged him down atop her. As it was, she burned for him in the worst way. The way his nostrils flared and his tattoos went bright with a fresh burst of phosphorescent blue light only fanned the flames of her desire. She wanted to command him to touch her . . . to kiss her. Her gift of Persuasion flared, bringing the words and the magic to the tip of her tongue.

By C.L. Wilson

C. L. WILSON

THE SEA KING

AVONBOOKS

An Imprint of HarperCollinsPublishers

THE SEA KING. Copyright © 2017 by C.L. Wilson. All rights reserved. Printed in the United States of America. No part of this book may be used or reproduced in any manner whatsoever without written permission except in the case of brief quotations embodied in critical articles and reviews. For information, address HarperCollins Publishers, 195 Broadway, New York, NY 10007.

First Avon Books mass market printing: November 2017

Print Edition ISBN: 978-0-06-201898-4
Digital Edition ISBN: 978-0-06-219811-2

Cover illustration by Judy York

Avon, Avon & logo, and Avon Books & logo are registered trademarks of HarperCollins Publishers in the United States of America and other countries.
HarperCollins is a registered trademark of HarperCollins Publishers in the United States of America and other countries.

FIRST EDITION

HB 04.15.2024

To Michelle Grajkowski.
For everything, all these years.

Acknowledgments

As always, a huge thanks to all my friends, family, and fans who have been and continue to be so supportive and encouraging. I especially want to thank the Starfish Club: Christine Feehan, Kathie Firzlaff, Sheila English, Susan Edwards, Karen Rose, and Brian Feehan. Our brain-storming retreats are the highlights of my year. Thanks to my mom, Lynda Richter; my sister, Carole Richter; and my daughters, Ileah and Rhiannon Wilson, for beta reading my work, and a very special thanks to my niece Kayla Dickens for being my social media guru.

Special thanks to my editor, Tessa Woodward, and the folks at Avon Books for all you do.

Finally, thanks again to Judy York, artist extraordinaire. I love all my covers, but this one is especially lovely! You're the greatest!

For My Readers

Thank you so much for picking up this book! Your support means the world to me. I hope you enjoy Gabriella and Dilys's story.

Be sure to visit my website, www.clwilson.com, to sign up for my private book announcement list, enter my online contests, and scour the site for hidden treasures and magical surprises.

I'd love to hear from you. You can find me on Facebook at www.facebook.com/authorclwilson, tweet me at @clwilsonbooks, or e-mail me at cheryl@clwilson.com.

CHAPTER 1

Sunset Beach, Isle of Calberna

"Higher, Dilys! Higher!" Pangi Mahilo's high-pitched squeal pealed out across the pink sand beach.

"Higher, eh?" Laughing at the squirming boy in his arms, Dilys Merimydion, Prince of the Calbernan Isles, cast a quick glance at Pangi's mother, who rolled her eyes at the son Dilys had been tossing in the air but still nodded her permission. "All right then," Dilys told Pangi, "higher it is. And you'd best hold on to your belly!" With a grin, Dilys tossed the gangly little boy several feet into the air over his head. Since Dilys stood seven feet tall, that meant the child flew a good ten or more feet above the ground.

Pangi's piercing shrieks of laughter startled a flock of seabirds hovering near the Calbernan Islanders who had gathered on the pink sand of Sunset Beach to celebrate the marriage of one of the sailors in Dilys's fleet.

"Me next! Me next!" came the chorus of childish pleading as Dilys set Pangi down.

"You've started something," murmured Dilys's cousin, Arilon Calmyria, with a grin for the horde of clamoring children.

"I always do." Dilys loved children, loved interacting with them and making them laugh. Maybe it was because he'd never had brothers and sisters of his own. Or maybe it was because he longed for a wife and children of his own with a ferocity of emotion that even among passionate, larger-than-life Calbernans was rare. "I have a particular talent for entertaining the little ones," he added.

"True. That's why you're the party favorite."

"*Ono*—no—" he corrected with a grin, "I'm the party favorite due to my good looks and charm. Isn't that right, Beno?" Dilys directed the question to one of the four-year-olds clinging to his leg like a barnacle.

"Right!" Beno cried.

Dilys rewarded the boy by plucking him out of the crowd and tossing him high into the air.

Nearby, another of Dilys's cousins, Ryllian Ocea, laughed and said, "The veracity of answers provided in exchange for personal gain is questionable at best." Ryll was studying law in preparation for his pending retirement from the sea and the mercenary work all adult male Calbernans performed until marriage.

That change of career would be happening within the year . . . for all of them. Ryll would take his place in his mother's law practice. Ari would be working with his parents at House Calmyria's shipbuilding business. And Dilys would begin his training to take over the daily operations of House Merimydion's vast shipping and agricultural empire.

Because tomorrow, Dilys, Ari, Ryll, and every marriage-worthy son of the sea who'd sailed with them last winter to the Æsir Isles—the northern archipelago that included the kingdoms of Wintercraig, Summerlea, and Seahaven—would be returning to those shores to court and claim wives from among the unwed and widowed women of Wintercraig and Summerlea. And once they were wed, their mercenary days were done.

As if reading Dilys's thoughts, Ari draped an arm across Ryll's broad shoulders and pointed his chin towards the bride and bridegroom, both clad in shimmering sea blue, with circlets of fuchsia and yellow flowers on their heads, their necks draped in plump stoles made from dark green *tili* leaves dotted with tiny, delicate white *merimydia* blossoms. "Just think, cousins, before the year is out, that will be us standing on the beach beside our *lianas,* grinning like we just won the All Isles Cup." The All Isles Cup was Calberna's most coveted prize in competitive sailing.

"Speaking as a former All Isles champion," Dilys said, "I can promise you I'll be grinning much, much more on my wedding day."

"I know that's true," Ryll agreed. It was no secret among Dilys's close friends just how impatient he was to close the youthful, unwed chapter of his life and move on to the next.

Four years ago, Dilys had earned his *ulumi-lia*—the tattoo curling across his right cheekbone that proclaimed him a man worthy of taking a wife. Most Calbernans wed within a year, two at most, once they earned that mark, but not Dilys. And not by his choice, either. He'd been sailing the sea, fighting other people's wars, for more than fifteen years now. He was more than ready for the comfort and joy of a wife and family.

Unfortunately, because his mother was both the *Myerial*—the ruling queen—of Calberna and the Matriarch of House Merimydion, one of Calberna's oldest and most venerated royal Houses, and because Dilys was his mother's only child, his marriage had become a matter of state.

He carried great power in his pure Calbernan blood—power that should have been merged with the pure blood of another great Calbernan House, not diluted by marriage to an *oulani*—an outlander—but the death of his childhood betrothed, Nyamialine Calmyria, had ended those hopes. And because any son of Calberna who wed an outlander remained a part of his mother's House rather than joining his wife's, marriage between Dilys and an *oulani* woman opened the door for a half-blood daughter to become the next *Myerial* of Calberna and the next Matriarch of House Merimydion.

A committee of the Queen's Council, led by Dilys's uncle, Calivan Merimydion, had therefore spent years investigating the bloodlines and magical gifts of Mystral's most powerful families to select a suitable bride for their prince. The committee, which Dilys's cousin Ari had jokingly labeled "the Bridehunters", had concluded that Dilys should wed one of the daughters of the Summer King, but before the marriage could be arranged, Prince Falcon of Summerlea ran off with the Winter King's betrothed, murdered that same king's heir while making his escape, and threw Wintercraig and Summerlea into three long years of war.

It was only now—after two negotiated treaties and four years of war, rebellion, and a ferocious battle to prevent the return of a dread god who would have cast the world into endless winter—that Dilys was finally setting off to claim his outlander bride. Not all Calbernans were happy this day had come. A group calling themselves the Pureblood Alliance had been quite vocal in their opposition to Dilys taking an *oulani* bride, and they'd gained the support of quite a few powerful Houses.

"Is Spring still the Season of choice?" Ryll asked.

Dilys tossed another boy high in the air, caught him, set him down, and shrugged in answer to Ryll's question before picking up the next boy and sending him flying up into the air. "If my uncle has his way."

Spring Coruscate, eldest of the late Summer King's daughters, was the wife Uncle Calivan and the Bridehunters had decided upon for Dilys. She was wise, capable, and from all reports, possessed the strongest magic of the three princesses known as the Seasons of Summerlea. Even though Summerlea's weathergifts never passed down to children outside the kingdom's direct royal line, Spring had other gifts—including a substantial talent for growing things, a gift that would benefit House Merimydion's agricultural enterprises nicely. She would make an acceptable mother for Calberna's next queen, they had decided. Assuming, of course, that the gods blessed the union with a treasured daughter for House Merimydion while Alysaldria lived. After the marriage, Dilys was also expected to combine the strength of Spring's weathergift with the power of his own seagifts to reassert Calbernan power in the Olemas Ocean, where a band of pirates had been causing trouble and disrupting trade for the last year.

Ari cast him a sly grin. "Any chance you might win Autumn instead? Just, you know, by accident?"

Dilys laughed. Autumn Coruscate, the youngest of the three Seasons, was widely recognized as one of the most beautiful women in the world—if not *the* most beautiful. Her weathergift was no insignificant talent either. "Anything is possible, cousin."

In fact, of the three Seasons, the only one who had been ruled out by the Bridehunters was the middle daughter, Summer. So far as the Bridehunters could discover, she possessed no magic beyond a weak weathergift that she used primarily to keep cooling breezes flowing during the hottest summer months.

Not that Dilys intended to let the Bridehunters make the final decision about which princess he should wed, but in the case of Summer Coruscate, he had to agree with their assessment. From all reports, she was unsuitable. Her temperament too gentle for the mother of Calberna's future queen. Though many Calbernans found great peace and joy wedded to sweet-natured *oulani* women, Dilys needed a wife who would command the respect of his people, not simply claim his devotion. His daughter—their daughter—would need a mother sharp and strong enough to be an asset at navigating the political undercurrents of Calbernan court.

One of the fathers walked over to retrieve his sons from the crowd around Dilys. "Food's ready, my sons. Come eat."

The boys pouted. "But, *Dede,* we haven't had our turn yet."

A hint of sternness stole some of the indulgence from Dilys's expression. One of the lessons Calbernan sons learned early was obedience to authority. As they grew older, their lives might depend on responding with alacrity to another's command. "Do as your *dede* says, boys. I'll fly you later, after you eat."

"*Tey,* Dilys," the boys agreed glumly. They trudged off after their father with slouched shoulders, but Dilys was pleased to see that they both perked up and pasted happy smiles on their faces before joining their mother, a soft-spoken *oulani* woman with creamy skin and pale green eyes. They snuggled next to her, telling her something that made her laugh and kiss them both. Good. Until he was wed, a Calbernan son's first duty was to honor his mother and to bring her joy in all things.

"Dilys." Ari nudged him with an elbow.

"What?" Dilys followed Ari's gaze towards a familiar Calbernan approaching from the city. One of the *Myerial*'s personal assistants, was walking briskly towards the beach.

"Sorry, little fry. Looks like I'm done for the day." Dilys freed himself of the crowd of children and quickly closed the distance between himself and his mother's assistant.

"*Moa Myerielua.*" My prince. The queen's assistant thumped his right fist over his heart in a Calbernan salute. "Please, forgive the interruption. The *Myerial* requests your presence."

"What's wrong?" Dilys's mother wasn't the sort to recall Dilys from a wedding without a very good reason.

"Forgive me, *moa Myerielua,* but I cannot say. I was

commanded only to locate you and escort you to the palace."

"Of course. Just give me a few minutes to take my leave of the bride and groom."

"What's up, cuz?" Ari asked as Dilys tracked down the newlyweds to congratulate them on their union and apologize for his need to leave.

"Where are we headed?" Ryll added.

The instant, unquestioning way they followed him made emotion squeeze hard. They always had his back. The three of them had become more like brothers than cousins since that horrible day when Dilys's childhood betrothed, Nyamialine, had died in the same terrible accident that had claimed the lives of Calberna's queen, *Myerial* Siavaluana II and her sole heir and daughter, the princess Sianna. That one terrible day had forged Ari, Ryll and Dilys's brotherhood in bonds of shared grief. Nyamialine lost to her brother Ari and her betrothed Dilys. Sianna lost to Ryll's elder brother Ruluin, and Ruluin lost to Ryll when Ru committed *kepu* with so many others because of that terrible day.

"It's all right, you two," he told them. "The *Myerial* sent for me, that's all. Stay here. Enjoy the day, and dance the *calipua* for the bride."

"Are you sure, Dilys?" Ari asked.

He wasn't. Something was definitely up, but he smiled with reassuring confidence. "I'm sure."

Cali Va'Lua, Royal Palace of Calberna

Half an hour later, Dilys strode into Calberna's soaring throne room. Sunlight filtered through the clear blue waters that surrounded the submerged glass chamber, illuminating the schools of fish, dolphins and other sea creatures that swam in the depths of Cali Va'Lua's central lagoon. At the far end of the room, on a golden throne that rose from a bed of scarlet coral, sat Calberna's revered and beloved *Myerial,* Alysaldria I, Treasure of Treasures, Queen of the Calbernan Isles.

Dilys's mother.

As always, she looked beautiful and regal, draped in cool, seafoam-green silk. The long swaths of her obsidian hair were piled high and decorated with brilliant pink, fuchsia, and scarlet anemones, while a single wrist-thick cascade of hair, gathered every foot with gleaming pearl bands, spilled over her left shoulder. She also looked tired. Dilys tucked his concern carefully out of sight before approaching the throne. He stopped at the base of the coral steps and dropped to one knee, bowing his head in greeting and submission.

"*Moa Myerial.*" My queen. Had they been alone he would have called her *Nima,* Mother, but this was no informal meeting, not with the Lord Chancellor of Calberna, the matriarchs of five royal Houses, the High Priest of Numahao, and half a dozen high-ranking officials all gathered in the room as well. "You sent for me?"

His mother did not smile in greeting as she usually did. Whatever this was, it was bad. But of course, he'd already surmised as much, both from the manner of the summons and the throne room's high-ranking assemblage.

"The Shark attacked the convoy we were escorting to Ere," a brusque masculine voice replied at his back. Dilys turned to face his mother's twin brother, Calivan Merimydion, Lord Chancellor of Calberna. "Your cousin Fyerin's ship, the *Spindrift,* was sunk. There were no survivors."

"*What?*" For one long, frozen moment, Dilys couldn't believe he'd heard right.

For the last year, pirates led by a mysterious figure known only as the Shark had been harrying ships sailing through the Olemas Ocean northwest of Calberna. The attacks had become so frequent and increasingly brazen that Calberna had begun offering armed military escort to ships sailing anywhere in or near the Olemas. But while the pirates could—and had—attacked even ships sailing under the Calbernan flag of protection, the idea that they would confront a Calbernan-crewed ship of any sort was beyond comprehension. Calbernans ruled the seas! There were no better shipbuilders. No better naval tacticians. And thanks to Calbernan seagifts, the oceans themselves obeyed Calbernan command. To confront a Calbernan on the sea was suicide. Or so it had been for millennia.

One time—and one time only—a massive armada comprised of the naval fleets of a dozen nations had assembled against the might of Calberna. Had attacked them not just on the seas but in their own waters. Outnumbered more than one hundred to one, not even the greatest magic Calberna had ever possessed had been enough to rout the invaders. At least not before Calberna had been dealt a blow from which they were still struggling to recover, twenty-five hundred years later. The Slaughter of the Sirens, that invasion was called. Or to native Islanders, simply, the Slaughter. A bloody, vengeful act that had nearly caused the extinction of the Calbernan race.

But this? A single pirate had not only attacked but sunk a heavily armed Calbernan military vessel? Such a thing had never happened. Ever.

"There must be some mistake. That's simply not possible."

"Word of the attack came from Prince Nemuan, who found and searched the wreckage himself. The convoy was looted and sunk as well." Calivan's expression was grim. Nemuan was the son of the former *Myerial*. Though he and Dilys were far from the best of friends, as a prince of Calberna, his word was beyond dispute. "There were no survivors."

Dilys cast a concerned glance at his mother. Now he understood the weary sense of frailty about her. She had loved Fyerin as deeply as Dilys. Everyone had loved him. Fyerin was the sort of Calbernan who drew people's affection as surely as a blossom drew honeybees. Ari was much the same way. Full of laughter and courage, brimming with loyalty, daring, joy, a truly vibrant spirit.

"And Nemuan's sure it was the Shark?"

"He's sure. He found Fyerin's body in the hold of the ship."

Dilys sucked in a breath and quickly veiled his gaze to hide the telltale flare of golden fire as emotion-fed power bled into his eyes. The Shark was careful not to leave behind witnesses to his crimes—that was one of the reasons he hadn't yet been hunted down and stopped—but he clearly wanted credit for his kills as well. The captain of every ship he sank was found locked in the hold of his sunken ship, gutted like a fish, tongue and eyes missing, forehead branded with the symbol of a shark. The horrifying consensus of those who had examined the Shark's victims was that they'd been alive for the process. The thought of Fyerin dying such a death made Dilys's battle fangs descend and his claws spring out from the backs of his nail beds, the sharp points biting into the palms of his hands as he curled his fingers into fists.

He shoved the pain down and chained it with cords of adamantine steel. Loss hurt, but as the commander of Calberna's First Fleet, his task now was not to mourn, but to prevent further losses.

"Sir." Dilys turned to the admiral of the Calbernan Navy. "Until we bring these murderous *krillos* to justice, I suggest we reroute all nonessential Denbe Ocean trade around Cape Stag or through the Straits of Kardouhm." That would cost Calberna a pretty penny. Circling around the Ardullan continent by way of Cape Stag would add weeks or even months to most voyages, and while the Straits of Kardouhm provided a shorter route from Calberna to the Denbe Ocean and all the rich markets of the east, the Omar of Kardouhm charged a high tax on every vessel sailing through his waters.

The admiral nodded. "The Council approved that measure not ten minutes ago, Commander. I've also sent word that every merchant ship sailing within a hundred miles of the Olemas Ocean should have a military escort. Two battle galleys to every merchant. Half a dozen to guard every convoy."

"I will, of course, cancel the upcoming voyage to Wintercraig," Dilys said.

"*Ono.*" No. The sharp denial came from Calberna's queen. "You will do no such thing."

"Alys . . ." Calivan's use of his sister's pet name told Dilys that this was an argument they'd been having for a while. He never called the *Myerial* "Alys" in front of members of the court unless she was out-stubborning him.

"*Ono*, Calivan. And I mean it. There are more than enough young men in our navy to deal with these pirates. Dilys and every Calbernan who has earned the right to seek a wife from among the women of the Æsir Isles will sail to Wintercraig next week, as planned."

"He should at least know he has the opportunity to wed an *imlani* and keep the bloodline pure." This came from Dessandra Merimynos, distant cousin of the late queen and current Matriarch of House Merimynos.

Alysaldria pressed her lips tight, and her golden eyes flashed with irritation.

Dilys glanced around at the high-ranking officials assembled in the room and realized that the pirate attack and Fyerin's death weren't the real reason he'd been summoned here. "What *imlani*? What are you talking about?"

Calberna's acting Minister of Internal Affairs stepped forward. "Loto Sami was aboard the *Spindrift*. As you may know, he was betrothed to Nyree Calagi's daughter, Coralee."

"They want you to marry Coralee Calagi," Alysaldria interjected.

"It's in the best interest of Calberna to keep the royal bloodline pure," the minister said.

"It's not in my son's best interest," she snapped. "It's

not in House Merimydion's best interest. Coralee is fifteen years old! Even if the betrothal contract could be dissolved, my son would have to wait at least another five years to wed her—who knows how long it would be before she could bear a child—let alone a daughter—if her grief for Loto makes her unable to claim her mate as she should?"

"Alys . . ." Calivan murmured.

She glared at him, her great golden eyes flashing with irritation. "Don't take their side, Cal. You know my feelings on this matter. Dilys has waited long enough—at your insistence, no less! And theirs!" She jabbed an accusatory finger in the direction of the other matriarchs.

"I don't understand," Dilys interjected, hoping to calm his mother's temper. "The betrothal contract between House Sami and House Calagi was signed in blood and salt. It is inviolable. I couldn't marry Coralee even if I wanted to."

The Slaughter had robbed Calberna of the magic of the Sirens, a loss that had not only weakened Calberna's might but also resulted in a dangerous drop in birthrate of *imlani* females, especially truly gifted ones. That was the reason families like House Merimydion and all the other royal Houses had standing betrothal contracts negotiated decades, even centuries, before the birth of a pureblood *imlani* daughter. The had been meticulously cultivating the royal bloodlines to pool the greatest magics of Calberna into their female offspring in an attempt to bring back the long-lost power of the Sirens.

"So we have all believed," the minister replied. "But the high priest has been researching the subject for months." The minister gestured to the High Priest of Numahao, standing beside him. "It was, in fact, your justification for breaking the contract with the Summer King last winter that gave him the idea."

The high priest nodded. "When you broke the contract with the Summer King to save Calberna and Mystral from the threat of the Ice King," the priest said, "that got me wondering if a betrothal contract had ever been dissolved for similar reasons. I had to go back nearly to the time of the Slaughter, but there is precedence for dissolving a betrothal contract if, by doing so, such a dissolution will prevent harm to the line of *Myerials*. House Sami has already agreed to step aside in the best interests of Calberna." He bowed in the direction of the Matriarch of House Sami.

Alysaldria gripped the arms of her throne and said, "I will confer with my son and the Lord Chancellor in private."

The assembled personages bowed and exited the throne room.

"You know this is a good offer, Alys," Calivan said when the doors closed behind them. "An *imlani* bride from a royal bloodline? It's the finest marriage Dilys could hope for."

"It would have been, had the betrothal taken place while Dilys and Coralee were still children. They would have had time to form the emotional ties necessary for a proper claiming. But Coralee has had fifteen years to bond to Loto. You saw them together, same as I did. Their ties were strong and deep. Her grief will be, too."

"And we will all be here to help her overcome that grief. You sell Dilys short, Alys. If he stays here in Calberna for the next five years, and spends that time with Coralee, I have no doubt he can win her heart as fully and completely as Loto Sami ever did. He is your son, after all. His gifts are many and great."

"Dilys could charm gold from a dragon. That's beside the point."

"No, that *is* the point. If anyone can heal Coralee's heart and form a bond with her strong enough to sire the daughters we all need, it's Dilys. And do not forget, Coralee will be *Donima* of House Calagi one day. Even if she bears only sons, they will be sons of a pure and powerful royal bloodline, guaranteed *imlani* brides of their own."

"And what is House Sami getting in return?" Her eyes narrowed. "My uncle Aleki's daughter Aleakali Maru will be the next *Myerial* if Dilys has no daughter while I live. I have heard rumors that Aleakali is expecting a daughter. I'll wager House Sami has surrendered the contract for Coralee in exchange for a betrothal contract to Aleakali's daughter. Why wed a son of House Sami to a Calagi when that son could wed a future *Myerial* instead?"

"If that's true, then why do we not approach Aleakali ourselves and propose that Dilys should wed her daughter?"

"Don't be ridiculous!" Alysaldria snapped. "Dilys earned his *ulumi-lia* four long years ago. I don't want him waiting *five* more years for a wife, and you suggest making him wait another twenty?"

"Perhaps you should ask Dilys what he wants. Perhaps he would not mind waiting a few more years for an *imlani* bride? Perhaps he would even prefer to betroth himself to a future *Myerial* of Calberna."

"And perhaps pigs will grow gills and swim with the kracken."

Under any other circumstances, Dilys would have been fighting to smother a laugh at that sharp-tongued remark. As large and loving as his mother's heart might be, she also possessed a ferocious temper, an iron will, and a wit that had fangs and battle claws of its own.

"Betrothing Dilys to an infant not yet born is out of the question," his mother continued, "but as for the Calagi girl, never let it be said I made this decision without considering my son's wishes." Alysaldria turned to Dilys. "*Moa elua,* my son, you have a chance to wed an *imlani* bride from a fine, strong House. And though I am impatient to see your future settled, five years is not twenty. Coralee Calagi is a beautiful girl, with many gifts. She will become Matriarch of House Calagi when her mother is gone. You and your children will want for nothing, and your blood—our blood—will make House Calagi even stronger than it is today. It is, as Calivan has pointed out, a fine and advantageous match, better than I could have hoped for after the death of our dear Nyamialine. If you want her, say the word."

"Well," he replied guardedly, "if I waited and wed an *imlani,* that would eliminate the friction between you and the other *Donimari,* who fear a half-blood inheriting the Sea Throne."

"I don't care about that." His mother waved impatiently. "The ones objecting the loudest have a vested interest in seeing the Sea Throne go to my cousin Aleakali. They've seized upon Loto Sami's untimely death as an excuse to grab the power they crave. Where were these concerned citizens when Nyamialine died? Did any one of them offer to surrender their own House's betrothal contracts to the son of the new *Myerial*? *Ono,* they did not. So, I'm not asking what they want, I'm asking what you want."

Dilys hesitated. It wasn't the delay that gave him pause. He'd already waited four years after all. Five more years wouldn't be such a long time. But he had loved Nyamialine, his childhood betrothed. Even though they'd only been children together, her death had stolen the joy from his heart for years. He knew that Coralee, who had spent her whole lifetime loving and being loved by Loto Sami, would not mend the wound of that loss in five short years. Not even if Dilys gave up the sea and spent every moment by her side. Perhaps it was wrong and selfish of him, but he wanted a wife capable of loving *him,* not mourning the betrothed she'd loved and lost.

"*Nima,*" he finally said, "I will do whatever you feel is best for Calberna and House Merimydion. If you wish me to wed Coralee Calagi, then I will do so with proper joy in my heart."

"But?" his mother prompted.

"But if the choice is mine, then I would sail for Konumarr tomorrow, as planned."

Alysaldria sat back and smiled. "Your desire is mine as well. It is decided, then."

"Alys—" Calivan started to object, until his twin's commanding gaze silenced him.

"Lord Chancellor," the *Myerial* said formally, "please recall the others so that I may give them my decision."

The queen had spoken. Clearly realizing further protest was futile, Calivan bowed stiffly and gave the guards at the door the order to open the throne-room door. He and Dilys both stood beside the throne, presenting a united front as the others entered. To Calivan's credit, no matter what his personal opinions on a matter might be, once the queen decided a course of action, not by word or deed did he ever make his objections known to another.

"Sealords, *Donimari*," Alysaldria nodded to officials and the matriarchs. "The decision has been made. The prince and his men sail tomorrow for the winter lands to court the wives they have earned the right to seek."

"*Moa Myerial!*" the Minister of Internal Affairs protested.

She held up a hand to silence him. To the matriarchs, she said, "My son is twenty-nine. He earned his *ulumi-lia* four years ago, yet still he is unwed. At your behest." Alysaldria turned to regard her Minister of Internal Affairs sternly. "Five—almost six—years ago, you and Calivan convinced me and my Council that Dilys should wait to choose his *liana* so that we could investigate all potential brides and select a union that would best serve Calberna and House Merimydion. Four years ago, Calivan assured me that a Season of Summerlea was that best union. Now, you come to me saying a Season of Summerlea will not suit and that we must rob House Sami of their long-awaited joy and force my son to wait five more years until Nyree Calagi's daughter is of age to marry?"

The high priest spread his hands. "*Moa Myerial, please . . .*"

Alysaldria's golden eyes flashed with temper. "Are you so afraid that this Season will bear a daughter for House Merimydion? Or is it that you think me incapable of ensuring that a daughter of House Merimydion will be born a true *imlani* capable of ruling from the Sea Throne? You suggest I am too weak to make it so?"

The minister and the high priest both flinched.

"We have heard enough." The *Myerial* stood before her throne, her eyes glowing like golden suns. She didn't often speak from the Sea Throne, using the royal "We," but when she did, it meant she was speaking as the Power of Calberna and that her decision was irrevocable. Recognizing the command for what it was, Calivan, Dilys, the *Donimari,* and the others all dropped to one knee and bowed their heads in submission, keeping their gazes fixed on the floor.

"Ministers, *Donimari,* We thank you for your concerns and your efforts to do what you believe to be in the best interests of Calberna. But We will not ask House Sami or House Calagi to break a contract signed in blood and salt. Nor will We deprive Our son, the *Myerielua,* his right to seek without further delay the happiness and peace he so richly deserves. And should Numahao grace his union with an *imlani* daughter for House Merimydion, she will be born with gifts great enough to honor the Sea Throne upon which she will sit, even if We must give Our own life to make it so. So We have spoken. So shall Our will be done."

The gathered courtiers murmured in unison, "So You have spoken. So shall Your will be done."

"You are dismissed."

The group rose and backed out of the room, bowing as they went.

When they were gone, and the throne-room doors closed behind them, Calivan turned to his sister. "Alys, what have you done?"

She rubbed her temples wearily. "I did what had to be done. I cut the legs out from under the Pureblood Alliance and ensured that my son can leave war behind him and finally claim the peace he has earned many times over."

"But to vow the sacrifice of your own life—from the Sea Throne, you swore it." Calivan's horror was clear. Every *imlani* child—especially every daughter—was born with seagifts because both the *Donima* of their House and their closest female *imlani* relatives passed on a measure of their own gifts before that child was born. But the great power stored in Calberna's native-born women was not limitless. An *imlani* female could drain herself unto death, just as the *Myerials* did on their deathbeds as they passed their power on to their successors. And Alysaldria had just sworn an unbreakable vow to do just that, if she could not gift Dilys's half-blood daughter with sufficient power any other way.

"*Nima* . . ." Dilys was as horrified as his uncle. "*Nima,* you cannot do this. I won't allow it. I will accept the betrothal to Coralee Calagi. I will wait ten years or twenty if I must."

"It is too late for that, *moa elua.* I have Spoken."

"Then I will not wed. I will live as Calivan does, bound to you and no other."

Her head jerked up. Blazing eyes met and held his. "You will do no such thing. I will see you wed and settled before this year is out. I will see my son—my only child—made happy."

"How can I ever be happy to wed an *oulani* if the price for that choice is your death?"

She made a sound of disgust and flung herself to her feet. "How? The same way I have found happiness without your father. Because you must. Because duty to House Merimydion and to Calberna means that you and I both must always find a way to be strong for others, even when we cannot be strong for ourselves." Then her expression softened. "Dilys, *moa elua,* tomorrow you will sail to the Æsir Isles, and you will bring home a daughter for House Merimydion, a daughter to fill my soul with joy and gladness, a *liana* you will love with your whole heart. And she will bear sons and, Numahao willing, a daughter for our

House and for Calberna. And your children will be fine, gifted Calbernans who will bring honor to our House, and our country, and our people. So I have Spoken. So shall my will be done."

Tears filled his eyes. He blinked them back with effort. His voice was choked as he bowed his head in submission and said, "*Tey, moa Myerial.*"

"Good. Then come here and kneel before me, my son. I will give you my blessing now, rather than tomorrow."

He ascended the coral steps and knelt before Calberna's pearl-encrusted throne. His mother leaned forward to cup his face with both hands. "My strong, brave, beautiful son," she said. There was a tremor in her hands that made him frown, but before he could remark on it, her large, heavily golden eyes flashed sun bright.

His body jerked. Power raged through him like a hurricane. The golden trident birthmark on the inside of his left wrist burned and throbbed, glowing the same yellow gold now blazing from his mother's eyes.

"Let my love bring you strength that you may conquer whatever challenges come your way," she whispered, and then she placed a kiss on his *ulumi-lia,* the iridescent blue tattoo that curled from the corner of his right eye across the ridge of his cheekbone.

His eyes rolled back. His muscles locked, else the energy that shuddered mercilessly through his body would have felled him. When she released him, he collapsed before her in dazed breathlessness. His lungs heaved and his racing heart stuttered in his chest.

She guided his head to her lap with one hand, and he laid his head upon her knees in a gesture of love and devoted submission, an acknowledgment that for all his dominance on the seas, his victorious ferocity in battle, and his intimidating height and build, he derived his true strength and greatest magic from this small, slender woman who had borne him. She loved and ruled him as ferociously as she loved and ruled her nation. And like every devoted son of Calberna, he just as ferociously loved, served, and defended her.

Dilys closed his eyes as his mother gently stroked the soft, obsidian ropes of his hair. The power she'd poured into him raged like a tempest inside him, filling his body so completely, his skin felt stretched and on fire. He fought to assimilate that power, to contain it and store it in his cells, to be called upon in future.

Gradually, his thundering pulse slowed and his breathing returned to a calm, unhurried rhythm. Alysaldria gave his locks one last maternal stroke, then released him.

He rose on trembling legs, humbled by his mother's tremendous gift. "*Moa nana, Nima.*" My thanks, Mother. "But you should not have given me so much."

Her eyes still shone pure molten gold, but she looked weary and drained. Pale beneath the deep bronze of her skin.

He was about to express his concern when Alysaldria's eyes rolled back and she collapsed into the cradle of her throne.

"*Nima!*" Dilys lunged for her, catching her slight, slender body and lifting her out of the throne. "Uncle Calivan!"

"Get the healer!" Calivan snapped to one of the guards standing by the throne room. "Dilys, this way. To the antechamber." Swiftly, his face etched with concern, Calivan led the way down the stairs behind the throne to the antechamber below. "Put her on that chaise." He pointed to the long, cushioned lounge set against the wall of the private chamber beneath the throne room and went to fetch a cool cloth and a glass of chilled, salted water while Dilys set his mother down.

She had already come around by the time Calivan returned with the cloth and the water. She waved off their hovering concern, though she accepted both the drink and the damp cloth. "It's all right. I'm fine."

"You're not fine," Dilys argued. "You fainted."

"And it's my own fault," she said. "Calivan has been

telling me I'm not eating properly. I suppose I should have listened to him."

Dilys cast a concerned look at his uncle, who snapped his fingers at one of the guards who'd followed them down to the antechamber and ordered, "Have the kitchens send up something for the *Myerial* to eat. Immediately. Tell them to send whatever they have on hand. No delays. They can make something more substantial for her later."

"*Tey,* Lord Merimydion." The guard bowed and hurried out.

Dilys turned back to his mother. She struggled to sit up, only to collapse weakly back against the chaise. A cold hand of fear squeezed Dilys's heart.

"*Nima,* it is more than not eating. You are not well." Her paleness today. That tremble in her hand before she'd given him her blessing. She was beginning to Fade, that loss of strength that befell some Calbernans, particularly after great tragedy or heartache, when their sorrow became too great to bear. To Calbernans, love and happiness were not simply emotions. They were as essential as air and water. A Calbernan could not live without them.

"*Nima,* you cannot ask me to leave you now. I won't do it. I won't go." He would devote himself to her entirely, pour upon her all the love in his soul to keep her strong. He would do whatever it took, no matter the cost to himself.

"*Tey,* you will." She shook her head. "I will allow no further delay. You will travel to the winter lands and you will bring back a daughter for me to love, a daughter to mother my grandchildren. I will hold your child in my arms."

And suddenly her decision to Speak from the Sea Throne made perfect sense. No wonder she had sworn an unbreakable vow to give her life to make his daughter strong. No wonder she'd commanded him to sail tomorrow to Wintercraig and claim his wife. She'd known she was beginning to Fade.

"Then I will stay, Alys," Calivan said, reaching down to stroke his sister's hair.

She grasped his wrist and shook her head again. "*Ono*. You and I have already discussed this. There is no one I trust more to protect my son's back amongst the *oulani* than you."

"*Nima—*"

"Alys—"

Dilys and Calivan protested in unison, but Alysaldria would not be swayed.

"*Ono*. Dilys, you will go tomorrow, as planned—*with* your uncle and with no more fighting between you. You will court this Season your uncle and the Council have chosen for you and you will win her love. Then you will bring her home to Calberna and give her children to bring you both as much joy and pride as you have brought me. That is what will make me happy. That is what I need from you."

"*Nima*." His throat was so tight his voice came out hoarse. He took her hand, pressed his lips to her palm. "As you require, so I shall provide, *moa nima*."

The sun was still low on the eastern horizon the next morning as Dilys headed to the palace docks, where a glossy blue canal boat was waiting to take him to his ship. He and his Uncle Calivan had shamelessly browbeat his mother last night until she had agreed to let her twin stay with her until she was stronger. Dilys would go on ahead, to begin his courtship of the Seasons, and Calivan would join him in a month or so, once Alysaldria had regained a measure of her strength.

As Dilys reached the perimeter of the palace gardens, a Calbernan stepped out from behind one of the mani-cured hedges.

"So, you're off to claim your *oulani*."

Dilys's body tensed. His mood—already troubled—grew

darker, and he turned slowly to face his cousin Nemuan, the son of the previous *Myerial*.

Tattoos covered Nemuan's body from neck to toe, with hardly an inch of unadorned bronze skin showing anywhere between, but unlike most Calbernans, whose tattoos were inked with the iridescent blue created from royal anemone, mother of pearl, and crushed silverfish scales, half of Nemuan's markings had been drawn in matte-black squid ink. Records of all the years he'd spent on the seas, not seeking gold and glory, but absolution and revenge for the loss of his sister, Sianna, and his mother, the *Myerial* Siavaluana.

Only two years older than Dilys, Nemuan had been a boy of eleven when the accident had claimed the lives of Sianna and Nyamialine, and ultimately Siavaluana as well. Too young to seek his own death for his family's honor, but not too young to go to sea. For ten years, he'd sold his sword without profit, facing battle after battle, mission after mission, to prove his strength, his skill, his command of sea and the ships that sailed it. To free himself from the stain of his family's failure to protect its women. Only after those years had he turned his mind to gold and glory, his desire towards earning a *liana* of his own. Unfortunately for Nemuan, those years of rage and fury had left their mark on more than just his skin. Though he had amassed gold and glory enough for a *liana* of his own, he had yet to win one.

He was waiting, he said, for a *liana* worthy of the son of a *Myerial*. And just like his cronies in the Pureblood Alliance, Nemuan made it clear he thought Dilys should do the same.

"Nemuan," Dilys greeted his cousin without enthusiasm. "I thought you were still at sea."

His cousin smiled, but no humor lightened the flat, dark gold of his eyes. "And miss the day a *Myerial*'s son sails off to fetch an *oulani* bride?"

Dilys's lips tightened. "What's done is done, cousin," he said. "No amount of sacrifice will ever bring your mother, Sianna, or Nyamialine back to us. It is time for you to set aside your fury and your grief. Claim a *liana* of your own to give you children. Seek what happiness this life yet holds for you."

"I do not forget so easily as you," Nemuan spat.

Dilys's lips tightened. "I forget nothing. But I cannot change what is, only what will be. And I choose life, for me and the children my *liana* will bear me."

"A *Myerielua* worthy of the name would say it was better to see House Merimydion die than sully Calberna's royal line with *oulani* blood. In Numahao's name, Merimydion, act like the Prince of the Isles you're supposed to be, not some spineless, self-serving weakling without the will to do what's right."

Dilys's eyes narrowed. The points of his battle claws pressed against his fingertips, wanting out. "Careful, Merimynos."

"You were given the chance to choose what was best for Calberna—to keep the bloodline of the Sirens pure. And you turned your nose up at it."

"I was offered the chance to wait five years before wedding a girl grieving for her lost love. I chose instead to seek a powerful daughter for House Merimydion, a daughter for my *nima* to love, one whose heart is not drowning in grief."

"A choice that's good for you and no one else."

"The *Myerial* does not agree."

"The *Myerial* is—"

"*Mua!*" Silence! Dilys's hand slashed through the air. His expression went hard as stone. "Your insults to me, I can let pass, but do not speak words about my mother that I will be forced to make you regret."

Nemuan's lips curled. "As if you could."

A split second later, Nemuan lay flat on his back, Dilys's

hand at his throat. The face of the former *Myerial*'s son was turning a satisfying shade of puce.

"I could," Dilys said. "I could very easily. And you'd do best to remember it, *pulan*." His mother had given him more than a little power. She'd all but drained herself for him, making him more than a match for his motherless, sisterless cousin.

Dilys released Nemuan and rose in one swift, smooth motion. Leaving his cousin lying there, Dilys crossed the coral slab of the dock and stepped aboard the glossy blue canal boat. "Don't bother coming to see me off," he said.

At the back of the boat, two Calbernans shoved long poles into the clear water of the canal, pushing away from the courtyard dock. As the boat moved down the canal towards the harbor, Dilys could feel Nemuan's narrowed black eyes boring into the back of his head. The two of them had never been particularly friendly—not at all since the deaths of Sianna and Nyamialine—but their shared blood had always kept them civil. Clearly, those bonds held no longer.

Dilys knew that in Nemuan, he now had an enemy.

CHAPTER 2

Konumarr, Wintercraig

"Calbernans, who claim to be the favored race of the goddess Numahao, all possess seagifts that enable them to manipulate currents, commune with creatures of the sea, and swim without needing to surface for air. They are rightly called Sealords, as the oceans of the world obey their commands." The small, golden-skinned boy standing at the head of the small schoolroom gripped the edges of the leather-bound book in his hands and turned expectant eyes towards his teacher.

"That was excellent, Jori." Gabriella Coruscate, the Summerlea princess known more commonly by her gift-name Summer, smiled at the young boy and took the book from his hands.

The seven-year-old beamed proudly. "I been practicing with Mam."

"You *have* been practicing with your mam," she corrected kindly, "and, yes, I can see that you have. You've made excellent progress, Jori." The boy's cheeks flushed a sweet, red-rose beneath his golden skin, making the smattering of white freckles across his cheeks glow like stars. He looked so earnest and adorable, with his big blue eyes and the sheafs of straight white hair slanting across his brow, and so proud, too—his spine straight, his narrow shoulders squared beneath his threadbare but pristinely washed, starched, and neatly mended shirt—nothing like the timid, painfully shy child who'd first stepped into her classroom two weeks ago. Unable to stop herself, she reached out to ruffle his hair, and was rewarded with another beaming smile and a palpable pulse of joy that suffused her with soothing warmth.

Summer let herself bask in that warmth for a moment, then stepped back from the lure of Jori's affection and turned to return the book to the neatly ordered bookshelf standing against the wall.

"All right, class. That's all for today. There will be no school tomorrow so everyone can attend the welcoming celebrations for the Calbernans. So, I'll see you again next Modinsday, when we'll start the next chapter in Tanturri's *History of the World*."

She laughed at the chorus of groans from the students. They much preferred reading adventures and heroic epics like *Roland Triumphant: Hero of Summerlea* or *The Great Hunt*—a predilection shared by Summer's sister Khamsin, the Queen of Wintercraig, who had founded Konumarr's new public school—but while those texts made for an exciting read, they didn't expand students' knowledge of geography and history beyond the shores of the Æsir Isles. Khamsin was determined that the graduates of her experimental new public school should emerge with the ability to read, write, do arithmetic, and have a useful foundation of knowledge in history, geography, and commerce, which is why she'd pressed her sister Summer into teaching this first semester. Children naturally flocked to Summer—and what parent would refuse to let their child attend a class taught by the most beloved princess in the Æsir Isles?

Summer wasn't entirely convinced that these children—many of whom would go on to join their parents in farming, fishing, sheep herding, or trapping—needed an education that went beyond basic reading, writing, and arithmetic, but Khamsin insisted. Who knew? Maybe she was right. Summer's own tutor had been fond of history, proclaiming, "A wise man learns from those who came before so that he may duplicate their successes while avoiding their mistakes." Even if the children never needed to know why long-dead kings had plunged their nations into war or how the battles had affected the world, the part about avoiding the mistakes of one's forebears was probably a lesson worth learning.

Certainly, it was a lesson Summer had taken to heart.

In any event, Tanturri's *History* was the students' least favorite text. Summer secretly agreed with them—she'd always found it a dead, dry read—but since Wintercraig's queen had included it in the curriculum, Summer would plow through it all the same. Hopefully, she'd found a way to make the material more interesting, both for her own sake as well as the students'.

"Lily"—she nodded towards the pregnant young woman at the back of the class—"suggested you might enjoy Tanturri more if we made costumes and acted out some of the historical events. What do you think of that?" When a small chorus of cheers replaced the groans, she smiled. "Excellent. Costumes it is. We'll plan our costumes for the first chapter and go to the store on Turinsday, where you can all practice your arithmetic by deciding how much of each fabric you'll need and how much it will all cost."

She stood by the door as the children filed out, saying good-bye and offering each one a personal word of encouragement for their continued efforts in class. In response to her praise, their joy washed over her like a swell of nourishing warmth. She watched them scatter—some racing home, some racing off to play in one of Konumarr's many parks, the younger ones skipping into their waiting mothers' loving embraces—and forced herself to keep smiling despite the ache of bittersweet longing that burned in her breast.

After they were gone, Summer stood in the schoolhouse doorway, closed her eyes and turned her face up towards the sun, letting the soothing radiance soak into her skin, bringing with it a surge of potent energy that slowly eased the ache in her heart. As a royal princess of Summerlea, she and her sisters all had a particular affinity for the sun—a trait which, as they recently discovered, was owed to the blood of the Sun God, Helos, that ran through their veins.

There was a small sound behind her. "Your idea was a hit," Summer murmured, without opening her eyes.

"Yes, ma'am."

"I hope you know you're going to help me with all the sewing the children don't do themselves—and I have no doubt that will be the bulk of it."

There was a short, uncertain silence, then a small laugh. "Yes, ma'am."

Gabriella turned to smile at Lily, the pretty young Summerlander who'd arrived in Konumarr only a few days after Summer's own arrival two weeks ago. Lily's husband had died in last winter's rebellion, leaving her pregnant and alone. She'd heard about the Calbernans coming to court willing women, so she'd walked and hitched rides from her home in Summerlea's northwestern province, the Orchards, all the way to Konumarr. She'd arrived with a burgeoning belly, no place to stay, and only a scant handful of copper *pisetas* to her name. Khamsin had offered her free room and board at the school in exchange for helping to clean the school and prepare the classrooms each day, but after the second time Gabriella had found Lily standing in the hall outside one of the classroom doors, listening to the lessons, she'd convinced the girl to assist her in the classroom instead.

"You have a good way with children," Summer said. "You're going to be a wonderful mother."

"Thank you, Your Highness." Lily smiled shyly and stroked a hand over her rounded belly. She was a lovely

girl, Summerlander dark, with wavy black hair, beautiful
dark-chocolate eyes, and deep, lustrous brown skin, but it
was the earnest sweetness of her spirit that Summer found
her most attractive quality. From Lily's telling reluctance
to speak about her life in Summerlea, the way she jumped
at loud noises or sudden movements, and the shadows that
sometimes haunted her eyes, Summer gathered the girl
had seen more than her share of rough times, but Lily
hadn't let those times harden her gentle heart. That took
strength. The kind most people missed because it was so
subtle.

Abruptly Lily flinched, gave a muffled grunt, and
clapped one hand to her right side. "Ow. Little sprout here
has quite a kick." She laughed and patted a spot on her
belly that was visibly moving as the child in her womb
stretched and turned inside her.

Summer's gaze fixed on that movement and the ache
in her heart surged back to excruciating life. With it came
a trembling deep inside and a feeling of terrible pressure,
like the rumbling of a volcano preparing to erupt.

She turned abruptly away to pluck her shawl from the
peg by the door. "I should go," she said. "My family will
be waiting tea for me. I'll come in on Helosday and we
can review your plans for the children's costumes." Not
waiting for a response and without risking another glance
in Lily's direction, she headed for the door. "Enjoy your
weekend, Lily."

What was happening to her?

Summer took deep breaths as she walked briskly
through the streets of Konumarr, heading for the bridge
that crossed the wide, deep Llaskroner Fjord to connect the
city to the palace on the fjord's northern shores. Ever
since coming here three weeks ago, the wall of calm,
serene control she'd spent a lifetime building around her
magic had been crumbling. And not just with small, minor
cracks either, although that would be bad enough. No, the

foundation of her self-control, her ability to sublimate her own desires, had suffered a major seismic shift.

Was her father's legacy of madness finally starting to manifest in her?

Gabriella was terrified that was the case, and even more terrified of what she might do to the people around her if it was. What she might do to the people she loved.

She knew everyone thought she was the weakest of the Seasons. She knew everyone thought she was so sweet and kind and gentle that she would never hurt a fly. That's what they were supposed to think. That was the face her mother, the late Queen Rosalind, had taught her to show to the world, the mask she'd taught Gabriella to wear so well it had become second nature to her.

Even now, though her mother was long dead—nearly two decades dead—Summer could still hear her voice, so gentle and yet so firm, pulsing with a magic that Queen Rosalind's Seahaven ancestors had long ago labeled Persuasion.

You were born with great power, my darling. Not just from your father but from me as well. You must learn to control it. If you don't, you could hurt a great many people, and I know you would never want that. You must control it, Gabriella. You must. *Your father and I will help you any way we can. But to start with, you must learn to always remain calm. Stay away from people and situations that upset you. Practice sending goodness, kindness, and happiness out into the world, so that you only get goodness, kindness, and happiness back.*

And that was exactly what she'd done. She'd avoided conflict entirely at first. Anger, hatred, violence: those emotions stung her senses like nettles, feeding darkness into her until her own darkness roared in response. As she got older, she'd eventually learned how to defuse conflict rather than run from it. She'd mastered the Persuasive gifts she'd inherited from her mother and her Seahaven ancestors, though she was always careful not to "push" too hard with those gifts, for fear of unleashing her other, more dangerous magic.

She'd thought she'd succeeded in caging her deadliest gifts and escaping the madness that had consumed and destroyed her father, but since coming to Konumarr, her hard-won and painstakingly-maintained serenity had all but evaporated. The beast that dwelt inside her had begun rousing at the simplest provocation.

It didn't even take anger or violence to shake the foundations of her control anymore. All it took was for her to want something, badly, and that hungry, wild, ferocious *thing* inside her roared to life, ripping and tearing at her control, threatening to break free.

Like seeing Lily's baby move and wanting—needing! *Craving*!—a baby of her own to love, even though that was the last thing she should ever have.

She'd reached Ragnar Square, the central plaza of Konumarr. Two dozen villagers were hard at work, twining blossoming vines around lampposts and stringing cables for the lanterns that would be lit tomorrow night for the celebration welcoming the Calbernans to Wintercraig. Several of the workers saw her and paused in their work to doff hats and bow or curtsy.

"Your Royal Highness."

Gabriella forced a smile, somehow managing to summon the Sweet Princess Summer mask they all expected to see. "Please, that's not necessary. Don't let me interrupt your work." Unbidden, a strong thrust of Persuasion pushed out along with her words. The workers—all of them— immediately went back to their tasks as if she wasn't even there.

Rattled by her unintentional use of power, Summer tucked her chin down and hurried past. This wouldn't do. This wouldn't do at all!

She didn't dare return to the palace just yet. She needed peace and quiet and a place to center herself, to shore up the crumbling foundation of her control. Rather than turning to cross the bridge leading to the palace, she continued walking briskly down the Konumarr's main road. She wanted to break out into a run, but that would draw attention to herself. Attention meant people would be bombarding her senses with their curiosity and alarm, and she wasn't prepared to risk any further damage to the barriers that kept her magic in check.

Just before the city gates, Gabriella turned left down a stone-paved path that led to her favorite place in Konumarr: a small, mossy grotto tucked away behind the misting waters of Snowbeard Falls. There the air was cool and damp, and the roar of the falls drowned out all noise from the city. It was the one place in all of Konumarr where she could feel well and truly alone—alone enough to find the peace she so desperately needed.

Gabriella sat down on the stone bench in the center of the grotto and closed her eyes as the misty spray from the foaming white veil of falling water dampened her face. The chilly moisture evaporated quickly on her hot cheeks, but she gripped the sides of the stone bench with both hands and remained where she was until the speed with which the water evaporated slowed down to something approaching normal. Only then did she open her eyes, and with hands that shook only slightly, she unclasped the charm bracelet secured around her right wrist and held it in her palm.

Small jeweled charms dangling from the bracelet's silver links winked up at her, each tiny shell, starfish, and sea creature paved with a different colored gemstone.

Your mother would have wanted you to have this. She could still hear her father's voice, before the madness had him fully in its grip, before she and her other sisters knew their beloved father had become a monster. He'd given Gabriella her mother's bracelet on her eighth birthday, less than a year after her mother's death. *You're so like her.* She remembered the feel of Papa's big, broad hands petting her black curls back off her face. *Like a little piece of my Rose, still alive for me to love.*

Summer gave a stifled sob and pushed away those memories, reaching instead for the memory of her mother unclasping her bracelet and putting it in Gabriella's small hands, teaching her how to find the calm within. *Pick a charm, darling. Any one of them. How about this little blue dolphin here? Such a happy fellow, don't you think? This one was always my favorite. Now, I want you to focus on it. Focus on this little blue dolphin.*

In a ritual that she'd done so often it had become instinct, Gabriella poked through the charms with one finger until she found the small sapphire-studded dolphin. Pinching that charm between her thumb and forefinger, she focused intently on the blue glitter of its gems.

Imagine him swimming in the ocean, laughing and leaping in the waves. Good, that's good, baby girl. Now keep imagining that happy dolphin until everything that makes you angry or upset fades away. There's my girl. There's my sweet, kind, good, beautiful girl. I love you, Gabriella. I love you so very, very much.

The little blue dolphin charm grew blurry. Gabriella blinked and wetness much warmer than the mist from the falls trickled down her cheeks.

"Oh, Mama," she whispered. "Oh, Mama, I miss you so much."

"You're late," Gabriella's eldest sister, Viviana, better known by her giftname, Spring, greeted her as she stepped out onto Konumarr Palace's western terrace. Spring frowned, her bright green gaze sweeping over Gabriella intently, missing nothing. "Is everything all right?"

Her mother's bracelet clasped back in place around her wrist, the fractures in the fortress containing her power once more tightly sealed, Gabriella summoned a blithe, sunny smile and, with the ease of a lifetime of practice, chose a lie she knew her sisters would believe. "Of course. Everything's fine. It was just such a beautiful day, I just had to take a little detour on the way home. I didn't think you'd mind."

King Wynter, Summer's brother-in-law, had promised her and her sisters that come spring his country would transform into one of the most beautiful places on earth, and he had not been wrong. With the long, bright days of northern Wintercraig's summer well underway, the ice and snow of winter had retreated, leaving picturesque waterfalls pouring down from the mountainsides, creating perpetual rainbows in the mists. Konumarr, built at the headwaters of the Llaskroner Fjord valley, was nestled in the very heart of that beauty, surrounded by green cliffs, lush forests, and abundantly blooming life. In certain parts of the city, you could even glimpse the glacier-capped peaks of the Skoerr Mountains to the north.

"Well, I don't mind," Spring said, "but a few more minutes, and I feared Autumn might start gnawing on her own arm."

"Not my arm, Vivi," retorted Autumn, the youngest and most beautiful of the three princesses known as the Seasons of Summerlea. "I was thinking about gnawing on yours." With a laugh and a toss of her bright auburn curls, Autumn stuck out her tongue and headed for the wide table where a full afternoon tea had been laid out for them.

As usual, the palace staff had outdone themselves. Tiered plates of sandwiches, savories, delicate iced cakes, and a variety of other sweets had been tucked amidst artfully arranged flowers and greenery, giving the impression of nature offering up a bounty of delectable treats. Autumn snatched up a plate and began to help herself to the goodies.

Gabriella glanced around the terrace, but apart from two guards and a servant standing off at a discreet distance, the three Seasons were alone. "Where's Storm and Wynter? I thought they were joining us."

"Khamsin took ill again right after lunch."

"Ah. Poor thing." Their youngest sister, Khamsin, hadn't had the most uneventful pregnancy, that was for sure. Even eight months into it, bouts of queasiness would still take her unawares at any time of day or night, a fact that had left her husband, Wynter, hovering over his beloved wife until she threatened to shoot a lightning bolt up his unmentionables if he didn't leave her in peace. "I hope Tildy brewed up something to help her feel better."

"She did, and it must have worked. We haven't seen Kham or Wynter for almost two hours." Spring winked and they both laughed. "So how was school today?" Spring asked. "Did the little sprouts learn heaps and heaps?"

"Heaps and heaps," Summer confirmed. She glanced past Spring to the tea table and tried to hide a smile as she watched Autumn pile her plate high with three savory meat pies, eight tiny sandwiches, four small iced cakes layered with fruit filling, and two small pastry cornucopias filled with sugared fruits.

Seeing the smile, Spring turned, then scowled. "Sweet Halla, Autumn! Could you leave some for everyone else?"

Autumn arched a haughty auburn brown and sniffed. "Oh, hush. There's enough here to feed an army. No one's going to be shorted because I chose to indulge myself. Which I'm going to do more of, now, just to irritate you." Blowing Spring a kiss, she added another meat pie and three large sugar cookies frosted with cream-cheese icing to the tottering pile on her plate. "So there."

Spring scowled. "You are incorrigible."

Autumn popped a tiny iced teacake in her mouth, grinned, and executed a wildly extravagant bow, complete with waving flourishes of her free arm. It was a credit to Autumn's natural grace that not a single item toppled from her teetering, overfull plate.

For the first time since her earlier lapse in control, Gabriella's fear evaporated completely, and genuine laughter bubbled up inside her over Autumn's antics. She tried to stifle a giggle because she knew Spring wouldn't approve, but succeeded only in giving an unladylike snort of amusement. That earned her a grin from Autumn and a dark look from Spring.

"Honestly, Gabi, must you encourage her?"

Gabrielle's smothered giggle turned into an outright laugh. "I can't help it. She's funny."

"She's ridiculous." Spring planted her hands on her slender hips. Her spine was rigid, her green eyes snapping. The long sheath of stick-straight black hair that feel to her hips didn't so much as twitch. "I hope you will be better behaved tomorrow with the Calbernans, Aleta Seraphina Helena Rosalie Violet Coruscate."

Autumn rolled her eyes, plopped into a chair at the table, then attacked her food with the ferocious focus of a general commanding the invasion of a small country.

"She's nervous about tomorrow," Summer murmured as she and Spring turned back to the tea table to fill their own plates with less than a fourth of what Autumn had taken. "You know how she gets when she's nervous."

Even on a normal day, most people who saw the amount of food Autumn put away were shocked, and when she was nervous, she ate at least twice what she usually did. By all rights, the sheer quantity of what she consumed should have left her as fat as a farmer's prize porker, but instead she maintained a perfect figure, slender of waist and limb but generously curved in all the right places. There was something about holding the sun in your soul that tended to burn calories like kindling.

Still, if Summer ate the way Autumn did, her curves would be so generous they'd be popping the seams on all her clothes!

"I'm nervous, too," Spring muttered, "but you don't see me trying to stuff the whole palace larder down my gullet!"

"No," Gabriella agreed. "But I do see you trying to control something you know you can't. And maybe obsessing just a little? How many more times did you read that report on the Calbernans last night?"

Spring flushed. "Summer the Sweet, sometimes you're a little tart."

Proving she was still listening even from her spot at the table, Autumn turned in her chair to crow, "Vivi! You made a pun!" She gave Spring two thumbs up. "I'm so proud of you!"

Spring rolled her eyes. Gabriella smothered a laugh, then said, "And since you didn't answer my question, I take it to mean you read the report at least—what?—two more times?"

"Four," Spring admitted grudgingly, "but only because I couldn't sleep!" They returned to the table and took their seats next to Autumn. "Of course, as usual, Gabriella, you don't look even the slightest bit nervous about tomorrow."

"Why would I be?" Gabriella reached for the silver teapot. "It's not like Sealord Merimydion is going to be paying me much attention when you and Autumn are here."

"Gabriella . . ."

Summer laughed with genuine amusement. "It's true and you know it. And I honestly don't mind. Quite the opposite, in fact. I don't have to worry about whether I'm making a good impression, or twist myself in knots when my potential husband turns out to be a loathsome toad or an intolerable gas bag. Instead, I get to just sit back and enjoy the show."

That comment pulled Autumn away from her food. "Hah," she said. "You weren't enjoying the show last week with that Vermesc ambassador. He really took a shine to you. All the Vermese do. They think you're their type. All soft and sweet and accommodating."

Summer blinked big, innocent blue eyes and gave her sister a beatific smile. "I *am* soft and sweet and accommodating."

Autumn laughed. "And sneaky. And stubborn. And subversive."

"Don't be unkind, Leta," Summer chided. But she couldn't stop the tiny smile that curled up the corners of her lips. Her sisters knew her better than anyone. They knew about the masks she showed the world. What they didn't know was how often the face she showed them was a mask as well.

Her smile dimmed a little at that thought, and to hide it she reached for the large silver teapot set out in the center of the table. Hefting the pot, she poured a stream of hot honeyrose tea into a crystal tea glass cradled in a beautifully carved silver holder. After adding two small flower-shaped cubes of sugar from the bowl, she handed the glass to Spring along with a tiny silver spoon.

"Speaking of the Vermese," Spring said. "I want to apologize again for abandoning you the way I did. I shouldn't have left you to cozy up to that cretin all on your own."

"As I've said before, there's no need to apologize. Cozying up to cretins is my specialty." Like her mother before her, Summer was considered the palace peacemaker. It was a role that usually suited her quite well. Gabriella sighed. "Unfortunately, that time, I don't think it did much good."

Two weeks ago, an apoplectic Galil beda Turat, ambassador to Maak Korin beda Khan, Mystral's wealthiest and most powerful emperor, had stormed out of Konumarr Palace, furious that the Great Maak's tenth marriage proposal since Autumn's thirteenth birthday had been refused. Only unlike the many times their father had refused the Maak's offers, Wynter had not only refused, he'd done so in a way that made it clear no future offers from the Great Maak would ever be welcome.

Gabriella had done her best to calm down the outraged ambassador, finally resorting to a push of Persuasion. His reaction still troubled her. The ambassador hadn't merely been outraged, he'd been afraid. One thing she'd learned over the years was that frightened, furious men could end up causing all sorts of trouble. And even though the ambassador was no threat, the same couldn't be said for his master, Maak Korin beda Khan.

"You did more good than I would have done," Spring said. "If I had to bite my lip one more time so as not to offend him with my bold, unfeminine ways I would have wrapped my hands around his skinny neck and strangled the life out of him. But that's still no excuse for leaving you to face him all on your own. I know the Vermese make your skin crawl."

Like she was buried in spiders, cockroaches, and every other manner of creepy-crawly, but all Gabriella said—mildly—was, "They are among the few visitors we've received over the years that I've never been able to make myself like."

"Can you imagine if one of the Verminous Vermese took Summer as a wife?" Autumn interjected. "He wouldn't know what hit him. Within the year, she'd probably have Verma turned into the next Calberna!" She laughed.

Summer repressed a shudder at the thought of being married—or rather, enslaved—to a Vermese man. "Some things are beyond even my powers of Persuasion." And what she might do to the Vermese, were she ever put under their control, would be neither as amusing nor as nonviolent as what Autumn had suggested. Suppressing another, deeper shudder, Gabriella reached for a fresh tea glass and poured a cup for herself.

No one—not even her beloved sisters—knew the true extent of Gabriella's magical gifts. They didn't even know about the magical gift for mind control that she'd inherited from her mother and their Seahaven relatives. They simply thought that she—like their mother before her—was so naturally kind and charming she could soften even the hardest heart.

"Thankfully," Spring said as Summer prepared her tea, "I doubt any of us need ever fear being married off to a Vermese. After the manner in which Wynter refused the Maak's latest offer, I feel safe to say that particular door has not only been closed, it's been welded permanently shut."

"Thank holy Halla, home of all good gods," Autumn said with heartfelt sincerity. Widely acclaimed as one of the most beautiful women in Mystral, with her dark Summerlander skin, pansy purple eyes, and rich, auburn hair, Autumn had been the object of the Vermese emperor's relentless marital pursuit since the day she turned thirteen. "Given the price Maak Korin offered this time, I thought I was doomed for sure."

"Wynter wouldn't do that to you," Summer said.

"Wynter is a king," Spring said. "Kings do that sort of thing all the time."

As princesses of Summerlea, now wards of Wintercraig, the three of them had always known their fate was to be married for the advantage of their monarch. In Summerlea as in Verma and Cho, men still ruled—both the kingdom and their families—although Summerlanders at least considered women to be people, not property. Here in Wintercraig, society was even more egalitarian on the gender front. The harsh conditions bred not just physical hardiness but fierce independence. A woman who had to chop wood, tend her farm, and keep her family and livestock safe from hungry predators while her husband was out hunting and trapping didn't take kindly to being bossed around by anyone. But just because Wintercraig women were independent didn't mean kings cast aside the rights of their rule.

"Not this king," Summer said staunchly, then ruined her show of unwavering support by adding, "Khamsin wouldn't let him."

Autumn grinned. "True," she agreed. "The Winter King has well and truly melted. And a year ago, who'd have believed we'd be saying that?"

The three of them laughed in shared delight. One of the most astonishing—and endlessly entertaining—aspects of living here in Wintercraig these last months was the opportunity to watch the fierce and fearsome Wynter of the Craig, terrifying Bogeyman from the north and conqueror of Summerlea, dote on their youngest sister. Khamsin didn't exactly have him wrapped around her finger—Wynter was too much his own man for that—but there wasn't much she truly wanted that he wouldn't move Halla and Mystral to provide for her.

"Be that as it may," Spring interrupted, "the fact remains the three of us are going to have to marry someone. And Wynter, no matter how much he dotes on Khamsin, is going to make sure that someone will benefit Wintercraig. So, which of us is going to take the pirate?"

"Sealord Merimydion isn't a pirate," Summer said.

"He's a mercenary who sails the sea, selling his services to the highest bidder," Spring countered. "That's close enough to a pirate for me." Setting her tea aside, she leaned back in her chair to regard her sisters. "Still, I suppose even a pirate is a better potential husband than a Vermese."

"Who wouldn't be?" Autumn muttered.

"Sealord," Gabriella corrected. "They call themselves Sealords."

Spring leveled a cool, grass-green stare Summer's way. Not quite a glare, but close. A definite warning. Spring wasn't as volatile as their sister Storm, but she could work up a decent tempest when it suited her, and it looked like it was about to suit her.

Considering Summer's earlier lapse in control, the last thing she needed was to have Spring's temper tearing at the mental walls she'd just repaired.

"Here, have a little mint in your tea." Gabriella crushed a sprig and leaned over to drop the fragrant leaves in Spring's tea glass. "It's very soothing for when you're out of sorts."

"I'm not out of sorts," Spring snapped. Then she realized the tea in her glass was starting to boil, and she grimaced. "Or maybe I am. Sorry. Entertaining that Vermese ambassador for three days put me on edge, and now we have to spend three *months* entertaining the pira—the *Sealord*."

"Well, Storm promises he's very engaging, at least," Autumn said. "And handsome. Nothing like that dreadful Prince Rampion Papa was courting on our behalf before the war."

"Prince Rampion was a nice man," Summer reproved.

"He was a deadly dull, skinny as a stick, and couldn't dance worth a *piseta*. And he had a big nose and spots." Autumn grimaced at the memory.

Summer sighed. It was true, Prince Rampion hadn't been particularly attractive, but there'd been a kindness and vulnerability beneath his stiff pride that garnered her sympathy. "He was very intelligent," she said. "And he grows roses."

Spring rolled her eyes. "No wonder you liked him."

Gabriella smiled. She'd inherited their mother's looks, her gift for Persuasion, and her love of flower gardening. Though Spring was, hands down, the best gardener in the family, she preferred turning her gifts in a more practical direction: the cultivation of fruits, vegetables, and grains. "Flowers are all well and good," she would say, "but they won't feed a family in winter." Summer was the one with their mother's passion for flowers. There was something very soothing about tending flowers on warm summer days, the rich smell of loamy earth, the heady scent of fragrant blooms, a fresh breeze on her face. Gardens were peaceful, and Summer loved them for that.

But Spring was wrong. Summer and Rampion's shared interest in gardening wasn't why he had appealed to her. He was, quite simply, a gentle, kind man she absolutely would never fall in love with.

And that had made him perfect husband material in Summer's opinion.

Unfortunately, Papa had not agreed. Rampion wasn't rich enough, his father's kingdom not influential enough.

Papa had been determined to wed his three beloved daughters to the wealthiest, most powerful kings on Mystral—and for the best, most advantageous marriage contracts. Oh, he prettied it up, of course, when talking to them. Saying things like, "I only want the best for my daughters," and that was true enough, else Autumn's fierce objections wouldn't have stopped him from accepting one of Maak Korin's previous offers.

But Summer had also always known that as much as her father loved his three, beautiful Seasons, in the end, he'd loved power even more. Had their brother Falcon not forged an alliance with the Calbernans two years ago for an army of mercenaries in exchange for the island prince's pick of the Seasons, Autumn already have become Maak Korin's forty-first wife.

It wasn't that their father had been a bad man—at least, he hadn't started out that way. It was simply that Verdan of Summerlea's truest, deepest, most giving love—and he had once been capable of truly great love—had died with Mama. Then that love had turned to grief, and grief had turned to rage and an insatiable, ravening hunger for power, for wealth, for anything to fill that yawning emptiness once filled by his love for his wife.

Or so Summer had decided this last year as she'd tried to come to terms with the madness that had consumed her father so completely that he'd destroyed his son's life, thrown his kingdom into war, and sought to kill his youngest daughter on multiple occasions—only to lose his own life in her stead on the last attempt.

And as horrible and awful as King Verdan's descent into madness had been, Summer was perhaps the only one of his daughters who truly understood it. Because, despite everyone's belief that Summer was like her mother in all ways, the truth was, she the one most like Papa when it came to how deeply and unreservedly she loved, and how completely those emotions could consume her.

And that was precisely why, no matter what, Summer

Coruscate, who longed for a true, deep, passionate love, would never marry any man who could lay the slightest claim on her heart.

She closed her eyes briefly, clamped unyielding chains around the caged monster in her soul, then opened her eyes again and pasted on a pleasant smile.

"I'm sure you'll both find Sealord Merimydion much more to your taste than Prince Rampion," she said. She was pleased that not a hint of her inner struggle showed in her voice or expression. Her meditation in the grotto had done its job.

"That's not saying much," Spring grumped. "I'd find eating ceiling plaster more to my taste than Prince Rampion."

"At least he wasn't Korin beda Khan," Autumn pointed out.

"Point taken." Spring steepled her hands before her. "Now back to the p—*Sealord*. Reports aside, what do we really know about this Dilys Merimydion?"

"We know that he's wealthy, he's a skilled warrior, he's handsome, charming, and helped save the world from a dread god who would have plunged the whole of Mystral into unending winter," Autumn added. "Not to ruin your determination to find something wrong with him, Viviana, but that last one tells me all I need to know. The man literally helped save the world." She shrugged. "I can spend three months of my time being nice to him for that."

Spring sighed. "Yes, yes, but in the reports I've read, there isn't one bad thing about him listed. Not one, and that's just not normal."

"You're complaining because the reports say Dilys Merimydion is a good man?" Summer shook her head.

"Not just good. Too good. As in too good to be true. I'm just saying, something smells fishy to me."

Autumn laughed. "You know, there's a good joke in that remark."

Spring rolled her eyes. "Don't. Please. Spare us." In addition to her addiction to food, Autumn possessed a terrible love for pranks, puns, and bad jokes. Which, of course, she took inordinate glee in inflicting on her family.

Autumn sniffed with mock indignation. "As if I would cast my pearls before swine. What were we talking about again? Oh, yes, Dilys Merimydion. The Scrumptious Sealord."

"Oh, dear gods," Spring groaned. "You've nicknamed him. Alliteratively."

"I thought about Delicious Dilys. Or Manly Merimydion. After all, from what Storm said, he's very easy on the eyes. I don't know about the rest of you, but after ten years of being pursued by the Verminous Vermese, I'm looking forward to being courted by a handsome, young suitor who actually respects women and considers them— *gasp!*—real human beings. Like men, but without the dangly bits. Shocking, I know, but there you have it."

Summer couldn't help it. She started laughing.

Spring glowered. "Stop that! Don't encourage her!" She turned the glower on Autumn and said, "Aleta Seraphina Helen Rosalie Violet Coruscate, can you please, for one moment, take this seriously?"

"You're taking it seriously enough for the three of us, dearest Viviana." Autumn lowered her voice and boomed sternly, "He wants to marry a Season so he must be investigated. Something about him smells fishy." Cupping a hand over her mouth, she quipped to Summer in a loud aside, "I dunno, do you think maybe it's—you know—the *gills*?"

Summer covered her mouth with both hands and spluttered with laughter.

Spring regarded them both with disgust. "Talk about pearls being cast before swine. I'm telling you in all seriousness that I've been looking at this from every possible angle and something about this situation just doesn't add up. The Calbernan made not one but two contracts, risking thousands of his men in war, specifically to claim—or have a chance to claim—a Season for a wife. Why not some other, less costly bride? There are other princesses out there—even some with magic that's at least on par with ours. Why us?"

"The Maak of Verma and Cho just offered the largest bride price in history to claim Autumn," Summer pointed out. "Maybe Sealord Merimydion wants the same thing."

"Perhaps, but if that was the case, don't you think Khamsin would have told us Autumn was the one he wanted? He's interested in our weathergifts—Kham said he admitted that—but he didn't care that they wouldn't be passed on to our children." The divine gifts bestowed upon Summerlea's royal family by the Sun God, Helos, never passed out of the immediate royal family. Though Spring, Summer, and Autumn all inherited their gifts from their father, only Khamsin, now the ruling Queen of Summerlea and Wintercraig, would pass on those gifts to her children.

"I think you're seeing suspicious motives when none exist," Autumn said. "Calbernans *do* rule the sea, after all. I assume they want to rule the weather as well for a while. What sailor wouldn't? Guaranteed clear skies and fair winds? Maybe stir up a few storms to belabor the competition. Even a single generation of that would give them a considerable advantage."

Summer reached for a perfectly iced tea cake topped with a sparkling sugar snowflake and took a delicate nibble. The tangy sweetness of the redberry jam filling, sweet almond icing, and delicate lemon cloud cake filled her mouth with delight. "Oh, sweet Halla, that's good." She pushed the plate towards Spring. "You really should try one of these tea cakes, Vivi. They're delicious."

"Seriously?" Spring regarded her two sisters in disgust. "Aren't either of you the least bit interested in getting to the real truth about our future bridegroom? I can't believe you're both being so cavalier."

"Not cavalier, Vivi. We're being sensible," Autumn replied seriously. "First of all, Sealord Calbernan will be the future bridegroom of only one of us. And second, Storm made it clear that the choice to marry him or not would lie with us—not him. So, he won't be bridegroom to any of us if we don't wish it."

"And third," Summer added, "it's a beautiful day in this beautiful city. And for the first time since we got here, we have the whole afternoon to ourselves, without a single Verminous Vermese or Perturbingly Perfect Pirate"—she sent a grin Autumn's way—"in sight, which means, after I finish tea, I'm going to walk along the banks of the fjord past all those gorgeous waterfalls and just enjoy the day. You should both come with me."

"Ooh, that sounds delightful," Autumn said. "Count me in." They exchanged a smile.

"You two go on without me," Spring said. "You both might think I'm being ridiculous, but I know there's more to this than meets the eye and I'm determined to find out what it is. The folk here in Konumarr have traded with the Calbernans for centuries. Maybe there's someone here who can help shed some light on their motivations."

"Vivi, you're starting to obsess," Gabriella warned. Spring didn't often get riled up about anything, but when she did, she was like a dog with a bone. She wouldn't let it go. Dilys Merimydion's reasons for wanting a Season for a wife had clearly become one of these things. Gabriella wanted to be sure Spring's worry didn't progress beyond a healthy concern. Because Summer wasn't the only one who'd inherited one of their father's more dangerous traits.

Spring opened her mouth to object, then snapped it closed. After a silent, scowling moment, she plucked two iced tea cakes from Autumn's plate, popped them into her mouth one after another, then drank down the rest of her mint-infused honeyrose tea.

"You're right," she said, setting her empty tea glass on

the table, "the cakes are divine, and the mint makes the tea very soothing. I think I'll join you two for a walk after all."

The three sisters smiled at each other with shared love and understanding. Daughters of a mad king they might be, but they had vowed they would always help each other, as they'd not been able to help their father or their brother, Falcon.

CHAPTER 3

With the sea breeze ruffling his hair, and his ship rocking rhythmically in the warm tropical waters of the Varyan Ocean, Mur Balat, Mystral's most infamous, feared, and obscenely wealthy slaver, regarded his guest over a steaming cup of star blossom tea.

The tea was steeped from petals and stamen of flowers that bloomed only once every ten years and only in the highest reaches of the Chitzkali Mountains, in the heart of cannibalistic despot Gulah Zin's territory. Prized for both the rarity and difficulty of acquisition of its main component as well as its fabled healing properties, star blossom tea was Mystral's rarest and most expensive beverage, an indulgence that cost a staggering two hundred golden *coronas* per half ounce. But Mur Balat was a man wealthy enough and connected enough to feed such indulgences.

He liked the taste and effects of the tea well enough. But he liked more the message it sent to those with whom he shared it.

Here is a man who can obtain whatever your heart desires, that cup of pricey, pale nectar declared. *No matter how rare, no matter how priceless, no matter how difficult to acquire.*

Provided, of course, that you could pay his fee.

"Sugar?" he asked politely. Born the bastard son of a Balalatika enchantress and a royal prince of a kingdom that had long since fallen into ruin, Mur Balat prided himself on his good manners. Bastard, thief, slaver, and whoremonger, he might be, but his mother had seen to it that he'd been raised, clothed, and educated as well if not better than his father's legitimate sons. At his father, the prince's expense, of course.

In the years since his mother's death, Balat had come to the conclusion that she truly had loved her handsome, devoted royal prince. If she hadn't, she would never have bothered to murder the prince's wife. And then, she wouldn't have laid such a devastating curse upon her lover and his father's kingdom as she stood on the pyre to be burned for her deed.

Balat's parents were gone. The once thriving kingdom that had been his childhood home was a shattered ruin of its former self, having been torn apart by war and conquest, its indigenous people murdered or enslaved. His mother's brilliant mind and most of her life's work had been destroyed by the king's men when they came for her. Not the most important treasures of the Balalatika bloodline, thank Halla, but her personal spell book, the one she had begun for herself as a young girl. And for what? Love?

Love makes you weak. And foolish. That was the lesson he learned from his mother's death. It was a lesson his current guest had, to Balat's continued enrichment, never learned.

Irritation flashed in Balat's guest's eyes, but was quickly smothered. He leaned forward to pluck two shell-shaped lumps of sugar from the bowl and drop them into his cup, then sat back to stir the tea with a tiny golden spoon. After taking a sip, he said brusquely, "Delicious, as always."

Balat smiled and leaned back in his chair, unoffended by his friend's curt demeanor. Theirs had been a strained friendship for quite a number of years. "It is my pleasure to indulge you, my friend." He made a point of sending his friend a small box of star blossom tea every year. As much a reminder of their past as a reminder of the power Balat held over him.

They'd first met years ago when they'd both traveled Mystral in search of the world's magical secrets. After the fourth time their paths crossed, Balat made a point of be-friending his fellow magical scholar. But although he and his friend had kept in contact over the years—Balat never lost touch with a useful acquaintance—it had been several years since they'd last met face-to-face. His friend found it difficult to leave home for any length of time.

That was part of the reason Balat had agreed to meet him here, at sea, rather than at Balat's primary home—a mighty fortress built on the cliffs overlooking Trinipor, the bustling slave capital of Mystral. Leaving home for the time necessary to travel to and from Trinipor would have roused too much suspicion for his friend, and given how close Balat was to finally unlocking the greatest magical power in the history of Mystral, this was not the time to invite unnecessary scrutiny.

"So," Balat prompted, "I take it you have reconsidered my offer?"

"I have. And you've brought what we agreed upon?"

"Of course." Balat snapped his fingers. A servant hurried forward and, with a deep bow, held out an ornate golden serving tray bearing a pitcher of water, two glasses, and a small box. Balat set the pitcher and both glasses on the table and lifted the lid of the box to reveal a tiny crystal flacon filled with a deep purple liquid.

"You'll find it much more powerful than the batch I brewed up for you before." Balat unstoppered the flacon and poured a single, scant drop of the purple liquid into the pitcher of water, stirring it with a glass rod the servant produced from an apron pocket. "Even this is a much higher concentration than is advisable. To avoid detection, I recommend diluting a single drop in two gallons of water every two or three months and dispensing it no more than a quarter cup at a time. Would you like to sample it yourself?" At his friend's nod, Balat poured two glasses from the pitcher, offering one to his friend and keeping the other for himself. Balat tossed back the contents of his own glass first, knowing his friend would not drink until after he did. He didn't take offense. His friend's suspicious nature was, in part, exactly why Balat liked him so well.

After waiting a few seconds to observe the effect of the drink on Balat, Mur's guest sipped at his own glass experimentally, and his eyes widened.

"That's far more potent than before. This is like drinking youth itself."

"Yes, I've learned the trick of separating out the toxins so I can distill the potion to a much higher concentration, which greatly amplifies its effect and eliminates the side-effects you worried about before. The potion won't bring the dead back to life, mind, but it does an excellent job of revitalizing whatever absorbs it. Short of drinking from the Fount of Æternis itself, nothing could do more to hold death at bay. This small flacon should supply you for twenty years at least."

Balat corked the flacon, molded soft gold wax over the stopper to seal it tight, and tucked it back into its box. "As we agreed, I am including the recipe for making more." He displayed a folded card, the inside of which was scrawled with alchemical notes. After laying the card atop the flacon, he closed and latched the box with a flick of his thumb, then handed it to his friend.

Balat's guest immediately went to open the box, but the instant he touched the latch, bright yellow sparks shot out. Snatching back his smarting hand and shaking it against the shock he'd just received, he favored Balat with a scowl. "A protection spell?"

Balat smiled. His friend wasn't the only one with a suspicious nature. "Simply a bit of insurance. I am giving you the extract as a show of good faith. When I have what you promised, I'll send you the key to remove the spell. In the meantime, my servant here will bottle up the contents of the pitcher. That should be enough to last the summer."

His friend regarded him with open bitterness. "After all this time, I'm hardly likely to betray you, now am I?"

Mystral's most infamous slaver shrugged and gave another small charming smile. "Caution has always served me well. So, do we have a deal, my friend?"

Calivan Merimydion reached across the table to shake his hand. "We do. Before summer's end, the Seasons of Summerlea will be yours."

An hour after the sails of Calivan Merimydion's ship disappeared over the horizon, a new set of sails appeared, these from a ship approaching from the north. Balat dined on a succulent feast of lobster, saffron rice, grilled vegetables, and glistening fruit as he waited for the ship to draw near.

When it did, an enormous, scary brute leapt aboard and headed straight for the dining table, ignoring Balat's icy disapproval as he plopped down at the table and reached over to snatch a handful of grapes from the serving platter.

"You there." The man known as the Shark, Mystral's most feared pirate, snapped his fingers at one of Balat's servants and pointed to the empty tabletop before him. After a hesitant look to Balat—who nodded—the servant bustled off and returned a few seconds later with a fresh table setting for the pirate. "I received your message. I take it your friend decided to come through for you?"

"He did."

"We could do this without him, you know." As the Shark spoke, a parade of servants came by, offering a wide selection of fine delicacies from the sea and local farms. He helped himself to three large reef lobsters, a salad, spiced cucumbers, roasted taca root, and a bowl of warm, crusty rolls swimming in melted garlic butter. "That spell you taught me has been working well. We can take the Seasons without additional help."

"Perhaps, but I've done the calculations and consulted with my seers. Taking the Seasons without his help adds unnecessary risk. This is too important an opportunity for me to leave anything to chance. I want the Seasons spirited away without the slightest trail leading back to either of us or to any of my clients."

"The Winter King will suspect at least one of your clients. The Maak hasn't exactly been subtle in his pursuit of Autumn Coruscate."

"Suspicion is a far cry from certainty. Without proof, they won't dare start a war with the greatest military power on Mystral. And taking all three Seasons instead of just the one will help allay suspicions that would otherwise go naturally in the Maak's direction."

"And who would be the second person they'd suspect? I'm thinking Mystral's most infamous and influential slaver." The Shark gave Balat a pointed glance.

"True. But that's why I have you—to give them other, more inviting trails to follow."

"Hmm." The Shark pulled off the tail of largest of his lobsters and cracked the shell with a flex of his massive hand. Pulling out the succulent meat, he drowned it in the bowl of butter and consumed it in three large bites. "And once you have the Seasons, I get what I want?"

"As soon as my transactions for them are safely completed, I'll give you everything you need to destroy your enemies."

"Then we have a deal." The Shark shook back the long coils of his green-black hair and cracked one of the lobster claws with his teeth. "Shame those witches of yours can't whip up a scry spell for me. I'd give anything to see that *krillo* Merimydion's face when he discovers all three of his precious *oulani* princesses are gone."

Konumarr, Wintercraig

"Holy Halla, home of all good gods!" Summer muttered the mild curse beneath her breath and tried not to gape at seemingly endless mass of perfect male humanity striding boldly down the crowd-lined streets of Konumarr.

Yesterday, Gabriella had been telling the truth when she assured her sisters she wasn't the least bit nervous about the Calbernans coming to Konumarr, but today that same statement would have been a flat-out lie.

Beside her, Spring gave a stunned, wordless noise, while Autumn grabbed Summer's hand and whispered, "I know what you mean. I think I've died and gone to Halla."

The Calbernans had arrived. Fifteen ships full of men: a literal invasion force. Only this time, instead of being greeted with swords and arrows as they had this past winter, the invading Calbernans marched down the streets of Konumarr beneath a celebratory shower of flower petals.

Summer found herself shrinking back as the Calbernans, tall, dark, barbarically handsome, drew closer to Ragnar Square and the royal party that had assembled to greet them. She'd always found the Winterfolk intimidating, with their broad shoulders and towering forms, but the Calbernans were even more so.

They were practically naked, clad only in bright, embroidered cloths that wrapped around their trim waists and fell to mid-calf, fluttering open to reveal flashes of long, muscular legs as they walked. Each man sported a wide, jewel-encrusted belt, gleaming golden bands at their ankles and upper arms, and wide golden torques at their necks. All also sported iridescent blue tattoos that curled in curious patterns across their heavily muscled, hairless bodies, and all bore an iridescent blue tattoo that curled from the corner of their right eye across their right cheekbone. Their feet were bare. Their long, green-tinted black hair hung down their backs in springy ropes. Bells on their ankle bands chimed with each long-legged stride.

As if they needed chiming bells to draw anyone's attention! Good gods, a woman could be deaf, dumb, and blind, and still be drawn to the Calbernans like a moth to a flame.

Summer's stomach curled up tight. The Calbernans were shockingly primitive, their fierce, powerful, unrelenting maleness utterly and unsettlingly displayed for all to see. And try as she might, she could not tear her eyes from the biggest, strongest, handsomest of them all . . . their prince, Dilys Merimydion, Sealord of Calberna, son of the Calbernan *Myerial*, Alysaldria I.

He was huge. A few inches shorter than Khamsin's husband Wynter, but nearly half a head taller than almost every other Calbernan or Winterman. Power radiated from him, fierce and unmistakable.

And he was beautiful. She could think of no other word for it. The long ropes of his hair were a glossy black that glinted deep, mysterious green in the sunlight, framing a face that was breathtaking in its symmetry, strength, and uncompromising lines. From the firm blade of his nose to the full, sensually sculpted lips, to the strong jaw, high cheekbones, and the deep-set, mesmerizing eyes of a bright, glittering gold. Even the exotic tattoos that swirled across his burnished bronze skin were beautiful, swirling patterns that sparkled in the sun and drew attention to every impressively carved muscle in his arms, broad shoulders, massive chest, and taut, rippled abdomen. More tattoos circled his equally impressive legs, teasing her with flashes of shimmering blue and bronze each time he took a step.

His bright, golden eyes fell upon her, she blushed and looked away, embarrassed to be caught staring, but the moment she felt the intensity of his gaze move away from her, she hazarded another peek.

Sweet Halla preserve her. He was magnificent.

The red rose-shaped birthmark on her inner right wrist—proof of her royal Summerlea heritage—warmed and began to throb, pulsing with the accelerated beat of her heart. Beneath the many bright, jewel-toned layers of her sumptuous court gown, a fire sparked inside Summer's body, a hot, restless, hungry fire that burned hotter with every rhythmic stride of the Calbernan's long, flashing legs.

Calberna's prince was too big. Too male. Too unsettling. Too appealing. Too . . . everything. And for her, that made Dilys Merimydion pure, deadly poison wrapped up in a dangerously tempting package.

Summer Coruscate, the princess who could never allow herself to love, would choose a million lackluster Prince Rampions or consign herself to a life alone before she ever risked her heart and her sanity by wedding a man like Dilys Merimydion.

Leading the same army of *Calbernari* who had sailed with him to conquer Wintercraig and Summerlea, Dilys strode boldly down the streets of Konumarr to a much different welcome than the one they'd received only a little over six months ago.

Instead of swords and arrows and armed defenders, the city was decked out for a celebration. The streetlamps were twined with garlands of greenery and blossoms, and festooned with ribbons of ice blue, white, and deep, rich rose. Wreaths and blossoms hung from every door and window. Wintercraig flags—the white wolf's head on a field of ice blue—waved at every doorway. And every plaza had been transformed into a feast hall set with massive wooden tables and chairs. The aroma of roasted meats and vegetables filled the air.

Winterfolk and Summerlanders alike lined the way four and five deep, and it pleased Dilys immensely to note that women and children outnumbered the men ten to one. They watched the Calbernans march past with wide eyes, and more than a few of the younger women nudged each other, blushing and giggling behind their hands the way girls often did when trying to catch the eye of a handsome man. That pleased Dilys as well. It was good to know his men would find a warm welcome here among the ladies of this land.

He knew the men following behind him were casting their own gazes across the potential wives gathered for the next three months of courtship—all while also keeping a careful eye on the heavily armed and armored Wintercraig guards stationed along the procession route, of course.

As per the conditions of his negotiated agreement with Queen Khamsin of Wintercraig, not one of the Calbernans carried a weapon, but no Calbernan—even unarmed—was truly vulnerable. They carried protection with them in their bones—the sharp, deadly battle claws and teeth, currently hidden from view but ready to snap into lethal place at a moment's notice. And that was the least of their natural defenses.

Dilys eyed the deep, cold waters of the fjord that ran alongside the procession route all the way back to the enormous palace built into the steep mountainside. The brave young Winter Queen had either been very wise or very foolish in choosing this spot for the Calbernan's visit. Where there were large quantities of water, be it river, lake, or ocean, Calbernans would always hold the upper hand. Dilys even more than most, bearing his mother's great gifts inside him as he now did.

As much as he liked Khamsin of the Storms, Dilys hadn't survived a lifetime of mercenary work by being a gullible fool. If today ended up being an ambush rather than a warm reception, blood would flow like wine.

It wouldn't all be Calbernan blood, either.

When none of the Wintercraig guards drew a blade, he concluded that wisdom had guided the young queen, choosing the location specifically to put Dilys and his men at ease. And in that, she succeeded. Their procession to Konumarr Palace proceeded without incident, and though not as raucous as they might have been for their own kind, the gathered throngs cheered the Calbernans as they marched past.

He supposed that shouldn't surprise him as much as it

did. Dilys and his men had, after all, helped defeat the Ice King and his dreadful army.

The city's main street led to a wide plaza that Dilys's Wintercraig handler informed him was called Ragnar Square, and there, the procession stopped. Only Dilys and his officers crossed the plaza to approach the blossom-and-vine-festooned landing where Wintercraig's royal family and Dilys's future bride awaited.

Dilys let his gaze roam with undisguised appreciation over the three Seasons gathered just behind Wintercraig's king and queen.

The reports and artists' renditions of the three dark Summerlander princesses had not done them justice. Each one of them was beautiful beyond words, with dark, silky skin, big, thickly-lashed eyes, and full, shapely lips made for passionate kisses. Each wore form-fitting, jewel-toned gowns in shimmering silks that exactly matched the color of their eyes.

Two of the Seasons—the auburn-haired beauty, Autumn, and Spring—watched his approach with bold, unflinching gazes. The third, a lovely, blushing *myerina* with tumbling waves of blue-black curls spilling about her shoulders, was more shy. She hung back between her sisters, watched him with wide, shocked blue eyes when she thought he wasn't looking, then hurriedly glanced away from him whenever he tried to meet her gaze. That would be the little honeyrose, then. The sweet, sunny-tempered Season called Summer, beloved for her exceedingly kind heart and gentle ways.

He returned his attention to the two Seasons the Bridehunters had approved for him. Though he hadn't believed it until just now, the odes to Autumn Coruscate's beauty were no exaggerations. If anything, they did not do justice to her vibrant, stunning perfection. She was entirely exotic and utterly intoxicating. From her pansy-purple eyes and long, extravagant curls of deep auburn hair that reminded him of a spectacular ocean sunset, to the lush curves displayed to perfection in her deep amethyst gown. The fact that she was watching him with undisguised interest bode well for the coming months of courtship.

Although Spring—the princess the Bridehunters had decided would be the best match for him—did not possess quite the same jaw-dropping exquisiteness of the youngest Season, she was still any man's definition of lovely. Her eyes a clear, piercing green, her hair a long, straight fall of inky silk that draped down to her waist, her body slender and shapely. Best of all, in Dilys's opinion, was her cool, bold, challenging stare.

Calbernans didn't fear a woman's strength. They celebrated it. Admired it. Wed it, if they were lucky enough. There was no greater treasure than a bold, brave, fearless wife who would pass on that bold, brave, fearless blood to her daughters and sons.

Just looking at her, Dilys could tell Spring would give him one Hel of a chase before he claimed her. Of course, she would think the claiming was all her idea, and he would be pleased to let her think so. He smiled broadly at the thought.

Dilys crossed the final distance of the plaza and came to a halt before the raised dais. His captains and their officers filed in to fill the space behind him, while the remainder of his men stood in neat formation in the main road.

The Winterman who had met Dilys at the docks to instruct him and his men on the protocols of the day now stepped forward and swept a deep bow to his king and queen.

"Your Graces, I present to you the Sealord Dilys Merimydion, son of the *Myerial* Alysaldria I, Lord Protector of Calberna, Keeper of the Golden Isle of Cali Kai Meri, Admiral of the First Fleet, Commander of the Seadragons, the most celebrated battlegroup of the Calbernan Navy, and Captain of the *Kracken,* flagship of the Seadragons."

Dilys stood proud as his titles rolled off the tongue of the Winterman announcing him. When the introduction was concluded, he put his right fist across his left breast and bent slightly at the waist, keeping his head high, his gaze fixed on the Winter King. To bow deeply was to expose one's neck, to offer vulnerability in a gesture of both trust and submission. Dilys and his men bowed that way to no man.

"Sealord Merimydion." Wynter of the Craig, the White King, returned Dilys's greeting with a nod of his own. "Six months ago you came to these shores as invaders, but today, my queen and I welcome you and your men to Wintercraig as honored guests. It is our hope that this day should mark the beginning of a long and prosperous friendship between our two nations." The Winter King's ice-blue eyes were cold and steady. A flurry of white swirled in those eyes, and the air around Dilys grew instantly frigid.

Most men—especially those dressed as lightly as Dilys and his *Calbernari*—would have turned blue with cold and begun shivering. But Calbernans, who lived and swam in all the depths of every ocean on the planet, were arguably the hardiest race in all of Mystral. They could regulate the temperature of their blood, and beneath their bronze skin grew a thin layer of insulating flesh that kept them cool in summer and warm even in the iciest depths of the sea.

So, as the temperature around him plummeted, Dilys's body reacted instinctively, blood heating to counteract the effects of the cold. All the while, he held Wynter Atrialan's gaze without fear. A small smiled played at the edges of his mouth.

He understood what was going on. The Winter King was just making sure Dilys knew that, though the Ice King had been defeated, the infamous power of the Ice Gaze was still Wynter Atrialan's to call upon.

He inclined his head in acknowledgment of the warning. The snow faded from the Winter King's gaze, and the air warmed again swiftly.

"Peace and friendship between our lands is my hope

and the hope of the *Myerial* as well, Wynter of the Craig,"
Dilys replied. His gaze fell upon the small, dark beauty
standing beside Wintercraig's king, and his small smile
spread to an open grin of appreciation. She was resplen-
dent in pale buttercup yellow, the mound of her advanced
pregnancy clearly in evidence.

To her, he bowed deeply, an elegant, respectful, admiring sweep, and bared his neck. "And you, Queen Khamsin.
Love and motherhood suit you even better than bravery
and battle. You are exquisite. *Doa akua,* your husband, is
a lucky man."

"Thank you, Sealord Merimydion." Wintercraig's young
queen smiled, even as the husband at her side gave Dilys a
dark, suspicious look and edged closer to his wife.

Just to prick the Winter King in retaliation for his earlier icy warning, Dilys held his warm, deeply admiring
glance a few seconds longer. Then he drew back, becoming all business as he introduced his fellow captains and
their first officers.

"This handsome fellow is my cousin Arilon Calmyria,
descendant of the great *Myerial* Siesulania V, Keeper of
White Bay and the Sister Isles, Fleet Commander of the
Stormriders, and Captain of the *Orca*." Dilys and Ari
could easily have been twins, they looked so alike. The
only truly notable difference between them, besides Dilys's
slightly more impressive collection of tattoos, was that Ari
stood three inches shorter than Dilys.

Ari bent slightly to Wynter, then gave a full, sweeping
bow of Calbernan respect to Khamsin. As he rose, he met
her gaze, his eyes sparkled with even more deep admiration and masculine appreciation than Dilys had shown for
her womanly gifts.

"It is my pleasure indeed, Queen Khamsin of the Storms,
to make your acquaintance." Ari spoke in a sensual purr,
his voice set on full simmer. "My cousin's considerable
praise these last months did not do you justice." In last
winter's invasion, Ari had remained with the ships just

off the coast of Wintercraig, protecting the beachhead and the invaders' flank while Dilys and his men met up with Falcon; thus Ari had not fought the Ice King nor met Khamsin.

Khamsin's cheeks turned a dusky rose as Ari focused his considerable charms on her. "The . . . ah . . . pleasure is mine, Sealord Calmyria," she replied in a somewhat breathless voice. A faint growl rose in Wynter's throat, which only made Ari's warm smile widen and grow warmer.

Dilys gave him a subtle kick in the ankle as he moved to introduce the next Calbernan nobles who had accompanied him up to the terrace. "And this fine son of the sea is my cousin Ryllian Ocea, descendent of the *Myerial* Kailuani III, Keeper of Silversands Isle, Fleet Commander of the Wavedancers, and Captain of the *Narwhal*." Ryll was as dangerous and fearsome a Calbernan as they came, as well as being a master sailor who could steer a galleon through rocky shoals in a dense fog without receiving the tiniest scratch on the hull of his vessel. He had an uncanny sense of waves and currents and exactly how they would react at any given time. Dilys could control the seas, but Ryll could become them.

Though Ryll could be every bit as provocative as Ari or Dilys, he'd obviously decided they'd pulled the wolf's tail enough. He bent his spine to Wynter, bowed deeply to Khamsin, but kept his considerable masculine charms under tight wraps as Dilys continued to introduce the rest of their fellow captains and first officers.

"Welcome, Sealords," Khamsin said with a smile when he was done, "and it is my pleasure to introduce you to my sisters, the Seasons of Summerlea. Their Royal Highnesses, the Princesses Spring, Summer, and Autumn Coruscate."

"*Myerialannas,*" Dilys let his expression show his profound appreciation for each of them. "It is with great joy I greet you." He tried—and failed—to catch the little honeyrose's eye, but the other two met his gaze and nodded their acknowledgement of his greeting.

"Sealord," said Spring, her tone as cool as a frosty morning.

"Sealord." The exotic Autumn arched one haughty brow and looked down her slender nose.

He grinned at them both.

"Sealord," whispered Summer, her eyes fixed upon his Adam's apple.

She really wasn't much smaller than her other sisters, he realized. She was just so slender and slightly built that, coupled with her timid demeanor, she seemed much more delicate and fragile. And he clearly made her nervous. The pulse in her neck was fluttering like a trapped bird, and she was doing everything in her power not to attract his attention.

Taking pity on her, he turned his attention back to Wintercraig's young queen. Now here was a woman who had proved her mettle in every way possible. Had she not already been wed and to a man she loved when they first met six months ago—he would not have left Wintercraig without her.

"It is our pleasure to welcome you and your men as our guests for the next three months," Khamsin said. "Sealord Merimydion, as we discussed in our previous communications, we have prepared accommodations in the palace for you and your officers. Are you certain you prefer the rest of your men to remain quartered on your ships?"

"I do." It seemed wiser. His men had, after all, last come to Wintercraig as invaders. Keeping them aboard ship at night seemed the safer course, in case any of the Winterfolk held a grudge. He did not want violence to mar this opportunity for him and his men to find *lianas* and forge ties with Wintercraig.

"Very good. The folk of Konumarr have prepared a celebration to welcome you and your men to Wintercraig. Sealord Merimydion, if you will come this way to help us start the festivities." She turned to her husband and held out her hand. Together, with Dilys beside them, they walked to the edge of terrace overlooking the city.

They looked out over the gathered throngs of Calbernans, Winterfolk, and Summerlanders, and in a carrying voice, Wynter began to speak. "Six months ago, Sealord Dilys Merimydion of Calberna and the men accompanying him today came to the shores of our kingdom. They came as invaders, unaware that Rorjak the Ice King had arisen. But Queen Khamsin, wise and brave beyond her years, convinced the Sealord and his men to fight with us rather than against us. Thanks to our queen's wisdom, courage, and weathergifts, the bravery of our own people, and the Calbernans' renowned skill in battle, the Ice King was defeated. Together, Winterfolk and Calbernans— led by Queen Khamsin and this man, Sealord Dilys Merimydion—saved me, saved Wintercraig, and saved the whole of Mystral."

A raucous cheer went up, and this time there was no doubting the genuine enthusiasm sent up by Winterfolk, Summerlanders, and Calbernans alike.

"In thanks, we have invited the Calbernans who participated in that victory to return today and live among us for the next three months as trusted friends. It is the custom of Calbernan men to seek wives from among the women of other lands, and the privilege of courting wives from those of you willing to entertain the possibility of such a union was one of the tokens of gratitude Queen Khamsin agreed to in return for the Calbernans vital assistance in defeating the Ice King."

Now Khamsin stepped forward, and her voice rang out, carrying on a controlled breeze. "For the next three months, these men will live among us. Use this time to get to know them. Wedding a foreigner, leaving your home and all that you know is a big decision, not to be undertaken lightly. Take your time. Make the choice that is right for you, but make it freely. To wed or not is your decision."

"My queen is absolutely right," Wynter added in a firm voice. "These men were guaranteed three months to court a wife, not the certainty that they would find one. If any of you feel pressured in any way, come to me or the Queen immediately, and we will put a stop to it." His hard gaze swept over the Calbernan horde.

Standing beside Wynter, Dilys arched a brow, amused rather than offended by the suggestion that a Calbernan would ever need forceful means to win his *liana*. If a woman was unattached and in possession of a pulse, she would not long remain unwilling in the face of a determined Calbernan's courtship.

"Above all," Wynter continued, "know that whatever you choose, you will always have a home here. There is work, food, and shelter in Wintercraig or Summerlea for any woman or child who desires it. Those of you who choose to wed and leave, know that you go to Calberna with our blessing. And to any Calbernan who takes a wife from among the citizens of Summerlea or Wintercraig, know that should you so desire, you would be welcome to stay here, with your wife, as a citizen of this kingdom."

Dilys kept his easy smile. No true Calbernan would abandon his homeland to become *oulani*. Calberna was built on the devotion of its sons and the strength of its women. And while fate had necessitated that most sons of Calberna find their mates from among the other peoples of Mystral, a Calbernan and his *liana* returned to Calberna—always.

Khamsin glanced up at him. "Sealord? Would you like to add a few words of your own?"

He nodded and stepped up to the balustrade to address the crowd. "First, I wish to thank King Wynter and his brave and gracious *liana,* Queen Khamsin, for their kind welcome. My men and I look forward to our time among you, and to returning to Calberna in three months' time with *lianas* of our own by our sides. My men are well capable of speaking for themselves, but on their behalf—and

my own—I will just say this. In Calberna, our women—
all women—are treasured. A Calberna's devotion to his
liana is unwavering and eternal. Your joy is our joy. Your
happiness and comfort our sacred duty. No woman has
ever regretted taking a Calbernan to mate, nor ever will.
The decision to wed is your choice, but if your choice
is to wed a Calbernan"—he turned to direct his last words
to the Seasons, and for the first time caught gentle Summer's startled blue gaze full-on—"you will never make a
better one."

Her eyes were like the clearest waters. A pure, deep,
sparkling blue, shimmering with light and warmth and inviting waves. They called to him, those eyes, as surely as
the sea itself, and for one instant, the world fell away and
he was diving deep and fast, into endless, magical, beautiful blue. In that instant, he felt a perfect peace, a sense of
rightness he couldn't explain. Like finding home after a
lifetime of wandering.

A loud wave of sound crashed over him, dragging him
back to the surface, to reality. He sucked in air, as breathless as if he truly had dived deep, and turned to see the
crowds cheering, and the celebration begun.

Queen Khamsin was saying something. He frowned
and tried to focus his rattled brain into some semblance
of coherent thought.

"—a feast prepared for you and your officers at the
palace." She waved a hand towards the wide stone bridge
that crossed the fjord to the sprawling palace on the northern shore.

He forced a smile. What had she said? Something about
following her to a feast? She was looking at him expec-
tantly, her body half turned as if to leave. He took a step,
and knew he'd chosen correctly when she smiled, took her
husband's arm, and began to lead the way.

He glanced back at the Seasons, but where there had
been three, only two remained.

Summer was gone.

* * *

Summer Sun!

Gabriella leaned against the cool stone wall, behind a stack of boxes piled in a shadowed alley off Ragnar Square, and pressed a hand against her frantically beating heart.

What in Helos's name had just happened? The Calbernan had turned unexpectedly and caught her gaze upon him and then . . .

She dragged in a breath, then another. Ragged. Shaken. She couldn't even begin to describe what had happened. It was as if, with one look, he'd dived into the deepest, most secret parts of her soul, places no one—not even she— had ever been.

Then he was gone, as abruptly as he'd come, and now there was something inside her that hadn't been there before. An empty, aching void. As if part of her was missing. A part that *he* had taken—and that only he could give back.

Shivering, hot and cold all at once, she wrapped her arms around her waist.

Was it possible he'd worked some sort of enchantment on her? Would he dare? Had he just stood beside her sister and her sister's husband, agreed that all women would have the freedom to choose whether to take a Calbernan husband, and then cast some sort of spell on her to make her want him so desperately?

As soon as the last thought formed in her mind, she laughed at her own absurdity. Why would she assume he'd taken one look at her and decided she was the one he wanted, through fair means or foul? When she was surrounded by her two far more desirable sisters?

No. No, it was much more likely that the shocking sensation that had swept over her when their eyes met was a product of her own imagination and her astonishingly powerful attraction to him.

She'd never in her life looked at a man and felt like a

starving beggar standing before a sumptuous feast. She'd all but licked her lips at the sight of him! Even now, just the thought of all that bronze, shimmering, tattooed skin, corded muscles flexing with the slightest movement, made hot blood pool in every one of her womanly parts.

One thing was certain. She could never—ever—allow herself to be alone with him. Helos only knew what she might do.

"Summer?"

The sound of Spring's voice made Summer jump and leap out from her hiding spot.

Her older sister regarded her with concern. "Are you all right, dearest?"

"I'm fine."

"It's just that you disappeared so abruptly." Cool, too-observant eyes did a short but thorough scan, not missing the hectic color in Summer's flushed cheeks. "Are you not feeling well, sweeting? Should I summon Tildy?"

"No!" Sweet Halla, the last thing Summer wanted was their childhood nurse, Tildavera Greenleaf, examining her. The canny old woman had an unnerving knack for divining exactly what ailed a person.

Aware that her protest was more a bit too forceful, Summer smoothed her hair back off her face and forced her nerves to calm. "No," she said again in a much more subdued voice. "I'm fine. Something from breakfast didn't entirely agree with me, but I'm already much better." The lie fell easily from her lips, and she dragged her customary serene mask firmly back into place. "We'd better get going before our suitor thinks we've run off."

"I doubt he's even noticed our absence." Spring's mouth quirked. "Autumn is with him."

Somehow, Summer managed to summon a grin and a laugh. That seemed to allay any of Spring's remaining suspicions, and the pair of them walked arm in arm back to the palace, hanging back a far enough distance from

Calberna's prince that Summer managed to get her panic under control.

As they walked, Konumarr City came alive with music and laughter and took on a carnival-like atmosphere. Jugglers, acrobats, fire dancers, and musicians took to the streets, providing entertainment from every corner and plaza. Already, scores of women bold enough to mingle with the Calbernans found themselves surrounded by openly admiring men, each vying for attention. Summer watched a brave child approach one of the men and reached out to touch his shimmering blue tattoos. When he knelt down to show them off, a dozen children and almost as many young women flocked round. People were smiling, food and alc was flowing. The ice had been broken.

The reception Khamsin and Wynter were hosting across the fjord in the palace's western gardens was slightly more subdued than the celebrations of the city, but no less welcoming. A small orchestra played from a candlelit grotto, tables overflowed with the bounty of Summerlea and Wintercraig, and scores of nobles, wealthy merchants, and tradesmen, as well as unattached ladies of both noble and gentle birth had gathered to make the acquaintance of Calberna's officers.

Summer's gaze scanned the gathered throng, stopping as it passed over one particular Calbernan. His back was to her, but she knew it was him. The long, greenish-black ropes of his hair hung down his back, drawing her eyes to his muscled shoulders, the line of his spine that disappeared into the flowing skirt belted at his trim waist. Her belly began to flutter. Her skin felt flushed. She drew a shuddering breath.

"Vivi?"

"Yes, Gabriella?"

"Do you think we could convince them to start wearing actual clothes?"

Spring laughed.

CHAPTER 4

The little honeyrose was avoiding him.

Standing alone in the shadows, Dilys surveyed the torchlit beauty of the palace's terraced western gardens. It was midnight. The sun had set an hour or so ago, though its light was still a glow on the horizon, and the reception was in full swing. Music was playing. Food and drink flowed without any sign of cessation. His officers were clearly enjoying themselves, and even though here at the palace, they weren't as outnumbered by potential *lianas* as their brothers across the fjord, there was no shortage of engaging feminine companionship.

Wintercraig's years of war had left their share of widows even among its gently-bred and noble families.

Truth be told, Dilys was still surprised by the warmth of their reception. The Calbernans had, after all, landed on these shores last winter as enemy combatants. But so far as he'd been able to tell, none of the women who had gathered here at the palace had lost a loved one to a Calbernan blade or trident. He was grateful for that. War was war, and the price of it dear, but joy would be elusive in any marriage where one party had suffered grief on account of the other.

That made Dilys wonder if perhaps the little honeyrose was avoiding him because she blamed him for her father's death. The garm—not the Calbernans—had slain King Verdan, but maybe she thought that without the Calbernans and their army to aid him, there would have been no rebellion, and therefore the king would still be alive.

Or perhaps she begrudged him the contract he'd broken with her brother, Falcon. Summerlea's prince had spoken fondly of all his sisters—but most especially of the gentle-hearted one he'd called "our sweet Summer Rose." Perhaps they'd shared a close-knit bond. Maybe she had wanted her father and brother to take back their homeland, and blamed Dilys for Falcon's exile.

Whatever her reason for avoiding him, her sisters didn't share the sentiment—or at least were much better at hiding it, if they did.

Autumn had started off a bit haughty and distant. He'd expected that. A woman as beautiful as she was undoubtedly used to men fawning over her, so he'd made a point of approaching her not as a man dazzled by her beauty but as a boon companion. And once he'd discovered her love of food and laughter, indulging her with both had brought her barriers down.

Spring was a tougher nut to crack. Every bit as cool and keenly intellectual as the reports on her had stated, she wasn't easily charmed. But Dilys didn't mind a challenge. After spending perhaps an hour in her company—during which he'd talked to her mostly about several papers she'd written on agricultural techniques and a new breed of pest-resistant crops—he'd taken his leave and wandered off to mingle with the other guests. His departure had surprised her as much as his choice of conversation, and he'd felt her eyes on him numerous times since. Mission accomplished.

The little honeyrose, however, remained elusive. He'd caught glimpses of her as the night progressed, but whenever he tried to make his way to her location, she was always gone before he got there. Now, instead of trying to seek her out, he found a quiet, sheltered spot that provided him an excellent view of the gardens and observed from the shadows as she worked her way through the gathered throng.

As he watched, he could see how naturally people responded to her, their smiles genuine, their expressions gentling when she was near. Occasionally someone would say something that made her soft laughter burst forth. When it did, she lit up, her joy incandescent, and people gravitated towards her even more readily, moths orbiting a radiant flame.

His own men weren't any more immune to her effortless charm than the Winterfolk. Every time she stopped to smile and chat with one of them, their spines straightened and their chests swelled from the attention she lavished upon them.

His men's reaction wasn't what surprised him. Calbernans thrived on feminine attention. It was the sweetest food for the soul. What surprised him was how much he resented his men for being the recipients of Summer Coruscate's attention.

If he didn't know better, he'd say he was jealous, but of course, that was ridiculous. His planned "courtship" of King Verdan's gentlest daughter was to be nothing more than a polite pretense. As such, her obvious desire to avoid him should have been a welcome relief—one less distraction to interfere with his determined pursuit of the regal Princess Spring or the beautiful Princess Autumn. And yet, the more Summer Coruscate smiled and charmed his men, the more she poured her bright incandescence upon them while blatantly denying him even the tiniest fraction of her regard, the tenser and more irritated he became.

He told himself he should let it go and just stay clear of her. Yet when he watched her wander to the edge of the crowd, then slip away when she thought no one was looking, Dilys followed.

The garden paths were illuminated with lanterns, but Gabriella kept to the shadows, preferring the peaceful anonymity of darkness as she walked down the hill to the shores of the Llaskroner Fjord. The moon was a large, silvery crescent in the sky, its light glittering on the night-dark waters, and the relative silence as the raucous sounds of merriment faded soothed her ragged nerves.

All evening long, she'd been acutely aware of Dilys Merimydion's presence, almost as if there were some sort of invisible thread connecting them, tugging at her and setting her senses trembling each time he drew near.

Keeping her distance had proven shockingly difficult. The Calbernans were every bit as charming and amusing as they were reputed to be, and that was doubly—nay, triply, quadruply!—true for their leader. Everything about him appealed to her. When he spoke, the low, rich timbre of his voice made her pulse pound. When he laughed, the sound sank into her skin, and the flame that lived at her core flared bright and hot and hungry. And when he'd bent his head to murmur something to Autumn or Spring . . . sweet Helos, she'd actually been jealous . . . *jealous*! Of her own beloved sisters! Over a man she'd barely even met.

She'd never felt anything like it, and she couldn't explain it. She must have spoken to at least a hundred Calbernan officers this evening, and not a single one of them—not even Ari Calmyria, who was the spitting image of his cousin Dilys—affected her even remotely the same way. Oh, the Calbernans were all handsome and charming enough, to be sure, but they didn't set her blood to simmering just by breathing the same air.

The only upside to her bewildering hypersensitivity to Dilys Merimydion was that she'd known exactly where he was the entire night. That allowed her to take evasive maneuvers each time she sensed him heading her direction.

That small boon notwithstanding, the whole evening had left her nerves rattled, her serenity shattered. Hence, the solitary walk to the fjord by way of the garden's quietest, most shadow-kissed tracts.

The terrace on the shores of the fjord was raised about eight feet above water level, with stone steps curling down on either side to a stone landing and the wooden pier that jetted out into the fjord. A dozen small boats were moored along the pier, including three small sailboats. Pleasure craft that had been brought out of dry dock for the enjoyment of the court, in case they or the Calbernan officers should desire to row or sail on the fjord.

Summer walked to the end of the pier, scowling a little at the piles of coiled ropes and anchors that had been carelessly left lying near the pier's edge. She knew the workers were still bringing boats out of dry dock, and giving each a thorough refitting as they did, but honestly, couldn't they have cleaned up their workspace at the end of the day? This was a hazardous mess.

She planted a slippered foot against one of the abandoned anchors and shoved it closer to the edge of the pier to give herself more room, when a voice announced from behind:

"It is a beautiful night."

The sound of Dilys Merimydion's already all-too-familiar voice made Summer jump and whirl around. One foot slid into the pile of coiled rope, and she had to fight to keep her balance.

How he had managed to sneak up on her without her notice when she'd been so acutely aware of his every move all night? She didn't know how or why her hypersensitivity to him had failed her, but there he was, standing at the other end of the pier.

Just as it had all evening, her heart began to race.

"Forgive me, *myerina*," he said. "I didn't mean to startle you."

No, just to intrude on my privacy, she thought sourly.

When the Calbernan froze for an instant, looking taken aback, a tide of red-hot mortification flooded her cheeks.

Merciful gods! Had she just said that out loud?

She *had*!

"Forgive me," she muttered. It was one thing to avoid a guest of the king. It was another to be rude outright. As a royal princess and a ward of the crown, her behavior reflected directly on Wintercraig's king and queen. "It's been a very long day."

Instead stomping off in a fit of offended male pride as many other suitors would have, the Calbernan prince merely lifted his brows. Then the corner of his mouth curled up in a wry smile. "So you *have* been deliberately avoiding me all evening. I thought it could be no accident."

Under normal circumstances, when safely tucked behind one of her usual masks, Gabriella could have managed a smooth response that gave nothing away. Instead, being flustered, she snapped, "You didn't seem to be lacking for company," then wished the ground would open up and swallow her when Dilys's smile deepened.

"Ah, *myerina* . . . I'm flattered that you noticed. It is true your countrywomen have made my men and I feel very welcome, but those women are not the ones I sailed halfway around Mystral to court."

He had to know just how dazzling his smile was, all those straight white teeth and those gleaming gold eyes, such a vivid contrast against his bronze Calbernan skin. He was probably used to getting his way in all things. Flash that smile and those eyes, flex those impressive muscles, and most women would fall like ninepins.

He began to walk down the pier, closing the distance between them. With his every step, she became increasingly aware of his height, his beauty, the essence of fierce maleness that wafted off him like steam from a kettle. And of course, all those hard, rippling muscles flexing beneath the acres of warm, dark, satiny skin displayed so disturbingly by his scanty Calbernan attire. The iridescent sheen of his blue tattoos shone with an otherworldly beauty in the moonlight, as if he'd been sprinkled with stardust. The sight was strangely and strongly compelling.

She dragged her gaze away before her eyes followed the glimmering pattern of those tattoos to places she didn't want to go. Everything about this man was dangerous to her, and since avoiding him didn't seem to be working, it was time to try something a little more straightforward.

"Please, Sealord, let's be honest with one another. You didn't sail halfway around Mystral to court *me* either. You came to court my sisters."

That stopped him. Truth often had a way of doing that to a man. But she had to confess, this time it hurt a little to know he was no different from the others.

"Why would you say that?" he asked.

"Seriously?" She rolled her eyes. "Do you know how many men have come to court the Seasons of Summerlea? Spring did the math last week. Seven hundred and ninety-two. You make seven hundred and ninety-three. Kings, emperors, princes, dukes, nobles and sons of nobles, even the occasional merchant king, anyone with wealth, power, or an ancient name. Autumn's the Season most of them come for. She is the most beautiful, after all. The suitors who value intellect over beauty come for Spring."

His head tilted to one side. His golden eyes gleamed in the moonlight.

"And who is it that comes for you?" he asked softly.

Gabriella could have kicked herself. She wasn't usually so careless with her tongue. Or so honest.

"That wasn't an invitation for pity," she snapped. "And it wasn't a solicitation for your attention, either," she added quickly, lest he decide she was a wallflower in need of care.

But he wasn't watching her with pity or with the look of a man whose impeccable manners or innate generosity demanded that no person in his sphere feel slighted. Instead, he was regarding her with an expression she could only define as *thoughtful*.

Oh, no. No, no, no, no. No.

She was not going to be "interesting" to him. She was not going to be a puzzle he felt compelled to solve. She was not going to be anything to him at all except that third Season he didn't really notice or think about.

Summer Coruscate! Get your head on straight, and send this man away! Right now!

"Sealord Merimydion—"

"Dilys," he interrupted.

"*Sealord Merimydion,*" she repeated with a warning look, "I invite you most wholeheartedly to concentrate your courtship on Their Royal Highnesses Spring and Autumn. I'm quite sure neither is opposed to entertaining a match with Calberna's prince."

He took a step forward. "And Her Royal Highness, the *Myerialanna* Summer?"

His eyes truly were the most amazing gold. Almost metallic. Glittering with light.

She swallowed hard and took an instinctive step back.

Unfortunately, she'd forgotten two facts: (1) that her right foot was still tangled in the coils of rope, and (2) that she was standing very close to the edge of the pier.

Thanks to the foot tangled in the rope, she lost her balance. And thanks to her proximity to the edge of the pier, when she hopped further backward on her unencumbered leg in an attempt to catch her balance, she found all but the very tip of her slipper landed not on solid wood planking but insubstantial ether.

Arms windmilling furiously and entirely ineffectively, Gabriella gave a startled shriek and fell backward into the fjord.

The coils tangled around Summer's ankle went taut, and the anchor that earlier she'd shoved close to the edge of the pier toppled into the water after her.

The next thing Summer knew, she and the coils of rope and the anchor were plummeting rapidly towards the bottom of the fjord.

The shock of her fall and the breathtaking cold of the water left Gabriella stunned for a moment, then the need to breathe snapped her to her senses. Her instinctive scream when she'd fallen left her with barely any air in her lungs. Kicking and flailing, she tried to swim back up to the surface, but the anchor tied to her ankle proved too heavy. Instead of going up, she continued to sink deeper.

There was a splash overhead as something big hit the surface. She paid it no mind. Her entire being was focused on freeing herself from the anchor that was dragging her to her death. Her lungs began to burn as the need to breathe became dire.

She tore at the rough, swollen rope tangled around her ankle, but the weight of the anchor kept the knots tight. Desperate, she grabbed the rope a little below her ankle in an attempt to relieve the tension so she could loosen the knots and get free.

When something grabbed her, what little air she still retained in her lungs left in an instinctive shriek that sent up a flood of rapidly rising bubbles. Water poured into her mouth and throat. She coughed. More water flooded in, and a few seconds later the strangest sense of calm washed over her.

Dimly, she realized she was drowning, but she couldn't move her arm or legs anymore. She also realized the "thing" that had grabbed her was Dilys Merimydion, who must have dived in after her.

He caught her arm and tugged. When she didn't move, it took him half a second to realize her predicament. He didn't try to unravel the knots tying her to the anchor, he simply swiped a hand down below her feet, and the weight of the anchor disappeared.

As he spun back around and reached out to grab her, his left wrist slid across her right. The red rose birthmark on her inner wrist—proof of her royal Summerlea heritage—flared with sudden, almost explosive heat, and the tattoos inked across Dilys Merimydion's body lit up with a bright, blue phosphorescent glow that illuminated him, her, and the dark water around them.

His gaze, wide, shocked, golden, bored into hers as their weightless bodies went rigid in the cold depths.

The edges of Gabriella's vision went blurry, and the world went dark.

The next thing she knew, she was lying flat on her back on the wooden pier. Dilys Merimydion was crouched over her, crooning, and what seemed like a veritable ocean of water poured out of her throat as he literally sang the water out of her lungs. A moment later, he placed his lips against hers and blew into her a breath that tingled with warmth and potent magic, and every nerve and cell of her body came roaring back to electric, wildly pulsating life.

When he pulled back, she drew in a long, shuddering breath of her own and stared up into his dark bronze face. His tattoos were alive with otherwordly beauty, the whorls and patterns emitting a phosphorescent glow, as if blue starlight danced across his skin. The stylized wave that curled from the corner of his eye across the crest of his cheekbone seemed to ripple like the surface of the water.

Despite their recent swim, he was completely dry and so, she realized, was she. Her hair was a mess, pins lost, curls spilled out around her, but every bit of her was perfectly dry.

Calbernans, it seemed, were masters of more than just the waters of the world's oceans.

He was still crouched over her. All that smooth, delicious skin a scant arm length away, fragrant with decadent, tropical aromas and earthy richness that not even their unplanned plunge into the fjord had been able to wash away. Did he always smell thusly? Good enough to eat? Her tongue hungered for a taste and her palms itched to flatten against the swell of his pectoral muscles, to discover if his skin felt as delicious as it smelled.

"Are you all right?"

His voice was low, husky, rough in all the right ways. She shuddered as every feminine muscle in her body clenched tight. Her fingers flexed.

Don't touch him! Don't touch him! For Halla's sake, Summer, don't touch him!

She wet her suddenly parched lips. "F-fine. I'm fine," she somehow managed to stammer. Sweet Helos! Dilys Merimydion wasn't just a terrible danger to her; he was a potently appealing poison she longed to consume. Every moment he sat there, crouched over her, edged her closer to the abyss.

He reached for her right hand, ran a thumb over the slightly raised rose-shaped, red birthmark on her inner wrist, then turned over his own left wrist to reveal a golden, trident-shaped mark.

It was not uncommon in Mystral for children of a particularly gifted—usually royal—bloodline to bear proof of that gift on their inner wrists. Females were born with the mark of their birthright on their right wrist. Males on their left. Wynter, Khamsin's husband, for instance, bore a white wolf on his inner left wrist.

Summer had never given her Rose a second thought, except when it grew hot and warned her of an impending breech of her inner barriers. But she recalled something odd happening at Wynter and Khamsin's wedding. Something powerful and elemental when their marks met.

Something not too unlike what had just happened in the water between Dilys and herself.

Something, Khamsin had admitted to her sisters in a giggling afternoon of girl talk, that still happened between them in private moments with the most scandalously delicious results. She had decided it was some sort of proof of compatibility between mates—sort of a divine confirmation that "this is the one for you"—as well as a little extra "oomph" to help certain things along, she confessed with rosy cheeks.

Intrigued, Spring had insisted on conducting a series of preliminary experiments to test the theory. Nothing happened when the sisters touched their marks to one another. Nor had anything happened when Spring "inadvertently" brushed her mark against Wynter's. Autumn had tried it, too, with the same lack of results. They'd tried to get Summer to do the same, but by then, Wynter had become a little unnerved by his new sisters randomly bumping into him and rubbing their arms against his and Summer found it a bit disturbing to test for sexual compatibility with her youngest sister's husband, so she'd declined.

Now, however, Gabriella had a sinking suspicion that Khamsin's theory might be correct.

She tried to tug her arm out of Dilys's grip, but he didn't let go.

"You can get off me now," she ordered, mimicking Autumn's haughtiest tone.

He didn't move. Instead, he locked his gaze on hers and, with slow deliberation, laid his left wrist flat against her right.

Summer sucked in a breath and went rigid beneath him as a fresh surge of energy shot through her. Only this time, instead of an electric thunderclap that stunned the senses, this surge fired up every sensual cell in her body. If Dilys hadn't been straddling her, she would have wrapped her legs around his waist and dragged him down atop her. As it was, she burned for him in the worst way. The way his nostrils flared and his tattoos went bright with a fresh burst of phosphorescent blue light only fanned the flames of her desire. She wanted to command him to touch her . . . to kiss her. Her gift of Persuasion flared, bringing the words and the magic to the tip of her tongue.

"Your eyes have gone gold," Dilys murmured, and there was something about the way he said it the stopped her cold. A sort of dazed confusion and wonder. All the Coruscate siblings' eyes changed when they drew upon their power. Khamsin's eyes went a shifting silver, sort of like swirling storm clouds. Spring's turned an electric green. Autumn's looked like flames. And Summer's went golden—the more power she summoned, the brighter and more obvious the gold. Her sisters had always likened it to the sun shining from her eyes, a mark of Helos, but Dilys, clearly, found it significant in some other way.

The shocking moment when their gazes had first met . . . that explosive moment in the fjord . . . and now, again, her uncharacteristically powerful sexual hunger just from the brush of his mark against hers . . . suspicion hardened to certainty.

Khamsin was right. The reaction of marks *did* mean something.

Summer suspected it didn't just mean she'd found someone compatible with her . . . she suspected it meant she'd found *the* someone most compatible with her. Her life's mate. The man with whom Gabriella could have the sort of love Khamsin had found with Wynter.

The sort of love her mother had found with her father.

A love the loss of which had driven Verdan of Summerlea so mad with grief he'd destroyed himself, his son, his kingdom, and very nearly the whole world.

Gods help her.

She wanted it—oh, not the destruction and misery her father had caused, but the love he'd had. The love Khamsin and Wynter had. That perfect, deep, consuming love. She wanted it so badly the hunger was a burning fire inside her soul.

And here it was. Hers for the taking.

"Dilys," she whispered, saying his name for the first time, and his eyes glittered bright as a gleaming gold idol atop a god's altar.

It felt right to say his name, right in a way nothing had ever felt before. The syllables whispered across her skin like a warm, languid caress, sinking into her flesh, into her very bones. As if his name was a lost part of herself that had finally found its way home. The hunger for him burned brighter, becoming a sweet and terrible ache.

There was a voice in her head, crying out a warning,

but it was only a dim echo, the caution drowned out by a seductive song that beckoned to her, ensnaring her soul in golden bands of honeyed light.

"Call me," the song whispered, only it didn't speak in words but rather in powerful swells of emotion, warm currents so strong she could feel resistance being drained away. A man's song. *His* song. "Sing my Name. Claim me as thine own. For I am thine before all others."

And deep inside, a powerful voice welled up inside her, whispering urgently, *Claim him. Make him yours.*

Certainty flowered in her soul. She could do it. She could bind him to her for all eternity. Every part of her being wanted exactly that.

Her hands rose, splayed fingers sliding across the intoxicatingly warm, deliciously soft skin of his lean cheeks, cupping his face.

Her eyes never left his as she gently and inexorably tugged his face down and guided his lips to hers.

She'd never kissed a man. She'd wanted to a few times before, but she'd never allowed herself to do so. Now, the instant his mouth touched hers, she knew she'd never want to kiss any man but him for the rest of her life. He was her one and only. He was everything she would ever want, everything she could ever need.

His lips were smooth and firm and warm against hers. Velvety soft to the touch. She licked at them gently with the tip of her tongue, tasting him.

He shuddered, and his lips parted, opening against hers as his head tilted and he deepened the kiss. His legs stretched out, his long body lengthened, pressing down against hers, a delicious, heavy, warm weight supported by the powerful arms that flattened against the dock to frame her. The long, silken, fragrant coils of his hair spilled down to dance along the tops of her shoulders and caress her cheeks. They—like he—smelled of sultry, tropical nights and warm sea breezes, sweet, spicy, exotic, and he tasted like the answer to every wistful, aching dream she'd ever dreamt in the long, lonely dark of her aloneness.

She gave herself up to the kiss, luxuriated in it. Her hands slid around the hot, sleek, hardness of his muscled chest, learning every swell and hollow, every texture. Satiny skin. The nubbly velvet of hardened nipples. The trembling steel of clenched muscle.

She could pet him like this for a lifetime and never grow tired of it. She dragged her nails down the bumpy line of his spine and reveled in the way he sucked in a sharp breath, shuddered against her, then ravaged her mouth with a kiss gone wild, licking her, tasting her, breathing her in. His fingers dove into the mass of her unbound curls, cupped her skull and pulled her closer, tighter into his kiss, and if by sheer strength and desire, he could drag her into his body and make her part of him.

He kissed her until she was dizzy and gasping for air, until he was gasping too. And when he finally pulled away to catch his breath, his eyes were dazed, his expression stunned.

"Blessed Numahao," he whispered. "How can this be? You are . . . you are . . ."

She stared up at him, drinking in the sight of him, saturating her soul with the bittersweet wonder of this moment, committing every tiny detail to memory. Her thumbs slid across his skin, caressed the glowing blue sigil shining on his cheekbone, traced the planes and angles of his beautiful face.

And then she smiled with aching gentleness, her heart savaged by the knowledge that if she let herself, she would love him as she would never love another soul . . . love him as no other being in Mystral could ever or would ever love another.

And she told him softly, the powerful gift of her Persuasion pulsing in her voice, "Nothing. I am nothing to you." She had to wrap her fingers around the back of his neck and hold on tight as he tried instinctively to pull away, to reject the command threaded through each word she spoke. "You came here to court my sisters, not me. I am not the wife you need, and you will not pursue me."

Her smile trembled, then broke. Unable to stop herself, she kissed him again, one last time. Kissed him with all the desperate longing that clawed her from the inside out, kissed him until tears of regret and sorrow spilled from the corners of her eyes. And then she pulled away to say, with an unwavering surge of even stronger Persuasive power, "You will not remember this. Not that you came to me, not that you saved my life, not that we kissed. *You will not remember. And you will* not *pursue me.*"

On the palace terrace, beneath the soft light of the stars and the glow of hundreds of candlelit lanterns strung about the garden, Ari Calmyria was enjoying the company of Lady Fern Goldenbanner. Bright-eyed, erudite, and admirably independent, the Summerlander Lady Fern had shocked her family and community by taking the small fortune her father had bequeathed to her upon his death and heading north to seek a future mate from among the Calbernans rather than wedding the dull-witted son of her closest neighbor after her family lands and titles had passed to a distant cousin.

"Or rather, wedding my money to him," Lady Fern confessed with a wry twist of her lips. "It wasn't until after the war put a sizable dent in their coffers that Lady Alder, Salix's mother, even remotely considered me a potential match for her son."

"I'm sure it wasn't only your money that he was—" Ari broke off in mid-sentence as every cell in his body suddenly snapped to sharp attention. Something rippled across his senses, a whisper that resonated with power. A Voice. Female. Full of magic.

Before he could track the Voice back to its origin, it fell silent.

"Sealord Calmyria?"

The warm hand on his arm pulled his attention back to the slender, bespectacled Summerlander at his side. She was regarding him with obvious concern. "Forgive me, *myerina*. Where was I? Ah, yes, the foolish neighbor who could not see the true treasure before their eyes . . ."

"Never mind that," Lady Fern exclaimed. "Are you quite all right? What just happened? You looked as if you'd been struck by lightning."

He had, in a way, but it was nothing he was willing to discuss with *oulani*. Ari forced a smile. "It's nothing. I thought I heard something, but I must have been mistaken."

Lady Fern wasn't so easily dissuaded. "What is it you thought that you heard? And why does it seem your countrymen all heard the same thing, while the rest of us appear to have heard nothing." She gestured to the other guests with a wave of her hand.

Ari glanced around the terrace. Sure enough, the other officers looked as stunned as he felt and were doing an even worse job than he was in hiding it.

He caught Ryll's eye and raised his brows in silent question. Ryll's response was a shake of his head and a shrug. He didn't know where the Voice had come from either.

Ari turned back to Fern and gave her a potent smile full of disarming charm. "The reason we heard something the rest of you did not is easily explained, *myerina*. Calbernans, you see, have extremely acute hearing. One of our many gifts from the sea. In fact, I have a rather humorous story about the time I tried to sneak past my father when I was a boy. . . ."

As he launched into his tale, not giving Lady Fern a chance to get a word in edgewise, he exchanged a speaking glance with Ryll over the top of Lady Fern's head.

The situation here in Konumarr had just become exponentially more interesting. Because whoever owned that Voice they'd all just heard was in possession of a gift Ari had never run across outside of Calberna.

A great, magical gift. A power the greatest Houses of Mystral had spent millennia hoarding, consolidating, interbreeding in the hopes of bringing it back to its fullest potential: a vocal magic known as *susirena*.

Siren Song.

Leaving a dazed Dilys Merimydion sitting alone on the pier, Summer made her way back through the gardens. She was careful to keep to the shadows, and she slipped into the palace via one of the side doors, taking one of the narrow, servant staircases to reach the second floor where her chambers were located. With her hair spilling down her back in unkempt curls, and her lips red and swollen from passionate kisses, anyone who saw her would have no doubt what she'd been up to. She wasn't up to dealing with rampant speculation and scandalized whispers behind her back.

She also wasn't certain how well the Persuasion she'd used on Dilys would hold up against rumors that Princess Summer had been kissing someone tonight.

Her maternal grandmother, Seahaven's Queen Rosemary, with whom she'd corresponded over the years had warned her that the Persuasive gifts she'd inherited from her mother weren't without limits. The gift worked best when trying to Persuade people to believe something they were inclined to want to believe anyway. In such cases, even a mild push could cement a person's views so strongly nothing short of an apocalyptic cataclysm would shake their belief in whatever they'd been Persuaded to believe.

A strong push of Persuasion, like the one she'd used on Dilys, could erase blocks of time or entire tracts of memories, but depending on the strength of the memory or emotional significance of what was being erased, sometimes even the strongest push could only cloud the mind with a surreal haziness. In such cases, the person being Persuaded might remember everything, but believe it to be no more than a dream or a figment of his imagination. Unfortunately, those hazy figments could easily begin to feel a lot more real if everyone around him started speculating about the reasons a certain princess had been spotted with mussed hair, flushed cheeks, and bee-stung lips.

That she couldn't allow. No matter what, Dilys Merimydion must not ever remember what had passed between the two of them tonight.

That she would never forget was her burden to bear.

It already hurt, of course. She had no doubt it would hurt even worse over the next weeks and months as she was forced to watch the man she now knew to be her own court her sisters—and worse, fall in love with one of them. Marry one of them. It would burn her soul like fire to think of him kissing one of her sisters the way he'd kissed her, to think of him lying his warm, heavy body atop Spring or Autumn, gazing into her eyes with the wonder and tenderness and devotion that should have been Summer's. To think of him sharing that body with her sister, giving her the children that should have been Gabriella's own.

The Rose on Summer's right wrist began to burn.

She clamped a hand over the hot, red birthmark, turned her thoughts away from their dangerous, angry, jealous path and hurried down the hall to the safety of her room.

She didn't bother calling her maid to help her undress. Her temper was too close to the surface to risk having another person nearby. Removing her evening gown and layers of undergarments was no simple task, but she managed, and when she was done, she threw the pile of clothes onto a nearby chaise and donned her favorite nightgown, a lightweight linen that felt cool and soft and soothing on her skin. She then sat down at her vanity, closed her eyes and brushed her hair well over the usual hundred strokes. The soothing tug and pull of the brush helped settle her nerves, so she kept brushing while she meditated on peaceful, happy things.

When she was calm again, Summer rose from the

vanity and walked around the room, blowing out the lamps her maid had left burning. Despite the late hour, Wintercraig's summer-night sky was still light on the horizon, the sun not far enough below the horizon for full dark. And already it was growing lighter again. Dawn would be breaking soon. As she went to the windows to pull the night blinds, she saw Dilys Merimydion walking up the steps to the brightly lit terrace below.

Just that quick, all her meditation-reinforced calm, all her determination to block him from her heart and mind, went up in a puff of smoke. She couldn't tear her gaze from him. He was so beautiful. It was as if the gods had created him to be her personal Halla, the walking, talking, breathing embodiment of everything she'd ever wanted, everything she would ever need or wish for.

Everything she could never have. Which made him, she supposed, more her personal Hel than Halla.

She'd deliberately misled him earlier, when she'd implied no suitor had ever come for her. They had. Scores of them—and not only suitors who knew they'd have no chance with Autumn and Spring. There'd even been at least a dozen of them she'd thought she could love. She'd sent each one of them away with a push of Persuasion. It always hurt. Sometimes more than others. But never had sending them away felt like this—like a white-hot knife to the chest—as if by turning away from Dilys Merimydion she was cutting out her own heart.

Below, he stopped in the middle of the terrace and pressed a palm to his chest. He glanced up, frowning. With a gasp she sank back into the shadows of the night drapes. His gaze searched the windows and balconies, coming back to her balcony several times, then fixing upon it as if he knew she was there, watching him. As if some invisible thread tied them together, linking them with some innate awareness of the other.

Her fingers tightened on the drapes until her knuckles turned white.

"Nothing," she whispered, her voice the barest thread of sound. "I am nothing to you, and you will not pursue me." And she kept whispering it again and again, until one of his men standing nearby called his name and finally pulled Dilys's attention away. Before he could turn back in her direction, she yanked the night drapes closed and hurried to her bed.

Sweet Halla, if just the sight of him weakened her will and unraveled her calm this badly, then she would have to make it her mission to stay as far from him as possible. It would be difficult. Konumarr wasn't exactly an enormous place. But she would succeed.

She'd spent a lifetime learning how to walk away from people and situations that threatened her self-control. Always before, even when it hurt terribly to turn from what she wanted, she simply remembered the time she had not, and then, walking away was easy.

It wasn't easy this time. Not by a long shot. But walk away, she would.

Because when Gabriella ran from her desires, she wasn't tucking tail.

She was saving lives.

CHAPTER 5

"Dilys! Thank Numahao, there you are!" Ari hurried across the garden terrace, Ryll close on his heels. As soon as they drew near, Ari grabbed Dilys's arm and hauled him into the shadows of the garden, out of sight of the terrace where the welcoming party was still in full swing. "Did you find her?"

Dilys regarded his cousin in bewilderment. "Did I find who?"

"You know who. The woman who was using *susirena*."

"*Susirena?*" Bewilderment changed to shock. "One of these women was using *susirena*? Are you sure? Who was it?"

"We don't know. She Spoke just for an instant, and her Voice was gone too quickly for any of us to get a lock on the origin. But all of us heard it." Ari tilted his head to one side, his golden eyes narrowing. "I'm surprised you didn't. Where were you?"

"Taking a walk down by the fjord." Dilys absently rubbed the golden trident on his left wrist. "Any possibility the *susirena* could have come from one of us? Maybe someone decided to show off, hoping to impress a female?"

Ari snorted. "It wasn't one of us. I know a woman's Voice when I hear it, Dilys."

"Ari's right," Ryll concurred. "It was a definitely a woman. And considering how quiet it was and how quickly it was gone, it still packed quite a punch. I'm really surprised you didn't hear it."

"Perhaps it came from further inland and I was just out of range. We can ask the *Calbernari* in the village tomorrow if any of them heard anything. For now, let the other officers know to keep their ears open. If there's a female here with the gift of *susirena,* we don't want to return to Calberna without her. And we will want to trace her lineage, find out where she comes from." If there was somewhere else in Mystral where *susirena* was manifesting, the *Myerial* would want to know about it, and Calberna's sons would most definitely want to seek wives from such lands. "For now, let's head back to the party. I don't want our hosts to think we are unappreciative of their hospitality."

The three of them slipped back into the crowd on the terrace with casual ease. It was 3 A.M., and the sun was already rising, but the party showed no signs of stopping. Dilys had to hand it to the Winterfolk. They certainly knew how to host a celebration. He couldn't remember ever partaking in such an extravagance of feasting and entertainment. Food and alcohol flowed with never-ending abundance, and the music and dancing continued without cease.

If the celebration was a test—if the Winterfolk were expecting the Calbernans to descend into drunken revelry—they were disappointed. Calbernans, with their extremely high metabolisms, rarely became intoxicated. Alcohol and drugs of any sort burned off so quickly as to render them ineffective. Even had that not been the case, Dilys and his men had come to Wintercraig to find wives, a task no Calbernan undertook lightly.

Though Dilys and his men remained alert and watchful, the woman who had uttered that whisper of *susirena* did not use her Voice again. Finally, around six in the morning, the revelers began to seek their beds. Dilys waited until he received word that all his men had made it safely back to their ships before he retired to the rooms provided for him in the palace. There, he drew the black-out shades and poured a veil of water over every door and window before curling up on the bed for a few hours of sleep.

His sleep was not restful. He tossed and turned, his dreams plagued by images of golden eyes, sunlit seas, and a song that wound around his heart, filling him with desperate yearning and a sense of loss he couldn't shake off.

He woke about half past ten to find the bedsheets twisted around his body and his hand wrapped around a huge erection.

"Sweet seas, Merimydion," he muttered. "They tell you some woman whispered *susirena,* and you dream of Sirens all night." With a pained laugh, he freed himself from the sheets, took care of the erection, then treated himself to a long soak in the spacious, claw-footed tub in his suite's bathing chamber.

Winterfolk, thankfully, were of similar height and build to Calbernans, so he was able to stretch out to his full length in the tub and completely submerge himself, a rare treat for a Calbernan away from home. A collection of fragrant soaps and bath salts had been set out on a table beside the tub. He sniffed them all, then chose the ones that suited his mood. He poured the salts into the water and submerged himself in the tub, enjoying the sensual, silky feel of the water against his skin. Water was the life-blood of Calberna, as essential to its people as food and love.

As he lay cocooned in luxuriant, wet warmth, he tried to plan the siege and conquest of Spring and Autumn, but his mind rebelled, coming back again and again to the mystery of woman who'd Spoken *susirena* and also—inexplicably—to the elusive third Season, Summer Coruscate.

That he kept thinking about a female with the gift of a powerful Voice made sense, but Summer Coruscate?

Why couldn't he stop thinking about her? And why did her blatant desire to avoid his company bother him so greatly?

He massaged his left wrist and pondered the mystery of the gentle Season's apparent dislike of him. It was possible that something had happened to her to make her leery of men. He'd met more than his share of abused women over the years. One didn't sail the oceans of Mystral for more than a decade, visiting some of the most dangerous ports and grimmest slave markets in the world, without having seen the hollow-eyed casualties of Mystral's darkest shadows. In fact, given the way Verdan Coruscate had tried to murder his own daughter last winter, Dilys wouldn't have been surprised to learn that the late king's cruelty had extended to more than his youngest child. And yet, Dilys was fairly certain no such mistreatment had ever occurred. First, because had anyone ever dared hurt the gentlest and most beloved of the Seasons, the whole of Summerlea would have been up in arms. And second, because Summer herself had avoided no man last night but Dilys. Not even Ari—who was as close to Dilys's identical twin as a Calbernan could get.

Yet she acted as though Dilys were a wolf, and she a helpless lamb he would devour if she strayed from the safety of the flock. He didn't understand it. He was a big man and as fierce a son of the sea as any ever born, but he would never harm a woman. Especially not a woman he'd come to court.

Especially not her . . .

The mere thought that she might consider him capable of such a thing made his battle claws pop out and his fangs descend, ready to shred whatever demons had instilled that fear. He snarled, releasing a string of air bubbles that floated up to pop on the surface of his bath, then he sat up so abruptly that water sloshed over the tub rim.

"You're being an idiot," he muttered to himself. "Why does it matter whether she likes you or not? Or fears you, for that matter? She is not the one you're here for. She's nothing to you. *Nothing*."

What man, when presented the opportunity to court two lovely, compelling women who welcomed his suit, would tie himself in angry knots over a third who obviously didn't?

Only a narcissistic fool.

Dilys was neither narcissist nor fool.

Whatever this mad obsession for Summer Coruscate was, it ended now. He was here to wed Spring or Autumn, and that was exactly what he was going to do. What did it matter that for all Autumn's stunning beauty and all Spring's brilliance and regal reserve, nothing inside him cried, "She's the one!" about either of them. He was a Calbernan. No matter what woman he married, once wed, she would become the center of his life and he would devote himself to her happiness for the rest of his days.

And his inexplicable fixation with Summer Coruscate?

He reached for the sea sponge and soap.

Best forgotten.

Thirty minutes later, garbed in a bright blue-and-white *shuma* secured in place with a belt encrusted with foaming waves fashioned from sapphires and diamonds, Dilys had put his disturbing thoughts of Summer Coruscate firmly behind him and focused his mind on the task at hand. He had come to claim a worthy, *strong* wife, strengthen Calberna's ties to Wintercraig, and forge business alliances that would benefit both their countries.

Time to get to it.

He'd already concluded that the fastest path to Spring's heart was through her love of horticulture and intellectual pursuits. Since agriculture was one of House Merimydion's main industries—shipping being the other—there was ample room to find common ground and establish a friendly rapport and a solid foundation of mutual respect.

Autumn, he would continue to entertain with laughter

and a little adventure. As was only natural for a woman who'd been sought after by men her whole life, she wasn't particularly forthcoming with insights on how to engage her interests, but what bird in a gilded cage did not long to fly free? He thought she might enjoy sailing and hiking, pursuits that got her away from the court where she was always being observed and emulated and pursued by hopeful suitors.

He also hadn't missed the admiring glances both princesses had given him and his men. That was why he'd chosen the blue-and-white *shuma,* and why he'd exchanged yesterday's belled ankle-rings and golden armbands for ones of beaded platinum that sported the same crestingwave pattern as his belt. The pale metal, brilliant diamonds, and pure white cloth contrasted dramatically with his dark bronze skin and the long ropes of obsidian hair spilling free and unadorned down his back and over his shoulders.

He looked exactly like what he was: a rich and valorous Sealord of Calberna, strong, powerful, battle-tested. Confident in all things and easy on the eye. A man even a wealthy, beautiful, magically-gifted princess would be pleased to call her own.

With a wave of his hand, Dilys removed the water veils from his doors and windows and exited his room.

He met Ari and Ryll coming out of their own rooms, freshly bathed, sharp-eyed and smiling.

"D'you think they will be serving food?" Ari asked. His belly rumbled, making them all laugh. They'd all eaten heartily throughout the celebration, but Calbernan metabolisms burned food as quickly as they did intoxicants.

"If not, the fjord is just a dive away," Ryll said.

A dive in the fjord and a brisk, watery hunt for breakfast sounded beyond good on a visceral level, but Dilys shook his head. "We eat like *oulani* for now."

Ryll sighed. "I hope at least they'll have salmon. I like salmon."

They turned the corner and Ari nearly mowed over

a young maid who was rushing down the hall with an armful of linens. The maid gasped. The linens tumbled to the floor. Instead of rushing to pick them up, the maid stood there, gaping at Ari.

He smiled, his teeth white and dazzling, which only seemed to addle the girl more. "Here, let me help you with that, *kali mana*," he said. The girl stood frozen in her tracks as Ari collected the fallen linens and stacked them neatly back in her arms. His smile grew warmer, his gaze holding her captive. "We're on the hunt for something to eat." His throaty voice and appreciative gaze made it sound like he wouldn't mind dining on her, and in a way that would more than satisfy them both. "Can you direct us to the nearest breakfast chamber?"

The girl's throat worked but no sound came out. She swallowed, balanced the linens in one arm, and pointed a trembling finger down one of the nearby corridors.

"*Moa nana, kali mana.*" My thanks, little jewel. With a last, lingering smile, Ari turned and headed in the direction the maid had indicated.

Shaking their heads, Dilys and Ryll followed.

"You really shouldn't do that," Ryll muttered.

"What?"

"You know what. Poor girl probably won't get a lick of work done today."

Ari grinned and glanced back over his shoulder. The little maid was standing exactly where he'd left her, watching him, linens tilting precariously in her lax arms. "I just gave her a little something to brighten her day."

Dilys rolled his eyes. "Ryll is right. Save your charms for your future *liana*." Ari hadn't used *susirena* to dazzle the maid—even though all *imlani*, including all males—possessed the gift in some degree. No true warrior of the Isles would even contemplate using magic to make a woman want him. Learning to court and win a woman was as much a part of their rigorous training as their battle and sailing skills. A Calbernan male could entice with his voice, his touch, his eyes, even the smallest motion of his body. And *that* was what Ari had just done.

"You're just jealous because the *myerinas* like me better than you." Ari arched a brow. "Including a particular sweet, summery little blue-eyed beauty."

Dilys ignored the quick, violent clench of his gut and laughed. "If you're talking about the Princess Summer, I wouldn't exactly call getting ten words out of her a sign of affection."

"That's ten more words than she gave you."

"She's shy."

"She wasn't shy about talking to everyone else last night. In fact, it seemed to me like she was making a point of visiting every table but ours and talking to every Calbernan but you. Because she talked to me. And she talked to you too, Ryll, didn't she?" He didn't wait for Ryll to answer. "Why, yes. Yes, she did. And she must've liked what she heard because she spoke to you again at great length, didn't she? That was you cozied up to her for half an hour on the terrace this morning, wasn't it?"

Ryll scowled. "Leave me out of it, Arilon Calmyria."

Dilys frowned at his cousin. "You spoke to *Myeri-alanna* Summer for half an hour this morning? About what?" Suspicion reared its head. "You haven't set a line for her, have you?"

Ryll drew himself up, clearly affronted. "I have not," he bit out, each word solid as a rock. "The three Seasons are off limits. We all know that."

"But you spoke to her for half an hour."

"I ran into her this morning coming back from a swim. She wanted to talk. What was I supposed to do?"

"Wanted to talk about what?"

"Wait," Ari interrupted. "You went swimming this morning?" He glared at his cousin. "Went hunting, you mean! You've already eaten!"

Ryll shifted his weight guiltily. "I just had a couple of salmon. And nobody saw."

"And you didn't invite me? You selfish—"

Dilys cut off Ari's bluster. "You say *Myeriulanna* Summer wanted to talk? About what?"

"Her brother, Falcon, for the most part."

"Oh." Dilys settled back a bit. A sister asking after her brother was no cause for alarm. But, then . . . "What about the least part?"

His cousin's expression turned confused. "What?"

"You said she wanted to talk about Falcon for the most part. What about the least part? What else did she talk about?"

"Oh, er . . ." Ryll began to look distinctly uncomfortable. "Ryllian . . ."

"She was just being polite. It's the *oulani* way."

"*What* is the *oulani* way?"

"Asking about a visitor's interests, about his culture and experiences."

"And his *ulumi*," Ari interjected with a smirk and an air of triumphant retribution, as if pointing that out were as much payback for his cousin going hunting in the fjord without him as it was a teasing prod at Dilys.

"She asked about your *ulumi*?" Dilys's voice rose. Despite his earlier decision to put Summer Coruscate from his mind, Dilys's battle claws sprang free in an instinctive territorial response.

Ulumi were the iridescent tattoos that covered every experienced adult male Calbernan's body. In Calberna, when a *myerina* asked a man to recount the tales of the victorious exploits inked across his body, it was a sign of intimate interest. Of course, they knew that a similar expression of curiosity from *oulani* females didn't necessarily mean the same thing, but nevertheless, when any unattached woman inquired about a Calbernan's tattoos, the speculation, sly winks, and rampant, shameless wagering began.

Seeing Dilys's claws, Ryll winced and held up his own, claw-free hands. "It wasn't like that."

"What was it like?"

"She wasn't asking about my *ulumi* in particular. She was asking about the meaning of them in general."

"And what was your answer?"

"I told her the *ulumi* are the personal record of every Calbernan male's victories in battle, and that if she wanted to know any specifics, she should ask you."

Dilys stared hard at his cousin. "She didn't ask me."

Ryll did not wilt. "You were still in your room. A royal princess is hardly likely to come knocking at her suitor's bedchamber door."

"You know, Dilys," Ari drawled, his eyes alight with mischief, "for a man who spent more than one evening on the voyage from Calberna telling us how little the Princess Summer would suit you, you've certainly got your *shuma* in a knot thinking she might be interested in Ryll instead." He cast a pointed glance at Dilys's hands and raised his brows.

Dilys grimaced. "I am merely surprised she has taken such a liking to Ryll."

"Thank you," Ryll said dryly.

Dilys grimaced. "I didn't mean it like that. Any woman would be lucky to be your *liana*." He was being ridiculous. Stung pride aside, Summer's obvious fear of him and marked preference for his cousin should have suited him perfectly.

Does suit him perfectly, he corrected himself sternly. In fact, if Ryll had a chance to win Princess Summer, Dilys shouldn't stand in the way.

Dilys took a deep breath and forced himself to do the generous thing. "This," he said, showing his claws, "is just instinct, not claiming." To prove it, he forced his claws to retract. It took considerable effort—far more effort than it should have—but the sharp, obsidian talons slowly drew back into the sheaths behind his nailbeds. "There you see?" No mature Calbernan male gave up a coveted prize without a fight. Especially not when it came to potential *lianas.* If he'd truly meant to stake his claim, his claws wouldn't have sheathed until he'd won. That they kept pressing against his fingertips was something Dilys was determined to ignore.

"The Queen's Council and I all agreed that of the three sisters, Princess Summer was the least likely to suit me. She is beautiful, of course, and seems as gentle and sweet-natured as all reports of her professed. But the *liana* I wed will have fire in her soul, like her sister Khamsin and the other two Seasons. She will, seas and stars willing, mother our next queen."

"You are seriously not interested?" Ari pressed.

"Not at all," Dilys lied. He was plenty interested. What man worth his salt wouldn't be? But he had been sent to choose the strongest princess to be his bride. Summer Coruscate didn't fit that bill. She was not the one he'd come for. *He would* not *pursue her.*

And he would keep his claws sheathed no matter how ferociously Summer's obvious preference for Ryll stung him.

"So then it wouldn't bother you at all to hear that *Myerialanna* Summer also asked Ryll what it means when a Calbernan's *ulumi* glow blue?" Ari asked.

And *sproing!* went the claws again. Dilys curled his hands into fists to hide them. She had asked *Ryll* about Calbernan mating rituals? A shudder went through him, as hazy images from his dreams flashed across his mind. *The blue phosphorescence of glowing* ulumi. *Golden eyes burning in the darkness of night-shrouded waters. Fire tingling across every nerve of his body. And a Voice singing softly, calling to him . . .*

The vision winked out as Ryll shoved Ari hard enough to send him stumbling into Dilys. "Storms sink you, Calmyria! Quit making it sound like I'm after his princesses!" Turning to Dilys, Ryll held out his hands, palms up in entreaty. "It's nothing like he's making it out to be, Dilys. Our paths crossed by accident. She said she's been reading up on Calbernans so she could teach the village

children about us before our arrival. She teaches at the
queen's new public school in town. Anyway, she said
she'd come across mention of glowing *ulumi* and wondered what the significance was. And I told her if she was
curious about it, *she should talk to you*." He said the last
through gritted teeth, glaring at Ari as he did.

Ari, the unrepentant mischief maker, just grinned and
said, "And yet you were the one she chose to ask, not
Dilys." He laughed and danced away from the fist Ryll
swung in his direction. "I'm just saying!"

Usually, Dilys would have found Ari's antics amusing and shrugged the jabs off with a laugh and a smile.
Teasing between males was common during the early
stages of Calbernan courtships, as was good-natured
one-upmanship as they vied for a woman's attention—
especially if the woman had not yet made her preference
known. Things didn't get serious until a Calbernan's *ulumi*
glowed blue, meaning *liakapua*—the mating ritual—had
begun in earnest. Once that happened, not even Ari would
have dared to tease Dilys the way he was doing. Because
to a Calbernan male in *liakapua*, even lighthearted teasing could be interpreted as a challenge, and all too
often, challenges at such a time sparked brutal battles
for dominance. Considering that Calbernan males were
armed with razor-sharp battle fangs and claws, such battles usually ended in serious injury or death.

But Dilys's *ulumi* had not glowed blue. He was not in
liakapua.

Which is why it made no sense that Dilys was currently
fighting the urge to go for Ryll's throat.

"That's enough, Ari," Dilys said a few moments later,
after beating back the savage impulse to cause Ryll bodily
harm. "You've had your fun, so leave poor Ryll alone.
And to answer your question, no, I'm not in the least bit
bothered that *Myerialanna* Summer feels more comfortable with Ryll than she does with me, or that she chose
him to ask about our *ulumi*. You know why I'm here. You

know what I'm looking for in a wife. And you know she is not it. Put it this way," he summed up, determined to put an end Ari's teasing, "Princess Summer is a soothing cup of milked tea, but I'm thirsty for a strong Summerlean fire brandy. For hospitality's sake, I will court her as I do her sisters for these first two weeks, but after that, if Ryll wants her, he should feel free to pursue her."

They turned the corner and nearly collided with two of the Seasons: Spring, majestic in cool iced blue, and Summer, looking delectably feminine in deep, soft rose.

Momentary concern flitted across Dilys's conscience. The two princesses had to have overheard him. His only saving grace was that he and his cousins had been speaking in Sea Tongue, the language of Calberna, rather than the common tongue, Eru. Hopefully, the princesses of Summerlea had not understood him.

Spring smiled with regal grace, nothing in her expression indicating that she'd comprehended Dilys's dismissal of her sister as "milked tea" or the too-casual way he'd offered her up to his cousin for courtship. "Sealord Merimydion. Sealord Calmyria. Sealord Ocea. Good morning."

"Good morning, Sealords." Summer offered shy smiles to Ari and Ryll, and a more forced one to Dilys. Her gaze never rose higher than his chin and quickly skittered away. Her cheeks turned a dusky rose. And despite his determination not to pursue her, that charming blush roused every protective and covetous male instinct he possessed.

His battle claws threatened to spring forth again, so he forced his gaze back to Spring. Tall, cool, beautiful Spring, who even after a long night of celebration and precious few hours' sleep held herself like a queen. He could easily see her sitting on their daughter's Queen's Council, offering advice, guiding their daughter with wisdom and strength.

"You three are up early," Spring continued. "That is quite rare for folk unused to a Wintercraig celebration. We didn't expect to see all of you up and about until at least noon."

"Calbernans require very little sleep," Ryll informed her.

Ari's stomach rumbled. "What we do require, however, is rather a lot of food." He accompanied the words with such a pleadingly hopeful look that shy Summer actually laughed.

The sound was light and musical, like the wind chimes that blew in the ocean breeze outside Dilys's bedroom back home. Dilys's scalp tingled, and the ropes of his hair coiled tight at the sound of Summer Coruscate's laugh.

"We were just going down to breakfast ourselves," she told Ari with a smile. "We will be happy to show you the way."

Ryll and Ari immediately took up her invitation, moving into position beside her so swiftly she laughed again, looped her arms through their proffered ones, and started down the stairs. Aware of Spring's cool, watchful gaze upon him, Dilys smoothed away the crease between his brows, summoned his most charming smile, and held out an arm in offer of escort to the woman who very well might be the future mother of his children.

The five of them made their way downstairs to a banquet hall not far from the garden terrace used for the feast and dancing last night. The banquet hall was large and ornate and had already been set up with three long tables laden with food, including chilled, marinated meats and vegetables, smoked salmon, and a variety of hot foods served in silver chafing dishes. Dozens of dining tables had been placed all around the room to allow Konumarr's visitors to dine and converse in smaller groups.

"Please, help yourself to the buffet." Spring gestured to the tables overflowing with food, while Summer went to speak with one of the servants attending the breakfast guests.

"My apologies, Sealord," Spring said, calling his attention back to her. "Summer, Autumn, and I won't be joining you this morning. We thought you would still be abed, so we have a previous breakfast engagement."

"You will be missed, *Myerialanna* Spring," he replied sincerely. "I thoroughly enjoyed your company at last night's festivities. I hope we shall see more of one another later today?"

"I'm sure that we shall. Ah, here is water for you." The servant Summer had spoken to earlier approached the table, carrying a tray of filled glasses. "Lightly salted, as you prefer your first morning beverage."

Dilys smiled. "You have studied our ways."

"My sisters and I all have. We thought it only prudent."

The servant placed the first glass before Ari, who took an experimental sip, nodded his approval, and tossed back the entire glass. Ryll followed suit.

"Enjoy your breakfast, Sealords," Spring murmured with a smile as Dilys curled his hand around the small water glass and gulped it down.

His eyes went wide. His salted water wasn't water.

Dilys choked and sputtered, eyes watering, as the potent glass of pure, crystal-clear, Summerlean fire brandy he'd just unwittingly gulped down scorched the lining of his throat.

"Oh, dear," Spring said with an exceedingly credible expression of surprise. Then she ruined it with a smile, and a too sweet, "Was that not to your liking, Sealord Merimydion? One moment. Let me get you something soothing." She waved over another servant and whispered in his ear. A moment later, the servant returned with a tea service. Spring filled the cup half-way with tea, then poured a generous portion of milk, and handed the milked tea to Dilys. In perfectly accented Sea Tongue, she said, "There, you are. Milked tea. Drink that down. It's sure to make you feel better. And now, if you'll forgive me. I'm already running late. Please, Sealords, do enjoy your breakfast. Our salmon is, in fact, quite excellent. But for you three, I recommend the dogfish. Or perhaps some roasted boar's ass would suit you better." She offered a last, syrupy smile, and sailed away, disappearing after her sister Summer through a door on the far side of the room.

Dilys, with one last cough to clear his scorched throat and windpipe, leaned back in his chair and roared with appreciative laughter.

"Now that's what I'm talking about, my friends! Gods, what a woman!"

"Insufferable, arrogant ass!" Summer scowled and paced the parqueted wooden floor of the empty ballroom that connected to the banquet hall. "The nerve of him, pawning me off on his cousin, as if I'm some . . . some . . . some booby prize to be regifted to his friends!"

"Calm yourself, darling." Spring wrapped an arm around Summer's shoulders. "I didn't think you liked him anyway. You spent the whole of last night avoiding him, after all."

Summer flushed. She hadn't meant to be quite so obvious about avoiding him at the welcome celebration, but after the shocking way she'd responded to just one simple look, she'd been running scared. And considering what had happened later down by the fjord, she'd been right to do so.

"I don't like him," she lied with perfect credibility. "Or rather, I don't like him for me. You or Autumn would doubtless be a much better match for him."

"So, you should consider his lack of interest a good thing, then." Spring chucked a finger under Summer's chin and regarded her with a too-observant green gaze. "It *is* a good thing, isn't it, Gabriella?"

"Of course it is! It's just that . . . oh!" She pressed her hands to her hot cheeks. "I think I'm more prideful than I ever knew. No man has ever been quite so blatant about finding me lacking before." Even though she'd Persuaded him to forget her, to believe she wasn't the right woman for him, she hadn't Persuaded him to compare her to something as insipid as milked tea! As ridiculous as she knew it to be, that stung! Especially since what little sleep she'd managed to get last night had been plagued by the disturbing dreams of Dilys Merimydion floating in a dark sea, his body illuminated with phosphorescent-blue tattoos, his golden eyes glowing bright, his hands outstretched—to her. And all the while, a voice had been singing a wordless song of such terrible longing that she'd awakened to a tear-stained pillow, clenched fists, and a painful, aching emptiness inside her.

"I'm afraid Dilys Merimydion's dismissal of my charms has put quite an unattractive dent in my vanity," she confessed.

"He's a pig and a fool," Viviana said stoutly, positioning herself firmly in the Defense of Summer camp. "And I wish I'd been the one to think of switching his salted water for Summerlean fire brandy. That is what you had served to him, wasn't it?"

Summer bit her lip and nodded.

"Ha! I thought so! Once I realized what you'd done, I served him a cup of milked tea!"

Summer's mouth fell open.

"Oh, and they know we speak Sea Tongue—or at least they know I do. I made sure to speak it when I suggested they give the dogfish or some roasted boar's ass a try this morning."

A bark of shocked laughter spilled out without warning. Gabriella clapped a swift hand over her mouth to stifle it and cast a nervous glance towards the closed door to the dining room. She'd met enough prideful foreign princes over the years to know that they didn't take kindly to being laughed at—especially not after being pranked. "You didn't!"

"Indeed I did. That's the least of what he deserved." Spring looped her arm through Summer's. "Come on, little sister. Let's go get some breakfast."

"You go on ahead," Gabriella said. "I need to make a quick stop. I think one of my garters is coming undone."

"All right, but don't be long." Spring kissed Gabriella's cheek and headed out to the terrace where the rest of their family was waiting.

The moment Spring was out of sight, Summer spun on her heel and headed for the nearest garderobe as quickly as she could manage without drawing attention to herself. No one crossed her path, which was good. Her hold on her customary serene mask was tenuous at best.

Once she was alone, the door to the well-appointed relief chamber closed and locked behind her, even that shaky mask fell away. She slumped against the wall and covered her face with her hands.

"Sweet Helos, Gabriella! What is wrong with you? Switching his water for fire brandy! Were you deliberately trying to unravel the Persuasions you put on him last night?"

If Spring hadn't realized what Summer had done and acted so quickly, Dilys Merimydion's suspicions would have been drawn to Summer—the one who'd had a private word with the servant who'd brought the "water" to the Calbernan's table. If that had happened—if he'd seen shy Summer acting so out of character from the timid, "milked tea" image he had fixed in his mind—the surprise would have loosened the ties binding his memories.

And since the Calbernans had apparently detected the strong push of Persuasion she'd used on Dilys last night—a little fact Ryllian Ocea had let slip earlier this morning, when she'd run into him in the gardens—there would be no way to rebind those memories without drawing the attention of every Calbernan in Konumarr.

Knowing the Calbernans had detected the strong Persuasion she'd put on Dilys was troubling, to say the least. Thankfully, they seemed as oblivious to basic Persuasion as everyone else. Certainly, Ryllian hadn't seemed to notice the soothing, "You can tell me anything. Your secrets are safe with me," whispers she'd been using on him this morning when she'd tried to pump him for information.

And although he'd had no trouble resisting her push when she'd asked about glowing blue tattoos, he wasn't immune to her gifts. That he'd told her about the strong push of Persuasion the Calbernans had all detected last night proved that.

Still, in retrospect, asking Dilys's cousin about glowing blue tattoos was its own special brand of stupid. If he mentioned her inquiry to Dilys, it could undermine her Persuasions as surely as letting Dilys see her acting out of character. She'd only attempted it because sometime during the long, restless, insomnia-laden hours of the night she'd come to the staggeringly brilliant conclusion that Dilys Mcrimydion must have worked some sort of secret Calbernan magic on her to make her want him so badly.

Now, she realized how ridiculous those suspicions were. Dilys's "milked tea" remark made it humiliatingly obvious that without the force of whatever had passed between them last night clouding his judgment, he wasn't even remotely interested in her! He'd offered her up to his cousins, for Halla's sake!

The sound of sizzling yanked her out of her agitated thoughts, and not a moment too soon. All the scented water left out for guests to wash their hands had boiled away. The rose petals that had been floating on the water's surface were now crisped bits of char at the bottom of the empty bowl, and the air in the room was hot and dry. A few minutes more, and the room would have burst into flame.

Horrified, Summer clamped down hard on her magic.

She'd very nearly lost control—something that hadn't happened in almost twenty years. And considering how many layers upon layers of binding spells and controls she'd spent a lifetime constructing and strengthening to keep her magic suppressed, no stupid offhand remark Dilys made to his cousins—no matter how hurtful—should have been able to rip through her shields so effortlessly.

The fact that it had meant something was terribly wrong with her.

Something that had nothing to do with Dilys Merimydion. Something that explained all the disturbing spikes of emotion she'd been experiencing since coming to Konumarr. The ferocious desire for a child of her own. The bursts of Persuasion she hadn't meant to use. The crazy, driven way she'd responded to Dilys Merimydion. And of course, her uncharacteristic fury over Dilys's dismissal of her charms.

Gabriella gripped the counter and stared at her reflection in the mirror hanging over the now-empty wash basin.

Dear gods. It had begun.

She was going mad, like her father.

CHAPTER 6

It took a full quarter of an hour of meditating on the jeweled charms of her mother's bracelet before Gabriella was satisfied that she'd shored up the controls binding her most dangerous magic. She spent a few more minutes ensuring that her customary serene mask was firmly back in place, then exited the garderobe and made her way out to the private garden on the side of the palace where Khamsin, Wynter, Spring, and Autumn were already seated. Back in Gildenheim, Valik, Wynter's second-in-command, and Krysti, Khamsin's young ward, always joined the family for breakfast, but the two had not come to Konumarr. Valik had remained behind to oversee the rebuilding of Wintercraig's armies after last winter's battle with the Ice King, and Krysti had stayed with him to serve as Valik's page and to begin his training as a knight.

"Ah, there you are, darling," Spring said as Summer took her seat. "I was just explaining that that we were late this morning due to our engagement in . . . um . . . foreign relations." She smiled and poured a cup of jasmine tea from the pot on the table and passed it to Gabriella.

"The Calbernans were awake, were they?" Khamsin lifted her own cup to her lips and regarded Spring and Summer over the rim.

"Surprisingly enough," Spring said. "And looking none the worse for the lack of sleep or copious amounts of drink they imbibed last night. I understand their leader, Sealord

Dilys, has a great fondness for Summerlean fire brandy." She flicked a smirking glance Summer's way. Gabriella quickly lifted her cup, pretending to hide a smile.

Wynter regarded his sisters-in-law with narrowed eyes. "Hmm," he said.

"So"—Khamsin jumped in—"what do you think of the Calbernans now that you've spent a little time with them?"

"Well, I don't know about Spring and Summer, but so far, I'm not disappointed," Autumn said and launched into a series of amusing anecdotes about her adventures at last night's welcome reception.

Gabriella let the conversation flow around her as she considered her predicament. Now that she knew she was going mad, she needed to formulate a plan. She couldn't stay here and put her family in danger. Her magic, unbound, was far too dangerous. And as protective as her sisters were—and Wynter was showing signs of outdoing all three of them!—she couldn't very well admit the truth to any of them. They would insist on keeping her close, trying to find a way to fix whatever was wrong. She couldn't allow that.

Thankfully, Dilys Merimydion's declared lack of interest provided the perfect excuse to make herself scarce. She'd just wait a few days until his preference for Spring and Autumn became too marked to be missed, then a few big, damp-eyed blinks, a little quaver in her voice, a tiny push of Persuasion, and her new brother-in-law would probably jump at the chance to help Gabriella put a little distance between herself and the latest suitor to reject her. As to where she'd go, well, she'd been wanting to travel north to the Skoerr Mountains to see the sun that never set. Once there, she'd Persuade one of the guards Wynter sent along to take her someplace else—someplace remote where her family would never find her and where there was no one around for her to harm.

"Helloooo. Gabriella?"

Summer blinked. Autumn was waving a hand before Summer's face. "Oh, sorry." Gabriella blushed. "I was lost in thought."

"Clearly." Autumn's auburn brows rose and her mouth quirked in a teasing grin. "Those Calbernans certainly do wreak havoc on a woman's concentration."

Summer smiled serenely, refusing to rise to the bait. "Do they? I hadn't noticed."

"Ha! Liar!"

"I confess," Khamsin said, "if I weren't a married woman, I'd seriously consider a Calbernan suit. Dilys Merimydion and his men are quite easy on the eye."

Her husband Wynter stiffened beside her, his brows drawing together. "I'm sitting right here, wife," he growled.

She smiled and patted his hand. "I know, husband, and you are all that I could ever want or need." As he started to settle, she added, "But I can still enjoy a nice view."

He scowled, then abruptly switched to a smile. "Ah, so you are saying I should find a view to enjoy, as well?"

Now it was Storm's turn to scowl. "I wouldn't recommend it."

Wynter laughed, a deep, hearty sound and with startling speed, scooped Storm out of her chair and into his arms. She squealed as he stood.

"Wynter! Are you mad? Put me down this instant!"

"I think not. Clearly, I've not seen to you well enough, if you feel the need to admire the view of other men." He bowed to the Seasons, holding his squirming wife with ease. "Ladies. Enjoy your breakfast."

The three of them watched in amusement as Wynter Atrialan, the fearsome Winter King, carted off their sister.

"Did you ever think, even once, that we'd ever see a sight like that?" Autumn said as Wynter paused to gaze down at his wife in open adoration, kiss her thoroughly, then disappear into the building.

"Never," Spring replied.

"I never dreamt he could even be likable," Autumn

confessed. "Let alone lovable. But it's obvious she loves him."

"And just as obvious he loves her."

Autumn sighed and put her chin on her hands, gazing at the now-empty doorway through which Wynter and Khamsin had disappeared. "What are the odds the rest of us will be so lucky?"

Spring reached for her teacup. "Slim to none, so don't waste your time pining for it."

Autumn grimaced and turned to scowl at her oldest sister. "Must you always be such a pessimist, Spring?"

"Being realistic isn't the same as being pessimistic."

"How strange, because it always sounds that way when coming from you." Autumn stuck out her tongue and tossed her head. "On a more *optimistic* note, the Calbernans are famous for showering devotion on their wives. That's close enough to love for me. Besides, I can think of many worse sights to wake up to than Dilys Merimydion." She plucked a small bunch of grapes from the fruit basket and popped one in her mouth.

Heat spiked in the Rose on Gabriella's wrist at the thought of Autumn waking up next to Dilys. To distract herself, she snatched up her silverware and began attacking her breakfast.

"While it's true he's certainly as handsome as any woman could want," Spring admitted grudgingly, "I don't like the way he was so dismissive of Gabriella this morning."

Autumn frowned and leaned closer towards Gabriella in an instinctive shielding gesture Summer doubted she was even aware of. "He was unpleasant to Summer?"

As Spring caught Autumn up with this morning's encounter with Dilys Merimydion, Gabriella polished off her plate of food and plucked a blueberry scone from the basket in the center of the table. She spread a dollop of clotted cream on the scone, added a smear of jam, and took a bite. Treating herself to something sinfully delicious was another one of the tricks she'd learned to keep her emotion-fed power from building up to lethal levels. She savored the meltingly delicious flavors of the scone, cream, and jam, focusing her attention on the pleasure of the delightful tastes rather than the tense, jealous anger bubbling inside.

"So, let me get this straight," Autumn said as Spring finished bringing her up to speed. "You pranked the Royal Prince of Calberna, swapping out his water with a straight shot of fire brandy that leaves him choking and sputtering in front of his men and an entire room of servants, and his only response is to laugh and applaud your temerity . . . and you think this is a character flaw? Do you even remember that dreadful Prince Berong's reaction when I snuck the teensiest dose of itching powder into his laundry? He turned purple and ran around the palace threatening to behead people!"

Spring scowled. "Did you miss the part about the cavalier way Sealord Merimydion dismissed Summer as a potential wife? He'd made his mind up about her before he even met her!"

"He came with a plan," Autumn corrected. "I thought that would appeal to you."

Spring opened her mouth, closed it, took a thoughtful sip of tea, then admitted. "All right, yes. I do appreciate that he did his homework and came with a plan. That shows a degree of preparation and thoroughness that I find appealing. It's a quality every leader should have."

"And he's got a good sense of humor, and a willingness to laugh at himself, which makes him even more appealing to me. And you—" She turned an admiring gaze on Summer. "Apart from my disappointment over you pranking a visiting prince without me"—Of all three Seasons, none loved a good practical joke more than Autumn—"all I have to say is, Well done, sister! I had no idea Gabi the Good had that sort of mischief in her!"

Summer blushed and took another bite of her scone, mumbling, "He made me mad" as she chewed.

Autumn gave Summer's back a couple of congratu-latory thumps and grinned. "I feel like a proud mama watching her fledgling take flight for the first time. All my pranking lessons over the years haven't gone to waste."

Spring cleared her throat and leveled a repressive look on the youngest Season. "Back to Sealord Merimydion. You might be ready to throw caution to the wind, but I'm not."

Autumn's grin became a scowl at her sister's criti-cism. "There's a difference between throwing caution to the wind and admitting that I found the man personable, witty, and charming—which I did. I'm just saying, we've had far more objectionable suitors paraded before us over the years. Honestly, Spring, why do you always have to look for the worst in people?"

"Because the worst is what most people try the hardest to hide, and I don't like unpleasant surprises. I'd rather know the total truth—all the bad as well as the good—before I decide to bind the rest of my life to someone else's."

The irritation faded from Autumn's expression. She reached for her tea glass, took a sip, and nodded. "Fair enough. You've always been the one who makes decisions with her brain. Gabi makes decisions with her heart." She cast a fond smile in Summer's direction. "But I've always trusted my instincts, and my instincts say we could all do a lot worse than ending up with a man like Dilys Merimy-dion. So, if neither of you are interested, I'm more than happy to keep our suitor entertained for the duration of his visit." She reached for a fresh cluster of grapes from the fruit bowl in the center of the table, popped another glistening grape in her mouth, and smiled as she chewed.

Summer's fingers curled tight. Autumn was a dazzling creature. If she set her sights on Dilys, he was as good as hers.

And that was all for the best, the rational part of her mind insisted.

But the mad, voracious, dangerously primitive part of her wasn't listening. The tea in her glass was starting to steam again.

"I need to go," Gabriella announced. She clung to her calm, congenial mask as she stood up. "I have loads of work to do before school starts up again on Modinsday. Lily had the wonderful idea of doing a dress up to get the children more interested in their history, but there's an enormous amount of planning and preparation before we can get started." She was intending to have the children use their math and problem-solving skills to plan the design, purchase, and construction of their costumes, but she needed to do all the calculations herself before assigning the project. A teacher should always know the answer before asking the question.

"I can lend you a hand, if you like," Spring offered. "Seeing as how Autumn has volunteered to keep the Calbernan busy."

"Very busy." Autumn grinned and waggled her eyebrows.

Heat surged inside Summer's skin. She turned from Autumn quickly, before the urge to turn her into a redheaded pile of cinders grew too strong to resist. "No, it's all right, Vivi. I'm sure you have other plans for the day."

"I don't actually. At least, not at the moment. I'm hoping to get a package from Uncle Clarence soon, but it hasn't arrived yet." Uncle Clarence was their late mother's brother and the current Crown Prince of Seahaven. Though their elderly maternal grandfather, King Eustace, was still technically the reigning monarch, Uncle Clarence had taken over most of the daily governance of the kingdom.

"Package?" Autumn, who was slathering clotted cream and jam on a pair of scones, stopped what she was doing to look up. "What sort of package?"

"Nothing that would interest you. Just some books."

"Why is Uncle Clarence sending you books?"

Spring shrugged. "Because I asked him to, of course."

She smiled at Summer and looped an arm through hers. "Shall we go?"

"Wait. Why are you being so evasive?" Autumn was now standing with her hands on her hips, scones forgotten, eyes narrowed. "Exactly what sort of books is Uncle Clarence sending you, Viviana?"

Spring lifted her eyes towards the sky in a silent appeal to the gods of Halla, then heaved a sigh and released Summer's arm to turn around. "Fine, if you must know, he's sending me copies of everything the Seahaven royal archives have on Calberna and its people. Havenfolk have been mariners for thousands of years. I thought if anyone was likely to have useful information about the Calbernans, it would be them." Small Seahaven's economy was almost entirely tied to the ocean, unlike Summerlea and Wintercraig, whose primary industries were land based. "And before you chastise me about obsessing again, I sent the request weeks ago. Though, to be honest, I'd do it again." She looked towards Summer as if seeking support. "I know I don't have any proof, and I know you two both think I'm being ridiculous and obsessive, but I can't shake the feeling that there's something the Calbernans aren't telling us. And I'm determined to find out what that is. *Before* one of us decides to marry their prince."

Gabriella bit her lip. "Well, that's a little embarrassing. I sent an eagle to Uncle Clarence yesterday before the Calbernans arrived, asking for essentially the same information." She shrugged and smiled sheepishly at Spring's astonishment. "Just because I wasn't all worried like you doesn't mean I didn't trust your instincts. You were so convinced something about the Calbernans was . . . erm . . . *fishy,* I figured it would only be prudent to help you investigate."

Autumn began to laugh. Her initial low, quiet chuckles rapidly rose in both volume and exuberance, until she was soon clinging to one of the chairs, and laughing so hard tears were running down her face.

"Honestly, Aleta," Spring scolded, "it isn't that funny."

"Oh, it is," she sputtered between laughs, "but not for the reason you think." She caught her breath long enough to say, "I sent an eagle to Uncle Clarence this morning! For exactly the same reason as Gabi!" Then she exploded with fresh mirth, laughing until her knees gave out and she collapsed on the terrace with a plop. Her eyes widened briefly in surprise, but the fall only set her off into fresh gales of laughter.

Gabriella and Spring stared at her, then stared at each other, then they were laughing as helplessly as Autumn.

They laughed and laughed and laughed. And that laughter did for Gabriella what no amount of meditation could have: it stole every scintilla of heat from the jealous anger that had been building inside her and washed her temper away on a flood of happiness and sisterly love.

The sound of the three princesses laughing with such abandon brought smiles to the faces of the passing nearby servants and brought more than one Calbernan—Dilys among them—out of the banquet room and into the hall, seeking the source of the delightful sound.

There was nothing quite like the sound of a woman's joyful laughter. A child's laughter had its own, special magic—filled with innocence and youth. But a woman's laugh . . . the sound of a woman's happiness warmed a Sealord's heart and gifted him with a special spark of rejuvenating energy. It was one of the sweet rewards Calbernans enjoyed for ensuring a woman's—any woman's—happiness.

For some reason, the sound of the Seasons' laughter resonated especially deeply with Dilys, gifting him almost as strongly as a physical touch. He closed his eyes, smiling, and let the radiant warmth of their joy wash over him.

"D'you think maybe they're laughing over the firebrandy joke?" Ari murmured beside him.

Still drinking in the magical sound of the Seasons'

happiness, Dilys shrugged. "I don't know. Maybe. I hope so, if it brought them this much enjoyment." Other men might have found themselves nursing wounded pride at the idea of a woman laughing at their expense, but not a Calbernan. At least not so long as the amusement was not mean-spirited, which this was not. He swayed a little as a fresh burst of laughter sent even more power coursing through his veins.

"I think perhaps I didn't give the Bridehunters enough credit for choosing my *liana*," he said, feeling almost drunk on the laughter-borne rush of energy. "If a simple laugh from the Seasons is this powerful, Numahao only knows what great gifts a bond with one of them will bring."

"What do you mean?"

Dilys opened his eyes and turned to Ari with a smile, thinking his cousin was teasing, but there was no spark of amusement in Ari's eyes, only honest curiosity. "You don't feel that?"

"Of course, I do. I'm not deaf. They have a rich laugh, but we've enjoyed laughter almost as rich before."

Dilys grabbed Ari's hand, but instead of the surge of fresh, electric power like that which sparked through his own cells, he found only tingling warmth. Slightly more powerful than the mild boost one usually received from a woman's laugh, but nothing like the raw energy he was receiving.

A quick glance around told Dilys that the rest of his officers were similarly unaffected. After basking in the warmth of feminine joy for a few moments, the other officers were already heading back into the banquet hall to return to their morning meal.

"Interesting," Dilys murmured.

Ari's eyes narrowed, then he gave a bark of laughter. "Ha! I don't believe it. Here less than a day, and already you've formed a of connection with one of them!"

"I hadn't thought so." Dilys turned back toward the sound of the laughing Seasons. "Perhaps one of them formed a connection with me?" He'd had numerous *oulani* women form emotional connections with him before. Quite a few before he had earned his *ulumi-lia*. Quite a few more afterwards, while he'd waited for the Bridehunters to finish their work. But none of them had ever either formed a strong enough connection or possessed enough power to give him this much energy from just a rich laugh. Only his mother had ever been able to do that.

"My money's on Autumn," Ryll said. "I could swear I saw a little of that haughtiness she wears start to melt last night."

"Maybe." He knew Autumn found him attractive. All Calbernans were attractive to the opposite sex. It was part of their biology, a lure designed to attract the emotional connections they needed for strength and survival. But as much as Autumn admired his looks, he hadn't sensed anything that went deeper than the expected physical interest. Not with Spring, either. And the little honeyrose had avoided him so completely, there was no possible way *she* could have formed any sort of connection to him.

Unless . . . it was possible the connection had come from him. He thought about his inexplicable anger earlier this morning when Ari had teased him over Summer's marked preference for the company of Ryll. Blessed Numahao, had her blatant preference for the company of other men caused him to unwittingly forge a territorial connection to her just to prevent anyone else from doing so? Was that what had haunted his dreams, destroyed his peace, and left him so ferociously possessive of her this morning? He had never been so petty.

Then again, he'd never been on a mission to win a *liana* before, either.

For all their affability and good humor, Calbernans were ferociously primitive when it came to claiming a mate. Once a Calbernan entered *liakapua,* woe betide anyone— especially any male—who tried to interfere. Every fighting skill a Sealord learned during his years of seeking gold and glory would be brought to bear to defeat any interlopers, thus proving himself worthy of his *liana*'s claiming bond.

Still, Dilys didn't want to be the kind of man who put himself and his wants and needs before all others. That wasn't how his father had been. That wasn't the sort of son his mother had raised.

"Or maybe there is no bond between me and any of the Seasons," he speculated. "Maybe the reason their laughter powers me more strongly than it does you is because something in their bloodline is particularly well-attuned to something in mine." He liked that explanation better that the possibility that he was being territorial over a woman who wanted nothing to do with him. Regardless, he needed to know what sort of connection had been formed and who had initiated it. If one of the sisters had forged an emotional tie to him, he needed to pursue it. On the other hand, if he'd inadvertently forged a territorial claim on Summer Coruscate, he needed to undo it so she would be free to explore her interest in Ryll. Whatever the case, Dilys should be able to determine the source of the connection simply by talking to the Seasons and taking each princess's hand.

He clapped Ari and Ryll on the shoulders. "You two go on back and finish your breakfast." They'd already filled and consumed three plates of food each, which meant they had a good two or three plates left to go. He started down the hall that led to the terrace from which the laughter of the Seasons was emanating.

"Where are you going?" Ari asked.

Dilys turned around, summoning a grin as he continued walking backward towards his destination. "To find out just how good an impression I made last night."

Summer and her sisters were still laughing when they stepped through the door that led from the terrace back into the palace. The instant Gabriella crossed the thresh-

old, her "Dilys sensors" started to ping. Her laughter died
in her throat. She began looking frantically for a quick
escape route, but it was already too late. The tall, devastat-
ingly handsome Sealord had caught sight of them and was
heading their way with purpose.

Gabriella took a quick step back behind her sisters as
Dilys Merimydion stopped before them and swept a deep,
graceful bow.

"*Myerialannas. Myerialanna* Autumn." Turning to
Autumn, he graced her with a dazzling smile, took her
hand, and bent over to press a kiss on the backs of her
fingers. "Thank you so much for the pleasure of your company last evening." Dilys released Autumn's hand and
turned to take Spring's. "*Myerialanna* Spring." Another
bow. Another kiss delivered to the backs of Spring's slender fingers. From another man, the hand kissing might
have seemed contrived or overdone. Not with Dilys Merimydion. Like everything else about him, his gesture came
across as charming, sincere, and self-assured. "And thank
you for your company as well. I thoroughly enjoyed our
discussion and look forward to an opportunity to continue
it. And *Myerialanna* Summer . . ."

As those golden eyes turned their focus upon her,
Gabriella shrank back and dropped her gaze, doing her
best to appear nervous, uncomfortable, and a little afraid.
It wasn't difficult. She *was* nervous and uncomfortable,
and she was a *lot* afraid.

She clenched her hands together so tightly all the blood
left her fingers.

". . . We did not have the chance to get to know one another a little better," he was saying. "But I hope that shall
soon change?" He reached out a hand in invitation.

She flinched and stepped back, unclenching her hands
only long enough to thrust them behind her back. Touching him right now—or ever again, for that matter!—would
be a very bad idea. The monster that her shared laughter
with her sisters had put to sleep was rousing once more.

And it wanted Dilys Merimydion. It wanted him more than it had ever wanted anything. She didn't dare lay claim to the smallest part of him—not even by so simple and innocent an intimacy as a touch of hands. Because if she did, she would never let him go.

"Ah," he said. A wash of strong emotions stung her raw senses. Remorse. Guilt. Piercing shame. All his.

She realized that he had interpreted her flinch as something more along the lines of a battered woman shrinking back from a threatening blow. He saw her as fragile—the shy, sheltered rose everyone believed her to be. He thought he'd hurt her tender, defenseless heart with his earlier incautious words, and he despised himself for it.

She should have jumped on that belief and played it up for all it was worth. Instead, she found herself overcome by an instant and overwhelming desire to soothe him and set his mind at ease. Only with great effort did she manage to keep from throwing aside the powerful weapon he'd unwittingly given her. Playing the fragile, wounded flower gave her the perfect excuse to avoid him.

"Forgive me, *Myerialanna* Autumn," he said quietly, "but might I have a moment to speak privately with and *Myerialannas* Spring and Summer?"

Before Autumn could answer, Spring said coolly, "There is nothing you need to say to us, Sealord Merimydion, that requires greater privacy than this. Besides, Autumn already knows what occurred this morning."

"Ah," he said again. But rather than squirming in embarrassment as some men might, Dilys nodded and said, "So be it. *Myerialanna* Spring, *Myerialanna* Summer, to my shame, you both overheard a conversation that should not have taken place. My cousins were trying to get a rise out of me over *Myerialanna* Summer's marked preference for their company last night, and to my shame, they succeeded. My poorly chosen words were naught but a crude shield for my own wounded pride. I came here to court three of Mystral's most admired and desirable princesses:

the Seasons of Summerlea. I led my men to war and stood against a risen god for that honor. To be clear: the opportunity to spend time in the company of any of Your Royal Highnesses is a priceless gift, one I do not intend to squander. I apologize sincerely for any wound my prideful foolishness may have caused, and I beg you both, most humbly, for your forgiveness. If you would, please, I would start anew."

She could feel his gaze upon her like a physical touch. Every word he spoke rang with sincerity, and the sound of his voice set her senses aflame. The low, melodious cadence was like a drug to her, gorgeous, deep, velvety. She wanted to sink into the sound and wrap it around her. She wanted to lay naked in the sun and have him whisper that seductive magic across her skin. Every cell in her body ached to believe him, to forgive him, to begin anew, to—*wait!*

Was he . . . *Persuading* her?

She nearly started out of her shoes. Holy Halla! *He was!* Since coming to adulthood, she'd never met another person—not even the most gifted of her Seahaven relatives—who could actually Persuade *her.* But if the Calbernans possessed a strong enough gift to influence her mind, it would explain why they had sensed the strong push of Persuasion she'd used on Dilys last night.

Well, this put a whole different spin on everything. *Calbernans possessed the gift of Persuasion.* No wonder people everywhere (especially women) found them so charming, so impossible to resist. No wonder they'd been willing to fight a war for the chance to wed their prince to one of the Seasons of Summerlea. Somehow they must have found out about the strong Persuasive gifts that ran through Seahaven's royal family—a gift her mother's family worked hard to keep secret, for obvious reasons. Most likely, her father had revealed the information himself as a way to convince the Calbernan mercenaries to support his efforts to retake Summerlea, though obviously he hadn't mentioned which of his daughters possessed the magic.

Maybe this was the secret ulterior motive Spring had been obsessing about. This courtship wasn't about claiming a bride with weather magic to help with Calberna's shipping industry. Dilys Merimydion and his men were seeking to strengthen their own ability to influence and control minds!

The dirty sneaks!

Of course, the fact that *she* had been using her gift to influence and control minds all her life was completely beside the point. She'd never done it for personal gain. If anything, she'd used it to keep herself from being a danger to others.

Obviously Summer wasn't the only one feeling Dilys's Persuasion. Spring was actually smiling at Calberna's prince as she accepted his apology with an uncharacteristic warmth. "Thank you, Sealord. That was a most gracious apology."

Silence fell . . . stretched out. Still smiling pleasantly, Spring stepped back and deliberately trod upon Summer's slipper-clad toes. The sharp pain in her toe snapped Summer to full attention.

"Yes, thank you," she muttered. She lifted her gaze as far as Dilys's nose before the peripheral gleam of those golden eyes sent the blood thundering through her veins. Her gaze skittered away. Considering what had happened to her yesterday, the first time she'd met Dilys Merimydion's gaze, it was possible the Calbernans could Persuade with their eyes as well as their voices. She wasn't going to risk it. "Most gracious of you."

Another silence stretched out, then the Sealord cleared his throat and said, "I invite the three of you to join me aboard the *Kracken* this evening for dinner and a sail down the fjord to watch the sunset at sea. There are storms out in the western Varyan, so it should be spectacular."

Autumn and Spring both accepted the invitation, but

Summer shook her head. Refusing him took effort. The seductive lure of his Persuasion curled around every word he spoke, making it nearly impossible to deny him. She'd had a lifetime of learning how to deny herself, though, so she managed. "It sounds lovely, but I'm afraid I must decline. I teach at the queen's new school in town, and I am quite behind on preparing the lessons for next week."

Thankfully, the Sealord didn't insist on pressing further. With a final, deep bow and a promise to collect Autumn and Spring at eight o'clock, he excused himself.

Summer didn't breathe easy again until he disappeared from view.

"Well," Spring said, "You have to give him credit. He doesn't beat around the bush. What do you think, Autumn?"

"Hmm?" Autumn murmured absently. "What?" She dragged her appreciative gaze off Dilys's departing backside, paused to admire a group of Calbernans who were lifting heavy objects for the delight of several other female onlookers, and wiped a hand over her lips as she turned to Spring. "I have to say, Storm wasn't exaggerating when she warned us these Calbernans were walking erotic dreams. Check my face. Did I miss any drool?"

Spring rolled her eyes. "You're incorrigible."

Autumn gave a small laugh. "At least now I feel a little more sympathy for those poor sods who walk into lampposts around me." Not that any of the Calbernans would know how sincerely and appreciatively Autumn was ogling them. To those who didn't know her well, she would appear every inch the haughty princess. She'd perfected that mask years ago and wearing it had become second nature.

Their oldest sister huffed a long-suffering sigh and directed her attention to Summer. "And you, Gabriella. What was with the flinching and cowering just then? Are you really that upset about his stupid remarks earlier, or did something happen between you and Sealord Merimydion last night that you haven't told us?"

Summer stifled a wince. Spring had a habit of seeing much more than most people wanted her too, including Gabriella. "No, it's not that," she lied. "But he made his preference clear, so I thought I might as well use that to my advantage. I truly am busy with the school, so since he already thinks I'm no bolder than a cup of milked tea, I might as well live down to his expectations. That way, he won't feel compelled to waste his time or mine with a courtship doomed to go nowhere."

Autumn's pansy-purple eyes widened. "That's really good thinking, Gabi." The wide-eyed look of admiration turned to narrow-eyed accusation. "What a shame it's also a total pile of horse *shoto.*"

Summer's cheeks went hot.

"*Aleta!*" Spring hissed.

"What?" All humor fled Autumn's face. "It's true and you know it. Gabi runs away from every man there's even the slightest chance she might feel more than friendship towards. And she does it for the same reason you try to find the deep, dark secret they're all supposedly hiding."

"Like we're the only ones? What about you and the way you've been objectifying these men?"

"Yes! I do it, too! I admit it! We may have different methods, but we all do the same thing. For all the same reasons. Because we're all afraid of falling in love and ending up like *him.*"

The three of them shared haunted looks.

"I don't know about you two, but I'm tired of being afraid," Autumn continued. "We all have dangerous gifts. Some more dangerous than others." She held her palm over a lit candle on the table, close enough that the heat from the flame should have scorched her flesh, but she didn't flinch. She closed her hand slowly, and the flame died. Then she opened her fist with a sharp flick, and all the candles in the room flared to sudden life. She met her sisters' gazes. Her purple eyes were flickering with fiery lights. "But Storm and Wynter have gifts every bit as dangerous as ours, and that hasn't stopped them from finding love."

"That's different," Spring said.

"Why? Because she didn't have a choice and we do?" Autumn stood up and gave her skirts a shake to smooth out the wrinkles. "This is our chance, sisters. Everything we know, everything we've read, everything we've learned says Dilys Merimydion is an honorable, noble man who comes from a country famous for how well they treat women."

"He's a mercenary," Spring reminded her.

"And an obscenely wealthy merchant, and a landowner, and a prince," Autumn shot back. "And a freer of slaves. And as handsome as any woman could ever want. And charming, too, with a surprisingly excellent sense of humor. Your objections, Viviana, are just obstacles you keep throwing in your own path out of fear. Khamsin likes him. That goes a long way with me. So, you two can keep making excuses to avoid him and not let yourselves like him, but barring any dreadful revelations once the information from Uncle Clarence gets here, I intend to welcome his courtship and see what comes of it."

It took Summer hours alone in her room, focusing all her attention on planning the children's costume project, before she finally managed to extinguish the fires of possessive fury that Autumn's parting declaration roused. Even then, when the threat of a deadly loss of control had passed, she knew it was only a temporary reprieve. Her defenses were shaky at best, and when it came to anyone else laying claim to Dilys Merimydion's attentions, they were virtually nonexistent.

Worse, that ferocious desire to have and keep him for her own was no false desire manufactured by the Persuasions he'd tried to manipulate her with earlier. No, that craving was entirely hers. In Dilys Merimydion, it seemed, her deepest lifelong desire had found its focus. She could not shift nor sway it, no matter how she tried.

As for Autumn's brave claim that Wynter and Khamsin had found and embraced love despite their dangerous mutual gifts, she was right, but Summer's parents had been happy too—blissfully so—until Queen Rosalind's death.

Dangerous power and deep emotion did not go well together. Period. As happy as Khamsin and Wynter were today, that love skated on the crumbling edges of disaster.

So, while Autumn was right that Dilys Merimydion was potentially the best husband any woman could hope for, that was the problem. With him, marriage would lead to love, and love would leave the door open for disaster.

The only reason Autumn thought she could love without putting herself or others at risk was because, although her gifts could be quite dangerous, she'd never killed innocent people with them.

Summer had.

CHAPTER 7

Dead Man's Cove, Crow Island

In the tattered sewer of a town called Dead Man's Cove—home to pirates and landless scum from all walks of Mystral—the Drowned Maiden pub was an infamous watering hole, frequented by those from whom light itself quailed in terror.

Conversations were low and guarded, weapons large and prominently displayed. The wenches who slouched from bar to table, taking orders and serving drinks and whatever slop passed for a meal that day, had long since passed their primes. Hair frizzy, flaccid breasts propped up by tight, grimy stays, paint bleeding around tired eyes and grim lips, any beauty they'd ever possessed had long since fled. Not that the equally scurrilous patrons of the Maiden seemed to care.

Flint Grumman, the grim, muscled barman and owner of the Drowned Maiden, poured ales and whiskey with a burning, well-chewed cigar clamped between blackened teeth. Every once in a while, ash from the tip of his cigar would fall into whatever drink he was pouring. He'd serve it anyway and charge extra for the privilege.

Not a single patron ever objected.

Light bloomed briefly in the shadowy pub as the door

opened, only to be blotted out the next second by the enormous figure that crouched down to cross the threshold. The growling whispers of conversation amongst the pub's patrons fell silent.

Every black-hearted pirate and reprobate in the Maiden watched in uneasy silence as newcomer approached the bar and signaled for a drink. Flint's hands shook as he poured, and a flick of ash fell from the tip of his cigar into the glass. Flint blinked, and in a move that surprised none who recognized the newcomer, set his cigar on the edge of the bar, fetched a new glass, and poured again. He shoved the second pour towards the newcomer and pocketed the man's coin with a trembling hand.

"I've come for a ship and men to crew her."

Silence.

Those watching from the corners of their eyes fixed their attention on their own tables and held their breath. None wanted to call the attention of the pirate known as the Shark.

Boot heels clapped on worn wooden treads. The Shark fixed his dead, black gaze on three men seated at one of the Maiden's scarred tables.

"I said, I've come for a ship and men to crew her."

The largest of the three men at the table—Bloody Jack Malvern, captain of the pirate ship *Reaper*—began to shake, tremors shuddering down his arms, making his beefy, thick-fingered hands rattle against the tabletop.

"I've decided yours will do," the Shark said.

As if abruptly released from invisible bonds, Bloody Jack exploded out of his chair, dual swords unsheathed and swinging.

The Shark dipped back, and Bloody Jack's swords skimmed past their target. Gleaming eighteen-inch blades shot out from the sleeves of the Shark's jacket into his waiting hands. The blades swung lightning fast, a silvery blur in the darkened room.

Bloody Jack was known for his speed and gleeful, homicidal skill with swords. It was said he could decapitate a man and filet the flesh from his bones before the corpse's head hit the floor.

The Shark was faster.

Bloody Jack's head, wearing an expression of stunned surprise, hit the floor treads with a meaty thump, landing beside the piles of sheared flesh and bloody bones that had been his body.

The Shark pinned his soulless gaze on the remaining two men at the table. "You, what's your name?"

Bloody Jack's first mate swallowed hard. "Tunney. Red N-Ned Tunney."

"Congratulations, Red Ned. You're the new captain of the *Reaper*." The Shark slipped his eighteen-inch fileting knives back in their spring-loaded wrist holsters and tucked them back up under the sleeves of his coat. "Summon the crew and provision the ship. You sail tomorrow on the morning tide."

Without waiting to see if his orders were obeyed, the Shark pivoted on one bloody heel, stepped over the pile of meat and bone on the floor, and ducked through the Drowned Maiden's door.

Konumarr, Wintercraig

His skin was so delicious to the touch. Heated velvet beneath her fingertips, brimming with sensual, energy. Summer's palms skimmed along the swells of Dilys's sun-warmed bronze skin, tracing the whorls and patterns of iridescent blue tattoos that told a mysteriously compelling, tactile story meant just for her. The tattoos lit up in the wake of her fingertips, coming alive with bright, phosphorescent blue light and sending waves of breathtaking, erotic heat tingling through her body. His eyes gleamed lambent gold beneath a thick veil of inky, obsidian lashes.

He lay naked against the lush, opulent silk, velvet, and

embroidered satin of her bed linens, a dark temptation. She knelt atop him, straddling his hips. Everywhere their skin touched, her flesh was suffused with a pleasure so deliciously intense, a connection so pure and deep, she never wanted it to end.

She drew in a shuddering breath and arched her back. The loose coils of her unbound hair spilled over her shoulders and danced across the bare skin of her back, tickling the curve of her buttocks. Her naked breasts thrust forward into his waiting hands, and he guided her to his mouth, laving her nipples with the hot, rough silk of his tongue. He caught one taut peak between his teeth. Fire shot through her, and a soft sob of pleasure broke from her lips.

She grabbed his head, thrusting her fingers into the thick, coiled ropes of his hair, holding him fast and shuddering in delight as his mouth worked its decadent carnal magic upon her and his fingers danced across the damp silk of her heated flesh.

"Dilys. Sweet Helos, Dilys!"

Her breath came faster, shallower, and her hips rocked in an instinctive rhythm as a delicious pressure of heat, tension and aching pleasure built up inside her. Her body ached for a release that somehow she knew only he could give her. She stood on the precipice, waiting for one final flick of his fingers and rasp of his tongue to send her flying over the edge.

Then, abruptly, the scene changed.

The woman straddling Dilys's naked body and sobbing his name as she rocked against him was no longer Summer. It was Autumn. And Summer stood, frozen with fury, in the doorway of her bedroom.

A roar of rage and betrayal ripped from her throat. "You dare?" Her voice shook. The glass window panes rattled. "You dare claim what is MINE?"

Autumn and Dilys turned to face her in shocked surprise.

Autumn held out a hand. "Summer . . . wait! Wait!"

But it was too late. The Rose on Summer's wrist went white hot and flames licked at the edges of her vision. Her barriers shredded as magic held long-dormant erupted with cataclysmic fury.

Autumn's eyes widened, then turned blood red as every tiny blood vessel in her eyes burst. Her mouth opened on a strangled scream as her body began to convulse. And all that gorgeous famously red hair turned to flame of almost the exact color.

Gabriella came awake with a cry, skin hot, heart pounding, her body aching with unsatisfied need so sharp it was a physical pain.

The distinctive smell of smoldering fabric made her swear and leap to her feet. She ripped the sheet from her bed and plunged it into the basin of water she'd left by her bedside for just that purpose. When the immediate threat of fire was gone, she held up the sodden sheet and regarded with grim dismay the charred marks that, when wadded together, formed the unmistakable shape of her hands clenched tight around the linen.

Swearing to herself, Summer folded the wet, scorched sheet and stuffed it the bag she was using to collect scraps of fabric and trim materials for her school's costumed history projects. This was the second time this week that she'd set fire to her bed while dreaming dreams that had become both increasingly erotic and increasingly violent, and while her maid, Amaryllis, had believed Summer's story about accidentally dropping a lit candle on the first burnt sheet, she was unlikely to believe the same excuse a second time.

Gabriella grabbed a fresh topsheet she'd pilfered from the laundry yesterday and began quickly remaking her bed to hide the evidence of her accidental flame.

"Damn it. Damn it. Damn it," she muttered as she worked.

In the ten days since the Calbernans' arrival, she'd successfully managed to keep her power under control during the day, but her barriers were clearly no longer strong enough to keep her magic in check while she slept. And it wasn't just burnt sheets Gabriella was worried about. Her sisters—Autumn, in particular—had died numerous times in numerous gruesome ways in her dreams. It didn't take much analysis to figure out why. All this week, Dilys Merimydion had begun to show a marked preference for Autumn's company. Summer's subconscious clearly considered Autumn a threat in need of elimination.

Afraid of manifesting that violence in real life, Gabriella had taken to avoiding Spring and Autumn as well as Dilys, a fact that had not gone unnoticed by her sisters. They weren't at all happy about it, but their concern and dismay only unsettled her further and made her avoid them even more.

Summer's plan to expose Dilys's use of Persuasive gifts—and thereby eliminate him from her and her sisters' lives—had come to nothing. The enormous wagonload of books and papers Uncle Clarence had sent from Seahaven's royal archives contained nothing that even hinted at Calbernans' ability to manipulate minds. And although Uncle Clarence had sent Summer a private eagle with a clear warning to keep her powers hidden around Calbernans because they did possess those gifts, the actual message itself—"I know for a fact that Calbernans can be very Persuasive, so I urge you and your sisters to be cautious around them."—was too vague to be of use against them.

It was just as well. Had Wynter thrown the Calbernans out of Konumarr for using mind-controlling magic— which he most definitely would have done—she wouldn't be able to use Dilys's obvious preference for Autumn's company as an excuse to get away from Konumarr. And now that she was far enough gone into madness that she'd begun burning her bedsheets in her sleep, leaving her family was no longer a future possibility, it was an immediate necessity. The longer she stayed, the more dangerous she would become. She'd never forgive herself if she hurt her sisters or Wynter—or anyone else, for that matter.

With her bed now remade and rumpled to look as if she'd slept on the new linens, she flung open her balcony doors to let in some fresh air and spritzed a bit of perfume on her bed to mask the slight charred scent that lingered in the fabrics. Then she rang for Amaryllis to help her get dressed.

Just hold it together a few more days, Summer, she told herself as she waited for Amaryllis. *Just a few more days.* She'd already planted the seed with Wynter, making him aware that Dilys's preference for her other two sisters was the latest in a long line of rejections, and leading him to believe those rejections had caused her a deep emotional wound that was becoming too painful to bear. Tomorrow she would once again mention her desire to visit the Skoerr Mountains and see the sun that never set, only this time she would include a little push of Persuasion—one subtle enough to escape the Calbernans' detection—to help Wynter realize that a solitary trip to the icy, remotest reaches of Wintercraig was exactly what Summer needed to help her get over this latest suitor's rejection.

Once there and away from the Calbernans, with their Persuasion detection, she would use the full force of her gifts to arrange some sort of tragic accident that would claim her life. Before, when she'd contemplated going away and not coming back, she'd thought she would fake her death and live out the rest of her life in seclusion. But now, considering how quickly the madness was claiming her and the way her fury had fixated on her sisters, her plans had changed.

Even if she isolated herself in the remotest reaches of Mystral, there was no way to guarantee that in her madness she would stay there or that the people she loved would be safe from her. Khamsin had been sent away to Wintercraig, after all, and their father had still pursued her there and tried to kill her.

No, there was only one way to make sure she never harmed anyone. She no longer intended to fake her death. She meant it to be real.

After a morning spent sailing the fjord with Spring and Autumn Coruscate, Dilys lay on his bunk in his ship the *Kracken*'s spacious captain's cabin, staring up at the well-fitted beams of the deck overhead while he tried to make sense of the feelings that had cast a pall over a day he should have thoroughly enjoyed.

"Dilys?"

Dilys turned his head as the door to his suite opened, and his cousin Ari entered, ducking his head to clear the doorway.

"They told me I'd find you here." With a casual intimacy that bespoke a lifetime of friendship, Ari snagged one of the cabin chairs, flipped it around and set it down beside the bed. He straddled the chair and rested his arms along the back. "What's wrong, cousin? You were very quiet this morning and then you left the palace after dropping off the *myerialannas* this afternoon and came out here."

Dilys stifled a grimace. He should have known his odd behavior today wouldn't get past his cousins.

"What happened? Are things not going well with *Myerialannas* Spring and Autumn?"

"*Ono.*" If only his problem was so simple. "I mean, things with them are going just fine. That's not it."

"Then what is it?"

Dilys linked his hands behind his head and stared up at the ceiling. Calbernans were, by nature, very social. They needed the close connections with friends and family, the confidences and interactions that built intimacy and nourishing emotional ties. But Dilys hadn't confided his growing disquiet to Ari or Ryll all week, and that wasn't like him. Maybe it was time he did. Maybe talking about it would help solve the problem.

"Spring was the Season that was chosen for me. You know this."

"*Tey.* Or Autumn. Lucky son of the sea."

"*Tey,* very lucky," he agreed without any particular enthusiasm. "It only makes sense that Spring would be the Council's choice for me. Having met them, she is clearly the leader of the three. She has the bearing of a queen."

"But you find yourself more drawn to Autumn."

"No. I mean yes, but no."

Ari lifted his brows. "Well, that clears things up."

Dilys bared his teeth and growled. "Yes, I find Autumn the more appealing. She's warmer and more approachable than her reputation suggests. I enjoy her company immensely. She makes me laugh more than any woman I've ever met. And she has made it clear she would not refuse an offer of marriage from me. That's not the issue."

"You find the most beautiful woman in the world more appealing than you thought possible, the Queen's Council has approved her as a potential *liana,* and your courtship of her is going well. I'm sorry, cousin, but I really don't see the problem."

"Of course you don't. Because there shouldn't *be* a problem." Beset by sudden frustration, Dilys sat up and scrubbed his hands over his face. "Argh! What is it about her? It makes no sense. I'm a fish on the hook, only I never saw the bait and I still can't see the hook! I just know it's there."

"Autumn has you on a hook?"

"No! Not her!"

"Then Spring?"

"No, not her either!" Dilys flung himself out of the bed and began pacing the width of his cabin. "If it were either of them, would I be clawing the walls? They're the ones I'm here for. The ones I was sent to court."

"Ah." Ari pushed several long ropes of hair over his shoulder. "So I take it the 'she' wielding the hook in question is the little sweet one, Summer."

Dilys threw his hands up in the air. "I told you it makes no sense!"

Ari shook his head. "Of course, it makes sense. She's beautiful. She's kind. After fifteen years of fighting other people's wars, coming home to her would be like escaping to paradise. Who amongst us *wouldn't* find that appealing?"

"Appealing has nothing to do with it. I need a strong, powerful, *fearless* wife capable of mothering Calberna's next queen, and she's a coward!"

"That's a little harsh."

"Oh? What would you call it, then? She runs the other direction every time she sees me. She hasn't spoken more than two words to me since the day we arrived."

"Now, that's not true. I've counted at least a dozen."

Dilys's stopped his pacing and turned to glower at his cousin. "I'm going to take your skull and smash it into the wall until your brains are soup."

Ari laughed, utterly unafraid. "You'd have to catch me first."

"My point is," Dilys said through gritted teeth, "she's not even close to what I need. She clearly wants nothing to do with me. So why is she the one I can't stop thinking about? And my dreams . . ." His voice trailed off as he remembered in vivid detail the erotic dream turned nightmare that had ripped him out of sleep this morning.

"What about your dreams?" Ari's voice had lost its teasing tone.

Tension shot through Dilys. His first instinct was to snarl and snap. The dreams of Summer, her hands on his flesh, his on hers . . . the seductive, silken feel of her nakedness against his . . . those were intimacies that belonged to him and him alone. Not to be spoken of. Not even with cousins he loved like brothers.

"She's in my dreams every night," was all he finally admitted. "She has been from the start." He refused to tell Ari how erotic those dreams had become, how in his sleep he made love to Gabriella Coruscate over and over and over again, how it felt like the most right and perfect thing he'd ever done. Or how, lately, those dreams had begun ending each night with fury and violence. How this morning, he'd come awake shouting, torn from a nightmare so vivid he could still smell the acrid stench of Autumn Coruscate's burning flesh, still see Gabriella standing in the doorway wearing an expression so ferocious and deadly only a fool with a death wish would dare cross her.

"It's almost like she's gotten inside of me somehow. And even though she's been avoiding me from the start, it's getting worse, not better. Every time I close my eyes she's there. I can feel her beside me, I can smell the perfume of her hair, but when I look, she's gone. I can hear her . . . but not. And the whole time I'm with Spring and Autumn, all I keep thinking is, 'This is wrong. I shouldn't be here.' Like I am *betraying* her somehow by courting her sisters. *Betraying her!* A woman who clearly wants nothing to do with me!" He pressed his face against the cool glass of the sterncastle windows. "Ugh. I told you it didn't make any sense."

"I'm not so sure about that. It sounds like sorcery to me." Ari's expression had gone grim.

Dilys flipped around to press his back against the window. "Come on, Ari. They're weatherwitches, not spellcasters."

"They're one of Mystral's most powerful families, and they've been wedding into Mystral's other most powerful families for thousands of years. Who knows what kinds of magical abilities they've accumulated and passed down over the years? Or what kind of magical services they might have hired?"

He opened his mouth to refute Ari's charge, then closed it. Of course centuries of intermarriage with other magically gifted families would have resulted in offspring who possessed more than just their weathergifts—like Prince Falcon's control over birds. That was one of the reasons the

Bridehunters had chosen a Season to be his wife. He also knew that many wealthy families kept hired spellcasters on their payroll to deal with situations that required talents the family didn't possess.

Dilys considered the possibilities for a moment, then shook his head. "No, it doesn't make sense. Summer has made it clear she wants nothing to do with me. Why would she or any of them bespell me so that she was the only one I desired?"

"I can think of plenty of reasons, starting with the fact that we *invaded* them this winter. We may not hold grudges against the people we're hired to fight, but that doesn't mean those people don't hold grudges against us."

That was certainly possible, but . . . "I don't get that sense at all. Not even from King Wynter. Calberna is a better ally than enemy, and he knows it."

"So maybe it wasn't the family. Maybe it was someone who doesn't want you to wed any of them. Don't forget we never found the woman who used *susirena* that first night. Maybe she did something to you." Ari gripped the back of the chair and stared at Dilys with a look of dawning suspicion. "The pirates . . . do you think they could have planted a spellcaster here to keep you from wedding a weatherwitch to use against them? Our trip has been planned for months, and our purpose in coming here has been no secret. They've got to know that wedding you to a Season will give us a powerful weapon to use against them."

Dilys thought about it briefly, but shook his head. "I wouldn't put it past them, but every move they've made against us has been direct and obvious and brutal. This is far too subtle for them . . . and not nearly bloody enough." He sighed and threaded his fingers through the ropes of his hair. "Honestly? I'm beginning to think I'm doing this to myself. Maybe I'm not as ready for marriage as I thought. Maybe the part of me that belonged to Nyamialine is still not ready to let another woman into my heart, so I'm sabotaging my chances to wed a Season. Or maybe I'm so used to women who would be mine for the asking that the only one I find truly interesting is the one who doesn't want me."

"First of all, winning over a woman just to prove you can make her want you is the sort of shallow challenge that only *oulani* men enjoy. It's definitely not your style. As for Nyamialine . . ." Ari's voice grew soft. "My sister loved you very much. Had she lived, your bond would have been unbreakable. As true a mating as ever there was. But you were still both children when she died. The love you shared, the bonds you forged, were those of friendship and affection, not the deep bonds of *llana* to *akua*. She would not want you to live your life alone. She wouldn't want that for any of us."

"I know that." In fact, now that he'd suggested out loud that he might still be harboring some sort of connection to her, he realized that those once-strong ties had been completely severed. No part of them remained. How could they, when his inexplicable attraction to Gabriella Coruscate had infiltrated every part of his being?

Ari rocked back a little. "So," he asked, "what are you going to do? Are you going to court Summer and see where it goes?"

At that suggestion, Dilys gave a humorless laugh. "How do you suggest I do that? The few times I've actually gotten within twenty yards of her, she starts shaking like I'm a hungry tiger and she's a defenseless rabbit I've decided to eat for snack. She'd probably scream and faint if I showed the slightest hint of desire for her." A desire which, after the constant erotic dreams he'd been having about her, he'd be hard-pressed not to reveal.

"She handles herself around Ryll and I just fine."

There it was again. That instant aggression. "Do me a favor, Ari. Don't keep bringing that up." He held up a hand, showing the tips of his partially unsheathed battle claws. "I'm serious. No joking around. Because whatever is making me think she's the only one I should be courting doesn't have a sense of humor when it comes to you two cozying up to her."

Ari raised his open palms in surrender. "I won't say another word about it. I swear."

"Thanks."

"You know what I think?"

There was a look on Ari's face that made Dilys wary. "Whaaat?" he replied slowly, drawing out the word.

"I think that if you are still feeling that strongly about Summer Coruscate—and if you're sure your feelings aren't the work of some spellcaster—that you're doing disservice to yourself and all the Seasons—including Summer—if you don't pursue her."

"Have you not been listening? She. Doesn't. Want. Me. And she's not the one I was sent here to wed anyway."

"*Fark* who you were sent here to wed. If your instincts are telling you beyond a shadow of a doubt that Summer Coruscate is the one for you, then I say listen to them. As for her not wanting you . . . in my experience—which, in all modesty, when it comes to courting women, far exceeds your own—when a woman runs from a potential husband as hard as Summer Coruscate has been running from you, it isn't him she's running from. And it isn't because she doesn't want him." He raised his brows.

"You're saying you think she's more interested me than she's letting on."

"I may have seen her looking at you a time or two when she thought no one was watching . . . and she wasn't acting like she didn't enjoy the view."

Was it possible? "Even if that's true, I already told Ryll he should feel free to court Summer himself."

"Seriously?" Ari looked pointedly at Dilys's hands, where his battle claws were already extending at the mere thought of Ryll pursuing Summer. "Like that is ever going to happen."

Dilys curled his fingers into fists. Strangely—or per-

haps not so strangely—hearing Ari scoff at the idea of him
or Ryll even considering a romantic interest in Summer
relieved all sorts of tension and aggression inside him. His
claws were already retracting—and not because he was
forcing them.

"So, it's settled then." Ari got up, spun his chair around
and put it back in its place. "Tonight, you are going to
spend the evening with Summer Coruscate, and you are
going to court her. And you aren't going to take no for an
answer. Agreed?"

Dilys hesitated. He'd never pursued an unwilling woman.
He'd never had to. But Ari was right, if everything in him
was saying Summer was the one, he was being an idiot
tying himself into knots trying to ignore his instincts.

"Agreed," he said.

"Good. And if she tries to run, Ryll and I will be there
to cut off her escape and drive her back your way."

"For goddess's sake, Ari, it's a courtship, not a hunt."

"Ah. That, my dear cousin, may be the real root of your
problem. You think a courtship and a hunt are two separate things." Ari grinned, showing gleaming white teeth
with battle fangs fully extended. "They're not."

"You're doing fine, Lily." Gabriella encouraged the young
Summerlander as Lily stumbled over a word in the book
she was learning to read. "Just sound it out." With Gabriella doing her best to avoid the Calbernans staying at the
palace, she had been staying late at the school every night,
sewing the historical costumes for the children and tutor-
ing Lily in reading and writing.

"No, not a long A." Gabriella corrected as Lily mis-
pronounced the word again. "This one makes the short A
sound, like 'cat' and 'hat.'"

Lily scowled. "Summer Sun! Could this be any more
confusing? If the letters make different sounds, why didn't
someone come up with different letters?"

Gabriella smiled, not taking offense at the girl's irritation. "I don't know. That would seem to make more sense, wouldn't it?"

Lily was not assuaged. "Maybe my father was right, and I'm too stupid to learn," she muttered. "Maybe working in the orchards is all I was ever meant to do."

"Don't say that." Gabriella leaned forward to take Lily's hands. "Don't ever say that. You aren't stupid at all. You've already come so far in just a month."

"This is all useless anyways," Lily said. "No job I can do needs me to know reading or writing."

"Perhaps not the jobs you've done in the past," Summer agreed, "but what about all the other jobs you'll be able to do once you learn to read and write?"

"Like what?" Lily lifted her black brows. Her skin was a much darker brown than Summer's, tanned a deep, rich tone by a lifetime spent outdoors in Summerlea's orchards, picking fruit and pruning trees. Her eyes were a warm shade of chocolate brown that sparkled in the sunlight.

"Like teaching, for one. Or working in a shipping warehouse, helping with inventories and stock reports. Or even running your own seamstress shop—just think how much easier it would have been this week if you'd been able to make a list of what we needed instead of calculating everything and remembering it all in your head."

Lily sniffed. "That wasn't hard. Lots easier, in fact, than all this." She tossed her book on a nearby desk.

"You thought that was easy because you're smart and you have an amazing memory," Gabriella said. "I couldn't have kept all those fabrics and yardages and whatnot in my head for two minutes, let alone several days, like you did."

Lily's scowl faltered a little. "Truly?"

"Yes, truly. I was very impressed . . . and more than a little envious." Lily's mouth fell open. Clearly, it had never occurred to her that a princess of the realm could envy her anything. "What I'm saying is that reading and writing opens all sorts of doors. It will give you many more options to support yourself and your baby." Gabriella hesitated, then added softly, "That's what you want, isn't it? To make a safe home for you and your baby, and give yourself options enough that you won't ever have to stay in a bad situation again?"

Though Lily never had much to say about her life in Summerlea, Gabriella knew something bad had happened back there. The girl had constantly flinched and cowered at sharp noises when she'd first arrived, and constantly glanced over her shoulder as if expecting to see someone hunting her. There were scars on her wrists, back, and arms that she kept hidden beneath long-sleeved gowns. Gabriella only knew about them because she'd come to the school early one morning this past week and walked in on Lily getting dressed in the school washroom.

Lily flushed and glanced down, biting her full lips. "Yes," she admitted in a hoarse whisper. "That's what I came here for."

"Well, I promise, I will help you do that as best I can. You learning to read is an excellent first step." She knew Lily had really come here hoping to wed a Calbernan, but Lily found the big, bare-chested Seafolk a bit intimidating. (Who could blame her?) She hadn't worked up the courage to approach one yet, and because there were so many other women who'd flocked to Konumarr for the opportunity—many of them widowed or orphaned by the war—that meant she hadn't yet caught any Calbernan's eye. More than once, Gabriella had found her staring out the window, sighing at all the laughing, happy women walking out with their foreign suitors.

"Do you really think I can do this? Learn to read?"

Gabriella gave her a quick squeeze. "Of course I do. You were determined enough to get here all on your own, weren't you? I know that couldn't have been easy."

"No," Lily agreed.

"Well, if you could do that, you can do this, too. You're smart. You've already picked up so much in the short time you've been here. You just need to keep at it and don't give up."

"No, ma'am. I mean, yes, ma'am." Lily grimaced and took a deep breath. "I mean, thank you, Your Highness, for all your help. I never knew a lady so kind as you."

Gabriella smiled. She'd come to care about the plucky young girl. Lily was good-natured, hard-working, and kind: qualities to be admired wherever they were found. And in Lily's company, especially this last week, she had found a measure of genuine peace. Even the sight of Lily's unborn baby kicking and moving in her belly didn't rouse the beast the way it had two weeks ago—probably because the beast had locked its focus on Dilys Merimydion and her sisters.

"Let's finish this page and make it an early night," Gabriella suggested. "I understand there's going to be dancing in the plazas tonight. I think you should go."

Lily cast a longing glance out the school windows, where the sound of laughter from courting couples wafted in through the open panes, but then her wistful expression closed up, and she said, "Oh, I don't know. It's been a long week. I was thinking about just catching up on my sleep."

"Don't be silly. Go. You'll have fun." Gabriella hated for Lily to be stuck here, holed up in the school, when she really wanted to be out in the village, dancing and meeting handsome young men.

"Er . . . well, maybe I will," the young woman muttered.

Gabriella, who'd made prevaricating her life's work, could smell even an accomplished lie from a mile away—and Lily wasn't close to being an accomplished liar. "That means you won't." She held up her hands to forestall any insincere protests. "At least tell my why you won't go when you clearly would like to? It can't be because of the baby. There are at least a hundred expectant mothers here looking for husbands."

Biting her lip and blushing a little, Lily admitted, "It's just that . . . well . . . I don't know anyone. Between working at the school and studying at night, I don't get out much. Not that I'm complaining!" she rushed to add. "Not at all. I'm so grateful for the school and the work and a place to stay. More grateful than I can possibly say—"

"But you haven't had much time to do anything else."

"Which is fine!" Lily exclaimed. "I have so much more here than I ever dreamed possible."

Gabriella laid her hands over Lily's and smiled. "It's all right. I understand completely. And it's my fault. I've been thoughtless, so wrapped up in my own life, I haven't paid attention to how little time I've left you to live yours."

"Oh, no, ma'am. Not at all. Please, don't think that. It's just that—well, I know I made my way from the Orchards to here on my own, but contrary to what you believe, that was desperation, not bravery. I'm really a big coward. Especially when it comes to going places and doing things without someone I know as company. I had plenty of time before we started making the costumes to go out and meet the folk around here, but I didn't. It was easier—more comfortable—to keep to myself."

Gabriella hadn't gauged Lily to be a shy wallflower. Probably because the girl was so good at helping out and getting things done. And because she was so good with the children—decisive and authoritative while remaining kind and approachable.

Now, Gabriella felt guilty for not paying more attention. She'd been so preoccupied with her own concerns that she'd been completely blind to Lily's. That wasn't like her, and she hated that she'd been so self-absorbed, but this, at least, was an oversight she could rectify. Summer was no stranger to shy wallflowers. Entertaining them, drawing them out of their shells, helping them meet and make friends had, in fact, always been one of her most common roles. (Cozying up to cretins being her other most common role.) Even if Gabriella couldn't stay in Konumarr long enough to see Lily's future settled, she could at least see to it that Lily got out of the schoolhouse, met some Calbernans, and made friends who would not let her hide away.

And she could start by seeing that Lily got out of the schoolhouse and had a little fun tonight.

"I think dancing in the plazas is just what you need," Gabriella said. "To be honest, I was hoping to go with you and do a little dancing myself." The sudden flare of hope that lit Lily's eyes made Gabriella feel even guiltier for not seeing how lonely she was before now.

Then Lily's brief spurt of hope faded. "You? A fine lady? Dancing in the plazas?" Lily shook her head. "Oh, I don't think so. That wouldn't be right." Like most Summerlanders, Lily had been raised with a very definite idea of social classes and who belonged where. It was one of Gabriella's least favorite aspects of her homeland. Here in Wintercraig, there were still nobles and peasants, but surviving in the harsh climate made them much more codependent, frequently blurring the lines between social classes, or erasing them altogether.

"I wasn't planning to go as a fine lady," Gabriella said, thinking fast. "You and I are close to the same size. I was hoping you could loan me a dress to wear, and maybe one of your scarves."

"I—are you sure?"

"Completely," Gabriella said. Actually, the more she thought about it, the better the idea sounded. One of the calming techniques her mother had taught Gabriella was to get away from whatever was upsetting her and distract herself with something fun and lighthearted whenever she felt herself getting too wound up. Gods knew, she'd been wound tighter than a coiled spring since the Calbernans had come. Dancing—a pastime she'd always enjoyed— would probably do her worlds of good. And since neither

Calberna's prince nor her sisters were likely to join the common folk for tonight's festivities, accompanying Lily to the party in the plazas was probably one of the safest places she could be tonight.

Lily bit her lip. "Well, I've got the dress my mother made. It would suit you, I think. It's my best."

"Oh, no, I can't wear your best dress. You should wear it."

"Can't." Lily gave a rueful smile and patted her thickening waist. "It doesn't fit me anymore."

"Ah. Then, of course, I'd be honored to wear the dress your mother made you."

CHAPTER 8

Lily's mother's dress needed only a few minor alterations to fit Gabriella. Since a princess could hardly disappear for an entire evening without raising the alarm, Summer left Lily to make the alternations and returned to the palace to establish her alibi for the night. After a small dinner with the family, she announced that she wasn't feeling well and headed for her rooms, dismissing Amaryllis with instructions that she should not be disturbed. After that, sneaking out of the palace was a simple matter of using the side doors and whispering a few words of Persuasion to make the guards look the other way as she passed by.

An hour later, wearing a very pretty lilac dress with full, lightweight sleeves and a ruffled hem, Gabriella exited the school with Lily by her side. Lily had changed into a high-waisted yellow gown that provided a stunning contrast to her dark hair, skin, and eyes. Both of them wore clean white linen scarves that covered their heads and tied at the back of their necks beneath the long, loose flow of black hair. They looked like two country girls from Summerlea on their way to a local dance.

"We could be sisters," Summer said as they made their way down towards one of the city's many large plazas. She and Lily had the same build. Their hair was the same color and length. Lily's skin was darker, but unless the pair of them stood side by side, it wasn't that obvious.

"Yes, I suppose so, Your Highness."

Gabriella stopped in her tracks, grasping Lily's arm. "No. None of that 'Your Highness' stuff. Tonight, I'm not a princess or a Season or a noble lady. You must call me Gabriella."

"I—I couldn't."

"Of course, you can. Try it. Gabriella."

"Gabriella," Lily whispered, then she clapped her hands over her mouth, her eyes wide and horrified.

Summer made a show of looking around and up at the sky. Then she grinned. "There. You see? And you didn't get struck by lightning!"

After a shocked moment, Lily giggled.

"Say it again," Summer told her.

With a little more confidence, Lily did. "Gabriella."

"Excellent." She looped her arm though Lily's. "And since we look so alike, if anyone asks, I think you should say I'm your sister. Would that be all right with you?"

"I—if that's what you wish, Your . . . er . . . Gabriella."

"It is."

Together, arm in arm, the two of them strolled down the stone side street and out onto the main thoroughfare. The sun was still shining brightly, though the plaza clock chimed nine o'clock in the evening as they approached. A band of drummers, fiddlers, and pipers were assembled on the balcony of one of the plaza buildings, playing a merry tune while scores of Calbernans and brightly garbed laughing women spun about the square.

Lily watched them with a strange mixture of happiness and sorrow. "Tomis always promised me we'd go dancing one day," she said. She rubbed a hand on the slight swell of her belly. "We never did."

"Tomis . . . he was your husband?" Lily had never mentioned him by name.

Lily glanced at her, eyes shimmering wetly, then quickly looked away. "He would have been. Truth is, we never got married proper like—just said the vows to ourselves."

She looked down at the ground and scuffed her shoe. "He joined up with the soldiers to make money so we could have a real wedding. Then, after Tomis died and I found out I was gonna have a baby . . . well, my da isn't a nice man. It would've been bad."

So, the abuser had been the father. It was a shame Gabriella couldn't risk taking the time to track him down and serve a little justice on him. She wouldn't mind unleashing her monster on a man who would abuse his own daughter—especially a daughter as kind-natured as Lily. "So, you came here."

Lily nodded. "I heard about these Seafolk coming here to look for wives, and I figured, why not? I heard they were good to women, and at least my baby would have a chance for a better life than me." She shook her head and swiped at her tears. "I'm sorry for lying to you, Your—" She stopped herself before saying the title, and took a ragged breath. "I'm sorry," she said again in a low voice, not looking at Summer. "If you want me to leave the school, I'll understand."

"Leave the school?" Gabriella regarded her in genuine surprise. "Why would I want you to leave?"

Amber eyes blinked solemnly. "Because I lied to you, ma'am."

"Gabriella. You agreed to call me Gabriella."

"That was before."

"Before what? Before you confirmed what I already suspected?" Summer smiled. "Don't be silly. You've a home here, Lily, if you want it. A place to live, a job, an education. We're going to the plazas tonight to have fun, and so you can meet the Calbernans to see if any of them suit you, but if you'd rather stay in Konumarr and raise your baby on your own, there will always be place for you, if not at the school, then at the palace."

"Yes, ma'am—Gabriella. Thank you."

"There's just one more thing I need to know."

"Ma'am? I mean, what is it?"

"How old are you, Lily, truly? I suspect you aren't the twenty years you claimed."

Lily bit the inside of her cheek. "I'll be seventeen the first Freikasday of next month."

"I see." So young. "Tell me, are you really interested in marrying a Calbernan? Or did you come here just because you thought marrying one of them was the only way to provide for your baby?"

Lily looked around at the towering, muscular, tattooed men laughing, dancing, and talking with the women of Wintercraig and Summerlea who'd come in search of husbands. "Well, they are just about the prettiest men I've ever seen."

"They are that."

"And like I said, I heard they're kind to their womenfolk. A girl could do worse, I expect."

"I imagine she could, but you shouldn't feel pressured to marry."

Lily sighed. "You know, I really did love my Tomis. We grew up together. But he's gone, and I don't want to spend the rest of my life alone. I want a father for this baby. And I want more babies after that. I need a husband for that." Lily turned to Gabriella. "I just want a good one. Not one like my da."

"All right, then." With a smile, Summer draped an arm around Lily's waist. "If a Calbernan husband is what you want, let's go find you a good one."

She wasn't there.

Dilys felt Summer Coruscate's absence the instant he stepped foot on the palace terrace, where his officers and the ladies of the court had gathered for the evening's entertainment. After gearing up for the hunt, having his quarry thwart his plans by not showing up at all left him feeling both bereft and more than a little surly.

When Spring and Autumn stepped out onto the terrace to join the festivities, he made a beeline for them, barely remembering to paste on a welcoming smile as he drew near. He forced himself to indulge in the usual pleasantries before asking about the whereabouts of their sister. His effort at subtlety must have fallen shy of the mark, because both Autumn and Spring looked a little taken aback.

The two Seasons shared a speaking glance, before Spring informed him, "Summer sent word that she wasn't feeling well this evening. She retired early and asked not to be disturbed."

"Did something happen between the two of you?" Autumn asked. There was a tone in her voice Dilys couldn't quite place.

"*Ono*," he denied. "Nothing happened." His curiosity rose. "Why? Did she say something had?" He hadn't managed to get within a hundred feet of Summer in several days, but after the way he'd put his foot in his mouth that first morning, he'd scrupulously avoided saying or doing anything any of the princesses might take offense at.

"No, of course not."

"Then did any of my officers said or do something to upset her? Because if they did—"

"Your officers have been perfect gentlemen," Autumn assured him. "I didn't mean to imply anything of the sort. I simply thought your inquiry might indicate that you and she had . . . um . . . decided to spend more time together."

Dilys hesitated. It belatedly occurred to him that indicating an interest in Summer might not exactly endear him to the two princesses he had been courting since his arrival. For a man trained since birth to understand and anticipate the desires of women, it was a particularly egregious oversight. But since neither one of them appeared put out at the possibility, he cautiously admitted, "I had thought perhaps we might begin to do so."

Another look passed between the two sisters. Dilys recognized that one. It wasn't a good look. And it meant he'd completely misread the two Seasons' response to his inquiry.

"Is that so?" Spring said. Black brows arched high over chilly green eyes.

"I thought you preferred someone with a little more fire to her," Autumn said. "Someone a bit less like"— she turned to her sister Spring—"what was that he called Summer again?"

"Milked tea," Spring supplied, her frosty gaze pinned on Dilys's face.

"Right. Milked tea." Autumn turned back towards Dilys and smiled.

That smile very nearly made him take a step back. He stopped himself just in time. There were creatures in the world to whom a man dare show no fear if he hoped to survive an encounter with them. Women—particularly angry women who thought they were protecting a beloved sister—were among the most dangerous of such creatures.

"As I already explained, that remark was a show of prideful idiocy that I regretted as soon as it left my lips. I didn't mean it. I never meant it, and I have already apologized for it. An apology which," he reminded them, "all three of you accepted."

"Well, there's forgiving," Autumn said, "and then there's forgetting."

"Two entirely separate things." Spring moved to her sister's side, effectively putting a wall of bristling femininity directly in Dilys's path. "Judging by the fact that Summer has made such a point of steering clear of you, I'd say she hasn't forgotten anything."

"And the forgiving is still pretty iffy too." Autumn's smile was so sharp it was a wonder he wasn't bleeding from multiple lacerations.

"I am aware I have much work to do to earn my way back into your sister's good graces. That's one of the reasons I was hoping to speak with her tonight. To start making amends."

"And?" Spring's eyes hadn't warmed in the slightest.

His brows drew together in confusion. "And what?"

"The other reasons you wanted to speak with her." Autumn elucidated crisply. "What are they?"

Dilys had faced enemy armies less fierce than these two women grilling him about his intentions towards their sister. His admiration for them grew exponentially, as did his interest in the woman who had inspired such ferocious love and loyalty.

He had come here to court the three Seasons of Summerlea, and to choose from them a *liana* who was strong, wise, and capable enough to mother Calberna's next queen. Everything he knew, everything he'd personally come to know about Autumn and Spring said they, not their sister, were the right choice to fill that role.

And yet every instinct and every cell in his body was telling him that Summer, rather than either of her wise, capable, strong sisters, was not just the woman for him, but the *only* woman for him.

Her sisters wanted to know his intentions towards her. A cautious man would hedge his bets now. Even if he wanted to follow his instincts to see what might come of them, he would keep his options open—court all three sisters, as per his agreement with Khamsin of the Storms—in case his instincts turned out to be wrong.

But Dilys had been in enough battles to know that sometimes a bold, direct, all-or-nothing attack was the only path to victory. Considering that his desire for Gabriella Coruscate had been growing stronger every day, despite the fact that she had turned avoiding him into a masterful talent, this battle was one where caution was the wrong choice.

"Forgive me, but my other reasons are personal. I will not do her the disservice of sharing them before I have a chance to speak with her privately." He bowed gravely first to Spring and then Autumn. "*Myerialanna* Spring, *Myerialanna* Autumn. Thank you both for the honor of your company these last ten days. You have made me feel truly welcome. Any man would be graced by the gods to call himself your *akua,* your husband. And now, if you will excuse me, as *Myerialanna* Summer will not be joining the festivities this evening, I will take my leave of you."

As he walked away he heard Autumn say, "Did he just . . . *dump* us?"

"You know," Spring responded in a thoughtful tone, "I believe he did."

Autumn's voice dropped to a whisper, which Dilys's acute hearing picked up as easily as if she'd been talking full voice right into his ear. "I knew there was something going on between the two of them! I *knew* it! I told you she was lying about it! I told you she was lying, even to us."

"It would seem so. The real question is . . . why?"

And that was the question Dilys was still pondering several hours later as he wandered through the shadowy, twilit gardens towards the shores of the Llaskroner Fjord.

Why would Summer Coruscate work so hard to avoid a suitor she was attracted to—assuming her sisters were right about her interest? Why would she make such an effort to make him believe she not only didn't like him, she was *afraid* of him? And why, when by all accounts she shared an extremely close bond with her fellow Seasons, would she lie about her feelings, even to the sisters she loved and trusted above all others? It made no sense.

The thick, soft garden grass beneath Dilys's feet gave way to the hard stone terrace and stairs leading down to the small pleasure-craft dock where several row- and sailboats had been moored for the use of the palace guests. Dilys descended the steps and stepped out onto the wooden dock. The moon had risen. Its silvery light glittered on the night-dark surface of the water.

For an instant, he thought he saw a woman standing at the far end of the dock, her slender form silhouetted by the moonlight, but when he turned his full attention towards her, she was gone. He frowned and stopped in his tracks. The vision felt odd, like a flash of memory or a hazy fragment of a dream swimming up from his subconscious. It had to be a dream. He'd never been down here on this dock, at night, with a woman. His evening sails with Autumn and Spring had been aboard the *Kracken,* not these small pleasure boats, a decision he'd made specifically so he would be able to concentrate on entertaining the princesses rather than handling ropes, sails, and the boom. As for his daily swims in the fjord, he'd restricted those to the early-morning hours, when most of the palace and village were still asleep but the sun had already risen.

And yet, this place . . . this *now* . . . seemed so familiar.

Dilys squeezed his eyes shut and rubbed his temples, trying to figure out where the memory was coming from. He'd been standing here, or in a place eerily similar to here. Only the dock wasn't as clean and tidy as it was now. There should have been coils of ropes and several anchors lying about near the edges of the pier . . . because the woman . . . she had stumbled on those coils of rope. She had . . . fallen. He could hear the splash. Then the silence when she didn't resurface. It dragged on one second . . . two . . . He could feel the slap of the night-damp wood against the soles of his feet as he'd run down the length of dock and launched himself into the still, dark water of the fjord . . .

His chest felt tight. Dilys lay a hand over his heart, pressing clawed fingers into the thick flesh of his pectoral. She'd been drowning. He'd tried to save her. He could see her there in the water, dark hair spread out like skeins of sea silk floating about her face. Golden eyes shining up at him in the darkness from a face shrouded in shadow.

Golden eyes, not blue. Not Summer Coruscate, then. But who? Why couldn't he remember?

Through sunset and into the twilit darkness of the short summer night, Lily and Gabriella laughed and danced and chatted with handsome Calbernan men. Lily flirted shyly. Gabriella did not. Several of the islanders tried to engage her, but she told them she was already spoken for and had just come to keep her sister company.

Tables overflowed with free food provided by the king and queen. More tables flowed with wine, ale, and mead for only a copper *piseta* a glass. Lily stuck to the free sweet punch until the attentive young Calbernan who had danced with her multiple times bought her a glass of ice wine, then another after she thirstily drained the first. Before Lily reached the bottom of her second glass, Gabriella realized the wine was a mistake. Either because she hadn't eaten much that day or because she had no head for alcohol, the strong wine went straight to Lily's head.

"Uh-oh, time to get you home," Gabriella announced when Lily started giggling and swaying on her feet.

"I will accompany you to your dwelling," said the young Calbernan who'd bought Lily the wine. He seemed sincerely distressed that his gift had impaired her.

"It's not necessary—Talin, was it? We're staying not far away." She'd had a nice night of anonymity and a very good time. But Talin and Lily had hit it off and she didn't want him to find out they'd lied about who she was just yet. If he came with them to the school, he might see Princess Summer leave—because Summer couldn't very well go back to the palace wearing Lily's best dress.

"The sun has set, and Lily-*myerina* is not herself," Talin replied. "I will accompany you."

Gabriella's approval of him went up another notch. Protecting the vulnerable was an admirable trait. But he still wasn't coming with them. "Really Talin, it's not necessary. With a whole Calbernan army here and the White Guard patrolling the streets, Konumarr is currently the safest city on Mystral." She smiled to soften her refusal. "Which ship are you on, Talin?"

The young man's chest puffed out slightly. "I sail aboard the *Kracken*, Gabriella-*myerina*."

Dilys Merimydion's ship. It figured. Talin was *definitely* not walking them back to the school.

"I'll see to it Lily finds you there tomorrow," she said with a tiny push of Persuasion. "All right? Wonderful. Have a good night, then." Without giving him time to object or shrug off her subtle command, she wrapped an arm around Lily's waist and headed for the road.

After a few wrong turns to make sure Talin hadn't gotten it into his head to follow them, Gabriella steered Lily down one of the side streets that ran parallel to the main road and headed for the school.

"Come on, Lily, let's get you home."

Lily blinked at her and smiled drunkenly. "I'm not Lily. You are. See?" She clutched at Gabriella's pink frock. "You're wearing her dressh." She poked Summer in the chest. "You're Lily. I'm Gabriella." Her head fell back and she laughed.

Summer sighed. "All right, Gabriella. Let's get you home. And no more ice wine for you."

Lily pouted. "But I like eyesh wine."

"I can see that," Gabriella said dryly.

"I liked Talin."

"Yes, he seemed very nice."

"He liked me, too."

"It definitely seemed so."

"You're such a good friend, Lily." Lily threw her arms around Summer's neck, dislodging the headscarf holding back Summer's hair, and smacked a loud, sloppy kiss on her cheek. "I wish you really were my sister. This was the best night of my life." Then she laughed, spun out of Summer's reach and ran up the street towards the school. She whipped off her own headscarf and threw it in the air, twirling in circles. "I love Talin. I love you. I love *everybody*!" She danced and skipped up the stone steps of the school, disappearing into the shadowy alcove of the recessed door, and began singing off key, "Lily, Lily is my friend. The nicest girl in Winterland." And she burst into drunken giggles over the rhyme.

Summer sighed and laughed ruefully as she pulled the dislodged scarf off her head and bent to retrieve the one Lily had tossed in the air. Definitely no more ice wine for Lily ever again.

The sky was dark now, and the moon had ducked behind a bank of clouds. Oil lamps burning every block kept the side street well lit, but several of the narrower alleys between buildings were impenetrable. Later, Gabriella would berate herself for not paying more attention as she walked past the darkened alley nearest the school.

The punch to her ribs caught her utterly by surprise.

It slammed into her like a hammer. She heard a crack, felt a searing flash of pain, then she was weightless, flying off her feet.

Her body slammed sideways into the gray stone bricks of the street. If not for her outflung right arm, her head would have slammed into the bricks as well. As it was, she was still left dazed when her arm smacked the stone, and her head slammed hard against her arm. Her unbound hair spilled over her face, blinding her as she lay there, gasping for breath.

"Did you think I wouldn't find you, you stupid slut?" She heard the crunch of boots on stone, then something hard slammed into her side. The little breath she'd managed to recover whooshed out of her again as a new, even more searing pain tore across her chest. The beast had kicked her!

She wheezed in pain, then gave a strangled scream as a meaty hand reached down to grab the front of her dress and haul her off the pavement.

"You thought you could just run away? You thought I wouldn't follow?"

The backhand caught her across the jaw. Blood filled her mouth as her teeth snapped together hard. She gasped and coughed on blood. The last blow had knocked most of the hair out of her face, allowing her to see at least the outline of her attacker. A big, hulking man, looming over her, his face cast in shadow. She blinked up at him, squinting against the light from the nearby streetlamp.

The man stiffened. He hauled her closer, pulling her into the spill of lamplight so he could see her face. "Who the *fark* are you? Where's my daughter? Why are you wearing her dress?"

And then, from the direction of the school, came Lily's scream. "Da!"

"Lily!" Gabriella's attacker released her, delivered one last, brutal kick, and took off in the direction of the school. "You stay right there, you worthless cow!"

Lily screamed again. A few moments later, Gabriella heard a blistering spate of swearing interspersed with the sounds of fists and booted feet battering against a closed door. Thank Helos, even drunk, Lily must've had the presence of mind to run into the school and lock the door behind her.

Summer rolled over to her hands and knees. A white-hot poker shot through her chest. She gasped, then doubled back over and coughed up blood. She was having trouble breathing, as if there were a heavy stone pressed down on her chest. He'd broken her ribs with one of those kicks, then must have driven that rib into her lungs with another.

The crash of the school door giving way brought her surging to her feet despite the searing pain. That brute was going for Lily. Pregnant Lily. One punch or kick like the ones he'd slammed into Gabriella, and Lily would lose the baby she'd run away to save.

Summer wrapped an arm around her torso and staggered towards the school. She'd seen the scars on Lily's back and arms. She knew this monster must have been the one to have made them, and she'd be damned to the frozen fires of Hel before she let him lay another finger on the sweet, shy girl she'd come to care about.

She ran through the splintered doorway into the school. The halls were dark. The lamps were unlit, but she followed the sound of running feet and shrill cries and swearing. Up the stairs. Down the hall past the second-floor classrooms. All of the doors were closed except one towards the back of the hall. It was open, the door's large glass viewing pane shattered.

Inside the room, desks lay overturned, haphazardly shoved aside like a jumble of child's blocks. Lily's father had her pinned by the neck against the stone wall, and his fist—that massive, hammer of a fist—was drawn back, ready to plow into her belly.

The pain of Gabriella's ribs gave way to a different, familiar pain. The hot, tight stretch of terrible power roaring to life inside her. She hadn't unleashed her most dreadful magic in almost twenty years. Not since the day she'd done murder.

She unleashed it now.

It roared out of her like a savage, untamed beast bursting from its cage. A violent, hot, incinerating firestorm of a beast. A fury that burned away pity, compassion, mercy.

"Get your hands off her!"

In Konumarr's plazas, where the music was still playing, and the dancers were still dancing, every Calbernan suddenly stopped in his tracks with a shudder. A split second later, every one of them roared, a sound that tore through the peace of the night, brought the musicians to a shocked halt, and sent the waters of the fjord into a frenzy of wild waves.

Battle claws sprang forth. Battle fangs descended.

As one, they abandoned the dance, their companions—their veneer of civilization—and raced down the street.

In Konumarr Palace, Ari, Ryll and the rest of the fleets' officers strolled the torch-lit garden paths and danced on the lantern-lit palace terrace, enjoying yet another cool, pleasant evening in the company of the lovely, accomplished gentlewomen who might be their future mates.

Then came the sound. A Shout the likes of which they'd never heard before. It tore through their beings. Pierced them to the core. Ignited a wild, furious flame that burned beyond all imagining.

As one, to the shock of their companions, they roared. Their voices shattered the night.

The water in the fjord rose up in response, cresting waves slamming against the banks.

Claws out, fangs down, they ran. Some raced across the bridge into Konumarr city. Others dove into the raucous, unsettled waves of the fjord, riding powerful jets of seawater to the other shore.

For she had Called. And they must answer.

Dilys stood on the edge of the dock, trying without success to remember the face of the golden-eyed woman in his visions.

And then his whole world turned on its head.

A Voice slammed into him with the force of a tidal wave. A Shout that emptied the seas, tore the fabric of the universe, exploded the sun. Claws and teeth of white-hot fire clamped tight around his soul.

Inside him, a cold, hard kernel dormant in him since birth erupted into fiery life. A nascent volcano ripping through the mantle of his soul. Spewing heat and flame and burning stone. Transforming.

Awakening.

He'd been asleep his whole life and never knew it.

That Voice. *She* had Shouted. And all the world fell away, leaving only the need to answer . . . to serve . . . to protect.

The roar ripped out of him, exploding from his throat. Raw. Pained. A thundering cry of bliss and fear and fury. An answering Shout of exultation and of warning.

The waters of the fjord went wild, the surface ragged with crashing, foaming waves. His knees bent. Strength gathered in his thighs. Exploded in a burst that sent him diving into the spout of water that rose up to meet him. The water carried him across the width of the fjord and delivered him onto the village docks within seconds. He hit the ground running.

There was no need to search. No need to wonder where he was going. Earlier today, he'd told Ari he felt like a fish on a hook. But that feeling was nothing compared to this. *This* felt like he'd been impaled by a whaling harpoon. And the invisible line attached to it was reeling him in faster than his feet could run.

He flew through the streets of Konumarr. Around him, thousands of others were running, too. Every single Calbernan in Konumarr . . . following the same invisible line.

He bared his battle fangs and snarled. He would fight them if he must. To the death—theirs or his. His claws were sharp. His body strong.

They had gathered, his potential rivals, around a tall stone building a block off Konumarr's main thoroughfare. He barked a Word he'd never known before. It spewed up from that newborn volcano inside him, filled somehow with more than just the vast power his mother had gifted him. His would-be rivals staggered back, clearing a path that led to the stone house.

He took the stairs three at a time. Raced through the splintered doorway. He'd never been in this building before, but he found the stairs without a thought and vaulted up them. There were others inside the stone building already. Crowding the hall between him and *her,* the one so inexorably drawing him to her side. They had heard her Shout, and they had come, like him, to answer that wordless call. Males hungry to be claimed, ready to prove their strength, their speed, their ferociousness in battle.

The tendons in his neck stood out like steely cords. He roared a challenge. Eyes hot, fangs bared, a few roared back, but the flash of golden fire in his eyes and the terrible

Word that he spat from his lips and drove them to their knees made them bare their necks in submission and let him pass.

It was good that they did. He would have shredded their flesh and painted the stone walls with their blood.

At the end of the hall, another shattered door stood ajar. Beyond it, a room with many desks piled against the wall. Calbernans crowded in the space remaining. The ones who had been closest when she Shouted. Unlike the ones in the hall, these parted and let him pass without challenge, though there was rumbling in more than a few chests and more than a few bared fangs.

The acknowledgment of his dominance settled him. The hot rush of his blood calmed, no longer drumming through his veins so loud it deafened him.

Only then did he hear the muffled sound of sobbing. A female. Frightened.

He shouldered past the last line of Calbernans into the small ring of space at the back of the room, where he found a slender young female in a yellow dress sitting on the bloody floor, clutching the prone body of another female, this one clad in torn and bloodstained lilac. Both of the females had come from some Summerlea farm or village, judging by their dark skin, black hair, and the style and quality of their clothing.

Blood covered them both in scarlet spatters. Covered the wall behind them. The floor around them. A thick, wide swath of scarlet led away from them to the opposite wall, where what looked like a pile of butchered meat lay in a heap against the wall.

It took Dilys a moment to realize the pile of meat was the remains of a man. His chest had burst open from the inside out, ribs splayed and bent back, organs liquified. His head and limbs had separated from the torso. Popped off like a cork from a bottle.

Dilys turned back to the weeping female huddled over the lilac-clad one. Was this sobbing Summerlander *her*?

The one who had Shouted with such force she'd ripped a man to bloody shreds and summoned every Calbernan in the city?

How was that possible? No one but the rarest of Calberna's native-born daughters could have given voice to that particular magic. Dilys should know. His and every other great House in Calberna had been trying to bring that great, long-lost magic back to their land and their bloodlines for millennia.

It couldn't be this Summerlander. The one who'd Shouted must surely be Calbernan. But what Calbernan parent would ever let her daughter—especially a daughter with that particular gift—leave the protection of the Isles? And how could such a daughter have been born in the first place and not be known?

It was impossible. It simply couldn't be.

And yet, without a doubt, a woman of great, long-lost Calbernan power had Shouted with a Voice that had not been heard in Mystral in more than two thousand years.

"Who are you?" he asked the crying Summerlander. "Where do you come from? Where is the woman who did this?" He pointed to the pile of meat.

He had not meant to sound threatening, but his reaction to the Voice that had summoned him was still so strong his words came out as a deadly growl. Coupled with his fully extended battle fangs and claws, he must have looked and sounded terrifying.

Certainly he did to the weeping girl in the yellow dress, because in response to his inquiry, she clutched the lilac-clad female's body more closely to her chest and began tearfully sobbing for him not to hurt them.

Behind him, the rest of his men began to rumble. They'd initially submitted to his dominance and given way, but this girl's reaction to him—a clear rejection—had just opened the door for challenge.

Dilys was torn. On the one hand, he needed to calm down and retract claws and fangs so he could calm the hysterical girl enough to get some answers. On the other hand, with thousands of Calbernan warriors at his back, all of them riding the killing edge, he needed to remain battle-ready until he put an end to the mystery, determined who had Shouted—and find out where she'd gone if she wasn't one of these Summerlander farm girls.

Which, surely, she couldn't be.

Then came a realization that tied his guts in knots. It didn't matter who the owner of that Voice had been, because he was bound by contract to exclusively court the Seasons of Summerlea for another ten weeks. To break a second contract bound in blood and salt would brand him forever as an oathbreaker and make him unworthy of the woman who wielded that Voice.

Which meant, no matter who she was, he had no right to court her at this time.

No right to be claimed by her, until the Seasons made their choice.

Blessed Numahao.

He was still reeling from that realization, when someone pushed his way forward from the back of the room.

"Lily?"

Dilys whirled, aggression rising in instinctive response. He recognized one of his men from the *Kracken.* A ballista operator named Talin.

"You know these women, Talin?" It was impossible to keep the growl out of his voice.

"*Tey, moa Myerielua.* Well . . . only a little. I met them tonight. Lily and her sister Gabriella, from Summerlea." Talin inched forward, watching Dilys carefully as he called, "Lily? It's me, Talin. Are you hurt?"

The weeping one in the yellow dress looked up with a gasp, but when she caught sight of Talin, she burst into fresh tears and start babbling incoherently in Sun Tongue, the native Summerlea dialect, confirming Dilys's earlier guess as to the girls' origins.

Talin started to go to her, but a warning growl from Dilys stopped him in his tracks.

Dilys gave himself a shake and forced the aggression down. He had no rights here. None at all.

"Sorry," he muttered to the still-frozen Talin. "Go to her."

Even after granting Talin permission to approach the women, the moment the ballista operator knelt beside them, Dilys's clawed fingers flexed, aching to rend something. Preferably Talin.

"Lily," Talin was saying. "Can you tell me what happened? Are you hurt? Does any of this blood belong to you?"

The girl shook her head wildly and said in Eru, the common tongue, "No. I'm not hurt. He tried, but she stopped him." And then she started babbling in Sun Tongue again.

"Who stopped him? Who did this? Where did she go?" Dilys asked. This time, the sound of his growling voice didn't make Lily scream. It made her shudder, clam up, and cringe back against Talin, clearly seeking his protection.

Talin shot him a sharp glance which, under the circumstances, was, admittedly, warranted. He'd clearly established enough of a rapport with Lily that she felt comfortable seeking his protection. That gave him the right to provide it, even to protect her from his prince.

Dilys bit back a snarl and curled his fingers into fists. It was a gesture of peace—albeit an uneasy peace—a sheathing of claws that he could not force to retract.

Talin turned back to his female. "Lily, who stopped him?"

"She did." She clutched the bloody body of the other Summerlander closer. "But he was going to kill me."

"Are you saying your sister did this? Gabriella stopped him?"

Lily buried her face in Talin's neck, nodding and sobbing, her whole body heaving as Talin gathered her close.

Thunderstruck, Dilys stared at the bloodied form of the unconscious woman in the lilac dress. The Shout had come from *her*? A Summerlander farm girl? How was that possible?

Her face was turned away and there was too much blood and hair covering it to make out her features. One arm lay limp at her side, slender, fine-boned, the palm looking so slight and vulnerable. Her palm was scraped. Her gown was bloodied, torn, and soiled with mud and dirt. That had not happened here, in this building. And it hadn't happened by accident, either. There were several muddy boot prints on the waistline of her gown.

Someone had kicked her. Stomped on her.

He glanced at the pile of meat that had been her attacker. Gauged the man's size by the length of his femur and the meaty hand still attached to the remains of his arm. A big, full-grown man. Hulking, by the mass of him. Not as large as a Winterman or a Calbernan, but compared to the women, plenty large enough.

He turned back to the Calbernans crowded behind him. Spotted Ryll in the midst. "Ryll, send for a healer. Quickly."

Talin was rocking Lily, trying to soothe her as she sobbed in Sun Tongue against his throat. After a few minutes, Talin looked up with a frown. "Forgive me, my prince. My Sun Tongue is not the best. She keeps saying something about the princess. That she's killed the princess."

It took a moment for that to process.

And then, for the second time, Dilys's whole body froze as that fiery, newborn volcano at his core erupted all over again.

This place—his gaze flew around the room, touching on the jumbled desks piled up against the walls—it was a school. The queen of Wintercraig had founded a school in Konumarr. She was very proud of it and had spoken of it often since his arrival. One of her sisters taught at the school—had, in fact, used it as her excuse to stay away from the palace since his arrival.

The Seasons were known by their giftnames, but they all had another. Ridiculously long Summerlander names. He knew, because he'd memorized them all before coming here. Including the name Gabriella Aretta Rosadora Liliana Elaine Coruscate.

Gabriella.

The Season known as Summer.

Dilys lunged forward, dropping to his knees on the blood-soaked floor.

Every Calbernan in the room snarled at him.

He didn't snarl back. He *roared*. He didn't even have to use a Word this time. The mere force of his furious warning was enough to choke their threatening snarls into discontented rumbling. Still unhappy, but no longer verging on challenge.

Dilys reached for the fallen, unconscious woman. His hands were shaking. He stopped. Stared hard at them. Then concern for her managed what will alone could not: his battle claws retracted, disappearing into his fingertips so as not to risk the slightest nick to her precious skin. Only then did he let himself touch her, brush back the blood-matted hair from her face.

"Gabriella," he called softly. "*Myerialanna* Summer . . ."

He heard Talin's sharp intake of breath. The ballista operator hadn't made the connection. Apparently none of them had, because the others in the room fell abruptly silent and the tension dropped by a significant, palpable measure. As well it should.

If the fallen woman was, indeed, Summer Coruscate, then both by dominance and by contract signed in blood and salt, the right of courtship belonged to Dilys. *Without challenge*.

He turned the woman's face towards his and wiped

away the scarlet spatters, revealing delicate, warm brown skin and serenely beautiful features. Her eyes were closed, but he didn't need to see their deep, beautiful blue to know.

Dilys bent his head, drawing in a ragged breath of both relief and stunned wonder.

It was her.

Summer Coruscate. The Season who had haunted his dreams since his arrival. The shy, fearful, reputedly powerless princess of Summerlea who somehow—by some impossible, incredible miracle of fate—spoke with the legendary Voice of a Siren.

CHAPTER 9

"*Myerielua* . . ." Talin said, his voice oddly shaking. "*Myerielua* . . . your *ulumi* . . ."

Dilys glanced down at himself. Every tattoo on his body was lit up as if from some inner fire, shining a bright, phosphorescent blue.

At the sight of those shining lines, something snapped inside his brain and memories—clear, true, and irrefutably his—flooded into his mind. The woman standing on the dock in the moonlight—that had been her. The eyes—blue that turned to gleaming gold when she used her most shocking gifts—those were her eyes. The fingers tracing the shining, illuminated blue lines of his *ulumi*—hers, as well. Her voice saying his name with wonder and longing as she recognized the nascent bond between them. Her lips cementing that bond with a kiss.

There was no mistaking what was happening to him—what had begun that first night, on that dock in the moonlight, when he'd dived into the fjord to save her and emerged a man bound in *liakapua*.

He had begun the mating ritual of his species . . . with her, Gabriella Coruscate. The Summerlea princess who had used her magic to manipulate his mind.

The *Siren* who had used her Voice to make him forget that he belonged to her, body and soul.

Before he could begin to process that, her body convulsed in a wracking cough. Blood splattered across his face. *Her* blood.

"Where's that healer?" he roared. "Get her here *now*!"

He laid Summer gently on the floor and pressed his palms against her chest. "You will not die, *moa kiri*. I will not let you." His mother had gifted him with her strength—almost all her strength—before he left Calberna. He carried it inside him now, a powerful, tremendous life force, raw magical energy, a vast ocean of it, from which he drew his own strength and powered his own gifts.

He had no power over flesh and bone, but blood . . . that was a different matter.

Blood was, primarily, water. Part of the ocean that had given life to all things. Part of Numahao that every living creature carried within itself.

And over water, Dilys ruled.

He closed his eyes, blocking out the press of anxious bodies, focusing on the blood—the water—that flowed through Summer's veins. She was in a bad way. Her ribs had been broken, her lung punctured. One lung had collapsed. The other was rapidly filling with blood. There was also a rapidly growing pool of blood in her abdomen where her attacker's booted foot had lacerated her kidney. She had other injuries as well, but those were the most severe. He focused on the lungs first. If she ceased to breathe, no other wounds would matter.

He found the punctures in the delicate lining of her lungs where tiny rivers of blood were pouring through. One by one, he blocked those flows, capturing the crimson currents with his magic and forcing them to turn, to follow a different path, using his magic to replace torn and ruptured cell walls with invisible barriers that routed her blood back into her veins.

The wounds inside her were many. Controlling them all was difficult. Dilys could move an entire ocean of water with a minor flex of his sea gifts, but every broken blood vessel, every tear in a vein, was like a separate ocean to be controlled. Controlling oceans was, in fact, far easier, because this work was so delicate, requiring intense concentration and finite control. And no matter the severity of the wound, each ruptured blood vessel required the same amount of effort to control. The task taxed his abilities to their limits. And still she needed more.

Her heart was stuttering. Her body shutting down. Even working as swiftly as he could, she was dying faster than he could save her. Her life force was draining with every passing second.

He gave her his.

There was no hesitation. No question. His life had belonged to her from the moment she'd kissed him on the docks that first night. Everything his mother had given to him and all the life his own cells possessed, he poured into to her now, trying to keep her alive until the healer came to repair the damage he could not.

"You will live, *moa kiri*. I will not let you die."

Her need was great. He drained himself, giving her everything except the magic he needed to keep commanding the blood in her veins and the life force he needed to keep breathing from one second to the next, and still there was no sign of the healer. He would have given her more—he would have sacrificed his own life to save hers without a second thought—but until the healer arrived to repair the damage to her organs, the only thing standing between Gabriella and death was Dilys. And Dilys was not going to last much longer without aid. He needed more energy and fast.

"Ryll, Ari, to me! I need your help!"

They had the closest connections to him, the strongest ties of love and blood. They could give him what he needed more quickly and with better results than the rest of his men, but he would drain every last drop of life force from every last Calbernan in Konumarr before he let her die.

Hands gripped his shoulders. Fresh energy—strong and

powerful, life and magic freely given—poured into him. He channeled it down his body and into Summer, siphoning only enough to keep the holes and tears in her veins dammed up and keep him working to seal the rest.

Someone was still sobbing hysterically. The girl. The witness.

In Sea Tongue he snapped, "Talin—the girl, Lily . . . you have a connection with her?"

"*Tey, Myerielua.*"

"She knows too much. You must take care of it. Is your connection strong enough or do you need help?"

A hesitation, then . . . "*Ono, Myerielua.* I can do it. No aid needed."

"Then do it. Now. Before the healer arrives."

A moment later, he heard Talin murmuring softly to the pregnant girl, Summer's friend, and a swell of *susirena* filled the room.

"I was the one to kill her attacker," Dilys instructed. "Tell her that. I am not sorry that I did, only that I did not get here sooner."

He heard Talin murmuring in Eru, his voice rich with *susirena* as he erased Lily's memory of Gabriella Shouting their attacker to death and replaced it with the memory of Dilys ripping the brute apart with his bare hands.

Mind control, used in this case for memory manipulation, was one of the most secret gifts left to native-born Calbernans. It was a gift Calbernans kept even from their *oulani* mates. A lesson they had learned the hard way back in the days of the Sirens. People rightly feared magic that could control their minds, and when enough people regarded the source of that magic with enough fear, those people became dangerous. That was why for the last twenty-five hundred years, Calbernan sailors had made a point of seeking out and destroying all record of the Sirens, their abilities, and their fate, and spreading misinformation specifically designed to cast doubt on any surviving accounts. And why, for thousands of years, while secretly and tirelessly working to bring the full magic of the Sirens back to Calberna, Calbernans had been systematically and equally tirelessly working to turn all outlander knowledge of that magic into myth and legend.

And they had succeeded. Though Siren-lore still existed, the Sirens had become mythological creatures, rarely, if ever, associated with Calberna. And although modern Calbernan magic didn't hold a candle to the power the Sirens of ancient times had wielded, the people of the Isles had restored enough of their ancestors' *susirena* gifts that all *imlani* could influence thoughts and—with enough of an emotional connection to their target—even erase and supplant memories.

But Siren's Song—true Siren Song—a Voice so powerful that it could not only control minds but also shatter solid objects and more—that was a magic that hadn't been seen since the Slaughter.

Not until now. Not until Gabriella Coruscate.

And she was dying faster than he could work to keep her alive.

He had just managed to contain the worst of the bleeding into her lungs, when a sudden drop in blood pressure pulled his attention to her lacerated kidney. One of the large veins had torn open, sending a river of blood coursing into her abdominal cavity.

"*Calbernari*! To me now! We are losing her!" Desperation and fear forged a band of steel that squeezed tight around his chest, making it hard to breathe. Dozens more hands slapped down against his flesh, flooding him with power. Scores more formed chains connected to Ari and Ryll, flooding them with power that, in turn, flooded into Dilys as well. He took everything they gave, and channeled it into his efforts to stop Gabriella's internal bleeding and keep her heart pumping. "Damn it! Where is that healer?"

"Here!" A voice called from somewhere near the back of the room. "I'm here!"

Bodies jostled as the Calbernans crowded in the room squeezed together to clear a path.

Tildavera Greenleaf, the old, gray-haired nurse he'd seen hovering around Queen Khamsin, hurried through the throng, carrying a satchel. The White King himself stormed in close on her heels.

"What the Hel is going on? Who did this?" Wynter Atrialan's ice-blue eyes, already turning white with wintry flurries, pinned on Dilys. The temperature of Dilys's body dropped rapidly. "Did *you* do this?"

"Not the time," Dilys snarled through battle fangs that shot down in response to Atrialan's insulting question. What he really wanted to say was "*fark* off," but that would have started more trouble than it was worth. He switched his attention to Tildavera Greenleaf. "You. Nurse. Her kidney . . . the vein burst. Can you fix it?"

"Yes. Let's get her up on a flat surface so I have room to work."

"Can't." Every word was rapidly becoming an effort that took more energy than he had to spare. He forced the explanation out. "If we move her, she dies. Work where she lies. Right kidney." He jerked his chin to indicate Gabriella's right side. "Hurry."

Without a word, nurse dropped to her knees beside Gabriella and opened the satchel she'd brought with her. She rummaged through the contents of the pack and pulled out a wrapped bundle that she unrolled to reveal a selection of surgical implements. Then, she pulled out a second bundle that contained a series of needles of various sizes and strands of what looked like dark thread.

Using a small pair of scissors from the bundle, she cut through the waist of Summer's lilac dress and the white linen chemise beneath and bared Summer's abdomen, which was mottled with dark bruising from the attack and swelling from the internal bleeding.

"I'll need the growing lamps," she said as she worked. "A dozen of them. Set up in a circle around us."

The Winter King turned around and started barking orders.

The lamps arrived a short while later, and within moments, Dilys, Nurse Greenleaf, and Summer were surrounded by a ring of blazing miniature suns that turned the area around them as warm and bright as full day. Nurse Greenleaf bathed Summer's skin with a pungent salve then picked up a small, wickedly sharp blade. Dilys had to fight back an instinctive surge of protective aggression as she cut into Gabriella's flesh.

"Oh, dear," she whispered when she parted the incision to reveal the damaged kidney.

"Fix it. Quickly." He was holding the pool of Summer's blood in a bubble of magic, feeding it back into her veins, but with the amount of blood pouring out, the task felt like bailing water with a sieve.

Setting her jaw, Tildavera Greenleaf went to work.

Dilys had to hand it to her. The elderly nurse was a swift, efficient, and divinely-gifted healer. She made short work of stitching the ruptured blood vessels and lacerated kidney while Dilys blocked Summer's blood from the area where Nurse Greenleaf was working. When her needlework was done, the Nurse sprinkled a greenish powder on the stitched wounds, murmuring softly beneath her breath as she went. A pulse of power emanated from her hands. Connected as he was to every molecule of Summer's blood, Dilys could literally feel the wounds sealing themselves in the wake of Nurse Greenleaf's ministrations. Tentatively, he released his hold on the blood circulating through Summer's kidney. He breathed a short, shaky sigh of relief when both the stitches and whatever binding magic Nurse Greenleaf had employed held in place.

"You have a gift, Nurse," he said.

"A little herb magic. A temporary measure only. She'll still need plenty of rest, sunlight, and healing to ensure it holds." Leaving the surgical wound open, she directed the light from one of the sunlamps onto the exposed kidney, then turned her attention to Summer's broken ribs and collapsed lung. She clucked her tongue against the roof of her mouth. "Now, this is going to take more doing than a bit of thread and some herb magic. I hope the cursed bastard who did this to her died a painful death."

"He did."

The Nurse flicked a glance up at him. "Your doing?"

"*Tey.*" The lie fell without effort. Not that it was much of a lie. He would have joyfully ripped the *farking krillo* limb from limb had Summer not beaten him to it.

Tildavera Greenleaf's mouth compressed in a brief, grim smile. "Good." The smile disappeared as she directed her attention back to Summer's ribcage. "You don't happen to control air as well as water, do you?"

"*Ono.* Alas, I do not."

"We'll do it the hard way then."

For the next half hour, they worked. Nurse Greenleaf made another incision to relieve the pressure on the collapsed lung and to repair the broken ribs. Several shards of bone had broken off to pierce Summer's lung in multiple places. The healer removed each tiny piece, stitched up the larger tears in the delicate lung tissue, and then realigned the broken ribs, sprinkling green powder and magic as she went.

The whole time she worked, Dilys crouched over Summer, stroking her face, her neck, her hair, filling each tender caress with energy and strength, whispering into her ear in his most beguiling tone. "You will be fine, *moa kiri*. You are strong. Life and magic and strength flows through your veins. You are a wellspring of power, a queen of all waters. All the life and energy and vitality in every ocean, every sea, every river, lake and stream lives in you. And if you need more, then take it from me. What is mine is yours without question or limits. So long as there is breath in my lungs, you will never stop breathing. So long as my heart beats, yours will never stop. Whatever pain you have, let me bear it for you. I offer my strength and magic and life force to nourish your own. Stay with me, *moa kiri*. Live for me."

As a Siren, Gabriella carried within herself the great, vast power of the seas, but it was the love provided through a trusted network of deep, emotional bonds that kept her alive. It was love that allowed her to tap that power, to master and share it. The bond between mates was a Siren's greatest source of strength, followed by maternal connections to her children, then bonds of family and friendship.

Despite the gravity of the situation, Dilys felt true hope blossom in his heart. Because, although Summer had made a master's art of avoiding Dilys and running from their bond, the link not only existed . . . it was already extremely strong. Strong enough to accept the flood of live-saving love and devotion Dilys poured through it. Awake, Gabriella might fear what he was to her. Her subconscious, however, not only recognized his right to protect her and tend to her needs, but accepted his care without hesitation, drinking down his devotion and responding to his voice and his gifts the way an *imlani* female responded to her chosen mate.

That knowledge set his mind and his heart at ease. Whatever her reasons for wiping his memory, it had nothing to do with lack of desire for him or their compatibility as mates. They rest they could work through in time.

One by one, Dilys felt the demands on his magic diminish as Nurse Greenleaf repaired Summer's lungs and stopped the worst of the bleeding. One by one, Dilys cautiously released his hold on each of the damaged blood vessels until he had drawn back all but an observational connection to Summer's blood. He maintained the connection, following the flow of blood through her veins to be certain no life-threatening leaks remained. There weren't, and Dilys could already feel Summer growing stronger.

He bent to press his lips close to her ear. "You did it,

moa kiri. I knew you could." With the immediate danger to her life past, he was able to focus all his remaining strength and send it pouring down their bond. "A gift, *moa kiri,* freely given. Whatever you need, so shall I provide." He stroked her hair and closed his eyes, resting his forehead against hers and sending up a silent prayer of thanks to Numahao.

Beside him, Tildavera positioned several growing lamps to shine on Summer's chest before returning her attention to the open surgical wound near the kidney. The results must have pleased her, because she stitched up that wound, administered more green powder and magic, then came back to close the incision along Summer's ribs.

"That's the best I can do." The healer sat back on her heels and regarded King Wynter, who had remained a silent, glowering presence throughout the surgery. "She needs rest and sunlight. I'll keep her under observation in case of infection, but she's in the gods' hands now."

"Can she be moved now?" Wynter asked.

"As long as it's done very carefully. Barring any abrupt jostling, the herbal seals I applied should hold." She glanced over in Lily's direction. "I'll take a look at the girl before we go."

Wynter gave a curt nod and barked orders to his men to bring a stretcher. As Nurse Greenleaf went to check Lily and the Wintermen rushed to obey their king, Dilys turned to clasp hands with his cousins and the others who had laid hands upon him to feed their magic and strength into him.

"My thanks," he told them. "You saved our lives."

"No thanks needed, cousin," Ryll said.

"You should all go get some sleep. You two, in particular." He gave Ari and Ryll an exhausted grin. "You both look terrible."

"Ha." Ari snorted. "Look in the mirror."

"Ah. Well, I guess it's a good thing my future *liana* has yet to awaken . . ."

His cousins laughed, and the three of them clapped each other on the back. The Wintermen with the stretcher arrived. Dilys hovered until he was certain Gabriella had been safely lifted from the floor and placed on the conveyance with no ill effects, then pressed a final kiss to Summer's brow. He would have followed them to wherever they were taking her, but a massive hand clamped down on his shoulder and kept him from getting to his feet.

"No need to accompany her. She'll be well looked after." Wynter fixed Dilys with a look of frozen steel. "For now, you and I need to have a few words."

Normally, the curt order would have made Dilys bristle, but he was so drained and so happy Gabriella was safe that all he could do was nod wearily. Besides, in all fairness, although Wintercraig's king wasn't known for his patience, he had held all his questions, kept his anger in check, and not interfered until after Gabriella had been healed. That earned him enough goodwill to keep Dilys's battle claws sheathed.

"Of course, Your Grace." Dilys accepted Ryll's outstretched hand to help him rise, then laughed a little as he stumbled dizzily. He'd been kneeling on the floor for at least an hour, and his legs had gone numb. "I'm at your servi—"

His voice broke off as the numbness in his legs spread to every part of his body and a heavy black wave crashed over him. Then he was falling, weightless, and his ears were ringing with the echoes of Ari and Ryll shouting his name from far, far away.

The next thing Dilys knew, he was waking to the soothing sound of running water and the warmth of sunlight on his face.

For a moment, as he lay there with his eyes closed, he couldn't quite place where he was. Not on the *Kracken*. The bed beneath him smelled of spruce and juniper rather than salty sea air or the familiar tropical scents of the

Isles, and it wasn't rocking with the rhythm of the sea. A small fountain burbled somewhere nearby.

He peeled one eye open, squinting a little at the glare of sunlight shining through the unshaded windows near his bed. He lifted a hand to shade his eyes and groaned softly as a sharp pain shot through him. His arms—his whole body—felt heavy as lead, and bruised, as if someone had taken a bat to him. He was especially tender around his ribs and back.

A rustle of cloth made his ears twitch. There was a soft patter of feet, the click of a door latch, then a woman's quiet whisper. "Tell the king he's awake." Feet took off running. The door clicked again, and the room fell silent. The woman—whoever she'd been—had left. Voices were murmuring in the hall outside. The language foreign but familiar. Ice Tongue.

Konumarr. He was in Konumarr. In his bedroom in the palace.

And with that realization, the dam burst and memories came flooding back. Konumarr. Courtship.

"Gabriella!"

He sat bolt upright in bed, threw the covers off, and leapt to his feet.

Then promptly grabbed for the closest solid object as dizziness assailed him and his legs started to buckle. Goddess, he was weak. And starving. And parched.

He reached a hand towards the small stone fountain that someone had placed near his bed—the source of the running water he'd heard upon waking—and called the water to him. His sea gifts flickered like a sputtering candle. The water continued tumbling over the pyramid of glossy stones, not responding to his call.

Dilys stared at the fountain in mute consternation. He was drained. Completely. That hadn't happened to him in years. Not since he was a boy just learning how to wield his magic. He'd given Gabriella everything he had, holding nothing back for himself.

With a sigh, he shuffled over to the fountain and shoved his hand into it. He stood there, eyes closed, absorbing the revitalizing energy of the water as it flowed over his skin. What he really needed was an ocean pouring over him, but since he barely had the strength to crawl across the room, this would have to do. Slowly, he felt his body strengthen until his legs no longer felt like they would collapse beneath him.

Someone had left a large pitcher of water and an empty glass on the dressing table against the wall. Ignoring the glass, he lifted the pitcher to his mouth and drank the contents down. It was lightly salted, and draining the pitcher helped significantly more than putting his hand in the fountain. By the time it was empty, he felt worlds better. Still not ready to move oceans, but at least able to walk without feeling like he was going to fall over with every step.

He wouldn't be a great deal of use to Gabriella in this state, but whatever she needed, he was determined to provide.

With that in mind, he made his way to the wardrobe containing the selection of brightly colored *shumas* he'd brought with him from Calberna and pulled out a turquoise blue reminiscent of the tropical ocean waters that surrounded his family's isle, Cali Kai Meri. With that he matched a set of emerald, coral, and turquoise bands dotted with small gemstone reef fish.

Dilys was just securing his *shuma* around his waist when the door to his chamber opened and Wynter Atrialan strode in.

"Good. You're not dead. I was not looking forward to telling Calberna's queen that her only son had perished in my kingdom."

It was a measure of Dilys's state of mind that his first words weren't a cheeky, "What? King's don't knock in Wintercraig?" but rather, "Where is Gabriella? I need to see her."

White brows rose over cold blue eyes. "Do you? Well, I need to get some answers. Starting with a thorough explanation of what happened two nights ago."

"I'll be happy to discuss all of that with you once I see Gabriella."

"And I may let you see her once I'm satisfied I know what transpired."

Aggression flared. Battle claws pressed against the tips of Dilys's fingers. "I insist you take me to her," Dilys persisted. He tried to summon *susirena,* intending to make Atrialan step aside, but the magic didn't respond to his call. The water had replenished some of his physical strength, but not his magical stores.

"Is that how it works in Calberna? Foreigners bark orders at your mother, the Queen, and she obeys?"

Despite his agitation, Dilys felt his cheeks grow hot. Atrialan was right, much as Dilys hated to admit it. The *Myerial* would be ashamed at her son's lapse in protocol. He took a breath and forced himself to calm down. "Forgive me, Your Grace. My concern for *Myerialanna* Summer has made me forget myself. You know how badly she was injured. She may need my help again."

"She doesn't. Her recovery has been nothing short of miraculous. In fact, while you've been lying in bed doing your best imitation of a death sleep for the last two days, she's been awake and outside soaking up the sun. She's already almost fully recovered. Tildavera tells me we owe Summer's life and a good portion of her swift recovery to you, which is why I'm going to overlook your impertinence just now. But that's where my goodwill ends. Until I get some answers, you're not getting anywhere near her."

Atrialan's teeth snapped together in a sharp, cold smile. "So what's it to be, Your Highness? Do you want to stand here arguing, or are you going to stop wasting both our time and explain to me exactly what the *fark* is going on? Including why you and every Calbernan in Konumarr ended up in the queen's school with a dead man and my wife's sister beaten nearly to the grave, and why your men have taken it upon themselves to post guards and erect *that*"—Atrialan jabbed a finger towards the window at Dilys's back—"around my palace?"

Dilys turned to see what Atrialan was pointing at, and his jaw dropped a little. A shining wall of water shimmered a few inches from his balcony, so crystal clear it was almost completely transparent. A sea veil. Similar to the protective veil of water he put around his room each night as he slept, only much stronger. He couldn't believe he hadn't noticed it.

"Ah." Dilys rubbed his jaw to hide his discomfort. "I didn't realize they'd done that."

"Done what? What is it?"

"It's a sea veil. A protective ward. Nothing dangerous." That wasn't entirely true. The sea veil did offer protection against attack and intrusion, but it also allowed the Calbernans to identify everyone who passed through the veil, and to trap or drown any or all of those people, should the situation warrant. Atrialan didn't need to know that, however. "I can only assume my men thought it best to add Calbernan protections to your own, given my weakened state and the attack on Gabriella. I wouldn't know for sure, as I only just awakened and you're the first person I've spoken to." He blinked innocently and offered a small, congenial smile.

"And the Calbernans who seem to think they have some right to set themselves up as Princess Summer's personal guard?"

They would have. Of course, they would have. They'd stumbled across the first Siren born in twenty-five hundred years. Every Calbernan in Wintercraig—in all of Mystral, for that matter—would die to protect her. Just as, to a man, they'd also die to protect the secret of what Summer was.

"I am their prince. I intend to make Gabriella my *liana* and the mother of Calberna's future *Myerial*. My men know this. They therefore protect her as they would their own princess."

"*Summer* is the Season you plan to marry?" Atrialan's voice dripped with disbelief. "Wasn't she the one you dismissed out of hand your first day here? What was it you called her? Oh, yes,"—his eyes narrowed—"*milked tea*."

"Does *everyone* know about that?" Dilys groaned and scrubbed his face. He was never going to live that down. "I apologized to all three Seasons for that bit of stupidity the day it happened. The apology was accepted."

Atrialan raised his brows. "And they say Calbernans understand women."

Dilys grimaced. He deserved that. But how it stung to be lectured about dealing with women by Wynter of the Craig.

"We'll come back to the situation between you and Summer later," Atrialan announced briskly. "I still have more questions about what went on the night she was attacked. Witnesses say you and your men all started running at exactly the same time—even those of you over on this side of the fjord—and every one of you ran straight for the school. How is it possible that every Calbernan in Konumarr realized Princess Summer was in trouble at exactly the same instant? And how did every one of you know exactly where to go?"

That one was easy to answer without evasions or lies. "We are gifted with acute hearing. We heard her scream. When a woman screams the way she and her companion did, Calbernans come running. It's in our nature."

"Princess Summer's attacker was literally reduced to a bloody pile of meat. You claim you did it, but you have no injuries—not even a scrape on your knuckles—and the only blood on you belonged to Summer. How is that possible?"

"Did you see what that filthy *krillo* did to Gabriella? I

slaughtered him so fast, he didn't have time to fight back. As for why there wasn't a drop of his blood on me, the healer—Nurse Greenleaf?—has no doubt already informed you my sea gifts—the ones that grant me dominion over water—also grant me at least limited control over blood, including the ability to remove it from my person, which I did before I laid my hands on Gabriella. And before you ask, I used that same ability to stop Gabriella's internal bleeding and keep as much of her blood pumping through her veins as possible until the healer completed her work and Gabriella was no longer in danger of bleeding to death." He met Wynter's gaze full on and told him with complete sincerity. "Had it been necessary for me to give my life to save hers, I would have done it without a second thought."

"Hmm." Atrialan grunted. He appeared slightly mollified, which meant Dilys hadn't yet contradicted anything Ari, Ryll, or the others might have already told him, but also still clearly suspicious. He possessed a much stronger instinct for sussing out lies and evasions than Dilys had realized. But it was also clear that he had recognized the ring of truth in Dilys's last statement. "You have spent every day since your arrival courting Spring and Autumn. In fact, my sources tell me you and Summer have avoided each other since day one. So how is it, Sealord, that you suddenly decided the woman you want for your wife is the one woman you made a point of disdaining from the start? You haven't shared more than a dozen words with her since the day of your arrival, and now suddenly no other woman will do and you are so devoted you'd give your life for her? A woman you know nothing about. A woman you made clear you were not interested in courting. How exactly does that happen?"

"I was never not interested in Gabriella."

"You have a funny way of showing it."

Dilys bit back a sharp retort. He told himself Atrialan had every right to be protective of the women in his

family. The quality was an admirable one. Highly Calbernan, in fact. It was just a pain in the ass to be on the
receiving end of that bristling, intrusive protectiveness.

"You want the truth? Fine. Here it is. I am the only
child of Calberna's queen. When I marry, my daughter—
should Numahao grant my wife and I the blessing of a
daughter—will become the next queen of Calberna. As
with every other nation on Mystral, it behooves Calberna
to have a strong ruler. Which is why, before I left the Isles,
I was instructed by the Queen's Council to marry either
Spring or Autumn. The opinion was that they were the
two strongest of the Seasons and therefore the best choices
to mother Calberna's next queen. I am a dutiful son. Despite my attraction to Gabriella—which contrary to your
belief, was both instant and strong—I tried to do what the
Queen's Council expected of me. But as the days passed,
it became increasingly clear that while duty required me
to pursue Spring or Autumn, my heart kept leading me
back to Gabriella. It's true, she has been avoiding me. I do
not know why. But I intend to spend the rest of my time
here getting to the bottom of that mystery and convincing
her that I am the right and only man for her."

Dilys leaned back against the dressing table and crossed
his arms. "Now, please, Your Grace, I've answered all
your questions. I need to see Gabriella. I need to make
certain with my own eyes that she is as fully recovered as
you say." He smiled tightly. "It's a Calbernan thing." And
it was. He'd been separated from his future mate for two
days, and the need to be near her, to touch her, to make
sure she was all right, was beginning to claw at him.

"We're not done yet. I understand Calberna is having
trouble in the Olemas Ocean."

Dilys scowled. "Even if we were—and I'm not saying
we are—what bearing does that have on my going to see
Gabriella?"

"It has whatever bearing I say it does." Atrialan arched
one arrogant white brow. "As I said, if you want to see

Princess Summer, you will answer my questions. I did not put any restrictions on what those questions would be about."

Dilys's back teeth ground together. "There is a particular pirate making a nuisance of himself in the Olemas. It's nothing we can't handle."

"That's not the impression I got. The ambassadors from Verma and Cho were here not long before your arrival. He told me a large band of pirates have allied together and all but brought Calbernan trade to a halt in that part of the world. He said the Calbernans had—let me see, what were his exact words?—ah, yes, 'gotten their stones handed to them.'"

"The ambassador from Verma and Cho was here to make another offer from Maak Korin beda Kahn for *Myerialanna* Autumn, was he not?" Dilys didn't wait for a confirmation. Everyone knew about the Maak's obsession with making Autumn his. "No doubt he knew of my trip here and the reasons for it and was doing his best to undermine me in your eyes."

"He's not the only source. Word from Seahaven is that anyone who wants their goods to pass safely through the Olemas these days has to pay a toll to the pirates and can't use either Calbernan ships or Calbernan escorts—or even have a single Calbernan on board, lest they find themselves targeted and sunk. They also say the pirates have sunk more than one Calbernan ship."

Dilys swore silently. He'd hoped the true depth of the problem hadn't become common knowledge.

"All right, yes," he acknowledged. "We have a problem there. We are addressing it."

"Hmm." Wynter leaned back against the wall. "How does one sink a Calbernan vessel anyway? I thought you folk controlled every wave on the ocean."

"We do. Sinking one of our ships is next to impossible, which means these pirates are no ordinary renegades. They have powerful magic on their side."

"And they seem to have it in for Calberna. Sinking the ships of the undisputed masters of the seas." Wynter arched a white brow and drawled, "It's got to be a huge embarrassment."

"Embarrassment isn't the word I would choose, Your Grace," Dilys informed him coldly. "My cousin Fyerin— beloved by my mother and me—was murdered by these pirates, his ship and all hands aboard, lost to the sea."

Every bit of smug amusement wiped from Wynter Atrialan's face, leaving sober sincerity behind. "I didn't know. Forgive me. Losing someone you love is no laughing matter."

"*Ono,* it isn't. As you may know, Calbernans breathe underwater. Drowning us is no easier a task than sinking our ships. Yet these pirates managed it." He felt the scrape of his claws digging into the top of the dressing table and forced his hands to relax. The rest of him, however, remained stiff as a board.

"It has been suggested that perhaps one reason for your interest in wedding a Season has to do with using her weathergifts to aid your navy. Possibly even to help battle the pirates."

"I fight my own wars, Your Grace. And I'm hired by others to fight their wars as well, because I'm damned good at it." Dilys gave a grim smile. He wasn't just a mercenary. He was leader of one of the world's most feared fighting forces.

"So if you marry a Season—and I'm not saying you will—there's no way you'll use her magic to take on pirates? Because, if you were hoping to use Gabriella that way, you can get back aboard your ship and sail home to Calberna right now. There's no way in Hel I'd let you marry her so you use her or put her life at risk fighting pirates."

It was Dilys's turn to narrow his eyes. "You insult me most gravely to suggest I would ever put my *liana*'s life at risk. And like so many of Mystral's male population, you seem to suffer from the misconception that women are somehow in need of a man's governance. They aren't. My *liana*'s choices once we wed will be her own—not mine, and not yours either."

"I think women are in need of—" Wynter broke off to give a bark of incredulous laughter. "Have you *met* my wife? Oh, wait. You have. On the *farking battlefield*!"

"Point taken, Your Grace. Wintermen do tend to value the contributions and capabilities of women more so than most others."

As quickly as it had come, Wynter Atrialan's laughter ended, and Dilys found himself staring once more into the frosty, ice-blue eyes of the Winter King. "My answer to your using any of my sisters—but especially Summer—to fight pirates is no. I haven't said anything before now because your courtship of Autumn and Spring hadn't progressed to a point where I considered it necessary. But since you seem to have settled on Summer, that has changed. All the Seasons were gently raised, but Summer especially is too innocent and too gentle to be put in such a position. So, I'm telling you right now, I will not allow you to put her or any of the Seasons in harm's way. And that decision has nothing to do with valuing their abilities or believing they need governance, and everything to do with protecting my own. Which I assure you, Sealord, I fully intend to do."

"Yet I stood beside your pregnant wife on a battlefield as we faced down the Ice King together," Dilys reminded him gently. Wynter's eyes started to swirl with white flurries. Dilys pushed away from the dresser and folded his arms. "I understand your concerns, Your Grace, and I appreciate your determination to protect the women in your family. But per my contract with your wife, I have the right to court the Seasons of Summerlea—*all* of the Seasons of Summerlea, which includes Gabriella. A contract, may I remind you, that I paid for with many Calbernan lives. Now I have patiently submitted to your inquisition, and I have answered all your questions. If you have any others, they can wait until later. Right now, I am going to see Gabriella. Then, I am going to court Gabriella. And when she consents to become my *liana*—which I assure you, Your Grace, she will—I'm going to marry Gabriella. As for what happens after that, she will choose her own battles and follow her own conscience. Whatever she chooses, I will give my life and the lives of every man under my command—every man in Calberna, if necessary—to keep her safe."

"Well?" Scarcely two seconds after Wynter returned to his office on the other side of the palace, the door near his desk opened, and Khamsin swept in. "What do you think?"

He eyed his wife, noting the cobwebs clinging to her white-streaked black curls. "I think you're in no condition to go snooping through dusty secret passages to spy on palace guests."

"Oh, pooh. What's the point of having secret passages if you can't use them to snoop? I was very careful and perfectly safe. Don't try to change the subject. What do you think of Dilys?"

"I think I still don't like him." He turned his chair and opened his arms to gather his wife on his lap.

She laughed and kissed him and ran her hands down his cheeks. "You will, once you get to know him better."

"I doubt it. I think he's planning to use Summer's magic to fight his enemies, and I don't like it."

"I fought your enemies."

"Not because I planned it that way. I would have stopped you if I could."

"It's a good thing for all of us that you didn't. And Dilys Merimydion did everything he could to keep me safe. Including sacrificing far too many of his best men. He did what was right and he helped save all our lives. Which is a damn sight more than my brother or father or many of my own countrymen did."

"Still not a fan. And Summer isn't you. There isn't a mean bone in her body."

Khamsin pulled back to give him an offended look. "Did you just call me mean?"

"You know what I mean. You know how to win a fight. Summer doesn't even know how to pick one."

"Hmmm." She reached for one of the plaits dangling from his temple and began twining it around her finger. "I think you may be underestimating her. She is a Season of Summerlea, after all. The blood of the Sun God runs through her veins, same as it does mine."

"Maybe so, but there's a reason everyone who meets her is so protective of her, and it's not because she's so strong and intimidating."

"Now you're saying I'm intimidating?"

"Absolutely. Halla knows, you keep *me* quaking in my boots."

"Ha. I wish." She had the end of his braid now and was idly brushing it back and forth against his cheek.

Wynter smiled and let her pet him to her heart's content. She was wearing a pretty green frock that was quite fetching. His gaze snagged on the silky expanse of plump breast displayed by the gown's square neckline. Pregnancy had filled more than his wife's belly—much to his delight. He bent to kiss her plump bits—only the two soft ones on top, since he couldn't bend far enough in the chair to reach the hard little mound of her belly.

Well, not so little anymore. He splayed his hands across it, measuring with a slight frown. "How much longer?"

"Another three weeks. Can you believe it?"

"Three more weeks? That can't be right. They can't be growing anymore in there. There isn't any room!"

Khamsin laughed. "Tell the babies that!"

She squealed when he scooped her up out of his lap and lifted her so that he could press his mouth to her belly. "Time's up, my lads. Come on out, now."

His response was a tiny thump in the mouth as one of the babies either kicked or punched him.

He grinned at Khamsin and set her back down in his lap. "Did you see that? Not even born yet, and one of them is already giving their father a whack on the chin. He's a fighter."

"Or *she* is."

His grin softened. "Or she is. Like her mother."

Khamsin looped her arms around his neck and smiled at him, her gray eyes shining bright against the dark frame of her lashes and her Summerlander brown skin. "Dilys is right, you know. No matter what we think, in the end, Summer, like each of my sisters, will do what she believes is right—including using her weathergifts to help her husband fight pirates."

"She's not married to him yet."

"And never will be if you keep standing in the way. I know you want to protect her—everyone does—but you have to let her live her life. You can't protect her forever."

"Watch me." He smoothed the hair back off her face, loving the silky feel of it against his fingers and the streaks of white that shot through it like lightning in a night sky.

"Wynter."

"Khamsin." He kissed her, thoroughly, then smiled at the sight of her hazy, heavy-lidded eyes, pleased with the results of his kiss. "I wouldn't sell Autumn to that Vermese *griss* for all the gold in Mystral, and I won't sell Gabriella to this Sealord for him to use, either."

"Nobody's talking about selling my sister to Dilys Merimydion. And this is surprisingly righteous talk coming from the man who claimed a warprize wife and threatened to work his way through all four of my father's daughters until one of us gave you an heir."

"You showed me the error of my ways," he declared piously.

"Ha. I think this is more a case of 'Do as I say, not as I do.'"

It was. It totally was. But he sniffed and said, "I'm only looking out for Summer's best interests."

"I think marriage to a man who can love, respect and appreciate her *is* in her best interest, don't you?"

"Not if that man intends to use her to fight pirates. He's a Calbernan mercenary. He values money first and foremost, and the pirates are cutting into Calbernan profits."

"Money isn't all that matters to Calbernans and you know it. And he didn't say he was planning to use her gifts to fight pirates."

"He didn't say he was not planning to either."

She slipped a hand inside his tunic to stroke the smooth skin of his chest. His lashes lowered, and he all but purred. He loved the feel of her hands on him. She was always so warm, her storm gifts a literal fire burning away inside her flesh.

"Wyn," she said in an equally warm murmur. "Give him a chance." Her lips sought and found his throat, nibbling little kisses along his slowly increasing pulse.

"A chance?" Wyn smiled. He knew he was being managed, but as long as she kept kissing and petting him, he didn't mind.

"Mmm. We owe him more than we can ever repay. Besides, he's a good man, and he'd be a much better husband to Gabriella than most of the suitors who've come calling over the years. Calbernans are fiercely loyal and loving and protective of their women."

"Sounds like a good dog."

She drew back to glare at him. "Oh, really? Aren't you fiercely loyal, loving, and protective, too?"

He grinned. "Woof."

She smacked his chest with an open palm and snorted in amusement. "Frost brain."

When she didn't immediately go back to kissing and petting him, he frowned. "Aren't you trying to seduce me into doing what you want? It hasn't worked yet. I think you need to coax me with more sexual favors."

"Oh, really?" One black brow arched expressively. "And will that work, do you think?"

"I don't know. Let's try it and see." He leaned back in his chair and offered himself up to her. "I'm all yours, *min ros*. Seduce away."

She got the most adorably determined look on her face, said, "All right," and to his delight, hiked her skirts and straddled him.

"Mmm," he approved. "So far, so good."

"Hush." She laid a finger across his lips, then replaced it a moment later with her lips and kissed him senseless.

Well, not entirely senseless. He still had a handful of thoughts floating around and colliding randomly in the blissful vacuum of his brain.

"Don't stop," he muttered when she lifted her head. "I think that's working."

"Good." She dragged his hands around to the laces at the back of her gown, and as he fumbled blindly to work them loose, she went back to kissing his neck. "As I was saying," she murmured against his skin, "Dilys Merimydion is a good man. I want all my sisters to be as happy in their marriages as I am, and I think he can make that happen." Her tongue darted out to lick the same skin she'd just kissed. "I've never heard of an unhappy Calbernan wife. Ever."

"She doesn't like him. She's made it clear she doesn't like him."

"That's not what Autumn and Spring think. They think she likes him so much it scares her. That that's why she's been running away from him so hard. I think they may be right. Back in Summerlea, when the suitors came calling, Gabriella never made herself scarce around the objectionable ones. In fact, the more awful a suitor was, the more solicitous of him she would become. It was only the charming ones who showed an interest in her that she tended to avoid. And I've never seen her avoid anyone the way she's been avoiding Dilys Merimydion." She'd found his ear and did things with her breath and her tongue that made him shudder and nearly shred her laces in his haste to get them undone.

"You know what I think?" he growled as her bodice loosened, freeing her pregnancy-plumped breasts to his plundering mouth.

"What?" She gasped and arched her back to give him better access.

"I think I don't want you talking or even thinking about other men at a time like this." He pushed a hand up under her skirts, finding the soft warmth of her thigh. He stroked softly, working his way higher until he found a different soft warmth, then stroked that until her head fell back and her eyes took on that glazed, silvery cast he knew and loved.

"Other men?" she moaned. "What other men?"

He smiled. "Precisely."

CHAPTER 10

"He's asking to see you again, ma'am."

Summer, who lay basking in the warm sunlight on the royal family's private terrace, scowled. "Tell him I'm resting. I'll *be* resting all afternoon, and I don't want to be disturbed."

"Yes, ma'am. I'll let him know." The palace servant who'd brought the message curtsied and hurried away.

When she was gone, Summer flopped back down on the lounge. "Carry on, Lily," she commanded the young Summerlander who had been practicing her reading at Gabriella's bedside these last several days. As Lily resumed her halting reading of *Roland Triumphant,* Gabriella closed her eyes, flung a hand over her eyes, and tried to empty her mind.

Peace, however, remained elusive.

Dilys Merimydion was simply refusing to take a hint. In the two days since he'd regained consciousness, he'd made no less than ten requests a day to see her. She'd rebuffed each one, claiming she was still not up to visitors, but she wasn't going to be able to hide behind that excuse much longer. Tildy's healing skills, herb magic, and the blessings of the sun had already restored Summer to better health than she'd enjoyed *before* the attack. In fact, despite having just mended from injuries so severe they should have killed her, Gabriella felt better than she had *in years.* She was brimming over with energy and strength, and for the first time in a long while, she wasn't having to constantly fight to keep her magic contained.

Not that she trusted her control to last, of course. The way she figured it, the explosion of magic that had ripped out of her and torn Lily's evil brute of a father to shreds was the magical equivalent of the eruption of an active volcano. It relieved pressure that had been building up, but the reprieve was only temporary. Another eruption was inevitable.

Still, for now, she was no longer an immediate threat to her family or anyone else. And she was feeling so good that, if not for Dilys Merimydion, she would already be back at the school teaching classes. Instead, she was confined to her rooms and this terrace. Because the minute Gabriella stopped playing recovering invalid, she lost the one shield that kept Dilys Merimydion at bay.

Summer sat up so abruptly that Lily broke off reading in midsentence.

"I'm so sorry, ma'am," the girl apologized in a mortified whisper. "I know I read some of that wrong, but I just don't know all these big words."

"What?" Realizing that Lily thought Summer's abrupt movement was a show of irritation, Gabriella hurried to reassure the girl. "Oh, no, Lily, you're doing splendidly. I'm so proud of the incredible progress you've made. I'm just finding it difficult to concentrate today. Instead of reading today, why don't we just chat instead?"

Lily blushed and ducked her head. "Er . . . all right, Your Highness, if that's what you wish. Though I'm not sure what you'd like to talk about."

"Well, you can tell me what you and Talin have got planned today." Lily and the young Calbernan she'd met had been seeing quite a lot of each other ever since the plaza dance.

"We're going sailing down the fjord . . . and taking a picnic out to the point." Lily smoothed her hands over the sleek, polished linen of her gown. Gone were Lily's simple, threadbare country clothes. Once Gabriella had regained consciousness, she'd insisted on having Lily as her companion for the duration of her convalescence and had seen to it that Lily received a complete new wardrobe of gowns fashioned from fine, beautiful fabrics that wouldn't have looked out of place on the daughter of any well-to-do merchant or gentleman. She'd kept the styles of her dresses simple, but the fabrics, though sturdy enough, were top rate.

Gabriella's gesture wasn't just generosity (or a not-so-subtle attempt on the matchmaking front). She honestly liked the girl. She liked her spirit and the courage she'd shown trying to make a better life for herself and her baby. Having felt the wrath of Lily's father firsthand, Summer had an even greater respect for the young woman's resilience. So keeping Lily close, continuing to encourage her reading and self-improvement, was the best way Gabriella could think of to help Lily achieve her aims.

But also, spending her waking hours teaching Lily to read gave her something to occupy her mind. Something other than the constant thoughts of Dilys Merimydion that had been haunting her ever since she'd awakened after the attack.

"That sounds delightful," Summer said to Lily. "I've never been sailing. Mama was afraid of the water." It had always struck Gabriella as ironic that the princess of a seafaring kingdom was so afraid of the sea. The few times their family had ventured to the coasts of Summerlea, Mama had steadfastly refused to visit the beach.

"Hello, dearest Gabriella. How are you feeling today?" Dressed in bright, sunny yellow, Autumn ran lightly down the terrace steps, carrying a beautiful arrangement of cut flowers. "Here. These are for you. And here's the note." She thrust the flowers into Summer's hands, and turned to smile coolly at Lily. "Hello, Lily. Heading off to see your young man, are you?"

Surprise tinged with wariness flashed across Lily's

face and were quickly hidden as she bowed her head and bobbed a curtsy. "Yes, Your Highness. Thank you for asking."

"Oh, don't thank her," Gabriella said. She set aside the note without a glance and laid the flowers on top. "She's just keeping up with palace gossip. Aren't you, Autumn?"

Autumn arched a brow. "Well, clearly you're getting better. You've entered the cranky stage of healing."

Gabriella flushed, immediately consumed with well-deserved guilt. "Sorry."

Autumn smiled, and it was like the sun coming out from behind the clouds, brilliant and beautiful. "Not to worry. I forgive you. I am unbelievably saint-like, that way." She plopped down on the chair Lily had vacated and reached for the book Lily had left on the table. "*Roland Triumphant*?" She laughed. "Of course, that would be Khamsin's reading primer of choice, wouldn't it?"

"Of course." Roland Soldeus was Summerlea's most famous historical figure—and the demigod ancestor from whom the Summerlea royal family descended. "She's determined to correct the shocking lack of hero worship for him throughout Wintercraig—one new reader at a time."

"How deliciously subversive of her." Setting the book back down, she directed the power of her smile in Lily's direction and said, "Have a wonderful time today, Lily."

Clearly dismissed, Lily glanced uncertainly in Gabriella's direction for confirmation, then bobbed a quick curtsy and hurried away.

"I wish you wouldn't play princess with her," Gabriella chided when she was gone. "She's a sweet girl."

"Who got you nearly killed."

"Not her fault. If you'd seen her scars . . ."

"I heard all about them." Autumn rolled her eyes at Gabriella's surprise. "Hello? Seamstresses. They talk. Besides, I wasn't playing princess. I was hurrying her along out of the kindness of my heart and a perverse new compulsion to play matchmaker. Her young man is downstairs wearing a hole in the stone with all his impatient pacing. Aren't you going to read your note?"

Gabriella glanced at the edge of the folded, sealed envelope peeping out from beneath the discarded flower arrangement. "No."

"You can hide out here until doomsday, but it won't do any good. He isn't going away."

"I'm not interested."

"I just do not believe this," Autumn muttered. "For the first time in my life, there's a man I'm actually interested in. Young, gorgeous, wealthy, a prince, not a conceited ass, and—did I mention?—gorgeous. In short, everything a woman could hope for. And who does he want? You! I could be moldy bread for all the interest he has in me. Isn't that just a slap in the face?"

"Precisely why I should stay away from him. He had plenty of interest in you before. He will again."

"Oh, no. Don't even use me as your excuse. The Princess Autumn of Calberna ship has sailed. It will never be. The same with Spring. He made that crystal clear even before you were attacked—in the kindest possible way, of course." She shook her head. "Look, Gabriella, I understand that what he did to that awful man who hurt you must have been horrifying to witness, but in my opinion, he deserves a medal for it. That brute deserved to be eviscerated. If I'd been there, I would have burned him alive."

Gabriella's lashes came down to cover her eyes. When she'd awakened after her attack, she'd learned that Dilys Merimydion and his men had claimed responsibility for the slaying of Lily's father. And she'd let him, not wanting her sisters to regard her with the same fear she'd seen in her parents' eyes the first time she'd murdered someone with her magic.

As to why Dilys Merimydion had proclaimed himself the killer, she didn't know. At first, she'd thought he'd done it to elevate himself in the eyes of Autumn and Spring—

after all, it would only be natural for them to think even more kindly of the man who'd saved their sister from certain death. But then she'd learned he'd already ended his courtship of them and made clear his plan to court her instead.

"Dilys is a good man," Autumn continued.

"Oh, so it's Dilys now, is it?"

"Yes, it is. And here's another first for you. He and I have become good friends—and I'm telling you, my friend deserves a chance." Autumn didn't have men friends—especially not young, attractive, in-their-prime men friends. Truth be told, apart from her sisters, she didn't have many friends period. Men wanted more than she was willing to give, and women didn't like Autumn constantly drawing all the male attention.

"He saved your life," Autumn pressed. "Not just by killing that awful man, but later. Even Tildy says you might have died without that Calbernan woo-woo magic he worked on you. The least you can do is see the man and thank him. You owe him that much."

"Aleta!" Gabriella snapped. "*Stop.* I've already said I'm not going to see him today, and that's the end of it."

"Well, that's too bad. He's on his way up now."

"What?" Gabriella sat up straight.

Autumn rose, graceful and serene, and altogether too pleased with herself. "Lily's young man wasn't the only one wearing a hole in the stone downstairs. When I offered to deliver Dilys's flowers and note, I told him to give me five minutes, then come on up."

"Oh! I don't believe you! How could you do that to me?" Gabriella threw off the light blanket Tildy had insisted on draping over her and jumped to her feet. She pretty much had been milking her wounded status the last day or so. Coruscates tended to heal quickly with the help of sunlight, and she was no exception. "Well, since you invited him up, you can just stay here and entertain him yourself! Because I'm leaving!"

The threat of running into Dilys Merimydion in the palace halls kept her from fleeing indoors. Instead, she went hurrying through the castle gardens, hoping to sneak out the eastern gate and go hide in her favorite grotto behind Snowbeard Falls.

As Summer's rose-pink skirts disappeared around a garden hedge, Autumn turned to Spring, who was stepping out onto the garden terrace. Autumn gave her a smug, triumphant smile.

"Told you she'd run."

"You did." But Spring didn't look smug, like Autumn. She looked worried. "I'm still not sure about this. What if we're wrong?"

"We're not."

"But what if we are?"

Autumn put an arm around her oldest sister's shoulders. It wasn't like Spring to vacillate after making a decision. She was too much a leader for debilitating self-doubt. They'd been discussing the Summer-Dilys situation since the day Summer was attacked, and they'd agreed that they couldn't keep enabling Summer's fear of emotional commitment. Spring was just letting maternal instincts and a lifetime of protecting Sweet Summer get in the way of what was best for her.

"Toughen up, mama bird," Autumn told her, giving Spring's shoulders a squeeze. "Time to push your little chick out of the nest."

Gabriella made it all the way to the far edge of the east garden without running into a single Calbernan. She was just starting to congratulate herself on making a clean escape when the one Calbernan she most wanted to avoid stepped out from behind a hedge, directly into her path.

One moment she was alone, rushing towards the haven of her favorite quiet spot in Konumarr. The next, she was running headfirst into the hardest, hottest, most shockingly silky expanse of naked male chest she'd ever encountered.

He'd appeared so suddenly in her path that she didn't even have time to put her hands up. Her face mashed into one rock-hard pectoral muscle. His arms came up around her, one hand splayed across her back to steady her, the other gripped the back of her head. He was as warm as a furnace. His skin was incredibly soft and oh so fragrant, filling her nose with scents of coconut, frangipani, and warm, tropical ocean nights. The scent of him seduced her. The feel of him made her yearn for more.

As it had since the first time she'd touched him.

Summer planted her hands against that wall of hard, burning skin, and shoved. Dilys Merimydion released her, and she stumbled back several steps, her heart pounding madly in her chest.

"I beg your pardon, Sealord Merimydion. I didn't see you there." She tried to dart around him to his right.

His hand shot out, his massive palm engulfing her right elbow in a light but unyielding grip.

"Don't go," he said. "We need to talk."

"I—er—" She cast a glance towards the garden gate and the walk just beyond it. Escape was so close.

"*Ono, Myerialanna* Summer," he said, clearly reading her intentions. "The time for running is over. As is my willingness to wait patiently for you to find your courage. You've been awake and well enough for visitors for days now, yet despite my numerous requests, you have refused to see me. Why?"

Her skin was tingling where he touched her. She gave her elbow a tug, but his grip remained ironclad. Rather than humiliating herself struggling against his greater strength, she forced herself to go still.

"Talk to me." His voice dropped, becoming a husky, beguiling murmur. "Whatever you're afraid of, I can help, but you need to talk to me." His eyes shone with a golden light so soft, so tender that she ached to sink into his arms and surrender herself and all her fears into his keeping. One big hand lifted, and he reached out as if to caress her cheek.

She flinched back. She was afraid that if he touched her with even a fraction of the breathtaking tenderness shining from his eyes, she wouldn't be able to stop from flinging herself into his arms.

He misinterpreted her flinch. The hand on her arm tightened, and he growled—*growled*!—at her. "Don't you dare shrink away from me like you're afraid I'm going to hurt you, Gabriella! You know better than that!"

For a moment, she could only stand there, gaping stupidly at him, stunned by the realization—the absolute certainty—that she'd not just angered him, she'd *hurt* him. Then stunned again by the realization that hurting him was like driving a knife into her own heart.

A moment after that second realization, her well-developed sense of self-preservation kicked in. With it came a surge of righteous indignation. Had he just attempted to Persuade her again? She wasn't sure, but she couldn't think of any other rational explanation for what felt like a deep emotional attachment to him. Especially since she'd done such an expert job of avoiding him specifically to *avoid* forming such an attachment.

More furious now than fearful, she yanked her arm out of his grip and snapped, "Let go of me! How dare you manhandle me? And how dare you address me in so familiar a way? You haven't the right!"

"Oh, yes I do," he snapped back. "You gave me that right the moment you kissed me that night on the docks."

The bottom dropped out of her stomach. Oh, sweet Halla, he remembered that kiss! The Persuasions holding back his memories were breaking!

"I have no idea what you're talking about." Hoping to shore up her weakening hold on his memories—or at least cast enough confusion in his mind to make him wonder if those memories were real—she took a deep breath, filled her voice with Persuasion, and said, "Look, they tell me Tildavera couldn't have saved my life without you. For that you have my gratitude."

Dilys's eyes narrowed a little, as if he could sense the pressure on his mind to believe her over his memories. She didn't want his suspicion to override her efforts, so she pushed a little harder. "And if you're the one who saved Lily and me from her father, you have my gratitude for that, too. He was a vicious brute who would have killed us both if he could."

That extra push seemed to be working, as his expression had changed from narrow-eyed suspicion to a sort of intent blankness. "So, thank you, Sealord Merimydion, for your great service to me and my family. Now, I'm sure you are looking forward to spending the day courting my sisters, so don't let me keep you from it. I know how important it is that you bring one of them home to Calberna as your wife. And I'm sure whichever of my sisters you marry, the two of you will be very, very happy together." With a final push of Persuasion and coolly regal smile, she turned away and started for the garden gate.

She'd taken two steps when he started to laugh.

"Oh, *moa myerina*! How in Halla's name have you managed to fool everyone all these years—how did you manage to fool me!—when you are such a truly terrible liar?"

Despite her plan to make a quick exit, Summer's mouth dropped open and she turned to glare at him. She wasn't a terrible liar! She was an excellent liar! "I'm sure I have no idea what you're talking about." She sniffed.

"Of course you do." He smiled. Grimly. "Fair warning, *moa kiri*: if you *ever* use your Voice to try and make me betray my bond to you again, so help me Numahao, I will turn you over my knee and paddle your backside until those sweet cheeks of yours are as red as the Rose on your wrist! As your *akua*, I may be bound to you body and soul, but my mind is my own, and not yours to manipulate."

It took her a few moments to get past the shock of his spanking threat to realize that not only had her efforts at Persuasion failed miserably just now—all her previous Persuasions had been utterly shattered as well.

He remembered *everything*.

Shoto!

Time to make a quick escape.

"Good day, Sealord." She whirled around and rushed towards the gate.

He darted around her with shocking swiftness. One moment he was several paces behind her, the next he stood between her and freedom. His laughter was gone. "Enough, Gabriella."

"I told you not to call me that."

"And I told you that right is mine, given and accepted, and I will use it. As for who killed the man who hurt you, we both know it wasn't me—even though I would have happily shredded that worthless *krillo* with my own claws had you not destroyed him with your Voice."

"My—? You think I killed a man with my voice?" She didn't even have to pretend shock this time. Even she'd never made that particular connection! She'd always said it was the beast—the great and deadly power that made its home inside her—but now that he'd suggested it, she could see he was right. The power pulling from every part of her, leaving her body on a terrible roar—a *shout* of killing rage. Dear gods. "Even if such a thing were possible, I can assure you I would never have *m-murdered* a man in cold blood." Her tongue tripped over the word as her mind filled with the vivid memory of Lily's father—mouth open, eyes bulging and filled with terror as he realized he was going to die—and her own hot, savage satisfaction at knowing that she would be the one to end him, to destroy his ability to ever hurt another person again. Gods, how the fury had raged through her. The Summer Rose on her wrist had burned hotter than a forge—as if a piece of the sun itself had lodged itself in her flesh.

"What you did was justice and self-defense, not murder, *moa halea*," Dilys said. He reached for her hands. She managed to sweep her left hand behind her back, but he caught the right. His fingers traced the lines on her palm. His thumb brushed across the red Rose on her inner wrist. "And there was nothing cold about it."

Her mouth went dry. Her skin tingled everywhere he touched, and her Rose warmed rapidly, the heat throbbing in time with her escalating pulse. "If you think I have it in me to kill someone—even a man as horrible as Lily's father—you're sorely mistaken. Everyone knows I'm the least powerful of all the Seasons." The words came out hoarse and shaky. She gave her wrist a tug, trying to free herself, but his grip remained ironclad.

"Another lie. One you have clearly spent a lifetime building. Don't get me wrong. It was wise of you to hide your true power from the world. There are those who would kill you if they knew what you could do. There are others—far more than I care to count—who would stop at nothing to gain some sort of control over you, to force you to use your gifts for their gain. But between us, *moa kiri*, this constant lying really must cease. Anything less than absolute truth weakens the bond between *akua* and *liana*, and I will not have you hurting yourself that way."

"I'm not your *liana*. You are not my *akua*. And I'm not lying!"

"You know what I think? I think you've been lying so long to so many people, you don't even know how to speak the truth anymore. I will help you with this. From now on, for every lie you speak to me, we will share an intimacy of my choosing. Nothing too much. Just a small kiss or caress, received or given depending on the needs of the moment."

Her jaw dropped. "Why on Mystral would I ever agree to a bargain like that?"

He gave her a smile full of steely determination. "Ah, *moa kiri,* I was not asking for your agreement. I was explaining how I intend to help you keep our bond as pure, untainted, and powerful as possible so that I may best see to your needs, as is my duty and my right."

She glared at him, rubbing her wrist (although in truth he'd not hurt her at all). "Look, whatever you think there is going on between us, you are wrong. Once I took your memory of what happened on that dock, you made it perfectly clear you had no interest in me—or have your forgotten how you prefer the taste of Summerlean fire brandy to milked tea?"

He winced. "This foolishness I spoke . . . it wounded you."

"No, it didn't," she lied. "I'd actually have to *care* about your regard to be bothered by the lack of it." Since he was still blocking the way to the eastern gate, she spun away and started walking back towards the palace.

"*Tey,* clearly it did, and I regret it." He kept pace with her easily. "I was an idiot. A fool. I spoke without care, out of injured pride. You are not milked tea. You are so far from such blandness I cannot believe the comparison ever entered my mind. You are fire, without a doubt. Not the bright, blazing fire of your sister Autumn, or the controlled burn of your sister Spring. Nothing so small as that for you. You are the volcano deep beneath the sea. A power so vast, yet so well concealed most would never have known of its existence. Even I did not understand what you were until you killed that man."

"Oh, I see. You're attracted to me now because you think I possess some sort of terrible power you can use."

"*Ono.* As you well know, I was attracted to you from the first. Deeply, powerfully attracted. To you before all others."

She stumbled, his words too reminiscent of that voice resonating deep inside her. *Claim him. He is thine, before all others.*

She pushed that memory and the feelings it roused away and resumed walking briskly. "You have a funny way of showing it."

"You made it clear you did not welcome my attentions. Besides, I was under orders from my queen's council to marry your sister Spring or Autumn."

"And I don't see that any of that has changed. So go do your duty, Sealord."

"*Everything* has changed. And I'm trying to do my duty—to you." He caught her arm. "Gabriella, please, hear me out."

She snatched herself free. "Don't touch me! And don't call me that, either!"

"Do you even know what a great power it is that you wield?"

"I am a weathermage of Summerlea. Nothing more. And not a particularly strong weathermage at that." Maybe if she said it often enough, he'd start believing it again.

"What you are, Gabriella, beyond a shadow of a doubt, is a Siren—and you wield the greatest and most ancient power of Calberna."

Her mouth dropped open. Of all the things she'd expected him to say, "You're a Siren" wasn't remotely one of them.

"Have you been into the Summerlean fire brandy again?"

He scowled at her. It made him look dangerous. "This is no joke."

"You're either joking or crazy. Everyone knows there's no such thing as Sirens. They're a myth—fantastical sea stories made up by mariners long ago."

"No, Gabriella. The Sirens were real. They were slaughtered twenty-five hundred years ago by evil men who attacked the Isles. No Siren's Voice has ever been heard again—not in Calberna, not in all of Mystral—until the night you killed that *krillo*."

"I keep telling you I didn't kill that man," she protested.

"You mean you keep lying about it," Dilys retorted.

"But kill him, you did, and with a Voice that Called every Calbernan in Konumarr to your side. Every. Single. One. There is only one magic that could have done that: *susirena*. Siren Song. And given what you are, everything else makes sense. The attraction between us. Why I haven't been able to stop thinking about you. Why, sometimes when you look in my eyes, it's as if you dive into my very soul. Because you do. Because from the first moment, you recognized me as a *sirakua*—a Siren's mate."

"I did no such thing."

"The Siren in you did." He took her hand, and she was so stunned by his declaration, she didn't protest when he laid her palm over his heart. "I am yours to claim, Gabriella."

Good gods, his skin was so warm, so soft. "I-I don't want to claim you."

"This is because of my foolishness at the start. I did not recognize you for the *myerial myerinas* that you are, and I wounded you with my prideful words."

No, it was because right now all she could think about doing was letting her hands roam over the intoxicatingly touchable expanse of his smooth, muscular, naked chest. She snatched her hand back before she humiliated herself by giving in to the temptation. Sweet Halla, it was as if his entire body was a weapon—one specifically designed to smash through her defenses.

"You have every right to expect better from your mate." His voice held an edge of irritation. "My only excuse is that you are the first Siren born in thousands of years. I didn't recognize the signs. But I will atone for my initial blindness, Gabriella. Before these next two months of courtship are done, I will prove to you that I am a mate you can be proud of, an *akua* you will never regret claiming."

The muscle beneath his so-soft skin looked hard as stone. The layered textures of him fascinating. She visually traced the outline of one swirling blue tattoo, aching to trace it with her fingers as well. What was he saying? Something about two months? That was far too short a time. If she spent a lifetime exploring him, it would not be enough. Then the rest of his words started to register. "Wait . . . what?"

He frowned at her. "What?"

"Two months of what?"

"I vowed to spend the next two months of our courtship proving myself to you."

"Courtship? You had no interest in courting me before, and as far as I'm concerned nothing has changed."

"Everything has changed."

"Not for me. So I suggest you focus your attention back on my sisters, because my answer, Sealord Merimydion, is no." Yet even as she said no, she found herself swaying forward. His scent—fresh, tropical fragrances, underlaid with the warm musk of man—filled her nostrils, dizzying her senses. The long ropes of his obsidian hair gleamed with rich health in the sunlight. And his skin . . . that endless expanse of warm, bronze skin shimmering with the mysteriously compelling patterns written upon it in iridescent blue ink. There was a story there . . . a story meant for her . . . a story she would understand if only she could touch it, trace each curving line and symbol with her hands . . . her lips . . . her . . .

Gabriella caught herself just before her empty, reaching hands landed on his body. She practically leapt backwards to put more distance between them.

"Summer Sun!" she snapped, driven beyond endurance by his inescapable presence and the terrible, burning ache he roused in her. It was like every part of him was a drug designed *exactly* to intoxicate her senses and addle her wits. "Don't you have some actual *clothes* you can put on?"

Shocked silence surrounded them both.

Then, in a voice that sounded oddly choked, he said, "My manner of dress . . . disturbs you, *Myerialanna*?"

"How could it not disturb me?" she cried. "You're running around half naked, for Halla's sake!"

"My garb is no different than that of all my countrymen. Or are you saying they disturb you as well? Do my cousins Ryll and Ari disturb you? I have seen you speaking with them on more than one occasion."

The last statement ended in a growl that sent tremors racing across her body. The lightning that had sparked when she'd touched his flesh struck all over again at the audible sign of a territorialism he couldn't hide.

Later she would tell herself that running full bore into Dilys Merimydion's hard, naked, shockingly seductive chest had made every rational part of her brain seize up and cease to function. That was the only explanation. Because if the rational part of her brain had been working properly, she would have died before admitting what she admitted next. Especially to him.

"Of course they don't disturb me! Why would they? They're completely different than . . . than . . ."

"Completely different than what?"

"Than this!" Her hands flung out, indicating his chest, his shoulders, his arms, everything beneath that colorful scrap of cloth wrapped around his waist. "Than you!"

His scowl cleared, replaced by the first hint of a smug, male smile. "You are saying that only *I* disturb you, *moa halea*?"

His voice had dropped to a low, husky note that sent fresh shivers shuddering up and down her spine. Her skin pebbled. Oh, yes, he disturbed her all right. Far too much. And she was having none of it!

"This conversation is over. *Don't* follow me anymore. There will be no courtship between us." She spun on one heel and took off towards the eastern garden gate. This time, to her surprise, he didn't try to stop her.

Dilys watched Summer's retreat with narrowed eyes. The beautiful, blue-eyed Season had spent the weeks avoiding him like the plague, and it was clear she thought he'd let her keep doing so. He watched her hurry through the garden gate and down the path that ran alongside the fjord, trying to put as much distance between them as she could.

At least now he understood why she had been avoiding him. Understood why she'd been so cold and standoffish to him, while treating his cousins to her generous warmth. At least now he understood why she flinched from his touch and trembled in his presence.

Summer Coruscate hadn't spent the last month trying desperately to escape his presence because she feared or disliked him. She hadn't avoided him at every turn because he left her cold or because she hadn't forgiven him for insulting her that first day.

No, Summer Coruscate fled from him because he *disturbed* her.

Ryll, the tough, stern, often scary sub-commander of the Seadragons didn't disturb her. Ari, the cousin who was Dilys's mirror image, didn't disturb her. The thousands of other Calbernans wandering about Konumarr in their *shumas* didn't disturb her.

Just Dilys.

And he didn't just disturb her a little.

He disturbed her a lot.

Moreover, there'd been nothing shy or timid in her voice when she told him so. Instead, there'd been fire. Snapping, sparking whips of it. Underlaid with a sound that made his toes curl and his body sing with tense anticipation.

That hook and line that had pierced him from the first moment of their meeting? The same hook and line that had grown to the size of a whaling harpoon when her Siren's voice had dragged across an entire city to her side? Still there.

Now burning like a freshly stoked forge.

He'd been worried when she'd continued to refuse to see him even after she'd Called him and every other Calbernan in the city. He'd begun to think that somehow he'd made a mistake. That he wasn't hers. That the feelings eating him alive were not reciprocated.

But now he knew that wasn't the case. That what he felt wasn't a misunderstanding made in the heat of a wild, shocking moment when a Siren's Voice rang out for the first time in more than two thousand years.

He was hers. He was hers and she knew it.

And she was his, too. She was just fighting it, as he had initially done.

Because that hook and line? Apparently, it worked both ways.

He watched the bright, sky-blue flows of Summer's long skirts disappear through the garden gate.

A slow smile curved his lips.

Any one of his cousins or his men would have recognized that slow, determined, predatory smile in an instant, just as they would have recognized the honed purpose carved into his features as he raced down the terraces of the palace gardens and dove into the Llaskroner Fjord.

Dilys Merimydion was going hunting.

CHAPTER 11

The cold water of the fjord slid over Dilys like a lover's caress as he swam beneath the surface. Had he been a cat, he would have been purring. Water—like love—was a vital nutrient to Calbernans, but apart from an occasional nighttime swim when the rest of the palace and city was sleeping, Dilys had kept his need for the sea under tight wraps since coming to Wintercraig. He'd come to woo an outlander bride, and he'd not wanted to appear too foreign or off-putting to his future wife.

All that had changed now. Dilys was no longer court-ing a mere *oulani* princess. He was in pursuit of a Siren, one who thought she could outrun her own desires by denying them—and him. He intended to prove otherwise, and he would need every advantage he could muster to do so. Including the strength and revitalization he derived from the sea.

She was walking—all but running—towards the grotto under the waterfall. It was, he knew from Ari and Ryll, one of her favorite places to go.

In the water, the thin membranes grew between his fin-gers and toes, a translucent but highly tensile webbing that gave him speed in the fluid world of the sea. The muscles in his body flexed and pulled as he swam. He could out-swim a dolphin, if need be, but for now he maintained an even, leisurely pace. He swam on his side beneath the water's surface and watched Gabriella's bright blue skirts as she hurried down the beautifully landscaped walkway toward the waterfall grotto.

She wanted him. So badly she could hardly keep her hands off him. So badly, she would flee him rather than face the truth.

That knowledge was a potent aphrodisiac that roused every predatory, territorial, and possessive male instinct he possessed. And every one of those sharply honed instincts was now fixed, entirely and immutably, on the princess Summer Coruscate.

Time to see exactly how hot her fire burned.

He swam deep enough to hide himself from view. He didn't need to surface for air. The gill slits that had opened along his ribs filtered oxygen from the water itself. Still, every hundred yards or so, he swam closer to the surface just to get a better view. Each time he did so, he was careful never to disturb the water in a way that would betray his position.

Calbernans knew how to hunt in the sea.

The roar and turbulence of the falls grew closer, and Dilys slowed. His prey had reached the grotto.

Summer Sun! Gabriella paced across the damp, moss-covered stone floor of the grotto tucked away beneath Snowbeard Falls, the main feeder river that carried runoff from the snowcaps and the glaciers of the Skoerr Mountains into the Llaskroner Fjord. A westerly breeze blew the cool mist from the fall back into the grotto, bathing Summer's hot cheeks, but the normally refreshing mist burned off the instant it touched her skin.

Tension coiled tight inside her, dread snaking around the nervous knots. Why had she opened her mouth back there in the gardens and snapped at him over his manner of dress? What maggot had invaded her brain, and caused her to cast away an entire lifetime of self-preservation with a few foolish, unthinking words? She'd doomed herself as surely as a doe leaping out of the brush into the direct path of a hunter's bow.

Gabriella wasn't a hunter. Summerlanders, in general, weren't. They were farmers, gardeners, nurturers. But she'd spent the last several months in Wintercraig. Hunting was a way of life here. Every man a natural-born predator. And she'd come to understand a more than a little about their natures. She'd seen that subtle tension that gripped them all when they sighted their prey. Sensed the electric thrill that rushed through their veins as they stalked. Heard the eagerness and satisfaction in their voices when they spoke of their hunts.

And she had just roused those exact responses in Dilys Merimydion.

Why, oh, why, hadn't she just kept her mouth shut and kept whimpering and flinching away from him until she'd made a clean escape? When he thought she feared him, she'd been safe. Both his pride and his protective instincts would have seen to that.

But now he knew that her fear wasn't of him but of what he made her feel.

And that, as they said here in Wintercraig, was an entirely different kettle of fish.

She stamped her foot and spun around, pressing her palms to her hot face. "Scorch me for a foo—"

Her voice cut off, her lungs suddenly and completely bereft of all air.

For the life of her, she couldn't move.

She'd thought she'd bought herself some time. The rest of the day. A few hours at the least. Time to clear her head and plan a course of action.

She should have known better. Dilys Merimydion wasn't a lethal mercenary feared the world over because he gave his opponents time to regroup and shore up their defenses. When he discovered a weakness, he went for it full bore. With heavy artillery.

And Dilys Merimydion was very, *very* heavy artillery.

He rose from the fjord like some magnificent god of the sea, stepping through the frothing, white deluge of Snowbeard Falls as if it were a veil of falling flower petals, his sleek, dark, powerfully muscled body unbowed by the pounding weight of water that would have crushed another man. His gaze locked on hers, and with slow, deliberate, fluid movements, he climbed up the wet, black rocks tumbled at the base of the falls, pausing to crouch on the large boulder at the top of the pile like some majestic jungle predator preening in the sun.

The effect was . . . spectacular. If she hadn't desired him beyond all reason before, this moment would have done the trick.

Water streamed down him in rivulets, sliding over satiny skin, drawing her longing, ravenous gaze down the length of his sculpted body. The folds of his wet *shuma* clung to him like a second skin, all but transparent, molded to the heavy, rippling muscle of his thighs, the scandalous bulge between his legs that beneath her hot, hungry gaze began to pulse and grow, lifting the damp length of his *shuma*.

"Keep looking like you want to eat me up, *moa halea*, and I'll let you." His voice was a hard, rough rumble.

The throaty sound scraped across her senses, but it was the other, underlying tone that made every hair on her body stand on end. Not so much a sound as a deep vibration tuned precisely to every erogenous zone in her body. It rippled across her skin as he spoke and made her nipples clench into hard, painful points. Heat pooled in the suddenly swollen, throbbing folds between her legs. Her body began to shake with fine tremors.

Halla help her. This was another kind of Calbernan enthrallment. An erotic Persuasion. It had to be. Men couldn't bring a woman to the brink of shattering ecstasy with a just few words spoken in a throaty voice. No matter how deep, velvety, and darkly seductive that voice might be.

Not that Gabriella had ever allowed herself close enough to any man she found attractive to know what shattering ecstasy felt like, of course, but Khamsin had been a font of information these last months. Determined that her sisters would not go into marriage ignorant and unprepared, Kham had told the Seasons exactly what went on in the marriage bed, what their future husbands would expect, and—equally as important, in her opinion—what they had a right to expect from their future husbands in return. The conversation had been accompanied by plenty of wide eyes, gasps, and giggling, but plenty of avid interest, too. Spring had even taken notes.

In any event, this shivery, hot, shaking, tight, her-whole-body-was-about-to-explode feeling seemed very similar to the shattering ecstasy Khamsin had described. One more word from Dilys, and Gabriella feared she might tumble over the brink.

The side folds of Dilys Merimydion's bright white-and-blue *shuma* parted. One long, muscular leg slid forward with fluid grace, clearing the surface of the boulder and stepping lightly on the damp flagstones of the grotto floor. Every move was like a sensual dance, slow, deliberate, seductive. He crossed the short distance between them and came to stand before her, so close she could practically feel the warmth emanating from his skin.

She knew she should flee. This man was dangerous to her. The wild sexual attraction was only the tip of the iceberg. If she let him close—if she acted on the feelings he roused—she would fall so hard, so fast, there would be no coming back. No hope to save herself. She tried to make herself turn and run, but her trembling body seemed deaf to the commands of her brain.

Afraid she would not be able to resist again if she fell into that sunlit sea once more and heard that voice commanding her to claim him, she dragged her gaze down, away from his eyes, and fixed it on his mouth. But then, all she could do was think, *My gods, what a beautiful mouth!* and remember the many scandalous ways Khamsin had said a loving husband could put his mouth to use.

"S-stop this r-right now," she stammered.

"Stop what?" His head bent.

"You know w-what." His nearness overwhelmed her. "Stop trying to s-seduce me."

"Is that what I'm doing?" The words feathered across her cheek like kisses, trailing a warm path towards her mouth.

She swallowed hard. Her heart was slamming against her chest. "You know it is."

His mouth hovered over hers, so close his lips brushed against hers when he spoke. "If you want me to stop, you have only to Command me . . . *Sirena.*"

She opened her mouth to tell him to stop, but the words caught in her throat when his palm came up to cup her cheek. Her skin burned where he touched it.

"No more lies, Gabriella," he murmured. "Give me the truth. What do you fear so much, that you would run so hard from what you want?"

"I don't know what you're talking abou—"

The press of his mouth against hers cut off her lie and swallowed it down, stealing it from her lips. He curled one arm around her waist and pulled her close, tightening his embrace until the full length of her body was pressed against him. His other hand tunneled through her hair, fingers curling around her skull, holding her fast. All the while, his mouth moved upon hers. Soft as silk, hot as fire. As relentless as the sea.

Just when her knees were about to buckle, he ended the kiss and pulled back.

"I told you the price you'd pay for each lie," he said. "Try again, *moa kiri.* And this time, tell me true."

She thought his voice sounded a little strained, but

it was hard to tell. Her brain was swimming in dizzied circles and she was having trouble putting two thoughts together. Summoning the mental coherence necessary to analyze his state was utterly beyond her.

"I don't know what you're—"

He kissed her again, cutting off her lie earlier this time. The dizzied circles in her brain became a whirlpool. His lips parted hers, his tongue licked inside her mouth and stroked her tongue. Gods, he tasted like chocolate and whipped cream and caramel cookies and honeyed fruits . . . every luscious, delectable dish she'd ever savored that had left her craving more.

She almost wept in protest when he pulled back a second time.

"Try once more," he told her. His voice was definitely rough this time.

"I don't—"

She barely got out two words before his lips found hers a third time. It was too much. Her quavering knees buckled. She fell against his tall, hard body, helpless to refuse him any longer, helpless to deny her own desires. Her arms lifted to encircle his neck. Her fingers thrust into the silky ropes of his hair, gripping tight. She took a deep, ragged breath, then shuddered as the intoxicating taste, scent, sight, touch, and sound of him invaded and overwhelmed every one of her senses. She closed her eyes to block at least one of those senses, but that only heightened the others.

The hand at her waist slid lower. He cupped her buttocks and lifted her with effortless strength. Her feet left the ground. He pressed her hard against him, holding the secret vee of her sex against the hard, hot shaft of his. Sliding her up and down until a terrible, delicious tension twined tight inside her.

She shuddered again and arched in his arms, tearing her lips from his to cry out against the tempest of his kiss, the mad, wild sensations he roused in her body.

Her head fell back, and she moaned as his lips kissed a trail of fire down her throat. How was it possible that something as mundane as a *neck* could be so sensitive? But hers was—at least to him. He did something near her ear that made her shudder and clutch his shoulders, digging her nails into his flesh.

"What are you doing to me?" she gasped.

"No more than you are doing to me," he muttered against the pulse in her throat. His lips dipped down to the plump curves of her breasts. His teeth nipped at flesh no man had ever touched. Teasing the skin bared by her gown's neckline, teasing more that the rich fabric still shielded. "You want me, Gabriella. Do not make of yourself a liar by trying to deny it."

"I'm not lying," she insisted. "I—" Her voice broke off as he whirled around, crossed the short distance to one of the grotto's stone benches, and laid her down on the hard surface.

To free both his hands, she realized a dazed moment later as he straddled the bench and leaned over her, letting his hands roam as his mouth returned to cover hers. He kissed her into moaning bonelessness then sat back and guided her hands to his body.

"You are lying, and there is no need. You are not alone in this. Touch me, *moa kiri*. Can you not see—can you not feel—what you do to me?" He dragged her hands across the hard ripples of flesh that cobbled his abdomen, up to the bulging pectoral muscles, and pressed her palms over his pounding heart. "Feel how fast my heart beats. That is for you and no other. I did not understand it myself until you Called me to your side, but now it all makes perfect sense."

Still holding one hand to his heart, he dragged the other to his face. "Do not fear this," he said and pressed a kiss into her palm. "Do not fear me." Then one by one, holding her slitted gaze the whole time, he took each of her fingers into his mouth, surrounding them with damp heat, stroking them with his tongue in a darkly sensual caress and voicing a stirring vow after each one.

"I will never hurt you," he promised after releasing her pinkie finger. "I will never betray you." Her damp ring finger trembled against his lips. "I will stand between you and all danger." The caress of her middle finger made her breath come in shallow pants. "I will devote myself to your happiness." Her index finger was next, followed by her thumb. "Whatever you need, whatever you desire, I will provide." Pulling her thumb free of his mouth, he nuzzled the soft skin of her palm and licked down the soft skin of her inner wrist. "For I am yours, before all others, Gabriella Aretta Rosadora Liliana Elaine Coruscate."

With her gaze locked to his, he said, "Claim what is thine." His lips closed over her Rose, and his tongue swept across the mark's red, slightly raised surface.

It was as if he'd touched her body with a whip of fire. Her Rose flared hot. Her body clenched, back arching. Lightning shot through her veins, traveling in an instant from the Rose on her wrist to her breasts and her groin. She shuddered violently, wracked with waves of intense pleasure that built and built to a terrible, ferocious, burning ache.

Dilys stared down at the Siren writhing before him on the stone bench of the grotto. She was the most beautiful thing he'd ever seen, with her rich, dark, Summerlander skin dewed by the mist from the falls, flushed from the passion that left her trembling uncontrollably in his arms. Her eyes, blue as the sky and deep as the sea, were wide and dilated, brilliant against the lush, midnight frame of her thick, curling lashes. Her full, lush lips were open as she panted for breath.

His fingers slid into her hair. Such soft, silky, jet-black hair. Like waves of ink curling in the ocean's current. His hands curved around her neck, slid up to cup the sweetly rounded contours of her skull.

The small, sweet tip of her pink tongue swept out between her parted lips, dampening the plump flesh, making it glisten. "Dilys, I-I—"

The sound of his name falling from those sweet lips made his blood go hot and his body grow rigid with desire. She hadn't Called his true Name, not the one that would claim him, but that didn't matter. The sound of his worldly name spoken in her husky, desire-thickened voice was like eating *arras* leaf—one of Mystral's strongest aphrodisiacs—straight from the tree. He pulled her legs up over his thighs and yanked her groin tight against his. His mouth dove down, claiming those glistening lips in an abrupt, fierce kiss that was all wild hunger and shocking dominance.

From earliest childhood, Calbernan boys were taught to sail, to fight, and to use the sea to protect Calberna and the women in it so that one day, they could amass sufficient gold and glory to claim a *liana* of their own.

But there was another skill—one unrelated to war and wealth—that every Calbernan male pursued upon reaching manhood. *Ililium*. The study and mastery of the sensual arts.

Every Calbernan male who bore the *ulumi-lia*—the blue tattoo on their right cheekbone that proclaimed them worthy of a *liana* of their own—had not only won sufficient gold and glory to honor his chosen bride, he also had mastered every possible way to drown that bride in carnal pleasure, and bring her time and time again to the heights of rapture.

Calbernan males who bore the *ulumi-lia* were masters of the sea, masters of war, and masters of the sensual arts.

And yet now, with Summer Coruscate in his arms and the taste of her on his lips, every seductive skill he'd ever learned evaporated from his mind, leaving only the instinctive need to feed his ravening hunger for her. He wanted her naked, in his arms, skin to skin, his body sliding into her. The sweet, hot friction of sex. Claiming and being claimed. Body and soul becoming one, binding the two halves of them together for all time.

His head slanted. His mouth opened, forcing her lips apart as well. His tongue swept into her mouth, tangled with hers. Invaded. Laid claim to. She tasted of sunlight and honey and hot, elemental magic. She burned him. Scorched his soul.

He bit at her beautiful, full lips, with light, raking nips of his teeth that made the tender flesh swell and warm against him. Instead of pulling away, she matched every needy bite, every thrust of his tongue, every hungry, demanding growl, with her own passionate responses. Her slender palms slid up the bare skin of his chest, over his broad shoulders, arms clinging tight. Her nails dug into the flesh of his back, raked at him. The sting of pain—proof of her own unleashed passion—only enflamed him more.

He clamped her body to his as if by the sheer force of his embrace he could crawl inside her soul and anchor himself there for eternity.

His sex was hard, heavy, the skin stretched near to bursting. Each brush of the soft fabric of his *shuma* all but destroyed him, sensitizing the tip of his sex until he feared he might come right then, just from a kiss.

She squirmed, her dangling legs moving restlessly, and the motion nearly sent him to his knees.

"*Moa kiri . . . moa myerial myerinas . . .* put your legs around me." His voice came out choked, rasping. Each word forced through a throat so tight he could scarcely breathe, let alone speak.

She obeyed without a word, legs sliding around his waist, ankles clamping tight in the small of his back. Her grip was hard, fierce, and his mind went up in flames thinking about all the other ways and parts of him she could clasp so tightly.

His sex was wedged between her fully open thighs, blocked from the gates of Halla by his *shuma* and the much-too-plentiful layers of her full skirts. Need and hunger pounded through him. He had to get inside her. The need was ferocious, overwhelming. A primal instinct immutably etched into every cell of his body. The same sort of primitive, relentless, mate-or-die dictate that drove so many creatures of the sea.

She whimpered and sobbed against him, arching her back, hips undulating in an instinctive rhythm that drove him even wilder for her. Her plump breasts strained against the confines of her bodice.

"I need to see you," he rasped. Without thought, his battle claws snicked out, sliced through the ties at the front of her bodice. Fabric parted. Her breasts spilled free. Beautiful, lush, firm globes, silky skin like chocolate cream, topped by dark, tightly beaded nipples. Numahao bless him. She was exquisite. More perfect than he'd ever dreamed a woman could be. Everything about her seemed to have been fashioned specifically to drive him wild.

He reached for her, filled his palms with her breasts. "You are so beautiful, *moa kiri*. So soft, sweet . . ."

With a short, choked cry, she grabbed his wrists, tried to pull his hands away.

He caught her hands, tangled her fingers in his. "No, Gabriella, please. Let me see you. Let me touch you." Gently, inexorably, he drew her hands out to her sides and dipped down to capture one straining nipple in his mouth. She gave a sharp cry and arched up against him.

As she did so, the fiery hot Summer Rose on her inner right wrist slid across the pale golden trident on his left.

It was like being struck by lightning.

He reared back, roaring, every muscle trembling. Her body arched, rising up from the bench as if tied to him by invisible strings. A cry ripped from her throat. Her bright blue eyes flashed purest gold.

Dilys had sailed through his share of hurricanes—some so violent the waves alone would have sent any other vessel to the bottom of the sea. He'd felt the sting of rain.

The punch of wind so strong even a Calbernan could not stand against it. The electric crack of lightning that sizzled through the air and raised every hair on his body. Relentless forty-foot waves slapping at his ship like a child batting at a toy in his bath.

That raw, unbridled power was nothing compared to the force that drove through him now.

It roared through his veins, turning blood to molten lava, making him quake with deep, racking tremors. His sex went hard as stone, stretched near to bursting. Need became punishing agony, a hunger so fierce it was a living, writhing thing inside him. Had he not been straddling the bench, the enormity of what he felt would have driven him to his knees.

With a cry of surrender, he fell upon her, suckling her beautiful breasts, reaching for her tangled skirts. Trying to fight through the layers of bunched, blue fabric. Hating them. Needing to feel her skin, naked flesh to naked flesh.

"Sweet Helos!" Gabriella clutched Dilys's head to her chest, awash in indescribable sensation. The shocking pleasure that had engulfed her when he'd laid his hands—his mouth—on her bare breasts was nothing compared to the inferno of need that consumed her now. Her arms and legs clung to him like vines. Her hips were rocking against him in a desperate rhythm. She needed. Ached. Burned. Hungered, ravenously, beyond all reason. Only Dilys Merimydion could give her what she craved.

And he was taking too long!

She dragged his head away from her breasts, snarled, "Hurry, damn you! Hurry!" Then she fused her mouth to his, feasting on him, all but attacking him. She bit his tongue, tasted the sweet, metallic savor of his blood. He groaned, slanted his head, and kissed her more deeply than ever, as if through a kiss alone he could crawl inside her and fill up that empty place screaming for succor.

Some distant, shocked part of her mind whispered,

What are you doing? But her body paid it no heed. It was as if some wild, primitive force had possessed her.

And that primitive force wanted *him*—Dilys Merimydion—in ways Gabriella had never even dreamed of.

A breath of cool air wafted across her backside. He'd finally fought his way through the tangle of her skirts. Her back arched as his hand curved around her buttocks.

A furious snarl rumbled in his chest as his fingers encountered yet another shield of cloth standing between his hand and her naked flesh. She felt a tug, heard the rip as linen sundered, then tore her lips from his and arched her back as broad fingers slipped across bare skin that had never known a man's touch.

Without hesitation, those fingers dove between the rounded mounds of her buttocks, seeking and finding the softer, even more intimate skin between.

Yes! Yes! She arched her back more, thrusting her aching breasts up. His hot mouth ate a scorching path down the line of her throat, found the mounds of her exposed breasts once more, bit at the hard, aching nipples until she cried out and writhed against him. Her fingers dove into the thick, soft coils of his hair, clutching his head to her. The hand between her legs stroked her slick, overheated flesh. Each brush of fingertips against skin ratcheted up her need.

Then, abruptly, he drew back, pulling away from her breasts, stilling the fingers that had been working their delicious, feverish magic.

"No! Please," she wept. Her hips convulsed, riding his hand, his fingers. She pushed herself against him, not knowing what she needed, but knowing that she needed it and only he could provide it. "Please!"

"My Name, Gabriella," he said, and in his voice was a sound beyond hearing that rippled across her body, sank into her skin, vibrated across every cell of her body. "Speak my Name."

"Dilys!" she cried, shuddering. "Dilys, please!"

"My true Name, Siren. Speak my true Name, and I will give you everything you want and more."

The terrible need she thought couldn't get worse peaked even higher. The magic in his voice whispered across her nerve endings, played upon her like a thousand lips, tongues, fingers, becoming a torment of exquisite agony, until she thought she would say anything, do anything to find the relief just beyond her reach.

A name trembled at the edges of her mind. The same name she'd heard before. Strange and foreign, a name that was both new to her and yet as familiar as her own skin. His Name, she knew. It rose in her throat, throbbed on her tongue, pushed to be Voiced. But she daren't. If she did, if she let him in, let herself love him with the wild, all-consuming abandon currently raging through every cell of her body . . . He was the flame that would light the world-destroying inferno inside her.

Her head thrashed from side to side. She was in an agony of need. She reached for him, fingers clawed. "Dilys, enough!" When he didn't immediately respond, desperation sharpened with spikes of anger. He thought he could refuse her? That he would torment her into bending to his will? "Enough!" she barked, and something very powerful from very deep inside roared up through her body and spilled out of her mouth, filling her voice with Command.

He shuddered as though she'd struck him a mighty blow. His eyes flared golden bright. His lips pulled back, baring gleaming white teeth that now included a distinct set of long, sharp fangs.

He dove down, taking one breast with his mouth, the other with his hand. The thumb beneath her skirts pressed hard on a spot between her legs that made her gasp and start to shake. He lifted his head, tugging her tight nipple up between his teeth, stroking the pebbled tip with his tongue until she wept and pleaded against for release.

And then he uttered, "*Ililia nua,*" in a Voice that penetrated every part of her being.

Sensation exploded across every nerve ending. A scream ripped from her throat as an ocean of pleasure crashed down upon her. It swept her up, tossed her wildly about, sent her tumbling, washed over her again and again and again until she was boneless and limp, her throat raw from her unbridled cries.

Dilys cupped her face with shaking hands. "Now, Gabriella," he urged in a harsh whisper. "Speak my Name."

She stared up into his fever-bright eyes, and found herself floating once more in that sea of sunlight again, heat and blinding radiance all around. And the voice was singing in her mind, a Siren's Song that promised endless happiness, love, complete belonging, an end to the loneliness that had surrounded her soul since birth. She wasn't meant to be alone. She was meant to be joined. To be part of another—part of *him*. Two halves of a whole, joined forever through unbreakable bonds that only she could forge.

"Speak my Name, *Sirena*. Claim me as your mate. Bind me to you for all time." It was Dilys's voice speaking to her in the sunlit sea, but the tones throbbed with a compulsion that worked on her like a thousand tiny chisels, chipping away at the wall of her will.

Despite the shattering release that had just torn through every part of her being, the power she'd feared all her life was nowhere near drained. Instead, it was bubbling inside her, rising like lava in the throat of a volcano, pressure building, making the shuddering ache of her pleasure-wracked body seem minuscule by comparison.

Claim what is thine. Speak his Name. Set us free.

The voice was like a sentience inside her, a caged beast fighting to be free, furious at the continuing shackles she placed upon it. It wanted Dilys with a wild, ferocious eagerness. Rejoiced at his nearness. Reached for him with all its considerable might.

And she, Gabriella, the Season who knew what horrors came from someone like her letting down their guard and surrendering to the madness of love, was all that stood between them.

If she gave in . . .

"No!" she cried. "No!" She sat up quickly, shoving at his chest with force enough to throw him off balance.

"Gabriella." He reached for her as she leapt to her feet.

That powerful wildness was still leaping hungrily inside her. If she let him touch her—seduce her—again, she would lose the battle to keep it contained. That couldn't be allowed to happen. "No!" she cried. "Get away." She shoved him away once more, and this time, unbidden, a burst of sharp power shoved with her.

There was a flash of light. The smell of something burning.

And Dilys Merimydion went flying backward through the frothing white curtain of Snowbeard Falls.

"Gabriella!" Dilys bobbed up, surfacing in the Llaskroner Fjord in time to see the Siren he planned to marry run out of Snowbeard Falls Grotto clutching the edges of her gaping bodice with both hands. "Gabriella, stop!" She paused, saw him there in the middle of the fjord, then took off running again, heading for the palace.

He swam quickly to the fjord's north shore and was about to climb out of the water when he realized his *shuma* was gone. The linen *gudo* he wore beneath was burned, and hanging in tatters from one hip. And there were scorch marks on his abdomen. He poked experimentally at the reddened skin and hissed a little at its tenderness. The blast of power that had sent him flying off his feet and into the drink had not only burned his *shuma* right off his body, it had done a good number on him as well.

A little lower, and she would have burned off something he'd miss a Hel of a lot more than his *shuma*.

And he would have deserved it!

He smacked the water's surface with the flat of one hand and sank back down into its depths, kicking off from

the shore to float out into the center of the channel. He
tracked the sky blue of Gabriella's gown through the gardens and back into the palace, where she slipped in a side
door and disappeared from view.

Only when she was safe inside did he drop beneath
the waves and dive deep into the cold, dark waters of the
fjord. The webbing between his fingers and toes expanded,
giving him greater speed as he swam the length of the
fjord and out into open sea. After what had just passed
between Gabriella and himself, he needed the comfort of
the deep, blue saltwater world that was his natural ele-
ment. He needed to think and regroup.

He had, without a doubt, made a gross tactical error.

Fury sizzled his veins, the bite of self-recrimination
sharp and painful. What had he been thinking? How
could he have made such a grievous mistake? All his life,
he'd trained for one ultimate goal: to forge a powerful and
lasting mating bond with the woman to whom he would
anchor himself, body and soul.

And yet, when that woman appeared before him, instead of courting her with the tools he'd spent a lifetime
preparing, instead of winning her trust and her love with
patience and skill, he'd bungled everything. From their
very first day, he'd alienated her. He'd dismissed her, insulted her, wounded her feelings, and now, after realizing what she was—*who* she was, both to Calberna and to
him—he'd rushed her. Instead of sliding into the chase
with the sleek confidence of the Calbernan prince he was,
he'd thrashed about with all the finesse of a frenzied shark.
Had his mentors witnessed his behavior, they would have
rightly turned their backs on him in shame.

If she refused to let him come within a thousand feet of
her ever again, he wouldn't be able to blame her!

His hands curled near his face, claws fully extended.
It was all he could do not to tear the *ulumi-lia* from his
own cheek in self-loathing. He wasn't perfect. He made
mistakes. Even now, despite his years of training. But not

once in his life had he blundered so many times and so badly as he had with Summer Coruscate.

His failure was all the more galling because his blunders had been with *her.*

He should never have followed her to the grotto. He'd known she wanted him. She couldn't hide that. Even if she hadn't lost herself almost as badly as he had in their kiss, he knew well enough how to read the signs of a woman's body to know that he aroused her on the most basic and primitive of levels.

He should have used that to his advantage. Been patient. He should have baited his hook and dangled it before her until *she* came to *him.* Instead, he'd cornered her, left her nowhere to run, overwhelmed her with his sheer physical presence and his own unbridled passion until she yielded.

And in doing so, he might just have lost everything.

There were some prizes brute force could not win. Some victories that required subtlety.

He needed to regroup, to set aside the wild, wave-tossed storm of emotion and desire and aching, painful *need* that battered him from the inside out. He needed to find or force calm enough to think.

He could not afford to blunder again. From this point on, his hunt had to be flawless or he would lose her altogether, and that was unthinkable.

The only thing that gave him any hope at all was the sweet, wild way she'd come apart in his arms, after she'd Commanded him to end her torment, and in return, he'd Commanded her to surrender to the *ililia nua,* the ocean of pleasure.

She was a Siren. He could not have compelled her just then with the weak shadow of *susirena* that Calbernan males possessed unless she allowed it. And she would not have allowed it from any male except one with whom she shared a bond of trust.

She might lie to him, try to deny him, refuse to Call

his Name, but at least on some basic level, the Siren in her recognized him as a male she could trust. Recognized him as a mate. As *her* mate.

He clung to that realization as the beacon of hope it was.

From this moment forward, he was going to make up for all his past wrongs. He was going to woo her as she deserved. Until he won her trust, proved to her that she had his complete devotion, convinced her beyond all doubt that he was the right—the *only*—mate for her. Until she Called his Name and bound him to her—and bound herself to him in return, body and soul.

This was the mission he'd trained for all his life. Gabriella was the victory he'd spent a lifetime working to achieve.

Filled with a renewed sense of purpose, Dilys shot for the ocean's surface, instinctively summoning his seagifts to speed him along. He shouldn't have gotten much of a response. Even though Ryll, Ari, and a number of his men had gifted him with enough of their own power each day that he was no longer struggling to make it through the day without collapsing, keeping Gabriella alive had drained away all the great magic his mother had given to him. He had no ability to replenish that power, and yet, now, he shot through the water at a speed that could only be powered by great magic.

That was when he realized that in their passion, the Siren in Gabriella given him power. A vast ocean of it. More power than even his mother had ever be able to share with him—and Alysaldria held within her the concentrated magic of generations of Calbernan queens.

He broke the surface of the ocean, leaping skyward, soaring weightlessly through the air. The warm golden rays of the sun enveloped him in a sea of light, and he gave a laughing shout of exultation before his body arched gracefully and speared back into the Varyan's welcoming blue waves.

She was his. Deny it all she would, but she was his as surely as he was hers.

She had accepted his passion, his care, his devotion, and given him in exchange trust, passion, and her glorious, Siren-born magic, filling him with crackling energy and more strength than he had ever known. In doing so, whether she had intended to or not, she had completed *makura ri*, the touch of giving and receiving, and committed herself to *liakapua*, the Calbernan mating ritual.

CHAPTER 12

Thanks to servants' stairs and a judicious use of Persuasion, Gabriella managed to make it back to her room without anyone raising an alarm over her disheveled appearance. Once safely behind her bedroom's closed and locked doors, she shed her torn blue gown and silk chemise, then stood there naked trying to figure out what to do with them. If there'd been a fire in the hearth, she would have tossed the clothes in and let them burn, but it was summer and the hearth was empty.

With no other obvious method of disposal available to her, she threw the dress and chemise in the corner of the room and began to pace with short, agitated steps. That lasted for perhaps five seconds before she groaned and covered her face with her hands.

Summer Sun! What had come over her?

He'd kissed her, touched her, and she'd lost all reason. He'd *suckled her fingers,* for Halla's sake! Then suckled something more scandalous than that. She covered her breasts with her hands, only to shudder as touching the still-sensitized tips made her muscles clench with remembered passion. She snatched her hands back and resumed pacing.

"It was magic," she muttered. "It had to have been."

There was no other explanation.

One kiss, one touch, and she'd practically begged Dilys Merimydion to ruin her right there on the bench in Snowbeard Falls Grotto!

She'd let him unlace her bodice, touch her breasts— *kiss* them! She'd wrapped her legs around his waist and rubbed the most intimate parts of her body against his. She'd let him put his hand up her skirt, let him stroke flesh so private not even the maids who tended her in the bath touched her there except through the barrier of a wash-cloth.

And, gods help her, she'd enjoyed every moment.

She'd wanted more.

Even now, after he'd given her a stunning release that was most assuredly the ecstasy Khamsin had told them all about, Gabriella wanted more. Much, much more.

A knock on the door made her gasp and whirl around.

"Gabriella?" Spring's voice. "Gabriella, are you in there? Are you all right, dearest?"

"J-just a minute!" Summer ran to her dressing room and snatched a robe off one of the hangers, pulling it on and thrusting her arms in the sleeves as she hurried to answer the door. Halfway there, she remembered the dress in the corner. "I'll be right there!" she called as she sprinted across the room to seize it. A frantic search of the room, looking for a place to hide the gown, offered up no more options than earlier.

"Gabriella, what's going on? Open this door!" More knocking. The knob rattled.

Summer ran back to the dressing room and shoved the dress into the corner, behind several other hanging gowns, rearranging them to hide the blue fabric.

"Gabriella!"

Summer ran for the door, tying the sash on her robe as she went. A lock of hair flopped against her cheek and she stopped in her tracks, her hands going to her hair. The neatly arranged coiffure that Dilys Merimydion had put in complete disarray. Gods! One look at that mess, and Vivi would have more questions than Gabriella was ready to deal with at the moment. She began pulling out pins, shoving them in her robe's pocket. When all the pins were gone, her hair tumbling down her back, she ran her fingers through the mass to smooth it, took a deep breath, then opened the door.

"Vivi. What's the matter?" She tried her best to look surprised and concerned. "Has something happened?"

Spring's eyes narrowed and swept the room as she stepped across the threshold. "One of the servants said they'd seen you running upstairs. I was concerned." She turned back to Summer. "I understand you ran into Sealord Merimydion in the garden." At the sound of Dilys's name, Summer flushed, and Spring's eyes narrowed more. "Gabriella, be honest. Is everything all right? Did something happen?"

"H-happen?" Summer heard the faint quaver in her voice and could have kicked herself. She'd have to do better than this if she didn't want Viviana learning every humiliating detail about Summer's indiscretion. "Don't be silly, Vivi. Yes, I ran into the Sealord in the garden. He tried to convince me to accept his courtship, I said no and I left. End of story."

Viviana was no fool to be so easily duped. "If that's all that happened, Gabriella, then why are you up here in your room, looking like you just rolled out of bed?"

Thankfully, being a recuperating invalid gave Summer the perfect excuse. "Going for that walk tired me out a lot more than I anticipated. I came back to my room to have a lie-down."

"And you didn't call a servant to assist you?"

"There wasn't any need. That particular dress is easy to get on and off without assistance." Way too easy. Dilys had managed it with one hand. She turned away, ducking her head to hide the furious blush that heated her cheeks. "What's with the inquisition, Vivi?" She put a scowl in her voice, hoping Spring would think she'd turned away to conceal irritation rather than secrets. "You're acting like you think I've done something wrong. I just wanted to be left alone! Can't you understand that?"

"Of course." Instantly contrite, Spring stepped behind her and wrapped an arm around Summer's shoulders. "I was just worried, that's all. You're my little sister. I've always looked out for you."

Summer felt like a worm. She turned and burrowed into Viviana's arms with genuine remorse. "I'm sorry. You have always looked after me, and I love you for that. I'm being short-tempered over something that's none of your fault."

Spring's hand smoothed down the length of Summer's unbound hair. "Do you really dislike him so much?" she asked softly.

"Oh, Vivi." All of a sudden there were tears in Summer's eyes. She wanted to wrap her arms around Spring's waist and sob out the whole, awful tale and ask for her sister's guidance.

Viviana saw the tears and her spine went stiff as a pike. "Something *did* happen, didn't it? What was it? *What did he do?*"

There was a martial light in Spring's eyes. A snapping fury she rarely showed. Seeing it made Gabriella gulp back her confession. If Gabriella told the truth about what happened in the grotto, Spring would march straight to Wynter and demand that Dilys Merimydion be brought to account for his actions. He'd taken husbandly liberties with her body—and it wouldn't matter to Viviana that Gabriella had not only failed to stop him, she'd urged him to hurry and begged him for more. Once Wynter—who was taking his role as male head of the family very seriously these days—found out what had happened in the grotto, he'd have Summer married to Dilys Merimydion before sunset.

"Nothing happened, Vivi," Gabriella lied. Despite the fact that Dilys Merimydion now seemed to possess an infallible Summer-tuned truth-detector, she was an exceptional liar. Had been all her life. Even without Persuasion. She pulled herself out of Spring's arms and wiped her eyes. "I'm just tired and not myself yet. My body may be fully healed, but I still don't have even half the energy I did before that horrible man attacked me."

She was also extremely good at manipulating people with emotional diversions. Like guilt. Guilt worked wonders.

Spring immediately backed off her interrogation. She blamed herself for the attack on Summer because she hadn't insisted that Summer be accompanied at all times by a personal guard when she went to work at Khamsin's school—a concession Summer had wheedled out of Wynter and Khamsin months ago. "Of course. How thoughtless of me." Instantly remorseful, and full of maternal care, Vivi dropped the subject and guided Summer to a chair. "Come sit down, dearest. I'll ring for some tea."

She went to the embroidered, beaded bellpull near the bed and gave it three sharp yanks. A handful of minutes later, Summer's maid showed up.

"Tea for Her Highness, Amaryllis. And some of those delightful iced cakes she loves so well."

"You aren't having any?" Summer asked as Amaryllis bobbed a curtsy and ducked out of the room.

"No. As you said, you're tired, so it's probably best I leave you to rest in peace and quiet. Besides, Autumn and I are going sailing this afternoon.

Summer's body tensed. The hands folded in her lap clenched together tightly. "With Sealord Merimydion?" Had Dilys declared himself her mate, taken those shocking liberties with her in the grotto, all while still squiring her sisters about in case things with her didn't work out?

She felt Spring's suddenly sharp gaze upon her.

"No," Viviana said slowly. "With Sealords Ocea and Calmyria. They promised to teach us how to sail a skiff."

"Oh." Summer's clenched fingers relaxed. "That sounds like fun."

"I'm sure it will be. Now that I've gotten to know them

better, I find Sealords Ocea and Calmyria to be quite companionable. Though Ari—I mean, Sealord Calmyria—and Autumn get into terrible mischief together, it's nice to see her laughing and so carefree. I do feel a little bad about taking up their time when they should be courting potential wives, but they assure us they have time both to court a wife and still entertain friends." Spring wandered over to the bookcase beside the vanity and leaned against it. She watched Gabriella's face as she added, "To be honest though, since Sealord Merimydion made it clear he's no longer interested in pursuing a potential union with Autumn or myself, I think they're spending time with us so we won't feel put out over being rejected by our suitor."

Gabriella hated the little jump of her pulse. A moment ago, she'd gotten instantly jealous and territorial at the thought of Spring and Autumn going sailing with Dilys. And now, her heart was thumping eagerly at the confirmation that he'd terminated his courtship of both Spring and Autumn?

"I'm sorry," she said. "I know you liked him."

"I did like him," Spring agreed. "I still do, and I'm perfectly content to keep liking him as a future brother-in-law."

"Well, he's making a mistake if he plans to spend the rest of his time here courting me. I wanted nothing to do with him from the start, and I still don't."

"Gabriella."

Summer glanced up and then swiftly away from Spring's intent green eyes. "What?"

"I know you and Sealord Merimydion exchanged a lot more than mere talk in the garden today. Don't bother to deny it." Spring held up a hand before Summer could speak the lie on the tip of her tongue. "Your lips are swollen and you have a little love bite just there." She touched her own collarbone.

Blushing furiously, Gabriella clapped a hand over her mouth and yanked the collar of her robe tight around her neck.

"And I have a confession to make. You didn't bump into him by accident. Autumn and I both knew you'd run away again rather than face him, so we told you he was coming to join us on the terrace, and we sent him to intercept you in the gardens."

Summer's jaw dropped. "You *lied* to me?" Hypocrisy, thy name is Summer Coruscate. "You *set me up*?"

"Yes," Spring admitted baldly, "we did."

"Why would you do that?" She was genuinely hurt. Her sisters had always had her back. Always. Summer might lie to them about some things (like about murdering people with her powers and about her true feelings for Dilys Merimydion), but she would never betray any member of her family—especially not Spring or Autumn. Never.

"We think you need to give him a chance."

"That's my decision, not yours!" Summer spat. "And, wait! Weren't you the one not five minutes ago who was getting all fired up at the idea that he'd 'done something' to me? If that's the kind of man you think he is, why would you want me to give him a chance? Why would you manipulate me into running into him?"

"Obviously, I didn't think he was the sort of man who'd ever force himself on you, and since you just swore to me he didn't, it's a moot point."

Summer clamped her lips shut. She couldn't argue there, unless she admitted she'd been lying earlier. And honestly, though she'd happily lie about some things, even she couldn't bring herself to claim he'd taken advantage of her, when she'd been the one to lock her legs around his waist and command him to "Hurry, Dilys! Hurry!" She pulled a swath of hair in front of her face and began brushing furiously to hide her hot blush.

"How is it that you've become such a loyal Dilys Merimydion supporter?" she muttered as she brushed. "Playing matchmaker this way isn't your style. Especially not with me." She met Spring's gaze in the mirror. "You know why I don't want to be with him."

"Almost losing you like we did changed my perspective."

"Spring . . ."

Viviana laid her hands on Summer's shoulders. "I know what you're afraid of, and I won't lie and say your fears are groundless. You have a right to be concerned. We all do. But we all also have the right to find some happiness in this life. I think Dilys Merimydion just might be yours."

He is thine. He is thine before all others.

Stifling a shudder at the memory of that voice and all the feelings that came with it, Summer put the hairbrush down and stood up. "I'm sorry, Vivi, I know you mean well, but I'm not going to change my mind on this. And now, if you'll excuse me, I'm really exhausted and I need to lie down." She swayed a little and reached out to grab the corner of the vanity, as if her legs had gone weak.

Instantly contrite, Spring slid an arm around Summer's waist. "Let me help you into bed."

Gabriella felt a twinge of guilt over using Viviana's love to distract her, but she shrugged it off before it could burrow in. The monster was already pushing her to accept Dilys Merimydion. Her wildly awakened hormones were pushing her to accept him. Autumn was pushing her. She didn't need Spring to start in on her, too.

She was strong, but even she had her limits.

Spring went into full maternal mode, tucking Summer into bed like she had when they were children and brushing her hair back off her face. "You just rest. I'll make sure no one disturbs you."

"Thank you, Vivi."

"Anytime, darling." Spring's arms slid around her in a final hug, but instead of releasing Summer right away, Spring loosened her embrace and pulled back only enough to look into Summer's eyes. "Just to be sure, before I leave, Summer . . . if Dilys Merimydion did more than just kiss you when he ran into you earlier, you would tell me, wouldn't you?"

Summer held her sister's gaze steadily. "Of course," she lied with perfect sincerity.

After a long, searching look, Spring nodded. "Good." She stroked Summer's hair and pressed a kiss to her temple. "I leave you to rest, then. I love you, little sister."

"I love you, too, Vivi."

"Well?" Down the hall, in her private library, Khamsin practically jumped on Spring as she entered and closed the doors behind her.

Spring sighed and shrugged. "She says nothing happened. She claims she was just tired from her walk and went to her room to rest."

"Hmm." Khamsin didn't believe it. One of the servants cleaning an upstairs bedroom in the east wing had reported seeing a huge splash in the fjord, then seeing Gabriella running back toward the palace with her hair mussed and her dress awry, while Dilys Merimydion shouted after her. "What do you think?"

Spring sighed. "I think she wants us all to mind our own business."

"So you think something happened."

"She's hiding in her room, her lips are swollen, and she has a mark on her neck that looks like someone took a nibble on her. Something definitely happened."

"But nothing serious enough for her to tell you about it." Kham hid her crossed fingers in her full Wintercraig blue skirts. Wynter was still stomping around swearing he wasn't going to let any of the Seasons step out of their bedroom without an armed escort. If Autumn and Spring's little matchmaking scheme had gone awry—if Dilys had let things get out of hand—there would be Hel to pay.

"Nothing that Summer thinks I need to know, in any case."

"Do you know why she's so dead set against Sealord Merimydion?"

Spring sat down in one of the ice-blue leather library chairs. "Because he makes her feel things she's not comfortable with."

Kham frowned. "What do you mean?" She'd spent most of her life in isolation, outcast from Summerlea's royal court, and cut off from her family. Her sisters and her brother had all made a point of sneaking away from the court to visit her when they could, but she hadn't spent half as much time with her siblings as they had spent with each other. These last months together in Wintercraig had brought them much closer, but the Seasons would always share a much deeper bond with each other than they would ever share with her. They knew each other's secrets.

"She's afraid she could fall in love with him."

"But that's a good thing, isn't it?"

Spring smiled sadly. "Not necessarily. Not for us."

"Explain."

And Spring did.

Half an hour later, still mulling over the fear she'd never realized each of her three sisters harbored, Khamsin entered Wynter's office.

"Well?" he asked when she came in. He'd heard the reports of Summer's race back to the palace, too, and only Kham's insistence that they let Spring talk to Summer and find out what happened had kept him from hunting down Dilys Merimydion and causing an international incident.

"According to Spring, she says nothing happened."

"Do you believe it?"

"Not for a minute."

Wynter's fingers curled into a massive fist. "I'm going to beat that fish bloody."

"No, you're not."

"Watch me."

Khamsin came around the corner of his enormous desk and put her arms around him. "You're not going to interfere. And neither am I. Not yet."

"Why not?" He remained rigid in her embrace, his eyes icy but free of the white flurries that would indicate he was drawing on the freezing power of the Ice Heart.

"Because." She laid a hand over his heart and petted him with small circular, soothing strokes. "This may just be one chance for Summer to have what we do, and I'm not going to jeopardize that. I'm not going to push her, and you're not going to pound him. We're going to sit back and let the two of them sort this out. At least for now."

"I don't like it."

"Of course, you don't. You're very territorial." He growled and she smiled up at him, loving him so much her heart felt like it would burst. "I don't know what went on in that grotto, but if Dilys deserved a beating over it, Summer would have said something to Spring. And she didn't. That tells me that even though she says she wants nothing to do with him, Summer isn't prepared to sic you on him."

"I'm going to sic myself on him."

"He saved her life, Wyn."

"So now he gets to do whatever he wants with her? Over my dead body."

Kham laughed. "It's not like his intentions are dishonorable. He would marry her tomorrow if she said yes."

"Fine. And he can keep his hands and other parts to himself until then." He brought both of her hands to his mouth, kissed them, then kissed her until her knees went weak. Then he set her in his chair and headed for the door.

"Where are you going?" she asked.

"To work on my international relations."

"Wyn."

He paused at the office door. "Don't worry, *min ros*. I'll be very diplomatic." He smiled, showing teeth, cracked his knuckles, and departed.

"Oh, wonderful." Khamsin sighed and got to her feet. It was probably best to give Tildy a heads-up that there were going to be bruises in need of healing.

After an uneventful day spent hiding in her room and yet another night spent tossing and turning to disturbingly erotic dreams, Summer woke the next morning tired and out of sorts. As she rose from her bed, a flash of color caught her eyes. She pulled back the sheer curtains covering the glass balcony doors and gasped.

Her entire balcony awash in flowers. Bright, vivid rainbow-hued flowers in all shades of red, pink, yellow, purple, fuchsia, orange, and blue. She opened the door, drew a breath, and hummed in delight. The scent was amazing. Even knowing who must have sent them, she couldn't keep herself from touching the soft petals, breathing in the gorgeous fragrances.

It was a ridiculous, romantic extravagance, this balcony full of fresh, fragrant blooms, morning dew still sparkling like diamonds upon their colorful petals.

And, despite everything, including her own sense of self-preservation, she loved it.

Dilys Merimydion had chosen one of the best possible ways to steal past her defenses. Flowers were one of her weaknesses, the others being children, pets, delicious food (especially desserts) and a shameful obsession with the decadent, sinfully rich chocolates created by Zephyr Hallowill, the master chocolatier who had emigrated from the distant kingdom of Windhaven fifteen years ago to become Summerlea's royal confectioner. All right, so those weren't the most unique set of secret passions for a woman, but Summer always had been the most feminine of Verdan Coruscate's daughters

Every blossom on the balcony was one of her favorites, which probably meant one or both of her fellow Seasons had probably helped him. He hadn't signed the two dozen small cards tucked in amongst the blooms, but the bold masculine scrawl and the message repeated on each of the cards left her in no doubt as to the person responsible for this floral munificence.

Claim me as thine, the cards entreated.

Summer drew another breath of intoxicatingly perfumed air and shuddered as she recalled the wild storm of ecstasy that had swept over her, wringing scream after scream of mindless pleasure from her. Gods help her, she wanted to experience that again. One taste of passion—of him—and she was already dangerously addicted.

But it was more than just the pure eroticism she craved. Yesterday, in Dilys's arms, she'd looked into his eyes and seen everything she'd ever wanted looking back at her. Everything. Even things she'd never known she wanted.

She looked at the cards in her hands, read the scrawl of black ink.

Claim me as thine.

Her jaw clenched. She ripped the cards in two and dropped the scraps on the surface of her dressing table.

Her maid, Amaryllis, came into the room with Summer's morning tea a few minutes later, her eyes widened at the sight of all the blooms. "I've never seen so many flowers in one place. They're beautiful. Did Sealord Merimydion send them?"

"The cards weren't signed."

If Amaryllis heard the curt edge to Gabriella's tone, she gave no sign of it. "Nobody told me you had deliveries this morning. But why did you have them put all the flowers out on your balcony?"

Summer whirled to glare at the glass-paned doors leading to her balcony. She'd been so seduced by the beauty and fragrance of the flowers, she hadn't even stopped to wonder how they had gotten there.

Dilys Merimydion had been on her balcony.

In the middle of the night.

While she was sleeping!

She clutched the lapels of her robe. Had he peered

through the glass? Had he come inside her room? Maybe stood beside her, watching her as she slept? Maybe even touched her. Cupped her breasts? Put his mouth on her while she, caught deep in the erotic wanderings of her dream, had slept on without waking?

Helos damn her for her depravity, but the thought made every intimate part of her flush and throb in heated response.

Angry at her arousal, she shoved the thoughts out of her mind and scowled at her maid. "It doesn't matter who sent them or when they arrived, Amaryllis. After you finish helping me dress, I want you to dispose of them."

"Oh, but—"

"All of them!" Summer snapped. "I don't care how. I don't want a single flower in this room when I return."

Amaryllis's friendly open face went blank with shock, then after a long moment turned wooden. She swallowed the rest of her objections and bobbed a stiff, obedient curtsy. "Yes, ma'am. As you wish."

"Good. And here." Summer swept the shreds of Dilys's notes off her dressing table and handed them to Amaryllis. "Dispose of these as well."

The shreds of notes disappeared into Amaryllis's apron pocket. "Yes, ma'am."

"Thank you, Amaryllis. I think I'll wear the white linen today." She poured herself a cup of tea while Amaryllis disappeared into the wardrobe.

White was cool and icy, untouched and untouchable. Hopefully, Dilys Merimydion would get the message.

Apparently, Calbernans didn't understand the language of colors.

Dilys Merimydion, who was waiting for her at the bottom of stairs as she headed down to breakfast, took one look at her snowy-white gown and, instead of keeping his distance, made a beeline for her. His gaze was fixed on her in a way that might have made her blood heat up all over again had she not been busy gaping at him in horror.

"Did I do that to you?"

His light blue *shuma* and silver torque did nothing to hide the mass of cuts, scrapes, and purple bruises that covered his body and made his iridescent tattoos practically glow by contrast. He had a dark bruise under one eye that ran all the way down to the *ulumi-lia* tattoo on his cheekbone, and another on his jaw.

"This?" He gestured to his battered frame. "*Ono, moa halea.* I was invited to partake in a wrestling match yesterday afternoon."

"A wrestling match with whom? Kukuna the Stone God?"

His grin flashed, then faltered as the gesture tugged at his split lip. "It was a very intense match. And you have been reading the legends of my people. You are curious about Calberna. This is good."

She grimaced. "Don't jump to conclusions. I read most of those legends *before* I met you so I could teach the children at the school about Calberna." Then, because curiosity got the best of her, she asked, "So which one of Wynter's men beat you to a pulp?"

His brows rose. "I am unpulped."

"Not from where I'm standing. Or are you saying the other fellow looks worse?"

He cocked his head to one side, as if considering, then gave that charming half grin again and said, "About the same. We declared it equal contest."

"Who did you leave unpulped then?"

"It is of no concern. We had our match. We tested each other's skill and resolve, and came away with a new understanding of each other." His easy expression sobered to something much more serious. "Gabriella—"

"Don't call me that."

He continued as if she hadn't interrupted. "I have been waiting for you here this last hour. I came to apologize to you yet again." He stepped closer and lowered his voice. "It seems that I am forever putting my feet wrong with you. I rushed you yesterday. I pushed when I should have been patient."

She could feel her cheeks growing hotter by the second. He was too close. His warm, tropical, masculine scent was enveloping her. She swallowed and stepped back. "Look, Sealord Merimydion—"

"Dilys," he corrected.

"*Sealord Merimydion,*" she reiterated, "there's no need for you to apologize to me for anything. What happened yesterday was a mistake, but it's over now. In the past. I've forgotten it, and so should you."

His brows rose. "You have forgotten? This, I do not believe." He stepped closer again. She retreated up another stair. "What passed between us was not forgettable. *I* am not forgettable. Not to you."

"You have a high opinion of yourself."

"No higher than deserved. But I know when a woman looks at me and likes what she sees. And I know when she wants more."

She did, gods help her. She was already melting, her hands itching to touch. She wanted to soothe his wounds, kiss them better. And then she wanted more of what he'd given her yesterday.

Summer retreated another step and, when he started to advance again, held up a hand as if to ward him off. "Is this your idea of not pushing?"

"I did not say I was not going to push. Only that I regretted pushing too much yesterday. Still, I know things between us happened faster than either of us anticipated. It has left you wary and me not as patient as I normally would be. So I retreat for the moment. You see?" He took two steps back and smiled disarmingly. "If you prefer, we can both pretend yesterday did not happen, and we will start anew, with today as the first day of our courtship."

"There isn't going to be any courtship."

"Of course there will be. That's why I came to Konumarr. So, *moa halea,* did you enjoy the flowers I left for you on your balcony this morning?"

"No," she said shortly. "I didn't. So don't send me any more. And we are *not* courting."

"*Tey,* we are."

"No, we're not."

"*Tey,* we are. How can you doubt it after what we shared in the grotto? I thought I knew all the secrets of *ililia nua,* but I doubt the gods themselves have ever known such incredible pleasure."

Her cheeks went beet red. "Would you stop!" she hissed.

He smiled tenderly. "There is no need for embarrassment. What happened between us is proof that our bond is strong. I should have led us there more slowly, but when I touched you and I kissed you, all I could think was . . . *more.* I think we both needed it, *tey?*"

"I certainly did not!" she exclaimed.

His brows arched. "An intimacy of my choosing is the price for each lie you tell me," he reminded her. "Since you keep lying, I can only assume you are asking me to kiss you again."

"You are impossible," she huffed. "Out of my way. I'm late for breakfast." She tried to skirt around him, but he caught her arm.

"Wait. Please." The easy affable smile left his face. "There is an important matter we must discuss. I meant to talk to you about it yesterday, but you distracted me so deliciously."

She arched her brows, trying to affect the same withering haughtiness Autumn had mastered. "I shall endeavor not to do so in future. Now, let me go this instant, or I will call the guards."

"Give me two more minutes of your time."

"This is not a negotiation."

"Two minutes. It's important. It's about keeping you and your family safe." When she sneered at him in disbelief, he said, "You're the liar, *moa kiri,* not I. Apart from my comment about milked tea, I've spoken nothing but truth since the day I arrived."

Well, that stung. "Oh, really? What about the lies you told Khamsin about killing Lily's father?"

His smile was filled with smug satisfaction. "So you do remember that it was you."

"Oh!" She couldn't believe she'd walked straight into that one. She glared at him. He was even sneakier than she'd thought. And if he wasn't using that sneakiness against her, she might even have felt a grudging admiration for it. "Fine. Let go of me, and you'll have your two minutes." She stared pointedly at the hand on her arm until he removed it. She folded her arms across her chest. "So talk," she commanded.

He moved a little closer and dropped his voice so low that no one within two feet of them could have heard it. "The power you wield—your Siren's gift—have you spoken to anyone about it since I told you what it was?" Gone was the charming, seductive suitor. This Dilys was all business, his expression grim, his tone brusque and no-nonsense.

"No," she admitted.

"Good. Don't. Don't tell anyone. Not even your sisters."

She didn't like the sound of that. "Why not?"

"Because if people find out what you are, you and everyone you love could be in grave danger."

"Well, it's a little too late to keep it a secret. According to you, every Calbernan in Konumarr already knows. And so does Lily."

"*Tey,* but my men would suffer the torments of Hel before betraying your secret. And I made sure Talin took care of Lily's memories. She remembers the same story I gave your family—that I killed Lily's father because he attacked you."

Summer's heart missed a beat, then started pounding furiously. She'd known Lily believed the story about Dilys

killing her father, but she'd assumed that was because of
the blow she'd taken to the head. "*Talin* 'took care' of Lily's
memories?" Her voice had started to rise and get louder.
He shushed her in alarm, and she lowered her voice back
to a harsh whisper. "You mean he can manipulate minds,
too? Can *all* Calbernans do that?"

"Nothing close to your degree, but yes. *Susirena* is one
of our gifts from Numahao."

A hand crept up to her throat. "All these weeks of
courtship . . . have your men been using magic to win over
our women? Have *you* been using it on *me*?"

"No!" The shock on his face seemed too genuine to
be faked. "A Calbernan would never use *susirena* to win
a *liana*. Calbernan males dedicate their lives to being
worthy of a woman's love. Do you think we—any of us—
would settle for some false pretense of it manufactured by
magic?" His hands slashed the air. "The mere suggestion
is an insult. Only a worthless *krillo* lost beyond all shred
of honor or redemption would take what must be given
freely."

"Yet you admit Talin used magic to alter Lily's mind."

"To erase the memory of a secret she should never
have learned. To protect you—and her." He drew in a
deep breath and visibly calmed himself. "Gabriella, you
must understand, what you are—what you can do—is a
treasure beyond price. Evil men once slaughtered tens of
thousands of my people and nearly drove us to extinction
because they both feared the gift you possess and wanted
its power for themselves. When they couldn't get it, they
stopped at nothing to destroy it. And they succeeded.
They wiped Sirens from the face of Mystral for over two
thousand years. You are the first born since the Slaughter,
Gabriella. The first Siren to Sing in twenty-five hundred
years."

"What does that mean, exactly, to be a Siren?"

"It means that you possess the strongest magic in all
Calberna. That, among other things, that you can kill with

your Voice, as you killed that *krillo* who attacked you, and bend minds to your will. As you did when you erased my memories of our first kiss."

His eyes were too intense. His words too disturbing. She looked away and gave a forced laugh. "Well, clearly, I'm no Siren then, since my efforts didn't work."

"As it happens, I have a measure of immunity against your power. Both because I am Calbernan, and because—though you insist on lying about wanting me—the Siren in you recognizes me as your mate."

"It's not a lie. I *don't* want you."

He moved so quickly she barely had time to gasp before he lifted her off her feet, fused his mouth to hers, and kissed her until her brain melted. Then he set her back on her wobbly legs and said, "That was for the lie. And for future reference, *myerina,* wrapping your legs around a man and Commanding him to pleasure you is not an effective way to illustrate your lack of interest."

Her face flamed. "I think your two minutes are up. Have a good day, Sealord Merimydion, but have it somewhere far away from me."

"Little coward," he said, but he held up his hands and stepped out of her way. "Fine. Run away again, if you must. But promise me you will keep everything we discuss about *susirena* to yourself. There are people who would stop at nothing to get their hands on you."

"Right now the only man who seems willing to stop at nothing to get his hands on me is you," she snapped.

"Oh, I want much more than just my hands on you. I thought we'd already established that. The difference is, with me you would be safe, protected, and loved. I would devote my life to your happiness. The men I'm talking about would use you—and use any means necessary to control you—including hurting you and the ones you love. So, please, promise me you will say nothing, at least not until we are wed and back in Calberna where I can ensure your safety."

"That's easy enough. I wasn't planning to say anything anyway, and since we will never wed"—she smiled sweetly—"I can honestly promise to take the secret of this so-called Siren power of mine to the grave." She stuck her nose in the air, whirled on one heel and marched down the hall to join her sisters for breakfast.

Her haughty exit lost a little of its dramatic effect when his laughter rolled out in her wake.

"Challenge accepted, *moa leia*," he called after her retreating back. "This is my solemn vow: before my time here in Wintercraig is up, you and I will be celebrating our forthcoming union. For now, enjoy your day. I will spend mine finding something besides flowers to tempt you with tomorrow."

CHAPTER 13

Rebuffing a determined Calbernan intent on courtship was much easier said than done. Especially when that determined, intent Calbernan was Dilys Merimydion.

In addition to the deluge of intoxicatingly fragrant blooms delivered to her balcony each morning, dozens of little notes and romantic gifts found their way into her presence. There was no telling when or where the gift would come, as no place in Konumarr and no time of day seemed off limits to Dilys Merimydion's campaign to win her over.

She'd go to pick a book from the library, and a card that read "Claim me as thine" would fall from the pages. She went to the garden to trim the roses and found a small, folded, perfumed note inside her gloves. The front of the folded note read, "Claim me as thine," while the inside of the card had been inscribed with a verse from one of her favorite poems. She went for a walk through Konumarr's shops, and a trio of charming children gathered on the street corner and began to sing as she drew near, their childish voices pure and crystal clear. Summer and everyone else who'd stopped to hear them sing clapped when they were done, but when Summer stepped forward to give the children a golden coin to thank them for their performance, each of them pressed a small card into her hand in return. Three more small cards, each bearing that now-familiar scrawl, "Claim me as thine."

And every morning at breakfast, there was a beribboned box waiting for her on the cushion of her chair. One morning, the box held a bracelet of the brightest, most beautiful sapphires she'd ever seen—each surrounded by a ring of oval diamonds shaped like the petals of a daisy. She closed the bracelet back up in the box and handed it to a servant. "Please see that this is returned to Sealord Merimydion."

The servant bowed and carried the exquisite gift away.

The next morning, another box awaited her when Summer came down to breakfast. This one contained a small golden pin shaped like a trident, symbol of House Merimydion. That, too, she returned. And on it went.

The sixth morning, thinking to thwart him, she had breakfast delivered to her room. But when her maid lifted the domed lids off the breakfast plates, Summer found not one but three brightly wrapped and beribboned gifts nestled amongst the muffins, fruit, and sitting alongside the small ceramic boat of creamy scrambled eggs. Each contained a tiny flower fashioned from perfect, sparkling gemstones mounted on a miniature golden stem. A fourth box, hidden in the sugar bowl, contained a crystal vase no bigger than her thumb, the perfect size to hold the three jeweled flowers.

Unable to help herself, Summer placed each of the three jeweled blooms in the vase and sat it beside her plate as she ate. Sunlight streaming in from her south-facing windows made the tiny blooms sparkle, and cast bright prismatic rainbows across the snowy white linen the maid had laid out over the table.

The exquisitely worked vase with its miniature jeweled blooms was the most enchanting thing she'd ever seen. But when she finished eating, Summer put each piece of the tiny arrangement back in its respective box and handed the boxes to her maid, Amaryllis.

"See that these are returned to Sealord Merimydion."

"Yes, ma'am," said Amaryllis, giving a short, bobbed curtsy.

The following morning, Summer rejoined her family on the terrace for their regular breakfast. And there, on the private family terrace, sitting on the chair reserved for her, was a large yellow box, about three cubic feet in size, its removable lid wrapped with green satin ribbon and a matching bow.

"That box is huge!" Autumn said. She gave Summer an eager grin. "Hurry and open it. Let's see what's inside!"

"You have to give it to Sealord Merimydion," Spring said. "When he sets his mind on something, he doesn't take no for an answer."

"Oh, I wonder what it is today," Khamsin said with a little clap of excitement.

Dilys Merimydion's daily morning gifts and the smaller cards and treats throughout the day had become a subject of marked interest to all of Summer's sisters. To the point where Summer suspected the servants took each rejected gift around to Spring, Autumn, and Storm for their viewing before returning it to the incorrigible Calbernan Sealord.

Wynter scowled, not at all pleased with Summer's persistent suitor, or his wife's interest in it. But in the face of Khamsin's open eagerness, Wyn gave an expressive roll of his eyes and settled back into his chair. "Open the blasted thing, Summer. Let's see what extravagance Merimydion wants you to send back to him today." He crossed his arms over his very impressive chest.

Her heart swelled with affection for him—and not just because he was the only one in the family who'd firmly allied himself with Camp Summer rather than Camp Dilys in the war of wills Autumn had taken to calling the "Courtship Siege." She would never forget the sight of Wynter's battered face greeting her at breakfast the day after Dilys had followed her to the grotto, or his gruff tenderness when he'd pulled her privately aside to make sure Dilys Merimydion hadn't done anything to her that required something more serious than a mere "wrestling bout."

Smiling at the memory, Summer reached for the ribboned top of the yellow box.

She expected the contents of the box to be exquisite and extravagant. While the little gifts throughout the day tended to be simple things, the gift that started off each day never failed to elicit gasps of appreciation.

Today was no exception.

When she lifted the lid on the yellow box, she didn't need to reach inside for its contents. This morning's gift flew—or rather, fluttered—out.

Hundreds of jewel-winged butterflies took to the air in a cloud of vivid, colorful beauty. Dozens of them alighted on the tableware after their release. Dozens more flitted about the surrounding garden, fluttering inquisitively around the blossoming flowers in search of nectar.

Summer and her sisters watched the beautiful creatures for several long minutes, then Autumn turned back in her chair with a smirk and said, "Well, there's no returning that gift, is there!"

Summer opened her mouth, closed it, then, despite herself, burst into laughter and admitted, "No, I suppose not." She had been well and truly routed.

Out of curiosity, she glanced into the box. A few butterflies still remained within. She reached inside, nudging her finger gently under their spindly legs and lifting them out to freedom. Two flew away, but the third remained perched on her hand, its gorgeous black and turquoise wings slowly opening and closing as she reached her free hand into the bottom of the box to retrieve the only thing left inside: a large folded card.

Claim me as thine, the outside of the card entreated once again. Inside, a painted paper butterfly popped up as she opened the card, spreading beautifully illustrated wings colored with bright rainbow hues. "Gabriella Aretta Rosadora Liliana Elaine Coruscate, *myerial-myerinas,* you make my heart take wing."

Conscious of the watchful eyes of her sisters and her brother-in-law, Summer closed the card and tucked it beneath her plate.

"I don't know what Dilys did that he has to work so hard to get into your good graces, but you've got to hand it to him. The man knows how to grovel." When Summer shot Autumn an accusatory glance, Autumn lifted her hands. "What? A sincere, satisfying grovel is a talent most men never really master. You could do a lot worse than wedding a man who knows how to apologize well."

"That's true," Khamsin agreed with enough emphasis to make her husband sit up straight in his chair. "Not that I have any complaints on that score," she added quickly, reaching out to give his hand a squeeze.

"Since I won't be wedding Dilys Merimydion, his mastery of groveling makes no difference to me one way or the other," Summer told them all, narrowing her eyes when Autumn seemed to be suppressing a smirk. "And since he was never in my good graces in the first place, he is not groveling to get back into them."

Autumn rolled her eyes. "Tell me at least that you aren't still holding that ridiculous 'milked tea' remark against him."

"No, of course not," Summer said, and her brows drew together in surprise as she realized she was telling the truth. Sometime between the interlude in the grotto and now, she truly *had* forgiven him. She couldn't even remember why the remark had cut her as deeply as it had. After all, she'd spent her life striving to *be* milked tea, to suppress every dangerous ounce of fire and passion she possessed. Hearing him call her that should have left her pleased with the success of her deception, not wounded and resentful because he hadn't seen straight through it.

"So if it's not that, then what is it?" Autumn persisted.

"None of your business, that's what!" Summer turned to Khamsin with a determined smile and said, "So, have you and Wynter decided on names for the babies?"

Khamsin and Wynter exchanged a look. For a moment, Summer thought they were going to pursue the inquisition, but instead, Kham laid a hand on her belly and said, "Well, we won't know what we're having until the babies are born, but we've agreed that, no matter what, our first-born son will be called Garrick, and our firstborn daughter will be Rosalind."

"What a wonderful tribute to our mother and Wynter's brother." Summer watched Autumn from the corner of her eye as she spoke. For a moment, she thought the youngest Season was going to start in on her again, but Spring gave a quick shake of her head and Autumn subsided back into her chair with a pout.

The name of Dilys Merimydion did not come up again.

All morning long, Summer saw butterflies. They were everywhere, flapping their gorgeous wings with lazy grace. Reminding Summer constantly of the exotic sea prince who'd sent them.

Autumn was wrong. Dilys wasn't groveling. Despite the hundreds of cards pleading for forgiveness, these extravagant gestures weren't apologies. They were planned attacks meant to weaken her defenses.

Ever since that day in the grotto, Dilys Merimydion had made himself both scarce and omnipresent. Never approaching her, keeping his distance, but making sure she remained wholly and completely aware of him every minute of the day. Parading around in the brightest of *shumas* clearly meant to draw her eye, his body oiled and gleaming in the sunlight. Stripping down to the very, very tiny linen undergarment all the Calbernans apparently wore beneath their *shuma* and swimming in the fjord beneath her bedroom balcony each morning and evening. (And, gods forgive her, she'd actually begun to look forward to those times.) Invading every part of her life—including her dreams, for Halla's sake!—until she couldn't go five minutes without thinking about him.

Groveling. Ha!

The day that man truly groveled would be the day fire reined in Rorjak's dominion of ice.

But . . . all right . . . the butterflies were beautiful. And romantic. And just about the loveliest gift she could ever imagine.

She walked down a hall that led past a row of wide, arching palladium windows overlooking the gardens. The windows were open to let in the summer breeze, and a gorgeous, rare blue lacewing butterfly was perched on the sill, airing its magnificent wings. Those wings were bursting with vibrant colors: royal blue, turquoise, periwinkle, teal, and countless shades in between, all interspersed with delicate tracings of purest black and bright, glimmering whispers of sunshine yellow. The wings fluttered open and shut, so fragile, almost ephemeral, their undersides dusted with pink and silver along the scalloped edges. The butterfly was impossibly beautiful.

Entranced against her will, she watched it sit there on the sill, basking in the sun, until the sound of childish laughter and familiar masculine voices yanked her back to her senses.

"Dilys! Dilys! Dilys!"

Dilys and his cousins and a dozen or so children were playing a game of kickball on the grass. She'd seen Dilys surrounded by children many times. They gravitated to him wherever he went. Probably because of the easy, wholehearted way he gave them both his time, attention, and affection.

He would make an exceptional father.

Outside, a young boy had stepped up to the kickball home plate. Dilys, who was acting as bowler, rolled the inflated leather ball towards home plate. The child gave the ball a mighty kick, sending it careening left, past Dilys and between second and third bases. The opposing team, which included Ari and Ryll, cheered as their players raced around the bases. In the outfield, two young boys on Dilys's team went chasing after the ball, but before they even reached it, the kicker had rounded third base and was heading home.

As Dilys turned to congratulate the kicker, he glanced over in Gabriella's direction. Their gazes locked, and they both froze. The laughter on Dilys's face faded to something warmer, deeper. Something entrancing and impossibly beautiful.

"Dilys! Heads up!" someone called a warning a split second before the leather kickball bonked Dilys on the head, sending him staggering sideways. The young outfielder who'd thrown the ball called, "Sorry, Dilys!" then ruined the apology by doubling over with laughter.

Instead of getting mad, Dilys let out a mock roar, snatched up the ball, and went chasing after the child, who squealed and started running.

Freed from the dangerous enchantment of Dilys's gaze, Summer drew back into the shadows of the palladium arches and watched the kickball game devolve into a laughing game of tag and tickle. When she realized she was laughing softly at Dilys's antics, she straightened up quick and gave herself a hard shake.

"Summer, you are an idiot. An easily manipulated idiot!" She scowled at the blue lacewing perched on the sill. "Shoo!" she said. She flicked her fingers at it. "Shoo!"

The butterfly just kept fanning its wings.

Summer could have lunged at it and scared it away, but she couldn't bring herself to do it. With a sigh and for her own weakness, she tucked her chin down and turned away.

The basket was waiting for her that evening when she returned to her room to dress for dinner.

A big basket, woven of thin brown reeds, covered with

a red-and-white checked cloth, perched in the center of her bed.

Telling herself she'd just have a look at the basket's contents before calling Amaryllis to take it away, Summer walked over to the bed. As she drew near, a sharp little bark broke the silence of her room, only slightly muffled by the checkered cloth.

Summer froze.

Another bark. Then another. The basket rocked as what lay within jumped from side to side beneath the cover.

Summer's heart slammed against her chest. Her fingers curled tight. No. No, he hadn't given her a . . .

"Arf! Arf! Arf!"

She whipped the checkered cloth off the basket and stared at the floppy-eared, golden-furred bundle of mischief leaping enthusiastically about inside the basket on four little paws.

Dilys Merimydion had given her a puppy!

A puppy!

The instant he caught sight of her, the little dog yipped and hunkered down, its little butt in the air, tail wagging. And then, with a happy, tongue-lolling grin, the puppy leapt up towards the rim of the basket, floppy ears flying.

The basket tipped over. The plump, milk-bellied little animal spilled out and would have tumbled from the high raised bed onto the hard floor had Summer not snatched him out of the air to save him.

Hard little claws scrabbled against her bodice. Delicate fabric ripped. The solid whip of the animal's tail thumped against her arm, and his little pink tongue slobbered all over her face in happy, excited, puppyish welcome. The warm little body wiggled and shook and wiggled some more, barking and yipping.

For one, long, yearning minute, she clutched the little body close and let her fingers run over his soft, golden fur as the puppy burrowed his nose into her throat and licked frantically at her pulse.

Oh, sweet Halla. She closed her eyes and nuzzled the puppy. So small. So warm. So loving and happy and alive. He would be her friend, if she let him. And he would be loyal, she knew. He would follow her everywhere, sleep on her bed, sit beside her, walk with her, play with her.

And she would love him.

So much.

Summer's eyes flew open. With ruthless will, she tamped down the long-buried pain and yearning inside her and placed the puppy in its basket, covering him back up with the checkered cloth.

This time, she ignored the puppy's yips and barks and bouncing as she stalked down the palace halls, basket in hand, to Dilys Merimydion's chambers.

Setting the basket down on the floor by her feet, she pounded on the door to Dilys's rooms. When no one answered immediately, she pounded harder. "Sealord Merimydion! Are you in there? Open this door!"

Doors opened up down the hall. Curious heads poked out. She ignored them.

"Open this door immediately!" *Bang! Bang! Bang!*

The door flew open. Dilys stood in the threshold, one hand holding a towel wrapped around his waist. Clearly he'd been bathing, and clearly he'd come running in answer to her shouts, not even bothering to magic away the water that was currently streaming down his bare flesh. It was a measure of her emotional state that she hardly noticed his near nakedness. His expression was full of concern.

"Gabriella? What is it, *moa kiri*? What's wrong?"

"Here." She reached down to snatch up the basket holding the puppy and thrust it in Dilys's direction, forcing him to grab it with both hands to keep the basket from falling. The puppy inside yipped and jumped about, dislodging the covering. The little black nose and dark brown eyes peeked out from beneath the checkered cloth. Seeing her, the puppy let out an excited bark and leapt against the side of the basket as if he was trying to reach her. Summer's heart twisted in painful yearning.

"I've had enough. You need to stop! I don't want your gifts, and I don't want you." The puppy poked his head out through the cloth and licked at her hand with its little pink tongue. She snatched her hand back. Her throat was closing up, the tears gathering. "I m-mean it!" she choked out. "No more!"

Her lips started to tremble, so she clamped them tight and spun around to march down the hall, leaving Dilys standing there, gaping at her, holding the puppy's basket, his damp towel crumpled at his feet.

Dilys stared after Summer's rapidly departing figure in dismay. He could have sworn he'd been winning her over with his daily gifts. From all accounts, the butterflies this morning had been a hit, but something had drastically changed between breakfast and now.

He stepped back into his room, kicking his towel inside with one foot, then pulling the door closed with the other. Dilys set the basket down and pulled out the little golden puppy inside, regarding the small canine with a frown.

"What happened to upset her so, boy?" he asked.

The puppy barked and yipped and licked his hand enthusiastically. Dilys cradled the dog against his chest and scratched his small chin.

The puppy was no mere mutt. He was a very expensive, very coveted purebred golden *malam*, a breed renowned for their intelligence, deep bonding, and fearsome protective instincts. Once the bond was forged, the *malam* would defend Gabriella with its life. The breed loved water, of course. Dilys would never have gifted his *liana* with any pet that did not.

When he'd chosen the dog, he'd thought about walking with Gabriella in the surf near Merimydia Oa Nu, her dog bounding in and out of the waves, making her laugh with his antics. Really laugh. Not that quiet, restrained laughter that was all most people ever heard from her, but the sort of laugh that cracked one open wide and poured out like sunshine through breaking clouds. A truly joyful laugh, like the one he'd heard the day after his arrival in Konumarr.

He'd also wanted Gabriella to have another, devoted protector besides himself—one capable of tearing the throats out of any *krillo* who even dared dream of causing her harm.

Golden *malams*, for all their small puppy size, would grow quite large. And unlike most large dogs, who rarely lived more than ten or fifteen years, it wasn't unheard of for long-lived *malams* to remain in good health well past their twentieth year. By then, Dilys would ensure Summer was surrounded by a circle of beloved friends, children, and other pets to assist him in absorbing her grief and giving back the love and joy she needed to thrive.

His mother's heart was as deep and wide as the sea, and she wasn't even a true Siren. Compared to her, Gabriella's heart was exponentially vaster, with an equally vast capacity to love, to grieve, to feel.

Autumn had been a good friend to him, helping to confirm his own observations about Gabriella's likes and dislikes, but it was clear she didn't know everything about her blue-eyed sister, or she would have advised him differently about the puppy.

It was time to seek counsel from the one person Summer confided in more than any other: her eldest sister, Spring.

He sought out Spring Coruscate in the greenhouse built half a mile beyond the edge of the palace's vast western gardens. The heavily glassed, freestanding structure had been designed and positioned to receive the most direct sunlight throughout the course of the day. The land around it had been cleared of trees so no shadows would block the sun. Probably quite important during Wintercraig's cold, harsh winter.

But these were the summer months, when everything was green and warm and still moist with ice melt from the Skoerr Mountain glacier fields. When he stepped inside the greenhouse, he found himself surrounded by warm, steamy air that made him glad for the customary lightness of his Calbernan garb.

His bare feet moved soundlessly on the dirt floor of the greenhouse. The structure was massive. At least a quarter mile long and half as wide, filled with neat rows, boxes, and suspended pots all overflowing with vegetation. The tall glass roof, steeply angled to shed heavy snowfall in winter, was supported by massive columns, around which grew trained limbs of fruiting trees and vines laden with grapes, tomatoes, and bean pods. Wintercraig's growing season might not be long, but this greenhouse had been designed to make the most of it. Dilys didn't doubt the produce from this building could keep the whole of Konumarr and its palace in fresh fruit and vegetables the year round.

Spring, clad in a light, unadorned green gown with a heavily-stained apron covering her bodice and the front of her skirts, was kneeling beside a bed of lettuces, plucking weeds and thrusting her fingers into the loose, loamy soil. She wore no gardening gloves. As Dilys drew near, his skin tingled. She was using her magic.

Not the weather magic that was the gift of every direct member of Summerlea's royal family—weathergifts didn't do much good inside a greenhouse—but something else. Growing magic of some kind. He took a breath. The magic tasted bright and grassy against his tongue. Like sunlight and springtime. No hint of danger.

"Princess Spring," he murmured. He kept his distance. Always wise to do with women of magic.

She kept plucking weeds and digging her fingers through the soil without responding.

He waited patiently. He was used to waiting for women to finish working their magics.

Five minutes later Spring drew her hands from the soil, wiped them absently against her dirt-stained apron, and got to her feet.

"Princess Spring," he said again, still keeping his distance.

She turned towards him, her brow furrowed in thought, then blinked in apparent surprise to find him standing there. "Oh, Sealord. Forgive me, I didn't hear you come in."

She had a streak of dirt on her cheek and another on her chin. Her normally piercing green eyes were soft and hazy, and her long, ruler-straight hair hung in two braided loops tied near her ears with green ribbons. The effect left Spring Coruscate, the eldest and most coolly regal of the three Seasons, looking surprisingly innocent and girlish.

"If you please, *Myerialanna*," he murmured, "I would have a moment of your time to speak with you about your sister Gabriella."

The hazy look left Spring's eyes, and so did the softness, leaving the intense, piercing green gaze he'd come to expect from her. "What about her?" A wealth of protectiveness curled around those words. A wall of thorns, just waiting to rip him to shreds.

His heart warmed with approval. Protectiveness was a trait he admired, no matter where he found it. "You know I have been sending her daily gifts."

One elegant brow rose, a sleek, black, expressive arch. "I could hardly miss it. Your gifts have become the talk of Konumarr."

Of course, they had. After having initially danced attendance on Autumn and Spring, he'd wanted to declare his interest fixed on Summer in no uncertain terms. Not just to convince Gabriella of his determination, but also to quash any thought that he'd somehow "settled" for her instead of choosing her outright. Summer Coruscate was the *liana* he'd chosen, the only Season he wanted, and he would not allow the slightest whisper to the contrary.

"This afternoon, I gave her a puppy. A golden *malam*.

She returned it, which I expected, of course, but when she did, she was visibly upset, even near tears."

"Ah," said Spring.

Dilys frowned. "'Ah' what? She loves animals. I know she does. I have seen how she smiles when the children in the village bring their dogs to the park to play. I have watched her pet those dogs, throw sticks for them. And I have seen the longing in her eyes when they depart."

"If you want to know why your gift upset her, perhaps you should ask her directly."

A loyal response. But he was a courting Calbernan who had somehow misread something vital about his chosen *liana,* and wounded her as a result. He needed answers, and he would not let Spring's loyalty stop him from getting them.

"If I thought she would speak to me, I would, but even if she did, it's unlikely she'd tell me the truth."

One sleek black brow rose. She fixed him with a cool, hard look. "If Gabriella doesn't want you to know, then I can't help you. The last time I let Autumn convince me to do so, Gabriella came back distraught and disheveled and shut herself away in her rooms. She claims nothing happened, but we both know that's a lie, don't we?"

Dilys's fingers curled. "What happened between Gabriella and me that day is not your concern—"

"I've been looking after my sisters since our mother died," she interrupted. "I consider their well-being very much my concern!"

He sucked in a breath, fighting back a hot retort. She was not Calbernan. She did not understand how gravely she'd just insulted him.

"Did you know," he said, "that Calbernan males must earn the right to claim a *liana*? And it is not some easy task. A Calbernan spends decades learning, training, and earning sufficient gold and glory to prove himself strong, brave, and skilled enough to be worthy of a wife."

One sleek black brow rose. Spring said nothing, but

her vivid green eyes watched him with unblinking intensity.

"Once a Calbernan has earned that right, there is no greater privilege or responsibility for a Calbernan male than to ensure the happiness and well-being of his *liana*," he continued. "There is nothing he would not do for her. Nothing he would not give to bring her joy. A Calbernan would rather cut off his own arm than cause his *liana* pain—even if she is not yet his in the eyes of the world." He let both his voice and his gaze harden as he said, "And if I ever assaulted a woman—any woman—in the way you're suggesting, my own men would slaughter me and throw my shredded remains to the sharks. And they would be right to do so."

"I see." Spring rubbed the back of her hand on her chin. A new, much larger smudge of dirt joined the one already there, turning almost her entire chin black.

Dilys touched a jewel on his belt, and the front of his buckle sprang open to reveal a small, waterproofed compartment. "Please. Gabriella was extremely distressed when she returned the puppy. I need to understand why." He extracted a thin, folded square of clean cloth from the belt compartment, shook it out, and offered it to Spring.

"Dirt on my face?" she asked, unsurprised.

"On your chin. And here." He pointed to a spot on his cheek that mirrored the location of the smudge on Spring's. As she scrubbed at her face, he said, "I would never ask you to betray Gabriella's confidences, *Myeri-alanna*. I only ask for guidance, so that I will not make another such mistake. Will you not help me?"

Her face now clean, the skin rosy from its brisk scrubbing, Spring handed Dilys back his cloth. He refolded the small square and returned it to the small compartment in his buckle. When that was done, his buckle once more clipped shut, he stood patiently waiting for Spring's response.

"I promised the head gardener I would look at some

ailing tomato plants for him," she said after a long silence. "You could keep me company, if you like. Perhaps we could chat to help pass the time while I work."

He could not have stopped his smile if he wanted to. "That would be my pleasure, *Myerialanna*."

Dilys followed her down the center aisle of the greenhouse. The smell of plants and soil was strong, the ground soft and warm beneath his bare feet.

"What were you doing with the plants and the soil back there?" he asked, curious about the Summerlander princess's magic.

"Oh, just helping things along," she said. When he cocked a brow, she added, "The nutrients in that patch of soil were running a little low. Now they're not."

"Ah. This is a gift all your sisters possess?"

"All Summerlanders have a basic talent for enriching the soil and making plants flourish. It's part of what makes our kingdom so valuable. In other lands, fields must lay fallow, but in Summerlea our growing season never ends, the nutrients in our soil never deplete, and our produce is the plumpest, ripest, richest in the world. Some of us"— she cast a look his way—"can grow other things, too. Our father, for instance. He could grow just about anything."

"Like what?"

She shrugged, and he wasn't particularly surprised that she didn't offer up more information. Calbernans didn't speak of their magic to outsiders either. But Spring was not a woman who made idle conversation. When she spoke, she spoke for a reason. Verdan had been able to grow things. Things that went beyond growing plants and enriching soil. So could others, including Spring and possibly Gabriella. Dilys filed the information away.

They passed by rows of broad green leaves shading bright yellow, green, and orange squashes, and a column completely enveloped from the ground to the impressively high greenhouse ceiling with leafy vines flush with plump green bean pods.

"This greenhouse wasn't here last year," Dilys said. He and his men had not landed at Konumarr. The defenses along the Llaskroner Fjord had been too strong. They'd chosen an uninhabited stretch of coastline a hundred miles further south. But he'd studied Konumarr none-theless, poring over maps and sketches provided by the merchant spies who sailed freely into the ports of foreign lands.

"The king had it built earlier this year. There's one near Gildenheim, too. It was another of my sister Kham-sin's ideas. She wanted to see if the greenhouses could supply sufficient produce to support a palace and its sur-rounding villages throughout the year. A way to lessen Wintercraig's need to import food from other countries, especially in the cold months."

"But Summerlea now belongs to Wintercraig. Food will never be a problem again."

Spring shrugged again. "Winterfolk prefer to be self-sufficient whenever possible. In any event, since the cli-mate here in Konumarr is milder than Gildenheim, and since we were coming here for the summer, the king de-cided to locate a second greenhouse here in Konumarr to see if this location makes a difference on production."

They had reached the plot of tomato vines. They looked perfectly fine to Dilys's eyes, with clusters of tomatoes in various stages of ripeness hanging amidst the pungent green leaves, but Spring frowned when she saw them.

"These plants are not healthy?" he asked. Agriculture was not his forte, but he was always willing to learn some-thing new.

"Not as healthy as they should be," she said. "The toma-toes should be larger, and there should be more of them." Kneeling, she thrust her right hand in the soil and began sifting it through her fingers. With her left hand, she reached out and began lightly stroking the thick, hairy main stalk of the tomato plant. "Hello, little friend," she whispered. "How are you feeling today? A little under the weather?"

He'd heard that Summerlanders talked to their plants, but until now, he had always considered the stories nothing more than a joke.

"I'm certain, if you tried, no other plant in all of Mystral could rival the size or quantity or ripe perfection of your fruit," Spring told the plant. "What do you think, hmm?"

As Dilys watched, the plant's vines thickened. New tendrils unfurled and climbed up and around the massive wooden pillar. The existing tomatoes plumped, while new, small yellow flowers blossomed all over the plant's new and old growth. Dilys's senses tingled like mad, recognizing the crooning words of encouragement for the commands they were. Spring Coruscate's magic wasn't only in her hands. It flowed from her voice as well.

Not the pure, powerful *susirena* her sister possessed, but something closely related.

"That's quite an impressive talent," was all he said.

"Mmm," Spring murmured in absent agreement. "One of the gifts I inherited from my father." Pulling her hand from the soil, she began running both hands over the tomato plant, inspecting its fibrous stalks and clusters of fruit the way a mother might inspect a child during its bath. Giving gentle caresses and whispering words of encouragement as she went. "Breeding is a funny thing. I could cross this red tomato plant with one of the varieties that produces yellow fruit, and I might end up with some plants that grow red tomatoes, others that grow only yellow, and some small percentage of plants that grow both red and yellow tomatoes on the same vine. Or, depending on their lineage, I could cross two red tomato plants and end up with a plant that produces yellow fruit."

Having finished with the first plant, Spring moved to the next. She thrust her right hand into the soil, stroked and caressed the tomato plant with her left, and began crooning her encouraging enchantment. As the plant shivered and responded, unfurling new vines and leaves and blossoms, swelling the fruit clustered among its leaves, she said, "Our father wasn't always as he was at the end." Her lips compressed. Her eyes darkened. She shot Dilys a shuttered look. "He wasn't always mad."

"I know," Dilys murmured. If they had known each other better, he would have laid a soothing hand upon her shoulder. But they did not, so he kept his hands to himself. "I met him as a young boy. My family and I sailed to Summerlea for Princess Autumn's naming day. It was clear how much loved his children and his queen. My father and mother were greatly impressed by his devotion. They found him almost Calbernan in that regard." It was the highest compliment a Calbernan could give an *oulani*. "That memory was one of the reasons we did not turn away your brother, Falcon, when he came to us for aid."

"Yes," she said. "When my father loved, he loved completely, with all the strength and emotion and magic within him. He held nothing back. He hated that way, too. And as I said, he had a gift for making things grow." Her voice trailed off, the hands sifting the soil and stroking the tomato plant slowed as her thoughts traveled down some invisible path. Then, with a brisk shake, she came back to herself. "My mother, on the other hand, was calmer. She loved with her whole heart, too, but that love never grew so strong it made her lose all reason. She was the perfect queen for my father. A cooling rain to his summer fire. She balanced him."

She tilted her head to one side. "Everyone always talks about how like our mother Gabriella and I are—Gabriella especially. I suppose it's only natural. We're the calm ones of the five of us. And in addition to inheriting our mother's looks, Gabriella is the kindest of us all, her heart the largest and most loving. Even you saw only her gentleness when you first met her and mistook it for weakness."

Dilys started to defend himself, then closed his mouth. He *had* been fooled by the face Gabriella showed the world. He *had* underestimated her strength, her passion, the vitality and the power she kept bottled up so tightly inside her. It wasn't entirely his fault . . . she'd run from him like a frightened rabbit from the very start.

Spring cupped one of the green tomatoes in her palm and bent to whisper to them. The fruit in her hand plumped and ripened. "But what those people forget about all the Seasons is that no matter how much any of us may look or act like our mother, the blood and magic of Verdan Coruscate runs in us, too. And none of us," she said, leaning back to reveal the bright, vibrant yellow tomato growing amid all the red ones, "is giftnamed Serenity."

"You're saying Gabriella is much stronger and potentially more dangerous than she appears," Dilys interpreted. "This, I know already. Calbernans do not fear a woman's strength—magical or otherwise. We celebrate it."

"Neither I nor any of my siblings fear what strengths we may have inherited from our father," Spring murmured. "It's the weaknesses that concern us."

And then, at last, he understood. Gabriella's habit of never letting any man get close, holding them at bay with soft words and that self-effacing sweetness that made her fade in comparison to her bolder, more vibrant sisters. Her fear of Dilys, of what he made her feel. Her pain when he'd given her a puppy to love.

The children of a madman would, naturally, be haunted by the specter of that madness.

Gabriella was a Siren. She felt everything more deeply than others. Indeed, her vast power came from the enormity of emotion that dwelled within her.

And she had spent her whole life trying to suppress that emotion, fearing to feel. Thinking the depth of her love, of her emotion, was proof that she was destined to follow her father's descent into madness . . .

"She is afraid to love?"

Spring stroked the pungent leaves of the plant in front of her. "You met my father. You knew him at the end. You've seen for yourself what can happen when someone with great power, who loves without restraint, loses what they love."

"Did Gabriella have a puppy when she was younger?"

"We weren't allowed pets as children. My father thought it prudent to keep children with potent magic away from fragile living creatures. He was probably right. Mama used to call Autumn and I her little thunderstorms. We were forever calling up storms whenever we got upset—which was shockingly often. We tended to emote a lot. Then Khamsin came along and put us both to shame." Her lips quirked in a wry grin.

"And Gabriella?"

Spring shrugged. "It's no secret she's always been the best-natured of the five of us."

She would be. As a Siren, she thrived on love—she required it, the way plants needed rain and fish needed water. Even as a baby, she would have instinctively behaved in whatever way resulted in her receiving the most of what she required. And receiving constant, loving attention would have, in turn, soothed her and fed her own happiness, making her a good-natured child others couldn't help but love.

"Of course," Spring continued, "I wasn't a particularly obedient child back then. Papa's no pets rule didn't stop me from sneaking out of the palace and going to play with the stable boy's dogs. It's a good thing I never got terribly attached. There was a horrible accident in the stables involving the puppies, and if I'd been there, I could have really hurt someone."

Dilys didn't have any older siblings, but he'd spent enough time around other people's children to know that where one child went, the younger ones were sure to follow. Spring was telling him that Gabriella had snuck out with her to the stables . . . that she'd gotten attached to the puppies . . . that she'd been there when something had happened to them. Gabriella, a young Siren, who would have been overwhelmed by her first taste of grief, who couldn't have known how to process it.

In Calberna, young *imlani* girls were pampered and sheltered, protected from all darker emotions until they could learn how to handle them, how to release sorrow and anger and grief in ways that caused no harm to themselves or others. Here in Summerlea, no one would know to take such precautions. And when dealing with a child of Gabriella's vast power, the results of such ignorance could have been catastrophic. It could have—no, it clearly *had*—left her with deep emotional scars.

"Thank you, *Myerialanna* Spring."

"For what?" Spring smiled obliquely and turned back to the tomato plants. "Be sure to close the door behind you on your way out."

CHAPTER 14

The Courtship Siege was over.

The morning after Gabriella had returned the puppy to Dilys, there was no carpet of flowers on her balcony to greet her with a riot of color or an intoxicatingly delicious perfume. There was no gift on her breakfast tray. Instead there was a simple card, tucked beneath her plate, that said:

Forgive me, Gabriella. My gifts were meant to please, not to distress you. To atone, I shall honor your wishes and refrain from sending you more.

Dilys

He was true to his word. In the five days since, she hadn't received so much as a single rosebud from him. She hadn't seen hide nor hair of him either. He no longer haunted the palace gardens. He wasn't at any of the meals. The Calbernans still played with the city's children on the palace lawn and in the city parks, but Dilys was no longer among them. And though she got up early and stayed up late to look, she no longer found Dilys Merimydion—scantily clad or otherwise—swimming in the fjord below.

She had done it, then. She had finally driven Dilys Merimydion away.

She told herself it was for the best. She had no future with him, no future with anyone. But the absence of his relentless attention—of *him*—made her feel bereft, as if she'd lost something precious.

Although she put on a serene face and carried on as if nothing was wrong, her customary mask felt strangely brittle and ill fitting, a feeling that intensified as the days passed. Her nights were restless, beset by dreams that alternated between erotic yearning and heart-wrenching loss that more than once dragged her from sleep to find tears soaking her pillow. As the days progressed, she became aware of an aching emptiness that had taken root in her chest and was slowly growing, becoming more aching, more empty, with each passing day.

This morning, six days after she'd returned the puppy, Gabriella couldn't stand it anymore. She broke down and sought out Ryllian Ocea to find out where Dilys had gone. She'd tried to be subtle about her inquiry, sneaking in the question between morning pleasantries, but she could have sworn she saw a glint of something—relief? Satisfaction?—in Ryll's golden eyes when he told her, "*Ono, Myerialanna.* The prince has not left Wintercraig. Well, he has, but only temporarily. There were matters demanding his attention, so he swam out to meet one of our ships at sea."

"Nothing serious, I hope?"

"Nothing the *Myerielua* cannot handle." Ryll smiled. "He should be back soon. I will tell him you were looking for him."

"Oh . . . erm . . . no, that's not necessary. I'm not. Looking for him, that is." She gave a small, nervous laugh and tucked her hair behind her ears. "I just wanted to make sure he was here—I mean *well*! Make sure he was well. That he wasn't suffering any sort of lingering ailment from . . . um . . . the thing with Lily's father . . ." She could feel herself sinking in a pit of her own making, so she said, "I'm glad he's in good health," clamped her mouth shut before she could make a bigger fool of herself, and hurried away.

She should have known Ryll would tattle on her, and that Dilys would take it as an invitation to resume his courtship. Which was exactly what must have happened, because that evening, just as Gabriella finished dressing for dinner, there was a knock on the door to her room. Amaryllis went to answer it and returned carrying a sealed vellum envelope.

"For you, ma'am," Amaryllis said, holding out the envelope and fighting a smile.

For almost a week now, Gabriella had been telling herself that the termination of Dilys Merimydion's courtship was the right and necessary thing, but the instant she recognized the same bold, masculine hand that had written, "Claim me as thine" on hundreds of cards, her traitorous heart did a giddy little dance. *He hadn't given up!*

She took the envelope, which Dilys had addressed using her full, formal title: *To Her Royal Highness, Gabriella Aretta Rosadora Liliana Elaine Coruscate, Princess of Summerlea, Duchess of the Vale.* Around her name swirled an intricate design of decorative loops and whorls, a pattern of growing vines decorated with dots of tiny, colorfully inked flowers. A beautiful design. One that must have taken him hours to complete.

A drop of ocean-blue wax stamped with the trident of House Merimydion sealed the back of the envelope. It popped free easily at the press of a fingernail. Inside, nestled in gold foil, a card written in a less elaborate version of court script announced:

Sealord Dilys Merimydion requests the honor of your presence at dinner in the Southeastern Garden Arbor. Seven o'clock in the evening. Follow the path of flowers.

"The path of flowers?" Gabriella murmured aloud.

"Out in the hall, Your Highness."

Curious, Gabriella headed for the door of her suite and pulled it open. Two parallel rows of potted and arranged flowers led from her door all the way down the hallway and disappeared around the corner. The space between the rows was strewn with a thick carpet of loose petals and whole plucked blooms.

"Did he denude every flower garden from here to Summerlea?" He probably had, damn him. She scowled at the resulting shivery thrill that shot through her at the romantic extravagance. "What time is it, Amaryllis?"

"Ten minutes 'til seven, ma'am."

She should refuse. The flowered path that led to Dilys Merimydion also led to immeasurable danger.

And yet, Summer found herself handing the invitation to Amaryllis and saying, "Please put this on my dressing table. And don't touch the ink."

"Yes, ma'am." No longer succeeding in hiding her smile, the maid curtsied and carried the salver into Summer's chambers.

Summer stood in the hallway for a long moment, breathing deeply, trying to quell the nervous knots tangling and twisting in her belly. "Oh, I am so going to regret this," she muttered.

And with that, Summer Coruscate put out her right foot and began walking down the flowered path that led to Dilys Merimydion.

Word of Summer's approach reached Dilys long before the woman he intended claim as his own came into view.

He stood in the dappled shade of the vine-covered arbor. The evening sunlight shone coolly upon him as a gentle breeze whispered across his skin, carrying the scent of the sea and the perfumed beauty of the garden.

Behind him, awaiting his lady's pleasure, sat a small, cozy dining table covered with pristine white linen, two comfortable, cushioned chairs, and a silver bucket freshly filled with ice to chill an uncorked bottle of the finest sparkling sweet wine from the cellars of Cali Va'Lua.

He'd sent for the wine the day he'd realized Summer's coldness towards him had nothing to do with lack of interest, and picked it up this week while planning the next stage of his siege to conquer the fortress that was Gabriella Coruscate's heart.

Now, as he stood awaiting her arrival, Dilys was aware of a strange tightness in his chest, an uncomfortable twisting disquiet in his belly. His hands, which should have been resting loosely at his sides, were opening and closing in fists.

Nerves, he realized.

He was nervous.

The was the first time she'd made the choice to come to him. The first time she'd indicated her willingness to consider his suit.

She might think she was coming to put him off. Knowing his skittish little honeyrose, that was exactly what she had in mind. But regardless of her intentions, she had made the decision to come to him. She had accepted his invitation and followed the path he'd laid out for her . . .

Keeping her here once she arrived would be entirely up to him.

He stood alone and silent as she approached, his hair spilling down his back. He wore a pristine white *shuma,* his belt pure platinum encrusted with diamonds. He watched her with unblinking eyes, drinking in her gentle, soothing beauty. She was garbed in soft lavender, a pretty pastel shade that gave her beautiful eyes a faintly violet hue. The thick, black mass of her hair had been artfully piled atop her head in a confection of curls and braids, with long curls left to cascade down her back to her waist. She wore narrow lavender slippers on her feet.

"You look exceptionally beautiful this evening, Gabriella. Lavender suits you."

"Thank you." Her voice was crisp, no-nonsense. "Sealord Merimydion, I thought I'd made myself perfectly clear that this—"

"Dilys," he corrected. "I am Dilys to you." He pitched his voice deliberately low, making his name a murmur so husky it was almost a purr. Bright, watchful eyes noted the tiny catch in her breath, the little shiver she couldn't manage to suppress. He hid a smile. Oh, yes, she thought she'd come to end his courtship once and for all.

He had no intention of letting her.

"Come, *moa leia*, sit." He walked to the waiting table set out beneath the arbor and pulled out a chair, but she made no move to take it.

"Sealord . . . Dilys," she modified when he flicked a warning glance her way. "This must stop."

"Of what do you speak, Gabriella?"

"The flowers, the notes, the gifts. This!" She waved to the beautifully set table beneath the arbor, to the servants waiting crisply for Dilys's command. "All of this!"

He lifted her hand. It was so slight compared to his, the slender fingers so delicate, almost bird-like. The creamy, burnished brown of her Summerlander skin was soft and satiny. Carrying that hand to his lips, he pressed a lingering kiss against the deliciously fragrant skin, then calmly told her, "No."

Her lips parted in surprise. Such soft, pink, delectable lips. He wanted to kiss them so badly.

"What do you mean, 'no'?" she demanded.

He kissed her hand once more—a poor substitute for her plump, moist lips, but better than nothing—and said, "I mean no, Gabriella. I will not surrender my right to court you."

"Your *right*?" Her nostrils flared. Her eyes flashed. He'd never seen her eyes go quite that shade of blue. More fire than sky, hot and electric. He loved it.

"If you think you have the right to any part of me, you are mistaken, sir!" Summer continued. "My sister, *Queen* Khamsin"—Her emphasis on the word "queen" almost made him smile. As if her sister's title could persuade him to alter his course. Him, the son of the *Myerial*, grandson of too many *Myerials* to count—"made it very clear that neither I nor either of my other two sisters are required to accept your suit. And I most definitely choose not to accept it. So thank you very much for the dinner invitation, but I must regrettably decline this and any such future invitations as you should desire to make." She gave her hand a tug, trying to free herself from his grip.

His fingers remained curled around her delicate wrist, the grip gentle but as unyielding as stone.

She yanked harder. Yanked again. Tried to pry his fingers off her wrist.

He remained a rock. The air around them grew warmer and the breeze kicked up. Summer didn't often manifest her weathergifts unintentionally—probably because she'd spent her whole life keeping her emotions and her gifts in tight check—but she was starting to manifest them now. The breeze made the fabric of his *shuma* flutter, but Dilys himself could have been a statue carved from bedrock. When she lunged back, putting the full weight of her slender body behind her efforts to escape, no part of him swayed even a fraction of an inch.

"Let me go!" she exclaimed.

He gave her a lazy smile. "No."

Sweet lady of the sea, she was lovely. Her face was flushed, her eyes starbright. Her beautiful breasts heaved from her exertions, the soft swell of her bosom pressing against the confines of her lavender gown as she struggled to catch her breath. If he thought for one instant that she would allow it, he would bear her down to the sweet garden grass this very instant, tear that gown off her body, and devour every soft, delicious, intoxicating inch of her until that volcano inside her erupted and she drowned him in all that beautiful, powerful, searing fire she kept so tightly contained.

"You have no right to keep me here," she told him.

The smile faded from his face. In complete seriousness and with all the tenderness in the world, he told her, "But I do, Gabriella. I paid for that right with the blood I spilled and the men I lost in the ice and snow of Wintercraig's battlefields."

She went still, her fiery passion momentarily banked.

"The contract I made with your brother gave me the right to take you as my *liana,* with or without your consent. I surrendered that right when I broke my contract with your brother, but my contract with your sister still guarantees me the right to court you. Three months to court the Seasons of Summerlea. That is what was I bought for myself when I joined your sister to defeat the Ice King. I have been patient, because I made so many mistakes with you from the start. But from this day forward, I intend to collect every day of courtship that is due me."

He'd spent the last seven days deciding how best to proceed with her. Now that he had a better understanding of why she was so determined to refuse him, he had come up with a different plan to win her. She was a Siren. All the gifts he had selected with such care and showered upon her had been reflections of his ever-increasing devotion, gifts of love, given freely, which had only fed her strength and enabled her to bolster her resolve to refuse him. He had, unwittingly, been reinforcing the very gates he was trying to break down. And he'd been doing it from afar— without the personal interaction and companionship that might have helped weaken those adamantine walls of hers.

So he'd changed tactics. He'd cut off the deluge, hoping to create a vacuum of need that would work for him rather than against him. Withholding himself from her this past week had been difficult in the extreme. He was already bound to her, and staying completely away—not even allowing himself a glimpse of her lest his own resolve crumble—was the hardest thing he'd ever done in his life. It physically hurt him to be away from her for so long while things were still unsettled between them.

But yesterday, when she'd sought out Ryll to ask if Dilys had left the city, he'd known the strategy had worked. And now it was time for the next phase of his new plan: forcing her to face her fears, with him by her side to help her through it.

He gestured to the chair beside him. "Please, *moa kiri*, sit. Your brother-in-law's chef, Ingarra, has prepared something special for us. You would not want her efforts to go to waste."

Summer sat. Some other woman might have plopped into the chair in a fit of pique, but Gabriella was, as in all things, exquisitely graceful. She sank into the chair with a smooth, effortless elegance that seemed totally at odds with the smoldering look in her eyes and the clench of her delicate jaw.

He ran a thumb across her hand in a final caress then reluctantly released her. With a brief nod to the waiting attendants, he took his own seat.

Court etiquette stipulated that his chair should sit opposite hers at the small table, but he didn't even want that slight distance between them. His chair sat at the quarter mark, close enough that when she plucked the folded napkin from her plate, he could have reached out to claim her hand again.

The first course was laid before them. A delicate, cold summer soup of fresh, pureed fruits and sweet nectar. Into the thin crystal flutes beside their plates, a crisply dressed servant poured sparkling golden wine.

She ignored both soup and sparkling wine and scowled at him. "Even though you won the right, there's no point in you bothering to court me," she told him bluntly. "It won't do you any good. I won't marry you."

"And yet, still, court you I shall. As provided for in my contract with your sister."

"You're just wasting both our time and squandering the opportunity you say you paid for so dearly. If you truly want a Season for your *liana,* you should concentrate your efforts on Spring or Autumn. They at least like you." She glared at him and added pointedly, "*I don't.*"

He wondered if she really thought that scowl of hers would frighten him off? That he would take her declared—and utterly false—distaste for him as anything but a chal-

lenge. For a moment, he was tempted to tell her how
beautiful—how utterly enchanting—he found her when she
was angry. But if he told her how much he appreciated her
temper, she would try to stifle it. The last thing he wanted
from her was that serene mask she wore around everyone
else.

So instead, he smiled calmly into her flame-blue eyes
and said, "Remember, *moa kiri,* the price for every lie
is an intimacy of my choosing." But instead of pressing
for another kiss, he said, "Try the soup, *shishi.* The chef
let me sample it earlier in the week. It's like nothing I've
ever tasted before. A sweet dream for the tongue." He
lifted his own spoon to his mouth and closed his eyes
on a hum of pleasure. "Even better than I remember. I'm
serious, Gabriella, you must try this." Just to tease her a
little and make those eyes flash some more, he refilled
his spoon and held it up to her lips in an intimate demand
that she give it a taste.

He had underestimated just how close to erupting the
dormant volcano of her temper really was.

She slapped at his hand, sending soup splattering
across the pristine tablecloth and his spoon clattering to
the paving stones.

"I'm not interested in the soup! And you can take that
contract with my sister and shove it up your—" Gabriella broke off the rest of her vulgar command, threw her
napkin on the table and started to rise. She was done with
Dilys Merimydion. So done.

Dilys's hand shot out to catch her wrist. She let out a
curdled scream of fury between clenched teeth and went
to yank her hand from his grip.

The look on his face made her freeze in her tracks.

For the first time since the prince of Calberna had
come to Konumarr, genuine anger glittered in his eyes,
turning them from warm molten gold to something cold
and hard and scary. Not scary because she feared he would

hurt her. Well, maybe a little. He was lethal after all. But mostly, the look in his eyes was scary because she realized she never wanted him to look at her that way again. Ever.

"My contract with your sister cost many lives—some so dear to me their loss is a hole in my heart that will never be filled. So, no, I will not dishonor their sacrifice of my Calbernans and my friends by throwing away the right they paid for with their lives." Each word was a sharp bite of sound that flayed her skin. "Nor will I let you dishonor your sister by breaking the conditions of her sworn oath, any more than I will let your insult your brother's chef by refusing to appreciate the meal she has spent the last week planning and preparing to please you. You are better than that, Gabriella Coruscate. Act like it."

Heat stung her cheeks. Her jaw dropped. The momentary pain she'd felt for his mention of lost friends—she understood the horrible ache of loss—dried up the instant he'd turned the whip of accusation on her. She couldn't believe he'd just reprimanded her—and with such razor-edged sharpness to boot! Biting her lip, she sank back into her chair and stared pointedly at the hand shackled around her wrist until he released her. She put the napkin back in her lap. "I thought Calbernans prided themselves on never losing their temper with a woman."

"I did not lose my temper, Gabriella. I would never do such a thing with you or any other woman. But I will not stand silent while you shame yourself by showing no care for the sacrifices, oaths, or efforts of another."

Stung, but unable to defend herself against a truthful accusation, she sat in embarrassed silence while the servants replaced the soiled tablecloth and spattered centerpiece, wiped clean the rims of the two soup bowls, and brought Dilys a new spoon. She felt like a rude, mannerless, misbehaving child. She didn't like the feeling one bit.

"Thank you," she said in a subdued voice when the servants finished cleaning up her mess.

The woman who had replaced the centerpiece with a fresh vase of flowers bobbed a curtsy. "My pleasure, Your Highness," she said.

The servants backed away to a discreet distance. An awkward silence fell.

Gabriella wouldn't look at Dilys. She stared at the garden, a nearby butterfly, the refreshed table setting. Her fingers traced the pattern of the silverware aligned perfectly at the side of her bowl.

He sighed. "Please, try the soup, Gabriella. Ingarra created it especially in your honor. She calls it Summer's Sweetness."

Summer didn't want to give in to him, but she wanted even less to hurt Ingarra by sending the soup back untouched—especially when she'd created the dish in Summer's honor. It never occurred to her to doubt Dilys's claim. If he said Ingarra had created the soup in Gabriella's honor, she had.

Gabriella dipped her spoon into the bowl and brought it to her lips. Exquisite flavors burst across her tongue.

"This is delicious," she admitted. Too good to hold a grudge because he'd made her try it. She sighed and let go of her simmering resentment.

"I told you, you would like it." The hard glitter in his eyes had already receded, leaving them warmly golden and fixed upon her with approval and something more that set off the butterflies in her stomach.

"What's in it?"

"A variety of fruits, nectar, spices, and I think a little magic. Ingarra would not admit it to me, but I am certain she is some sort of cooking enchantress." White teeth flashed.

The flutters in her stomach quintupled in strength. That smile of his should be outlawed. She bent her head quickly to take another spoonful of soup, and gave a wordless murmur of pleasure. Light, sweet, fruity, tart, filled with surprise and delight, Ingarra's concoction was amazing.

Perhaps Konumarr's chef truly *could* work some sort of enchantment with her cooking.

Or, perhaps, Summer thought as Dilys left off watching her to attend to his own food, the real enchantment at work was the man sitting beside her, close enough she could practically feel the warmth emanating from his fragrant skin. He smelled of exotic oils, rich and masculine and utterly enticing. The bronze of his skin was decadently dark and gleaming against the pristine white of the table linens and his equally snowy *shuma*. His hands were large and strong. Her gaze wandered up his arms, paused at the impressive bulge of his biceps, then swept across the even more impressive breadth of his shoulders and chest. *Everything* about him was large and strong.

A disturbing warmth unfurled in her belly. Since coming to Wintercraig, she'd grown used to being surrounded by giants. The shortest Winterman she'd met yet stood at least six feet tall, while Wynter himself towered well over seven, all of them as strong as they were tall, rippling with hard, powerful muscles. Yet none of them made her feel as small, as delicate, or as womanly as Dilys Merimydion did right now, just sitting beside her at a dinner table. She wanted to stroke her hands across all that naked, gleaming skin, to rediscover its silky softness and the hard swell of muscle beneath. She wanted to explore all those intriguing, iridescent tattoos, trace their swirling lines with her fingers. Taste them with her tongue. Take him inside her body again and again and again as she'd been dreaming all week. Summer squirmed a little in her seat, then glanced up to find Dilys's gaze fixed on her with such drowning intentness that her heart slammed against her chest.

She dropped her gaze, scolding herself soundly for her abominable lack of control around him.

Summer desperately cast around for some topic of conversation to stop him looking at her like he wanted to eat her up and blurted out the first nonsexual thought that came to mind.

"Tell me about your friends who died fighting the Ice King." Before the words had even fully left her mouth, she was flushing with equal measures of shame and horror. The Calbernan had unsettled her so badly, she'd forgotten how to make polite conversation! In no culture anywhere on Mystral was it considered acceptable to probe a guest about the recent loss of a loved one. She reached out instinctively to lay her hand upon his arm in apology. "I am so sorry! Please, forget I asked. It's none of my business."

Instead of taking offense, Dilys covered her hand with his own. "The question is no offense, *moa myerina*. Calbernans who die with honor would wish to be remembered, their victories celebrated. Besides, their deaths earned me the right to sit here beside you today, so why should you think they were none of your business?"

"I don't mean to cause you distress. It's clear you mourn them still."

"Of course. I will mourn them all my life." His thumb stroked the back of her hand, each brush a featherlight caress. "But a Calbernan's heart is large. Though his losses may be many, so too are his joys." He smiled. "Aanas Holokai was the oldest of my friends who fell that day. He and I were cabin boys together on our first voyage to sea. He had a bright smile and a voice that could sing birds from the sky. He had just earned his *ulumi-lia*"—with his free hand, Dilys brushed a finger across the swirling blue tattoo that looked like stylized waves across his right cheekbone—"and he was eager to find a *liana* of his own and start a family. He dreamt of a sweet, soft-spoken woman who would allow him to protect and pamper her. A woman to whom he could sing each day to bring her joy. He wanted a large family. As many children as his wife would wish to give him."

"If he hadn't found the *liana* he wanted here, would he have bought one off the slave markets?"

A shrug. "Probably. There are many women on the slave markets who are in need of devotion and care." His jaw tightened. "Sadly, Mystral is full of barbaric brutes who treat women no better than cattle. It brings us joy to free women from such places. Even those rare few who choose not to wed a Calbernan are offered safe haven in the Isles."

"You free the women you buy from the slave markets?"

His brows rose. "Of course. What did you think we did with them?" There was no offense in his tone, only curiosity.

"The obvious, of course. Your men want wives. They buy women from the slavers." She spread her hands.

He sniffed. "No Calbernan who has earned the *ulumilia* would ever take an unwilling woman to wife, no matter how much gold changed hands. All enslaved women are freed and courted and wed to the Calbernan they choose of their own free will. Or wed to none of us, if that is their desire."

"Yet you just told me your contract with Falcon promised you one of the Seasons in marriage."

"Yes, and whichever one of you I chose would have come to Calberna, where I could have courted you properly, and you would have accepted me freely before we were bound in marriage."

"Have you always been this arrogant?"

"Not arrogant," he corrected. "Confident. There's a difference."

"Not much of one, from where I'm sitting."

"I am a prince of Calberna. I have trained my whole life not only to lead our warriors to victory into battle, but also to serve and protect the women who are our heart and our true strength. I have spent years learning what women want and how to provide it to them, so that when the day came for me to find my *liana*, I would know how to be everything she needs. And, believe me, Gabriella, those were lessons I attended to very intently."

Her cheeks went hot as she remembered how well he'd provided what she'd needed during their interlude in Snowbeard Falls Grotto. Ducking her head to hide her blush, she took a last spoonful of Ingarra's Summer's Sweetness, then nodded to the servants who'd come to clear the table in preparation for the next course. "So what will you do when your three months are up and I won't marry you? Will you seek a wife on the slave markets?"

He tossed his head, sending the long, silky ropes of his hair flying back over his shoulders to stream down his back. "That is not a concern."

"Don't be so sure of that." She tugged her hand out from under his and reached for her flute of sparkling wine.

One sleek, dark brow arched. "Ah, *kalika u moa kiri*, sun of my heart, before my time here is over, you *will* freely choose me to be your *akua*. You will claim me and bind me as your husband, your lover, your life's mate, the father of your children, your helpmeet and your protector."

She forced the corner of her mouth to curl. "In your dreams," she scoffed and lifted the wine flute to her lips.

"Yes, Gabriella. In my dreams." His voice dropped to that low tone that sent shudders of fire through her veins. "And in yours, too, I suspect."

Her hand shook, making wine slosh over the crystal rim of the flute and drench her fingers. Her gaze shot to his. He couldn't possibly know about those dreams . . . *could he*?

His lips curved in a knowing smile. He took the wine flute from her unresisting fingers and set it aside. Then, holding her captive with those mesmerizing golden eyes of his, he lifted her hand to his mouth and slowly licked the wine from the fingers.

Each slow, warm, moist rasp of his tongue shot through her body like an electric current, sizzling from the sensitive pads of her fingers straight to her feminine core. Still holding her gaze, he dragged her hand down to press her palm against the hot, naked skin of his chest, curving her fingers around the massive swell of his pectoral muscle.

Her mouth went dry. Sweet Halla, he felt like sin, like

every wicked fantasy she could ever dream of. Rock-hard muscle beneath soft, satiny skin. Her fingers flexed and trembled against his flesh. Her whole body trembled. His mouth curved in a slow, simmering smile that made her squirm in her chair, and his golden, leonine eyes glowed with lazy, masculine satisfaction.

"Oh, yes, *moa halea*. You will be my *liana*. Of that, there is not the slightest doubt."

Gabriella pulled her hand back. "If you're serious about courting me, you need to stop that. There is more to marriage than sexual attraction."

It pleased Dilys to no end that both her hand and her voice shook as she pulled away. It pleased him even more that she acknowledged the attraction between them. The mention of marriage was, of course, just a ploy, a bait to manipulate him into surrendering one of his most powerful weapons in their war of wills. But he liked that she'd mentioned it all the same. The more often she spoke of marriage, the more used to the idea she would become.

"Indeed there is," he agreed, settling back into his chair to give the illusion of a small retreat. "I believe it is customary for couples to use their courtship to get to know one another better. Let's start with you. I already know that most people think you are honest, even though you lie whenever it suits your needs." She rolled her eyes, which made him laugh. "I know that you love beautiful flowers but only those with an equally beautiful fragrance, and that you are very generous—except when it comes to sharing Zephyr Hallowill's chocolates. Those you hoard, even from your sisters."

She gaped at him. "Who told you tha—" Her lips pursed in an exasperated scowl. "Autumn."

He grinned. "She and I have become good friends these last few weeks."

"Too good, it would seem," Summer groused.

"Her first loyalty is to you. She just happens to agree

that I would make an excellent husband for you." Before consenting to help him with his pursuit of Summer, Autumn had vowed to roast him like a sausage on a stick if he ever mistreated her sister in any way. She hadn't been joking. "My cousins and I thoroughly enjoy her company. I get the feeling it's rare for her to have male friends, especially attractive, unmarried males in their prime."

"Your modesty continues to leave me speechless."

He laughed. "I was actually referring to Ari and Ryll, but thank you. "

The servants delivered the second course, a salad of baby greens topped with sliced pears, candied nuts and apricots, and crumbled goat cheese. He waited for the servants to depart and Summer to pick up her fork before saying, "Tell me about your mother. What do you remember about her?"

Gabriella shrugged. "Not much. I was very young when she died."

"You were seven, I believe?"

She poked at her salad. "Yes."

Old enough to remember more than vague impressions. She had memories. She just wasn't sharing them. "I understand she was very kind and gentle, a calming influence on your father."

"She was."

"I've heard you are very like her."

"So people say."

He reached for his wine, took a sip, and regarded her over the rim of the crystal flute, until the silence made her stop shoving her salad around on her plate and look up at him. Gently and without recrimination, he said, "A conversation works best when both parties actually participate, Gabriella." Setting his glass aside, he reached across the table to take her hand. "Or should we dispense with getting to know one another and just go back to exploring our mutual sexual attraction?"

She yanked her hand back. "Yes, my mother was kind

and gentle. She was probably the kindest, gentlest, most loving person I've ever known. She had a way of smiling that was like the sun shining in your heart. And when she laughed . . . not even the most miserable person in the world could have clung to bitter feelings after hearing her laugh. I remember the day she died like it was yesterday." She rubbed a hand over her heart, as if it ached. "I miss her. Every day. There's a hole in my heart where she used to be, and nothing has ever filled it. I don't think anything ever will."

"She sounds wonderful."

"She was. And except for my looks, I'm really nothing like her at all."

"Oh, I doubt that."

She looked up at him, her blue eyes so bright against the black frame of her thick lashes and the Summerlander darkness of her skin. But for all their brightness, those eyes held many shadows, too. "No. I'm really not. Trust me on this one."

He wanted to wrap her in his arms and kiss away her pain until all those shadows disappeared. "There has never been a creature in all Mystral with a bigger heart or a greater capacity to love than the Sirens. The intensity of their emotions was a reflection of their power, the source of it, in fact. What they loved, they loved deeply, wholly, without restraint. No one could love like that without grieving the same way. Your feelings for your mother are a perfect example, though to be honest, it's a small miracle that you survived the grief of her death without manifesting your power in some violent way. Especially given your youth at the time. Your father couldn't have anchored you. He would have been too wrapped up in his own grief. And your brother and sisters were too young to be of much assistance."

"Then perhaps you're mistaken about me being a Siren."

He hid a smile. She was so quick to deny anything that unsettled her. So determined to cling to her masks. "*Ono, moa kiri*. There's no mistake. Just another mystery. From what I've been taught, most Sirens don't gain full control over their gifts until adulthood, but perhaps you somehow learned control much earlier." He took a bite of his salad and waited for her to follow suit, before asking, "Do you recall any other traumatic loss you may have suffered before your mother's death? Some occasion where your gifts may have manifested in such a way that the shock of it frightened you into repressing your power?"

If he hadn't been watching for her reaction he might have missed the way her fork paused in midair, trembling slightly as her hand shook at the memory.

"Not that I recall," she said. And there was that tone in her voice he had come to recognize. The little vibration that told him she was lying. Again.

He backed off. He'd confirmed that there had been an incident. One traumatic enough that Gabriella felt the need to lie about it even now, twenty years later.

He still needed the truth, though. He needed her to tell him about the demons of her past so he could help her exorcise them. He changed tack, trying to get at the root trouble from a different angle.

"Considering the gifts you possess, it isn't surprising that your father eventually went mad after your mother died. For you to possess the power you do, she had to have enough Siren's power in her to at least partially bind him to her. When that connection was severed . . . well, the fact that he survived as long as he did is a testament to his own strength. And to you. Of all of your sisters, you were the one he loved the most, weren't you?"

She set her fork down and looked up at him. "My mother wasn't a Siren, and I don't want to talk about my father."

Her refusal was disappointing, but not unexpected. Gabriella had become an expert and refusing to face her fears.

"What shall we talk about then? We have an entire evening to fill."

She scowled at him. "I don't know. Maybe I'll ask you all sorts of prying questions about *your* life."

She obviously meant it as a threat, hoping to stop his "prying," but he smiled with genuine delight. "That's an excellent idea." He spread his hands in invitation. "For you, *moa liana,* I am an open book. Ask me anything."

CHAPTER 15

Summer pressed her lips together in disgust. Once again he'd baited a trap, and once again, she'd walked right into it. Clearly, he wanted her to ask about him, to show interest in his life, his history, his likes and dislikes. Because he knew that remaining ignorant about him made it easier for her to keep holding him at a distance.

"Fine," she bit out. "Since you're so interested in fathers, let's talk about yours."

She'd hoped to jolt him out of his complacency, but he merely shrugged. "What would you like to know? His name was Dillon, born of House Ocea."

"Your cousin Ryllian's House."

"Ryll's mother was my father's sister. My father was a fine Calbernan. Excellent in battle, strong in heart. Wise in so many ways. Devoted to my mother, of course. They were betrothed from birth, and wed the day after he earned his *ulumi-lia*. They were expecting a second child—a daughter—when he was killed. My mother lost the baby. She would have followed him—their bond was very strong—but she had her twin, my Uncle Calivan, to help her survive her grief, and me as well, though I was still too young to be much help in that way."

"You mean she would have killed herself because he died?"

"No, that's not what I mean." Melancholy curled around the corners of his lips. "My mother isn't a Siren—not even now that she holds the magic of the *Myerials* as well the magic of House Merimydion—but she's close enough to one that were it not for my uncle, her bonds to my father would have killed her when he died."

"Sirens don't survive their mates?"

"According to our histories, that was one of the prices of the power. Mated Sirens could not live without their mates—nor their mates without them. Their bond, once forged, became a sort of symbiosis, necessary to the survival of each of them. That was how the Sirens were slaughtered. The attackers discovered the secret, you see. They burst their own eardrums so *susirena* could not compel their minds, and they snuck into our palaces and villas and murdered the Sirens' mates and children, severing their deepest links to the ones they loved the most. Even the greatest and most powerful of the Sirens—*Myerial* Maikalaneia—could not survive the slaughter of her family. It's why her family was targeted first. Even if the enemy could not hear her Song, she could have Shouted the flesh off their bones, splintered every ship in their armada. She could have Shouted continents back into the sea, so great was her gift. But all they had to do to destroy her was to kill the ones she loved." He reached across the table to take her hand. "I don't need to tell you this is another of those Calbernan secrets that you must never reveal to another."

"No," Summer murmured, reeling at the thought of what those ancient, evil men had done to destroy the Sirens they feared. No wonder Dilys was so adamant that she should never reveal the truth of what she was to anyone—not even her family. "Your father . . . how did he die?"

"Thieves broke into House Merimydion's warehouse. We keep a tight restriction on who sails into our harbors, but these thieves were smart. They smuggled themselves in aboard one of the vessels of our most trusted trading partners, then waited until most of the city was at the birthday celebration of our princess. My father and I were on our way back to our ship to sail home."

"You were with him when he was killed?"

"He left me sleeping with our guards while he went into the warehouse to get a gift that had come in for my mother. He'd been having treasures brought in from all over Mystral in preparation for the celebration of my sister's birth. That's what drew the thieves—the many priceless items he had acquired. He walked in on them. They were armed. He had only his battle fangs and claws. He still managed to kill six of them before he died." The words were matter-of-fact. The tone was anything but.

"How old were you?"

"Eight."

Her heart squeezed. So young. Barely older than she'd been when Mama had died, and she still remembered that horrible day as if it had happened yesterday.

"I'm sorry. I know how awful that must have been." She reached for his hand in an instinctive gesture of compassion.

He clasped it gently and laid his other hand on top of them both so that her hand was surrounded with his warmth. His lashes were lowered, hiding his eyes, but when he looked up a few moments later, there was a gleam of something that made the emptiness inside her tingle and start to hum.

"Thank you," he said, and the tingle became a hum, resonating inside her. Soothing the ache. As if the resonance helped to fill the emptiness.

She pulled her hand back. He did not attempt to stop her, but neither did he open his hands. His fingers applied the slightest pressure, so that drawing away from him felt like a slow, reluctant release. Even after she was free, it felt as if there were tiny filaments still tying them together, tugging harder at her the farther back she pulled.

"In any event," Dilys continued after a moment, "my mother very nearly didn't survive my father's death. She lost their baby, which made her grief even worse. Sometimes I think that even with my uncle and me there to anchor her, she would have Faded completely had the *Myerial* not died the following year."

He fell silent as the servants approached to clear their salad plates, and then came the parade of salver-bearing servants carrying out the various main courses of their meal. The dinner was a culinary delight. Not as over-the-top as a dinner of state, but just as exquisitely prepared. There were two selections of flavorful fish, a fruit-and-nut stuffed fowl, and a minced lamb pie with a perfectly baked golden crust. For vegetables, Ingarra had prepared light, crisp sea cucumbers tossed in a delicate sauce, roasted summer squash, a coconut and calava root soufflé, tiny roasted potatoes drizzled with garlic oil, and a tangy seaweed dish that Dilys said was a favorite among Calbernans.

The minced lamb pie, squash, and potatoes were three of Gabriella's favorite dishes. The others were Calbernan specialities she'd never tried before. Though Dilys did not push her to do so, she accepted a small portion of each of the Calbernan foods. Each time she did, a surge of warmth whispered through her veins. It took her a few minutes to realize the sensation was coming from Dilys— that she could physically feel his pleased approval flowing into her. It felt . . . nourishing, invigorating. Like rain falling after a long drought.

She wanted to accuse him of working some sort of enchantment on her, but whatever this was didn't feel wrong. It felt right. So incredibly right she didn't want it to stop. The tension that had wound her up so tight this last week was flowing out of her.

She took a bite of the first of the fish dishes, a lightly battered snapper in a delicious three-flavor sauce. The combination of sweet, sour, and spicy flavors, coupled with the crispness of the batter and the moist flakiness of the mild fish, was a complete delight to her taste buds.

"This is gorgeous." Her praise won her one of Dilys's wide, approving smiles and another surge of melting warmth.

"I am very glad you like it. I chose only foods I thought you would enjoy."

"You chose? You mean Ingarra didn't prepare the menu?" She was surprised. Ingarra was quite particular about who she allowed in her kitchen, and even more particular about the dishes she would and would not prepare.

"She chose the soup and salad courses, but for the main course, I wanted to give you a taste of Calberna. We use many different foods and spices than you do in the Æsir Isles, but I selected the ones I thought you'd find most appealing based on the local cuisine you seem to enjoy most. The selection of your favorites I included in case you weren't feeling adventurous."

"You chose well," she murmured after giving all the other new foods a try. "It's all delicious."

Waves of warmth lapped against her senses. "It is my pleasure to give my *liana* happiness in all things."

"I'm not your *liana*," she retorted. But for the first time, the rejection felt more like a flimsy lie than an unshakeable truth.

"You will be."

A choked laugh barked out before she could stop it. "Are you always this sure of yourself?"

He smiled, golden eyes gleaming like a great hunting cat's. "I am Calbernan."

"Ah . . . yes. Calbernan is the Sea Tongue word for arrogant, isn't it?"

His low, husky chuckle rolled across her skin, making her shudder. "As I've told you before, I have spent every day of my life since I was five learning the skills necessary to protect and provide for a wife." One long finger flicked out to brush a long, soft curl of black hair behind her ear. His voice dropped to a sensual purr. "And every skill necessary to keep her happy in all ways."

Her mouth was suddenly parched. "Truly?" Her mind filled with all manner of images of Dilys keeping his woman—keeping *Gabriella*—happy in all ways. If what had happened between them in the grotto was anything to go by, he had mastered those lessons. Color and heat flooded her cheeks. She cleared her throat, shoved the erotic images out of her mind, and tried to force the conversation back on a safer path. "You've trained every day since you were five?"

"As do all Calbernan boys. The day after my fifth birthday, I moved from the home of my parents to the training villa on our property and I resided there, under the care of my instructors, until I went to sea at age twelve."

"What sort of training did you receive?"

"The usual. Military, naval, and survival training, of course. Hunting, sailing, fighting, land- and sea-based military strategy. Basic business skills such as how to read and negotiate contracts. How to use my seagifts. One day of every week was devoted to *myeriasu,* the arts of courting and caring for a *liana.* How to converse with her, how to put her at ease. How to understand what she needs and provide it for her."

Gabriella cleared her throat again. "When did you have time to be just a boy?"

He shrugged. "There was plenty of time for that in the first five years of my life."

"That's horrible."

"Far from it. I enjoyed my training, and excelled in every discipline." A mischievous light entered his eyes. "Including my training in the erotic arts, which began when I reached seventeen years of age."

She blushed—violently—and quickly looked to see if the servants were close enough to have overheard his last remark. They weren't. In fact, there weren't any servants around at all. At some point after serving the main courses of the meal, they had disappeared, leaving Dilys and Summer alone in the garden.

The sun was still several hours from setting, but it had descended far enough to cast this part of the garden in the shadow of the palace. The dining table beneath the arbor suddenly felt so much more intimate than before. Much more like a stage set for seduction.

And though she'd unbent enough to share this private meal with him, she wasn't ready for a repeat of what had happened in the grotto.

"Sealord Merimydion—" she began.

"Dilys," he interrupted, his tone pleasant but insistent.

She sighed, then decided this was one battle not worth fighting and surrendered. "Dilys, then. If you're going to attempt to seduce me every time we're together, I will make certain all our future meetings take place in the company of my brother-in-law."

He pressed a hand to his chest. "Ah, *moa kiri*, you wound me."

"I should be so lucky," she grumbled under her breath.

"Very well. No more demonstrations of or discussion about my outstanding talents in the erotic arts, until you decide otherwise. A great loss, to be sure, but I will abide by your wishes."

Against her will, laughter spluttered from her. Gods. The man was entirely too sure of himself.

With obvious reason, a traitorous little voice whispered deep inside.

No. She wasn't going to be charmed by him. She wouldn't be charmed.

He smiled at her. Charmingly.

Her heart began thumping against her chest.

Picking up her fork, she dug into her meal. This time, she deliberately concentrated on the non-Calbernan dishes to avoid rousing any more will-weakening waves of approval.

"I have to say," she said after sampling the extremely delicious roasted potatoes, "I don't approve of your country's customs at all." Her tone was belligerent. Picking a fight seemed much safer than letting her insides go all gooey and weak.

His brows arched in an expression of mild curiosity. "Oh? Of which customs do you speak?"

"All of them. Forcing all men into military service. Taking a child away from his mother at age five." She scowled. "I thought yours was a race dedicated to the happiness of its women. Surely the Calbernan mothers can't be happy to have their babies ripped from their arms at so early an age." To drive her point home, she met his gaze full on and told him, "I know I could never be. Never."

I will never be your liana. *I will go through the courtship motions if I must, but that is never going to change. You are wasting your time.* She willed her eyes to say the words, willed him to give up and turn away.

He did not.

His smile disappeared, but that wasn't the reprieve she'd hoped for. His dark, exotically handsome face became sterner. Stronger. Danger and strength and steadfast resolve wedded together in lines that looked much less approachable and yet more compelling than ever.

Laughing, roguish Dilys charmed her. Stern, somber Dilys frightened her a little, even as his palpable aura of power and command drew her like a moth to a flame.

"The women of my country understand what our men must be, for the benefit of us all." His voice was low, soft, a dark whisper that set every nerve in her body jangling.

She reached for her wine with a shaking hand and took a hurried sip. "Which is?"

"Strong. Fearless. Capable." He leaned towards her, invading her space with his raw power and overwhelming presence. "Willing to die for what's most important to us."

Her pulse was pounding in her veins, throbbing at the base of her throat. "And what's that?"

"You've read about Calberna, about our history, our legends. You already know."

She swallowed and wet her lips. "Your women."

"Our women," he agreed. The words breathed across her skin like a spell. His eyes gleamed, golden, mysterious, hypnotizing. "Our mothers, our sisters, our daughters. Most of all, our wives. The *lianas* who complete us. Many *oulani* believe there is no bond greater than that which exists between a mother and her child. Perhaps for them, that is true. Perhaps it is even true for the women of my own country. I do not know. But for a Calbernan male, there is no bond greater, no tie more vital, than the bond between a Calbernan and his *liana*. Whether she is *imlani* or *oulani* makes no difference to him. Only with her can he give everything that he is. Only from her can he receive everything in return."

It was there, in the dark magic of his voice . . . the promise that promised . . . *everything*. Everything she feared. Everything she yearned for. Everything that ached inside her like a terrible, gaping wound in the fabric of her soul, empty and unfulfilled.

She took a breath, a gasp that shuddered in and shuddered back out.

Just that quick and she was drowning again in that sunlit sea. Every word from his mouth was like a stone tied to her body, weighting her down, dragging her through the darkest depths of the sea, to that frightening place at the core of her soul. To the volcano. That fiery sun that blazed in the center of her being, that molten inferno that moved inside her like a wild, caged thing, a dragon locked behind a lifetime of stony will.

Call him. Claim him. Speak his Name. Make him thine before all others.

The lure was so strong. To give him everything of herself . . . to share the burden of that frightening, deadly gift that lived inside her. To receive everything of him back in return: his strength, his fearlessness, his confident certainty that he was a master of the world in every way that mattered. To trust that he was strong enough to protect her, against even herself.

What would it be like to live without fear? What would it be like to love so wholly, so completely? To love without restraint, without holding back the truth of herself?

It would be madness.

A beautiful insanity of self-indulgence.

She knew whose blood ran in her veins. She had seen, firsthand, the madness that had befallen Verdan Coruscate when he lost what he had loved so dearly, so deeply.

Dilys claimed that Sirens could not survive without their mates—but what if he was wrong? She wasn't just a Siren, if indeed that was one of her gifts. She was a weathermage of Mystral, a descendent of Helos the Sun God. What if the rules and limitations that had governed the Sirens of old did not apply to her?

What if she gave herself to him, let herself love him, only to discover that their bond did *not* destroy her upon his death?

Summer knew her father's madness was but a dim shadow of what would come if ever grief roused the monster that lived in her soul.

She tried to free herself from the arcane magic of Dilys Merimydion's voice. It was impossible with him so close, looking so seductively solemn and strong. The best she could manage was a weak, flimsy challenge.

"And you think a Calbernan's desire for a wife justifies taking a child from his mother's arms at so young an age?"

"Not the desire, no. But the bond? Yes. That is worth everything." His words rang with unwavering certainty. "Our women—our wives—are the heart of Calberna. Without them, Calbernan males could not function. We would die. Just as you would die without the heart that beats in your chest."

He reached out slowly, laid three fingers lightly on the thin fabric that covered her left breast. Her breath caught in her throat. She stared at him in shocked silence. She made no attempt to move or to remove his hand. There was nothing sexual or teasing about his touch this time. It stunned her all the same.

"But for all its strength, the heart is a vulnerable thing," he continued. "It needs must be surrounded by a cage of bone to protect it. At all cost, at all times, the heart must be protected." His hand turned over. Now it was the back of his fingers that caressed her skin just above the neckline of her gown, the touch featherlight, impossibly gentle. "Calberna's sons are those bones. We are the spear, the sword, the unbreakable shield that protects Calberna's vulnerable heart. It's why we are born. It's what we live for."

Her body started trembling. Did he sense the battle waging inside herself? Did he have any clue how close she was to throwing herself into his arms and begging him to be her unbreakable shield?

"I still couldn't bear to surrender my child to someone else's keeping," she told him. Her voice came out a rasping whisper. "I would never let anyone take my baby away from me." The fire locked deep down inside her flared at the mere thought of it.

At last she found the strength to lean back and put a little much-needed distance between them.

He frowned down at his hand, still outstretched in the now empty, his loosely curled fingers moving ever so slightly, as if still caressing her skin. His hand closed in a fist, which he drew back to his side.

Then, as quickly as it had come, his odd solemnity disappeared, replaced once more with the charming, easy smile she'd come to expect from him. And she could breathe again. Think again. She pressed a shaking hand to her lips.

"My mother felt much the same as you." He took a small forkful of the second fish, this one a flounder stuffed with sautéed mushrooms, green onions, and herbed breadcrumbs. "But I was betrothed at a young age to an *imlani* daughter of royal blood. It was imperative that my training begin as early as possible. Still, my mother had her way." His smile grew affectionate, the love in his eyes clear to see. "Most sons are trained at the academy in Cali Va'Lua. My mother would not permit it. She allowed me to move to the training villa on the family estate, but forced the instructors to come to me. It was her way of keeping me close, long past the time when other boys would leave their family."

Summer barely heard anything beyond the word "betrothed." Her breathless yearning evaporated. A violent flare of something that felt suspiciously like possessiveness welled up in its place.

"You were betrothed?" There'd been no mention of a betrothal in the reports she'd read about him.

"*Tey,* when I was four. It was a long-standing betrothal contract, forged decades before I was even born."

There was a story there. Not a good one, judging by his fading smile. The savagery in her soul calmed slightly. Rationality resurfaced. He would not be here, courting her now, if he had a wife waiting for him back in Calberna. Unlike the Vermese, Calbernans did not practice polygamy. And considering the way Calbernans felt about the inviolability of their contracts, a betrothal between two of the queendom's greatest Houses would not have been broken by choice. "What happened?"

"She died in the same accident that killed our crown princess, Sianna. Our queen followed her daughter in death a few days later. That was how my mother came to be *Myerial.*"

"I'm so sorry."

"Thank you." He traced a finger across the snowy white linen tablecloth. "But the wound is not as painful as it once was. Nyamialine and I were only children when she was taken from me, and our bond wasn't fully formed."

Nyamialine. His childhood betrothed's name was Nyamialine.

He gave the long ropes of his hair a quick shake that

sent them dancing across his back, and blasted her with a soft, warm smile that stole her breath. He leaned over in his chair, reaching down to pluck a single, creamy flower from a nearby bed, and offered it to her. "Enough sad talk. Let us speak of happier things as we enjoy the rest of our meal."

"All right." She took the flower and lifted the blossom to her nose, inhaling the lovely fragrance. The sadness, the awkwardness, the inexplicable flare of jealousy, all faded in the face of his encouraging smile and the warm glow in his golden eyes.

"Excellent. You can tell me about your work at Queen Khamsin's school. I have seen how the students adore you."

They stuck to safer, less emotion-laden topics for the rest of their meal. To her surprise, Summer found Dilys a genuinely entertaining companion: smart, witty, observant, full of both amusing and poignant anecdotes from his many travels. He was also a skillful interrogator. He coaxed more information out of her about herself than she would ever have intentionally offered up.

When the meal was done and Ingarra's splendid dessert—a small, iced cake covered with exquisitely rendered sugar flowers—was naught but crumbs, Dilys escorted Summer back to her rooms and bid her good night.

He did not try to kiss her. Not on the lips, not even on the hand. He merely stood before her, so tall and strong, and offered her one last gift: a single, perfect rose. Only the rose he gave her this time wasn't one of the local cold-hardy blooms that grew in Wintercraig. It was one of her mother's most fragile and most exquisite hybrid blooms. A rose created and cultivated exclusively in the carefully-tended greenhouses of Vera Sola in Summerlea. A tender pink bloom with edges of soft rose and a surprising golden center, named Queen Rosalind's Radiant Beauty.

Tears rose to her eyes as she accepted the flower. Even

had she still been in the mood to return every one of his courtship gifts, she wouldn't have returned this rose. It was like holding a little piece of home—a treasured memory of her mother—in her hands.

"It occurred to me," he said, "that having been away from Summerlea so long, you might be missing your home, so I thought I'd bring a little home to you here."

She stroked the soft, velvety petals of the flower, then looked back up into his darkly handsome face. The gold eyes gleaming softly, framed by thick black lashes and dark bronze skin. The shimmering blue stylized waves curling along the bridge of his cheekbone. Tenderness welled inside her.

"Thank you," she whispered. She didn't know if one of her sisters had told him of her particular attachment to her mother's roses, or if he'd just made a lucky guess, but of all the gifts he'd showered upon her, this one touched her the most deeply.

Never had he appealed to her so completely as he did now, this very moment. He stood before her, a haven of strength and otherworldly beauty and beckoning welcome. Everything about him called to her senses. The soft drape of his pure white *shuma* circling narrow hips, his feet bare on the marble floor, the broad, muscular expanse of his chest and shoulders—shoulders that looked strong enough to bear the weight of the world. Most of all the dark, warm, silky skin shimmering with hypnotic swirls of iridescent ink and fragrant with the exotic oils that made her ache to snuggle close and breathe him in like the flowers she loved so much.

It was as if every part of Dilys's being was standing before her, murmuring softly, "I am everything you've ever wanted. I am all that you will ever need. I can keep you safe—even from yourself—if you will just let yourself love me."

The Rose on her wrist pulsed warm against her skin. It was so hard—so dreadfully, painfully hard—to be alone when everything in her cried out with the need to feel complete.

If he leaned down right now to kiss her, as the soft light in his eyes told her he wanted to do, she would let him. And she would kiss him back.

But instead, with one last, faint smile, he bowed his head and stepped back. "Good night, princess. May your dreams be sweet."

Then he was turning . . . walking away . . . and then he was gone.

Gabriella stood beside her doorway for a long time, staring at the empty space where Dilys had been. It occurred to her that, apart from her initial resistance and the rough start to their dinner, she'd never enjoyed a more wonderful, perfect evening in her life. She'd never lost herself in conversation with any man like she had tonight—never revealed as much of herself to anyone either.

Never felt such a perfect sense of peace. Of belonging. Of coming home.

Long after Amaryllis had helped her change into her nightclothes, Gabriella lay awake in her bed, staring at the Summerlea rose she'd placed in a bud vase and set on her nightstand. Throughout the few brief hours of Konumarr's short summer night, she seriously thought about Dilys Merimydion, contemplated what life with him might be like, imagined letting herself love him. And she waited for the familiar sense of terror to rise up and clamp its jaws around her. Waited for the monster to roar with triumph and claw for its freedom.

But for the first time in her life, the terror didn't come and the monster didn't rouse.

CHAPTER 16

Every day for the next week, Dilys spent several carefully planned and frugally apportioned hours in the company of the woman he planned to wed.

He was careful to keep his desires tightly checked. The more he wanted her, the less he allowed himself to touch her. He had made his desire for her clear. Now it was time to let that knowledge of that desire work upon on her.

That she wanted him as desperately as he wanted her, he did not doubt, but she was still too skittish, too ready to bolt if he came at her directly. Forcing her to admit her desire hadn't worked. She'd only accused him of using his magic against her and then run away. Seduction hadn't worked. She'd only resented him for the ease with which he'd broken down her will to resist him. Absence *did* work, but he couldn't make himself stay away—at least not completely. With both of them bound in *liakapua*, they needed to spend time with one another, to share emotions, to share touch.

So he saw her every day, for a few short hours. He abandoned all the seductive techniques he'd spent a lifetime learning in order to win the bond of his chosen *liana*. Instead, in the time he and Summer spent together, he offered her simple companionship. Friendship. Laughter. Even a little adventure—something to break up the sheltered monotony of her gilded royal cage. One day he took her hiking up the mountains. Another day, he took her out on one of the local Winterfolk's small skiffs and taught her how to read the wind and work the sails. And just yesterday, they had gone cloudberry picking with several dozen other couples and children, then joined the group in one of the plazas, where they spent a laughing hour or two making and baking cloudberry pies with the fruits of their excursion. Gabriella—who'd never baked anything in her life—ended up wearing almost as much flour as went into the pie crusts, but the day was delightful, the pies delicious, and he could have sworn she was sorry when the afternoon ended and he escorted her back to the palace.

There were weddings daily, as Summerlander and Winterfolk women chose their mates from among the Calbernans. Dilys attended several of the ceremonies with Summer—including the marriage of her friend, Lily, to his ballista operator, Talin. And even though Summer fretted that Lily had chosen too fast and was acting recklessly, it was clear that Talin doted on his new *liana,* and that the Summerlass had blossomed in his care. Lily was still shy—she probably always would be—but there was a new confidence about her, a greater readiness to laugh and smile. As for Talin, he strutted around in his new *obah,* grinning like a *koku* fish and bragging about his impending fatherhood with as much pride as if he'd done the deed himself.

Each time Summer and Dilys were together, he tried in dozens of different ways to get her to talk about the terrible event in her childhood that had frightened her so badly she had spent a lifetime walling up her emotions, caging her power, and damming up the driving, Siren-born need to love and be loved in return.

She hadn't confided in him yet, but his patience was beginning to pay off in other ways. She'd become less guarded in her conversation. She'd stopped constantly lying to him . . . well, for the most part. She'd stopped trying to put as much physical space between them as possible, too. Now, in fact, she frequently chose to close the distance between them rather than widen it. And yesterday, when he'd taken his leave of her, she'd leaned towards him, a slight flush in her lovely cheeks, and he'd known he could have bent his head and kissed her and she would not have stopped him.

But passive acquiescence was not what he wanted from her.

The next time he kissed her, it would be because *she* initiated it.

He only hoped that time would come soon, because being with her but withholding himself from her was killing him. Each moment in her company was an exquisite torment that kept him lying awake in his bed every night, racked with need and longing.

He took comfort from the knowledge that the most precious of victories were always the hardest won. When his Siren finally claimed him, every sleepless night, every painful moment of self-denial, would be worth it.

Or, at least, that's what he told himself each time he had to wrestle his desire into submission and don the increasingly torturous mask of Dilys the Patient Suitor before heading out to meet the Siren whose claim he was determined to win.

Dilys grimaced at his reflection in the mirror as he arranged the fall of his green, blue and gold *shuma,* then gave his emerald-and-sapphire-encrusted belt a final, unnecessary adjustment and headed downstairs to collect his future bride for today's adventure.

Summer and Dilys shared a light afternoon tea, complete with dozens of the delicious little iced cakes that she loved and a full tray of sinfully delicious chocolates from Zephyr Hallowill's shop. Summer couldn't decide between the two, and ended up eating far too many of both her favorite confections. Dilys didn't seem to mind her gluttony. He only smiled at her with indulgent delight and offered her more iced cakes and chocolates, seeming to thrive on her pleasure as if it were his own.

"You will not find this so amusing when I double my weight," she warned him.

He only laughed softly and drained his tea glass. "Come walk with me then, if it worries you. I've been wanting to try the labyrinth in the western garden. Ryll tells me there's a pretty fountain at its center."

She took his arm and allowed him to escort her through the terraced gardens towards the large four-acre spruce maze that ran along the shores of the fjord west of the palace. The maze was a delight, designed several centuries ago by one of Wintercraig's queens. In addition to the many twisting paths, it included half a dozen covered bridges built of stone and painted timber that rose up above the tops of the tall spruce hedges, crossing over paths below, to give maze walkers an elevated glimpse of the maze from various angles.

As they walked the maze and chatted, they somehow ended up on the subject of Dilys's childhood betrothal. Gabriella wasn't entirely sure how the subject came about, but once it did she found herself growing tense and slightly irritable. Dilys, of course, noticed instantly.

"What's wrong?"

She plucked a fragrant, soft-needled branch from the spruce hedge, and glanced down as she twirled in in her hands. "Nothing. I don't know . . . I just can't imagine you betrothed." She tossed the branch away.

He bent down to retrieve it. "Perhaps, *moa leia*, it isn't that you can't imagine me betrothed to another, it's that you don't like to imagine it."

She looked up at him sharply. "I'm sure that's not it."

He gave a wry smile. "You are still so quick to deny me at every opportunity. Why is that?"

"I told you from the beginning I would not marry you."

"You did," he agreed, "but you've never told me why.

What makes the prospect of being my wife so unappealing? I am not a cruel man, nor an ill-favored one. We enjoy each other's company and are never at a loss for things to talk about. And, of course, sexually, we couldn't be any more compatible."

She blushed and gave him a warning glare. He merely grinned and continued listing all the reasons why he was such an excellent husband material.

"I am Calbernan, so you know I would never hurt you or be unfaithful. Nor would I ever try to control you."

"No, you'd only seduce me into doing whatever you wanted."

His eyes gleamed with warm golden lights. "A man has to have some way to keep the woman he loves from walking all over him. How could she ever love him back if he didn't?" He brushed the soft needles of the spruce wand against her lips, a gentle caress that made her gasp a little and back away.

"You don't l-love me." She stammered over the L word. "You can't."

"Can I not?" He lifted the branch to brush its soft needles against his own lips. She watched with rapt attention. It was almost like a kiss. From her lips to his, with the small, fragrant spruce wand as the messenger. "I think I can."

"You don't know anything about me!"

"I know a great deal more about you than your father knew about your mother when they wed, I imagine. Besides familiarizing myself with the information prepared by the Queen's Council, I have spent the last month learning everything I can about you. Your likes and dislikes. How to make you smile, even when you don't want to. How to tell when you're lying—which you do with abominable regularity, by the way. At least when it comes to subjects you don't want to talk about. I know that you like children, and womanly things. I know that you would follow Hekane

herself into Hel if she but baited a trail with Zephyr Hallowill's chocolates. I know that you like me—more than
like me—even though for reasons you will not share with
me, you are determined to deny it. And I know, Gabriella
Coruscate"—he brushed the small, fragrant wand against
his lips again and leaned closer to caress her mouth in the
same manner—"that you are all that I could ever desire,
all that I have ever needed, all that I can imagine when I
think of my life bound to another's."

"What a pity you shall be so sorely disappointed,
then." She meant for the quip to come out lightly, a saucy
rejoinder to show that his declaration meant nothing to
her. Alas, her throat was too dry and too tight, and her
voice sounded more like a shaken whisper than a teasing
riposte.

"What a pity if we should *both* be so sorely disappointed," he corrected. He tucked the little spruce branch
into the band on his right arm, as if it were a memento
he meant to cherish. "I can give you everything you ever
dreamed of, Gabriella, if only you will let me."

"I already have everything I need." She turned away
and started down the garden path. It was dangerous to
stand for long in the company of a tall, dark, unrepen-
tantly masculine Calbernan intent on seduction.

He followed close on her heels. "Untruth," he murmured, his lips so close to her ear, she nearly jumped out
of her skin. "You want a husband. You want children. You
want love. I can give you these things." His voice whispered down her skin, making her flesh pebble and her
breasts grow full and tight.

Helos help her. She did. She wanted all of that. She
wanted *him*. She wanted to fall into his arms, promise to
give him everything he asked for, take everything he offered. She wanted to bind him to her for all times and
so securely that he wore her possession like one of those
iridescent tattoos on his skin, openly, permanently, for all

to see. So that no other woman would ever again know the teasing, seductive glint in his eye or the sound of her name whispered in his dark velvet voice.

"The price is too high," she bit out.

"The price of what?"

She'd taken a wrong turn in the labyrinth and come to a dead end. Trapped, she whirled around and spat the truth, hoping that might grant her a reprieve. "Love!"

He put his hands on either side of her head, boxing her in loosely between himself and the hedge at her back.

"Tell me about the love that hurt you so, Gabriella. There is a wound in your soul, a sorrow you do not speak of. I know this, for I have known loss and sorrow too. It helps if you talk about it."

There it was again, that tug deep inside. That yearning to open herself up and bare her soul to him. She shook her head. "No, it doesn't."

"Try. Talk to me, Gabriella. Lay down the burden you insist on carrying. Give it to me. I am strong enough to bear both our troubles. Let me help you."

"I'm fine," she insisted. She refused to look into his eyes. If she did, she would give in. She knew it.

"Then shall I tell you about Nyamialine, instead?"

She shrugged, risking a quick, darting glance up at his face. "If you wish." If her will was stronger, she would have said no. She should have said no. But that part of her that found him so appealing was hungry to know everything about him—including the story of his lost love. He hadn't spoken of his childhood betrothed since the night of their dinner in the garden.

"Her name was Nyamialine Calmyria. She was Ari's sister."

That surprised her. She looked up without thinking, and was instantly trapped by his golden gaze. "Ari?"

"*Tey.* It is one of the reasons we are such close friends. There was more than our parents' blood to bind us." He straightened slightly, taking one hand off the hedge to lift a long black curl off her shoulder and twine it around his finger. "We were betrothed on the day she was born. I was four years old."

"That's very young."

"In Calberna, *imlani* daughters are so rare and so precious that betrothal contracts are written decades—in some cases even centuries in advance. As I told you before, the contract between Nyamialine and me was such a one. Made long before my grandmother's birth."

"Not even your parents had a say?"

"What would they say? House Calmyria is a fine House, very powerful, descended from queens and ancient Sirens, as is my own. To wed a son into House Calmyria is a great honor. Ari and I would have become brothers in truth, not just in heart."

"But to have your life mapped out for you before you are even born—"

"You mean, like your life was?" He shook his head. "Gabriella, you were born a princess of Summerlea, and Heir of the Rose. I know the customs of your people. Eventually, when your father was ready to let you go, you would have been wed to a prince of a neighboring land to benefit your family and Summerlea. Do you deny this?"

She scowled. "No." Of course that would have been her fate. That was what princesses and second sons were for—human capital to be used for political, economic, and diplomatic gains.

"And so here I am, prince of a neighboring land, offering marriage that will benefit your family and both Summerlea and Wintercraig, and a guarantee that I will devote myself to your happiness and joy. Why does this frighten you?"

She'd had enough of being trapped between him and the hedge. She ducked under his arm and started walking briskly back towards the next intersection of the labyrinth.

He caught up with her before she'd taken four steps, his long stride easily outpacing hers. But he didn't press further. "The daughters of Calberna are raised with love and indulgence, *tey,* but they are also raised to rule. To rule their families, to rule their Houses, even to rule the Queendom of Calberna. You insist on thinking of marriage as a trap imposed by men upon women because that is so often how it is used in the rest of the world. This is a crime, and a custom we Calbernans find repugnant. The strength of Calberna flows from our women. We protect them, we love them, but we do not cage them."

"And if Nyamialine had decided she didn't want to wed you?"

"That would never have happened. I would have been whatever she needed me to be."

"What about what you need?"

"What I need, Gabriella, is a wife of my own to love. A companion as devoted to me as I am devoted to her. I need to have the emptiness inside me finally filled."

She swallowed hard. For all his cockiness, his swagger, his strength, that last, hoarse admission revealed a deep vulnerability she hadn't realized existed. He was a lonely man, with a heart that yearned for love, for his own place to belong.

"You shouldn't need another to make you feel complete."

He blinked . . . and then he laughed. There was nothing mocking or sarcastic in the laugh. It was more a laugh of surprise. "But I do, Gabriella. I am Calbernan. We require the completeness of a mated union the same way we require air to breathe and food to eat. As I've already told you, Calbernans are symbiotic people. Just as our women cannot survive without the love of their mates and family, neither can our men survive without the strength and love of our women. It is from our women—our *imlani* females—that our magic flows. That power inside you— the one so vast it frightens you?—that power was never meant to be contained. It was never meant to be bottled up inside you. It's meant to be shared with your mate, your children, your nation. That's what it is to be a Siren."

There was something breathtakingly beautiful about the life he was describing. The idea of being part of something greater than herself. Something compellingly whole and complete. She could almost feel his need and his love lapping at her like waves on a beach, pulling from her love and strength, giving back the same, a perfect rhythm of life. Of peace.

She could almost feel the monster inside her relax, no longer fighting against its cage or threatening destruction, but rather feeding its strength to him and to others—nourishing instead of destroying. No longer fearing love but embracing it.

What a dangerously appealing dream.

She turned away and began walking again, turning right when the path intersected another. He jogged after her.

"What is it?" he asked when he caught up to her. "What are you running from now?"

"How did Nyamialine die?" she countered.

He sighed at her blatant dodge but told her nonetheless about the accident that had claimed the lives of so many. "The *Myerial*'s mate and every unmarried male of House Merimynos and House Calmyria above the age of fourteen took their lives in grief," he said in conclusion.

"What?" She gaped at him in horror. "That's barbaric!"

"It is the Calbernan way. The death of *imlani* females from two of the most powerful Houses of Calberna was no small loss."

"So your people's answer is more death?"

He drew a breath, exhaled in such a way as to make her think he was holding on to his patience. "Have I not just told you of the nature of Calbernans? The sacrifice was a measure of our grief, yes, but also necessary to prevent weakening House Merimynos and House Calmyria beyond repair. We have no Sirens, Gabriella. Even one with a power like yours could have provided strength enough to make the sacrifice of so many unnecessary. The *Myerial*'s mate would still have perished, but the others . . . many of them might have been saved. *You* could have saved them. Your power—that gift you fear so badly you can't even bring yourself to speak of it—that power could have saved them."

She stared up at him. She'd never thought of the monster as anything more than a danger to be contained. "You don't know that. You don't know anything about my power. You don't understand what it can do."

"So tell me, Gabriella. Tell me what it can do. Tell me why you fear it so."

Dilys wanted to reach for her, to hold her, to help her face the demons of her past. He would battle them himself if he could. But she hadn't given him that right . . . and she'd made it clear she would not thank him for taking it. So he stood before her, silently willing her to finally open up and trust him with her truths, with her secrets. To share with him, as he had shared with her.

For one, gut-wrenching instant, he thought she'd rebuff him yet again, but then she began to speak.

"You know about my father. How he died. The things he did." Summer plucked a spruce branch from the hedge and began denuding the twig of its soft, fragrant blue-green needles. "Storm tried to keep the worst of it from us, but I overheard her talking with Wynter once. I know our father tried to kill her more than once. I know he nearly succeeded." Her brow creased as emotion welled. "Our father—m-my father—was a monster."

"He was not well," Dilys agreed softly.

"He was insane." She crumpled the remains of the spruce wand and let it fall. "He loved my mother so deeply, that when he lost her, he lost his mind." Her beautiful eyes were swimming with tears. She tilted her head back to look at the sky and blinked rapidly, but they leaked from the corners of her eyes to trickle down the sides of her face into her hair.

There was no way he could keep his distance. Not when her sorrow was spilling from her eyes. He caught her in his arms. "I'm sorry, *moa leia*. I am so sorry for your pain. But what happened to him has nothing to do with you."

She wrenched away. "I'm just like him! Don't you see? I'm just like him!" She turned and took off running.

He chased after her. Because she was headed for the center of the maze rather than one of the exits, he waited until she slowed before catching up to her. She was calmer then. Her tears had stopped.

"You're nothing like your father, Gabriella. You couldn't be. You are a Siren. Your heart is filled with love. You could never become obsessed with hatred and a lust for power the way your father was at the end. It's not in your nature."

"What proof do you have of that? Siren, I may be, but if I am, I'm the first of my kind. A Siren born of royal Summerlander blood—not Calbernan. How many of your ancient Calbernan Sirens carried the power of the Sun and who knows how many other forms of ancestral magic in their veins, as I do?" They had reached the center of the maze. She paced across the grass to the fountain and stared hard at the falling water. "You think I'm a Siren. Everyone else thinks I'm like my mother. You all think I'm loving and calm and gentle, that I would never hurt anyone—that I would never do anything horrible . . . But you all think that because that's what I want you to believe. If you knew what I was really like . . ."

"Gabriella . . ."

"I am my father's daughter."

"No, you aren't."

Her face creased with an expression of anguished affection, as if she both loved and hated how swiftly and stoutly he jumped to her defense.

"Yes, Dilys, I am. The monster that lived in him lives in me, too. You saw what I did to Lily's father."

"I did. And if you hadn't killed that worthless *krillo,* I would have. Your brother-in-law would have. Every one of my men, every one of your brother's guard, even your own sister Khamsin would have. Would you stare at us all in horror and call us monsters, too?"

"Lily's father wasn't the first person I've killed, Dilys."

CHAPTER 17

There. She'd said it. Admitted it. That horrible black stain on her soul.

Summer stood before him, fists clenched, chest heaving as if she'd run a hard race.

"Tell me," he said. And he reached for her hands. There was no horror in his eyes, no fear, just warmth and compassion and acceptance. One at a time, he peeled back the tightly curled fingers of her hands, kissed each palm, and pressed her hands to his chest, pressing his own hands atop them to anchor them there. All the while, he kept his eyes locked with hers. Steady. Accepting. Unwavering.

"Tell me," he said again.

And as she stared up into the endless sunlit sea of his warm, golden gaze, she could almost hear him singing softly, his voice a sweet enchantment, *Give me your pain, moa kiri. Let me bear it for you. Let me set you free.*

Her mouth trembled. Gods, she wished she could. Never had she wanted so badly to be the sweet, loving, gentle woman the world thought she was. Never had she wanted so badly for her soul to be unstained, for the monster to be gone. If she was everything she'd spent her lifetime pretending to be, she could have thrown herself into his arms, surrendered herself to the promise of paradise. She could have accepted his courtship, his love. Let herself love him in return.

The mere thought made her want to weep.

There was a terrible, tight, pain inside her. A child's voice crying out in a high, thin, keening wail. Other voices, screaming, high-pitched. Men and horses. Desperate. Frantic. The sounds of mindless, abject terror all creatures made when death came with a violent, agonizing hand.

She would have clapped her hands over her ears to drown the screams out, but Dilys held her fast.

"Tell me, Gabriella."

She closed her eyes, flung back her head, strained back so that only the anchor of his hands holding hers to his chest kept her from falling. "I killed them. I killed them all."

"Who, *moa kiri*?"

"A man and three boys. Back in Vera Sola." Beneath his anchoring hands, her fingers curled into claws, dug into the solid flesh of his muscular chest. The visions from a thousand nightmares rose before her eyes. Eyes wild and terrified. Mouths open, screaming.

"Who were they, Gabriella?" His voice called her out of the past. Dragged her back to the gardens of Konumarr Palace. To him.

Her eyes snapped open. She stared up at Dilys. "The stable master and his three sons. Everyone thinks they died in the fire, but they didn't. I killed them the same way I killed Lily's father."

If she thought he would flinch, she was disappointed. He remained steady as a rock. Calm and patient. Waiting for her. "Tell me," he said, his voice as soft as the wings of those butterflies he'd given her that one morning but as relentless as the sea. And like that ocean, he could wear down even the strongest of stone. Day by day, hour by hour, he'd been pounding away at the granite walls she'd locked around her past, and now, with one final shudder of protest, they crumbled, and the answers he'd been digging after all these weeks spilled out like water pouring through the breached dam.

"I wasn't allowed pets. None of us were. Papa said it was a bad idea. As it turns out, he was right." She could feel the powerful heart in Dilys's chest thumping against her palm. Slow, steady. "The stable boy's dog had puppies. Spring snuck out to play with them, and I followed her. I was four. I fell in love the first moment I saw them." She blinked up at him. "I've always felt everything so much more deeply than Falcon or my sisters. Mama always said I got that from her, but that I got my temper from Papa. It isn't a very safe combination."

Even as a very small child, anger made her chest burn, and her stomach hurt, and her hands clench in tight, hot fists. Anger made her throat go raw and tight as it boiled and spewed and bubbled inside her heart.

The feeling was terrible and uncomfortable. Summer was the sweet, sunny-natured princess. The others could rage and storm about—especially their youngest sister—but Summer never did. She didn't like for people to be upset. It made her skin prickle and her bones ache. She wanted people to be happy. She was like Mama in that regard. The two of them thrived best in a calm, loving environment. They soaked up kindness the way a rose soaked up sunshine. It nourished their souls.

But when Summer got angry, she could actually feel fire roaring away inside her. Violent. Dangerous.

Mama knew about that fire, of course, the same way Mama knew everything about all her children.

"Look at me, Gabriella," Mama would say in that gentle, implacable voice that brooked no disobedience, willful or otherwise. Most of the time Mama called Summer by her giftname, just as everyone else did, but when she used Summer's birth name, it meant that whatever came next was meant to be heard and heeded. Sometimes what was meant to be heard and heeded were words of love and pride, precious drops of golden sunlight that soaked into Summer's soul. "I love you, Gabriella, my darling girl." "The gods blessed me, Gabriella, to give me such a sweet, caring daughter." "You make me so proud, Gabriella."

But sometimes, what was meant to be heard and heeded were words of instruction or gentle admonishments. As was the case whenever the angry fire blazed so hot in Summer's heart that she thought she might explode.

"Look at me, Gabriella," Mama would say at such times. "Look at me now, my darling. Let it go, Gabriella. Be calm. There's my girl. There, now. You're such a good girl." Then, when the fire was safely banked, and the Rose-shaped birthmark on Summer's right wrist no longer burned like a white-hot coal against her arm, Mama would enfold Summer in her arms, and the cool, sweet, nourishment of her love would surround Summer in a world of peace and calm and gentleness, and everything would be set to rights.

Only Mama hadn't been there that day in the stables, and Summer—protected, pampered, surrounded by love—had never known grief or horror, or the consuming fury that would erupt when she lost what she loved.

"What happened to the puppies you loved, Gabriella?"

She blinked up at Dilys a little hazily, her thoughts still mired in memory. "They died, of course. But you knew that."

"*Tey, moa leia.* I suspected so." The fingers clasped over hers were stroking lightly, soft, gentle, undemanding caresses. "Talk to me, Gabriella. Tell me what happened." His voice was as calm as a still mountain lake. Somehow, that made the words easier to say.

"It wasn't anyone's fault. But they were puppies and they shouldn't have been in the stables. Papa had bought a new stallion. Very expensive. Very high strung. And the puppies got out of their stall. The stable master and his eldest son were bringing the stallion in, trying to calm him . . . but the puppies must have startled him."

To this day, she didn't like stallions. She couldn't be

near them. She rode, of course, but only on gentle mares or placid geldings. And she hadn't stepped foot in a stable since.

"Mama and Papa and the rest of us were just coming back from an outing when it started. I heard the screams and the barking and went running into the stables before anyone could stop me. Several of the puppies were already dead by the time I got there. The stallion was out of control, rearing, stomping everything in sight, and so were half the other horses in the stables. The mother dog was savaging him, trying to protect her puppies. Who could blame her? The stable master and his sons were trying to calm the stallion, but the puppies were everywhere, barking, getting underfoot, making things worse. Everything happened all at once. The mother dog got hold of the stallion's foreleg and the horse went down. The older boy kicked one of the puppies so hard I heard her spine snap. And then I snapped, too."

Gods, the fire and the fury that had roared up inside her. The shaking, howling scream of rage that had erupted from her thin, four-year-old chest.

"The one he kicked. She was the one I loved most. I was going to smuggle her into my rooms and keep her. And they killed her. So I killed them."

She looked at Dilys and remembered what she'd felt like after that rage had come pouring out her. After the stable master and his three sons and the wild-eyed, terrified, injured stallion had fallen, writhing, to the floor as every bone and organ in their bodies had exploded inside their flesh, leaving flaccid, bloody bags of skin. She'd stared at them, the living beings she'd killed, and for the first time in her life, she hadn't felt *anything*. She'd felt hollow, as if her insides had been scooped out, leaving her an empty, paper-thin shell.

"I don't know what started the fire. Maybe that was me, too. Or maybe a lantern got kicked over. Or maybe it was Papa after he saw what I'd done. In any case, he and Mama let everyone believe the fire was what killed them."

"As well they should have. You were just a child, Gabriella. You were not to blame."

She ignored his absolution. It didn't change what had happened. And she didn't deserve it. "Papa banished all pets from Vera Sola after that. Every dog and cat and small animal in the city was taken away. I wasn't allowed in the stables again, and they made sure, when I rode, I never had the same horse twice. So I couldn't get attached. I wasn't allowed to play with other children until I proved I could control myself. Mama worked with me every day."

Summer remembered the feel of Mama's hands holding her small face. She remembered the way Mama's eyes fixed on hers and never wavered, cooling the fire that raged in Summer's soul.

"There is great power in you. So you must—Gabriella, you *must*—learn to control it. Do you understand, darling? You must control your emotions, or you could hurt someone again. And I know you would never want that."

So Gabriella had learned how to control her anger and push the bad, hot, violent feelings away. For Mama. Because Mama was Summer's anchor in the storm, just like she was Papa's. Gentle, steadfast, unwavering.

"It was very difficult for me after Mama died," Summer told Dilys. "But I saw how Papa despised Storm—even as a baby—for not being able to control her gifts, and the thought of him ever hating me the way he did her was more than I could bear." She shrugged. "So I learned to stay away from things that made me feel too much. I learned how to avoid extreme emotion, how to make the people around me happy so I could stay happy too."

"And then I came along."

"And then you came along."

"What do I make you feel, Gabriella?"

She looked up at him. Traced the strong, beautiful lines of his face with her eyes.

"Too much," she admitted. "Far, far too much."

Emotion broke across his soul like sunlight breaking through the clouds after a fierce storm at sea. It suffused him with the same relief and satisfaction and sense of a fight well won, the same profound sense of awe that left him marveling at the beauty and the challenge of this wondrous world. Of this woman who had somehow, in so short a time, become his world, and no less wondrous than the one whose seas he'd sailed most of his life.

"And if I could promise you need never fear your power again, *moa kiri*? Would you let yourself love me then?"

The fingers splayed across Dilys's chest trembled. Or maybe that was him doing the trembling. He couldn't be sure.

"You can't promise that," she said.

"But if I could? If I could promise you'd never hurt anyone by accident ever again, would you still refuse me?"

Her eyes were so wide, so deeply blue. Her soft mouth trembled. She looked so uncertain. Fear and hope teetering uncertainly on a delicately balanced fulcrum. He'd never wanted to kiss her more.

He didn't. She had to come to him. She had to make the choice.

"No." She spoke in a whisper so low he had to strain to hear her. "No, I wouldn't refuse you."

"And would you let yourself love me? Could you? Love me?"

Her lashes fluttered down. Her head bowed, leaving him looking down at the neat part and glossy black curls of her artfully arranged hair. As silky and dark as any *imlani* females. "If it wasn't a danger to everyone around me? Could I love you then? I suppose so." She tugged at the hands he held pressed to his chest, pulling with enough force that he had to let her go. "But it doesn't matter," she said. "You can't change what I am."

He half expected her to walk away. To put as much distance between them as she could. She was a turtle without her shell, vulnerable, and she was an expert at running from people and situations that made her that way. But she didn't run, and his heart nearly burst with pride and soaring hope and love so strong it made tears sting his eyes.

"There is no part of you I would ever want to change, Gabriella Aretta Rosadora Liliana Elaine Coruscate," he told her huskily. "You are perfect, just as you are."

Her gaze shot up, startled, and he had to smile at her surprise.

"Think about it, *moa kiri,* you just spoke to me of the most painful experience in your life. A memory so terrible you have spent your life cutting yourself off from even the possibility of love. You just relived every horrible moment of that experience in your mind—even the bits you didn't tell me about—and yet the power you fear so much did not overwhelm you."

Her jaw dropped. She turned over her right hand, staring in shock at the red Rose-shaped birthmark on her inner wrist. She touched it with shaking fingers, then pressed a hand to her chest.

"How?"

He reached for her hand slowly. Unfurled the slender, delicate fingers. Laid her trembling palm over his own heart.

"You gave your pain to me. You let me take it from you and give you my love back in return."

"I don't understand."

"You weren't born to stand alone, *Sirena.* You were born to love and to be loved. To share what's inside you. And whether you want to admit it or not, your heart knows you can share it with me."

He could see her doubt, feel the fear trickling into him

through the filaments of trust and need that had multiplied and strengthened these past weeks, binding them ever closer. But beneath the doubt and fear was a sweet savor that set his senses soaring. Hope.

Numahao bless him. Earlier, when she'd told him about the horrible incident in her childhood and she'd unwittingly let him bear her anguish, that subconscious gift, that sharing of emotion, had come with ragged surges of magic that had filled every corner of his being with tingling energy. But this—this hope—even fragile as it was, was like a blaze of brilliant light illuminating the night, a river of pure power, pouring into him. And she wasn't even aware . . . wasn't even trying to share her gift with him.

He could scarcely imagine what it would be like once she actually claimed him as hers and forged bonds of love even stronger than what tied them together now.

"Let yourself love me, Gabriella Aretta Rosadora Liliana Elaine Coruscate."

She stared up at him, and though all his life he thought the wide, golden eyes of Calberna's *imlani* females were the most beautiful eyes in the world, he measured by a different standard now. There could be no eyes more beautiful than those of clear, deep sapphire. Blue as summer skies and the prettiest seas he'd ever sailed.

"Why do you do that?" she asked.

"Do what?"

"Call me by my full name. Are you trying to work some sort of Calbernan magic on me?"

He smiled. "Not in the way that you mean."

"Because I know that some folk believe names have power. That by speaking the true name of a thing, you can bind it."

His smile broadened. "Names *do* have power—true names, at least—and I do aim to bind you to me in every way possible. But *you* must claim *me* first before I can."

"How do I do that?"

"You already know my true Name. Speak it, and you

make me yours forever. And when you speak it, I'll know your true Name too. Until then, I call you by your full name because that's the truest name for you I know." He shrugged, feeling a little shy as he admitted, "It makes me feel closer to you."

He traced a finger down the side of her face. "I call you other names too, all of them true in their own way. *Moa leia.* My flower. *Moa halea.* My love. *Moa kiri.* My heart. *Myerial u moa kiri.* Queen of my heart. *Moa liana.* My wife, my beloved, my life's mate."

Her lips were parted. Her eyes a little dazed. And sweet, hot energy was pouring into him, wave after wave. It was the most marvelous feeling. Like food for a hungry soul. And he hadn't realized how badly he'd been starving. She nourished parts of him he'd never even known existed. And, like any starving man set before a feast, he wanted to gorge himself. He wanted to take everything she had to give him so that he'd never be hungry again.

But he wasn't hers yet. She hadn't claimed him as hers and invited him in. Until she did, that dazzling bounty of love and power wasn't his. To take what must be given was the worst sort of crime. Punishable, in Calberna, by death.

He bent his head, shuddering against the aching need she roused within him. He clasped her hand more tightly to his chest and willed her to hear his silent plea.

Claim me, Sirena. *Speak my Name. Make me thine.*

But she didn't, and so, with deep regret and no little effort, he released her hand and stepped back to break the connection between them. The abrupt loss of her sweet succor made him groan. To leave her, to leave the Halla of that communion, pained him in ways he'd never known. Nothing less than the fullness of her love, the utter completeness of her claiming, would ever assuage the hunger that burned in him now.

If she didn't have him, he would Fade. Or rather, he would do the Calbernan male's equivalent. He would give himself up to the ocean and swim the depths until no strength remained in his body except that which the fishes could claim from his lost and lifeless corpse.

He tried to smile in answer to her questioning gaze, but the effort was too much for him.

"Come, *moa kiri*. I'll take you back to the palace."

As they exited the winding paths of the labyrinth, a familiar six-blast call of a Calbernan conch-shell horn rang out in the distance.

"What's that?" Summer asked.

Dilys, who had halted to listen to the sound, took the closest set of terrace steps three at a time and turned to look out over hedge maze to the fjord beyond. He raised a hand to shield his eyes and gaze at the Calbernan ship sailing round the bend towards Konumarr.

"Dilys, what is it?" Summer joined him on the top step and turned to follow his gaze.

Three familiar flags flew from the mainmast of the approaching ship: the green-and-blue flag of Calberna, the curling blue-and-white waves of House Merimydion, and atop them both, the small white-and-gold crown on a field of coral red. The pennant flown by royal envoys of the *Myerial* of Calberna.

"I think my uncle is here."

"Your uncle?"

"My mother's twin, Calivan Merimydion. He was originally planning to accompany me, but my mother . . . fell ill and he stayed behind to assist her."

She went still beside him. "Your mother is ill?"

He cursed himself for saying anything when he heard the tremor in her voice and knew he had reminded her of her own loss. Still, he had spoken, she had asked, and now there was nothing for it but to give her the truth.

"She Fades," he told her honestly. "I told you that Sirens don't survive their mates, *tey*? Well, my mother has enough Siren in her that my father's death nearly took her, too. But then the *Myerial* died, and my mother inherited the queen's gift." He stared out at the horizon, not seeing his uncle's approaching ship, but the memory of his mother's pale, thin face the day before Nyamialine's death. "Sometimes, I used to think it was only the queen's gift and the duty that came with it—not the love of me or my uncle— that kept her with us."

A warm, slender hand touched his arm. A gentle touch of comfort and sympathy. With it came another astonishing wave of power, sparkling with compassion and strength.

He laid a hand over hers and smiled. "I came here seeking a wife not only for my own joy but also to bring her a daughter to love, and the promise of a grandchild to look forward to. Joy enough to keep her with me for a while longer." His smile tilted towards self-deprecating as he admitted, "A man grown I may be, but I am not ready to lose my mother."

"Of course you aren't." And there was a note in her voice so sweet, so full of kindness and understanding, that he wanted to snatch her up in his arms and never let her go.

Instead he lifted a hand to cup her face and ran his thumb along the crest of her cheekbone, tracing the path where the mate to his *ulumi-lia* would, Numahao willing, soon reside. "You, *moa kiri,* truly are a *myerial myerinas,*" he told her huskily.

She didn't pull away, merely stood, looking up at him. "What does that mean?"

"A treasure of all treasures. A pearl of all pearls. The queen of all queens. It means you are a woman without equal."

"Ah." Her cheeks turned a dusky pink beneath their Summerlander brown. "I wouldn't go as far as all that."

"I would."

She stared up at him, rosy-cheeked, plump lips parted, her eyes a wide and endless blue, and it was all he could do not to kiss her. Then she blushed a deeper shade of pink and pulled away with a small, self-conscious laugh.

"Well, um . . . shall we go greet your uncle?"

He grinned. He liked that she'd said "we," making the two of them a couple. "If you like. Are you up for an adventure?"

She hesitated. "What sort of adventure?"

His grin grew wider. Holding her hand, he ran towards the edge of the terraced garden. As they reached the edge of the terrace, he wrapped a powerful arm around her waist and cried "Hang on, *moa leia*!"

Summer screamed as Dilys wrapped an arm around her waist and leapt off the garden terrace into the dark waters of the Llaskroner Fjord. She kept screaming as he propelled them rapidly through the water towards his uncle's approaching ship. She was still screaming as he shot them both upwards on a wide spout of water and stopped only when he dropped them lightly onto the polished wooden deck of his uncle's ship.

She should have been drowned or at least soaking wet from head to toe, but he'd somehow made the water of the fjord flow around her, keeping her surrounded by a cone of breathable air as he swum them towards the boat. And though the spout of water that had delivered them onto the ship's deck had soaked her slippers and the skirts of her gown, he'd evaporated the moisture with a wave of his hand.

She was still gripping the arm he'd clapped around her waist; her fingers dug into his muscular forearm in a death grip. With effort, she pried each one free and turned to glare up into his laughing, golden-eyed gaze.

"A little warning would have been nice."

He only laughed. "Where's the fun in that?"

She grimaced. "Show-off," she muttered, and she stepped away to give her skirts a firm shake. Only then did she realize they were surrounded by unfamiliar Calbernan warriors, every one of them clad in gleaming musculatas and dark green loincloths, every one of them holding a polished, wickedly sharp trident and a long, coffin-shaped shield.

Standing beside the top deck railing was an older Calbernan male. He was also clad in a loincloth, but his musculata was worked in gold with raised designs of sea serpents and foaming waves covering the chest. And where each of the other warriors wore a dark green cloak clasped about their shoulders, the older man wore a loose-fitting, wide-sleeved robe of fine fabric that hung down to mid-calf. He was watching her with narrowed golden eyes and an inscrutable expression.

"*Myerialanna* Gabriella Coruscate," said Dilys, "it is my honor to introduce you to His Excellency, Calivan Merimydion, Lord Chancellor of Calberna."

She blushed to the roots of her hair. "Your Excellency."

"Your Royal Highness," the Lord Chancellor replied, offering a polite bow. "Forgive me. I would offer you refreshments or a comfortable place to sit, but I was not expecting visitors until some time after we made dock." He flicked what looked like a reproving glance in Dilys's direction. Her interpretation of the look was confirmed a moment later when he added, "My nephew can be impetuous at times."

If Dilys took offense he did not show it. Instead he said, "I was surprised to see your ship, Uncle. You sent no word of your impending arrival. *Moa nima* is well?"

Calivan Merimydion switched to Sea Tongue and said, "She is much improved. I would not have left her otherwise. But you should not speak of such things before *oulani*."

"I have no secrets from my *liana*," Dilys replied in the same tongue.

Calivan's whole body tensed. "Your *liana*?" He speared Summer with a narrow-eyed gaze. "She has already bound you to her?"

"Not yet," Summer replied in perfectly accented Sea Tongue. Calivan looked startled, but Dilys only gave her an amused glance. He'd clearly suspected she was as fluent in his native tongue as Spring.

Gabriella didn't like the way Calivan was speaking to Dilys—a seasoned warrior who had, quite literally, saved the world. Although Dilys was more than capable of fighting his own battles, she nonetheless found herself springing to his defense. "Your nephew believes in the power of affirmation," she continued in articulate Sea Tongue. With a smile much fonder and more intimate than she had ever given Dilys before, she laid a hand on his arm, gazed adoringly up into his eyes, and said, "He is convinced that if he says a thing often enough, it will become true. I confess, the tactic is an effective one. He has been wearing down my resistance."

Dilys's amused smile turned into a quickly smothered grin. He caught her hand in his and lifted it to his mouth to press a kiss against the back of her fingers. "My *liana* has the right of it. She hasn't made her claim final yet, but her growing affection towards me gives me confidence that she soon will."

"I see." Calivan switched back to Eru, the common tongue. "Well, this is good news. I look forward to the day when I may offer you both my congratulations. And, of course, the *Myerial* awaits the arrival of her new daughter with great anticipation and much joy."

The mention of Dilys's mother made Summer suddenly regret her impulsive pretense—what if Calivan Merimydion raised his sister's hopes for a forthcoming engagement?—but when she tugged on her hand to free it, Dilys did not let go. Unwilling to engage in an embarrassing struggle to get her hand back, Summer let him keep it and pasted a pleasant expression on her face.

"Thank you, Your Excellency," she said.

She stood quietly as Dilys and his uncle quickly caught each other up with the happenings in Calberna and Konumarr. As they spoke, she could see some small resemblance between Dilys and his uncle in the shape and color

of their eyes and the thick slash of their eyebrows, but
that was it. Had she met the two side by side, she would
never have suspected they were related. Though both
men were clearly fit, Calivan was leaner. Dilys had more
muscle mass. All those years of swinging heavy swords
and fighting other people's wars, she supposed. Calivan
also seemed a little cagier. Less open. She'd spent a lifetime living amongst palace intrigues. She recognized the
signs of a man accustomed to the ever-changing political
winds of court. He didn't strike her as one of those obse-
quious, oily politicians who curried favors, though. There
was too much steel in his spine, too much an aura of command about him. He wasn't the gadfly. He was the spider,
spinning his webs.

They both were lethal men, each in his own way. The
difference, she suspected, was that Calivan's was the knife
you wouldn't see coming.

Summer shivered a little, then smiled as Dilys glanced
down at her, his eyes filled with laughter over some story
he'd been relating about his cousins Ryll and Ari.

"Oh, they are terrible flirts," she agreed. "Half the
women in Konumarr are madly in love with them. I think
that's the problem. They're enjoying all the attention too
much to make up their minds."

"Their mothers will not be pleased," Calivan said.
"Houses Ocea and Calmyria both need daughters. Arilon
and Ryllian should settle down and tend their duty to
mother and House."

Was it her imagination, or was there another jab at
Dilys in that remark?

"I'm sure they will," Dilys said easily. "We've a few
weeks yet before our time here is done."

"Only if the King and Queen of Wintercraig agree to
postpone the rest of your visit."

For the first time since coming aboard, Dilys tensed.
"What do you mean?"

Calivan hesitated, frowning at Summer.

Dilys shifted a little closer to her. "I told you, I have no secrets from Gabriella. Whatever you have to say, you can say in her presence."

After another long pause, the Lord Chancellor of Calberna sighed. "I suppose she will learn soon enough anyways. I merely thought the news should go to the king first. A matter of diplomacy, you understand." The last remark, he directed towards Summer.

"Of course," she murmured.

"Does this have something to do with the reason you and your crew are sailing armed and armored?" Dilys asked.

"It does," Calivan affirmed. "Our friends in the Olemas Ocean have set their sights on the Denbe now. A Cantese convoy was attacked just east of the Milinas Strait."

The Milinas Strait was the western gateway to the Denbe Ocean from the Sterling Sea. Summer knew from her recent study of Calbernan commerce that the Milinas Strait was one of the main shipping channels used by Calberna and their network of trade partners. If the pirates successfully gained control of both the Olemas and Denbe Oceans, they would control two thirds of Mystral's northern hemisphere.

"There's more," Calivan continued. "The Cantese were sailing under the flag of House Merimydion. As were three other convoys attacked within the last month. Three of our trade vessels are missing, presumed sunk or commandeered. It's our belief that House Mermydion's ships and trading partners are being targeted specifically."

At Summer's side, Dilys had gone utterly still. The muscles beneath her hand were taut, and he was all but vibrating with contained emotion. Anger, she realized, when she cast a searching glance up at the handsome face that now looked carved from stone and the eyes that blazed with golden fire. She shivered a little. She wouldn't want to see that face coming at her in battle. There was no mercy in it at all.

"Which of our ships were taken?"

Calivan rattled off a short list of names.

"And the rest of our merchant ships?"

"The *Myerial* has recalled them all to Calberna. The captains were not happy about it."

"Better angry than dead. They should be integrated with the other fleets. If this is a direct attack on House Merimydion, we won't make our ships an easy target for these miserable *krillos*."

"*Tey,* well, as to that . . . we have a plan."

Calivan Merimydion's plan was simple. He'd already spread word that House Merimydion had a convoy on its way filled with magnificent treasures to celebrate Dilys's forthcoming marriage to a Season of Summerlea—a collection to rival the dragon's hoard of priceless gifts Dilys's own father had gathered in anticipation of his daughter's birth. Now, he just needed Dilys and his men to set a trap, using that convoy as bait. Pirates with a grudge against House Merimydion wouldn't let such a prize slip through their fingers, and Calivan's ears across the seas had already informed him that the Shark was making plans to personally intercept the convoy.

Later that night, after escorting Gabriella to her chambers, Dilys headed for his uncle's room. He'd known since the not-so-subtle jabs about doing duty to mother and House that his uncle would expect a full accounting of why Calberna's prince—who had been clearly told which Seasons he should marry—was courting the one Season who had been deemed unsuitable for a royal union.

Calivan answered the door on Dilys's first knock and waved him curtly inside. Once the door closed behind them, Calivan flicked a hand at the full basin of water on his dressing table and spread a water veil around the room for privacy. "So, Nephew, explain yourself."

Dilys bristled. Even expecting the inquisition, he took exception to his uncle's tone. It was one thing to be told which woman he should take to wife, but it was entirely something different to be addressed in such a scathing tone for choosing Gabriella instead. As if she was so utterly without merit as to be the worst possible match he could ever have made. The insult to her, though unspoken, made his hackles rise and claws come out.

"Speak carefully, Uncle," he hissed through fully descended battle fangs. "Do not dare to insult my *liana*. You will not be forgiven." Fury pulsed through him, and his *ulumi* flared bright in warning.

Calivan's jaw dropped. "You have entered *liakapua*? With her?"

"I have, and that is my answer to you."

"How is this possible?" Calivan dragged his fingers through the ropes of his hair. "She is not the one we chose for you."

"Perhaps not, but she *is* the one Numahao chose for me. And there is much more to her than your lengthy investigations revealed."

His uncle's eyes narrowed with sudden sharpness. "What do you mean?"

"I mean she is a Siren."

"A *what*?"

"You heard me."

Calivan stumbled back a step, completely nonplussed. Then his expression hardened and he folded his arms across his chest. "That's impossible. She can't be. An *oulani* Siren? No. *Ono*. You must be mistaken."

"There is no mistake. We all heard her Shout. Every last one of us in the city. We all came running. She is a Siren. The first in twenty-five hundred years."

"It cannot be. It's some other magic. Some sort of deception. A ruse to get you to marry the least gifted weatherwitch instead of the strongest."

Dilys grabbed his uncle by the throat, claws digging into the skin on either side of his windpipe. "Do not," he growled, "by word, tone, or deed, suggest she is anything but the treasure of treasures she is." With a snarl, he released his mother's twin and stepped back.

Calivan massaged his throat, eyeing his nephew warily for the first time. "My apologies," he said in a much more conciliatory tone. "It will not happen again. But if this is true about her being a Siren, why did you not send word immediately? I would have brought an entire fleet to protect her."

"I would not risk her safety sending word of her existence along even our most secure seaways. I do not know what sort of magics or spies the Shark has at his disposal, but I wasn't willing to let unfriendly ears learn what Gabriella is. I thought it best to keep what she is a secret until I could bring her home safe to Calberna. Even then, the truth of what she is can never be known to the *oulani*. There are more greedy, honorless *krillos* in the world today than there were at the time of the Slaughter."

"*Tey,* of course. Of course." Calivan steepled his hands and pressed them to his lips. "This changes many things. A Siren. No wonder you erected the sea veil around the palace." He shook his head and began to pace. "Her gift gives us a strong advantage against the Pureblood Alliance. They cannot refuse to the recognize the daughter of Calberna's prince and a Siren as Calberna's next queen."

Dilys crossed his arms. "You are still thinking my daughter will be the next *Myerial*? Uncle, Gabriella is a Siren, the first born since the Slaughter. The Sea Throne is hers. *Nima* can gift her the power of the *Myerials* and then retire to Merimydia Oa Nu. Without the weight of so many lives and the responsibilities of a queendom resting on her shoulders, we should be able to slow her Fade."

Calivan shook her head. "If Summer Coruscate were *imlani,* there would be no question of her becoming our *Myerial,* but she is not. However she came to possess the gift, she does not possess Calbernan blood. No *oulani*—not even a Siren—can sit on the Sea Throne. You should not even suggest it. The Pureblood Alliance has caused problem enough over the mere possibility of a half-breed becoming the next *Myerial*. What do you think they would do if House Merimydion tried to put the crown on the head of a foreigner?"

Dilys swallowed his retort. There was no point in arguing with his uncle. Calivan's first loyalty was to his twin. But if Calivan thought there would be no support for Gabriella to take the throne once Calbernans learned she was a Siren, he was mistaken. Calberna was a land whose people valued strength, and there was no stronger Calbernan magic than Siren Song. Already, Dilys's own men called Gabriella their future queen—and to a man they would die to protect and serve her, without a thought to her *oulani* blood.

"Still, she must be guarded as the treasure she is," Calivan continued. "Which men will you be leaving behind to ensure her safety?"

Dilys told him the names of the ten elite Calbernan warriors he had chosen to remain in Konumarr while he and the rest of the fleet were springing their trap on the Shark. He'd selected Synan Merimydion—a distant cousin from his own House—to lead them.

"Good. Very good. They are all fine warriors. You could not have chosen better. I would offer to stay behind myself, but I'm not comfortable being away from Alys for long."

"Give *Nima* my love, Uncle. And tell her about Gabriella. It will bring her joy to know her son will have a Siren for a wife."

"I will." Calivan reached out to clasp Dilys's arms, then dragged him into an embrace, thumping him affectionately on the back. "I am happy for you, Nephew. Dispatch these pirates quickly, so that you may return home to your mother with your magnificent new *liana*."

CHAPTER 18

"I still don't like this." Summer stood on the docks of Konumarr harbor and glowered up at the armored Calbernan Sealord standing beside her. "You came here to marry a weatherwitch because you wanted our help to deal with these pirates, and now you're going to sail off to confront them without our gifts to help you?"

Dilys smiled down at her. He always seemed to be smiling, damn him. If she didn't know better she'd say it was because he never took anything seriously. But she'd seen his face when his uncle had shared the list of Calbernan sailors from the missing vessels. People he knew, people under his protection—many of them—were presumed dead or sold into slavery. There'd been death in his eyes.

These pirates—whoever they were—had no idea of what they'd roused. No idea of what destruction they'd called down on their own heads when they set out to harm people under Dilys Merimydion's protection.

"You have the power to keep me from this fight, *moa kiri*," he told her. Sweet Halla, that smile of his was a weapon. Broad, dazzling white in his deeply bronzed face. "Just stake your claim. Make me yours, and I'll sail with you back to Calberna tomorrow alongside all the other *lianas* and *akuas*."

For the last two days, the married Sealords and their new families had been preparing to depart for Calberna.

Dilys and the rest of the unwed warriors had spent the time provisioning their ships and preparing for battle.

"You're just saying that because you know I won't do it. If I bound you to me five times over, you wouldn't let your men sail into this fight without you."

"Would I not?" His smile winked out. "Let's put that to the test. All joking aside. If you truly want me to stay, then claim me, Gabriella. Speak my Name and make me yours."

"Dilys . . ." Gods, what he did to her. When he spoke in that voice, when he looked at her that way—like she was Halla, and he was the poor soul locked outside its gates, begging to get in . . . "You know I won't do that. I—I can't." Summer couldn't afford to let herself be rushed into marriage. There was too much at stake. Her gifts were too dangerous, her control over them uncertain at best. One afternoon of controlling her gifts while recounting the most horrible day of her life did not constitute sufficient proof that she could risk releasing her emotions from a lifetime of fierce control.

"And I cannot let this challenge to my House go unanswered. Calberna cannot allow it." Dilys smoothed a hand across her hair. "At least give me your blessing before I go, Gabriella, since you won't give me your heart."

"You have it."

His lips curved with gentle amusement. "*Ono.* I don't mean words and kind thoughts. I ask for a Siren's blessing."

"I don't understand."

Taking her hands, he dropped gracefully to one knee before her, then cupped her hands around his face. "Bless me, *Sirena*. Before I head into battle, grant me the gift of your good wishes and whatever affection you bear me. If I am to die, let me die with that much at least."

The mere thought of Dilys perishing sent a jolt of panic ripping through her, followed by an instant, ferocious rejection. He couldn't . . . *die*. Not now. Not when she . . .

when she . . . The sudden swell of fierce emotion over-whelmed her. Heat suffused her. The Rose on her right wrist burned like a coal.

Dilys's fingers clamped tight around her wrists, clutched her hands to his face. His back arched, every muscle in his body went taut, and the tendons in his neck stood out like thick cables. He started to shake. A rattling groan spilled from his mouth.

Alarmed and horrified, she yanked her hands away.

The next thing she knew, she was free and standing six feet away from him, one hand pressed to her chest, breath heaving in and out of her lungs. Dilys had fallen forward, onto his hands and knees, and he was swaying, shaking his head drunkenly.

Then he began to laugh. The weak, breathless kind of laughter that came after surviving an unexpected brush with near death.

"Goddess, woman. Either you care for me a great deal more than you are willing to admit, or you *really* don't want me to die." He pushed himself up and sat on his heels, staring at her with golden eyes so bright it almost hurt to look at them.

"Did I hurt you?"

His eyebrows rose. "Hurt me? *Ono, moa kiri,* quite the contrary. But I think now I know what it feels like to be struck by lightning." He clambered to his feet and grabbed a nearby mooring post to steady himself. One hand still clinging to the post, he swept a low, wobbly bow. "Thank you, Gabriella. Your gift was great indeed." He dragged in a shaky breath and grinned. "Are you sure you don't want to claim me now?" He flung out his arms. "I am yours for the taking." He swayed woozily and had to grab the post again.

"Sit down before you fall down," Summer snapped.

He started laughing again and sat—or rather, collapsed—on the dock. "You are so bossy, *moa leia.* Has anyone ever told you that?"

Affronted, she put her hands on her hips. "They. Have. Not."

"I like bossy women." His eyes closed. His head lolled back. That smile stayed on his lips. "I like you, too. Very much. Come here." He waved for her to come closer.

She stayed where she was. "I don't want to come there. Are you *drunk*?"

"Only on your love." His lips parted in a grin. "Come here."

"No."

One eye peeled open. "Please." He waved again and held out a hand.

"Oh, for Halla's sake." She blew out a disgusted breath and walked towards him.

As soon as she was within reach, he grabbed her hand and gave a yank. With a shriek of surprise, she toppled her off her feet and into his lap. She struggled briefly, trying to get loose and back on her feet, but his arms were suspiciously strong, making her think his collapse was just an act.

"Let me up," she commanded, pushing against the hard, molded plate of his golden armor.

"No."

"This is undignified."

"Perhaps. The answer is still no." Her hair had come free of its pins. Brushing back a loose curl with his chin, he bent his head to nuzzle her neck. "You always smell so sweet."

She shivered as his tongue traced a line up her throat that his lips then followed with kisses. "Stop that."

"I don't want to."

"Dilys." She glanced around, blushing at the sight of all the Calbernans, Summerlanders, and Winterfolk watching them with open interest. "Everyone's looking at us. You're making a scene."

"Let them look. I want to kiss you, Gabriella. I want it so badly. But I vowed I wouldn't kiss you again until *you* kissed *me*." He pulled back to stare into her eyes. "Would you send me into battle without a last kiss from my love?"

She rolled her eyes. "How many women have you used *that* line on?"

"You're the first."

"I don't believe you. And I'm not your love."

"You are. The only love I'll ever have."

She blinked up at him, feeling her world tilt off balance. He was devastating to her equilibrium when he smiled, but he was even more devastating to it when he got all serious and intense and his voice took on that husky timbre that made every cell of her body leap to tingling life.

Then common sense reasserted itself.

"I told you before . . . you don't love me. You can't."

"I can and I do."

"No, I—"

He put a finger on her lips, silencing her.

"Siren though you are, you can't Command my heart." He traced the outline of her lips with a fingertip. "I do love you, Gabriella Aretta Rosadora Liliana Elaine Coruscate. And I will until the day I die."

Despite her doubts, that sounded like a binding vow.

"So, will you kiss me?"

She shook off whatever enchantment he was working on her and set her jaw. "No. Now let me up. Your men are waiting."

He closed his eyes and pressed his face against her hair for a second or two. Then he sighed and gave her a crooked smile. "You are a cruel, cruel woman, Summer Coruscate." He shifted his arm, planting a hand firmly beneath her bottom and gave her a shove that set her on her feet.

"Cheeky creature." She glowered at him for his familiarity, shook out her skirts, and set about repinning her fallen hair. But as she curled up her locks and shoved pins in place to hold them, she kept casting quick, troubled glances his way. What if he *did* die? For all his confidence and capabilities, he was still mortal. And these pirates had not only proven themselves both willing and able to kill Calbernans—they had a specific grudge against House Merimydion. Dilys would be sailing into battle with a target on his back.

He was on his feet and gave all signs of being completely recovered from his earlier disorientation. Her mouth curled in spite of herself. Idiot. He'd just pretended to be "drunk on her love" as an excuse to pull her into his lap and beg her for a kiss. She shouldn't find his antics amusing, but she did.

"*Alakua.*" Speaking the Sea Tongue word for "captain," one of the officers from Dilys's ship stopped beside him and clapped a fist to his armored chest. "Forgive me, *Alakua.* It is time." The other men had already boarded the ship. Dilys was the only member of the *Kracken*'s crew who had not.

"*Tey.* Thank you," Dilys said. To Summer, he offered a final, small smile. "This is good-bye, then. Time for me to take my leave of you."

"Yes." He had already taken leave of her family. Though Wynter, Khamsin, and Dilys's uncle had all said their good-byes at the palace, Summer had accompanied him to the docks to see him off. Spring and Autumn were further down the mile-long dock saying their farewells to Ari and Ryll and the other officers who'd danced attendance on them this summer.

"I will see you again when I return," Dilys told her. "You still owe me two weeks of courtship."

Kham and Wynter had agreed to let Dilys and his men continue the final days of courtship after they returned from dealing with the pirates. Assuming, of course, that they *did* return. Summer thought about Dilys's cousin, Fyerin, and his crew, all of whom had not survived their last encounter with these pirates. She clasped her hands together and squeezed her fingers tight.

"If you insist," she said.

"I do. I intend to hold you to every day of my contract." Dilys stood a little while longer, as if waiting for her to say or do something, then gave a wry smile and clapped a fist over his heart. In Sea Tongue, he said, "Until the seas bring me home to you, or we meet again in the presence of Numahao." And, with that, he turned and began walking up the gangplank.

Summer stood where she was. Her fingers squeezed tighter and tighter. Her jaw clenched. He was halfway up the gangplank. A few more steps, and he'd be aboard his ship. And then he'd be gone. Her hands started to shake. There was a strange buzzing in her ears. Everything faded except for the reality of Dilys walking up that gangplank . . . walking away . . .

"Dilys!" His name burst from her lips. "Wait!"

She didn't care that everyone was watching. She ran up the gangplank. As he turned to face her, she threw herself into his arms and slammed her mouth against his. She kissed him passionately, fervently, pouring everything she was into that kiss. Her arms wrapped around his neck. His arms pulled her tight against him. She kissed him, and it was . . . perfect.

When the kiss ended, Dilys lifted his hands to cup her face. He smiled, great, golden eyes gleaming. "Thank Numahao," he laughed softly. "It's a miracle." He kissed her again, long and deep, robbing her of breath. When he finally pulled away, she was dizzy. That made him laugh again, the sound rich and warm, and she realized that all he had to do was laugh, and her heart lightened.

"Be safe and don't do anything stupid," she told him sternly.

"You have my vow, *moa haleah*. I shall do no stupid thing."

"I mean it."

"As do I. Have you not just given me the greatest of all reasons to return to you safely?"

She rolled her eyes. "It was just a kiss."

"*Ono*, it was much more than that." He smiled and tenderly stroked the back of one knuckle down her cheek. "You just gave me hope."

Her throat tightened, and she had to blink against the sudden burning in her eyes. She turned her head to brush her lips across his caressing hand, then gave him a shove. "Go." Her voice came out rough, a little scratchy. "Your men are waiting." She hurried down the gangplank before she could give into the urge to throw herself back into his arms.

A few minutes later, the ships weighed anchor. The massive sails unfurled. Summer lifted a hand and summoned an easterly wind to speed them on their way. The sooner they were gone, the sooner they would return. Already her heart was aching at the thought of not seeing Dilys for weeks, possibly even months.

"I'm going to miss them," Autumn announced, staring after the departing ships. "They were such good company." She turned away. "I'm heading back to the palace. Do you two want to come with me?"

When Summer didn't answer, Spring said, "You go on. We'll head back in a while."

Autumn hesitated then stepped over to give Summer a hug. "He'll be all right, Gabi. Don't forget he fought the armies of a god and won. What's a few measly pirates compared to that?"

Gabriella nodded and somehow managed to shape her mouth in the form of a small smile. Autumn meant well, she knew. And Summer wasn't being particularly adept at hiding her worry.

"You care for him very much, don't you?" Spring murmured, after Autumn departed.

Summer watched Dilys's ship sail down the Llaskroner Fjord. "Much more than is wise."

"Do you love him?"

The ship rounded the bend and disappeared behind the

slope of the mountain. Summer sighed and turned to meet Viviana's softly searching gaze. "For all our sakes, I hope not." But she knew, even as she said it, it was already too late. That was her heart that had just sailed out of view. And if it didn't come back to her safe and sound, they were all in trouble.

As the remaining Calbernans completed their final preparations for departure, Calivan Merimydion summoned the ten warriors who would be remaining behind in Konumarr to guard Summer Coruscate.

"*Calbernari,*" he greeted as the ten joined him in his chambers. "Close the door, please."

Once the door was shut, Calivan veiled the room with not one but five layers of insulating water to capture all sound before it escaped the room. After making certain the veils were seamless and impenetrable, he turned to the assembled warriors.

"I have discovered how the Shark has managed to capture our warriors and drown them. He is using a very powerful spell, and at the request of the *Myerial,* I have spent the last several weeks devising a countermeasure. A protection rune that, with your permission, I will ink into your skin."

"You think the Shark will come here?" That came from Synan, the member of House Merimydion whom Dilys had left in charge. "Forgive me, Lord Chancellor, but aren't you expecting him to go for the wedding treasure?"

"I am, which is why Dilys and his men have already agreed to the procedure. But you ten will be protecting the future daughter of House Merimydion. Dilys insists that you be protected against enemy spells."

Synan gave a sharp nod of assent. "Of course, Lord Calivan. Whatever you and the *Myerielua* require."

"Excellent." Calivan withdrew a pot of specially formulated red ink from his bags, and used it to draw a circle of runes behind the right ear of each warrior. When he was done, he carefully repacked the pot of ink and the bespelled golden quill he'd used to apply it, then turned back to the gathered warriors and summoned his magic.

As the twin of Calberna's reigning queen, he had a more powerful command of *susirena* than most males, but even that advantage wouldn't have allowed him to overcome the natural resistance to mind control that all Calbernans possessed. Not, that is, without the spell he'd just inked upon these warriors' skin. That spell, taught to him long ago by Mur Balat, allowed him to bypass a Calbernan's natural defenses to plant commands in their minds with his magic. There were limitations to the spell. For instance, he couldn't Command a Calbernan to murder someone he would normally die to protect, but directives that didn't trigger those deep protective instincts were impossible for even the strongest bespelled warrior to refuse.

"From now until the day Dilys returns," he Commanded, "you will open a door on the southwest corner of the Sea Veil each evening after the sun sets, and you will leave that door open until sunrise. You will not patrol that section of the palace. Except for you, Synan." He turned to the young scion of House Merimydion. "You will stand watch each night at the southwest corner, and you will warn the men who come that they must silence the women and keep them silenced. The women know spells they can cast if they are allowed to speak. Do you understand?"

"*Tey,* Lord Chancellor," Synan confirmed in a monotone.

"Good. And each morning, all you men will remember that you patrolled the entire perimeter of the Veil, and that everything was secure and in order. You will not remember that these Commands were ever given to you. You will simply carry them out, and you will not remember having done so. You will not reveal nor remove the runes on your skin, nor will you remember that I placed them upon you. You will not see them upon yourself or each other, but if someone else draws the marks to your attention, you will remember that the runes are a protective spell against enemy magic that you received from an enchantress you met during your travels."

He paced around the room, stopped before each man to be sure his Commands had been imprinted and would be obeyed. When he was satisfied with the results, he released his power, and began speaking to the men in a normal voice.

"*Calbernari*, the security of the first Siren born since the Slaughter lies on your shoulders. My nephew hand-picked each one of you due to your dedication to Calberna and your unsurpassed abilities as warriors and Sealords of the Isles. Keep the *myerial myerinas* safe until your prince returns. If there is trouble, you will send word both to Dilys and to me immediately. Is that understood?"

"*Tey*, Lord Chancellor," the men confirmed.

"Excellent. Keep watch on the waters and stay alert, men."

"*Tey*, Lord Chancellor."

"You are dismissed. And thank you—each of you—for your dedicated service to the *Myerial*, and I rely on fine men like you to keep the Isles safe."

When they were gone, Calivan walked over to the wide, tall windows overlooking the palace gardens and the fjord beyond. The men who'd just left would die when Mur Balat sent his slavers to take the Seasons. A grievous loss. Each of the men came from fine families in strong Houses. But he was much more concerned about Dilys. Calivan hadn't anticipated that Alys's son would enter *liakapua* with one of the Seasons any more than he'd anticipated that Summer Coruscate would be a Siren. If Dilys did not survive losing his mate—and there was a good chance he wouldn't—Alys would suffer another devastating loss, but there was no help for it. Mur Balat's elixir would slow Alys's decline, while the advances Cali-van was making with magic-storing crystals would hopefully help reverse it. Calivan would be there, offering his unconditional love to help her over her grief. Also, contrary to what he'd told Dilys, if a Siren—even an *oulani* Siren—stepped foot on Calbernan shores, there would be many powerful voices demanding that Alys step down and pass the crown of Calberna to the one who wielded Numahao's greatest gift. Calivan, whose life was entirely dedicated to protecting and advancing his sister and her interests, wasn't about to let that happen.

So rather than shaking his resolve to aid Mur Balat, the truth about Summer Coruscate's astonishing gift cemented it.

Calivan glanced around the chamber where he'd been sleeping since his arrival. His belongings were already packed and loaded on the ship.

Time to head for home . . . and Alys.

Gabriella couldn't sleep.

Dilys had been gone four days now, and each one seemed an eternity. The nights were the worst. She'd become so used to spending her evenings with him, enjoying a peaceful stroll through the gardens, or a gorgeous sunset sail. So used to the thousands of small caresses that made her feel adored, the laughter that lightened her heart. Without that—without him—she could feel the tension and pressure building up again as her power pooled inside her.

She fell back on the practice of a lifetime, meditating to calm herself and strengthen her shields, adding layers to the internal wall that kept the monster caged.

The familiar mental chores were harder now, without Dilys there beside her. It was as if he had become her touchstone, replacing the little sapphire dolphin on her mother's charm bracelet. He centered her. For all that he loved driving her crazy—both with desire and with his constant teasing—his presence put the monster at peace.

Now he was gone, and the monster was no happier about it than Gabriella.

There was a noise outside her balcony. Gabriella narrowed her eyes. Even with Dilys gone, she still woke each morning to a balcony carpeted with her favorite fragrant flowers and no clue as to how they got there. Thinking to catch Dilys's cohort in the act, she crept over to the balcony doors and flung them open, crying, "Aha!"

But the man on her balcony wasn't anyone familiar. Not a Calbernan. Not a Winterman. Not a Summerlander either. He was, in fact, the most unsavory-looking man she'd ever clapped eyes on. Scarred, skinny, and swarthy-skinned, he was clad in a smelly, filthy amalgamation of patched, ill-fitting, and mismatched clothes that included a badly stained naval officer's jacket, an infantryman's black breeches, and what appeared to have once been an elegant gentleman's knee boots. The man caught sight of her and grinned, displaying a handful of blackened teeth and swollen red gums.

"Eren't ye a pretty one."

Gabriella stumbled back. Before she could scream to alert the guards, a hand clamped a coarse, pungent cloth over her mouth and nose, and a steely arm clamped round her waist, yanking her back against a second, much larger but equally smelly man.

Summer's eyes widened. She tried to struggle but her captor held her fast. She drew in a breath to scream but the pungent odor from the cloth filled her lungs and nostrils, carrying with it a strange, dizzying lethargy.

"That was easy," the man in front of her said.

She blinked, trying hard to focus. He was pulling something from a bag strapped to his hip. A coil of rope.

Summer drew another breath, tried to scream again. Tried to struggle. But she could not find her voice or make her limbs obey. Her ears began to ring. The lights from the garden below and the city across the fjord went fuzzy and haloed. The man holding her said something, but she couldn't make out the words.

The world went dark.

* * *

Wynter lay on his side, propped up on one elbow amidst the puddle of satin sheets, his ice-blue eyes focused intently on his wife's naked, swollen belly. One large hand splayed across the mound, resting feather light, as their unborn children shifted and moved about in their mother's womb.

"We could have twenty children, and I don't think I'd ever get tired of this," he said, his voice husky. Reverent.

Khamsin laughed, and one of the babies kicked hard, a strong pulse against Wynter's hand.

"Twenty? I love you, Winterman, but that's not going to happen. Not even close."

He glanced up then, his eyes bright and intent as they fixed on his wife's beloved face. "But think of all the fun we'd have trying." His voice dropped an octave and gained a soft, throaty growl that made her breath catch and her skin flush with sudden heat. He loved that about her. The passion she no longer even tried to hide. How easily he could rouse her desire with just a look, just a rumbling growl.

"You are so bad."

"That's why you love me so much."

Her lips curved in a sultry smile that made his body go hard and aching. "That's definitely part of it."

The hand on her belly slid up towards the single button that kept the edges of her silk robe fastened between her breasts. He popped it free with a flick of his fingers and brushed the silk aside to bare the beautiful satin-skinned mounds of her breasts.

Pregnancy had made those breasts much fuller than they'd been when they first wed. Her dusky nipples seemed larger and darker, too, and they were definitely much more sensitive than they had been. A fact that had provided them endless delight over the last months.

He thumbed one and reveled in her sharp gasp and the way she arched her back. He could spend a lifetime loving her. Ten lifetimes. An eternity.

"I adore you, *min ros*."

He bent to kiss her, to take those lush, full lips, the sweet warmth of her mouth, to taste the fire that had saved his frozen soul.

The sound of raised voices in the room outside their bedchamber made him freeze. A split second later, he leapt off the bed, flipped a sheet over Khamsin, snatched up his sword, and crossed the room in three ground-eating strides. He reached the door just as someone began rapping upon it, calling, "Your Grace!" in urgent tones.

Wynter flung the door open. "What's happened?"

The Steward of Konumarr stood beside Wyn's valet, a dozen White Guards behind him. "The princesses, my lord," he gasped, bending over to catch his breath. "The princesses are missing."

"What?" That sharp cry came from behind him.

Ice gathered in his eyes, while behind him he felt the electric snap in the air as his wife summoned her own deadly power.

CHAPTER 19

"Synan missed his check-in. That's two in a row."

Dilys turned from his position at the sterncastle rail to face his first mate, Kame Samatoa. It was eight in the morning. Synan had missed the three-o'clock check and now the seven as well, making it nine hours since his last communication.

One missed check-in could have been a dolphin pod interrupted or prevented from passing along the signal. Two in a row . . . that could only mean something was wrong.

And there was a sinking sensation in Dilys's stomach that told him what that something might be.

"Signal the fleet and come hard about. The Shark can have the treasure and choke on it—assuming he was even after it in the first place." More likely the thrice-damned *krillo* had baited a trap of his own, and Dilys had fallen right into it. "Set a course for Konumarr. And I want every seagift on this ship focused on the task of speeding us along."

"*Tey, Alakua.*" Aye, Captain. "Right away." Kame turned and began shouting orders.

The deck tilted beneath Dilys's feet as the *Kracken* circled sharply around and began heading north, back towards the Æsir Isles.

"Shall we send a signal back to Konumarr, *Alakua*?" asked Dilys's second mate.

"*Ono.* If there are unfriendly ears listening, I don't

want to alert them that we're on the way." Dilys stared grimly at the horizon ahead, the curvature of the world obvious as the Varyan ocean stretched as far as the eye could see. *Gabriella,* moa halea, *I pray I am mistaken and there is nothing wrong. But one way or another, know that I am coming for you, and that nothing will stop me from reaching your side.*

Summer woke to groggy, pain-filled darkness. For countless minutes, she lay conscious but uncomprehending, her drugged brain struggling to interpret the impressions gathered by her physical senses. Everything was black. She'd been blindfolded. She tried to raise her hand to remove the blindfold, but her arms were bound tight behind her back. There was a horrible taste in her mouth—not solely due to the disgusting cloth shoved in and tied in place—and her head was pounding.

She was on her side, laying on some sort of lumpy, swaying surface. The air smelled of salt, sweat, and that musty, moldy smell of a confined space not regularly aired out. The world was tilting and swaying in a rhythmic manner, and she could hear the creak of wood, the flap of fabric snapping in the wind, the shouts and movement of men overhead.

Shards of memory were slowly coming back to her.

She'd been kidnapped. Stolen from her room in Konumarr Palace. She'd been blindfolded, drugged, and trussed up like a roasted Harvest goose. And now she was on a ship, sailing gods only knew where. Far from the safety of Summerlea and Wintercraig, that much was certain. Far from the reach of Khamsin and Wynter's wrath. And if her captors possessed an iota of intelligence, far from Dilys as well.

Her body ached. She wasn't sure how long she'd been lying here, tied up and motionless, but the arm beneath her was numb and prickling. She tried to pull her hands

free of their bonds, but every attempt to wriggle free made
the cords cut into her skin, the knots completely ungiving.
Summer slid down the lumpy surface of her makeshift
prison bed and began using her bare feet to explore her
surroundings. Her toes made contact with a ribbed, verti-
cal surface. Wall? She moved her feet across it. Outrage
flared. No. Not a wall. They hadn't put her in a room but
in some sort of cage. Like an animal!

If she hadn't been gagged, she could have used Persuasion to command any guard within hearing distance to
release her, and then she could have taken over the ship,
one pirate at a time, but with her voice silenced, her options were limited.

This would have been the perfect time for some practical magical gift, like the ability to unravel binding ties or
send telepathic calls for help along with detailed information to help lead rescuers to her location. Or even something
as simple as the ability to slow her captors down. Dilys was
days away, but Wynter surely would have already sent a
rescue party after her. If she could slow the ship, it would
give her rescuers a chance to catch up.

Summer stilled.

She was on a ship at sea. She was in possession of a
weathergift. Storms at sea were no laughing matter. And
never was the threat of a storm at sea more troubling than
in the hottest months of the year, when the temperature
of the oceans reached their peak, and the air became a
volatile soup ready to explode with wild fury.

Gabriella wasn't Khamsin, able to summon a tempest on
a whim, but she was still the Season whose giftname was
Summer. She carried the fire of the Sun itself inside her.

The only problem was that, unlike Storm, whose magic
burst upon the world with every stray emotion, Gabriella
had spent most of her life suppressing the deadly fire inside
her. Afraid of losing control, she'd rarely used anything
but the smallest portion of her gifts to summon cooling

breezes and gentle rain to make summers pleasant rather than stultifying and to aid with the growing of bountiful crops.

Now, if she had any hope of slowing this ship, Summer needed more than a gentle breeze. She needed power enough to summon a strong headwind. Something with enough force to slow this magic-powered ship. That meant channeling more magic than she'd ever done on purpose.

That meant tapping the volcano.

She took a deep breath, pushing back her anger and fear over being kidnapped. Pushing back the anxious tension that coiled in her body like a hissing snake. *Stay calm, Gabriella. Stay in control. All you need is a little of what lives inside you. You want to summon a headwind, not a hurricane.*

When she was sure she'd released as much fear and tension as possible, Gabriella took another breath and reached inside herself to that hot, molten, fiery place that dwelled at her core. The one that lay hidden, trapped beneath so many layers of stony discipline and buffering calm. And there it was, the fuel at the heart of a flame. Sun bright. Sun hot.

The gift of Helos.

A portion of the god's power gifted to her, just as a portion of his power lay inside all who bore the red Rose. Those who—she now knew, thanks to Khamsin's discovery of Roland's sword—were the human descendants of Helos himself, through Roland, the son the god had conceived upon a mortal queen.

Helos, help me, she thought fervently. Her parched lips formed the words around the gag that silenced her.

And with deliberate calm, she peeled back the layers of control—the years of discipline and distance—that kept her power in check.

As she worked, she sent her senses outside herself, wafting out through the walls of her current prison, through the bowels of the ship, into the brisk, briny sea air. The sun was high in the sky, pulsing with light and power. So warm. Much warmer than it had been in Konumarr.

She could feel the great ocean of currents in the sky. Up rose the heated air. Down flowed the cooler air from the highest reaches. The rise and fall of the air generated a magnificent, endless dance of winds, energy stored in every molecule. And high above the dancing surface level winds roared the great invisible river that guided and pushed the lesser currents.

Summer reached out with her power, seeking a place ahead of the ship. Heating the sea and air with a controlled lash of power. Hot, moist air thrust up into the atmosphere. Cooler, denser air rushed into the void left behind. A gust of wind blew hard. The ship shuddered as the wind punched the sails and a large wave slapped the bow of the boat.

She fed more energy into the sea and the sky, drawing winds directly her way. Power crackled in the distance as the volatile air began to condense and clouds began to form. As she fed the storm, she tasted a familiar tang on the wind.

"Vivi?" Gabriella's garbled whisper came out little more than a muffled grunt of sound.

Spring's magic was there, in the sky with her own, adding more warmth to Gabriella's own, widening the circle of heated air and water. Helping her feed the storm.

Gabriella bit her lip, fear and love fighting inside her. If Spring was there in the sky, that meant she must be here on the boat, too. The kidnappers hadn't taken just Summer. They'd taken Viviana, too.

The ship lurched to one side as a powerful gust of wind struck hard. Gabriella cried out as the sudden roll of the ship lifted her body and threw her into the wall of the cage. Wood creaked and groaned. Men shouted above decks.

She grunted in pain as the righting of the ship smacked her facedown onto the lumpy, smelly pallet.

Summer was still struggling to roll over onto her back

when the door to her small prison slammed open. Heavy boots stomped across the wooden floor.

"Awake and causing mischief," a harsh, gravelly voice declared. "The captain is not amused."

There was the sound of the cage being opened. Then hard hands flipped her over with ease and a damp cloth covered her nose and gagged mouth. She tried to scream, tried to struggle, but the man was too strong for her to fight.

The familiar, pungent odor of whatever he'd poured on the cloth filled her nostrils. Her mind went lethargic, thoughts muzzy. The tension in her body faded. The effects of the powerful sedative slipped over her like a shroud.

Once more, everything went black.

"My future *liana* and her two sisters have been stolen, and you think I had something to do with it? Have you lost all reason?" Dilys glared at Wintercraig's king. Upon their return to Konumarr, Dilys and his men had been greeted by armed guards—not just guards on high alert due, but suspicious, angry, hostile guards. Dilys's men had been taken into custody, while Dilys himself had been escorted by a dozen armed and angry White Guards into the palace throne room, where both Wynter of the Craig and his queen were waiting.

"The princesses are missing and so are the men you left to 'guard' them," Atrialan shot back in a fearsome voice. "I'd say my reasoning is *farking* sound."

"Synan and his men were my strongest and most trusted warriors!" Dilys snarled. "If they are missing, it's because whoever took the *Myerialannas* killed my men and disposed of the bodies. There's no other possible explanation. Do you forget my men and I fought a god for the right to court the Seasons? What possible motive would we have for kidnapping the woman I plan to marry and her sisters?" Outrage, fury, and, yes, fear battered him, tearing away even the pretense of calm. Outrage that the Winter King would suspect a prince of Calberna of such perfidy. Fury that someone—anyone—dared kidnap his future *liana* and her sisters. And fear—icy, soul-consuming fear—at the thought of what the Seasons' abductors might do to them. Do to Gabriella.

If anyone touched his little honeyrose . . .

If they dared to hurt her . . .

Black, diamond-hard talons shot from his fingertips, ready to rend.

"What motive?" Wynter shot back. "I can think of several. Perhaps your courtship wasn't going as well as expected. Perhaps you decided the assurance of having three powerful weather witches in your control was more appealing than the possibility of winning one. Perhaps you decided you didn't like the bargain you struck last winter with my queen, so you broke it. You've certainly done that before."

Snow flurries swirled in the Winter King's eyes, and a distinct chill emanated from him. Uncowed, Dilys bared his teeth in a fierce snarl.

"I have only broken one contract in my life—and not without cause. As you well know. Or are you telling me now I should have left your queen to face the Ice King and his minions alone?"

Furious as he was, even Wynter of the Craig had to back down from that one. He did, but not gracefully. With a sharp oath and clenched fists, he turned away.

"If you didn't do this, then who did?"

"Release me, and I assure you I will find out."

Wynter merely curled his lip and said, "They came by sea, using fog to mask their movements. I've been down to the fjord. The air stinks of magic. Manipulating fog on the water is a seagift, is it not?"

Fog on the water was just an extension of the sea, water droplets suspended in the air. Calbernans could not affect the weather like the weathermages of Wintercraig and Summerlea, but manipulating fog . . . that, they could do.

"*Tey*, we can, but so can many others. In fact, if you cross the right palm with silver, you can buy such a spell on the black market." His chin lifted. He stared at Wynter of the Craig with unflinching eyes. "I am telling you, I did not do this thing. My men did not do this thing. But if these *krillos* who took the *Myerialannas* came by sea, then I am your best hope to hunt them down."

Wynter's lip curled again. "If you think for one second that I'd trust you to go after my wife's sisters, you are dreaming."

Dilys's temper flared. He subdued it with ruthless control. Fury would get him nowhere. Gabriella must come first.

He swept a hot, molten gaze over the cold, distrustful Wintermen lined up against him. Prideful, stubborn, suspicious idiots. They thought they could track a ship across open ocean. They would be wrong—especially if the ship in question belonged to the Shark. Without Dilys, without his men, Gabriella and her sisters were as good as lost. Before the Wintermen could do more than grab their weapons, he turned to their queen and dropped to his knee before her.

"I swear to you, Khamsin of the Storms, *Myerial* of Wintercraig and Summerlea, I swear to you on my life and the lives of my men and on the blood of *Myerial* Alysaldria I, my great and glorious mother, I swear to you I will find your sisters and bring them home or die trying. I swear it." He bowed his head, baring his neck to her in a sign of complete submission and vulnerability. "Give me my men and my ships, and let me hunt. Grant me this right, this honor. Lay your hands upon me and grant me the great gift of your trust. I will not betray you."

For one long, interminable minute, he thought she would refuse. His thoughts whirled. If she refused, what would he do? The Seasons—Gabriella—were out there, captured by gods only knew what manner of foul, corrupt soul. Dilys wanted to hunt with Khamsin's blessing in order to keep the peace between Wintercraig and Calberna, but if they tried to hold him—to stop him . . .

Someone—the Shark or some other rabid *krillo* of a pirate—had stolen Summer Coruscate. That someone—the vile coward!—had crept into her room, laid his foul hands upon her. Frightened her. That someone had stolen her from the safety of her home and her family and the Calbernan prince who had, in every way that mattered, already pledged his life and his heart to her.

That someone—and every living soul who had aided him—was going to die.

As would anyone who stood between Dilys Merimydion and his *liana*.

Khamsin had still not given him her answer.

He clung to his rage, using every ounce of the discipline he'd honed over a lifetime to keep it caged. But, gods, oh gods, it wanted free. It howled for release. Clamored for destruction.

It would be so easy. The sea was one of the most primal forces of the planet, and it would leap to Dilys's command. The sea would surround this city and swallow it whole—taking every living creature in the Llaskroner Fjord with it.

Only the certainty that Gabriella would never forgive him gave him the strength to keep that desire in check.

Gabriella . . . moa myerina *. . .* moa liana *. . . I will come for you. Whether they allow it or not, I will come for you.*

It would be better for all if they allowed it.

So he shed his pride like the useless skin it was and said, "Please, *Myerial* Khamsin." His voice shook, a testament to the power raging beneath his thin veneer of calm. "Send me with your blessing. Trust me to bring them back. I beg you." His claws dug into the stone floor.

At last, Khamsin gave him her reply. "Bring them back to me," she said, her voice low and thick. "Bring my sisters home."

She laid her hands upon his head. A shock shuddered through him. He lifted his head in stunned surprise, reaching for her wrists, holding her palms to his face as power—her power—poured into him.

Her eyes went silver, shining bright in the darkness of her face.

His back arched. What she gave him was like his mother's gift and Gabriella's, and yet so different. His mother's gift and Gabriella's felt like lava poured from the center of a volcano. This was crackling ropes of lightning called from the heart of some great storm.

It fed him and lashed him, roiling and clashing inside him, a tempest, angry and wild and deadly powerful.

Around him, the Wintermen yanked swords from scabbards and leapt towards him, shouting, "Release her, Merimydion!"

Ice crusted on his back. A roar, the enraged howl of a terrible beast, shook the room.

He felt them all—Wynter and his men—lunging towards him. The awareness was exactly like his sea sense, as if the air had turned to water and they were frenzied sharks darting in for the kill.

He released Khamsin's wrists and flung out his hands. His fingers splayed, and her power pulsed from his palms, rolling out from him like ripples in a pond. His attackers flew back, tossed away on that invisible wave.

They leapt back to their feet, and he crouched, snarling, prepared to destroy them.

"Stop!" Khamsin's voice lashed the room like a whip of lightning.

Dilys froze, panting. His body trembled with scarcely contained violence. The urge to kill was a red haze veiling his mind, but she who had given him this strange, electric power that roared through him had commanded him to stop.

"Dilys! Wynter! All of you! Stop it this instant! Put your weapons down. Now!"

Dilys was unarmed but not weaponless. With effort, he sheathed his claws and calmed the wild, mad, turbulent power boiling inside him.

As he did so, Wynter snatched Khamsin out of her chair and thrust her behind him, shielding her with his body. "Are you all right, *min ros*?" he asked in a harsh whisper. His eyes—now pure white from the deadly magic he had *not* tucked safely back away—remained fixed on Dilys.

"I'm fine," she assured him. Her slender brown hand stroked his arm in a calming caress. "It's all right, Wyn. I'm fine. He wasn't hurting me."

"Then perhaps he can explain"—Wynter's voice grew colder and more forceful—"what the *fark* he was doing?"

Dilys straightened from his crouch and forced his muscles to unclench. "She granted me her blessing to go after her sisters," he said. "And she shared with me her power so that I might use it to bring them home." He bowed respectfully in her direction, though she was still almost completely shielded by her husband. "My thanks, Khamsin of the Storms. Your gifts are powerful indeed. They will serve me well. I promise you I will find your sisters, and I will bring them home." To Wynter, he said, "Call off your guards and get out of my way."

"Wait just a frosted minute."

Dilys's temper snapped. His claws, which he had retracted, shot from his fingertips once more. "Enough! Every moment you delay, my *liana* and her sisters are at risk. Your queen has given me her trust and her blessing. I am going. I do not want war with Wintercraig, but war there will be if you do not get out of my way. Now, *MOVE*." The last word vibrated with Command.

In startled unison, every Winterman standing between Dilys and the door moved aside.

He rushed through the cleared path and out the door.

Behind him came the sound of swearing, then the clatter of boots on stone as Wynter and his White Guards gave chase.

"Merimydion! Damn it. Merimydion, you blue bastard, stop!"

Dilys paused at the door that led outside to the gardens. "No, I will not stop. I'm going to the fjord to make the sea give up its secrets, and then I'm going after Gabriella and her sisters. You release my men and tell them to meet me at our ships. We sail within the hour. I will not break my vow to your *liana*. But if it makes you feel more at ease, you may send men from your White Guard with me when we sail—up to a dozen per ship. I have seen them fight. They will not be a burden. Do not bother with your Ice Gaze and do not make further attempts to stop me. Neither will work. Your wife shared her gifts with me, and I will use them if I must."

The Winter King glared at him in a mixture of outrage, confusion, and fury. "What do you mean my wife shared her gifts with you? And what the *fark* did you do to us back there?"

Dilys tamped down the urge to strike out. The Winter King was wasting time Dilys did not have—time Gabriella and the Seasons did not have. "Free my men. Send them to my ships, along with what men you wish to accompany us." He hesitated, then to ensure that Wynter would leave him in peace, he surrendered the news that had come to him along with Khamsin Atrialan's power. "And tend to your *liana,* Atrialan. Your children have decided to be born now."

After a moment of shocked blustering, Wynter Atrialan barked out orders to free Dilys's men and dispatched several dozen White Guards to set sail with them. Then he fixed Dilys with a last hard look, his gaze sharp enough to cut glass.

"Do not fail us, Merimydion. Find the Seasons and bring them home."

Having won, Dilys decided he could spare a moment to be gracious. He inclined his head. "My men and I will track them to the farthest corners of Mystral if we must.

One way or another, Wynter of the Craig, we will bring your *liana*'s sisters home."

Wynter returned a curt nod, then spun on his heel and abandoned all pretense of calm to go racing back to his wife, his long legs making short work of the distance between them.

Just before Dilys ducked through the door to head down to the fjord, he saw the Winter King emerge from the room with his slight, very pregnant queen clutched in his arms. He was shouting for the royal healer, Tildavera Greenleaf.

Dilys turned away and headed for the fjord at a dead run. He ran for the same reason Wynter had run. Because his woman needed him.

No. No, that wasn't right. He didn't run for her need—although he would, without question. He ran for his own. Not because she needed him, but because he needed her. Because the slightest threat to her safety made his blood turn to ice and his heart pound so hard it nearly burst from his chest.

He didn't bother running all the way down to the water's edge. He dove from the garden terrace. For a long stretch of seconds, he soared, weightless, a diving seabird. Then his body pierced the sea like a sharp spear, and he was soaring again, but this time in the denser, still weightless world of the ocean.

Power roared up inside him. He pulsed it out. A beacon of awareness, of searching, that raced with electric speed from one tiny molecule of water to the next.

The pulse filled the breadth and width of the fjord in an instant then kept going.

As it went, he sent out a second, slower but stronger pulse of power.

If the first pulse had been the crack of an electric whip, a bolt of lightning leaping though the cells of the sea, this pulse was the rolling heave of some great colossus shrugging beneath the mantle of the earth. It rolled out of him like a tsunami, a wave of immense power shifting entire oceans as it went.

Every Calbernan was born with a seagift. All Calbernans could manipulate waves and currents to some extent. Even in the doldrums near the equator of Mystral, no Calbernan ship ever stalled, not even when the sea was still as glass and the sails hung dead-straight from the masts. Most Calbernan Houses could commune with one or more of the myriad species that dwelled in the oceans as well.

Dilys of House Merimydion could commune with them all.

Every creature, from the tiniest amoeba to the largest whale, to the wild, cold-blooded beast, the kracken, that great, deadly dragon of the sea that dwelled in the darkest abysses of the ocean.

As he floated, weightless, in the water of the fjord, sending his power out into the sea, the golden trident on Dilys's left wrist glowed sun bright.

"This is my mate," that second pulse called, carrying with it a vivid, sensory image of Gabriella that shared every sight, smell, sound, taste, and touch of her that Dilys knew. "Find her. Find the ones who took her. Show me the way."

Two hours later, Dilys stood at the helm of his ship, the *Kracken*, as it sailed out of Konumarr's harbor and down the Llaskroner Fjord towards open ocean. Ari's *Orca* and Ryll's *Narwhal* followed in his wake, along with the remaining three ships from Dilys's fleet.

He'd found his missing men—Synan and all nine others—at the bottom of Llaskroner Fjord, wrapped in sailcloth and weighted down with lead ballast. Dilys expected to find them drowned, their foreheads branded with the symbol of the Shark, but if they'd died at the hands of Dilys's greatest foe, the *krillo* hadn't had time for his usual torture. Instead, Synan and his men's throats had been slit and the right half of their faces, including their ears and a goodly portion of their scalps, had been sliced away. The grim finding helped put an end to any remaining suspicion that Dilys or his men were behind the abductions.

He'd also found a trail to follow. In response to his inquiries, the inhabitants of Llaskroner Fjord had shared with him images of a ship that had sailed into the harbor under cover of fog. The same ship had dumped the bodies of Dilys's men overboard as they departed. No doubt to cast suspicion for the abduction on Dilys and his men, a ploy that might have worked had not Dilys returned as soon as he had.

As it was, however, whomever had created the fog had been complacent in thinking Dilys was away from Konumarr, because while the fog prevented any pursuers from seeing or identifying the ship above the surface of the water, those precautions did not extend to the eyes below the water. And while most nonmammalian sea life didn't have particularly long memories or a particularly accurate sense of time, Dilys's swift return to Konumarr had enabled him to extract from the Llaskroner's many small, marine minds enough detail to piece together a reasonably specific description of the ship's keel. He'd sent that description out to pods of whales, seals, and dolphins and asked them to help him locate the ship he was seeking.

So far, none of the hunters had reported a live sighting of the ship, but he had received multiple reports of a mysterious, fast-moving fog bank that had traveled west across the Varyan several days ago.

Dilys had traded his *shuma,* belt, and bands for the Calbernan version of armor: the blue-green loincloth lined with rings of hardened steel; the protective chest, arm, and shin guards; and the thick leather belt that strapped two sheathed swords to his waist. His trident was belowdecks, hanging on the wall of his cabin along with his shield. The twelve White Guards Wynter had assigned to Dilys's ship were just coming back above decks after stowing their gear in the bunks below.

He regarded their plate-steel armor with distaste.

"You and your men should lose that armor," he told the Winterman, a commander of the White Guard named Klars Friis. "Plain furs are better than that."

"Oh?" Friis arched a white brow.

"*Tey*. If the ship goes down, my men and I can swim in our armor. You White Guards will drown in yours."

The Winterman paled a bit beneath his golden skin. "You expect this ship to sink?"

"Expect? No. But ships do on occasion sink—especially in battle. And given that whoever took the Seasons has powerful magic at their call"—it took powerful magic indeed to hide a ship on the water from Calbernan eyes— "you can be sure there will be a battle. A fierce one, I expect. Exchanging your armor for something that won't take you straight to the bottom of the ocean seems a wise precaution."

Friis blinked, then said gruffly, "I'll speak to my men."

Dilys nodded curtly. Off the port bow, a large blue-and-white whale leapt out of the water. Massive flippers slapped the air as the whale's body twisted. The creature slammed down on the surface of the water with a mighty splash.

Dilys turned the helm over to his second mate and walked to the port railing. He held a hand out over the sea. A spout of water rose up from the waves below and engulfed his hand, connecting him to the ocean and all the creatures in it.

Then he could hear the whale song repeating the tonal cries that had traveled through hundreds of miles of ocean from distant pods to the blueback whale that had just breached beside the *Kracken* to get Dilys's attention.

They had located the ship carrying the Seasons. It was already a thousand miles away. Whatever magic these pirates had at their call, it was damned powerful. Even among Calbernans, summoning an ocean current to speed a boat along that fast was a gift limited to those of royal blood.

Dilys closed his eyes and concentrated on the power stored inside his body—the bubbling, lava-hot sea- and weathergifts bestowed by Gabriella and the crackling electric storm gifts laid upon him by Khamsin Coruscate.

He channeled the seagifts into the ocean, reshaping the currents to his will. Spray misted over him, and the long ropes of his hair blew back from his face as the *Kracken* picked up speed.

The crackling energy of Khamsin's weathergift he called upon more cautiously. Her gift was wilder than his Gabriella's, and very powerful. He could feel it fighting for release, the energy whipping at him in frenetic arcs that set his temper on edge.

His admiration for Khamsin grew tenfold. How did she live with such a wild, fierce battle raging inside her every second of the day?

Dilys used every ounce of his training to keep that magic in check, loosening his hold just enough to let a few wild sparks leap out. The sails of his ship gusted, the canvases bulging as wind filled them.

The *Kracken* shot forward, cutting through the waves like a knife.

Behind him, riding the wind and current he was generating, the other ships of his fleet followed suit.

CHAPTER 20

Summer groaned as she roused to consciousness. Her head ached ferociously. Her mouth felt—ugh, best not think about what her mouth felt like. The disgusting gag was still in place. Her stomach was churning wildly. Whatever sleeping poison her captors had used on her, it didn't agree with her.

"Awake, are you, my pearl?" crooned a voice Summer didn't recognize. Foreign, accented, male. Eru, the common tongue, wasn't his first language. She tried to place the accent—some sort of western land—but her mind was too muzzy to properly identify it.

She considered keeping her eyes closed and pretending to sleep until a large hand slid with shocking brazenness up her leg, underneath her nightgown.

Her eyes flew open. She jerked away from the vile hand that dared to touch her.

No longer locked in some musty, smelly hold and no longer blindfolded, she was on a bed, in a ship's cabin. Her captor, his teeth a white slash grinning in a darkly bronzed face, watched her with unsettling black eyes.

"You are a soft, pretty little thing. Which Season are you?" That cold gaze roved over her with leisurely insolence before finally meeting her murderous, narrow-eyed glare. "Summer, I'd say, with those lovely blue eyes. Hmm?"

The man was tall, his dark skin weathered to a burnished teak. He wore his thick black hair in a simple queue and sported a neatly trimmed mustache and goatee. His clothes were impeccably neat and made from obviously expensive cloth. In fact, he might have passed for a wealthy nobleman in the right environment, but she would have feared him even then. There was a cold, predatory gleam in his dark eyes, a snake coldly sizing up its prey.

Whatever his plans for her, they weren't good.

And then he introduced himself. "Where are my manners? I am Mur Balat, purveyor of Mystral's finest and rarest goods."

Summer's stomach gave a sudden, queasy lurch. Her flesh went clammy, and her eyes went wide. Instinct had her rolling over, trying to raise up on her knees and lean over the side of the bed as her stomach spasmed.

Balat—Mystral's most infamous slaver—moved with unexpected swiftness, yanking free her gag and holding her head over an empty wooden pail as she was violently sick.

"Easy, my pearl. The *tzele* the men gave you to keep you docile has this effect on some. It will soon pass." His voice was gentle, crooning, almost soothing. As was the hand stroking the back of her neck.

Somehow that made him even more terrifying.

When she was finished, he wiped her face with a cool, moist cloth that smelled improbably of lemon and some exotic tropical scent she didn't recognize.

"Better?" He brushed a dark hand along the edges of her hairline, pushing back the limp curls. She flinched. He gave a small, good-natured chuckle. "I take it you've heard of me." The thought that she knew his name and feared him clearly gave him pleasure.

"P-plea—" Her abused throat closed up. She coughed— froze a moment when she thought she might be sick again—then swallowed painfully and forced the words out. Her voice was hoarse. "I am an Heir of the Rose, a princess of Summerlea. My brother-in-law is the Winter King . . . Whatever you are being paid for us, my family will pay double—triple—even more to get me and my sisters back." She tried to put a push of Persuasion in her voice, but her throat was too sore, and trying to focus enough to call her magic was like swimming through glue.

Balat regarded her with an unwavering gaze. "As a businessman, I'm normally quite open to a better offer, but in this case, as tempting as that sounds, my pearl, there's not enough money in the world to induce me to return you or your sisters to your family. You are simply far too valuable to me. Not, of course, in your current, filthy condition, but that's easily remedied." He clapped his hands and a door slid open on the side of the room, and three women entered carrying a basin, a large steaming ewer, and a basket filled with cloths and a variety of small bottles and containers. All three women were clad in pristine white skirts that were slit up to their thighs. Naked from the waist up, their blue-black skin was covered in a strangely beautiful, flowing design of gleaming silver symbols. Runes of some kind. Their hair was burgundy, their eyes peridot green, and each wore a silver collar around her throat.

"Clean her up," the man commanded. "And take care of this." His slippered foot nudged the pail beside the bed.

Wordlessly, one woman picked up the pail and carried it away while the other two approached Gabriella. Working in concert, they set the basin down on a small table beside the bed, filled it with steaming water from the ewer, and drizzled a thick blue liquid into the water. The third woman returned, and together, the three of them untied Summer's wrists, holding her firmly. She didn't resist them. The *tzele* hadn't fully worn off, but the infamous Mur Balat had made a vital mistake.

He'd put a daughter of the Sun in a room with windows. Uncovered windows. In broad daylight.

The sunlight was bright and warm and revitalizing. She could feel herself getting stronger, more lucid with each passing moment as the sun-born magic in her blood burned the remaining *tzele* out of her system.

"My sh-sisters," she murmured, the slurring only slightly exaggerated. Helos help her. That *tzele,* whatever it was, packed quite a punch. "Where are they? What have you done with them?" With effort, she managed to send a tentative tendril of power billowing outward, tasting the winds in an effort to locate Autumn and Spring.

"They are alive and unharmed, my pearl. Never fear. I pride myself on taking excellent care of all my treasures."

After removing the chafing hemp rope Gabriella's abductors had used to bind her wrists, the peridot-eyed women replaced it with loops of sturdily braided silk and pulled Gabriella's arms over her head, tying the rope to a post behind the headboard. Her ankles were next, but when it became clear the women intended to spread Gabriella's legs and tie each ankle to opposite bedposts, panic set in hard.

There was only one reason to tie her in such a manner. To make it easier for her abductors to rape her.

Summer's mind was still clouded with *tzele,* but that didn't matter. There was no way she was going to submit to rape without a fight. She began to struggle, bucking and kicking out.

"Get off me! Let go of me!" She tried to fill her voice with Persuasion, but her mind was still too blurred by drugs to muster the focus that power required.

Fire, however, was a different matter. Even though she'd spent her life hiding the true strength of all her magic gifts, Summer had the strongest affinity with the sun of all her sisters. When she called, all desperation and wild fear, the sun came roaring in response.

Summer gave a guttural cry as power pulsed through her, hot and fiery. Her Rose went white-hot, a searing ember against her skin. The ropes around her wrists burst into flame. The unlit oil lamps hanging from the ceiling burst into fire and shattered, sending flaming oil spraying across the cabin floor. The three slave women went flying, slamming into the walls and sliding down, hair singed, clothes smoldering. Every drop of moisture in the cabin evaporated, leaving the room so hot and parched, it hurt to breathe. Outside, the sea grew rough as storm clouds boiled across the sky, and the ship lurched sideways on a sudden gale-force wind.

Freed from her bonds, Summer lurched to her hands and knees, then nearly collapsed again. The remnant effects of the *tzele* had burned away in an instant, but the sheer force of what she'd just channeled left her dizzy.

Mur Balat took a step towards her. She drew a deep breath of the hot cabin air and focused on Balat—intending to scorch him to cinders—when her magic just . . . evaporated. One instant, her power was a palpable force inside her, the next it was as insubstantial as smoke—impossible to grasp, let alone wield.

A desperate, wrenching pain exploded inside her, as if her skin were being peeled from her body.

"Incredible!" Mur Balat exclaimed. He loomed over her, palms outstretched, eyes glowing furnace red. Rivers of glowing, golden light were flowing from her body into his, forming a shining halo around him. "Truly exquisite. One of the most delicious powers I've ever tasted. And nowhere near as insignificant as I was led to believe." He clucked his tongue against the roof of his mouth. "You, my pearl, have been hiding your gifts under a bushel."

She couldn't move, couldn't speak, couldn't scream. The three slave women gathered around her and, working quickly, tied her back up, hands above her head, legs spread and tied to the bedposts, and there was nothing she could do to stop them. When they were done, they hurried around the room, throwing sand on the fires she'd sparked.

Only once the fires were extinguished did the golden aura around Mur Balat begin to dim, then to blacken.

Then the now-shadowy aura sank into his flesh and was absorbed. His fiery red eyes went black once more. At last, Gabriella was free of whatever arcane hold he'd trapped her in, but she was so weakened she couldn't lift a hand or manage more than a whimpering protest as the three women cut away her nightgown and began to wash her with warm, scented water.

She tried reaching for her magic again, but nothing came to her call. Frantic, she pulled again, reaching deeper, and again

Balat had stolen her magic.

The slaver licked his lips and his gaze roved over her exposed body with open appreciation. "I must say, you are every bit as lovely as that magic of yours is delicious. Had I more time, I would gorge myself on you for hours. Alas, there is no time to indulge. I have an urgent task to attend to." He stroked a hand down the side of her face, ignoring her shuddering flinch. "Normally, after I've eaten someone's magic, they remain incapacitated and incapable of accessing their powers for days, but your sisters have already proven exceptional in their abilities to recover from my little indulgences. And therein lies my dilemma."

Sitting down on the edge of the bed, he skimmed a hand along the curve of her bare breast.

"I can't keep dosing you with *tzele*. You Seasons don't tolerate it well and the effects wear off too quickly. If I give you more, I run the risk of overdosing you—the results of which would be . . . well, unpleasant, to put it mildly. But as you have proven more than once, if given the opportunity, you'll use your magic to cause trouble. I must, therefore, employ a different method to control you until I return. Sadly, I don't think you'll like it very much." He squeezed her breast.

Terror and outrage combined gave her the strength to hiss, "Let me and my sisters go now. Let us go, and you may survive this. If you don't, Dilys Merimydion and

Wynter of the Craig will hunt you to the very ends of Mystral, and when they find you, they will destroy you."

Balat rose to his feet. "I wouldn't pin my hopes on that, my pearl. But if, by some miracle, they do manage to track this ship down, my friend here is more than capable of sinking any ship on the sea." He crossed the cabin and opened the door. A tall, dark massive figure filled the doorway. As the newcomer stepped out of the shadows of the doorway into the room, Summer felt the simultaneous blows of shock and dread as she realized Balat's "friend" was a Calbernan.

He wasn't one of the ones who'd come to Konumarr this summer. Of that, she was certain. This was a man who, once seen, you would never forget. He was tall, like all of his kind, his skin a deep, dark bronze. His chest and shoulders were broad and muscular, his build every bit as impressive as Dilys's. But where Dilys's and his men's *ulumi* were all iridescent blue, more than half of this man's tattoos had been inked in matte black, making it appear as if he were surrounded by swirling shadows.

"Your Royal Highness," Balat addressed Summer with courtly graciousness, "allow me to introduce you to the Shark."

Dilys smiled with grim satisfaction as a pod of dolphins sang out their news. Summer's kidnappers must either think themselves safe or whatever magic they'd used in Llaskroner Fjord had run out because the concealing fog surrounding their ship was gone. They were sailing full speed towards the coast of Frasia. The dolphins and porpoises riding the bow wave of the ship happily called out the details of the vessel as they swam, and Dilys's network of oceanic spies promptly fed those details back to him.

The name of the ship was the *Reaper*. A three-masted caravel, built for speed and maneuverability. The type of vessel favored by the pirates who had long-plagued the reefs and shallower waters of the Carmine Islands that bordered the southern Olemas Ocean and the western-most Varyan.

"Pirates?" Commander Friis echoed in disbelief when Dilys shared the news. "You honestly think a band of pirates would sail halfway round Mystral and invade Wintercraig to make off with the Winter King's sisters? No pirates I know of would ever dare such a thing."

"You weren't meant to think it was pirates," Dilys reminded him. "You were meant to think I did this—and you were all ready to believe just that, remember? It's only luck that I came back when I did and was able to prove what really happened." He cast a grim look in the direction of Frasia. "*Ono,* this was another targeted strike against House Merimydion."

"And the Seasons? What are they going to do with them?"

"I don't know. Use their weathergifts to take control of every ocean in Mystral. Or sell them. That's what I'm hoping for." He gave Friis a grim glance. "If they're being sold, their abductors will be more likely treat them gently, so as not to devalue the merchandise."

"So, what's the plan?" Friis asked.

"We catch up to them."

"And then?"

Dilys's battle fangs descended, and he gave Commander Friis a cold, savage smile. "Then I teach them the price of laying hands on a Calbernan's *liana.*"

After Friis left to check in on his men, Dilys folded his arms over the ship's railing and stared grimly out at the vast ocean.

If the *krillos* who'd stolen Gabriella and her sisters were minions of the Shark—and he was almost certain they were—then it was Dilys who'd brought that danger to the Seasons' door. Dilys who'd made Gabriella, Autumn, and Spring the targets of his enemy.

Even if the Shark wasn't behind the abduction, Dilys should have known that his much-celebrated bride-finding trip to the Æsir Isles would have drawn the attention of his enemies. Uncle Calivan was right. He should have brought extra ships and warriors who had not yet earned their *ulumi-lia* to provide security. He should have summoned an entire fleet the first moment he'd heard Gabriella's Siren's call. He should have gone to Wynter Atrialan, told him of the power Summer possessed, warned him that it would make her a target.

Most of all, he should never have left her side. Not for an instant. Not until she was his, and he was hers, and she had the whole of Calberna dedicated to ensuring her safety, her protection, and her happiness.

What was wrong with him? He was supposed to be a prince of Calberna, the spear that protected the ones he loved. And yet, when it was most important, when the ones he loved most were in danger, he somehow always seemed to come up short. His father, Nyamialine, Fyerin: all dead. His mother was Fading, and Dilys was helpless to stop it. Now, the woman he loved and her precious sisters had been taken . . .

If he couldn't stop that . . . if he couldn't save them . . .

His claws dug into the wooden ship's rail.

To the sky, on the air that somewhere Gabriella was breathing too, he whispered a solemn vow, "I am coming, *moa kiri*. No matter where they take you, no matter what happens, I will find you. Be strong, *moa halea,* and do whatever you must to stay alive."

To the sea he sent a prayer, "Numahao, guide me. Grant me speed and strength to find and free her. And, please, I beg you, watch over her until I do. Keep her safe from harm."

"I'll be back in a few hours," Balat told the Shark. "She's yours to enjoy until then. Don't leave any marks like you did on the other two, though. There won't be time to repair damages."

"No marks," the Shark agreed.

"And I expect her to be *fully intact* when I return. I promised to deliver a priceless royal virgin, not some randy pirate's leftovers."

The three collared slaves picked up their equipment and followed Balat out of the cabin, leaving Summer alone with the rogue Calbernan. The Shark crossed the room to sit on the bed beside her.

"Can you believe in this day and age, there are still so many men in the world who object to treading a path already cleared by others?" the Shark asked in a conversational tone. "As if a woman's greatest value lies with an insignificant bit of flesh. And they pay such exorbitant prices for the opportunity to be the first." He reached out and gently cupped her breast, ignoring her flinch as he circled the aureola with a featherlight touch. "It's good for my purse, of course, but does so interfere with my fun."

With shocking abruptness, he went from gently tracing her nipple to pinched it so hard she couldn't stop a pained cry. A cold, cruel smile curved his lips. "Not all my fun, of course." Holding her gaze, he leaned down and dragged his tongue over each of her breasts, laughing at her outraged gasp that ended as a snarl of vengeful fury.

Gabriella reached for her deadliest power, intending—for the first time in her life—to deliberately Shout a man to pieces, but the expected flood of terrifying magic never came. That firestorm of power that had swirled within her all her life was still. Mur Balat hadn't just eaten the magic she'd thrown at him. He'd somehow stifled her strongest and most devastating gift. What weak magic did rouse in answer to her call was drawn out of her the instant the Shark closed his mouth around her breast and suckled her in an obscene imitation of a lover's caress.

Gabriella gave a broken, gasp of realization.

This vile Calbernan was a magic eater, like Balat.

And she was helpless against him.

She was bound to this bed, stripped of her clothes, her dignity, and her ability to defend herself. For the first time

in her life, she was utterly vulnerable and completely defenseless. Tears welled in her eyes. She squeezed her eyes
shut tight and turned away. She couldn't stop the Shark
from violating her, but she didn't have to look at him while
he did. Her horror only seemed to feed his sick enjoyment.

"You all do that," he noted a moment later. "Close your
eyes. As if not seeing will make something not happen.
Your sister Autumn didn't at first. She glared at me the
whole time. Yes, just like that." He chuckled and released
one breast to give Summer's cheek a pat when she snapped
her eyes open and fixed him with an incinerating look.
The other hand continued to squeeze and stroke in a foul
mockery of a lover's touch. "I think she would have burned
me alive, if she could. I admired that about her. But even
she closed her eyes in the end."

The thought of him touching her sister, of breaking the
haughty pride Autumn wore as her mask to keep everyone but family at bay, made Summer ill. She would gladly
consign this despicable, gloating beast to the hottest fires
of Hel—and send him there herself, if she could. But she
wouldn't give him the satisfaction of her rage, as that only
fed more magic to him. Instead, she closed her eyes again
and concentrated on blocking as much of her power as she
could from him, trying desperately to shore up the fortress
that surrounded the fiery energy at her core. In that regard,
the lifetime she'd spent suppressing her powers served
her in good stead. Her internal barriers were strong, and
she had long ago learned how to separate her mind from
emotional triggers.

She couldn't keep everything from him, though. While
Balat had ripped her magic out of her without laying a
finger on her, the Shark drained it through physical contact. And he reveled in finding the most invasive, intimate,
obscene ways to take it, biting, licking, and sucking at her
flesh. Worse, with each lewd lave of his tongue and each
drawing pull of his disgusting mouth, it felt as if he stole
not only her magic but something else, something more

vital. He hollowed her out, bit by bit, leaving her dazed and despairing.

Hours later, Summer lay shivering convulsively, her wrists and ankles still bound, her head turned to one side. Heavy sheafs of her dark, unbound hair lay across her face, hiding red-rimmed eyes and the streaky remnants of tears she hadn't been able to stop herself from shedding. A broad, now-familiar hand stroked gently up one leg, and a fresh wave of convulsive shudders wracked her frame.

It had been hours since Mur Balat abandoned her to the Shark. Hours since Summer had braced herself for rape only to breathe a sigh of relief when Balat warned the Shark that he was not to damage her virginity. Hours in which the Shark had taught Gabriella just how naive that brief surge of relief had been.

Virgin, she still was, but there wasn't a single inch of her body that had not be used and degraded in every other way imaginable.

Her defiance was gone. The Shark had drained that from her long ago. He'd drained her of tears, too. He'd tormented her so long, so relentlessly, that now all she could do was lie there, dull-eyed, and endure, praying for her ordeal to end.

And then, at last, the cabin door opened.

"All right, I've let you indulge long enough," Balat chided as he swept into the cabin. "My girls have work to do. My buyers expect a level of perfection." The slaver stalked over to the bed and nudged the Shark with his foot. The three collared slave women stood several paces behind him, holding fresh wash water and an armful of what looked like strung pearls.

The Shark gave Summer a few, last leisurely licks before heaving a regretful sigh and rolling over to get off the bed. "You should reconsider your asking price, Balat," he said as he straightened to his full height. "There is much more to her than her reputation suggests." He trailed his fingers up and down her body. "I've barely had time to taste what she's made of, but it is much more rich and plentiful than we've been led to believe."

"I'm satisfied with the terms of sale. There's no need to quibble for a few more coins. Now, come away and let my women work."

Balat leaned over and cupped both hands behind Gabriella's head to lift her hair off her neck and fan it out above her head. Once her neck was bared, he slipped a cold metal collar around her throat. "Now this, Your Highness, is a containment collar tuned specifically to your very delicious, very unique magical signature."

The instant the collar's locking mechanism clicked shut, Summer's connection to the source of her magic splintered. The sunlight was still shining through the cabin windows and yet all she could feel was its mild warmth. No charge of magical energy. She slumped back against the bed and stared up at her captors in mute horror.

Mur Balat smiled. "Effective, isn't it? A little invention I designed to facilitate the storage, transport and sale of magically gifted merchandise." He turned away. "Come, my friend. You've had your fill."

"I know. There's just something about this one that keeps making me want one more taste." The Shark ran his fingers across Gabriella's eyelids, down the slope of her nose, and across her lips, then he leaned down and traced the same path his fingers had wandered with slow, languid sweeps of his tongue.

The Shark stood up with a sigh. "Barely even a whiff of anything tasty. Disappointing how well it works, isn't it? That's why I hate having to use Balat's collars instead of *tzele*. They never leave me much to snack on."

"Don't be so greedy," Balat chided. "You can glut yourself on the other two all the way to Trinipor. Now, come along, my girls cannot work with your great bulk lying all over my merchandise."

As Balat and the Shark headed for the cabin door,

Gabriella hissed after them. "He'll be coming for you, you know. Dilys will hunt you both to the farthest corners of Mystral, and when he finds you, he's going to kill you."

The Shark stopped, turned around, and laughed. "No one is coming, princess. We went to great pains to ensure that."

"You're wrong. You're on a ship in the ocean. No matter what you've done to hide your trail, you're mad to think Dilys won't track you down."

The Shark turned around, his hungry, predatory smile sharp as knives. "Oh, I hope he does. You have no idea how much I hope he does."

For the next several days, Gabriella was left to the ministrations of Balat's three peridot-eyed slaves. Every inch of her skin was scrubbed, waxed, plucked, polished and perfumed to perfection. Her hair was treated with hot oils, washed, trimmed, and brushed until it shone like satin. Her teeth were polished and bleached to pristine whiteness. Even the reddened marks on her neck, wrists and ankles where her bonds had chafed her skin were erased. The slaves, it turned out, had a gift of their own— one not hindered by their collars—for healing flesh and eradicating scars and blemishes. A useful talent for servants of a man who dealt in human merchandise.

She didn't feel her sisters' magic again, but considering that she couldn't feel her own, that didn't surprise her. No doubt they'd been drained and collared by Balat and his filthy companion before they'd gotten around to doing the same to her. She was, after all, widely acknowledged as the least powerful of the Seasons.

She hoped collaring and having their magic eaten was the worst that had befallen her fellow Seasons, but she remembered Balat ordering the Shark to leave no discernible mark on Summer because there wouldn't be time to erase it, as there would be with Autumn and Spring. She tried not to think of what sort of marks the Shark might be leaving on her sisters, or what he might be doing to create them.

Raging over their fate but being helpless to do anything about it made her despair, so she forced herself not to think about it. Despair would help none of them. Instead, Summer focused all her energy on observing her captors and testing the limits of her magic-inhibiting collar in the hopes of discerning some weakness she could exploit.

She was kept naked, collared, and bound. Partly, Summer surmised, that was to make it easier for Balat's slaves to work their relentless, beautifying efforts on her body, but she had no doubt her captors also meant to keep Summer feeling as vulnerable and defenseless as possible.

Every evening, after the three women finished their day's work, the Shark came to visit. He stayed with Gabriella throughout the night, subjecting her to intimacies no man but Dilys had ever been allowed—as well as some not even Dilys had claimed. But where she had received only wild, breathtaking pleasure from each caress, stroke and bite of Dilys's hands and mouth, the Shark's foul parody of lovemaking left her shaking in her skin, and not just from repugnance. There was something about what he did that stole from her more than her dignity and whatever magic Balat's collar had not completely suppressed. It was as if each touch of the Shark's loathsome hands, each stroke of his foul tongue, ate away at parts of *her*, not just her magic.

All the while, he whispered to her, "Did you let Dilys do this to you? Did you enjoy it? I know he did. One day soon, I'll make sure he knows just how well I've enjoyed you, too."

If she could have, she would have incinerated the Shark on the spot. She would have Shouted every cell in his body to liquid goo. And how ironic was that? All her life, she'd feared the dangerous magic she possessed, feared the harm she could do—had done—with it. She'd wanted to be free of her magic, so she wouldn't be able to hurt anyone. And now, thanks to Balat and his collar, she was.

And what did she want? To have every dangerous, lethal bit of her magic back so she could rain destruction and death upon her captors.

She tried to shut out the Shark's taunts, to show him no weakness and stay strong in the face of his abhorrent attentions. But the long, dark, torturous hours of the night ate away at her will as surely as his touch ate away at her magic, and by the time he left her each morning, she was a trembling wreck, flinching from the slightest touch, her face streaked with the tears she couldn't stop herself from shedding, her throat raw from the screams and pleading cries for mercy she couldn't keep trapped inside herself.

Begging was a victory she would rather die than give him, but as the days and interminable nights went on, she could feel even that will eroding.

The Shark could have dragged the magic out of her with any impersonal touch, but he chose to heap degradations upon her for his own sick entertainment and to exact some sort of twisted revenge on Dilys. She wasn't sure why the Shark hated Dilys, but whatever the reason, it was deeply personal, the hatred too obsessively virulent to be caused by anything else.

"Does Dilys know about this enchanting little freckle you have down here?" the Shark crooned one night. "I'm going to take great pleasure in describing it to him, letting him know how I've touched it, savored it in every possible way. How do you think he'll react to that? The great Dilys *farking* Merimydion once again proven incapable of protecting his women. Just as I've proven him incapable of protecting his House and his interests. Will he finally do the honorable thing and take his own life? A true prince of Calberna would."

That roused her fury enough to make her snap, "Dilys has ten times the honor in the tip of his little toe than you could ever hope have in your whole body. I don't know what kind of sick, shabby House you spawned from, but clearly, the gods must have held your mother in great disfavor to have saddled her with a piece of *garm shoto* like you for a son."

It wasn't the best insult she'd ever come up with—Autumn could no doubt have done much better—but it still did the trick.

The Shark's eyes blazed a bright, furious gold. He reared back and backhanded Gabriella hard across the face, snapping her head to one side, splitting her lip, and setting her cheek on fire.

"You will shut your mouth, or I'll shut it for you," he snarled.

She laughed and licked the blood off her lips. "The truth stings, doesn't it?" Scum-sucking pirate and magic eater he might be, but the Shark was still Calbernan enough to bear the same ferocious devotion to his mother as the rest of his countrymen did to theirs. She'd wondered about that.

And then, because she'd rather be beaten senseless than suffer one moment more of his filthy, degrading touch, she goaded him more. "Who's your father? Does your mother even know?"

Another slap. To the other cheek this time, and a much harder hit than the first. She rotated her jaw, feeling the twinge of protesting tendons as she did. Oh, yes, disrespecting his mother was most definitely an emotional trigger. He'd nearly dislocated her jaw with that blow.

"I'll take that as a no." She spat blood on the sheets of her bed. "Is that why you hate Dilys Merimydion? Because he's the son of a queen, while you're nothing more than some jealous, puffed-up get of a Houseless trollop?"

"*Oulani souss*! If you were a man, I would kill you for such slurs." The Shark's hand drew back, fingers curled into a fist.

Summer braced herself. This blow was going to hurt.

But before the Shark could swing, the door to the cabin burst open and Mur Balat stormed in shouting something in a language Gabriella didn't recognize. Her skin prickled with gooseflesh as magic rolled through the room.

The Shark froze in place, his fist clenched and drawn back, ready to strike.

"Idiot! Fool! Witless, undisciplined bastard! I told you not to mark her!" He marched forward and yanked the Shark's arm. The pirate's frozen body toppled over like a marble statue pushed off its base.

Gabriella watched in surprise, half expecting the Shark's arms to snap off when he hit the deck, just as a statue's would have done. Instead, whatever spell had frozen him seemed to wear off when his body and the deck made contact, and rather than breaking into pieces, he crumpled bonelessly against the dark wood and lay there, gasping for air.

"Get him out of here," Balat snarled, and two large men standing near the cabin door rushed in to grab the Shark by his arms and drag him out.

"Aneesh! Gulette! Ula!" Balat shouted. "Get in here and work your magic!" Mere seconds later, the three female slaves were ringed around Gabriella's bed, moving her face gently this way and that as they examined the swelling skin and developing bruises left by the Shark's blows. "You have less than twenty-four hours to repair the damage that idiot *pulan* has done. If she fights you, dose her with *tzele*. Whatever it takes to get the job done. She must be *perfect*. The buyer will balk if he finds a single blemish."

CHAPTER 21

Gabriella's buyer had arrived.

Gabriella, still a little woozy from being dosed with *tzele* for fighting Balat's slaves, swayed on unsteady legs as the hulking guard fastened a chain to her collar and led her like a prized dog up to the main deck of the ship. Mur Balat was greeting his guest, a noble-featured gentleman clad in robes of expensive silk brocades who had just rowed over, presumably from a ship anchored somewhere nearby, though she couldn't tell where that might be in this thick fog.

"Ah, here she is now," Balat announced as the guard walked Gabriella near. "What did I tell you, Your Excellency? Exquisite, is she not?"

Thanks to twenty-four hours of ice packs, magic, and gentle fingers that stroked her skin like fairy wings, the bruises on her face had all disappeared. Every inch of her had been washed, shampooed, curled, polished, and plucked, every tiny blemish banished, every pore shrunk to porcelain fineness, until she gleamed with the perfection of smooth, sun-warmed marble. She'd been draped in a long white sheet of fabric that was open on one side and held in place by a jeweled clasp at shoulder and hip. The drape was meant more to tantalize than cover, since as the fabric was so sheer that the dark coins of her nipples and the narrow, freshly-trimmed vee of black hair on her pubis were clearly visible. The slaves had rubbed her lips with scarlet paste, lined her eyes with black cosmetics, then curled her hair and pinned it up in a loose pile on the top of her head, fastening it in place with jeweled combs.

The buyer's eyes showed appreciation for their efforts as the servant holding Gabriella's leash walked her closer to the men.

The well-dressed man circled her once. "Very nice . . . but I would see all of her before we finalize our transaction. My lord is quite particular. He expects perfection."

"Of course." Balat clapped his hands, and one of the peridot-eyed women stepped forward to release the two clasps holding the drape in place. White, gauzy silk fluttered to the floor. Swift hands darted out to snatch the jeweled combs from her hair, and long black curls tumbled down to the top of her buttocks.

"Ah . . . beautiful." The man circled Gabriella again to view her from all sides. He put out a hand to touch her, then hesitated. "May I?" he asked Balat.

"Of course."

Gabriella tried to flinch back, but the hand on her collar held her firm. Thanks to the sunlight filtering through the fog, the last of the *tzele* was wearing off, taking with it the pleasant sense of being removed from her body. Now she was acutely aware of standing naked on the deck of Balat's ship, bare to the lascivious eyes of the crew. Rather than humiliating herself further by struggling against her captors, she lifted her chin and stared straight ahead. It wasn't as hard as it might have been. The hands of Balat's guest roved over her not with lust but with the impersonal touch of a buyer thoroughly examining a piece of merchandise.

She'd never really thought much about slavery. It wasn't a Summerlander custom, and the countries that practiced it were far from her small sphere of influence. But if she got out of this—no, *when* she got out of this—she was going to start a one-woman war against it. She might not succeed, but by Helos, she was going to do everything in her power to wipe slavery from the face of Mystral.

Starting with Mur Balat.

"A delight to all senses, just as you promised. She is certified pure?" Balat's client inquired as concluded his inspection.

"I confirmed it myself. You're welcome to verify, if you like."

"That won't be necessary. And her weathergifts?"

"Still intact. Just suppressed by the enchantments on the collar. Once your lord has broken her to service, I can adjust the enchantment for a small fee to keep her more dangerous gifts shackled while allowing her to access the ones he finds most beneficial."

"Excellent." The client reached into his robes and withdrew a small, wrapped parcel. "Here is the payment you requested."

Balat accepted the parcel, and with a hushed, almost reverent air, he unwrapped it to reveal a small, ragged book. His hands shook slightly as he opened the cover of the book and began ever so gently turning the pages.

Summer couldn't see very well from this angle, but the book appeared to be extremely old, the parchment pages curling at the edges. Balat turned to a page near the back of the book, placed a rune-etched gemstone atop in the center of an intricate drawing sketched on that page, and murmured a few words. The book glowed violet, and for an instant Gabriella could have sworn she saw a gleaming silver fountain rise up from what had appeared to be old but perfectly normal parchment pages. The image—and the violet glow—were gone in an instant, and Balat looked triumphant.

"I have been seeking this particular tome for a very long time," he murmured. "We do, indeed, have a deal. The Season known as Summer is yours." He snapped his fingers, and the servant holding Gabriella's collar handed her leash to Balat's client. "And may I say, Your Excellency, as always, it's been a pleasure doing business with you."

A few minutes later, Gabriella was aboard the small skiff, being rowed through the fog towards her buyer's ship. Her last sight of Mur Balat was of him striding towards the sterncastle, calling out for the crew to make sail. Then the ship that had been her prison—the ship still carrying her sisters—disappeared into the fog and was gone.

The *Reaper* had disappeared into a fog bank near the Vargan Banks, a series of wide underwater plateaus some two hundred miles off the easternmost coast of Frasia. But though the fog blinded the above-water eyes of the dolphins and whales, Dilys was still able to track their progress via his undersea spies.

When those eyes reported that the *Reaper* had weighed anchor in the fog bank, unease crawled up Dilys's spine. Fearing the reason for the strange behavior, he poured more magic into the sea, boosting the *Kracken*'s speed. Sure enough, less than three hours later, his eyes in the sea reported several other craft making their way towards the *Reaper*'s location, and he didn't need those eyes to tell him what was happening.

The meetings at sea were quick, taking less than half a day. When they were done, the fog finally began to dissipate. Five new ships were sailing in five different directions and the *Reaper* was speeding towards Frasia's port of Sau Lauro. There was no telling which of the five ships now carried Summer and her sisters. The *Reaper* had suspected they would be followed and had arranged countermeasures to protect against it.

Dilys sent Ari, Ryll, and the rest of his fleet after four of the fleeing ships, blasted a call along the seaways ordering the Calbernan navy to intercept the southern-bound fifth vessel, while he and his crew pursued the *Reaper*.

They were close enough now to use their seagifts against their quarry, pulling strong currents into the paths of the fleeing ships to slow them down. None of the five new ships had magic on their side, so by the end of the day, Ari, Ryll, and the rest of the fleet had captured their prey, all of which turned out to be decoys. There was no sign of the Seasons on any vessel, and even when Commanded with *susirena* to answer his questions truthfully, none of their crews knew anything about kidnapped princesses. They were merely local Frasian fishermen, making a little profit on the side by meeting the *Reaper* by the Vargan Banks to trade a few barrels of Allodyne brandy for several crates of lace and fine fabrics from the silk mills of Sheen.

That left the *Reaper,* whose magic-born speed was no match for the full force of Dilys's seagifts.

Dilys and his men boarded the pirate ship on a cresting wave, leaping from the foaming froth onto the deck, swords and tridents in hand, ready to rend. Their claws were out, their battle fangs down as they roared and attacked.

The fight was short, bloody, and merciless. No quarter given to the scum who had invaded Konumarr and stolen away Gabriella Coruscate and her two sisters.

The pirate's captain was still alive at the end of it. Pierced by Dilys's trident, sword hand hacked off at the wrist, and passed out from the pain, but still clinging to life.

"Bind that wrist," Dilys ordered one of his men. "I don't want him dying yet. The rest of you, get down below and start searching. Tear this ship apart if you must, but find them. I'll search the cabin of our fine captain here, myself." He lifted the corner of his lip, baring his fangs in a savage sneer.

Leaving the White Guards and his own men to search belowdecks, he leapt up the quarterdeck stairs and threw open the door to the captain's quarters. None of the Seasons were within, but as he ransacked the place, looking for clues, he discovered a strand of long, curling red hair and flecks of dried blood on the corner of a hanging lantern. His blood ran cold, then colder still when he found another hair of the same length and shade on the sheets of the captain's bunk.

Boiling with fear and fury, Dilys slammed out of the cabin and crossed the deck in long, ground-eating strides. The pirates had strewn sand across the planking to keep it from getting too slippery, and the grit clung to the bottoms of his feet, making raw, scraping sounds with each step.

He slapped the pinioned captain back to consciousness, then grabbed him by the throat, battle claws digging into the flesh on either side of the man's windpipe.

"Where are they?" he demanded, filling his voice with Command. "Where are the Seasons of Summerlea? Where is my *liana*, the princess Summer?"

The pirate, pale and clammy and dazed from his wounds, stared up at Dilys with dull eyes. Before he could answer, one of the Calbernans who'd gone to search belowdecks poked his head up through the hatch and waved.

"*Myerielua*! Down here!"

With a snarl, Dilys released the pirate captain and went below. The warrior who'd summoned him led him through the artillery deck, past the rows of ballistas tied into place, loaded and ready to fire. They hadn't gotten a single shot off. Dilys had battered the already wounded pirate vessel with a barrage of furious waves—several of which had carried he and his men aboard the Reaper. The *Kracken* had moved in for boarding after that, and Wynter Atrialan's White Guards had finished off any pirates that had escaped Dilys's men.

At the far end of the artillery deck were the officers' quarters. Small, private compartments built into the stern of the ship.

One of the rooms held a cloth-covered cage. Commander Friis was there, his golden skin and white hair spattered with blood, his pale blue eyes icy cold.

"There's another cage like this one the starboard side," Friis said. "One of my men is Snow Wolf clan. The scent is weak, but his nose tells him they were definitely here. Princess Summer in this one"—he gestured to the cage—"Princess Spring in the other. No sign of Princess Autumn."

"The captain of this floating *shoto* hole kept *Myerial-anna* Autumn in his cabin," Dilys said in a low voice.

A growl rumbled in the chests of the two Wintermen standing beside Friis.

"There's a bigger problem," the Wintercraig White Guard captain continued grimly. "My man says the Seasons haven't been on this ship in a while. Possibly not since a few days after they were taken. We've been tracking the wrong ship."

"*What?*" Dilys could feel himself shaking. He wanted to rip this ship to splinters. He wanted to slice its captain to ribbons, one tiny piece at a time, and drink the man's scream for days.

But first, he was going to get answers.

He returned to the main deck and hunkered down before the ship's wounded captain.

"We all came from the sea," Dilys told him in a pleasant voice. "Did you know that? And in us all, the sea remains. It's the water and salt in our flesh. It's the blood in our veins. And I am a prince of the sea. Of all seas." His eyes went cold and he seized the man's head in both hands. "Your blood answers to me."

The pirate grabbed Dilys's wrists. His pathetic, frightened whimpers turned to screams as his body started to convulse. The vessels in his eyes began to burst, turning the whites into pools of bloody red. And from his nose and ears, wet, glistening trails of scarlet trickled out.

"You will tell me, now," Dilys crooned. "You will tell me everything you did to her. You will tell me where she is, and who has her. You will tell me who hired you. You will tell me everything I want to know, and when you obey"—he smiled again, his fangs sharp as a shark's—"I will give you the death you'll be begging me for."

Fifteen minutes later, his body bathed in the remnants of a hot, scarlet mist, Dilys stalked to the stern of the ship to question the rest of the pirate ship crew. Commander Friis, pale beneath his scarlet-painted golden skin and wearing globs of bone and brain matter in his hair, followed close behind. The rest of the Wintermen who had been with Dilys while he questioned the pirate captain were still leaning over the side of the ship, puking their guts up.

He supposed it wasn't every day they saw a man's head literally explode.

But then, it wasn't every day Dilys Commanded every ounce of blood in a man's body to go rushing into his brain either.

The interrogation hadn't gone well.

The captain had possessed no useful information about what had happened to the Seasons. He remembered the Seasons being on board. He remembered keeping them drugged and compliant. As to Gabriella's fate, that was a blank.

The interrogation of the rest of the crew didn't go any better. No one—not one single man aboard the ship—remembered what had happened to the Seasons or how they had gotten off the ship.

"Gather your men," Dilys commanded Friis as he finished questioning the last of the pirates, a foul-mouthed bastard who'd tried to push Dilys into giving him a quick death by taunting him with all the depraved atrocities he and the crew had supposedly perpetrated upon the Seasons. "Get everyone back aboard the *Kracken*. We sail within the hour." He just had to find out where they would be sailing.

"And the *Reaper*?"

Dilys stood and, with one savage swipe of his clawed hand, ripped out the foul-mouthed pirate's throat, taking the lower half of his jaw with it.

"Leave her," he spat. He threw the bloody lump of flesh, cartilage, and bone over the side of the ship to the sharks circling below. "She'll sink soon enough. These worthless *krillos* can feed the fish—at least that will be one useful thing they've done with their miserable lives."

Friis glanced at the spurting arteries of the dying pirate's eviscerated throat, and he swallowed hard, visibly shaken by Dilys's savagery. "Yes, Your Grace."

"I am not Your Grace," Dilys corrected him brusquely. Stalking back to the mainmast, where the body of the pirate captain was still pinned, Dilys yanked his trident free. "I am *Myerielua*. Prince of the Sea." His men parted before him as he strode to the side of the *Reaper*. Trident in hand, he leapt to the top of the railing and dove into the waves below.

He swam down into the water until the cooling ocean depths drained the worst of the hot rage from his soul. He'd been duped from the start. Duped into taking all his men out of Konumarr and leaving Gabriella unprotected. Duped into following the *Reaper* long after the princesses had been taken off it. Duped again into wasting countless precious days and diverting his fleet from the Carmines to pursue decoy vessels and a ship full of pirates whose minds had been wiped of almost all useful information.

And he said "almost all" instead of "all," because everything about this kidnapping—the magical fog, the erasing of minds, and the fact that his sea-dwelling spies had reported no other vessels in the vicinity of the *Reaper* except the five decoys—were powerful clues on their own. He just hadn't been looking at them properly until now.

He'd been reacting. He'd been thinking with his heart, with his fear and his guilt. He'd been a boy again, shocked and shaken by devastating loss. Terrified of losing another person he loved—the one person who mattered even more than all the others. Terrified that he would fail her. That she would be taken from him like his father and Nyamialine and Fyerin.

This time, he set fear and guilt aside. He set all emotion—so strong a part of every Calbernan—aside. This time, when he sent out his call to his eyes in the water, he asked not for what they had seen, but what they had not seen.

Gabriella's kidnappers—or rather, the individuals who had hired the crew of the *Reaper* to abduct the Seasons—were masking themselves and had been from the start. Just as the crew of the *Reaper* had used magical fog to hide their presence in the Llaskroner Fjord, the real perpetrators of this crime had been hiding their presence as well, making themselves utterly invisible even to the creatures of the sea.

This time, when calling upon his ocean-borne spies, instead of asking about ships, Dilys asked about water displacement. Places where, in the absence of a tangible ship, the ocean should have been, but wasn't. Because he was now absolutely certain there was another ship. And even masked, that ship wasn't sailing on air.

As expected, the denizens of the sea came back with a barrage of information. He filtered through the memories and pieced together a tracking map. He'd been on the wrong track since leaving Konumarr. While he'd been heading west towards Frasia, the "invisible" ship had been heading southwest, towards the Carmines and the Olemas Ocean. And now, thanks to Dilys's rerouting Calberna's fleets to cut off the southern-bound decoy, the "invisible" ship had slipped past them and was well west of the Calbernan fleet, with nothing but open sea between it and a clean escape into the Olemas.

Dilys blasted a new order along the seaways, sending the coordinates of his quarry to the captains of the Calbernan fleet, and ordering every ship within five hundred miles to pursue them at the fastest possible speed. He and his four-vessel fleet did the same.

Dilys wasn't surprised when, within a few hours of his giving that order, the "invisible" ship sped up to a shocking—and very telling—twenty knots.

And that was when a possibility he'd begun to suspect solidified into near certainty.

The initial fog used to mask the kidnapping, the interference with the eyes of the sea, the control and erasing of *oulani* minds, the obvious interception of the message he'd sent to the Calbernan navy, and the incredible speed of the escaping ship: taken altogether, the clues led Dilys to believe that whoever was on that ship—whoever had orchestrated the abduction of the Seasons of Summerlea—wasn't using a series of expensive but purchasable magic spells, but rather a Calbernan seagift.

A *royal* Calbernan seagift.

As to who that person could be . . . well, the list was short enough to count on one hand. Someone had drawn Dilys and all the Calbernans out of Konumarr so the pirates could sail in, undetected, to steal the princesses. And by disposing of Dilys's men at the bottom of the deep fjord—a place no Winterfolk would ever have found them—the kidnappers had specifically intended to cast suspicion on House Merimydion—and Dilys, in particular, since it was his potential *lianas* who had been taken. Couple the clues together with a personal grudge against Dilys and an extraordinarily strong seagift, and one name, in particular, leapt to mind.

Inside his mind, Dilys's hand curled around that name like a fist, grinding its bones, crushing it to dust.

Nemuan.

The name of Gabriella's new captor was Solish Utua, and he was a purveyor of human treasures for the warlord king Minush Oroto. Solish, who was a eunuch, made it clear that his only interest in Summer was in training her to become the Most Favored Jewel in Minush's *cashima*—his pleasure palace—so that Solish could advance to a much more powerful position in his master's court.

"For the time being, you will be confined to this cabin. Once you have proven that you will not try anything foolish, you will be allowed to join me on deck to enjoy the fresh sea air while we continue your studies."

The possibility of earning a measure of freedom was too great a temptation to pass up, so Gabriella willingly donned the mask of a docile, obedient slave and dedicated herself to learning all Solish Utua could teach her about becoming Minush the Red's Most Favored Jewel.

The part wasn't too difficult to play, and Gabriella soon came to the conclusion that being bought by Solish Utua was probably the best stroke of luck of this entire ordeal. He didn't maul or molest her. He didn't starve or mistreat her. He didn't loose a magic eater on her several times a day. He even gave her real clothes—soft, loose-fitting gowns, and luxurious robes. So long as she remained docile and compliant, he treated her with an almost courtly courtesy, including answering the questions she asked about his acquaintance with Mur Balat (he'd known him ten years), the price he'd paid to purchase her (her weight in gold and diamonds, plus an ancient book reputed to be the grimoire of a famous, long-dead enchantress), and what he knew of Balat's plans for her sisters (nothing, although given the expense and risk of their kidnapping, he assumed Balat had extremely wealthy and powerful buyers lined up to purchase them).

Best of all, he made no attempt to block the strong, bright, sunlight that streamed through the large windows that lined the back of the cabin, utterly confident in the efficacy of Balat's inhibiting collar. Gabriella imagined that under most circumstances, that confidence would be well deserved, but as the ship sailed closer to Mystral's equator, Summer began to notice a familiar warmth gathering inside her. A warmth that grew stronger and more palpable with each passing day.

Magic—*her* magic—was coming back.

Elated, she made a point of sitting in direct sunlight as often as possible, trying to fan that warmth into hot flame. It was slow going. The collar prevented her from wielding her magic, but it also prevented her from actively calling the sun's energy to fill her magical stores. They *were*, however, filling. And without the Shark there to constantly drain her dry, there was soon a bright, hot pool of sun-fed power smoldering beneath her skin.

She also discovered that although the collar prevented her from accessing her power and wielding it, it didn't stop her emotions from affecting that power. Including—or rather, especially—that fierce, volatile fire at her core, that power she'd locked up so firmly that even Mur Balat and the Shark hadn't been able to reach it.

The one thing Solish Utua did not do was give Gabriella much time alone. He or one of his guards was at her side every hour of the day, and he slept in the same cabin, only a few scant feet away from the cot to which she was chained each night. A guard stood near the door, watching over her as Solish slept.

In those quiet hours each night, as Solish slept, Gabriella saturated her mind with thoughts of vengeance, rage, and violence. The more she did, the more she could feel the fiery inferno of the monster boiling madly inside her, trying to get out. The pressure inside her built and built and built until she passed out from the pain. And when she woke the next day, she soaked up as much sunlight as she could, so that each night, as Solish slept, she could push herself harder, and stoke the fires of her rage higher.

CHAPTER 22

"He's headed for the Kuinana," Kame, Dilys's first mate, pronounced grimly as Dilys and the Calbernan fleet closed in on the rapidly fleeing invisible ship.

"I know it." The Kuinana was a series of massive reef systems, riddled with caves, that surrounded the north-eastern tip of the Ardullan continent. A narrow, twisting channel though a forest of razor-sharp coral was the only navigable passage through the ocean-facing side of the reef.

For three days now, Dilys and the Calbernans had pursued the invisible ship across the Varyan into the warm, turquoise waters of the Sargassi Sea, closing the distance so rapidly that their prey had dropped their cloak of invisibility and concentrated all their magic on outrunning their pursuers. To sail that fast required tremendous magic, a fact that further solidified Dilys's suspicions that the Shark was his cousin Nemuan. But no matter how strong the Shark's magic, Dilys had the power gifted to him by both Gabriella and Khamsin of the Storms, and every ship in his fleet was speeding along on swift currents of both sea and air, all but flying across the ocean's surface.

The Shark's ship was clearly visible now, perhaps thirty miles ahead of the fleet.

"If he makes the Kuinana we lose him."

"I know that, too," Dilys said.

With its narrower lines, shallower keel, and smaller length, the Shark's ship would have no trouble navigating the passage through the reef, or sailing the long stretch of calm shallows that ran for two hundred miles between the reef and the Ardullan coast. Dilys's *Kracken* was at a distinct disadvantage. His ship was wider and longer, built for battle, not for racing through tight, curving passages lined with razor-sharp reefs.

"Who do we have near the south Kuinana Gate?"

Kame named two ships.

"Send them to block off his escape." Not that boxing the Shark's vessel behind the reefs would net him Nemuan. Even if Nemuan couldn't reach land and disappear into the dense jungles of Ardul, the reefs of the Kuinana were riddled with undersea caves. Nemuan and his entire crew could abandon ship, and Dilys might never catch them. It was much easier for Calbernans to hide themselves in the water than hide a ship . . . they could simply make the creatures around them think they were sharks or dolphins.

"I'll try to slow our quarry down before he enters the Kuinana, but if that doesn't work, you follow him in."

"Tey, moa Myerielua."

Dilys clapped a hand on Kame's shoulder. "If for some reason, I don't make it back, there's a message in my cabin for my Uncle Calivan. See that it gets to him immediately."

"Tey, moa Myerielua."

"Good." Although Dilys was almost certain it was Nemuan in that ship, he hadn't shared his suspicions with his crew. He wouldn't blacken the name of a Calbernan prince without incontrovertible proof. His crew wasn't stupid. They'd noted the same things Dilys had, but none of them would suspect a Calbernan of rank—especially a prince—of being the murderous pirate responsible for the deaths of so many of their own and the kidnapping of the three Seasons. They all thought the Shark was a powerful magician.

Leaving Kame at the wheel, Dilys dove over the side of the ship. The ocean here was as warm as bathwater. He let the clean, salty depths surround him, let his senses flow out.

With his pursuers closing in on him, Nemuan had dropped the invisibility enchantment on his ship. Either he was focusing all his efforts on maintaining his ship's high speed, or whatever spell he'd been using to mask his ship had run out. The now visible fleeing ship was not Nemuan's *Wave Dancer* but a different, unfamiliar vessel. Dilys didn't find that surprising. A prince of Calberna was hardly likely to commit grand treason in his own vessel.

Focusing on a fifty-mile swath between the swiftly cruising ship and the Kuinana reef, Dilys began pulsing fist after hammering fist of power into the sea. The ocean swelled up, then smacked down, swelled up, smacked down. Slowly, great waves formed, five foot, ten, twenty. Too high for Nemuan to risk a reef entrance through the Kuinana's treacherous northern gate. He would have to calm the seas before he could.

Calming the seas would take time.

Strong webs plumped between Dilys's fingers and toes. He gave a kick and speared through the waves swifter than a dolphin, continuing to send out those pulses of power before him as he went. Behind him, the *Kracken* and the rest of the fleet sailed on the same magic-fed current Dilys was using to propel himself.

As he swam, Dilys sent calls to every large sea creature within twenty miles of Nemuan's ship, ordering them to pursue the vessel and do everything in their power to slow it down.

It wasn't long before Nemuan's ship began to falter. Dilys's waves were churning the waters, disrupting currents and turning the entrance to the Kuinana into an impassible, frothing white explosion of huge, crashing waves. Whales and dolphins were harrying Nemuan's ship, slamming against the hull to slow its speed. Nemuan's crew had begun harpooning everything in sight, turning the sea around the ship bloodred.

The *Kracken* had caught up with him. Dilys rode a spout of water back aboard deck as he and the rest of his fleet closed in around the foundering vessel.

"It's over!" Dilys shouted, pitching his voice so that it could easily be heard by Nemuan's acute Calbernan ears despite the distance between them and the turbulence around his ship. "You have nowhere to go! Heave to and prepare to be boarded. Surrender the Seasons!"

Dilys calmed the waves and called off the attacking whales and dolphins as the Calbernan fleet closed in. The *Dancing Ray,* one of the shallowest-keeled vessels in his fleet, came abreast of the foundering ship and used grappling hooks to tether her in preparation for boarding.

Seconds later, there was a burst of powerful magic and the ship Dilys had chased halfway across Mystral exploded in a fiery ball, raining fire and molten shrapnel upon every ship in a two-hundred-yard radius.

For one stunned, horrifying moment, Dilys couldn't move, couldn't think, couldn't breathe. He could only stare in mute horror at the fiery inferno that had been Nemuan's ship. Then the shout of one of his crew brought him snapping back into himself.

"Gabriella!" Dilys howled her name and dove over the side of the *Kracken*. He pierced the water deeply and began swimming with desperate speed towards the burning wreckage.

The sea was aflame with a dreadful, unnatural fire. Heat scorched him when he surfaced, turned the tropical ocean's sparkling blue waters into a hellish red-orange sea when he dove. The shattered hulk of the pirate's ship lurched drunkenly on the fiery waves.

"Gabriella!" he howled her name again. Shrieked it.

There were men in the water, screaming and thrashing as the unquenchable flames stuck to their bodies and consumed their flesh. The water did not douse the flames. Instead, it almost seemed to feed them. Some of the burning men were pirates. But most were Calbernans. Sailors from the *Dancing Ray*.

He ignored them, his mind utterly possessed by the driving need to find Gabriella and save her. Nothing else mattered. Not even the agony of friends and countrymen burning alive in a flaming sea.

He summoned a spout of water, riding it up towards the broken shards of the ship's deck. "Gabriella!" he shouted. The whole craft was engulfed in fire, hardly an inch untouched by the hungry, licking flames. No place for him to stand, no way for him to search for her. Even here, beside the burning craft, the heat was so intense the water beneath his feet was starting to boil. Some distant part of his mind was aware that his own flesh was cooking, both from the scalding water bubbling at his feet and the fiery inferno burning before him, but he kept searching, kept screaming her name.

Something exploded nearby. Flaming debris struck his arm and flung him backwards into the sea. He surfaced quickly, aware of a sharp, searing bite of heat and pain. His arm was on fire, and his swift plunge into the sea hadn't doused it. He slapped at the flames with a bare hand, and cursed as fire spread to his palm as well. The fire was like burning pitch. Sticking to whatever touched it. He slammed his burning hand back over the burning patch on his arm and held fast, hoping to smother what water couldn't put out.

"Gabriella!" he screamed again. And despite the futility of it, too mad with horror and grief to admit that no one could still be alive in the fiery inferno, he swam again towards the burning wreckage.

"Dilys!" A small rowboat bobbed in the waves nearby. Ari was leaning over the prow. The tang of sea magic surrounded the small craft and its crew, a fresh scent wafting beneath the acrid smoke and stench of burning wood and flesh. They were using their seagifts to keep the fire away from their boat. "Get the Hel out of there!"

He ignored them and dove towards the fiery, sinking ship. Even here, beneath the waves, the fire was still burning, the heat overwhelming, but Dilys dove towards the shattered, sinking, flame-engulfed ship, no thought in his mind except the need to get to Gabriella. To find her. To save her.

Hands grabbed him from behind. He fought them, claws out, fangs snapping, roaring and thrashing, screaming her name. "*Gabriella! Gabriella!*"

Something hard smashed into the side of his head.

Before the magical, inextinguishable fire finally died away, seven ships of the Calbernan fleet were sunk. More than two hundred Calbernans were dead or missing. The *Kracken* and its crew had nearly been among them, until they discovered they could smother the fire by dousing it with sand.

After the flames finally died down, the grim business of recovering bodies began. Ari and Ryll had arrived with the rest of the fleet, and they, too, joined in the search. They searched throughout the rest of the day and on into the night, using the glow of their *ulumi* and the senses of the ocean's denizens to penetrate the darkness of the night-shrouded ocean.

A few hours before dawn, the Calbernans searching the wreckage made a chilling discovery: the remains of two women burned beyond recognition and torn apart so violently by the explosion, it was hard to identify all the pieces. But two parts were easy to distinguish. One was an arm, the other a charred, ravaged bit of once delicate skin—both bearing the distinctive raised birthmark shaped like a rose.

They had found the Seasons of Summerlea.

"No." Bereft, hollowed out as if his heart and every organ in his body had been ripped from his chest, Dilys stared at the gruesome remains, all that was left of two daughters of the Summer King. He refused to believe the truth before his eyes. "It isn't her. She isn't dead. She can't be. I would know if she were dead!" But would he? She'd never claimed him. Their bond wasn't complete.

"Dilys." Bleak-eyed, wan beneath his sun-bronzed Calbernan skin, Ari started to reach for Dilys's shoulder, only to let his hand fall away. There could be no condolence, no assuaging of grief. Not for this.

Helpless to lessen their cousin's pain, both Ari and Ryll regarded him with agonizing sympathy.

"It isn't her," Dilys said again. "It can't be her." Numahao could not be so cruel. To take not one but two *lianas* from a man in one lifetime. To strip him of all those closest to his heart. Surely not.

But the raised rose birthmarks on those charred bits of flesh made a mockery of his protests.

Numahao *could* be so cruel. He was living proof of that.

"Why? *Why*?" His voice was hoarse, shredding as the words scraped through a too tight throat. His claws dug deep furrows into the planking of the *Kracken*'s deck. "I couldn't save my father. I couldn't save Nyamialine. I couldn't keep Fyerin safe. And now G-Gabr—" His voice broke. He couldn't say her name. Couldn't add it to the list of his beloved dead.

And suddenly it was all too much. His grief too great to be borne.

Whatever it was, whatever the reason that his existence brought death and sorrow to the ones he loved, it must end now. And he understood why every unmarried adult male in House Merimynos had committed *kepu* when Siavaluana and Sianna had perished. Not for shame of being unable to protect their precious, adored women. Not to avoid burdening their House with too many sons. It was grief. Pain so deep, so unendurable, that ripping their own hearts from their chests was the only solace left to them, the only escape from the unquenchable, writhing agony of their loss.

Without Gabriella, there could be no Dilys. He could not live in a world where she didn't.

He didn't even want to try.

His claws sprang forth. Howling her name on a roar of anguish, Dilys drove his hand towards his own sternum with bone-shattering force.

Night had fallen, and Gabriella was once again pouring violent emotion into the cauldron of her captive magic. This time, the pain of what she was doing was worse than ever before. The monster was wild, furious, desperate to break free. It shrieked and raged inside her, turning her shackled magic into a volatile inferno that threatened to tear her apart. Despite her determination to keep quiet so as to avoid rousing suspicion, a low moan rattled in her throat.

Her collar vibrated against her neck. She didn't think anything of it at first, but as she continued to push herself and her pained whimpers became cries she muffled against her arm, the vibration in her collar increased as well.

Then came a snap, like a bubble popping against her skin. Shards of agony pierced her brain, and everything went black.

When she woke, the sky was still dark, the sun still several hours from rising, but for the first time since she'd been collared, she could feel a hairline crack in the barrier standing between herself and her magic. It was so small as to be almost imperceptible, but to a weatherwitch who'd been cut off from her gift for weeks, that hairline fracture might as well have been as wide as a canyon.

She opened her eyes and glanced around the cabin. Solish was sleeping. The guard at the door was playing a game of cards to pass the time, the lantern beside him burning dimly so as not to disturb the viceroy's sleep.

Gabriella fixed her gaze on the guard and for the first

time in weeks tried to put Persuasion in her voice as she whispered, "You are very tired. Your eyes are so heavy. You can't keep them open."

A few seconds later, the guard yawned and his head began to nod forward.

It was working!

Emboldened by her success, she pushed a little more. "You have to sleep. Your whole body is so weary. You cannot stay awake another minute. You have to close your eyes and sleep now, and you will not wake up until dawn, no matter what you hear."

The guard's head slumped forward, chin resting on his chest, and she heard the rumble of soft snoring.

Elated, Gabriella reached for her magic, calling for its vast power to flood into the collar around her neck, hoping to burn it out. The collar went red-hot. Her flesh went hotter still. The Rose on her wrist was a glowing ember. The pain of it was terrible, as if she were burning alive from the inside out.

Either she must have made some sort of sound or the smell of the scorching linens around her must have dragged Solish Utua out of his sleep, because he sat up in the bed, took one look at Summer, whose whole body was now glowing with the fire trapped inside her, and screamed, "*Tzele*! Bring the *tzele*!"

The door to the cabin slammed open. Three hulking brutes came rushing towards her.

All she could think was, *No!* She wasn't going to let them touch her. She wasn't going to let them drug her. She wasn't going to be held against her will. Not now. Not ever again.

And every ounce of violent, volatile, enraged emotion, every second of pain, anguish, and humiliation she'd suffered since her kidnapping, every tear she'd shed, every prayer for salvation and strength, every single powerful emotion that she'd ever known, she poured into the bubbling cauldron of her magic's heart.

And then she Shouted: "*NO!*"

And the collar cracked open wide.

And the magic she'd spent a lifetime caging burst free.

"*NO!*" she Shouted again. Time slowed, each instant stretching out, bringing every tiny detail into sharp focus. She watched the men rushing towards her turn into twin pyres of flame and ash. The man who'd bought her from Mur Balat met the same fate. Then the ship—Gabriella's floating prison, sailing her towards the barbarian who thought he could own a Season of Summerlea—bowed under tremendous force, wood bending, charring, then splintering outward into an explosion of a million shattered, flaming pieces.

Sound travels fast over water.

Gabriella's Shout—the scream of a Siren—traveled faster than any natural sound on Mystral. It raced across the Varyan. Shattered every window on the Calbernan Isles and every window for hundreds of miles along the eastern coast of Ardul. In its wake, dragged along by the great force of that scream, raced a massive wave, a *tsunami* speeding out from the floating pile of burning flotsam that had been an unwise warlord's ship.

Every Calbernan in the Isles—every Calbernan sailing the Varyan—heard that Shout.

Hundreds of miles away, aboard the *Kracken*, Dilys heard that Shout.

With it came the searing harpoon to his heart . . . not the death blow of his own clawed hand but sudden, savage joy as his *ulumi* blazed to blinding life.

"*Gabriella!*" he roared. He leapt to his feet. "Helmsman! Weigh anchor! Set a course for the source of that Shout!"

The command was unneeded. The ship's crew were already scrambling in the rigging, pulling up the anchor and preparing to set sail.

"She's alive." He turned to Ari and Ryll. "She's alive!"

He laughed, knuckling at the tears streaming from the corners of his eyes. His cousins clapped him on the shoulder and dragged him close for hugs.

"You should take Ryll and the rest of the fleet with you to get your Siren," Ari said. "My crew and I will stay here to finish the recovery efforts. We still have missing men, and families back home who will want to know we did everything possible to bring their sons home."

"*Tey*, of course." Dilys could hardly process. The wild upheaval of emotion had left him dazed. He hugged Ari close once more. "Thank you, Ari. Stay safe."

"Always." Ari jumped to the top of the ship's rail and dove into the sea.

It occurred to Gabriella as she was treading water amidst the shredded, smoldering debris of what had been Solish Utua's ship that Shouting her only means of transport to pieces might not have been the most brilliant move on her part. She'd left no piece of the vessel larger than the palm of her hand, which meant there wasn't even anything big enough to use for floatation, and she was alone in the middle of a vast, empty ocean.

She knew essentially where she was. Now that she was free of the collar, the location of the sun told her that. South of the equator, east of the continent of Ardul, and several hundred miles southwest of the Calbernan Isles. There was no land within swimming distance.

Perhaps half an hour after her Shout, she saw several dark fins cut the surface of the water nearby. At first she thought they were sharks drawn by whatever blood had been spilled by the shipload of sailors she'd just Shouted to pieces, and her heart started to pound. Her magic roared up instantly, without even a call, ready—almost hungry—to Shout away the ocean predators if they came closer. Before she could unleash it, inquisitive dolphin faces popped up, and the air filled with the sounds of high-pitched chirps and squeals. Several of the creatures began leaping into the air, arching and twirling about before diving back into the ocean with a splash. They ringed around her, chattering and chirping, and it became clear they meant no harm, that they meant, in fact to keep her company, and possibly to protect her. An hour after the dolphins arrived, a handful of swimming Calbernans arrived, too.

"*Sirena.*"

The sight of the unfamiliar men, with their gleaming gold eyes and sharp, fully extended white fangs set her nerves on edge. The swimmers were more likely Calbernan merchants or fishermen than villains in league with the Shark, but she wasn't ready to take chances.

"Stay away from me!" Without the collar or her own internal barriers to restrain her magic, her Persuasion cracked like a whip. "Don't come any closer!"

To a man, they jerked back as if she'd struck them. The confusion and surprise was plain on their faces, but not a single one swam any nearer.

"*Sirena,*" said the one who'd first spoken to her. "We heard your call. We've come to answer it."

"What's your name?" one of them asked.

"Where are you from?" queried another.

"Do you know Dilys Merimydion?" The Calbernans were speaking Sea Tongue, so she asked her question in Eru, hoping to keep an advantage in case they turned out to be an unfriendly bunch. "Can you get a message to him? Please, I need to find Dilys Merimydion. Di-lys Meri-myd-ion." She enunciated each syllable slowly and distinctly, the way people did when they didn't think you spoke their language.

"My friends, look at her," a fourth Calbernan muttered. "She is *oulani*. How can she be the Siren we heard?"

The first man gave the fourth a disgusted glance. "Don't be an idiot, Mahelon. The call led us here—all of us and all of them as well—" He gestured to the wide ocean all around them, where Gabriella could now see more than a dozen ships speeding quickly her way. "Besides, can you not see she is the one the prince has been searching for?" Turning to Summer, the first man smiled. The smile was much more charming and much less threatening with his long battle fangs retracted. In Eru, he said, "*Sirena,* I am called Amanu Susa. My family lives not far from Cali Kai Meri, the family isle of House Merimydion. My younger brother served on the *Kracken.* The *Myerielua* attended his wedding earlier this year. Let us escort you to Calberna, and we will send word to him. Please, *Sirena,*" he added when she did not immediately jump on his offer of escort. "You were on the sea when you Shouted. Most of the Varyan will have heard you by now—or very soon—which may include those who stole you from your lands. You will be safer in the Isles. Let us take you there."

"Where is your boat?" she asked, more to stall for time than because of any genuine curiosity. "You must have a boat? Surely you didn't swim all this way from Calberna?"

Amanu laughed, and the sound was every bit as charming as the good-natured laughter of every other non-Shark Calbernan she'd met. "Our ship is there—" He pointed to one of the fishing vessels heading their way.

The absurdity of her reluctance struck her. Who was she kidding? Of course she was going with them. What else was she going to say? No, leave me floating here alone in the ocean to drown or be eaten by sharks? "Very well," she agreed with as much regal dignity as she could muster. "I would be honored to accept your escort to Calberna."

"Wonderful!" Amanu issued a sharp whistle.

Gabriella gave a startled cry as two dolphins popped up on either side of her.

"Hold on to their dorsal fins, *Sirena.* They will swim you to our ship. Hold on tight. Ready?"

At her nod, Amanu whistled again, and the pair of dolphins flanking Gabriella took off. She gave a small, startled yelp of surprise and tightened her grip as the dolphins dragged her swiftly through the ocean towards the approaching fishing vessel. The Calbernans and the other dolphins followed alongside, leaping through the waves like flying fish.

It didn't take long to reach Amanu Susa's fishing boat, and they lifted her onto the deck by way of a magic-borne spout of water. Strong, bronzed hands were there to steady her as her feet touched the deck.

"*Sirena,*" the fishermen murmured, their expressions and their voices filled with awe that bordered on reverence.

Dilys had told her about the Sirens, about the terrible blow their loss had been to Calberna, but the truth of that loss hadn't fully registered until now, this moment, as she stood on the rocking deck of a simple Calbernan fishing vessel, surrounded by the near-worshipful faces of these Calbernans. Had the goddess Numahao herself stepped down from Halla to tread upon this very deck, these men couldn't have been more amazed or reverent. Her fear that Amanu and his men might be in league with the Shark evaporated in the face of their awe.

"Send word to the *Myerial,* and to the *Myerielua* as well," Amanu said to one of the other men aboard. "Tell them the crew of the *Blue Pearl* has found the *Sirena,* and we are bringing her home to the Isles."

CHAPTER 23

About fifty miles south of the shores of the westernmost Calbernan Isles, a familiar ship crested the horizon. Flying the colors of Calberna and House Merimydion, Dilys's flagship, the *Kracken*, was speeding across the deep, blue Varyan Ocean, on a direct course for the fishing boat carrying Gabriella, which was now accompanied by a fleet that had grown to more than two hundred vessels.

Aboard the *Blue Pearl*, Gabriella was beset by equal parts exhilaration, relief, and dread as she watched the *Kracken* draw near. Relief that Dilys was unharmed. Exhilaration that she would see him again after the last long weeks of torment and horror. And dread for the same reason.

Her stomach tied itself in knots, and her hands gripped the *Blue Pearl*'s railing so tightly her knuckles turned white. Her heart was slamming against her chest wall.

The *Kracken* was still easily a mile out when one of the Calbernans aboard leapt from the bow into the sea. She knew who it was long before she tasted the salty tang of his sea magic or saw the streak of blue light spearing through the water. Dilys, his *ulumi* glowing bright, swam towards her faster than even his magic-powered ship could sail. Moments later, he rose on a wave of water like a young god of the seas. He leapt from wave to deck with one lithe, agile movement to stand before her, so tall, so strong, and—even though his face was drawn to the point of gauntness and there were dark rings beneath his eyes—so beautiful her heart nearly broke to look upon him.

"Gabriella." There were tears in his voice, tremors in the hands that reached for her, then stopped, as if fearing she was a figment of his imagination.

She knew that feeling. She'd dreamed of him while in the clutches of the Shark and Mur Balat, tasted the bitterness of despair when she woke from the dream to find him nowhere in sight and the wooden walls of her floating prison still about her.

Then his arms were around her, solid and real, and it was his skin pressed against hers, soft, supple, so very warm, his scent filling her nostrils, a mix of aromas unique to him. And every part of her shuddered with joy and relief and . . . and love. Yes, love. Helos help her.

"Dilys, I—" Her throat closed up, tears threatening. She battled them back, afraid to let them fall for fear of not being able to stop crying once she started. It wouldn't do to fall so completely to pieces in front of an audience. Nor was it safe. These fishermen had come to her aid. The last thing she wanted was for some inadvertent, emotion-fed burst of power to cause any of them harm. Her barriers were gone . . . blasted out of existence by that Shout that had torn through her collar and disintegrated Solish Utua's ship. The fishermen aboard the *Blue Pearl* had been so awed by her they bordered on reverent, making it easy to hold herself in check around them, but with Dilys here, her fragile facade of calm had no chance of standing firm.

Dilys kept his arms around her, stroking her back and murmuring soft, soothing words against her ear. "It's all right, *moa kiri*. It's going to be all right. You're safe now. I will never let anything happen to you ever again." And even though she knew that "safe" was a word that could never again be applied to her in any context, the sound of his voice, the strength of his arms wrapped around her gave her a measure of comfort.

She clung to him, drawing strength from his closeness. Enough, at least, to help her keep her composure until the emotions bubbling madly inside her began to subside.

When she was relatively calm again, she started to pull away from Dilys, but he slid an arm around her, tucking her against his side, and turned to Amanu and his crew. "*Calbernari,* you have my deepest thanks. I will always be in your debt for coming to my *liana*'s aid. And I will personally dower every one of your unwed sons in thanks for the great service you have provided House Merimydion and Calberna. If any of you ever need anything—anything at all—do not hesitate to ask. If it is within my power, I will see it done. Which one of you is the captain of this vessel?"

Amanu Susa stepped forward and bowed low before his prince. "I am, *moa Myerielua.*"

"Susa? There was a Manelo Susa who served aboard the *Kracken.*"

"My younger brother, *Myerielua.*"

"A good man. I attended his wedding before leaving for Konumarr this summer."

Amanu beamed. "You did, my prince. My family was greatly honored."

"Captain Susa, make a list of your crew and their families and send it to me at Merimydia Oa Nu. So long as I live, your families will always be welcomed by mine."

Gabriella watched how quickly and completely the crew of the *Blue Pearl* fell under Dilys's spell. He was so easy with them, so naturally and effortlessly charming. And so sincere. That was the real root of his near-magical charm. He genuinely cared, genuinely took an interest in their lives. And not just because they were Calbernan. He'd been the same in Konumarr, to the Summerlanders and Winterfolk.

That was the difference between herself and Dilys. The face she had always shown the world was a lie, a mask she'd worn since childhood. Dilys's goodness, on the other hand, was the real thing. People loved him because he deserved it, not because he showed them a lie meant to manipulate them into loving him.

The *Kracken* had furled its sails and was drifting alongside the *Blue Pearl* now. Beaming Calbernans filled the riggings and lined the side of the ship, their smiles wide and dazzling, their joy so thick in the air each breath was a dizzying rush.

"*Myerialanna* Summer!" they called out, and, "*Sirena!*"

Their welcome washed over her, but instead of revitalizing her, their happiness and warm welcome began to sting her raw senses like nettles.

They all believed the lie of who and what she was. They didn't know. None of them. Not even Dilys truly understood. How could they? She hadn't truly understood either, until the Shark had laid his filthy hands upon her, and every thought in her mind turned to bloody, violent vengeance. A good person—one who was truly good at heart—didn't relish the thought of turning her aggressor's brain into soup, didn't dream of crushing every bone in his body, one at a time, and drinking his agonized screams like a fine wine.

Even now, though she was safe, free, and reunited with the man she loved, all she could think of was going after the Shark and Mur Balat, tracking them down, slaughtering them in the worst, bloodiest way possible. Helos help her, even the urgent, heartfelt need to rescue her sisters was secondary to the ferocious lust for vengeance that writhed inside her.

With a wave of his hand, Dilys summoned a spout of blue water from the sea. He swept Gabriella into his arms, said, "Hang on, *moa kiri*," and jumped onto the crest of the wave. It carried them up into the air, rising swiftly to the higher deck of the *Kracken*.

When they landed and Dilys set her on her feet, she stepped away quickly, out of his reach. She felt the instant, startled flare of concern, the wounded surprise, quickly stifled. She ignored both, plastering on her usual smiling mask as she girded herself to greet the members of his crew and assure them she was well and unharmed. More lies, from the princess of lies. They believed her without question, of course. Dilys didn't. He knew something was wrong. The whole time she stood there, greeting the crew and the Winterfolk who had sailed with them in search of her, his concerned gaze kept darting back to her again and again.

"I'm very tired," she told him softly when the reunions were done. "And I need a bath. Might I have one?" She'd bathed the day the fishermen had rescued her from the sea, but it hadn't been enough, not nearly enough, to wash the taint of the Shark from her flesh or make her feel clean again.

"Of course you can have a bath. Whatever you desire, *moa haleah,* so shall I provide." He called to one of the crew, issuing the command to have a tub and fresh, hot water brought to his cabin.

"The water doesn't need to be heated. I can do that myself." She smiled wanly and held up her wrist, where her Rose was a dark, warm red against her skin. It hadn't cooled since her barriers had broken.

He walked her to his cabin, where his men were already setting up the large copper tub and hauling in buckets of fresh water from their stores. Since, per Summer's request, the water didn't need to be heated, it only took a few minutes for the crew to ready her bath, laying out a washcloth, a jar of soap, and what appeared to be several neatly folded bedsheets.

"We don't have bath towels aboard," Dilys told her. "They aren't something Calbernans need, but the sheets should work almost as well."

"It will be fine, thank you."

"There are clean *shumas* in my dresser that you can use when you're done. I'm sorry. I don't have robes or gowns. I'll put a call out to the merchant vessels in the vicinity."

"It's fine. I can just wash what I have on and have you dry it for me when I'm done. It's what Amanu did after fishing me out of the sea." They were being so polite to each other, so stilted.

"If that is your wish." He started for the door, then stopped just as he reached it. "Gabriella . . ."

"What?"

He regarded her from the doorway, a rare look of indecision on his face, but then he shook his head. "Never mind. Have your bath, *moa haleah*. We will speak when you're done." He left, closing the door behind him with a soft click.

Gabriella's fingers curled into fists. She thrust them into the cool water in the copper tub. She'd hurt him. He'd felt her withdrawal as clearly as she'd felt the wound it dealt him. She would hurt him even more once he realized that her kidnapping had left her more resolved than ever not to marry him. Everything she'd feared and fought against her whole life had come to pass.

She regarded the now-steaming water in the tub, gallons and gallons of water that she'd heated to near boiling without even thinking about it.

To free herself from slavery, she'd freed the monster.

There would be no caging it ever again.

"What's wrong, Dilys?" Ryll asked. "You do not look like a happy *akua*-to-be, just reunited with the love of his life."

The *Kracken* was under sail again, its course set for Calberna. Ryll had left his own ship to join his cousin on the *Kracken*.

"I wish I knew. She isn't speaking to me."

"She needs to."

"I know." Pain held within, unshared, festered. "She's bathing now. When she's done, we will talk. I'll know better how to help her once we do."

"Do you think they—" Ryll broke off, looking shame-faced.

Dilys's mouth thinned. "Do I think they raped her? I don't know. Possibly not. Virginity is highly prized by those who would pay to have a princess stolen from her home. But if she was, we will get through it. Whatever she needs, so shall I provide."

"And whatever you need, so shall I provide," Ryll vowed, his voice rich with compassion, "and Ari, too, once he's done at the Kuinana."

"I know." Dilys laid a hand on his cousin's shoulder. "And I thank you. You are my brothers in every way that matters."

"Is there anything we can do for you now—or for her?"

"No, I—" Dilys started to refused, then broke off. "Wait. Actually, there is one thing. You're handy with a needle, aren't you?"

A knock sounded on the cabin door, making Gabriella jump.

"Just a minute!" She was still in the tub, where she'd been for over an hour, and the water was just as hot as it had been when she started. She'd had to add more water, in fact, to replace what had steamed away.

Not that the bath had truly helped. She'd all but boiled herself and scrubbed her skin raw, but she still didn't feel clean.

She climbed out of the copper tub, snatched up one of the sheets Dilys had left for her, and wrapped it around herself before calling, "Enter."

The latch lifted. Dilys stepped into the room and closed the door behind him. He was carrying a small parcel. "Ryll and several of my crew made you a few things to wear while you were bathing. I'll just set them here. You don't have to wear them if you don't like." He handed her the parcel and watched while she opened it.

The first item Gabriella pulled out of the parcel was a robe sewn from white silk. The second was a sleeveless gown in a beautiful shade of sea green, the skirt slit up the side to reveal a pristine white underskirt. Strands of large, perfect pearls hung in graceful arcs at the waist. There was another, simpler gown, too, blue and sleeveless, that laced up in the front.

"It's beautiful, beautiful—they're beautiful."

"The crew considered donating their *shumas* for the cloth, but one of the merchant vessels nearby offered some of the fabric in their hold instead."

"Please, thank them for me. The merchant ship as well as your own crew."

He nodded and eyed the still-steaming copper tub. "Are you done with your bath?"

"Yes."

"Then why don't you try the dress on, in case it needs alteration, while I take care of the bathwater." He gestured to a screened alcove in the corner of the cabin.

Gabriella picked up the simple blue gown and headed for the alcove. As she dressed behind the screen, she could hear Dilys moving around in the cabin. A month ago, she would never have changed clothes with Dilys in the same room, no matter how many screens stood between them, but there was something about being chained naked to a bed and subjected to countless indignities for days on end that had stripped away every last vestige of virginal modesty.

She pulled off the damp sheet, flung it over the top of the screen, and dropped the gown over her head, not surprised to find it a perfect fit. The gown had a modest scooped neckline and full skirts. She laced up the bodice and exited the alcove in time to see Dilys drawing the bathwater out of the tub and sending it out the window with a wave of his hand.

"That's a convenient trick," Gabriella noted. She rubbed one of the sheets over her hair until her curls were damp dry.

"*Tey.* There are a thousand and one practical uses for

my gifts. That is number two-hundred thirty-three. The tub, I'll have to physically carry out." He smiled a little.

She didn't smile back. Turning away, she picked up the hairbrush Dilys had left out for her, and sat down at his mirrored dressing table to begin pulling the brush through the wet tangles of her hair.

"Gabriella . . ." Dilys watched her in the mirror with eyes as careful as his tone. "Are you angry at me?"

The hand pulling the brush through her hair went still. The question honestly shocked her. "Why would I be angry at you?"

"Because I should have been there to stop them from taking you and your sisters."

"Dilys, I was taken from my bedroom at Konumarr Palace. If I was going to be angry at anyone for allowing that to happen, I'd be angry at the palace guards. Or Wynter, for that matter, since he's the king and was in the city at the time. But I'm not. It wasn't their fault. It certainly wasn't yours."

"You've been acting strangely since we boarded the *Kracken*."

She laughed a little without humor. "Have I? I suppose I have." She winced as the brush caught on a tangle in her hair. Grabbing a chunk of hair above the tangle, she started to attack it with the brush, but Dilys made a sound of protest and took a step towards her.

She froze. Completely.

Dilys froze, too. His hands came up, palms open and facing her. "I was just going to offer to brush out that tangle before you rip out half your hair."

She watched him warily, trying to still the rapid beat of her heart. "I'm sorry. I'm still a little jumpy."

"Don't apologize. Not to me. Not to anyone. I just wish I could have found you sooner . . . could have been there to stop it in the first place."

"I know. I just . . . I don't want to be touched right now."

"Gabriella, the people who took you, did they—"

"The Shark and Mur Balat," she interrupted. "That's who took me. Mur Balat is a slaver—"

"I know who Mur Balat is." His voice had gone hard, cold, his body stiff. "I suspected the Shark was involved. I even suspected Balat and the Shark had a mutual understanding not to interfere in each other's enterprises. But I didn't think the two of them were working together, and I definitely didn't think Balat would be stupid enough to declare war on Calberna and the Winter King."

"I don't think Mur Balat meant you to know he was involved, but I don't think he was concerned about the possibility either. If you or Wynter came after him with magic, you'd lose."

"What do you mean?"

"I mean I tried to use my magic against him, and it was a mistake. It was almost as if he . . . absorbed it somehow . . . then he made a collar that prevented me from using my gifts at all."

Dilys gripped the solid wood support beam that rose from the center of cabin. "Balat is a magic eater?"

"I'm vaguely familiar with that term, but he did say something about liking the taste of my magic. Is that what he was doing? Literally eating my magic? Like it was food for him?"

"It depends on the type of magic eater he is. That certainly helps explain how he managed to take control of the Trinipor Coast without an outright war. I always thought it was the witches he keeps in his employ who were his real secret weapon."

"Did you know that the Shark is a Calbernan?" She watched him closely, saw the way his battle claws sank into the wooden post.

"We knew he possessed seagifts. You don't sink Calbernan vessels or drown Calbernan crew without magic strong enough to counteract our own, but I didn't begin to suspect he was from the Isles until after you were taken. As we tracked his ship down, it became clear he was using powerful seagifts, not some purchased spell or weaker form of water magic."

"So, since you know the Shark is Calbernan, you wouldn't be at all surprised to hear that he's a magic eater, too. Would you?"

Dilys flinched, and that was answer enough.

"Are all Calbernans magic eaters?"

His head shot up, his eyes wide and shocked. "No! By Numahao, we are not! A Calbernan—and I mean a true son of the Isles, not that thrice-damned, rotten-souled *krillo* who calls himself the Shark—are nothing like those scum."

"But you all eat the magic of your wives, and especially your *imlani* women, to power your own. You've admitted as much. The 'symbiosis' you were telling me about."

"There's a difference, Gabriella. Magic eaters *take* what they want. Calbernans accept only that which is freely given, and we give back whatever our women need in return." He drew himself up. "Is this why you don't want me touching you? Because you think I would eat your magic the way Mur Balat did?"

"Wouldn't you?" she challenged.

His head snapped back as if she'd slapped him. "Have I ever done so? Even once?" Then his eyes narrowed. "But you know that. You're just trying to push me away again. I thought we'd gotten past that."

She hated that he was so adept at avoiding her every attempt to control their conversations, hated that he was so good at seeing through her lies and misdirections. "Between the two of them, I'd rather have my magic consumed by Mur Balat than the Shark any day. Balat drained me without laying so much as his little finger on me."

His expression went blank. The sort of blank that told her great and terrible violence was simmering just below the surface. He couldn't hide it completely. It rumbled in his voice as he said, "And the Shark? Did he lay a finger on you?"

"He took great pleasure in laying all manner of parts on me. And no," she added before he could ask again, "to answer the question that has you turning that post into toothpicks, he didn't rape me. Neither of them did. Royal virgins are apparently not as valuable once they've been . . . used."

He drew in a sharp breath, a muscle ticking at the hinge of his sharply clenched jaw. He glanced at the long furrows of splintered wood his claws had dug out of the support post and put his hands to his sides. "Gabriella."

She turned back towards the dressing-table mirror, grasped a thick hunk of her hair and began working the brush though the tangle. "It's funny," she said. Her voice cracked a little, and she had to stop, take a breath, and swallow past the lump in her throat. "It's funny, I always thought at heart I was a strong person."

"You are, Gabriella. You're the strongest woman I've ever known."

She laughed hollowly. "Then you must know some pretty spineless and pathetic women."

"I have known such women, yes, but you're not one of them. Not even when you were doing your best to pretend to be milked tea."

"Aren't I? You give me too much credit. The pirates, the Shark, Mur Balat—none of them did anything to truly harm me. In fact, there are those who could reasonably argue that I was actually pampered by my abductors. I was too valuable a commodity for them to damage. They kept me restrained, of course, but Balat had these women aboard who spent hours working to beautify me. Massaging lotions and creams into my skin, tending my hair, my nails. Trying to make his product as close to perfection as possible before the sale."

The brush had stuck on the tangle. She gripped her hair

in a tight fist and forced the bristles through, hearing the rip as strands of hair broke. Dilys made a sound of protest, as if the damage she was doing to her poor hair hurt him more than it did her.

"I've never been a thing before," she continued as she pulled the clumps of hair from the brush and attacked the knot from a different angle. "That was a strange feeling. I've never been truly helpless, either. There's nothing like being dehumanized and made completely helpless to strip away all the lies and masks and self-delusions a person hides behind and show them what they're really made of. Even though I spent my life keeping my magic bottled up, I always knew it was there. That gave me a certain bravery. I told myself I would never willingly use that power, but it turns out that's not true. It never has been. When it comes down to it, I will choose to kill whoever hurts me. I will kill them and take pleasure in it, and I won't care who else gets hurt in the process." She dragged the brush though the tangle again, tearing more hair free.

"Gabriella, stop. Give me that brush before you rip all your hair out." Not waiting for her permission he crossed the floor and reached for the brush.

She thought about fighting him for it, but the instant his skin brushed against her, longing surged up with the force of an erupting volcano. She released the hairbrush as if it burned and snatched her hand back into her lap.

Dilys scowled, his eyes flaring bright gold as he clearly misinterpreted her flinch. But instead of calling her out on it, he gripped the brush, drew the moisture out of her still-damp hair, and went to work on the tangle at the back of her neck. He was much more patient and gentle with it than she had been—much more patient and gentle than she deserved—carefully unraveling the knotted strands a little at a time, pushing them aside to get at the core of the knot underneath.

"You say none of your captors raped you? The Shark did. When a Calbernan turns his back on every tenet of honor that we hold dear and choses to become a magic eater, as the Shark did, he becomes the worst, most despicable kind of magic eater there is. He takes sick joy in draining his victims against their will, and he doesn't just take power when he feeds. He takes little bits of his victim's soul. The Shark—may Numahao curse him for all eternity—he might not have raped your body, *moa leia,* but he raped your soul." Tears welled in his eyes. "He did that to you, and I wasn't there to stop it. I will never forgive myself for not being there to stop it."

"Dilys—"

"You think that because you're willing to do whatever it takes to stay alive that somehow you're unworthy of happiness?" he asked softly. "You think because you want to hurt the people who hurt you that somehow *you're* the monster? Gabriella, every living creature has a right to defend itself."

"I did more than defend myself. There were innocent people aboard the ship that I destroyed. Servants. Slaves. I didn't spare a single thought for any of them before I Shouted that ship and everyone aboard it to pieces. How was that defending myself?"

"Would you rather still be a prisoner sailing towards a lifetime of being treated as an owned thing?"

"You're missing my point. I killed them. I killed every one of them. And I *wanted* to. That's how I managed to do it. I kept fantasizing about killing them over and over and over again, in the worst ways possible, until not even Mur Balat's collar could keep that part of me contained. I hungered for their blood, their deaths. I *relished* the thought of killing them."

Dilys had reached the stubborn knot at the tangle's core. He set down the brush and let his battle claws emerge just enough that he could pick apart the individual strands of the tangled knot.

"Listen to me, Gabriella, really listen to me. You have

nothing to be ashamed of, nothing to feel guilty about. As a Siren, no matter how you became one, you're a force of the sea, just as I am. And like the sea, from which we derive our gifts, we are wild at heart, and deadly when angered. You say there were innocents aboard the ship you destroyed. How long were you aboard that ship?"

"Almost a week."

"And in that time, did any of these supposed innocents attempt to free you or get a message to me or anyone who could come rescue you?"

He glanced in the mirror and saw her delicate brows draw together. "No."

"Then they were not innocents, and they deserved their fate. You did what you had to do to free yourself. Had I been there, I would have slaughtered every last one of them, and their deaths at my hand wouldn't have been as quick or as painless as they were at yours." He met her eyes in the mirror and bared his elongated fangs. "I am a warrior of Calberna and a son of the sea, and I make no apologies for my nature. You shouldn't either."

"Easy for you to say. Their blood isn't on your hands."

"It isn't on yours either. Their blood is on the hands of the Shark, Mur Balat, and the men who paid Balat to kidnap you and your sisters. Their blood is on my hands as well, before it's on yours. Had I done a better job of seeing to your protection, you and your sisters would never have been kidnapped. You would never have spent a single moment in the possession of those vile *krillos*."

"I told you I don't blame you for that, Dilys."

"Don't you? A *liana* should be able to rely on her *akua* to keep her safe from harm, and I failed to do so."

He had broken down the knot to its last few strands. With infinite care, he separated the last of the tangle and stared with aching sadness and a sense of vast emptiness at the smooth, vulnerable skin at the back of her neck, realizing at last what was at the core of the other tangle, the one wrapped around her heart.

"I failed you, Gabriella."

He had come into the cabin determined to tear down the barriers she'd begun erecting between them again, determined to uncover whatever wounds her abductors had inflicted upon her so that he could help heal them. But if the root of the problem was that she had lost her trust in him—that she no longer saw him as a male she could rely on to be what she needed—then she no longer saw him as a male worthy of being her mate.

And, honestly, could he blame her? Twice now, Dilys had been measured on the most important scales there were, and twice now, he had come up wanting, unable to protect the females he loved. First, as a child with Nyamialine. Now, as a man with Gabriella.

Calbernan customs were wrong, it seemed. Not every male who earned the *ulumi-lia* was truly deserving of a wife.

He picked up the brush and ran it through her hair, mostly to give himself an excuse to touch her one last time. He brushed her hair until it shone like smooth waves of black silk and the curls of it wound around his fingers and clung to his skin. Then he set the brush back down and took a knee before her, reaching out to clasp her hand as he looked into her beloved, beautiful blue eyes.

"Gabriella Aretta Rosadora Liliana Elaine Coruscate, I'm going to ask you one last time, and then never again. Will you Speak my Name? Wilt thou claim me as thine own?"

Her soft mouth trembled. The slender hands in his trembled. "Dilys—I-I . . ." She broke off, closing her eyes and clamping her lips tight. She took a breath, then a second. The fingers clasped in his squeeze him tight. Then they relaxed, her face relaxed, and her eyes opened, deeply blue and full of calm determination. She pulled her hands free of his. "No," she said. "I'm sorry, but no, I won't."

He bowed his head, absorbing the blow to his heart, accepting its fatal finality. "Accepted." Was that his voice?

So hollow and raw? There was no blood spilling from the invisible hole in his chest, but he could feel it pouring out of him all the same. With great effort, he forced himself to stand. "Your pardon, *Myerialanna*. I will take my leave of you now, and set the *Kracken* on a course for Konumarr. I promised your sister and her husband that I would find you and bring you safely home, and that is what I intend to do." He gave a final bow and started for the door.

"What?" Gabriella leapt to her feet. "Dilys, no!" She ran after him and grabbed his arm. "We can't go back to Konumarr yet. My sisters are still out there. Mur Balat and the Shark took them, too! I can't go home until I find them! Balat was planning to sell them, just like he did me. Everything the Shark did to me, he did to them. I can't leave them to that. I have to rescue them! You have to help me rescue them!"

Her frantic fear beat at him. She might no longer trust him, might have rejected him as a potential mate, but he was still bound to her by the unbreakable ties of *liakapua*. He had hoped to reestablish the closeness they had shared that day on the docks, when he set sail, hoped to use that connection to ease into the truth about her sisters' fate. But that option was gone now.

He drew himself up and squared his shoulders. "Forgive me, *Myerialanna* Summer. There is no easy way to tell you this . . ."

She drew back, every part of her closing off in instinctive self-protection. "Tell me what?"

"Your sisters . . ."

"No." She began to shake her head, backing away further still.

"We picked up the trail of the ship carrying your sisters over a week before your Shout. Every Calbernan vessel in the north Varyan joined the pursuit. We had them cornered. We were about to board them, when the ship . . . your sisters must have tried to use their magic to get free, and the ship exploded."

"No." She held up a hand as if as if to silence him, as if that could make his words less true. "No, Dilys."

He couldn't keep his distance, couldn't stop himself from catching her hand, threading his fingers with hers as if he still had that right. "I'm sorry, Gabriella," he said softly. "Your sisters did not survive."

CHAPTER 24

"No." Gabriella's trembling lips pressed together. Tears welled in her eyes, blurring her vision. "No, Dilys. My sisters can't be dead. They *can't* be." Her heart was breaking, the pain immense. They couldn't be dead. Not Aleta . . . not Vivi. They were her sisters, her family. They were everything. "You must be mistaken. Maybe they weren't on the ship. How could you be sure?"

Grief lined his face with deep furrows. "I'm sure. We found . . . we found—" He broke off and cleared his throat. "I saw the remains myself. There's no mistake. They were aboard the ship when it exploded, and they perished in the blast."

She stared up at Dilys, anchoring her gaze to his as the pain swamped her. She started to shake. She was scraped raw, her nerves lying so close to the surface, her control a thin, brittle shield, rapidly cracking now as the shocking news of her sisters' deaths rapidly escalated to an emotional agony the likes of which she hadn't felt since the day her mother died. The pain stole her breath and clenched around her heart like a steely fist.

This was precisely the sort of pain she'd spent her whole life trying to avoid ever feeling again, precisely the sort of pain that had made her fight so hard against letting Dilys into her heart. It hurt. It hurt so much.

Pressure built as her magic bubbled up, slamming against her fragile shields, seeking release just like the scream gathering in her throat and the tears gathering in her eyes.

She wanted to kill the ones responsible for her sisters' deaths. She wanted to hear them scream, as her sisters must have screamed, as her heart was screaming now. She wanted to watch them burn. She wanted to see the terror in their eyes and know she'd put it there. She wanted to watch their skin split, hear their bones shatter, feel the hot splatter of their boiling blood upon her face and know they would never hurt her or anyone else ever again.

Her whole body was shaking now. The Rose on her wrist was on fire. Every breath was a gasp of searing air. She was dimly aware of Dilys's arms around her, of her fingers grasping his upper arms, nails digging deep into the flesh. He was murmuring something. Words she could barely hear above the roaring in her ears.

The scream was on her tongue, filling her mouth, pressing against the backs of her teeth. It tasted of fire and destruction and devastating grief and the need to kill and kill and kill and kill until the ones who had hurt her were wiped out of existence and this agony inside her had poured itself out like lava from an erupting volcano.

She flung her head back and set it free.

The scream tore from her throat, a wail of unbearable grief, the sound of a heart breaking, of love dying.

The ship shuddered as if caught in the jaws of some great beast. The glass panes of the captain's cabin windows rattled loudly, and a dozen of them cracked. A dozen more exploded outward, spewing a cloud of shattered glass into the sea. One full shelf of books toppled to the floor, and the lanterns hanging from their hooks swung wildly while the flames threatened to set the whole cabin afire.

And then she became aware of Dilys, his body drawn tight, every muscle standing out in rigid relief. His eyes were ablaze. His battle fangs were fully descended. And in a choked voice, he kept saying over and over again, "Let it go. Gabriella. Give your pain to me, *moa haleah*. Give it all to me and let me bear it for you."

She drew in a shuddering breath. Her throat was raw, her lungs empty and aching from the force of her scream. Dilys's palms stroked across her back, leaving trails of soothing warmth in their wake. His murmuring voice softened the sharp, searing edge of her grief, and the screams still trapped inside turned into broken sobs and a flood of hot tears. Then she was in his arms, clutching him tight, crying with abandon.

She cried until there was nothing left, until the agony of grief faded to a sort of hollow numbness. The forlorn reality of loss settling in. Her body's trembling slowed. Exhaustion fell over her like a heavy cape, and suddenly all she wanted to do was sleep. She wanted to sleep so that she could wake up to find that all of this was a very bad dream.

But, of course, it wasn't.

Hiccoughing softly, Gabriella nuzzled the hard warmth of Dilys's chest, drying her tears against his silky skin. She frowned a little at the sharp, acrid scent that prickled her nose, a faintly scorched fragrance.

"Oh, no, did I catch something on fire?"

Instead of answering, he just kept stroking her back in that rhythmic pattern. And it finally dawned on her that something was wrong. He was as rigid as stone, yet shaking like a leaf.

"Dilys?" Slightly alarmed, she pulled back to look up at him.

His eyes were squeezed tight, and there were white brackets around his mouth, etched deep. He was panting softly, shallow breaths. And the scorched scent was coming from him.

"Oh, Helos!" She tried to yank away, certain she'd done him harm, but his arms were locked in place. "Dilys!" She reached up to clasp his face. His skin was hotter than she'd ever felt it. As hot as her own had been only a few minutes ago. "Dilys! Talk to me."

Sweet Halla, what had she done?

The cabin around them was dry as a bone. A single spark would send it up in flames. The floor was littered with broken glass and the ceiling overhead was cracked, the timbers bulging upward. Beyond the broken windows along the stern, the seas had grown rough, and the previously clear summer sky was dark with ominous clouds. Rain had begun to pelt down in sheets, while gusting winds howled across the ocean's surface and whipped the ship's sails. In the explosive fury of her grief, she'd nearly Shouted the *Kracken* to splinters and set it on fire and while simultaneously summoning a tropical storm, which was tossing the ship about like a cork.

She could have killed them all. She nearly had.

But Dilys had stopped her. Somehow—miraculously—he'd stopped her!

"Dilys?" She stroked his face with shaking fingers. "Dilys, speak to me."

He muttered something that sounded like, "Give me a minute," and his tone was more than a little cranky.

She bit her lip and tried not to feel offended. She had, after all, channeled the equivalent of a hurricane, a firestorm, and an earthquake into him in the span of a minute or two. And as she had observed over the years, most men went into attack mode whenever they were feeling tense, wounded, or vulnerable. Rather like Khamsin had always done. It was just a shock to see Dilys exhibit that behavior—especially towards her.

Hoping to soothe him, she began to stroke his back and murmur softly, "It's all right. It's all right."

But instead of being soothed, he went even more rigid. "Blessed *farking* Numahao!" he gasped. "Gabriella! Stop!" With a guttural roar, he grabbed her wrists and shoved her halfway across the room.

She grabbed hold of the splintered remains of his desk and gaped at him in shock. He'd just sworn at her and had practically thrown her across the room. As if her touch were anathema. The rejection struck at her soul. She didn't know whether to shout at him or cry.

Before she did either, he whirled around. And the scathing scold on her tongue died without a squeak. His eyes had turned white gold and there was steam coming off his skin.

"Forgive me," he bit out, and he dove through the stern windows of his cabin and into the sea.

"Dilys!" She ran to the shattered windows. Wind and rain pelted down, whipping her face. The ocean below should have been a churning froth of angry waves, but there was a marked circle of calm radiating out from the *Kracken* on all sides. The crew must have been using their seagifts to calm the area around the ship and keep them steady despite the storm she'd generated. The only visible sign of turbulence below was the small area of froth where Dilys had dived into the sea.

"*Myerialanna!*"

"Princess Summer!"

Behind her, the door to Dilys's cabin burst open. Commander Friis and Dilys's first mate, Kame, rushed in.

"Princess!" Friis exclaimed. His sword was unsheathed and held before him, ready to slay whatever threats he found within the cabin. "Are you all right? What happened?"

Kame was not armed, and he looked more concerned than aggressive. His bright golden gaze swept swiftly across the battered remains of Dilys's cabin, taking in all the signs of destruction. "*Myerialanna,* where is *Myerielua* Dilys?"

Her mouth started to tremble. She was verging on tears again and the power she'd just expended was starting to build back up. She'd done something to Dilys when her grief had made her lose control. He'd told her once that she couldn't hurt him, that of all people, he would be entirely safe around her even when her emotions got out of hand. But clearly that wasn't the case. Those blazing white-gold eyes . . . that steam rising from his flesh . . . the frantic way he'd dived through the glass windows to reach the sea far below. Oh, yes, she'd done something to him all right.

"*Myerialanna,* answer me," Kame prodded. "Where is Dilys?"

She clenched her jaw and wordlessly pointed a finger towards the broken window.

"Alive?" Kame barked.

She nodded. Then felt her soul quail.

There was a strange surge of power, muffled so that it felt like the pop of a soap bubble on her skin. Yet it made every hair on Gabriella's arms stand on end.

Kame's eyes suddenly went wide. "*Shoto!*" he cursed. "Grab something and hang on." Not waiting to see if she and Friis obeyed, Kame spun and ran back out onto the sterncastle, shouting in Eru so the White Guards would understand, "Rogue wave! Rogue wave! Brace yourselves!" Then, in Sea Tongue, "*Calbernari!* Spotters to the rigging! The rest of you to the rails, quickly!"

Gabriella grabbed one of the support posts and wrapped her arms around it.

Friis did the same. "What's going on?" he demanded.

Even as he spoke, they heard the shout from up above. "Astern! Astern!" Gabriella looked out the stern windows and in the distance, maybe a mile or two from the ship, the storm-tossed ocean surface rose as if being lifted by a tent pole. It grew higher and higher until it filled the entire expanse of windows along the back of Dilys's cabin

"*Calbernari!*" Kame's voice rang out. "Hard about! Quickly! He's sending it away from us. Don't let it get beyond our reach!"

She swelled of magic that had felt like a soap bubble popping on her skin grew exponentially stronger, and her mouth filled with a sharp, salty tang as every Calbernan aboard the *Kracken* directed his seagift into the ocean. The ship began to roll and toss as the Calbernans turned all their magic away from calming the ship's path and towards calming the monstrous wave that was racing away from them.

The ship heeled hard about, and she lost sight of the enormous wave. Ignoring Commander Friis's sharp cry of alarm, she released the support post and staggered across the now pitching deck towards the cabin door.

They were in the full fury of her storm now. The sails were whipping wildly as the wind gusted from multiple directions. Waves were crashing over the sides of the boat, forcing the deckhands to constantly stop and grab the nearest mast or railing to keep from being washed overboard.

The monster wave was in front of them, racing away faster than they could chase it, and all the efforts of the Calbernans didn't seem to be doing much either to shrink it or to slow it down.

One of the Calbernans spotted her in the doorway and tapped Kame on the arm, pointing and shouting over the noise of the storm.

Kame staggered across the deck towards her. *"Myerialanna,* get back in the cabin! It's too dangerous out here for you."

She shook her head. Rain plastered her hair to her face and soaked her gown. "The wave. It's going too fast. You're losing it."

"Tey, the storm is slowing us down."

She looked at the angry clouds overhead, the sheets of rain pelting down. "I can help with that." She pried one hand off the doorway to show him the red Rose on her wrist. "I am a Summerwitch, after all."

He grinned, and the heavy rain sluiced over his dark skin and dazzling white teeth. "So you are, *Myerialanna.*" He waved a hand at the roiling black sky. "By all means, then, your help is most welcome."

She didn't grin back. There was too much fear roiling in her belly. She wasn't nearly as confident of her abilities as she'd just implied. The barriers keeping her magic in check were utterly shattered, its full power unleashed for the first time in her life, and she had no idea how to wield it safely.

But this situation was all her fault—the storm, the wave, whatever she'd done to Dilys.

She'd literally exploded people with her magic before. What if she'd just done the same to him? What that was the reason he'd dived through the window and leapt into the sea—because she'd turned him into some sort of magical bomb and he was desperate to get as far away from the *Kracken* as he could before he exploded?

Her magic spiked with sudden ferocity, and with a gasp, Summer wrenched her thoughts sharply away from the idea of Dilys dying. She couldn't think about him right now. Her emotions were too fragile, the yawning abyss of grief-borne madness closer than it had ever been.

Focus, Gabriella. Focus.

"Kame, if I get the wind blowing in the right direction, can you calm the seas so we can put on some speed?"

"*Tey.*"

"Good. Let's do that."

Kame shouted orders. The Calbernans who had directed their magic towards containing the wave once more channeled their power into calming the seas before the *Kracken*. Summer sent her consciousness out into the storm. As she had done that first day when she'd awakened in that cage in the pirate ship, she heated certain sections of air before the ship, making it rise and creating low pressure that drew cooler masses of air in. Back then, the storm had built slowly, requiring her consistent effort and attention. Now, with her barriers down and her magic in full force, the clouds formed as swiftly as any storm Khamsin had ever called. The wind changed direction, blowing towards the areas she had chosen. The

Kracken's sails filled with a satisfying crack. The waves before them parted by magic, and then they were flying across the sea down a narrow channel of calm, pond-still ocean, gaining on the monstrous wave that was racing before them.

The surrealistic effect of the Calbernan magic—that calm valley between mountains of churning waves—left Summer both awed and elated and nervously optimistic. It was working.

They chased the massive wave nearly twenty minutes before catching up to it, and as they drew near, the Calbernans in the rigging gave an elated shout.

"*Myerielua!*" the spotters cried, and they pointed towards the crest of the wave. The Calbernans aboard the *Kracken* began to cheer.

Gabriella looked in the direction they were pointing, and the bitter dread that had been churning in her belly dissolved into breathless relief.

Dilys! Oh, blessed Helos, and thank the sweet mercies of all the gods! She hadn't killed him!

With his knees bent, his arms extended, and the long coils of his green-black hair flying behind him like pennants, Dilys was surfing the crest of the monster wave. His *ulumi* were shining bright, power radiating from him like a beacon as he rode the enormous wall of water. As she watched, the wave began to shrink, its crest sinking lower and lower as Dilys forced its rolling energy to dissipate.

Summer directed her attention to the storm, using her gifts to break up the low-pressure center and disorganize its energy. By the time she was done, the storm was over, the rogue wave had vanished, and Dilys rode a spout of water back aboard the deck of the *Kracken*.

"Well done, *Alakua!*" Kame crowed as Dilys strode towards them. "That was some kind of wave taming, my prince! I've never seen the like."

She wasn't feeling quite so thrilled about the show. "I thought I'd killed you!"

He didn't answer Kame, and he didn't pay any attention to her scold, either. Instead, he walked straight up to her, caught her face in his hands, and kissed her until her knees gave out and she collapsed against him.

"Dilys!" She gave a startled cry as he swooped her up into his arms and carried her across the quarterdeck to his cabin.

"You," he snapped at Commander Friis. "Out. Now."

Friis lifted a snowy brown and looked to Summer for instruction. "Your Highness?"

She stared at Dilys, at his fierce expression, the blazing gold of his eyes, and every part of her body, from the top of her head to the tip of her toes all but burst into flame. Lust swamped her. His as much as hers. Sweet Helos, she could all but feel him swimming through her veins, setting her afire from the inside out.

There was a song singing. Words she didn't understand, but they wrapped around her, tangling her up until she couldn't move, the song growing louder and more compelling with every passing moment.

"It's all right, Commander," she said, her unblinking gaze fixed on Dilys. Her heart was pounding. Her breath getting faster, shorter. "Do as he says."

"There. You heard her. Go." When Friis didn't move fast enough for him, Dilys set Gabriella down, frogmarched Friis out of the cabin, and slammed the door shut behind him.

When Dilys turned back around, Summer was still standing where he set her, watching him with wide, shocked eyes. Her face was flushed, her chest heaving.

In her shoes, he supposed he'd feel the same. The events of the last hour must have seemed more than a bit bizarre. But to him all the pieces of the puzzle had finally clicked into place, and for the very first time, everything made perfect sense. At last, he knew exactly what she needed from him. Exactly what he must do.

He couldn't form the words. There was still too much of that electrifying energy flowing through his veins. Too much of her inside him. Wild emotion. Raging grief over her sisters. Fury towards the ones who'd caused their deaths. The shame and humiliation of what the Shark had done to her, and ferocious desire to hunt him down and kill him in the slowest, bloodiest, most painful way possible. A soul-deep yearning for Dilys, coupled with a desperate, clawing fear of giving in to that yearning. Not just because of what the Shark had done to her but because of her terror of letting herself love. Fear of unleashing all that endless, raging power inside her upon the world. And underneath it all, an aching loneliness. A soul starved for what it needed most. A desperate need for something good to help erase all the bad.

He understood her now in ways he never had before.

It wasn't that she didn't trust him.

It wasn't that she didn't want him.

It wasn't that she didn't love him.

It never had been.

She was a great, vast, wild power. He was her greatest vulnerability. And that terrified her beyond all reason. She was afraid of hurting him. She was afraid of hurting others. Most of all, she was afraid of what she might do if anything ever happened to him.

He must have been staring at her too intently, because her expression turned from mild shock to genuine concern. "Dilys, you're starting to scare me now. What's going on?"

"This," he said, and he crushed her to him. His head swooped down to take her mouth in a raw, passionate kiss. Her initial startled gasp gave way to hesitant confusion, then melting warmth that changed quickly to growing heat as her passion rose to match his. He groaned into her mouth and gathered her close. His hands swept down her back. His fingers curled around her buttocks and pulled her tight against him. And when her arms twined like vines around his neck and she crushed her breasts against his chest, his heart nearly burst from pounding so hard.

Magic surged inside him, as immense and forceful as that rogue wave he'd blasted out into the sea. He'd already released so much of the power that she'd shared with him. First, with that initial, wild blast that created that enormous wave, and then the power he'd expended catching up to that wave and taming it. Yet despite all that he'd used, he was still so far from being drained he could scarcely believe it.

No wonder she'd spent her whole life terrified of unleashing the magic inside her. She didn't merely hold a strong gift. She held all the energy of the sun, all the untamed wildness of the sea. Vast, unimaginable power. And when she'd shared her grief with him, poured that power into him along with all the fear and pain and longing of her wondrous, magnificent, deeply loving and passionate soul . . .

Numahao bless him.

He tore his mouth from hers to gasp her name on a ragged inhale, then buried his face in her throat, kissing, nibbling, biting the sweet, sweet, oh-so-silky skin of her neck, the shell of her ear, the tiny, sensitive spot behind that ear that made her cry out when he laved his tongue across it. Her fingers thrust into the coils of his hair and gripped his skull.

"Dilys . . . sweet Helos, Dilys . . ."

The sound of his name on that ragged, breathless gasp filled him with satisfaction and pride. That was his name on her lips. Him she called to give her what she needed. His kiss, his touch that drove her sweetly out of her mind with pleasure.

Soaring hope and steely determination flared within him in equal measure. This was right. They were right. He was exactly what she needed, and it was well past time for him to prove it to her once and for all.

Her skirts bunched around them as she wrapped her

legs around his waist. He walked them blindly to his bed, kicking toppled books out of his path as he went. When he reached his bed, he lay her down upon the downy mattress and pulled back to look at the glorious beauty of her passion-flushed face. Her eyes had gone soft and hazy, her lips plump and red. Color stained the beautiful brown skin of her cheeks. And all her silky black hair lay fanned out around her head. She looked like a mermaid lazing in a warm tidal pool, all soft and dreamy and utterly inviting.

His claws sprang from his fingertips. He dragged them down the front of her gown, slicing the fabric from neck to navel, baring the dark perfection of the beautiful skin beneath. So smooth. So silky.

He slid his hands inside the torn edges of the gown, laid his palms against her flat, warm belly and slid them up, parting the shredded gown as he went until she lay bare before him.

There was hesitation in her beautiful eyes. Worry. Shame. A little fear. The Shark had befouled her with his disgusting touch, reveling in taking intimacies that only a trusted lover should ever have claimed. He'd left no inch of her skin untouched, no part of her free of his taint. He'd made foul what should only ever be beautiful.

That could not be allowed to stand.

Dipping his head down, Dilys set out to replace every awful, humiliating, degrading memory with something new, something joyous. Her lovely breasts with their dark, taut peaks rose and fell with each shallow, panting breath, and he caressed them first with his hot, hungry gaze, then with his hands, and finally with his lips and his teeth and his tongue until her back arched up to offer him her sweet flesh.

Bit by bit, inch by inch, he laved every morsel of her flesh with loving caresses, adoration, devoted care, wiping out even the smallest echo of a memory of what the Shark had done to her. And with each stroke of his fingers, every sensual, dragging lave of his lips, his tongue, he gave her back a hot, tingling flare of the magic she had given him. She clutched his shoulders, her nails digging deep, and his name fell from her lips with breathless urgency.

"Dilys!" She squirmed against him, her hips rocking against the hard length of his sex in blatant demand. "Come into me now. I need you inside me."

There was Compulsion in her voice. He had ripped her gown down to the hem and sliced through the folds of his linen *gudo* before he managed to shake off the Command he wasn't yet ready to obey.

"Don't speak," he growled. He rose up to kiss her again, deeply and thoroughly, while one palm rubbed the sweet, softly-furred mound of her sex until her parted legs began to tremble with the first of what he intended to be many orgasms.

"Dilys!" She clutched at his hips, trying to drag him closer. "I need you n—" Her voice broke off and her eyes flew open, wide with sudden fear, as he clamped a hand over her lips. They had gagged her. They had Silenced her Voice. He eased his grip, but didn't remove his hand. He would take that memory and remake it as well.

"No," he told her. "This is me, and you know I will never hurt you, and I will never take what you do not give. This"—he tapped his fingers against her lips—"is just a reminder, *moa kiri*. I want to give you what you need in my own way, at my own pace, without you Commanding me to rush when I want to go slow. I promise, you will enjoy it. Will you do that for me?"

Eyes wide over his silencing hand, she nodded slowly.

"Good girl." To reward her, he replaced his hand with his mouth, and while kissing her deeply, pressed a thumb to her clitoris and pulsed a throb of hot magic through his hand. Her eyes went even wider, and her body arched as if electrified, shaking furiously as the next orgasm crashed over her. Her teeth clenched tight as her muffled scream of pleasure tore from her throat.

He kissed his way down her body again, giving every

inch of her body the same, agonizingly thorough attention, pulsing hot, tingling flashes of magic as he went. For the next hour, he tormented her with slow, languorous pleasure, working his way down to her toes and back up, then turning her over to do the same again. She cried out again and again, and her nails ripped him bloody more than once. But even when she was sobbing and crying and pleading for release, she didn't Command him to hurry.

That deserved another reward. He drew her up on her hands and knees and kissed every inch of her sweetly rounded buttocks while one hand teased her dangling breasts and the other drove first one finger, then two, then three inside her quaking body, sending pulse after pulse of energy through his fingertips with each thrust until she shrieked in mindless pleasure and collapsed into shuddering unconsciousness on the bed.

As she began to rouse, he at last brought his mouth to her core. Her flesh was steaming, the soft black curls and delicate folds drenched with honeyed moisture. He waited for her eyes to flutter open. Her head lifted slightly, then fell back as if the effort was too much.

"Dilys," she moaned, "please. No more." Her voice was hoarse from her cries, and the low, husky rasp tightened everything inside him.

His own body was hard as a rock. His sex was so engorged, it was a wonder the tightly stretched skin hadn't burst. He had long ago passed the point of pain. When he finally allowed himself to enter her, he knew he wouldn't last long, but this wasn't about him. This was all about and for her.

She had poured herself into him—all of herself, holding nothing back—giving him her grief, her fear, her fury, her lust for vengeance, her pain. And he was giving her back every pleasure he could think of. More pleasure than she'd ever known before. More than she thought herself capable of taking. And he wasn't done yet.

"Yes," he murmured, his breath a hot fan against her

most sensitive flesh. "More." And with a wicked smile, he lowered his mouth and feasted until, screaming, she came again.

And then, at last, he slammed his rock-hard sex into her body with a single, powerful thrust. He groaned at the furiously tight grip of her body as he pulled back to thrust again. He went deep—ah, goddess! So deep—and she was so hot and wet and so *farking* tight, and his sex was like a raw, exposed nerve rubbing against her. Pain and pleasure shot through him in equal measure. His fingers dug into the soft flesh of her rounded hips. His muscles strained, the tendons in his neck standing out like ropes, as he drew back and thrust a third time. Her body clamped hard around his. She screamed. His control shattered.

Gripping her hips, he came in a fury of wild, staccato thrusts, filling her with his seed and his magic. Emptying himself until he had nothing left to give her. And then he collapsed beside her on the bed, pulled her into his arms, and they both fell into exhausted slumber.

CHAPTER 25

Gabriella woke numerous times in throughout the rest of the day and the night, pulled from sleep by dreams of loss and grief that made her magic flare and tears dampen her face. Each time, Dilys held her in his arms and took away her pain, giving her pleasure after ecstatic pleasure in return until at last, as dawn broke over the ocean, she woke to find her cheeks wet with grief for the loss of her sisters but no corresponding hint of dangerous magic.

He held her as the storm of tears rained down, then tenderly sipped the salty wetness from her face.

"I love you," he told her softly. "I am so sorry I was not able to save your sisters. I would give my life to bring them back to you. You know this."

Tear-reddened blue eyes regarded him through spiky black lashes. "I know. You aren't to blame for what happened. You did everything you possibly could."

"I did," he agreed. "But I still failed you. My death is yours, should you wish it."

It took several seconds for his words to register, and when they did, she rose on one elbow to glare at him. "Don't be ridiculous! You know how I feel about that barbaric custom. Even if I blamed you for not being able to save my sisters—which I don't—I would never want that. And I'll thank you not to even suggest such a thing to me ever again." Clearly irritated, she rolled away from him and sat up, dragging the sheet up over her breasts and tucking it beneath her arms to hold it in place.

He rolled to one side and slid a hand across the bed. Reaching the sheet she'd pulled up around herself, he gave it a tug. She tried to hold on, but he was persistent and kept tugging until the sheet slipped down to bare her beautiful breasts.

"If that is your Command, then so shall I obey," he vowed. Lust turned his voice thick and throaty. It didn't matter that he'd just spent the better part of the last fourteen hours claiming her body over and over and over again. All he had to do was look at her, and he wanted her again.

He came upon all fours and slowly stalked across the short distance of the bed until he could reach her nipples with his mouth. He licked them intently, loving the way they beaded on his tongue.

"I will never again offer you my death," he said, rising up on his knees to claim her mouth, and trailing heat and magic in his wake, "if you claim me as your *akua,* and bind me to you for all times."

"Dilys . . ." She pulled back, frowning at him, and pushed him away so she could scoot back. She leaned against the headboard and dragged a pillow across her lap and another across her breasts. "You are not going to seduce me into doing what you want. Not about this. It's too dangerous."

He scowled a little, but his irritation had less to do with her stubborn refusal to marry him than it did with her determination to hide her body from him. "No, it isn't too dangerous," he told her. "As we proved yesterday beyond a doubt."

"Proved?" She gaped at him then gave a harsh bark of laughter. "The only thing we proved is that I nearly killed you!"

"You're wrong, Gabriella. That may be how your *oulani* mind sees things, but it isn't remotely what happened."

"Oh, really?"

"*Tey,* really. I failed you. I couldn't save Spring or Autumn."

"I don't blame you for that."

"I know you don't. That's the point, don't you see? Given my inability to protect the ones you love, you had no cause to trust me with your pain. Yet you did. You trusted me to bear your grief, even though I failed your sisters and I failed you."

"And you think me sharing my grief with you somehow proves I'm supposed to claim you for all times with some sort of Calbernan woo woo?"

"*Tey,* it does. Because whether you want to admit it or not, the Siren in you has already decided that I am strong enough to be your mate."

"I think whatever happened yesterday must have scrambled your brains." She threw the pillows aside and jumped out of the bed, stalking across the cabin to snatch up the white robe the men had made her. "Do you even remember what happened?" she demanded as she thrust her arms into the sleeves and tied the belt around her waist. "I lost control of my power completely. I nearly killed us all!"

"But you didn't!" He jumped out of the bed and followed her, not bothering to cover his nudity. He caught her shoulders and spun her around to face him. "Look around you, *moa leia.* Are we dead? Has the ship sunk? Did any of us receive so much as a splinter yesterday because of your grief? No! Because you gave me your pain and let me bear it for you. And it worked. As I told you it would."

Her eyebrows shot up towards her hairline. "It only worked because you shoved me away before I could kill you, then dove through a glass window to get away from me and started a *farking* tsunami in the middle of the ocean!"

He blushed. He couldn't help it. "*Tey,* well, I admit I could have handled things better, but in my defense, you are the first Siren whose pain I've ever tried to ease. I wasn't properly prepared for the enormity of your grief, and then you started trying to soothe me. I should never have snapped at you and pushed you away the way I did. It's just that I was barely holding what you gave me, then you kept giving me more. It was too much."

"You think I'm upset because you snapped at me?"

"You had every right to be."

"I'm upset because you keep refusing to accept the truth. It's too dangerous for me to love anyone."

"Nonsense. Besides, you already love me. Refusing to claim me won't change that."

She trembled a little and took a wobbly step back, as if she'd just been thrown off balance. Her mouth opened, then shut, and her wounded blue eyes stabbed him to his heart before she turned away to gather her composure.

"No," she admitted, "it won't. I will always be a danger to others if anything ever happens to you, but I don't have to endanger you by staying close. You're safer without me. The only one who doesn't see that is you."

She admitted to loving him, yet in the same breath continued to reject him. Was there ever a woman so stubborn and hardheaded? Feeling exasperated, Dilys didn't know whether to shake her or kiss her. In the end, he did both. Grabbing her shoulders, he gave her a firm shake. "Gabriella Aretta Rosadora Liliana Elaine Coruscate, has anyone ever told you that you talk complete *shoto*?"

Her outraged gasp gave him the perfect opening to plunder her mouth. Pulling her close, he swooped down to claim her lips. She struggled against him, beating at him with her fists, but he was physically much stronger than she was. He held with effortless ease and kept kissing her until she stopped fighting him and started to kiss him back.

"I don't want to hear any more about how I'd be safer or better off without you," he told her when he finally lifted his mouth. "You are not and will never be a danger to me. What you are, *moa kiri*, is the woman I love, the woman I cannot live without, the woman I want to stand beside for the rest of my life."

"Then you're an idiot with no regard for your own life." She regarded him unhappily. "You may have managed to keep me from hurting anyone this time, but what happens when I get bad news and we're not on a ship in the middle of the ocean?" she countered. "What happens if we're somewhere you can't conveniently expel the excess power I give to you? What if we're in city or a palace or a schoolroom? What then?"

He stifled a sigh and reminded himself that her stubborn single-mindedness was precisely the trait that had enabled her to keep her magic under control despite not having a proper network to aid her. "Gabriella, my love, you are a Siren, and I should have prepared for that before trying to lessen your terrible grief. I didn't, and that fault is mine. I will not make that mistake again."

"What do you mean?"

"I underestimated the true strength of your power. I thought that I alone would be all you need—that I could provide for you as I have for my mother numerous times over the years. But you weren't born to power a single Calbernan, even if he is your mate. You were born with strength enough to power us all."

"That's precisely my point!" she cried. "I'm the forest fire, and you're standing there with a glass of water saying you can put me out. But you can't!"

He arched his brows. "Considering that I've spent the better part of last fourteen hours proving that I can, in fact, light your fire and put it out over and over again, I'm vaguely insulted by that remark."

"Aargh!" She clenched her fists and gave a strangled scream. "For Halla's sake! Would you please be serious!"

"Oh, but I am being serious, Gabriella." Letting every last vestige of humor fall away, he regarded her with sober, unswerving intent. "I have never been more serious about anything in my life. Tell me, is this fear that you will do some irreparable harm should I be injured or slain the last obstacle standing in the way of your marrying me?"

"Pardon?"

"You love me. You have admitted it. If I can prove to you that you need never fear losing control over your magic, regardless of your emotional state, would you finally agree to be my *liana*? Will you claim me as your mate?"

"The question is moot. There's no way for you prove such a thing."

"Answer the question anyway."

She scowled, then huffed. "Fine. Yes. If you could prove I that I will never lose control and hurt innocents—which you can't!—then I would marry you."

"And claim me as your mate."

She rolled her eyes. "And claim you as my mate."

"Good. I will hold you to that." He strode for the door and reached for the latch.

"Dilys!" Gabriella's strangled cry stopped him before he could throw the door open. "Where do you think you're going?"

"To prove beyond any doubt that you are no threat to me or to anyone if you do not specifically choose to be."

"For the gods' sake, put some clothes on before you go out there!"

Considering the quantity and volume of the screams he'd wrung from her over the last fourteen hours, there wasn't a Calbernan or Winterman on this ship—or any of the ships in at least a five-mile radius, for that matter—who didn't know exactly what the two of them had been doing or how often they'd been doing it. His nudity wouldn't exactly be a shock to anyone. But it mattered to her, so he paused long enough to grab a *shuma* and knot it about his waist.

"Better?" he asked, and he waited for her stiff, pink-cheeked nod before he flung open the cabin door.

"Kame!" he shouted to the Calbernans on the sterncastle. His first mate, who was standing at the *Kracken*'s wheel, turned around at his call. "Call the men. You and Kuota come here and lay hands on me. Then have the others form up behind you until we're all linked."

Soon every sailor aboard the *Kracken* had lined up to form a living web, all linked hand to skin. All linked, ultimately, to Dilys. He turned back to Gabriella and motioned for her to come to him. She did, reluctantly, and when she drew near, he took her hands and pressed them to his chest. "Good. Now, I want you to share with me again as you shared your grief over your sisters. Give me everything you possibly can."

"Dilys . . ." Gabriella was starting to see where he was going with this, but after what had nearly happened yesterday, she was squeamish about the idea of rousing anything even close to that much of her power again. "I really don't think that's a good idea."

He leveled a hard look on her. "You promised that if I could prove to you once and for all that you can love me without putting anyone in danger, you would marry me and claim me as your mate."

"Yes, but I never meant I'd put us all at risk again to prove it. I won't." Dilys stared at her long enough to make her squirm, but she didn't back down. "I won't do it, Dilys. I'm not going to endanger us all by summoning the full force of my magic. I won't." She crossed her arms and tried to ignore the disappointment in his eyes.

"I see," he said at last. "Very well." He turned towards the bridge. "Helmsman, set a course for Konumarr."

"*Tey, moa Myerielua.*" The helmsman began barking orders, and the ship that had been sailing towards Calberna set a more northerly course.

Gabriella scowled at Dilys. "What do you think you're doing?"

"Taking you home to Wintercraig, of course. As I told you yesterday, I promised Queen Khamsin I would bring her sisters home. Now that our search has ended, I'm honor bound to deliver you safely back into her care."

"I can't go back! I'm too much of a danger to anyone I love. You know that!"

"I'm sorry, *moa haleah*. It cannot be helped. You refuse to wed me because you fear your power, but you refuse to allow me to demonstrate that such fears are groundless. Right now, you are a subject of the King and Queen of Wintercraig, and I have no authority to refuse your sovereign's command to your return to your homeland. Had you agreed to wed me, on the other hand, our marriage would make you a daughter of House Merimydion and a subject of the *Myerial*. In such a case, were you to command me not to return you to the bosom of your *oulani* family, I would be breaking no vows or treaties by acceding to my wife's desires. Alas . . . you are not my wife, nor a citizen of Calberna, so . . ." He let his voice trail off and shrugged.

She narrowed her eyes. "Are you telling me you're shipping me back to Wintercraig—where you know I'll be a danger to my family!—unless I marry you? That's blackmail!"

"I prefer to think of it as negotiating from a position of strength." Behind him, a number of Calbernans and even a handful of traitorous Wintermen suddenly started coughing or scratching their noses and looking up at the sky to hide their smiles.

She whirled on Commander Friis, who was standing a few feet away on the quarterdeck, working hard to conceal his amusement. "Are you just going to stand there and let him blackmail me?"

Friis stood at attention. "Forgive me, Princess, but . . . ah . . . given the events of the last twenty-four hours . . . I . . . er . . . well, I"—he coughed into his fist—"I think the king and queen would prefer to see the two of you married as quickly as possible." His gaze strayed to a point beneath her throat. His cheeks and tips of his ears went pink and he glanced quickly away.

She looked down to see her robe gaping open to her navel. Blushing furiously, she jerked the edges of the robe together and tightened the sash with a yank.

She spun back towards Dilys, ready to blister his ears with a few hot words, only to find that he had come up behind her, blocking her from the view of his crew. She craned her head back to glare up at his great, hulking height, expecting more smug arrogance, but the teasing laughter had left his face, and his eyes gleamed with a soft, sympathetic light.

"It's all right, Gabriella," he murmured. One large hand slid around her neck, and his thumb gently traced the line of her jaw. "Trust me. It really is going to be fine. You won't hurt anyone. I promise."

Her chin started to tremble and she had to look away quickly.

"All right," she mumbled when she had herself under control. "All right. I'll give it a try."

He kissed her again, tenderly, and pulled her out onto the deck. "Kuota, Kame." He waited for the two Calbernans to lay their hands upon him, then he pressed Summer's palms to his chest. "Now, *moa kiri,* rouse your gifts."

Since yesterday's excitement had started with the news of her sisters' deaths, she let her mind tentatively turn to that for a trigger, but to her surprise, nothing happened. Oh, she still felt the pain of their loss and tears came to her eyes almost instantly, but the rush of grief-fired fury never came. Her magic remained quiescent.

She frowned in confusion. "Nothing's happening. I'm thinking of my sisters, but nothing's happening." A look flashed across Dilys's face: satisfaction. "Did you do this?"

"*Tey.* You gave me your pain. I gave you back love. You should be able to mourn them now without fear of accidentally unleashing your magic."

He appeared so matter-of-fact, as if he hadn't just given her one of the most incredible gifts imaginable. All her life, she'd held herself back, held her heart back, afraid to love for fear of what loss would make her do.

"My gods," she whispered. "You did it."

"What I did isn't a blanket cure," he said. "It only works for the one emotional path. Pick a different pain, and your power will rise as it always has. For the purposes of this demonstration, that's what I need you to do. Think of whatever you fear most."

She didn't even need to hunt for a fear. It came of its own volition. The thought of Dilys dying.

And just that quick, her power came roaring up, fresh and furious, ready to destroy anyone who even thought to harm him.

"Good," Dilys bit out, his voice gravelly. "Now, give it to me. All of it. Hold nothing back."

Two minutes ago, she would never have dreamed of releasing her power without restraint, but she was finally beginning to believe him when he told her not to fear hurting him with her magic. With only the slightest hesitation, she unleashed the torrent inside her.

Dilys's body stiffened as if electrified and his eyes flared a bright golden white. Behind him, an instant later, Kame and Kuota did the same, then the six Calbernans behind them, then the next line and the next. Her power chained through them, filling each one, then spilling over to the next.

By the time her power reached the last dozen men, she was having to forcibly push energy out to them.

"There, you see?" Dilys pulled her hands from his chest and kissed her fingertips. "Problem solved." Behind him, his entire crew was regarding her with a dazed wonder that bordered on reverence.

After a lifetime of clinging to her fear, so certain the happiness she longed for most could never be hers, it was hard to accept that she might actually be able to love, like any other person. "It seems promising, I'll grant you that, but I won't have a whole ship full of Calbernans following me around the rest of my life to stop me from killing innocent people whenever my emotions get the best of me."

"*Ono.* But you will always have me, and I will see to that you have a personal guard, chosen from the strongest among us, the ones who can help you the most. You can claim the happiness you hunger for. You can love with your whole heart, without fear."

She stared at him, and the yearning rose in her heart. Could it really be that simple?

"Believe it, Gabriella," Dilys told her. "Believe in me. I am the mate born to stand at your side."

Her fingers traced the outline of his mouth. The lips that had teased her, courted her, challenged, and defied her; enchanted, seduced and ultimately cast aside every objection, doubt, and fear, until all that remained was need and certainty.

In the end, the decision was really no decision at all. It was simply a truth she could no longer keep denying. That he was hers, and she was his. Always.

"I do believe in you, *moa akua.*" And softly, for their ears alone, she Spoke the Name that had imprinted itself upon her soul. Then louder, in a clear, ringing voice that carried the length and breadth of the ship, Gabriella said, "I claim thee, Dilys Merimydion. I claim thee as mine own. For thou art mine before all others, as I am thine."

A name he had never known but now recognized with every cell of his being suffused Dilys's mind. He Spoke that Name in a reverent whisper, binding her soul's resonance to his own, then raised his voice to say, "And I claim thee, Gabriella Aretta Rosadora Liliana Elaine Coruscate. For I am thine, before all others. As thou art mine."

There were no words to describe the feeling that settled over him. It was like opening his eyes and finding all the stars of the universe suddenly there, within his reach, and realizing that nothing was impossible, that he had just become part of a divine and greater whole. He was Calbernan. He'd never truly been alone. But until now, he'd never truly been complete, either. And in that single, perfect moment of communion, he understood the true face of joy, which for him could only come at Gabriella's side.

He closed his eyes and fell to his knees as Dilys, son of Alysaldria, became Dilys, mate of Gabriella. Tears tracked warm trails down his cheeks. He didn't wipe them away. Some things deserved the shedding of salt.

"Dilys, my brother." Kame reached over Dilys's back to hand him an unsheathed dagger.

The sharing of blood and salt was purely ceremonial, Dilys realized as he dragged the sharp edge of Kame's blade over his palm. He could not be more bound to Gabriella than he already was. She had Spoken his Name, and he had Spoken hers, and now every part of them, body and soul, belonged to each other.

Still, it was tradition. Blood and salt to seal the bond.

He rose on shaky legs and offered his *liana* the knife, holding out his hand, palm up, to display its line of glistening scarlet. She sliced her own palm, and as he clasped their palms together, mingling the blood in their veins, he said, "Blood to blood and salt to salt, we are one, Gabriella Coruscate, bound before all, never to be divided."

"We are one, Dilys Merimydion" she agreed.

And it was done. She was his *liana,* his wife and mate, in Name and blood and salt. And he was her *akua,* bound to her forever.

His crew cheered loud and long, their eyes bright, their joy palpable. The Wintermen cheered as well, though it was clear they didn't understand the full import of what had just taken place. To Dilys's surprise, a bright-eyed Kame produced a fine white silk *obah,* heavily embroidered along the edges with golden tridents and red roses sprinkled amongst a sea of green vines and blue waves.

"Ari and Ryll started working on it back in Konumarr,"

Kame said as they helped him into the delicate garment. "They gave it to me before we set sail for the Green Sea. The men and I finished it up a few days ago. Thank Numahao it will finally get some use!" He grinned and slapped Dilys on the back. "Now, my prince, let us sail the ship softly while you go tend to your *liana*. Your mother will be wanting a sweet, golden-eyed *Myerialanna*!"

The Calbernans roared with laughter and began singing songs about mating and making babies.

"You can't be serious," Gabriella protested when Dilys ushered her back into the cabin and locked the door. "We just spent fourteen hours in bed."

"Are you tired?"

"Yes!"

"Ah, well." He tugged loose the sash of her robe and pushed the fabric from her shoulders. It slid down her body and puddled at her feet. His gaze swept over her sweetly curved body, and his body came roaring back to life, ready for a new adventure. He might just have spent the last fourteen hours engaged in a marathon of vigorous, passionate lovemaking with Gabriella, his adored, but he had yet to spend a single second making love to Gabriella, his wife.

"You can just lie back, then, and let me do all the work."

Much, much later, Gabriella lay on the rumpled mess of Dilys's bed, boneless, exhausted, and sated beyond all comprehension. Good gods, the man had no quit. He'd brought her to climax so many times, she'd lost count. Again and again and again, until she was a sobbing, screaming, mindless mess, clinging to him as the sensual firestorm laid waste to her. The pleasure had been so intense, so completely shattering, that even now, just the memory of it made her aching flesh ripple with tiny aftershocks.

Dilys—her *akua*—lay sleeping beside her, one heavy arm flung across her waist. His iridescent blue *ulumi* were still glowing, albeit considerably more faintly than they'd been doing during the long, passionate hours of their love-making. She stroked fingers through the coils of his hair and marveled at how completely at peace she felt. He had done that. He had taken every fear, worry, and wound in her soul and laid them all to rest. Her father's madness, her fear of her terrible gifts, the horror of what the Shark had done to her, the devastating grief of losing her sisters—all had lost the power to hurt her. Because Dilys had taken the rawness of her pain and given her back such infinite, unstinting love, there was no holding on to grief, or rage, or terror. He had made himself her haven in the storm—even when was the storm was her own fears and insecurities.

He had freed her. Freed her to live. Freed her to love. Freed her to know what happiness truly felt like.

For the first time in a long, long time, Summer looked into the future . . . and felt hope.

She turned to press a kiss against his crown, breathing in the exotic, intoxicating fragrance of him. A smile played about her lips. After more than twenty-four hours of virtually nonstop sex, the pair of them should smell rank as a stable of goats, but they had paused once or twice to bathe along the way. And making love with a Sealord in a body of water—even a small one—well, that had come with its own set of surprises. She squirmed, remembering how he'd taken control of the water, used it to stroke and tease every inch of her skin inside and out, brought her to multiple screaming orgasms without laying a single finger on her.

Gods, how she loved what he did to her. She loved that almost as much as she loved *him,* and that was saying a lot.

A sudden, loud pounding on the cabin door ripped her out of her happy reverie. She jumped, and Dilys came instantly awake, leaping out of the bed and landing on the balls of his feet, sword in hand. Where had the sword come from? She hadn't even seen one within reach.

"Dilys! It's Ryll!" More insistent pounding. "Open up!"

Gabriella sat up, dragging the sheets up to her chest as Dilys flung open the door. "Ryll?" Dilys asked. "What are you doing here? What's happened?"

"The Shark didn't die in that explosion like we thought. He's still alive, and he has Ari."

CHAPTER 26

The *Kracken* sailed north towards the Olemas. Ryll's *Narwal* and the rest of the western Varyan fleet sailed close on the *Kracken*'s stern. The captains of those ships had gathered in Dilys's stateroom aboard the *Kracken* to discuss their option and come up with a plan to get Ari back and put an end to the Shark.

That Nemuan and the Shark were one and the same was no longer a suspicion but a certainty, one he shared with Ryll and the other captains as he called the meeting to order. Not surprisingly, they were shocked and disbelieving at first, but when Dilys asked Gabriella to describe the Calbernan who'd held her captive aboard Mur Balat's ship, her mention of the matte-black *ulumi* covering a good half of his body left Ryll and the other captains stunned but convinced.

"I had my suspicions before the Kuinana," Dilys admitted, "but I didn't want to slur a *Myerielua*'s name without proof. I regret my reticence now. If I'd been more open . . . if I'd shared my suspicions . . . perhaps Ari would never have been captured."

Gabriella, who was sitting beside him at the table, laid a hand over his. "We don't know that it would have made a difference." She pitched her voice low, her tone and her touch a soothing balm.

The guilt that had been beating him up since the news about Ari suddenly lost its power to injure. Her help wasn't necessary. He would have handled it. Warriors were trained from youth to compartmentalize their feelings and focus on the mission at hand. But it was nice that he didn't have to, nicer still that she loved him enough to save him that small hurt. He spread his fingers so that hers fell between them, and gave a gentle squeeze of thanks.

Their eyes met in a moment of silent understanding. Then she pulled her hand back and turned to the rest of the table. Her voice became brisk and authoritative. "And it doesn't matter one way or the other. Right now, the only thing we need to be thinking about is how to get Ari back."

Ryll's eyes widened a little, and he gave Dilys a look that was part admiration, part indulgent amusement, the sort you might express after watching a child display a new skill. Dilys realized Ryll had never seen Gabriella drop her Sweet Summer mask. Despite her considerable Siren's power, Ryll still thought she was that kind, shy flower who naturally faded into the background beside her bolder, brighter sisters. Amusement flickered through Dilys. Poor Ryll. He was in for a shock.

"What I want to know is why Nemuan would turn traitor?" That came from Anat Popolo, captain of the *Mermaid*. He and Nemuan had sailed together in their youth.

"I don't know," Dilys bit out, "and to be honest, I don't really care. For now, we just need to get Ari back and put an end to Nemuan's treason. He knows I'll be coming for him. That's why he took Ari: to make me come after him. And there's only one place the Shark would go: to his base of power in the Olemas. No doubt he thinks that will gain him the upper hand."

"Forgive me for saying so, *moa Myerielua*," Narun, captain of the *Windrunner,* pointed out, "but in the Olemas, he *does* have the upper hand. His pirates have already proven their ability to fight and defeat us. That's how they wrested control of that ocean from Calberna to begin with."

"Now we know why," Ryll put in bitterly, "a *farking*

traitorous prince of the Isles has been teaching them how to beat us!"

"It's not just that," Narun said. "According to our last estimates, he has at least two hundred pirates sailing his flag. He's built an armada. We should at least gather the rest of the fleet before we go after him."

"*Ono,*" Dilys said. "If we wait, we lose any chance of getting Ari back alive. You all know what happened to Fyerin." Poor, bright, trusting Fyerin. His brutally tortured remains "discovered" and brought home by Nemuan. Discovered? Ha! How that *krillo* must have laughed, accepting the weeping thanks of Fyerin's mother for bringing her son's body home.

"We're just ten ships."

"Nine," Dilys corrected. "I'm sending Gabriella and the *Dolphin* back to Calberna, to inform the *Myerial* of Nemuan's treason and let her know what's going on."

"What?" Gabriella sat up straight. "I'm not going to Calberna. I'm going with you."

He'd expected an argument. That's why he hadn't brought it up to her last night. "You are the first Siren born in two thousand five hundred years. Ensuring your safety has to be our first priority."

"Your *akua* is right, *Myerialanna,*" Ryll said. "You should listen to him."

Her brows snapped together. "Was I speaking to you, Ryllian Ocea?"

Ryll gaped at her for a moment, then clamped his mouth shut.

Gabriella turned back to Dilys. Her eyes were now snapping with golden sparks. "I'm not asking for your permission, Dilys. I'm telling you I will be sailing with you to the Olemas and assisting in the rescue of Arilon Calmyria. That's not up for debate."

The captains around the table shifted in their chairs and looked to Dilys, as if he could dissuade her. He scowled at them. Really. What did they expect him to say? She was a Siren and his mate and had just made her intentions perfectly clear. He couldn't very well Command her to return to Calberna.

"Fine. You're coming with me, but I will be the commander of the battle, and once it begins you will follow my orders."

"Agreed." She beamed at him. "You won't regret it. Nemuan may have eaten my magic, but—"

"What?" The captains regarded her in shock. "Nemuan *ate* your magic?"

Ryll turned to Dilys for confirmation. "He's a *farking* magic eater, too?"

Dilys forced his claws to stay sheathed. It was hard, whenever he let himself think of what Nemuan had done to Gabriella. "*Tey.* He is."

"The steaming pile of whale *shoto.*"

"I knew—I mean—it's clear he'd lost his way," Captain Sanu, of the *Star,* breathed, "but this . . . to sink to such foul depths. Sweet goddess, has he no soul?"

"Not one any of us can save," Dilys bit out. "Even death is more mercy than he deserves, but at least in death the gods can judge his crimes."

Gabriella laid a hand on Dilys's back, and her touch bled off the worst of his rage, as she had bled off his guilt over Ari earlier. It shamed him a little that *she* should be the one soothing *him* right now. But it also made him proud. He'd been able to give her that peace of mind. He'd been able to help her distance herself from the horrors Nemuan had inflicted upon her. He also remembered his parents, the way they'd constantly exchanged small touches. Sometimes hugs, sometimes tender caresses, sometimes just a brush of fingertips. He realized now they hadn't just been expressing their devotion to one another—although that was certainly part of it—they'd also been sharing their strength, soothing frayed emotions, being both balm and bulwark for one another. And he loved that he and Gabriella were already instinctively doing the same.

"As I was saying," she continued, her voice calm, "when the Shark ate my magic, I'd already been drained by Mur Balat. He suspects there's stronger magic in me than I ever let on, but my guess is he'll assume that was my Siren's magic, and that I'm as weak a Siren as I supposedly am a weatherwitch. That makes me the perfect secret weapon. Besides, I have a score of my own to settle with the Shark."

It was Dilys's turn to sit up straight. His brows snapped together. "You're not getting within a hundred yards of that magic-eating bastard, Gabriella. Siren and my *liana* you may be, but *that's* not up for debate."

She smiled. "Don't worry, *moa akua,* I'm not suggesting I should fight him in hand-to-hand combat. Unlike Khamsin, I never trained with swords. I also understand that you are a male and my mate, and therefore you feel driven to avenge what he did to me. That is your right, by virtue of our bond, and I wouldn't presume to rob you of it. But I do intend to see that it's a fair fight. Just you and he, Sealord to Sealord."

When she put it that way, how could Dilys refuse?

"So we're agreed? You'll take care of Nemuan, and I'll take care of the armada?"

"Forgive the impertinence, *Sirena,*" Narun interrupted. "We all know you're Siren's gifts are powerful enough to Shout one ship to pieces, but are you saying you can destroy hundreds?"

Gabriella shrugged. "I don't know. I've never tried. But what I can't Shout away, I should be able to eliminate with my weather magic."

"Forgive *my* impertinence," Captain Popolo said, "but are you saying your weathergifts are stronger than your Siren's magic? Strong enough to wipe out an armada two hundred strong? Forgive me, but my mother sits on the committee that researched potential brides for the *Myeri-elua*. I understood your weathermagic to be . . . er . . . my pardon, but negligible."

She gifted Popolo with an enchanting smile and told him gently, "That's what I *meant* for everyone to think, Sealord. But I come from the royal line of Summerlea, descended from the Sun God himself, and my giftname is Summer for a reason." Sweet Summer gave way to the Siren once more. "As for your other question, to be honest, I don't know which of my gifts is stronger. I've kept my magic locked away all my life for fear of hurting people with it."

"My friends," Dilys said, "no one—not even Gabriella herself—has yet seen the full extent of what she can do. She holds very powerful gifts from Helos and Numahao combined. Let me put it this way: when she poured so much magic into me that I had to jump into the ocean and start a tsunami just to rid myself of the excess? That didn't even make a dent in her stores. She was just venting what was too great for her to contain."

"Now it's my turn to say 'forgive the impertinence,'" Captain Sanu ventured, "but if the *Sirena* has never wielded the full measure of her gifts, should the first time be in battle against an enemy who has proven himself capable of besting even strong and experienced Sealords? More to the point, if her magic is as strong as you say, will it even be safe for her to use it at all?"

Beside him, Gabriella flinched. The movement was so slight the others would not have noticed, but Dilys was too attuned to her to miss it. He knew it was her greatest fear: that she would lose control of her magic and harm innocent people—or worse, those she loved. He slid an arm around her waist and rested a hand on her hip. His thumb slid gently back and forth in a small caress as he absorbed her fear and gave her back love and his utter faith in her in return.

"It will be safe," he said, as much to reassure her as his gathered captains.

She smiled up at him, then nodded to the others. "It will be safe."

That decided, the group of them settled in to hash out the details of their plan of attack. When they were done, the captains returned to their respective ships. After they departed, Dilys and Gabriella shared a quiet meal then went for a stroll above decks, stopping at the bow of the ship to look up at the stars and enjoy the feel of the wind and salt spray on their faces.

Dilys stood at Gabriella's back, his arms wrapped loosely around her shoulders. The stars of the equatorial night sky shone bright in the moonless night sky. Dilys found the familiar constellations of Helos and Numahao and chuckled softly.

"What's so funny?" Gabriella wanted to know.

"I'm just thinking about what a force of nature you are. All the power of the sun and the sea rolled into one."

"And that's amusing to you?"

"*Ono.*" He nuzzled her hair. "What's amusing me is the thought of the Hel on Mystral you're about to unleash on that bastard Nemuan."

"Hmm." She leaned a little more deeply into his embrace. After a few moments, her hips shifted against him, and she titled her head back to arch a brow. "That doesn't feel like amusement to me."

He smiled slow and wide. "I told you before. Strong women are *arras* leaf to me."

"Strong *women*? Plural?"

"Woman," he corrected. "Singular. You. Only you. As you know, I'm a one-force-of-nature kind of male."

She turned to face him, looping one arm around his neck and leaning back a little as she slowly traced a finger down his chest, trailing the heat of her magic in its wake. "Mmm. And just how much of an aphrodisiac is my particular force of nature to you?" Her finger dipped below his navel and continued tracking down the thin, silky line of dark hair that disappeared into his jeweled belt.

He shuddered and snatched her up in his arms. "Oh, *moa haleah*. It's like eating *arras* straight from the tree."

The *Kracken* sailed through the Sargassi Sea, the swath of warm, tropical waters separating the continents of Ardul and Frasia, and headed into the mouth of the Olemas Ocean. Gabriella stood at Dilys's side on the *Kracken*'s bow, her eyes gleaming pure gold as she tapped the vast well of her power. Ahead of their small fleet, a tropical storm whipped the seas and skies into a frenzy, a pocket of volatile weather created and guided by Summer.

With Dilys's aid, she'd spent their voyage to the Olemas learning to unleash and use her gifts. One of the things she'd discovered was that now that her magic was unrestrained, finesse had become a thing of the past. Delicate, targeted work was difficult, if not impossible. She could set a boat on fire, but lighting a single candle? That ability escaped her. She'd had hopes, for instance, of being able to target a Shout to a particular individual and snipe them from a distance, but her Shouts didn't work that way. The farther she was from a target, the wider the spread of her devastating magic. As for her weathergift, here in the summer, sailing already warm tropical seas, she could whip up a storm as quickly as Khamsin, but with all the energy of the sea and open sky at her fingertips, Summer's storms had an almost unlimited potential for growth . . . and devastation.

She hadn't come close to utilizing the full force of her gift yet. With nine ships and hundreds of Calbernan lives in such close proximity, she hadn't dared—not even with Dilys's help. And he had been a help. Every moment she'd practiced, he'd been by her side, offering advice and encouragement, bleeding off her magic when it threatened to surge out of her control. She'd fed him a lot of excess as she'd worked to learn what she could and couldn't do with her magic, and he'd used that power to extend his eyes and ears in the sea. His direct network now stretched throughout the Sargassi and a full hundred miles into the Olemas.

"He's got a hundred ships forming a blockade about fifty miles west of us. He's trying to mask their presence with fog."

Gabriella stretched out her senses. She couldn't detect the ships themselves, but she could sense the cooler air filled with moisture hanging over the water. The fog he was using to hide his ships. There was a definite tang of magic in that fog.

"I see it. Where are the rest of his ships?"

"He's got at least another two dozen ships sailing with him. I haven't found the others yet, but my eyes and ears in the sea are looking for all possibilities. If they sail anywhere within reach of my network, I'll spot them. Even if they're using the same invisibility spells he employed to mask himself from the last time."

They rounded the northernmost edge of the Kuinana. The Olemas lay before them. Nemuan's unnatural fog hovered across the water like thick smoke. She could see it stretching out on either side of her rain-dark storm.

"All right, *moa kiri*, are you ready?"

She pulled her attention from her storm to offer him a smile. "As ready as I'll ever be."

"Then do it."

She closed her eyes, reached for the heat of the sun, and poured energy and heat into the volatile core of the storm she'd been steering ahead of them. She thought building the storm would be hard, but it wasn't. Clouds boiled out across the sky and blackened with shocking speed. Wind gusted. The storm-tossed surface of the sea became a riot of devastating waves, forty feet from crest to trough. What had been a tropical storm intensified rapidly into a hurricane.

When she and Dilys had discussed her plan to summon a hurricane to defeat the armada, her biggest fear was that she might lose control of the storm she had created. But now, as her magic and her consciousness rode the currents of hot, moisture-laden air, she knew that fear was groundless. Khamsin had always been the one afraid of losing control of her storms, but Summer's whole life had been dedicated to controlling the storm within. Compared to that, keeping this hurricane leashed to her will was child's play. She thrust it into the fog bank, using her storm as a battering ram. Her gale-force wind and waves tossed the pirate ships aside like toy boats, clearing the fleet's path of would-be attackers. Aboard the *Kracken*, Dilys and his men used their seagifts to calm the waves before they could batter the Calbernan fleet.

A few of the pirate ships managed to ride out the storm and get close enough to begin firing shot filled with the same unnatural, unquenchable fire that had destroyed the ships in the Kuinana. One of the shots hit the *Mermaid*, which was sailing forty feet to the port side of the *Kracken*.

Having fought the fire before in the Kuinana, Popolo's men were prepared. They dumped buckets of sand on the blaze. As the pirates readied a second barrage of fire, a pod of blueback whales breeched directly off the pirate ship's starboard side. Waves swamped the ship. One of the blueback's heavy tails smacked the bowsprit. The blow brought the bow of the ship careening downward into the trough of a massive wave, just as another wave rose up near the stern. The ship capsized. Sailors screamed as the fire they'd been intending for the Calbernans now ignited the sinking hulk of their ship and the crew trying to swim away.

Aboard the *Mermaid*, Popolo's crew gave a loud cheer. Those bluebacks had been his. The waves had been generated by his men.

Another two pirate ships approached from the starboard side of Ryll's *Narwhal*. Ryll and his men capsized them before they got within firing range and sent them to the bottom of the sea.

Directly ahead of the *Kracken*, four ships had survived

Summer's storm and were now heading straight for them. Gabriella let out two controlled Shouts. The oncoming ships exploded into clouds of splinters. From the crew of the *Kracken* and the other ships of their fleet, a great, raucous cheer went up. Amid the cheers and chanting chorus of "*Sirena! Sirena!*" she caught snatches of awed voices. "Did you see that?" "She blasted those *farking krillos* right out of the water!"

"Well done, *moa kiri*." Beside her, Dilys beamed with pride. "You're getting good at that."

She blushed a little, then grinned back at him. "I am, aren't I?" To her surprise, she didn't feel one ounce of horror or guilt for destroying the pirate ships or the lives aboard. Instead she felt exhilarated. She'd defended the *Kracken* and the Calbernan fleet with her magic. She hadn't lost control even once, killing only the enemy and no one else. As for those enemies, they'd been bad, evil men bent on doing bad, evil deeds, and the world was a better place without them.

She wasn't conflicted over killing them. Instead, she felt . . . right. As if, after all these years, she finally understood her purpose, understood why she'd been born with such great and terrible gifts.

"Gabriella?" Dilys was watching her closely. "What is it?"

"I think I understand now. Why I am . . . what I am."

"What do you mean?"

"I always thought I was killer, a monster, a threat to everyone I love and all the innocent people around me. But I'm not. I can kill, yes, but I'm not a killer. I'm a protector. I was born to defend good people against the real monsters. That's why the gods gave me the gifts to do it."

He pulled her close and kissed her thoroughly. When they pulled apart, they were both breathless, their hearts pounding.

"Was that my reward for being such a good little force of nature?"

He laughed. "Just a small taste of your reward, *moa haleah*. The rest will come later." His eyes glowed brighter as he reached out with his magic to connect to his network of ocean spies. "Uh-oh. I think you, my secret weapon, aren't such a secret anymore. Looks like Nemuan was monitoring his fleet. He's starting to run scared."

"What do you mean?"

"He's broken off from the rest of his armada and is heading fast for Trinipor. Mur Balat has a fortress there. If Nemuan reaches it, Ari's as good as dead. The place is impregnable. We have to stop him before he gets there, but he's got a very substantial lead on us."

"Understood." Her voice was low and throaty, resonating with power. She closed her eyes and lifted her hands. Her hurricane strengthened. She poured more and more power into the storm, sending clouds boiling across the sky until they covered the sky from horizon to horizon. And still Gabriella poured her magic into the storm, forcing an explosion of rapidly increasing intensity. The whirling mass of stormclouds stretched out to cover the entire southern half of the Olemas Ocean and most of northern Ardul. The winds whipped to speeds exceeding one hundred miles an hour, one hundred forty, then faster still. The massive waves churning across the ocean's surface swelled to ninety- and hundred-foot monstrosities. Black clouds blotted out the sun. Lightning crashed and crackled across the crisply delineated edges of the storm's monstrous eyewall. And there, in the center of the ferocious, killer storm, Dilys's fleet sailed on smooth seas beneath sunny blue skies, chasing down Nemuan's ship faster than he could flee across what even to his princely sea gifts had become dangerous, unfriendly seas.

Closing the distance took a full day. Gabriella maintained the control and intensity of her monstrous storm the entire way, managing the upper levels winds to keep the tops of her storm's thunderclouds from shearing off and robbing the hurricane of its power, while steering the entire storm on a resolute, unwavering path towards the fleeing Nemuan. She didn't sleep except for a few brief five- and ten-minute naps snatched here and there in Dilys's arms, because unlike her initial storm, this great beast of a hurricane wanted its freedom. It bucked against her control constantly, requiring her complete concentration. But not once did Gabriella fear losing the upper hand, in large part because Dilys remained by her side, anchoring her in a way no else ever had—or could.

Not a single pirate Nemuan left behind to defend his flank survived the devastation of Gabriella's hurricane. As the Calbernan fleet closed the gap between themselves and the fleeing Nemuan, Gabriella began to disperse her storm, shrinking the feeder bands, breaking up the enormous clouds forming the center. She spun off a smaller low-pressure center and kept it focused over Nemuan's ship, harrying him with gusting winds and waterspouts to keep him from escaping. Dilys remained by her side, bleeding off any spikes of excess power and using it to fuel his own efforts against Nemuan, slamming the traitor's ship with wave after merciless wave. One of Summer's waterspouts got a little too close, striking the ship a glancing blow that ripped off the top of the foremast and the bowsprit.

The ship slowed, then limped to a halt.

As Dilys's fleet drew closer, Ryll and a small team hitched a ride with a pod of swift dolphins and headed for Nemuan's ship.

"Why dolphins?" Gabriella asked. "Can't Ryll and his team swim faster using their seagifts?"

"*Tey,* but Nemuan and his men will be looking for our magic in the water. By using the dolphin's natural speed to transport them, Ryll and his team are essentially invisible. Once they're close enough, I'll start slamming waves into the ship. That'll keep the crew busy and give our *Calbernari* a way to get aboard without being detected."

"Then I do my thing?"

"Then you do your thing."

"What if it doesn't work? What if Nemuan is expecting it and took steps to protect against it?"

"Then Ryll and his men with have to go with plan B."

"I hope he's not expecting it then."

Dilys grinned and dropped a quick kiss on her lips. "Me, too. But I wouldn't worry. You've been wiping the floor with these *krillos* since we started."

Twenty minutes later, Ryll and his team washed aboard Nemuan's ship on a massive wave.

Gabriella walked to the railing of the *Kracken,* looking out across the storm-tossed waters to the Shark's pirate ship, and began to sing.

It was a song like the one from her dream. A melody without words, but rich with emotion. Each tone carried intense longing coupled with achingly seductive promises of dreams fulfilled.

Come to me, the melody seemed to say. *I am all you've ever dreamed of, all you could ever wish for. Come to me and find the peace and paradise you've been searching for. I am love and family and prosperity and joy. I am the Halla you have always longed for. Come to me. Come.*

It wasn't Persuasion but pure Siren's Song that poured out of her on the wordless notes, soaring across the distance between the two ships. Despite their natural resistance to mind control, Nemuan's Calbernan crew fell under the spell of her Siren's Song and abandoned their posts to stumble blindly towards the railing of the ship.

Aboard the enemy vessel, Ryll and his men crept belowdecks and began searching for Ari. They, too, felt the pull of Gabriella's Song, but with wax plugs in their ears muffling the sound, they were able to resist the need to follow that song to its source.

They found Ari, tortured and unconscious, chained in the bowels of the ship. With the help of his men, Ryll loaded his cousin into a makeshift litter and carried him back above decks, where they slipped over the side to the waiting dolphin pod and hitched a ride back towards the Calbernan fleet, sending the all clear to Dilys once they were out of immediate danger.

"We've got him," Dilys said to the still singing Gabriella. "Ari's safe. They're bringing him back now."

Gabriella turned to him, her eyes still glowing gold, her voice still rich with the Siren's irresistible allure. "Then put an end to the Shark once and for all."

Dilys bared his battle fangs. "As my *Sirena* commands," he said, and he leapt into the sea.

Filling his sea voice with power, Dilys called out, "It's over, Nemuan. The shame you have heaped upon your House, the ruin you have made of your mother's name: it's all over. You can choose one of two ways to meet your death. My *liana* can obliterate you and your entire ship with one Shout, or you can meet me in the sea, and you can accept your death at my hands." He pulsed a location a few miles from where the Ardullan continental shelf dropped off into deeper ocean. "Just you and I, *krillo*. No weapons but fang and claw. And our ships weigh anchor where they are."

Silence. Then, curtly, "I will meet you. It will be my pleasure to rip out your heart and feed your body to the sharks."

"And mine to tear the entrails from your body and turn the ocean red with your blood," Dilys shot back, "but it won't be sharks I summon to feast upon your flesh. It will be the kracken."

A blast of fury shot across the ocean. Dilys smiled coldly and waited for the burst of magic that announced Nemuan's presence in the water before he began to swim.

As he swam, Dilys monitored his cousin to make sure he was, in fact, headed for the location Dilys had specified. He also tried to anticipate all the ways Nemuan would try to win the advantage. The shadow-stained—those Calbernans, like Nemuan, who were so beset by grief that they'd recorded their anguish on their bodies to be re-membered always—never wholly healed from their loss. The pain stayed with them, like the squid ink tattooed into their flesh. It made them a little mad. A lot unpredictable. Quick to anger, and savage when they attacked.

Nemuan planned to fight, but there would be nothing fair about it. The battle would be vicious, brutal, and to the death. Like any predator's attack.

Dilys had chosen open ocean for their fight, far enough away from either of their respective ships to discourage interference. If any of Nemuan's men had followed him into the sea, Dilys hadn't seen signs of them, and he'd kept an eye on every living creature swimming in his same direction.

The waters were clear, visibility high. The flat ocean floor lay one hundred feet below the surface. They were miles away from the cave-riddled reef system as well as the sharp drop-off of Ardul's continental shelf.

They met fifty feet below the surface. Two Calbernan males in their prime. Lords of the sea. Sunlight filtered down through the water overhead. It played across their bodies, illuminating the iridescence of their blue *ulumi,* making them shimmer. The long ropes of their hair and the drapes of their *shumas* floated lazily about them as they hung there, suspended in the ocean's liquid embrace.

"Merimynos." Dilys voiced the greeting not with power, but with the tonal phonemes of *Coa Anu,* Under-sea Tongue.

"Merimydion." Nemuan's lip curled back in a sneer, his teeth flashing blue white in the sunlit waters.

"What happened to you, cousin?" Dilys asked with genuine regret and bafflement. "You were a prince of Cal-berna, the honorable son of an honorable House. The son of a queen! How could you betray everything? How could you shame your mother's name this way?"

Nemuan's battle fangs descended, white and sharp and deadly. "What would you know of honor and honorable

Houses, *krillo*? You, who would foul Calberna's line of queens with inferior *oulani* blood."

"Inferior?" Dilys laughed without humor. "My *liana* is the first Siren returned to us since the Slaughter. You heard her Shout. You know it to be true."

Nemuan's lip curled. "I know there are many kinds of magic in the world. Including magic that can make the impossible seem true. But true Sirens are daughters of Numahao, born to the Isles."

"Is that what you told your men? How you got them to continue this madness of yours even after you all heard what she was?"

"My men live to serve a true queen of the Isles, not some *oulani* slut." Nemuan gave a sneering laugh. "Though I have to hand it to you, Merimydion. At first, I thought you'd picked the runt of the litter. I mean, compared to her sisters—especially that Autumn—little blue eyes wouldn't be my first choice. But then I showed her the joys of *Ililium.* Again and again and again. And she was begging me for more. You must be a *shoto* lover, Merimydion."

For an instant, Dilys saw red and nearly lunged at Nemuan in a blind rage, but at the last second, he saw the triumphant gleam in his cousin's eyes and realized that was exactly what Nemuan wanted. His cousin was no green boy. He was every inch a warrior of the Isles, just like Dilys. And if Dilys lost control, that gave Nemuan an advantage.

"I know what you did to her, magic eater. Even without all your many other crimes, that alone would have earned you a traitor's death. But enough of this." Dilys's eye flared bright gold, and his power boomed out, filling his sea voice with Command. "Confess your crimes, Nemuan Merimynos, and accept your punishment."

Nemuan's body went rigid. The tendons in his neck stood out like ropes pulled tight beneath his skin. His eyes went wide and filled with shock.

Before her death, Siavaluana's youngest son would

have been able to slough off Dilys's Compulsion with a sneering laugh. Even a few months ago, he might have been able to resist, despite his mother having been dead so many years. The last three *Myerials* had been daughters of House Merimynos, so despite the House's devastating losses, its surviving sons and daughters still wielded great power. But Dilys now carried in him the most powerful of all Calbernan magics: the gift of a Siren.

Nemuan's arm shot out and his wrist turned up, baring the small harpoon gun built into his wristband. The small gun fired, shooting a tiny streamlined dart through the water.

Dilys spun to one side and barely managed to avoid the projectile, which he was sure must be poisoned, given its miniature size. By the time he'd recovered and spun back around, Nemuan was racing away, swimming very fast towards the continental shelf. Clearly, he thought to lose himself in the darkness of the ocean's depths, where the eyes Dilys could access were few and far between.

Putting on a burst of seagift powered speed, Dilys followed.

Even without Gabriella's gift to aid him, Dilys was—always had been—the faster swimmer. He caught Nemuan a quarter mile from the shelf drop-off and attacked, claws extended and battle fangs bared. They tumbled through the water, limbs flailing, bodies twisting. Teeth and claws flashed as they fought in brutal silence, each struggling for supremacy. Dilys ripped slashes across Nemuan's chest, tearing hunks of flesh from his arms and legs, but Nemuan, a prince of Calberna, had lacked no training in battle. He managed to get in more than a few strikes of his own.

Blood spilled. Scarlet eddies wound around them like unraveling ribbon.

Nemuan swiped a clawed hand at Dilys's throat. Dilys felt the sting as his skin split but managed to twist away before Nemuan could slice his jugular. Another quick twist brought Dilys back around, and he raked his own claws deep and hard down Nemuan's side, ripping through his gill slits and shredding the delicate oxygen-filtering filaments beneath the skin.

Nemuan roared and coughed a mix of blood and water and air. Pressing the advantage, Dilys rammed a fist into the wound and raked the claws of one foot down Nemuan's thigh, gouging deeply. The sea around them was a mist of red now, and the sharks Nemuan had taken as his namesake began to gather.

Seizing them with his seagift, Nemuan drove three bull sharks towards Dilys. Though Dilys was the better swimmer, Nemuan had always been better at controlling sharks. Dilys spun away, evading the sharp, biting rows of teeth but losing a layer of skin along his calf to the sharp, dermal denticles of the predators' skin. A swift call on Gabriella's gifts gave Dilys the edge he needed to briefly override Nemuan's control and send the rest of the sharks skimming harmlessly past. But even without Nemuan's control, the blood in the water would keep them coming back and drive them into a frenzy of hunger.

Dilys dove for Nemuan again, driving sharp claws into his cousin's torn side and ripping out the exposed gill membranes. Nemuan screamed and convulsed in pain. The sharks darted in for a second pass. This time, Dilys grabbed his incapacitated cousin and shoved him towards the sharks' gaping maws. Only Nemuan's quick, barked Command saved him from losing a limb to the predators' snapping jaws.

Dilys locked his cousin in an unyielding grip, one taloned hand poised over Nemuan's unprotected belly, the other at his throat. "I can do this all day, *pulan*," he hissed near Nemuan's ear. "I'll feed you to them bite by *farking* bite if I have to."

"Go to Hel, *skuurl*. And take your whole cursed House with you."

"You first, cousin." Dilys pinched Nemuan's trachea and gave him a slight shake. "You've lost and you know it. You're going to die. There's no way around that. But out of respect for your honored mother, I'll give you a chance to preserve at least some semblance of honor. Return with me willingly to Calberna, testify against everyone who participated in your treason, and I promise the true depths of your depravity will not become public knowledge. You'll still die a traitor's death, but your House will be spared the shame of having their once-honored prince publicly branded a magic eater."

For a moment, Nemuan looked defeated, but then he bared bloody fangs in a mocking smile. "You want me to identify traitors? Just look in the mirror, *skuurl*." Nemuan laughed, then coughed up another bubble of air, seawater and blood. Eyes glinting with dull hate, Nemuan spat, "This much I will give you: my most fervent prayer to Numahao that you, too, may live to witness the destruction of your House and the loss of everything you hold dear."

Dilys's jaw hardened. He hadn't really expected Nemuan to cooperate, but some part of him had hoped he would. "And that is your final answer?"

"The only one you'll ever get from me."

"So be it." In one swift move, Dilys ripped open Nemuan's throat and belly. Then he locked an arm around his cousin's chest and swam towards the sharp drop-off of the continental shelf, calling out a Command as he went. He stopped at the edge of the shelf and let his body sink until his feet touched the sandy soil of the ocean's floor. "By the grant of Numahao, and as *Myerielua* of the Calbernan Isles, I declare you, Nemuan Merimynos, to be a traitor to Calberna, and in keeping with the laws of the Isles, I condemn you to meet the kracken."

Weak and dying from blood loss and his injuries, Nemuan turned his head to see around Dilys's body, and his eyes widened in sudden terror as he beheld the monstrous carnivorous leviathan slowly rising from the deep.

By the time Dilys swam back to the *Kracken*, Summer had dispersed the last remnants of her storm. He rode a spout of water up to the main deck, went to his cabin to have his wounds tended and change into a fresh, unbloodied *shuma*, then joined Gabriella in the cabin where Ari was recuperating. "How is he?"

"Not well," she admitted. "Unlike with me, there was no Mur Balat to keep the Shark from doing damage to poor Ari. He's got a broken leg, and hundreds of cuts and burns all over his body. There was a strange circle of runes drawn in red ink at the back of his neck. Whatever it was terrified him. When I asked him about it, he went wild and ripped his own skin off with his claws to get rid of it. He's sedated now, and I recommend keeping him that way until we get him someplace safe where he can be properly looked after. I tried sharing some of my magic with him, to help him to heal, but I don't know if it did him any good. If we were closer to Wintercraig, I'd say we should get Tildy to help him."

"When we get back to Calberna, Uncle Calivan should be able to help him. He's not quite as gifted an herbalist as your Tildavera Greenleaf, but he knows his way around healing potions."

"That sounds good. We should probably put him on one of your fastest ships and send him back to Calberna right away."

Dilys went still, his gaze suddenly very watchful. "You don't wish to sail to Calberna?"

She realized immediately that he'd misinterpreted her request. "I do. Of course I do. But there's something I need to do first. A vow I need to keep."

Less than twenty-four hours later, Gabriella stood on the deck of the *Kracken* looking out over Trinipor, the capital of Mystral's slave trade, and the massive stone fortress that loomed over the city from the clifftops above. What until a few hours ago had been Mystral's busiest, most profitable, and most deplorable slave port was now a ghost town. The thousands of men, women, and children who had been held for sale here were sailing towards Calberna, where the offer of safe haven or a small gold stake and transport to the port of their choice awaited them. The slavers themselves were either dead or in chains, preparing to be transported to several labor camps, where they would be put to work mining precious minerals until they earned enough money to buy back every slave they'd ever sold.

All that remained of Trinipor now were the empty buildings and slave pens, and the opulent, abandoned fortress of Mur Balat. Of Balat himself, there was no trace. According to witnesses, he hadn't been seen in over a month. His coven of witches had declared him slain in a fiery explosion at sea, then fled in the night, along with half of his servants and guards. A few of the more brazen remaining guards had decided to claim Balat's fortress and his slave trade for themselves. Most of them had perished fighting the Calbernans who'd come to put an end to Trinipor.

"It's time, *moa haleah*." Dilys touched her arm gently.

"Everyone is out, right? The city and fortress are empty?"

"*Tey.* Just as you ordered."

"Good." Her hands clenched tightly around the ship's railing. Scores of Calbernans floated in the water below, waiting. She took a deep breath, then another.

Gabriella had insisted on visiting her former captor's palatial home, to see with her own eyes the princely life he'd built for himself on the backs of his victims. She toured the holding pens, the cages, the locked rooms where he kept recalcitrant and magically gifted slaves, letting each new outrage fuel the molten kernel of fury bubbling at her core until the pressure had become so fearsome that holding it in felt like trying to stop a volcano from erupting.

She probably should have excused herself when the Calbernans discovered the rooms in Balat's palace that housed a dozen naked young women wearing magic-restraining collars and the blank, hollow-eyed look she recognized all too well. But even now, with her rage-fed power threatening to shatter her control, her heart also swelled with pride for Dilys's men, all of whom had been so gentle, so incredibly tender and compassionate towards those who had suffered so terribly. Feared mercenaries the Calbernans might be, but when it came to Mystral's most vulnerable, no one had a bigger heart, or a greater capacity for giving.

Dilys's hands clasped her shoulders, his touch warm and reassuring. "I am here, Gabriella. Do what you must. The men and I will make sure no one gets hurt."

She nodded, unable to speak. Her throat was tight, her magic swelling to a painful crescendo. She squeezed the ship's railing until her knuckles turned white, took a final, deep breath, then let out a Shout like no other. Magic poured from her throat, her fury, her vengeance, her grief, and her pain unleashed in a scream that blasted across the water and slammed into Trinipor like a hammer of the gods. Trees and buildings were ripped from their foundations. Stone shuddered and groaned. She Shouted and Shouted and Shouted, releasing all the rage and fury and grief inside her until Mur Balat's mighty fortress, the entire city of Trinipor, and several miles of the northern Ardullan coast crumbled and collapsed into the sea. In the water, the scores of swimming Calbernans absorbed the shock wave of the sudden collapse, taming the resulting tsunami before it could start, swimming fast away to disperse the energy in harmless bursts spread out across the Olemas.

When it was over, Gabriella leaned back into Dilys's strong arms. She felt drained and weary and sad, and the only reason she wasn't collapsing into broken sobs was because Dilys was there, his love and his strength pouring into all the empty places inside. Her sisters were gone, the men who'd hurt them and her were dead, she'd put an end to the Trinipor slave trade and wiped Mur Balat's base of power from the face of Mystral. She'd done all that she could to avenge her loved ones. It still wasn't enough—probably never would be—but it would have to be enough for now.

She turned to wrap her arms around Dilys's waist and pressed her face to his chest, letting the beat of his heart and the safe haven of his embrace soothe her raw emotions. "Let's go home, *moa akua*. To Calberna."

CHAPTER 27

The *Kracken* sailed slowly into the pristine turquoise waters of Cali Va'Lua's main harbor. Standing on the deck beside Dilys, wearing the sea-green gown his crew had made for her, Gabriella felt her stomach fluttering with a jumble of nerves and excitement.

Until the day of her abduction, she'd never traveled beyond the borders of the Æsir Isles. And except for a few childhood trips to Seahaven, to visit her mother's family, and her recent journey to Wintercraig, she'd never left Summerlea. In fact, after her mother's death, she'd rarely traveled beyond the walls of Vera Sola.

Calberna, with its crystalline waters, pink sand beaches, and swaying tropical palms, was the most exotic and beautiful place she'd ever been. Almost like a like a slice of Halla on earth. Everything was bright and beautiful, and the air was so thick with exuberant joy it was intoxicating to her senses. Thousands had gathered to welcome the first Siren to return to Calberna since the Slaughter. They lined the docks, as well as every ship in the harbor and every wall and walkway as far as she could see. Cheering, bright-eyed, sun-bronzed folk throwing flowers, and loops of blossoms and glossy green leaves as the *Kracken* sailed past.

"*Sirena!*" they cried, and, "*Myerielua!*"

"It seems the word about me is most definitely out," Gabriella murmured.

He grinned, his teeth white and dazzling in the dark bronze of his face. "*Tey.* Yours may well have been a Shout heard around the world."

He didn't look bothered by the idea, but still, she had to ask. "Is that going to be a problem for Calberna?"

"*Ono, moa haleah.* Most of those who will have heard your Shout won't know what it was. And of those who do, any of them foolish enough to invade Calbernan waters will find a harsh welcome." He bent to kiss her lips tenderly, which made the crowd go wild. That made him grin again and he pumped a massive fist in the air, to the further cheers of his countrymen. The sheer, silky fabric of his *obah* fluttered about him like a pennant.

She rolled her eyes. "You are enjoying this perhaps a little too much."

"No such thing. I am enjoying this every bit as much as I should. In fact, I think now, *you* should kiss *me* . . . may I suggest a great, lusty kiss so our people have no doubt that you have, indeed, claimed their prince as your own." He grinned. It was the sort of grin that was half dare, half amused certainty that she wouldn't take the dare.

Gabriella arched a brow. He'd been in especially high spirits all morning, teasing her, laughing, pulling the Siren's tail. She knew most of that was carefully orchestrated bluster to keep her nerves at bay. But part of it was because he thought he could tease her with impunity. Silly man. She hadn't spent a lifetime as the sister of Autumn Coruscate, the prankster princess, without learning how to answer a dare. Time for him to learn a little lesson about his new wife.

In a Voice filled with Command, she told him, "Bend down."

He was already bending before it even registered with him what she'd done, and when it did, his eyes went wide with surprise. But it was too late. She'd already caught him.

She gripped his head between her hands, plastered her lips to his, and proceeded to kiss the *shuma* off him.

As she did, she hummed softly in the back of her throat. The melody was one she'd only ever heard in those erotic dreams that had haunted her since the night at the Llaskroner Fjord when his *ulumi* had glowed blue, and it worked now exactly the way it had worked in those dreams.

Dilys shuddered and fell to his knees. His arms wrapped around her, his hands splayed across her back, gripping her tight as a sound that was half growl, half sob escaped him.

She kept kissing him and humming that tiny, powerful thread of Siren Song that was meant for him and him alone until every drop of his blood, every cell in his body, every thought, every breath, every beat of his heart opened to her, invited her in and begged for her claiming. She conquered him entirely, leaving no part of him untaken. And then she pulled back, meeting his stunned golden gaze with her own blazing one, and said against his swollen, trembling lips, "Thou art mine, Dilys Merimydion. Mine and no other's."

He swallowed hard, and his rasping, "*Tey*," was barely more than a scrape of sound.

She straightened, turned to the gathered crowds, and in a Voice backed with enough power to be heard by every ship in the harbor and every person in the city, declared in perfect Sea Tongue, "I claim this male as mine own. Before you all, I claim him. He is my mate, my male, my *akua*. Mine and no other's!" She repeated the claim in Eru, and then Ice Tongue as well, in consideration of the White Guards aboard her vessels.

For the next several seconds, a shocked, deafening silence ensued, broken only by the crack of the wind moving canvas sails, the sound of waves crashing on the shore, and the cries of seabirds wheeling overhead.

And then came the roar.

It welled up from every throat in the harbor. A great huzzah that was almost as loud as a Shout of their own. Suddenly, the air was filled with flowers and rings of glossy leaves and Calbernans leaping like dolphins in the waves and the chanting cries of *"Sirena! Sirena! Sirena!"*

Gabriella turned to Dilys, who was still swaying on his knees and staring at her like he'd never really seen her before. She grinned. "Was that lusty enough for you, then?"

He blinked and blinked again. "Er . . . *tey* . . . I think that did the trick."

She laughed and patted his cheek. "Good. Oh, and just so you know, it wasn't Spring who switched your water for Summerlean fire brandy that first morning."

The smile spread across his face, slowly at first, then bursting into a wide, dazzling grin. He surged to his feet in one fluid motion, sweeping her up in his arms. She thought he meant to kiss her every bit as senseless as she'd just kissed him, but instead he lifted her high and settled her on his broad shoulder.

"Sirena!" he cried, echoing the chants of his people. *"Sirena!"*

Behind her, every member of the *Kracken*'s crew was grinning wide enough to split their faces. The Calbernans leaping in the water began gathering up the floating blossoms and leafy wreaths and ferrying them to the ship, offering them to Gabriella and Dilys and everyone else aboard the ship until the *Kracken* was entirely festooned with bright flowers and greenery.

As they drew closer to the docks where the *Kracken* would make berth, Dilys took her down from his shoulder and set her back on her feet. He stood at her side, one broad hand resting at the small of her back. She liked that. She liked the oneness of standing side by side, liked the warm link of his skin against hers. She liked the joy pouring into her from all directions of this beautiful island nation.

She nestled against him and placed a hand over the swell of one hard pectoral muscle, sharing that joy with him. With it went a tendril of grief, still strong but no longer the raw, bitter pain it had been.

"I wish my sisters could have been here to see this."

"I wish that, too, Gabriella. More than almost anything I wish it. But the part of them that still lives in you *is* here."

It was a pretty sentiment, one she chose to embrace. The worst of what would have been her devastating grief was gone. The sadness was still there. Not taken away, but shared with him, and softened by the sharing. Without the grief, she could concentrate on the memories of all the loving, laughter-filled times she'd spent with her sisters, remembering the joy rather than the loss.

She stood there, nestled against him, smiling and waving to the exuberant, welcoming Calbernans and realized her mask was gone. Her smile was real. Her happiness genuine. For the first time in her life, the monster was at peace. Dilys had given her that, too.

They had reached the innermost part of the harbor.

"These are the docks and central warehouses of House Merimydion," Dilys said, pointing to the neat rows of large, aesthetically pleasing buildings gathered along the water's edge. "Half of all shipments in this hemisphere pass through this port. And thanks to many improvements my father and the other males of House Merimydion made over the years, a full third of that traffic travels on our ships and through our warehouses."

"You are telling me I've married into a House full of canny businessmen."

He smiled, revealing that creased dimple in his cheek. "*Tey.* Wealthy, too."

She laughed. "And modest."

"Most especially that." He lifted her hand for a kiss. The ship had come to a halt. Dilys's crew threw mooring ropes down to the waiting dockworkers. "Come, *moa liana.* My mother awaits." A swimmer had brought word earlier that *Myerial* Alysaldria had arranged a formal gathering at the palace to greet them. "To be honest, I am surprised she hasn't already sent a dozen couriers asking what's taking so long."

Mostly just to tease him, she said, "Maybe she isn't looking forward to meeting me quite as much as you've led me to believe."

"That's not true. I think she was even more impatient for me to claim a *liana* than I was."

Gabriella's brows lifted. "Oh, really?"

"*Tey.* She wants me settled, happily mated, with a family of my own."

"Even though I am an *oulani*?"

He smiled down at her with such tenderness it made her heart ache. "My mother was the one who insisted that I sail to Wintercraig to claim you even when others wanted me to wait for an *imlani* daughter to come of age." He smoothed a swooping lock of hair off her face and brushed the backs of his fingers across her cheek in a gentle caress. "I think she is glad, actually, that you are *oulani*. As such you become a daughter of House Meri-mydion, and I remain its son rather than joining the House of my *imlani* bride. *Nima* always wanted a daughter of her own, especially after losing my unborn sister after my father died. I am joyful that in wedding you, I can provide her the daughter she has always longed for."

Summer could hardly remember what it was to have a mother. She'd been so long without one. "Do you think she'll like me?"

He laughed, then scooped her up in his arms, sweeping her off her feet and kissing her soundly. "Like you? Oh, *moa kiri,* she will love you. Of that, I have no doubt. You are a woman of compassion and fire. You are brave and strong, but also gentle and understanding and good with even the most difficult of people." He set her back down on her feet and kissed her again. Then he straightened, puffed out his chest, and added, "And, of course, she will also love you because you have the good sense to love me, her only son."

Gabriella smacked him on the chest and rolled her eyes. "Arrogant."

He pretended to look wounded. "I but speak the truth. Or do you not love me after all?"

"Oh, I love you all right. In spite of the arrogance."

"Confidence."

"Arrogance."

He laughed. "Come now. Admit it. You already love me beyond all reason, just the way I am. You could not possibly love me more."

Her own smile faded. "*Tey*," she agreed seriously. "I do love you, *moa akua*. Beyond all reason. Just the way you are. I always will."

He kissed her again, thoroughly. He didn't pick her up this time; instead he bent down from his great height to meet her where she stood. His fingers thrust through the upswept waves of her hair, dislodging pins. He kissed her as if she were the essence of life and without her he would die. And to him, she was.

"As I love you, Gabriella Merimydion, *moa liana, moa haleah, moa fila*." My wife, my love, my life. The words felt like a sacred vow, whispered against her lips, breathed into her very soul. Her arms twined around his neck, holding him fast.

She stood up on the tips of her toes. Her back arched, body strained, as she met him kiss for kiss, vow for vow, love for love. "*Moa akua, moa haleah, moa fila*," she whispered back.

When Dilys lifted his head and straightened once more, it was to find all the Calbernans gathered on the docks watching him and Gabriella. They were grinning like thieves who'd just discovered a lost dragon's hoard. Dilys grinned back, and the crowd burst into raucous cheers, clapping and pumping their fists in the air.

Gabriella turned a deep rose beneath her brown Summerlander skin, but she didn't shrink back against him.

No, his sweet, brave *liana* lifted her beautiful chin and gave them all a regal—albeit very rosy—nod.

Still grinning, Dilys put a hand to the small of her back and started to usher her towards the end of the dock only to stop again at the sight of his uncle Calivan standing there, his shell-pink-and-ivory *obah* fluttering about him in the breeze.

"Uncle, there you are." Dilys smiled warmly.

Instead of returning the greeting or the warmth, his uncle's cool golden eyes swept over Gabriella and Dilys, settling on the silky white *obah* Dilys's men had made for him to celebrate his union.

"You spoke your vows? Without a priest? Your mother will not approve."

Dilys felt Gabriella stiffen at his side, and his own body drew tight with rising aggression. In a quiet voice, he said, "Uncle, you forget yourself. Do you not give welcome to my *liana*, Mystral's first Siren since the Slaughter?"

Immediately Calivan pasted on a smooth smile and an expression of warm welcome.

"Forgive me, *Myerialanna*," he said in crisp Eru, "Welcome to the Calbernan Isles. Warmest of greetings to your new home." He held out his hands, palms up.

After a quick, tentative glance up at Dilys, Gabriella placed her hands in Calivan's. "Thank you, Chancellor Merimydion."

"I was horrified, *leili*, to hear of the capture of you and your sisters, and devastated—as were we all—to learn of your sisters' untimely and tragic deaths."

"Thank you." Gabriella gave a flawless smile, gentle, understanding, serene. It was the smile Dilys had come to recognize as part of her "court face." Calivan's accusatory greeting had put her on edge, and she had retreated behind her most polite mask in response.

"The *Myerial* and the *Donimari* await us at the palace. I've arranged for a watercoach to take us. It's just over here." Calivan released one of Gabriella's hands and tucked the other on his arm as he turned and led the way. "I must apologize again for the rudeness of my initial greeting, *leili*," Calivan said as they walked. "It's just that I have spent a lifetime looking after my twin's happiness, and I know how much she was looking forward to planning and attending your wedding."

"I'm sorry. It was not my intention to have robbed Dilys's mother of a long-awaited joy."

Dilys didn't like hearing Gabriella apologize for wedding him, and he certainly didn't want her entertaining any regrets about it. "Our vows were spoken on the sea and bound in blood and salt," he said, "but I see no reason why we could not have a second ceremony at Cali Va'Lua or perhaps Merimydia Oa Nu. I'm sure *Nima* would enjoy it just as much."

"Of course," Calivan said. "That is what many of the *Calbernari* who returned with their *lianas* have already done."

"Problem solved, then." Dilys told himself he shouldn't bristle. His uncle had, after all, devoted his life to Alysaldria's happiness. And it was true Dilys's mother probably would be at least a tiny bit upset that her son had already spoken his vows on the sea, without the ceremony and celebration she had always envisioned for him. "I only have one son, and he will only wed once," she'd always told him when they spoke about her plans for his wedding. He had long ago resigned himself to a huge court affair, complete with parades, balls, fire ships, and more. Still, no matter what his mother wanted, that didn't excuse Calivan from voicing his displeasure in front of Gabriella.

"What reason did you give for evacuating the *oulani* from our waters?" Dilys asked to change the subject. There wasn't a single foreign ship in the harbor. That didn't surprise him. All *oulani* ships would have been sent away the instant Gabriella's Siren Shout had reached Calbernan shores.

"We told them there was a tsunami coming and that all foreign vessels needed to head out to sea."

"Ah." Gabriella's Shout had, in fact, generated a tsunami, so the warning hadn't been a lie. The Calbernans had simply dissipated the wave before it could make landfall. "And what will we say to keep them from returning?"

"The matter is still under discussion with the Council."

"You plan to isolate Calberna from the rest of the world?" Gabriella interrupted. "Why? Just because I'm a Siren?"

"Not just because you're a Siren," Calivan replied. "But because you're the *only* Siren—and the first born to this world in thousands of years. Your protection is of paramount importance. Especially given the recent unpleasantness."

"But my kidnapping had nothing to do with me being a Siren. Mur Balat and the Shark didn't know what I was. If they had, I doubt Balat would have sold me to Solish Utua."

"All the more reason to be extra cautious now. Calbernans have done everything in their power to erase all record of the Sirens and to dismiss the memories of them as fanciful folklore and myth, but it is possible there are those in the world who still know the truth, who would do you harm if they knew what you were. The Sirens were slaughtered precisely because Calberna allowed *oulani* into their lands and waters. We will not let that happen again. You are here with us now, and we intend to protect you in every way possible."

She pulled her hand off Calivan's arm and stopped walking. "You're proposing that I should be—what?—imprisoned here in Calberna for the rest of my life? Cut off from the outside world? Cut off from my *family*?"

"Of course not. Your sister Khamsin and her husband will always be welcome to visit. But do not forget that Dilys is your family now," Calivan said. "As are the *Myerial* and I."

Dilys recognized the flare of rebellion sparking in Gabriella's eyes and the determined tilt to her chin, and he grew alarmed. Calivan was making a muck of things. "No one is talking about imprisoning anyone, least of all you." He shot his uncle a hard look. "But my uncle is right about the danger *oulani* now pose to you. *Moa haleah,* you know about the Slaughter. You know why the truth about your gifts must never be revealed outside of Calberna. We cannot risk such a thing ever happening again. *I* will not risk such a thing happening to you."

"I understand that, and I'm not proposing that we run around shouting what I am to all corners of Mystral. But I just spent weeks being held against my will, and that will never happen again. I may be a Siren and I may have married you, but I will be returning to Wintercraig to visit my sister Khamsin and her husband and their children. And I also intend to hold you to your promise to show me the world."

"And I will keep my promise, as I keep all of them. We will return to Wintercraig within the week, if you like." Now that the Shark and Mur Balat were gone, the most immediate danger had passed. Others would need time to prepare before they dared launch an attack. But even if that weren't the case, if she needed to see her family, he would make it happen. He took her hands and pressed her palms to his chest, willing her to feel his sincerity, willing her to believe that no matter what his uncle or even his mother said, Dilys's first loyalty was to Gabriella now. Now and forevermore. "Whatever you want, *moa haleah,* whatever you need, so shall I provide."

"All right," she said. "All right." She took a breath and grew visibly calmer. "As for isolating Calberna from the rest of the world because of me, I believe that is precisely the wrong thing to do. People fear the unknown. If Calberna closes its harbors and no longer welcomes foreigners to its shores, all you will succeed in doing is rousing suspicion and distrust."

"I'm sure the *Myerial* and her Council would welcome your input as they decide the way forward, *Myerialanna*," Calivan said.

Gabriella looked as if she was about to argue more, but instead, she swallowed it back and gave another of her polite court smiles. "Then I shall be sure to speak with them, Lord Chancellor."

They began walking again, chatting about less volatile subjects as they went. Gabriella did not take Calivan's arm again, but instead remained close by Dilys's side. He liked that after the argument with her uncle her first instinct was to make it clear she and Dilys were a unit: Dilys and Gabriella, a mated pair.

"Ah, here we are. Your watercoach, *Myerialanna*." Calivan gestured to a lacquered blue-green boat, open at the front, and shaped to resemble a cresting wave, complete with silver fringe and accents made to resemble sea foam.

"How beautiful," Gabriella said as Dilys helped her into the fanciful canal boat. "I almost feel as if it should be pulled by along by a harnessed team of dolphins."

"That's only for when we take the coach for a spin on the open sea," Dilys said. Her eyes widened, and he laughed. "I'm joking, *moa kiri*. Although now that you mention it, such a mode of transportation would, no doubt, delight *Nima,* although she doesn't do as much sailing as she used to."

"Why not?"

It was Calivan who answered. "There are many demands on her time. Queendoms, like kingdoms, don't govern themselves."

"Well, perhaps that will change now that Dilys and I are married and can be here to help."

Dilys smiled and lifted her hand for a kiss, happy that Calivan's earlier, uncharacteristic blundering hadn't put her off the idea of making Calberna her home.

"Perhaps, it will indeed." Calivan nodded to the gondolier, and with an answering nod, the muscular Calbernan thrust his pole into the water and pushed off.

The city was clustered at the base of a great mountain peak that rose sharply into the sky, its steep surfaces forested in lush green foliage broken by dozens of tall cloud-fed waterfalls. The slender watercoach glided smoothly through the crystal-clear waters of the city canals towards a tunnel in the side of the mountain.

Schools of brightly colored fish swam in the crystalline waters beneath the boat. It was astonishing to Gabriella that any city's waters could remain so clear and unpolluted, even on Calberna. She started to say something about it to Dilys, but just then a Calbernan male and three small boys swam underneath the boat. They rolled over on their backs to grin and wave as they passed by.

Her mouth fell open. "My word."

Beside her, Dilys laughed. "Someone's showing off. That's another of my cousins, Maru Ocea, and his boys. They will meet you properly at the palace."

"Ocea? Any connection to—?"

"*Tey.* Maru is married to Ryll's sister."

She watched the man and his three sons, four dark shadows knifing swiftly and effortlessly through the waters, until they swam so far ahead she couldn't see them anymore. Not once did they surface for air. "So it's true that Calbernans can breathe underwater?"

He shrugged. "It's true."

"How?"

"A gift of our physiology. We have gill slits. Here." He traced a finger down the side of his ribs. "They seal when not in use, but when we swim, we can open them to breathe the oxygen in the water."

"Like fish."

"This upsets you, *moa kiri*?"

"No, I'm not upset. Maybe a little disappointed." She

bit her lip and smiled a little sheepishly. "I was sort of hoping it was more Calbernan magic. The kind you could work on other people, so I could go swimming like that, too."

"Ah." He was smiling again. Relieved. "I'm afraid not." Dilys laid a hand on her shoulder and squeezed gently. She leaned back against him and snuggled closer when his arms wrapped around her.

"Our children, will they be born like you? Able to breathe in water?"

His arms tightened a little at the mention of children and his lips found her neck for a kiss that made her eyes close in quiet bliss. "*Tey.* All *imlani* are. Does that thought disturb you?"

"No, not particularly. But how is it possible? Your people have been mating with outlanders almost exclusively for over two thousand years. Genetically, speaking, you should have bred out almost all Calbernan traits by now."

"I explained to you about the ability of Calbernan males to store and use the magic gifted to them by women of power."

"Yes."

"Well, native-born Calbernan females have a gift too. Not only can they fuel the magic of our males, but they can pass all or a portion of their gifts to others. Every female bearing Calbernan young will visit the *imlani* women of her House during her pregnancy, and the *imlani* will pass a portion of their seagifts to the young. The closer the blood ties, the more magic the *imlani* women will share with the unborn child—especially if the child is a daughter. It is how we survived after the slaughter of the Sirens. To keep our race alive, the strongest of our remaining women shared their power with the next generation, and upon their deaths, they gave what remained of their gifts to the *Myerial*. And every *Myerial* thereafter passed that power along with her own to her successor. My mother, when she inherited the throne, received all the accumulated power of *Myerial* Siavaluana II and all the *Myerials* that came before her. She would have passed that power to our daughter, but since you are a Siren, the Sea Throne and the *Myerial*'s gifts rightfully belong to you. And you can pass both to our daughter in time."

"What if we don't have a daughter?"

"If we have a son who marries and bears a daughter, you will pass the Sea Throne and your gifts to her. Should you perish without a daughter or granddaughter of your blood, then the throne and your gifts will go to my mother's uncle Aleki's daughter Aleakali Maru. None of Siavaluana II's children bore her female grandchildren while she was still alive, and Aleakali Maru is the eldest granddaughter of Siavaluana I, born while her aunt, Siavaluana II was on the throne, and thus granted a queen's gift while in the womb."

"That seems very confusing."

"Calbernan succession is always determined by which *imlani* daughter has the closest and most recent blood ties to the line of the *Myerials*. All *imlani* females who belong to the House of the current queen or the House of a previous *Myerial* receive a gift of power from the current *Myerial* while still in the womb. That power will be added to her own, thus making her and her daughters stronger in their gifts, and ultimately restoring the Sirens to Calberna."

"But I have no blood tie to the *Myerials*. Won't there be objections to my taking the throne?"

"You are a Siren. Those objections are moot."

"Hmm." Many a civil war had broken out over disputed royal successions. And as they'd been sailing down the crowd-lined canalways, Gabriella thought she'd seen more than a few native Calbernans who didn't appear quite as enthusiastically welcoming as the rest.

"Dilys is correct," Calivan said. "The families who

wanted Dilys to wed an *imlani liana* will hold their silence now. Tradition demands it."

People holding their tongues was a far cry from people embracing her in welcome, but she was no stranger to court politics. She'd won over diplomats from enemy kingdoms and garnered support for her father's initiatives on more than one occasion. She'd make a place for herself here, too. This was a land where women led. She was more used to being a subtle power behind the throne, but she'd been trained to be a queen who would do any kingdom proud. She'd do Dilys and House Merimydion proud, too.

"Then I will do everything in my power to serve House Merimydion well and prove worthy of the support and acceptance of Calberna's esteemed families," she said.

For the first time, Calivan smiled with genuine warmth. "Well spoken, Gabriella."

Dilys settled back in his cushioned bench, his arm still curled around her shoulders, one hand gently stroking the side of her throat. She liked his touch. It soothed her, that closeness, the tender intimacy, the knowledge that if she was near, he hungered for physical contact as much as she did.

Symbiosis, indeed. Since they'd wed, she couldn't go more than a minute or two without wanting to touch him. If Dilys's parents had shared a similarly deep bonding experience, she wasn't sure how *Myerial* Alysaldria had managed to survive all these years without her husband. Now that Gabriella claimed Dilys as her own, and been claimed in return, the idea of living life without him was anathema. She wouldn't linger on for years as her father had done, consumed by loss until love turned to madness. She would find a way to follow him.

The boat turned left at another curved intersection, and the rows of houses and grassy banks opened up to a spectacular final approach to the palace. Larger-than-life statues of muscled Calbernan males with flowing ropes of hair, their massive fists clutching tridents of pure gold, lined both sides of the canal, and arcs of water shot from the points of their tridents. The watercoach sailed beneath the canopy of jetted water into the cool, darkness of the tunnel. On the other side of the mountain, another formation of statuary greeted them, but these stony Calbernans were female, slender and shapely, with graceful arms lifted overhead, holding large conch shells from which spouted another crisscrossed canopy of glittering, sun-drenched water.

Beyond them, the canal opened to an enormous, crystal-blue lagoon ringed on all sides by steep, lushly-greened cliffs.

"How stunning," she breathed. "Is this—? Was this—?"

"A volcano?" Dilys supplied. "*Tey.* All the Calbernan Isles are. But this is the oldest and greatest of them all. Long since dormant, of course. Now home to the children of Numahao."

"It's magnificent." The water-filled crater of the volcano had been transformed into a massive, naturally-walled city, its only navigable entrance through that tunnel. At the center of the great lagoon rose the pink, gold, and ivory beauty of Cali Va'Lua, Calberna's royal palace.

The canal boat docked, and Dilys led Gabriella through the immaculate palace gardens into Cali Va'Lua's stunning coral and crystal foyer.

From the foyer, they passed through a wide gallery lined with paintings and statuary of the great queens of Calberna, then down a wide marble stair to a magnificent room that Dilys called the Hall of Waters. On either side of a wide marble walkway, clear sheets of water poured from pearl-encrusted fountainheads into the large pools. Abundant clusters of fragrant lilies covered the surface of the pools. Beneath their wide green leaf pads and trailing roots, bright orange, white, and purple fish swam in leisurely circles, while beyond the Hall's thick glass walls and reinforced glass roof, brightly colored tropical fish of the wild variety swam among vibrant coral reefs.

At the end of the Hall, a curving spill of stairs led to the throne room below.

"Wait," she said when the guards flanking the throne room doors started to open them.

Dilys regarded her in concern. "Gabriella?"

"I just need a moment." She took a breath. She was surprised at the nerves fluttering inside her. She'd spent her whole life at court, first her father's, then Wynter's. But it wasn't really the introduction to a new court that was making her nervous. "Are you sure your mother's going to like me?"

Dilys's expression softened. "My mother will love you. How could she not?"

There was such sincerity and assurance in his voice, such love beaming from his eyes. For her. She clamped down on her nerves and summoned a smile that only trembled slightly. *Courage, Summer. This is only the first impression that will affect the rest of your life.*

"All right," she said a moment later. "All right, let's do this."

Dilys nodded, and the guards opened the massive, gilded doors.

Everyone—and there were hundreds assembled within—turned to face the doors as they opened. There were so many golden eyes and burnished bronze faces in this room. Not a foreign face in the lot. Except for hers.

"These are the *Donimari*," Dilys whispered. "The heads of all Calbernan Houses, along with their *akuas*."

Gabriella's fingers tightened around Dilys's hand. His fingers squeezed back. The heat deep inside her lurched, pressure building. But before fear could rouse the volcano, Dilys's thumb stroked the inside of her palm. And in that instant, her fear fell away. Oh, it wasn't completely gone. She could still feel the fluttering jumps in her belly. But

Dilys was beside her, and she realized he would always stand beside her, no matter what. And with him at her side, she no longer needed to fear the violent power that lived inside her. Her chin lifted.

She pasted a serene expression on her face, and with Dilys at her side, sailed forth into the unfamiliar sea.

The *Donimari* moved aside as Dilys and Gabriella approached, clearing a path from the door to the throne, and Gabriella had her first glimpse of *Myerial* Alysaldria I, Queen of Calberna. Gabriella's new mother-in-law.

She was a tiny woman. Small boned, delicately formed. Perhaps the massive throne she sat upon made her appear smaller, but Summer didn't think so. Thrones tended to increase one's appearance of grandeur, not decrease it. The closer she and Dilys approached, the more apparent it became that Alysaldria was, indeed, a small woman. Probably several inches shorter than Summer herself. Yet she'd birthed a son who stood seven feet tall. Astonishing.

She was beautiful, too. Truly, enchantingly beautiful. As dark as her son, with huge, black-lashed golden eyes in a fine-boned face of delicate, ethereal beauty. Long skeins of silky black hair were piled atop her head. To a man, Calbernan males wore their hair in scores of long ropes. Not because they fixed it that way, but because that was the way it grew. The women, however, did not. What ropes there were had been put there, braided or curled. The rest was a silky mass of lustrous black strands. If Alysaldria brushed out her hair, it would probably spill down to her ankles.

She wore a crown that looked like the fronds of golden anemones, each curling spike crusted with diamonds and pearls. Pearls wound through her hair and draped across her chest, following the boat-shaped neckline of her stunning coral gown studded with pearls and diamonds and golden beads. Her slender hands were folded in her lap, the short, oval nails painted the same color as her gown.

"*Myerial*." Dilys dropped to his knee before the throne.

"*Myerial*," Gabriella echoed, and she sank into a smooth, deep court curtsy.

"Rise and be welcome, Dilys, *soa elua*," Alysaldria said. "Rise and be welcome, *Sirena* Gabriella, *soa Doalanna, Myerialanna kona Calberna*."

A loud, shocked murmur of protest rose from the court.

Gabriella sent a quick, questioning glance at Dilys, who looked both stunned and impressed. Behind him, Chancellor Calivan appeared dumbfounded. "What is it? What just happened?"

"My mother has just Spoken from the Sea Throne," Dilys murmured in her ear as they rose. "She has just welcomed you as a Siren and daughter and has declared you the rightful heir both to the Sea Throne and House Merimydion. She has made it impossible for any of the *Donimari* to challenge your position or authority."

The *Myerial* held out her hands. "Come closer, my children."

Summer followed Dilys's lead, climbing the coral steps of the throne's dais and taking the queen's hands.

"You are well, my son?" Alysaldria's sharp gaze swept over her son with a mother's attentiveness, missing nothing. "You were chasing those *krillos* so long that I began to worry."

"I am well, as you can see, *Nima*," Dilys assured her. "The *krillos* had help masking their trail. But they have been dealt with. As I mentioned in my report, the Shark is no more."

"Nor is the Pureblood Alliance. After your news, I summoned them all for a Questioning. There was more rotten fruit on that tree, but it has been plucked now. The traitor Nemuan has been declared *kado'ido,* a Houseless pariah whose name has been stricken from Calberna, all images and records of him excised. The others who confessed to plotting with him have already met the kracken. I have permitted the rest of the traitors' Houses to don white in mourning for their lost sons, but only on condition that they should immediately repudiate and dissolve the Pureblood Alliance and join me in welcoming my new daughter as the blessing of Numahao that she is."

"That doesn't appear to have gone over well," Dilys murmured, glancing around the room at the tight faces and barely leashed resentment from quarters that had previously been quite vocal supporters of the Pureblood Alliance.

"I don't care. They fomented rebellion and provided a breeding ground for traitors. They're lucky I didn't purge their whole Houses. A Siren has been returned to us. They can either accept her or meet the kracken like their treacherous kin. But enough nasty politics." In an abrupt change of subject, Alysaldria turned a golden-eyed smile on Gabriella. "You are not the Season we chose for my son."

Gabriella's lips curled wryly. "So I understand, *Myerial.*"

"*Nima,* my daughter. You must call me *Nima,* now. You may be *oulani,* but you are also a Siren bound to my son in blood and salt, and therefore bound to me by the same, my daughter and a daughter of my House. My joy is beyond measure." Her voice resonated with sincerity.

"*Nima.*" Warmth unfurled in Gabriella's chest. She'd lived most of her life without a mother. To have one again . . . it was more than she had hoped for since she was a child. "I am the one who is joyful. Dilys has told me much about you."

Alysaldria arched a brow at her son. "All good, I should hope."

"Of course." Gabriella wet her lips. "I know I am not the wife you would have chosen for him, but I promise I will make him happy."

The *Myerial's* full lips broadened in a smile every bit as dazzling as her son's, and in her cheek bloomed a dimple even more pronounced than his. "You are wrong, my dear. My advisors may have thought one of your two sisters would have been the best choice, but not I. I trusted my son to win the claim of the woman best suited to him. Do you love him?"

"Very much."

"Then he has exceeded my dearest wishes for him, for it is clear to me that he loves you as deeply as any *akua* ever has or could love his *liana*. That you are a Siren, bringing back to us the most ancient, powerful, and venerated of all Calbernan magics, is an added gift we could never have expected or hoped for, and proof that even the wisest of advisors can sometimes make mistakes." She cast a look towards a group of Calbernans standing to the left of the throne. The advisors, Gabriella deduced, when several of them began looking distinctly shamefaced.

"I am sure they had only Dilys's and Calberna's best interests at heart," Gabriella said, speaking loudly enough for those closest to the throne—including the advisors—to hear. She couldn't change the past, but she could do everything possible to smooth her way forward, including soothing the ruffled feathers of those who would have picked a different wife for their prince. "I spent a lifetime suppressing and masking my gifts out of fear of harming someone with them. Your advisors saw me exactly as I intended everyone should—as the weakest of the Summer King's daughters. But Dilys has convinced me that the power I have feared all my life need not be a danger to those I love, but a boon for his—for *our*—people. Thank you, *Myerial*—*Nima*—for your warm and gracious welcome. As I told your brother, Lord Chancellor Calivan, earlier, I shall endeavor to serve House Merimydion, Calberna, and all the folk of the Isles to the best of my ability."

"I am sure you will, *moa alanna*. We will begin preparations for your coronation immediately. I will, of course, abdicate the throne and pass to you the gifts that *Myerial* Siavaluana gave to me on her deathbed."

"Alys! *Ono!*"

Alysaldria speared her brother with a look sharp enough to silence his distraught outburst.

"As a Siren, Gabriella, the Sea Throne rightfully belongs to you," Dilys's mother continued. Her voice had a hard edge to it, a clear warning against further dissent. "It is not meet that I should keep the crown when Numahao has sent to my House a daughter bearing her greatest gift."

Gabriella could feel the scores of eyes boring into her back, but despite the tense silence of the throne room, no one uttered a sound. Calberna was a land steeped in tradition. And she was an outsider—an *oulani* stranger suddenly thrust into their midst. Calivan may have been the only one to verbalize his distress over his sister's decision to abdicate, but she doubted he was the only one to hold that sentiment.

"I am honored by your trust, *moa Myerial*," she began cautiously, "and I wish to serve Calberna to the best of my ability, but you are its queen, not I. I am, after all, a stranger to these lands, and to its people."

"That matters not. The law is clear. Sirens rule Calberna. You are a Siren. The Sea Throne is yours."

Gabriella bit her lip. First she had gotten into an argument with Calivan, and now the queen. She hadn't wanted to start her first day in her new home getting in fights with every member of Dilys's family, but the idea of suddenly becoming responsible for the governance of an entire nation was more than a little overwhelming.

"But must it be so right away?" she pressed. "So much has happened so quickly, *moa Myerial*. I need time to settle into my new home and become familiar with the ways and traditions of my new country. To give Calbernans a chance to get to know me, and I them. And also to work beside you, to learn to be a queen worthy of ruling of these great Isles."

"This is unnecessary. You are a Siren. Your worthiness is unquestionable."

Beside her, Dilys shifted his weight from one foot to another. The slight, nearly imperceptible motion made her aware of his growing unease. Gabriella's hackles rose. She laid a hand on Dilys's arm, and forced a pleasant smile. "I appreciate your confidence in me, *Myerial*. I suggest we discuss the particulars of the succession later, once my *akua* and I have had a chance to rest from our journey."

"Very well, but I must warn you, I will not change my mind on this matter."

"Then our discussion should be lively indeed, because neither will I. And Dilys can tell you how stubborn I get when I'm determined not to do something."

Dilys gave a laugh that sounded only slightly forced. "Oh, *tey*, my *liana* is the proverbial immovable object."

"Is she?" Alysaldria arched a brow, power vibrating in her voice.

Gabriella met the challenge of her mother-in-law's golden gaze head-on. "*Tey*," she replied with an answering rumble of power, "she is."

The two of them stood there for several, long, silent moments—the two greatest powers in Calberna—taking each other's measure, each refusing to be the first to look away. Summer had spent a lifetime soothing others and subtly Persuading them out of their snits, but the right to self-determination wasn't going to be a battle she won with charm. Not this time. Dilys's mother was clearly used to mowing down all obstacles in her path through the sheer force of her will and her power, but Gabriella was done being Sweet Summer. She was a creature of great power, and she would not be bullied into doing anything she did not wish to do.

Besides, if she ever *was* to take over rule of this queendom, she could not afford to let the *Donimari* see her back down from the very first challenge of her authority. That was one of the lessons she'd learned from her father: no one respects weakness.

Abruptly, Alysaldria broke into a wide, bright smile, the dimple flashing in her cheek. "Ah, my son, your *liana* will keep you on your toes."

Dilys let out the breath he'd been holding and answered his mother's dimpled smile with one of his own. "I know it well, *Nima*. And I thank Numahao daily."

His mother rose from the throne. "Come, *moa alanna*. Allow me to introduce you to the *Donimari*."

CHAPTER 28

The next several days passed in a whirl for Gabriella as she settled into her new life. Ari had roused and was on the mend, although due to all he'd suffered, his memory of his time in captivity was riddled with gaps. In Gabriella's opinion, the loss of those particular memories sounded more like a boon than a curse. There were a few of her own she wished she could forget.

Dilys was embracing his new role as a married man with relish. He'd resigned his commission in the Calbernan navy in order to take over the day-to-day running of House Merimydion's conglomerate of businesses.

Although Gabriella had remained steadfast in her refusal to take the place of Alysaldria as *Myerial,* the two of them had worked out a compromise. Alysaldria would continue to act as *Myerial* for the immediate future. In return, Gabriella agreed to spend five hours a day apprenticing with Dilys's mother, becoming acquainted with the current state of Calbernan affairs and the duties of its queen so that she could both assist the *Myerial* and prepare for the day she eventually assumed the throne. At *Myerial* Alysaldria's insistence, Gabriella also spent another five hours a day with Lord Chancellor Calivan, who had assumed the responsibility of bringing Gabriella up to speed with the history of Calberna, its royal families, and everything known about the Sirens.

"Ever since the Slaughter of the Sirens some twenty-five hundred years ago, Calberna has made a national mission of seeking out and either liberating or destroying all written records about the Sirens," Calivan informed Gabriella as they walked down a spiraling glass tube that led from the main, central hub of the palace to a smaller, completely submerged structure built some forty feet deeper in the volcanic crater. "Our primary goal was to erase all proof of their existence and their abilities—to delegate them to the realm of myth and legend. The hope was, of course, that when the Sirens finally returned to us, the world would have forgotten the true extent of their power. The world would, therefore, have no cause for alarm at their return, and no reason to ally against us, thereby allowing the Sirens to quietly increase their numbers and return their great strength and great gifts to our people."

"Dilys told me about the Slaughter," Gabriella murmured. "I can understand why Calbernans felt the need to take such precautions."

Although she paid complete attention to what Calivan was saying, her gaze drank in the sight of the undersea world just beyond the walkway tube's glass walls. The waters were darker here, in the depths of the crater. You could still clearly see the bright sunlight overhead, but below, the watery world became shadowy. The round glow lights running along the walkway's ceiling illuminated a different reef from the one in the brightness overhead. Fewer fish. The corals and the fish both darker and less colorful than the relatives that basked in the warm, sun-drenched waters above, but beautiful nonetheless.

Biross and Tarrant, two of Gabriella's new guards, walked behind them, their massive hulking presence making her feel comfortable. Four of the *Myerial*'s own guards accompanied them as well—two at the front and two in the rear. A protective detail that, Calivan informed her, had become standard ever since the deaths of the previous *Myerial* and her daughter.

"The histories of the Sirens have been preserved for

posterity in the private library of the *Myerials*," Calivan continued as they walked. "Documents describing the various gifts and great feats of Calberna's greatest Sirens. Histories of their battles and sacrifices. Personal memoirs of the Sirens, their mates, and their most trusted confidants and advisors. Fascinating stuff. The *Myerials* and Lord Chancellors through the ages have maintained this information in the hopes that it might be used to train future Sirens to manage their gifts."

Gabriella nodded. "You think there will be information there that can teach me how to better control my Siren gifts?"

"I know there is." Calivan smiled down at her. The sheer silk of his *obah*—a rich copper, today, that set off his greenish-blue *shuma*—swung about him with each step, making the scalloped fringe of pearls, aquamarine beads, and tiny oxidized copper discs that edged the *obah* sparkle and chime. "The study of magic has always been a particular hobby of mine, especially when it comes to magic that could aid or threaten a Siren. Alys—my sister—might not be a full Siren, but she has always been remarkably gifted—one of the strongest *imlani* born to our people since the Sirens. I set out from an early age to learn everything I could to protect her and prevent an attack such as the Slaughter from ever happening again."

"I can understand that." Gabriella thought of her own sisters, and all the ways she'd stifled her own magic in order to keep them safe from it. "Sisters are precious."

"They are indeed." There was a strange sadness in his golden eyes and a wistful melancholy at the corners of his mouth turned his expression pensive and slightly regretful. Then he smiled again, and the fleeting expression vanished. "And now that you have come to Calberna—Mystral's first Siren since the Slaughter—I can show you the skills and artifacts I've amassed over the years to keep Alys safe and strong."

"I look forward to learning anything you can teach me.

Dilys may have informed you that I've always been . . . afraid to use my magic. I haven't always been able to control it. That's why I insisted on bringing Biross and Tarrant with me today." She nodded at the two towering warriors walking behind her. "Since we're going to be doing magical exercises, they're here in case I call up too much magic and need someone to bleed off the excess."

Calivan arched a brow. "Dilys said you were quite gifted."

"Dangerously so. I've kept my gifts suppressed all my life. It's the only way I've been able to stop from hurting people by accident, but that's not an option anymore. My magic has become too powerful to be bottled up all the time, and it replenishes at such a fast rate, I worry about keeping the pressure from building too high." She regarded him hopefully. "Does that sound like a problem your magical studies can help me with?"

"I believe so. Just off the top of my head, I can think of several techniques we might try, and there are at least three ancient Sirens who were reputed to be extraordinarily powerful. We can probably find some mention in their journals about how they kept their gifts from harming those around them."

They had reached the end of the spiraling tube and stepped into a building that had clearly been carved through the coral and directly into the steep, volcanic rock of the crater. The dark, pitted stone had been left rough in places, and in others had been smoothed and inlaid with gorgeous detailed mosaics depicting what looked like scenes from Calbernan history. Men and women swimming and hunting among the fishes. Erupting volcanoes spilling rivers of orange lava into steaming oceans. Ancient, gold-eyed women standing tall and commanding atop great stone promontories, holding out their slender arms towards the enormous white, foaming sprays of crashing waves.

The entire lagoon-facing wall of the spacious room

was a bubble of clear glass, allowing for a spectacular underwater view of the crater, the expansive underwater portion of the palace, and the vibrant coral reef above. Near the glass wall, a wide moon pool carved into the floor provided direct access to the deep waters of the lagoon, so that Calbernans could swim in and out of the room at will.

Gabriella paused to drink in the underwater view of the lagoon. "This is beautiful."

Calivan paused beside her. "*Tey.* The sea is one of Mystral's greatest treasures. A secret world of unparalleled beauty that most *oulani* will never know." After a moment, he turned and gestured to a door carved into the volcanic rock. "This way, *Sirena.*"

She and her two guards followed Calivan through the door. Beyond the door lay a large, windowless room carved deep into the black rock of the extinct volcano. Bookcases lined every wall and formed long rows that spanned the entire length of the room, each one crammed with books, scrolls and piles of paper.

"The archives of the Sirens," Calivan announced. "This room contains every surviving historical record of the Sirens, including the texts from Calberna's own libraries as well as all the documents we have . . . ahem . . . liberated over the last twenty-five hundred years from libraries and private collections across the whole of Mystral."

"Impressive." She wandered over to one of the closest bookcases and plucked a book from the shelf, leafing through the surprisingly modern-looking pages. "This one seems relatively new."

"We have transcribed the older texts so their information is not lost. The most delicate of the original documents are kept in a special storage room in an effort to slow their inevitable decay."

"Mmm. Smart." She set the book back on the shelf and dusted her hands. "So, do we begin here, with you teaching me the history of the Sirens?"

"*Ono.* I will compile a condensed version of what information I believe you will find most useful. But first, I think we should begin by testing your magic, so I understand what we're working with."

Gabriella shifted her weight from one foot to another. It was ridiculous to be so nervous. Thanks to the Shout that had sent Trinipor into the sea, her magical reservoirs, while nowhere close to being empty, were still a long way from overflowing. She should be able to manage a few simple tests without endangering anyone.

Straightening her spine, Gabriella forced a smile to shove her nervous discomfort deep down inside. "Of course," she said, pleased with the calm, cool, collected tone that gave away none of her jittery fear. She glanced around the full library. "Considering how valuable all this information is, however, I don't think we should begin those tests here."

Calivan gave a short bark of laughter. "*Ono,* I should say not." A smile of genuine amusement curved his lips. "I have a private laboratory, where I do most of my experiments with magic. It's just this way." He began walking towards another door off to one side of the library, flanked by two of the four queen's guards.

Gabriella glanced over her shoulder to make sure Biross and Tallant were behind her, and followed Dilys's uncle.

"The Second Fleet will sail today. There's still cleanup to be done in the Olemas. As for you, Ryll"—Dilys held up a hand to forestall the objection he saw brewing in his cousin—"I promised Khamsin of the Storms I would bring her sisters home. Once Ari is on his feet again, I want the two of you to return to Konumarr with the remains of the Seasons Spring and Autumn. You will be my envoys to Wintercraig, offering Calberna's contract of alliance to our new family in the Æsir Isles. You will take the rest of our brothers with you. According to the terms of my contract, you are still owed a few weeks of courtship. My greatest wish is that you both will find *lianas* who can make your heart sing, as Gabriella does mine."

"Unlikely." Ryll smiled ruefully. "The *Sirena* is one of a kind."

"I wouldn't be too sure of that. Her Siren's blood came from somewhere, after all."

Ryll quirked a brow. "You think there could be more Sirens out there?"

"I think it's a definite possibility. Which is why, when you and Ari bring the Seasons back home, I want you both to begin investigating. After Gabriella's great Shout and our subsequent battle with Nemuan, we can't assume her secret is still safe. Which means if there are others like her, they won't be safe either. Many will want to claim that power for their own—and not just the magic eaters."

"Magic eaters." Ryll spat the words like a curse and paced beside the round window of Dilys's palace office. Beyond the thick glass, bright tropical fish swam lazily amongst the coral reefs that lined Cali Va'Lua's great lagoon. "I still can't believe Nemuan sank so low. I still can't believe he was the Shark, either! He was a Prince of Calberna—the son of a great *Myerial*. How could he betray us—betray his own mother! Betray everything he was raised to honor and protect!—in such a vile, unforgivable way?"

"He was grief-mad," Dilys said. "The thought of an *oulani* woman—even a Siren—sitting on the throne that had belonged to his mother was more than he could bear."

"It was more than just that," a familiar voice said from behind.

Dilys and Ryll spun around. "Ari!"

Their cousin listed in the doorway. His arms, left leg, and torso were thickly bandaged. His broken right leg was splinted from ankle to several inches above his bended knee, and he was leaning heavily on a crutch tucked under his left arm. His dark bronze skin had a sallow cast, and deep lines of pain were etched from his nose to the corners of his mouth. He'd pulled off the bandages that had swathed his face, revealing a jagged patchwork of angry red wounds, the edges of which had been stitched together with black thread. The healers had already informed Dilys they could do nothing to prevent scarring, that Ari's only hope of even minimizing it was to stay out of the sun for at least a year. As if that was going to happen. Though he and Dilys had once been mirror images of one another, no one would ever again mistake one of them for the other.

"What are you doing here?" Dilys jumped up and skirted around the edge of his desk, intending to rush to his wounded cousin's side, but Ryll beat him to it, sliding a strong arm around Ari's back and guiding him to one of the two large chairs in front of Dilys's desk.

"Sit, Ari. Sit before you fall."

Ari scowled, then winced as motion tugged the torn edges of his stitched wounds. "I'm fine, Ryll. Don't fuss."

"You shouldn't even be awake, much less up and wandering around. Calivan was keeping you sedated to speed your healing! How it is your mother even let you out of bed?" Ari's mother had been glued to her youngest son's side since the moment he'd been carried off Dilys's ship. No one—not even Calivan—had been able to pry her from her child's bedside.

Ari collapsed in the chair, grimacing at the clear proof of his own weakness. "*Nima*'s sleeping. I needed to speak to Dilys, so I slipped the tonic Calivan meant for me into her tea. They won't be happy with me, but at least my *nima* will get a few hours of rest instead of driving herself towards a Fade worrying over me." He shifted in the chair, stifling a groan as his wounds protested.

Dilys clenched his jaw. This was his fault. He'd made his cousin a target. Nemuan had taken him—tortured him—to get to Dilys. "I am so sorry, Ari. I never meant for this to happen. If I could take your pain and bear it myself, I would."

Ari blinked in surprise, then smiled gently. "Do you think I don't know that? What happened to me wasn't your fault. The only person to blame is Nemuan." His smile turned rueful. "And me for not smelling the stench of treason when it sailed right up to my ship and boarded."

"Nonsense. He fooled us all. Even after I knew he was my enemy, I didn't realize the extent of his treachery. He was the son of a *Myerial*, after all. Even grief-mad, he should still have the strength to uphold the honor of his House."

"In a very twisted way, that's what he thought he was doing. That's what I wanted to talk to you about." Ari grimaced as he stretched out his splinted leg before him. "Nemuan blamed House Merimydion for the death of his mother and sister. He said the cave-in at the ancient temple—the one that killed Nyamialine and the others—was deliberate. He claimed your House orchestrated the disaster to put your *nima* on the throne."

"That's absurd!" Dilys felt his temper shoot up, battle claws pressing against the tips of his fingers. He'd rip Nemuan to shreds all over again if he could. "That *farking* idiot betrayed his people, became a magic eater, murdered Calbernans, then kidnapped, tortured, and sold the Seasons of Summerlea because he thought my family murdered the *Myerial* and her daughter for the Sea Throne? My *nima* never wanted that burden! Blessed Numahao, ever since my father died, all she wanted was to join him. Every day was a torment for her! My uncle and I struggled constantly just to keep her from Fading! And that mad, treacherous, idiot of a *krillo* thought House Merimydion would conspire to add to her burden by laying responsibility for the whole of Calberna on her shoulders?"

"I know that, and you know that, but he was convinced."

"What about Nyamialine? Did he think my House conspired to kill her, too?"

"*Ono,* he believed her death was entirely accidental.

She wasn't supposed to be at the temple, remember? She was a last-minute addition to the group." Ari shifted in his chair. "It was because of Mia that Nemuan thought he could get me to join him in his insanity. He thought that since Mia was my sister I would want to avenge her and take my own justice on your House. I told him to go eat whale *shoto*. He told me I could either join him willingly, or he'd take over my mind and force me to his will."

"That's not possible." Ryll protested.

"That's what I thought. But to prove he could do it, he bespelled two of my men—drew some sort of runic symbol on their foreheads in red ink—and used his Voice to convince them I was responsible for the *Sirena*'s capture. Then he Commanded them to torture me. *And they did*." He gave a hollow, humorless laugh. "Most of these wounds, my own men gave me. Men I've sailed with for years. Men I trusted at my back. When he was satisfied he'd made his point, he Commanded my men to drown themselves. *And they did*. That's how he killed Fyerin and the others, and why they were all branded. He used the brand to hide the spell he'd put on them. Then he put the same spell on me."

Dilys looked at the bandage still adhered to the back of Ari's neck. "The runic circle Gabriella told me about. The one you shredded your own flesh to remove."

"*Tey*." Ari started to reach for the wound, but drew back before he touched it. "I don't know if the Commands he gave me still hold sway without the mark, so you need to take precautions. Lock me up where I can't hurt anyone. Because the whole time he was torturing me, he kept going on and on about how he would use me to destroy your House, so you would know the pain of what you Merimydions did to his."

"I'm not going to lock you up, Ari. The fact that you're here, telling me about this, is proof enough for me that Nemuan's spell is broken."

"You should still put me under guard. Just to be safe."

Dilys waved Ari's suggestion away. "Why was Nemuan so certain my House was behind the deaths of his mother and sister?"

"He said he'd seen the proof of it with his own eyes. And considering that he was in league with Mur Balat, I think we can guess where the proof came from."

"As if anything from Mur Balat could be believed."

"Balat may have been many things, but no one ever accused him of being dishonest."

"Probably because any who did ended up dead."

"True, but information brokers who market lies to powerful people don't tend to live long."

"So you think Nemuan hired Balat to find out who killed his mother and sister?"

Ari shrugged. "Either that or Balat came by the information some other way and simply used it when it was useful to him."

Dilys headed for the door.

"Where are you going?" Ari called after him.

"To see my mother. If there really is a traitor in our House, she needs to know about it."

Calivan Merimydion's magical laboratory was quite impressive. While the Lord Chancellor busied himself gathering up several items and storing them in a small pouch hanging at his waist, Gabriella wandered the spacious room, inspecting the books, the crystals of every shape and color, the numerous shelves filled with labelled jars of potion-crafting ingredients, and what appeared to be an extensive collection of magical artifacts.

"You seem to have made quite the study of magic," she said.

"*Tey.* It's always been a hobby of mine."

Calivan calling his interest in magic a "hobby" was a gross understatement. This was no hobby. This was an obsession.

"Why such an interest?"

Calivan shrugged. "I am a Calbernan. Just because I wasn't allowed to risk my life and my sister's happiness by seeking gold and glory like the rest of our warriors doesn't mean I didn't pursue other methods of protecting my people and the women of my House. Now, before we begin, I need you to share some of your power with me. Once I understand what your gifts are, I'll be better able to train you in how to use and control them." Calivan held out his hands.

She made no effort to take them. Ever since the Shark, the idea of touching any Calbernan but Dilys was anathema to her. Ari had been different, of course. She'd been trying to save his life, and he'd been too damaged to be any threat to her. She didn't think she'd be able to touch even her own guards except in the direst of emergencies—and they were men Dilys trusted implicitly, men he'd handpicked to protect her and absorb her magical overflow should her gifts threaten to overwhelm her.

Of course, once she became *Myerial* and *Donima* of House Merimydion, she'd have to get over her phobia of being touched. It was ridiculous to expect Dilys to serve as her conduit for every gift of power she'd be required to make. There would be too many. She was destined to be the engine that powered an entire nation. According to Dilys's mother, the pregnant daughters of House Merimydion would expect—no, require—her to share her gifts so their children would be born strong *imlanis* in their own right. The powerful daughters of the royal Houses would expect the same, so that more Sirens could be born. The sons of Calberna, heading out to war, also deserved every advantage her gifts could give them.

She could not regard them all with suspicion. Every man in the world wasn't a rapist lusting for a victim. Every Calbernan wasn't magic eater slavering to take by force what magic she would not share freely.

Still . . .

"Can I not just demonstrate my gifts, instead? Would that not give you a good idea of what I can do?"

"What you can do, yes, but not how you do it, or the amount of power you're capable of generating."

"I'm capable of generating quite a lot."

"That's only natural. You are a Siren, after all. However, it would be much more beneficial to understand exactly how powerful a Siren you really are. That will enable me to tailor my lessons to suit your needs."

His reasoning made perfect sense. Of course, he needed to understand as much as possible about her power so he could help her learn to control it. So why was she so hesitant? This was Dilys's uncle—the *Myerial*'s twin brother. He couldn't possibly mean her any harm.

And yet, still, her whole body throbbed with resistance at the idea of letting Calivan touch his skin to hers.

Mistaking the reason for her reticence, Calivan said, "You needn't worry about generating more power than your guards and I can contain. I have taken the liberty of preparing several crystals capable of storing any excess power." He pulled a shining, polished stone the size of a goose egg from the pouch at his waist. "One of my more recent discoveries in magical devices. The crystal can be imbued with magical energy from any source and used for a variety of purposes. It can store spells. It can be used to power magical artifacts. The energy can also be extracted and used by anyone with the proper knowledge and ability—Calbernans, for instance—with very little power loss."

"Are you intending to store my power in those stones?" she asked.

"I hope so. I would certainly like to do so. It would allow me not only to measure how much power you're capable of generating, but also to experiment on your magic without constantly needing you to be present."

"I need to think about that for a little while. What if

we start with a demonstration and work our way towards
having me share power with you or storing it in those
stones?" She flushed a little, feeling embarrassed by her
reticence. She didn't want this man to think she didn't like
or trust him. He was an important member of her new
family.

Thankfully, Calivan didn't appear to take offense. "We
could do that, of course, if that is what makes you most
comfortable. But I won't be able to truly understand what
we're dealing with until you share your gifts with me.
Every holder of great power wields that power slightly differently than anyone else. It's in those differences that we
find the true keys to control."

She flushed again, and bit her lip in shame for her own
cowardice. "Of course. That makes sense. It's just that . . .
well, after the Shark . . ." Her voice trailed off.

"I understand." His eyes were kind. His voice soft and
full of sincerity and compassion. "I'm so sorry. I should
have thought of that myself. If you'll follow me, I have a
reinforced chamber built deeper in the mountain, where
you can demonstrate your gifts without fear of causing
harm."

"Dilys? What's going on? Why are you ransacking Prince
Nemuan's office?" In a whirl of sheer silk and subtle perfume, Alysaldria entered the small palace office that had
been assigned to Nemuan Merimynos in his role as commander of the Fourth Fleet. Behind her, two of her guards
positioned themselves on opposite sides of the doorway.

"I'm looking for information." Dilys kept rifling
through the drawers. His mother had been in a meeting
with the *Donimari* when he'd first sought her out, so he'd
decided to search Nemuan's palace office for clues to the
traitor's identity while waiting for the meeting to end. "Ari
says Nemuan blamed House Merimydion for the deaths
of his mother and sister. I'm hoping he kept some sort of
journal that might give me a clue as to what he meant."

"If he did, he'd be unlikely to keep it here. Not that I'd put too much stock in Nemuan's claims anyway. The poor boy was clearly grief-mad."

Dilys ignored the fact that his mother called Nemuan, a man who'd spent the last two years terrorizing sailors across the Olemas Ocean, a "poor boy." To her, despite his treachery, Nemuan was still the son of a *Myerial*, and a cousin she'd watched grow from infancy. His treason was the final, regrettably tragic turn in a life derailed by suffering. Dilys's mother had a hard time seeing bad in the people she loved.

"So grief-mad that it took him almost twenty years to take action against us?" he replied instead. "Forgive me, *Nima*, but that doesn't track."

She laid a hand on his bare shoulder, warm power pulsing gently into him, a soft caress of energy shared instinctively through the bonds of maternal love. "We have no idea what was in Prince Nemuan's thoughts all those years, *moa elua*, nor do we know what set him off. Although," she admitted softly, "I think it's clear that your impending betrothal to an *oulani* woman was a factor."

"*Nima*." Finding nothing enlightening in the late prince's desk or filing cabinets, Dilys abandoned the search and rose to take his mother's hands and raise them to his lips. "According to Ari, Nemuan was insistent that House Merimydion was directly to blame for the deaths of Siavaluana and Sianna."

His mother made a sound of distress. "Such madness. As if any of us would ever wish harm upon another royal House—let alone the House of my father's beloved sister!"

"That's what I said. After all, what possible motive could any of us have? *Tey*, you became *Myerial*, but you didn't want it."

"No, I never did. I never even wanted to rule House Merimydion. My dream of a perfect life was your father and me and a cottage by the sea, loving one another and raising our children." She laid a slender hand along his cheek, gazing up at him with eyes shadowed by an old but still strong sorrow. "And then, he was gone, and simply surviving from one day to the next was almost more than I could bear. Even with you and Calivan there to keep me going, I could feel myself Fading. I'm ashamed to say I wanted it." Long black lashes swept down over her eyes. "As much as I loved you both, I wanted to join your father more."

His throat grew tight. "I know, *Nima*." He'd always known. It was, in fact, a secret fear that had long lived at the back of his mind: that his love, her brother's love, her duty to House and country wasn't enough to hold her to life, not when her longing for his father beckoned to her from the grave.

"Ironically," Alysaldria continued, "though I didn't want the Sea Throne, though I still don't want it, Siavaluana's death saved my life. She gifted me her power before she died. That gift stopped my Fade, helped me hold it at bay all these years since."

He frowned, "But it has begun again, hasn't it?"

Her smile was wan. "I still miss your father, Dilys. No number of years will ever change that. And you are settled now, and happy, with a *liana* who completes you, as your father completed me, a mate truly worthy of you, who brings you a joy I thought lost to you forever after our poor Nyamialine. I have been fighting for years, but now, at last, I can finally rest."

Alarm flared. His fingers clenched. She was planning to surrender to the Fade! "*Nima* . . ."

She pressed a slender finger to his lips and shook her head. "*Ono, moa elua.* We will not speak of it. Your poor uncle is distressed enough for the both of you. He does not want to let me go. Why do you think he tried to betroth you to an infant? Or threw such a fit when I vowed from the Sea Throne to ensure your daughter was born a true Calbernan, with all the gifts a *Myerial* would require?"

She sighed. "Poor Cal. It was no joy for him to be born my twin. He should have had a *liana* of his own to love. He is so strong, so loving, so fiercely devoted, with such a sharp, intelligent mind. He would have made even a Siren a worthy mate. And yet in a cruel twist of fate, all that love, all that strength and devotion, was shackled from birth to a twin sister instead of the mate he could complete and who could complete him."

"I've never heard him complain."

"Of course you haven't. He would never dream of hurting me by voicing even the tiniest regret over the high price of being born my twin. I doubt he even allows himself to consider any life but the one he has. That doesn't make it any less tragic that my beloved brother has been robbed of a *liana* and family of his own."

Dilys was astounded. He knew his mother missed his father. How could he not? Dillon Merimydion's death had stolen the radiance from her smile. But the rest . . .

"How long have you felt this way, *Nima*?"

"Truthfully? Since the first time I understood that my love for your father was so much deeper and more essential to me than my love for Calivan. That's the first time I realized what Cal would be missing, and the first time I realized that no matter how much I loved my brother, it was to Dillon that my heart—and my life—was irrevocably tied. I love my brother. I love him deeply. But that awful night in our warehouse—if those thieves had murdered Cal instead of my Dillon—I would have grieved, I would have mourned for years, a part of my heart would have died with him, but the Fade would never have laid its hand upon me. Your father would never have allowed it. He would have anchored me to life the way you anchor your Gabriella, the way she anchors you. That is the gift of a true Calbernan claiming. And it makes me weep that I am the reason my brother will never know that joy for himself."

"*Nima,* you cannot blame yourself. You were not the one who created the custom that bound Uncle Calivan's life to yours."

"Neither have I been the one to challenge it." Alys pressed her fingers to the inner corners of her eyes. She wasn't crying, but Dilys knew her well enough to know she was fighting to keep from it. She blinked quickly and took several deep, rapid breaths to compose herself. Once she had, she lowered her hands and lifted her chin in a familiar, regally decisive manner. When she spoke again, it was not Dilys's *nima,* but the *Myerial* Alysaldria I who said, "But enough of that. You came here with a far more immediate concern. Do you truly believe a member of our House was responsible for Siavaluana's death?"

"I believe Nemuan believed it. Oh, he might certainly have concocted the whole story as a way to win Ari to his side, but once Ari refused to betray us, Nemuan had no reason to keep up the pretense. Unless, in Nemuan's mind, it wasn't a lie."

Alysaldria nodded crisply. "Then let's proceed on the assumption that he was right, that a traitor to Calberna does, in fact, reside within our House. If Nemuan committed his suspicions to paper, he wouldn't have kept it here, in the palace, where the members of our House come and go so freely. Nor would he have confided in anyone in the palace, except possibly for the oldest retainers, the ones who had served House Merimynos before us. Or perhaps someone with ties to House Merimynos who works and lives within the palace walls? We did not supplant every member of the staff with our own people when we came." She tapped a finger to her lips thoughtfully. "The palace smith, for instance, was born to House Osa, who serve House Merimynos. He personally made the weapons for every one of Siavaluana's sons. He's someone Nemuan might have confided in."

"That seems as good a place to start as any," Dilys said, "but I recommend rounding them all up at the same time so they don't have time to agree on whatever story they think we want to hear. I'd also like to send someone to search Nemuan's private quarters both here in the city and in Cali Va'Mynos."

"Agreed." Alysaldria turned to her two guards. "Peris, gather two teams of your most trusted men. Send one to Cali Va'Mynos and another to House Merimynos's mansion here in the city. I want both dwellings searched from top to bottom, with particular focus on Prince Nemuan's rooms and offices. Bring back every personal journal, every scrap of correspondence, every note Prince Nemuan penned or kept. Andion, you will assemble the entire palace staff and identify every member of the staff with blood ties or particular loyalty to House Merimynos or a notable friendship with Prince Nemuan."

"*Tey, moa Myerial.*" Peris and Andion both bowed deeply. As they did so, the long ropes of their hair slid forward over their shoulders. A flash of red caught Dilys's eye, and every muscle in his body went taut.

"Hold!" he commanded, his voice vibrating with power. The two guards snapped to attention. "*Moa Myerielua?*"

"Andion, show me your neck."

"My prince?"

"Your neck! Show me your neck." He was already reaching for the long ropes of the unresisting guard's hair. Andion stood silent and still as Dilys bared the corded column of Andion's throat, revealing a small red circle of runes inked on the dark skin behind his ear.

"Where did you get this? Did Nemuan put this mark on you?" He held Andion's shoulder in a fierce grip.

"Dilys!" His mother's alarm, which normally would have stopped Dilys in his tracks, barely registered, so intent and all-consuming was his focus.

His claws slid out, piercing Andion's shoulder. Before the man could flinch, Dilys's free hand shot to the guard's throat, battle claws curled around his trachea in a raw threat. The sharp edge of one claw stroked the small red rune-circle near Andion's ear. "I'll ask one last time. Who gave you this mark?" Blood seeped out from beneath Dilys's grip on the guard's shoulder and trickled down Andion's *ulumi*-covered chest. Like all the queen's guards, Andion was a celebrated hero of many wars, but Dilys would rip out his throat without a thought if Andion were part of Nemuan's conspiracy.

"What's come over you, Dilys? Release him this instant!" Command throbbed in his mother's Voice. He felt it clearly, yet felt no compulsion to obey.

"You don't understand, *Nima*. Ari says Nemuan drew a mark like this on him and his men. It allowed Nemuan to control them with *susirena*. That's how Nemuan drowned my men—drowned Fyerin and the others. He inked that mark on them then Commanded them to drown, and they had to obey."

"That can't be true," Alysaldria protested. "That mark is a ward designed to *block* the power of adverse spells and magic."

"Who told you that? Because I suspect whoever did is our traitor."

His mother went pale beneath the bronze of her skin. "*Ono*." Her lips started to tremble, and her head shook from side to side in a sort of dazed denial. She stumbled back, away from Dilys, raising one shaking hand to cover her mouth.

And then he knew, of course. The realization made his heart slam against his sternum. In his veins, every drop of his blood turned to ice. Sweet Numahao.

Sweet, blessed, Numahao.

Calivan.

Dilys released Andion and lunged for his mother, seizing her arms in a tight grip. "*Nima*? Where is Calivan? Where is your brother?"

Alysaldria stared up at him in mute horror.

"He's with the *Sirena*." That came from Peris, whose eyes were grim, and whose lips were bracketed by tense, white grooves. "The Lord Chancellor offered to help her with her magic. Said he'd been poring over the ancient texts ever since he discovered she was a Siren, so he could be of assistance."

"Where did they go?"

"I'm not sure. I think I heard him mention something about his laboratory, the one below the Siren library."

Dilys turned and bolted towards the door.

"Dilys!" his mother cried after him. "Dilys, wait!"

He didn't slow one bit. "Send for Ryll," he called over his shoulder. "Tell him to meet me at Calivan's laboratory with as many men as he can gather. And make sure none of them bear that mark!"

CHAPTER 29

With Biross and Tarrant and the two queen's guards at her back, Gabriella followed Calivan and the other two guards through the door at the back of his lab into a glow-lit tunnel whose walls were covered with a smooth white surface that felt spongy to the touch. The door to the tunnel swung shut behind them, the sound of the latch clicking into place making Gabriella jump and turn in surprise. They were deep inside the mountain now, and Gabriella's connection to the sun was severed completely when the door closed behind them.

"You mustn't mind the automatic latch on the door," Calivan remarked. "It's a safety precaution, just like the energy-absorbing material covering the walls and the back of the lab door. Some of the spells I've tested have been quite potent, and even the smallest leak of magical energy could do a great deal of damage to my lab."

"Of course." She felt silly, being so jumpy when clearly she was in no danger. It was just that when the door closed and severed her connection to the sun, her sun-born weathergifts disappeared with it. The loss of the powerful, smoldering heat at her core brought back too many unpleasant memories of being collared and helpless. "I'm sorry. You must think I'm being ridiculous."

"Not at all. Considering the traumatic experience you suffered, you're doing splendidly."

At the end of the tunnel another door awaited. This

one opened to what looked like a large, round room entirely coated in the same energy-absorbing material as the tunnel.

"And this is my testing room," Calivan said. His *obah* flowed around him as he strode into the chamber. "Here you can demonstrate your gifts without worrying about causing harm."

Gabriella made it as far as the door—a door that housed heavy, retractable metal bolts that would extend into the surrounding wall to form an impenetrable seal when closed—before full-blown panic set in. There were no windows, no other doors in the testing room. No way in or out except the one door with its thick, retractable metal sealing rods. And the walls were designed to be impervious to even powerful magic.

She wasn't sure that even a room reinforced against magic could hold hers—after all, she had Shouted the entire Trinipor Coast into the sea, taking Mur Balat's fortress and the mountain on which it stood along with it. But if Calivan's testing chamber *was* capable of containing even her most dangerous magic, then stepping inside it would be like willingly clamping another of Mur Balat's collars around her own throat. The thought made her heart pound and her breathing turn rapid and shallow.

"*Sirena*?" Calivan turned when he realized she hadn't followed him into the room. "What is it?"

"I'm sorry." She shook her head, backing away. Her skin felt icy, the normal heat of her sun-fed gifts extinguished. Her other, far more lethal power was rousing fast in response to her panic. "I'm sorry, Lord Chancellor, but I've changed my mind. I don't think this is a good idea. Maybe later, when Dilys is available . . ."

Calivan might be Dilys's uncle, but the memories of her captivity were still too recent, too raw. And it was only Dilys that Gabriella truly trusted. Only Dilys with whom she would ever allow herself to let down her guard and become truly vulnerable.

Calivan's brow furrowed for a moment, then smoothed into an expression of understanding. "Of course, *Sirena*. Whatever you prefer. We'll head back now. Perhaps you'd be more at ease if you began by reading the journals written by the ancient Sirens."

"Yes." She dragged a polite mask into place, unwilling to show the genuine face of her fear to anyone but Dilys. "That sounds like a wonderful idea."

"Excellent. Let's head back to the library."

"I'm sorry," she said again as he drew near. "My gifts are still too unpredictable for me to feel comfortable using them in an enclosed space beneath the city." The excuse fell easily off her tongue, unburdened by even the slightest hint of remorse. It was true she was nervous about using her gifts, but that had nothing to do with why she wasn't going to follow Calivan Merimydion into an enclosed, magically warded place. Later, she would confess her lie to Dilys, and he would give that husky laugh that made her shiver in all her most feminine places, then demand a forfeit of his choosing. She went damp at the thought. What he claimed as forfeit had gotten far more intimate—and exponentially more enjoyable—since their marriage.

"No need to apologize. There's more than one way to catch a fish." Calivan smiled charmingly, was still smiling charmingly when he slung one arm around her throat, clamped a hand over her mouth, and ate down her magic in great, ravening gulps.

The attack was so sudden, so unexpected, it took Summer a full second to realize what was happening, and by the time she gathered her wits enough to cry out against Calivan's muffling hand and struggle to free herself, he had already drained her so deeply she had no strength to fight.

"My goddess!" Calivan breathed. "Such strength!" His voice was awed. And then, brutal with Command as he shouted in a Voice filled with stolen power, "Kill her guards!"

The four queen's guards converged on Biross and Tarrant so quickly Dilys's men didn't have time to clear their swords from their scabbards before they were impaled on the sharp points of the queen's guards' tridents. Their bodies crumpled, blood pouring from the holes in their chests.

"Quickly, throw the bodies into the chamber." The four queen's guards gathered up the fallen warriors and carried them the short distance to the spherical testing chamber, tossing their bodies inside like so much garbage. Outrage and horror clashed inside her. She tried twisting free, but Calivan only tightened his grip, crushing her arms against her ribs, making it hard for her to breathe. Without releasing his grip, he reached into the pouch at his side and extracted one of the polished, egg-shaped crystals. It began to glow brightly as he began feeding it the magic he was extracting from her.

"You should have returned home to Wintercraig instead of marrying Dilys and coming to Calberna," he chided, his tone surprisingly void of wrath. "Balat had what he wanted, the Winter King would have made sure Minush Oroto rued the day he ever dreamed of owning a Season of Summerlea, and Dilys could not have continued to pursue you once you publicly refused to claim him. If you had just gone home, everything would have been fine. I never wished harm to you or your sisters. I just couldn't have any of you marrying my nephew."

Summer stiffened as the meaning behind Calivan's words sank in. Sweet Helos. Calivan Merimydion was behind her kidnapping! He'd helped Mur Balat abduct Summer and her sisters!

"Alys vowed from the Sea Throne that any daughter of Dilys's union with a Season of Summerlea would be born *imlani*, with gifts worthy of a Calbernan queen," Calivan continued. "I couldn't run the risk of losing her. My whole life has been devoted to keeping her strong and safe and happy. And then not only did you come back and make Dilys your husband, but you're a Siren! You don't need

Alys's gifts to make your daughter *imlani,* but you'll still kill her all the same. You'll take her throne, and leave her nothing. She'll drain herself to give you her queen's gifts, drain herself so deeply that even the elixir I've been using to keep her alive will not stop her Fade."

Calivan shuddered, as if beset by some great and terrible emotion. Then he bent close to Summer's ear and hissed, "I won't let my sister Fade. I don't care what I have to do to prevent that."

There was a tone in that hissing voice. A note of wild ferocity she'd heard before. An obsession just like the twisted seed that had born such dreadful fruit inside her father. Anger flickered inside her, bringing a surge of fresh, wild magic.

The first crystal egg was shining so brightly it was blinding, like looking directly into the sun. Calivan exchanged it for a second. This one filled even faster than the first.

It wasn't just his hand in the kidnapping of Summer and her sisters that outraged her. It was his obsessive love for his sister that eclipsed his ability to consider anyone or anything but his own fear and grief. Even his own family.

Family should never hurt family.

Lily's father should never have beat his daughter until she felt driven to risk her life and that of her unborn child to escape him.

Nemuan Merimynos should never have let his anguish over the murders of his mother and sister drive him to murder his own innocent cousins in revenge.

Verdan Coruscate should have found the strength to survive his wife's death without letting grief and guilt drive him to madness and destruction. His kingdom conquered. His son disinherited and banished. One daughter sold into marriage to end a war. The other three scattered to the winds—two dead, one about to die. Every loss and tragedy utterly avoidable, had Verdan loved his family enough to put them first, as Alysaldria had done for Dilys. She had not set out on a reckless course of revenge. She had not driven herself mad over the loss of her husband and unborn child. She'd made herself stay strong for the child she had left.

And now Alysaldria's brother—her twin—would do to her son what a band of murderous thieves had done to her. Slaughter his mate. And if Dilys didn't follow her to the grave, he would torment himself every moment for the rest of his life. The brave, magnificent, larger-than-life warrior she had married would perceive her death as yet another personal failure, proof of his inability to keep his loved ones safe.

"Good goddess, is there no end to your magic?" Calivan replaced a second sun-bright crystal with not one but two more, and Gabriella sagged in his arms as the drain on her magic increased commensurately.

"CALIVAN!"

Calivan started in surprise as a familiar voice roared the Lord Chancellor's name.

"RELEASE MY MATE, YOU TRAITOROUS KRILLO*!"*

Dilys! The sound of her mate's voice caused a fresh surge of magic to well up inside Gabriella. His nearness, the knowledge that he'd come for her, that he would always come for her, brought the bonds of their union singing to life, acting like a catalyst on the source of her power.

Calivan cursed as the magic gathering inside her swiftly outpaced his ability to drain it from her. "You four!" he Commanded the queen's guards. "The Calbernan out there is trying to kill the *Myerial*! Get out there and stop him. Kill him if you have to!"

What? This vile man . . . this queen killer . . . would murder his own nephew? His own flesh and blood? *He thought to kill Dilys? Gabriella's mate?*

Over her dead body.

The wellspring of power renewed by Dilys's nearness became a roaring fountain geysering up inside her. Fierce and ferocious and murderously protective.

"My goddess! How much *farking* magic do you have?"

This time, Calivan's voice revealed dawning fear, as the flood of her magic threatened to overwhelm him. Another crystal filled, then another, and still her magic continued to surge.

She tried to draw a breath—just one was all she needed. The ocean of power pounded against her, needing an outlet—needing her Voice to free it. Like the scream that had sunk Trinipor, the Shout building inside her was a guttural cry of rage and retribution, but also a ferocious need to protect her mate from the murderous madman who shared his blood. All her Shout needed was a breath—just one—to set it free.

But the hand clamped over her nose and mouth denied her that. She clawed at Calivan's forearm, her nails digging so deep they drew blood. Her fingertips burned and throbbed from the ferocity of her grip.

"*Die!*" Calivan Shouted, using her own stolen magic against her. "*Die now!*"

The Command slammed into her with such force, it felt like every bone in her body shattered. What little breath remained in her lungs wheezed out in a strangled cry. Her heart slammed against her chest, then began to stutter, the rhythm faltering as the magic erupting inside her grappled with the powerful Command pressing down upon her.

Still holding her fast against him with the hand clamped hard over her mouth, Calivan freed his other arm, drew the dagger from the jeweled scabbard at his waist and slammed it into her chest.

Pain exploded inside her, scattering her wits and robbing her limbs of strength. Darkness swept in from the periphery of her vision, eclipsing her sight. Her body sagged against his.

Dimly, she was aware of Calivan dragging her back to his testing chamber and tossing her inside atop the bodies of Biross and Tarrant.

"Siren you may be," he said, "but you're no true daughter of Numahao. Even if you somehow survive my Command and my blade, you can still drown like the *oulani* you are!"

He turned a large valve in the corridor outside the chamber and seawater began pouring in through two large grates in the testing room's ceiling.

The door slammed shut, and Gabriella heard the sound of the steel bolts sliding home, sealing her and the bodies of Biross and Tarrant inside as the room rapidly filled with water.

Dilys dropped to his knees and slid under the sharp, glistening points of one of the guard's jabbing trident. He leapt back to his feet a split second later to deliver a driving blow to the guard's solar plexus. The guard gave a wheezing gasp as all the air in his lungs whooshed out, then dropped to the ground when Dilys followed up with a knockout punch to the bespelled male's jaw.

"Get him out of here," Dilys barked to one of Ryll's men. "Lock him up somewhere where he can't hurt anyone until we can free him from whatever spell he's under."

Around the room, Ryll and two dozen other warriors were subduing the remaining three ensorcelled queen's guards. Dilys would have killed them if he'd had to. Thankfully, Ryll had come with enough men to make bloodshed unnecessary.

The same wasn't going to be true for Calivan.

The minute four of his mother's most trusted guards had run into the room with weapons drawn and murder on their mind, Dilys's suspicions about his uncle had been confirmed.

Calivan Merimydion had betrayed his people.

He'd inked loyal, honorable men with the same controlling spell the Shark had used on Ari. The same spell the Shark had used to drown Fyerin and the other Calbernan's he'd murdered in his quest for vengeance against House Merimydion.

Calivan had inked them with a spell they could not resist and sent them to murder his sister's son.

Worse, he'd sent them to murder the claimed mate of the first Siren born in twenty-five hundred years. He knew exactly what Dillon Merimydion's death had done to his mate, Alysaldria—and Alysaldria wasn't a Siren. With the strength of her gifts—the strength of the ties that now bound them—Gabriella wouldn't be able to survive Dilys's death, any more than Dilys would be able to survive hers.

And for the harm Calivan intended towards Gabriella, Dilys would show his uncle no mercy.

With a savage snarl, Dilys raced across his uncle's laboratory, heading for the door at the back of the room. Half of Ryll's men departed, escorting the ensorcelled queen's guards out of the vicinity. The rest followed Dilys.

"*Moa Myerielua,* wait!" Three of Ryll's men put on a burst of speed, catching up to Dilys and blocking his path to the door. "It could be a trap, my lord. Let us go first."

"*Ono.* That's my mate in there."

"And our *Sirena,* our future *Myerial,* the hope for all of us. Who will not survive if you are slain."

Dilys tried to shove them aside, but three more grabbed his arms from behind while three more ran around them to throw open the door.

The instant they did, blinding light flashed and a powerful explosion rocked the room. Glass vessels shattered. Magical artifacts went flying. Dilys and his men were flung backwards by the force of the blast. When Dilys got to his feet, four men—those who had been closest to the door at the time of the blast—lay dead or dying, their skin bubbling and melting off their bones.

The sight drove Dilys's anger even higher, and not just because of the men murdered before his eyes. That explosion had been meant for him. Which meant Calivan hadn't even intended to give him a warrior's death.

"*CALIVAN!*" he bellowed. "You traitorous coward! Leave off your sorceror's tricks, release my mate, and come out and face me like a *farking* Calbernan worth his salt!"

"I don't want to kill you, Dilys," Calivan called out. "I didn't want to kill her either. But I can't let her take the Sea Throne! Alys will Fade!"

Dilys walked closer, careful to keep clear of the corridor opening in case his uncle had more unpleasant magical surprises in store for him. He gestured Ryll over to the opposite side. "It's over, Calivan. *Nima* knows what you've done. She knows you were involved in the deaths of *Myerial* Siavaluana and Sianna. Of Nyamialine. Even if you succeed in killing me, your life is forfeit. And without both you and me, *Nima* will Fade anyway. Is that what you want? To be responsible for your own sister's—your own twin's—death?"

"I won't be! I've seen to that. I found a way to keep her Fade at bay. Between an elixir to hold her to life and the power I've gathered in these stones, she'll have strength enough to live for decades—maybe even centuries!"

"And do you think that's what she wants? To live at the price of all the blood on your hands? Do you even know your sister at all?"

"*You don't understand!*" Calivan cried.

"I understand enough. Now, release Gabriella and come out to face me, Uncle. I will give you a warrior's death. A fight, just the two of us. Fang and claw only."

"You think you could take me fang and claw?" Calivan's voice was sharp. "You think because I was forbidden a warrior's life that I am easy prey?"

"*Ono,* Uncle. I know you are not. I merely thought to offer you the honor denied Fyerin and the others who died at Nemuan's hands because of you."

"I am not to blame for Nemuan's actions!"

"Are you not? You murdered his family. You destroyed his House. The loss drove him as mad as the fear of loss has driven you."

One of Ryll's men darted across the room. A blast of

magic erupted from the hallway. Ryll's man barely managed to dive to safety. The table behind him, however, did not fare so well. The spell—whatever it was—scorched the wood and shattered several sealed glass jars, liquefying their contents and spilling smoking, bubbling goo across the floor. Several of his men began to cough and wave at the noxious smoke.

"Be careful, Nephew. What's in my lab doesn't tend to react well when mixed together without care. I suggest you take your men and leave."

Ryll's man reached Dilys's side. "It's just him in the hall, *moa Myerielua*. The *Sirena* isn't with him. The hall is about twenty yards long, with a closed door at the other end. She must be behind it. There's nowhere to hide that I could see."

Dilys glared at the smoking mess on the laboratory floor. Enough was enough. "You want to kill me? Here's your chance. Because I'm coming to get Gabriella. The only way to stop me is to kill me. Then you can explain to *Nima* how you murdered her only child."

"I'm not going to murder you. There's no need. You're already dead. You just don't know it yet."

Dilys's blood turned to ice. Calivan's smug certainty could only mean one thing.

"What have you done to her? What have you done to my mate?"

Mindless of the threat of his uncle's magic, Dilys lunged through the doorway and ran towards his uncle. Just as Ryll's man had reported, Calivan was alone in the corridor. The door behind him—the only other way in or out of the corridor—was closed.

Dilys's battle fangs descended and his claws came out, but neither were needed. Calivan stepped aside without protest as Dilys shoved past. When Ryll and the rest of their men would have raced in as well, however, Calivan sent them careening backwards with a power Word and threw a vial after them, shouting, "*Ignetha!*" He slammed the hallway door shut against the resulting fiery blast and locked it tight.

"A Calbernan deserves the right to die by his mate's side," Calivan said. "That much I can offer you. Ryllian Ocea and your men, however, either leave my lab or die."

Dilys ignored him. He'd reached the door at the end of the hall and was straining to open it. The circular steel locking mechanism refused to budge.

"It's no use," Calivan said. "She'll be gone long before anyone manages to get through."

Now seemed a perfect time for fang and claw.

Dilys whirled, grabbing his uncle by the throat. "Open it! Open it now!"

Calivan regarded him with an almost pitying expression. "I couldn't even if I wanted to. The door is bolted shut with three-inch steel bars driven half a foot into solid rock, and I destroyed the mechanism to retract the bars."

"Then melt the bars!"

"It doesn't work that way, Nephew. Besides, even if I could, your *liana* would be dead long before I finished. The room should be entirely flooded by now. Gabriella Coruscate may possess a Siren's gifts, but she doesn't possess a Calbernan's gills."

Dilys squeezed his hand around his uncle's throat until runnels of blood seeped out beneath his claws. "Gabriella *Merimydion*, Uncle. A daughter of my *nima*'s House."

"A usurper. A threat to my sister's life." Calivan tilted his chin, his expression proudly defiant and tinged with triumph. "Go ahead and kill me, Nephew. The usurper will still be dead."

There was a screech of protesting metal, and the door to the laboratory flew off its hinges. Dilys and Calivan both spun towards it in surprise. Alysaldria stepped across the threshold, flanked by an ash-blackened Ryll and followed by a small army of grim-eyed warriors, many of them sons of Houses Merimydion, Ocea, and Calmyria.

"He's not going to kill you, Cal," Alysaldria said.

"You're going to stand before a Gathering, confess your crimes, and accept the Crown's judgment for the murder of *Myerial* Siavaluana, *Myerialuanna* Sianna, Nyamialine Calmyria, Fyerin Merimydion, and every other life brought to an end by your treasonous actions, and for the attempted murder of my son and his *liana,* the Siren and soon-to-be-*Myerial,* Gabriella Merimydion. And then, Cal, you're going to be executed. Noran"—she turned to one of the warriors behind her—"I want you to oversee the destruction of everything in this laboratory. That means every magical artifact, book, vial, jar, and implement, including whatever items the former Lord Chancellor has on his person."

"Alys, *ono*!" For the first time, genuine fear entered Calivan's eyes—but not for himself, and not for the execution awaiting him. He clutched the pouch at his side. "You'll die!"

"Then I will be free to join my *akua,* as I have longed to do all these many years since his death." Her eyes were cold, her face drawn and tight, but she didn't waver. "Take him into custody. And get that door open!"

Two men marched forward to grasp Calivan's arms while Ryll and half a dozen other warriors raced for the other end of the corridor, axes and crowbars in hand. They began hacking at the door and the surrounding wall.

Dilys didn't want to release his grip on his uncle. Everything in him demanded that he rip out the throat of the man who had threatened his mate. But it was more important right now to get to Gabriella. With a snarl, he shoved his uncle away and spun away to help Ryll and the others.

"Hold on, *moa kiri,*" he shouted. "I'm here. We're going to get you out of there!"

A shout and a sudden scuffle made Dilys spin back around. Calivan had Spoken a Word that sent the two warriors holding him to their knees.

Dilys bellowed a war cry and launched himself at his uncle. Calivan turned, but he wasn't fast enough to evade the fist that slammed into his temple. The blow dropped Calivan to his knees, and Dilys was on him in an instant. He wrapped one clawed hand around Calivan's throat, and positioned the other at the vulnerable flesh of Calivan's belly. All he needed was a single word from his mother, and he would eviscerate his uncle, ripping out both throat and belly in lethal wounds not even Calivan's considerable seagifts or his skills with foreign magic would be able to staunch.

Instead of fighting Dilys's hold, Calivan clutched his leather pouch to his chest and pled with his sister. "Alys, you can't let them destroy what's in here. You'll die, and everything I've done will have been for nothing!" His face was pale beneath its deep Calbernan bronze. "Please! Please, Alys! I've been trying to make things right for you again since Dillon died!"

Before Alys could answer, a burning pain erupted in Dilys's chest. He gasped for air. His lungs filled, but it didn't matter. He couldn't breathe! The burning expanded. His body convulsed.

His mother's shocked, horrified gaze, held his, the terrified knowledge in her eyes confirming what he knew was happening.

Gabriella.

She was dying.

CHAPTER 30

Bloody, drained, struggling for breath, Gabriella clung to life with every ounce of determination in her as the traitor Calivan Merimydion's testing chamber rapidly filled with seawater.

She wasn't dead yet. That was the one glimmer of hope she clung to.

Well, not the only one. Dilys was out there, fighting for her. So long as she was alive and Dilys was alive, there was hope for them both.

She pressed a palm weakly against the wound in her chest and tilted her back to take a painful gasp of air. When Calivan had knifed her, she'd managed to twist at the last moment, so that the blade meant for her heart had pierced a lung instead. Every breath was an agony and the wound was seeping bloody bubbles of air, but that was still better than the alternative.

Poor Biross and Tarrant had not been so lucky.

Their bodies floated nearby, rising alongside her as the water rose. She hated that they'd died for her. Their blood mingled with her own in the churning seawater, painting her with a debt she could never repay.

Already the water had nearly reached the ceiling of the small room. Another minute or two, and all the air in the room would be gone.

Just then, Biross gave a weak cough, the water around him splashing as his body jerked.

"Biross!"

Pain shot through her as she paddled the short distance towards him. The top of her head knocked the ceiling. Less than a foot of air left. And still seawater poured in through the large pipes in the ceiling.

"Biross, hang on." She reached for him, grabbing his limp arm and pulling him close. She might not possess an *imlani*'s native seagifts—might not know how to manipulate water the way Dilys had done when he'd saved her life—but she was still a Siren. Even drained as she was, her magic was already returning. Not fast enough for any hope of Shouting her way out of this room, but perhaps fast enough to save a life. "Biross, can you hear me?" She clung to his arm. "Take my magic. Use it to save yourself." She summoned what she could and sent it into him. She couldn't heal him. Even if she had full access to the full power of the sun, the only person she could have healed with it was herself. But if Biross could use his seagifts to control his bleeding long enough for Dilys to rescue them, he might make it to a healer in time. And maybe—just maybe—if she gave him power enough, he might be able to hold back the flooding of the room as well. The chance was a slim one, to be sure, but even a slim chance was better than no chance at all.

"Biross, I can't stop the water coming into the room. You can do it, but not if you die on me! Use what I gave you to save yourself, so you can save us!"

But Biross's blood continued to flow, and the seawater continued to pour in.

Five inches of air was all that remained. Gabriella's face was pressed against the ceiling now, each wheezing breath a frantic, painful gasp. Her chest was on fire, every breath a struggle, as if a three-hundred-pound rock was sitting on her chest. She could feel panic prying at her with sharp, scrabbling claws.

Two inches.

"Biross!"

One inch.

She took as deep a breath as she could manage and closed her eyes. When she opened them again, the room was entirely submerged in seawater. The roar of the water pouring relentlessly in had gone silent. Tarrant's body floated weightlessly nearby, bumping gently against Biross.

She shook Biross, pushing more power into the mortally wounded warrior, but if he was aware of it, she couldn't tell. His eyes were closed. His body limp. The only sign that he was still alive at all was the gill slits that had opened along his rib cage. They fluttered open and closed in a slow, shallow rhythm. He was still breathing, then. His body had recognized the change in their environment and instinctively adjusted to breathe water instead of air.

A useful ability her own body, unfortunately, did not possess. And the power that continued to flood into her, amplified by her growing fear and desperation, was all but useless. Without air she couldn't Shout. Without sunlight, she couldn't heal herself.

She was going to die. She was going to die and take Dilys with her. That knowledge kept her holding her breath until her chest was on fire. She couldn't die. Dilys was just outside the door. She could feel him there—his presence, his love, her love for him fueling a torrent of magic inside her. And she was helpless to go to him. Helpless to save herself, to save them.

A large hand closed around her shoulder.

Biross had roused enough to speak, though it was clearly a labor for him. Blood bubbled out of his mouth, a frothing, darkness that billowed like a foreboding cloud around him. Using the strength she'd given him, he willed every last measure of his magic and his lifeforce into her, and with it came the ephemeral whisper of his dying wish. A prayer. Not for himself, but for her.

Numahao, Mother of All Waters, save her. Save your daughter.

As the gift of his life flooded into her, every drop of

blood in her veins turned to molten lava. Nerve endings shrieked, her entire being immolated in a crucible of pain. Her back arched, and she gave a wrenching scream, the last of the air in her lungs escaping in a flood of bubbles.

It hurt. Good, sweet gods, it hurt!

Starved of air, her body instinctively tried to take a breath, only to suck in a massive gulp of water instead. She choked and coughed. Blood streamed from the wound in her chest and bubbles rushed from her mouth in a red-tinged flood. Her body began to jerk and spasm. Another involuntary breath brought a painful, burning, tearing feeling as her throat closed up.

She stared into Biross's now sightless eyes as the strength left her limbs, and a strange calm overtook her. She knew she was lost. She blinked once, slowly, as her consciousness slipped away. Her last thought, her one regret, for the strong, beautiful, loving man she'd claimed.

Dilys.

Dilys's shaken concentration was all the opening Calivan needed. He launched himself at his nephew, going for his throat. Dilys threw up an arm to block, then swore as his flesh tore beneath his uncle's claws and teeth. Dilys slammed a fist upwards, knuckles crunching against Calivan's jaw. His uncle staggered back, snarled, then lowered his head and plowed into Dilys, taking him down hard. The air whooshed out of Dilys's lungs, leaving him momentarily stunned. Calivan seized the opportunity to hammer steely fists against Dilys's ribs in a punishing barrage, each blow backed by powerful muscle. Calivan might have been forbidden from earning *ulumi* in battle, but he was every bit as skilled and strong as any other warrior of the Isles.

Dilys grunted in pain as his ribs broke with an audible crack.

"Cal!" Alysaldria cried. "Stop this insanity!" She lunged for her twin and grabbed one arm, wrapping her own arms tight around it and pulling back with all her weight. To the rest of Dilys's men, she cried, "*Calbernari*! Aid me!"

"*Ono!*" Dilys snarled when his men would have run forward to join the fray. He pulled back his lips, baring the sharp white menace of his battle fangs. "Aid Gabriella! Find a way to break down that damn door!" He maneuvered his arms between his uncle's body and his own, blocking the rib strikes, then brought the crown of his head ramming up into Calivan's chin. Calivan grunted and reared back. "*Nima,* help them. Shout the *farking* thing apart, if you can. Just get in there and save her!" Dilys sank his fangs into his uncle's shoulder and shook his head like a shark with captured prey. Blood spattered as flesh rent. Calivan roared and stabbed a clawed hand at Dilys's chest, aiming for his heart.

Dilys rolled to one side to avoid the killing blow, then rolled rapidly back to deliver a sharp elbow to the side of his uncle's head.

Calivan cried out as his head wrenched sharply to one side. A fist to the temple sent him toppling over. Dilys rolled over, rammed a knee hard into Calivan's groin. As his uncle howled and instinctively drew his body up to protect his throbbing stones, Dilys straddled his chest, pinning his arms to his sides, and began hammering his fists into Calivan's face. Calivan's lips split. His nose shattered. His teeth cracked and broke, and his eyes swelled shut. All the fight went out of him, but Dilys kept hammering. Again, and again, and again he struck, his mind a red haze of rage and bloodlust.

"Dilys, stop." Ryll's voice was cool and firm, backed with power that only fell slightly short of a Command. "He's down. He can't hurt anyone else. Gabriella needs you now."

It took a few seconds for the words to sink in. Panting, still boiling with unreleased rage, Dilys curtailed his punches. His uncle was unconscious, his face resembled a bloody lump of raw meat. It wasn't enough. It wasn't nearly enough to assuage Dilys's fury. But Gabriella needed him. She needed him to free her, not to keep pounding the man he'd already incapacitated.

He pushed off Calivan's body and staggered to his feet. As he did, his foot bumped against the pouch Calivan had strapped across his body. With a resonant, clinking sound, several brightly glowing crystals the size of goose eggs rolled free. Dilys put up a hand to shield his eyes and reached for one of the crystals. The instant he touched it, the powerful magic—*Gabriella's* magic—throbbed against his senses. Instinctively he opened for it, and the magic flooded into him in an unchecked rush that made him stagger back in surprise.

"Blessed Numahao." The stunned whisper slipped from his lips. Every *ulumi* on his body had lit up, a bright blue white. Dilys didn't know how, but his uncle had somehow drained Gabriella's magic and stored it in these crystals.

He sliced the strap of the leather pouch with his claws and yanked the bag free, kneeling to collect the crystals that had rolled free and shove them back into the pouch. When he had them all, he spun back towards the locked door of the testing chamber.

His mother and his men had hacked, clawed, and Shouted at the stone surrounding the door, but for all their efforts, they'd barely scratched the surface.

"*Nima*, try using this." He handed his mother one of the sun-bright stones. "Be careful. It's potent."

She grasped the crystal in her slender hands. A moment later, her body shuddered as if struck by lightning. Her eyes flared with a light almost as bright and blinding as the crystals. "My goddess!" she exclaimed in a whisper as stunned as his had been. "Is this what she holds inside her?"

"A small fraction of it. Try that Shout again now."

His mother turned to the door and Shouted "Open!" in a voice that shook with power.

The dense volcanic rock surrounding the door cracked, a spreading web of deep fissures.

"It's working! Shout again, *Nima!*"

"Open!" Alys Shouted again. "Open!" More cracks formed. Chunks of dark stone tumbled out onto the floor. Ryll's men leapt forward, ripping at the rock with bare claws.

Dilys put his hand on the stone. He could feel the pulse of the ocean behind the wall. Calivan had sealed Gabriella inside the room and flooded it. He grabbed one of the crystals, drained it with a thought, and took command of the near-limitless power of the ocean just behind those few inches of rock. Using the added power granted him by that crystal filled with Gabriella's magic, he slammed a ferocious wave of water into the wall around the door, concentrating all of the water's energy on a single spot weakened by the cracks his mother's Shouts had opened. He pounded that spot again and again, wearing away at the stone, eroding it until the crack was a leak, and the leak became a hole, and the hole became a fatal weakness in the structure of the wall.

The wall crumbled. Metal screamed and bent as the door was ripped from its moorings. Seawater poured out of the testing chamber in a wild rush that threatened to sweep them all away.

"Dilys!" his mother cried.

He clamped a firm magical hand upon the water and molded it to his will. Gabriella and the bodies of her two guards were still floating in the chamber. He summoned a current to carry them out to him and snatched Gabriella into his arms, clasping her to his chest.

"Take Biross and Tarrant," he commanded. "I'll hold this back until we're all out."

Everyone moved with alacrity, snatching up the bodies of the dead Calbernans and Calivan, and rushing for the door at the end of the tunnel. Dilys brought up the rear, holding back the tide of water until he was out of the tunnel as well. Only when the door was closed and sealed behind them did he release his hold.

The second the door was sealed, he turned the full force of his attention to Gabriella. Her eyes were open and glassy, her lips parted. She wasn't breathing. There was a telltale rip in the front of her gown, tinged with dark blood. He laid her on one of Calivan's laboratory tables and tried breathing into her mouth and compressing her chest to make her heart start beating again, but that only made what blood remained in her body gush from her wound. Her skin took on an alarming, chalky hue. Swearing, he plunged his magic into her, taking command of her blood as he had once before in an attempt to stop the hemorrhage. Oddly, the knife wound itself, though deep, wasn't the primary cause of her blood loss. The blade had pierced her lung but missed her heart and all major blood vessels. As he worked to force the water from her lungs, using her blood to form temporary seals across the tears of the delicate tissues, what he found left him stunned.

"Good Goddess." Dilys gave himself a shake and focused his concentration on the source of the bleeding inside her. Her lungs. Alongside her punctured and water-filled landwalker lungs, a second set of sea lungs had begun to form. Begun, and been stopped in mid-transformation, resulting in a maze of ruptured blood vessels and a torn patchwork of frilled membranes partially attached to her ribs.

Realizing that he'd have to find a way to help her body complete its transformation or watch her die in his arms, Dilys flew into a renewed frenzy of action. He seized Calivan's pouch and snatched one of the bright crystals from its depths, siphoning the stored magic from the crystal and shoving every last bit of it into Gabriella. "Stay with me, *moa kiri*! Stay with me!" He drained another crystal, then another and another, transferring all of the stolen magic back into her, giving her as much of his own as he dared as well. "Come on, *moa kiri*. You can do this." She remained glassy-eyed and unresponsive. He cast a frantic gaze at his mother. "*Nima!* Help us! She needs more magic!"

But when Alysaldria would have approached, Ryll and his men stepped in her way. "Dilys, my brother, *ono*. My heart is breaking for you, but if Gabriella is lost to us, we cannot risk losing your mother as well. You *know* that." Ryll didn't state the other obvious truth. There was no way Calberna's queen would survive the death of her son and the traitor's death awaiting her twin, so what magic she currently possessed had to be saved to be passed on to the next *Myerial*.

Dilys ground his teeth to hold back the roar of frustration rumbling in his chest. Anger would serve no purpose. Ryll was right. They couldn't risk losing the magic his mother carried.

He clutched Gabriella to his chest, trying to think past the terror that gripped his heart. What blood remained in her veins, he was keeping contained. Oxygen, however, was a separate issue. The abruptly arrested transformation of her lung tissue was preventing her from breathing either air or water. She was rapidly slipping away from him, the slender body in his arms more akin to a corpse than the vibrant woman who'd claimed him, her slight form so still and cold, her flesh chilled by the sea . . . all the sun-kissed warmth that he loved so much drained out of her.

Wait.

His mind seized on two small words.

Sun. Warmth.

That was it!

Gabriella was the daughter of the Summer King, descendent of the Sun God, Helos. When Lily's father had beaten Summer nearly to death, Dilys's aid and Tildavera Greenleaf's great healing skills hadn't been enough to mend Gabriella. Summer had spent days basking in the sun to complete her recovery. But here, tucked away in a cave a hundred feet below the surface, she was cut off from one of her greatest sources of power.

Praying that he was right, Dilys scrambled to his feet and raced out of the laboratory and through the library,

Gabriella clasped in his arms. When he reached the glass-fronted lobby area, rather than sprinting up the tube and through the palace to reach the surface, he dove for the moon pool. Gabriella wasn't breathing, so a swift swim directly to the surface couldn't hurt her any more than drowning already had. And swimming would cut his time to the surface in half.

The moment he hit the water, the webbing between his toes plumped and expanded, giving him additional speed through the liquid environment that was his second home. The massive muscles in his lower body flexed, sending him shooting upwards through the lagoon's clear waters, towards the shining sunlit warmth of the surface.

"Calbernari!" he shouted in Undersea Tongue as he swam, "To me! On the south palace lawn! The *Sirena* needs your help!"

He burst from the water like a porpoise, propelling himself through the virtually nonexistent density of the air to land on the soft grass of the manicured palace lawn. He found a spot where no shade blocked the sun's midday rays and laid Gabriella flat on the ground. The wet cloth of her dress clung to her. He shredded the fabric without a thought. He wasn't entirely sure how her Summerlander magic worked, but it seemed to him that the more of her skin available to the sun's direct rays, the better. If he was wrong and she got irate later over the ruination of her gown and the careless way he bared her to the eyes of their people—well, he'd wear a stupid, besotted grin and accept her fury without a peep of protest. Better a live, angry *liana* than a silent, dead one.

Calbernans were already pouring from the palace and leaping from the waters of the lagoon in response to his call. "She needs magic," he told the ones who reached him first. "As much as we can offer her. Anyone with a direct emotional connection to her, lay hands on her. The rest of you, network to me or the others. And for the gods' sake, do not cast your shadow on her. She needs sunlight as much if not more than she needs our magic." It was afternoon, the sun casting shadows from west to east, so Dilys positioned himself to Gabriella's right. He began channeling his magic into her, infusing it with all the wild, unfettered love in his heart. A dozen pairs of hands were laid upon him, and power flooded into him and through him to Gabriella.

"Let me through!" The growing throng parted as Ari, hobbling on crutches and scowling ferociously, shoved his way through.

Dilys met his cousin's eyes and after only a slight hesitation gave a nod of thanks. Ari was wounded, but on the mend. If he considered himself well enough to help, Dilys wasn't about to refuse his aid. A dozen of the Calbernans who'd accompanied him to Wintercraig joined Dilys and Ari at Gabriella's side, including Ryll and the young, newly-wedded Talin, with his pretty Summerlander bride by his side. The network of power multiplied exponentially. She absorbed so much power, so quickly, Dilys could only wonder how her slight body could hold it all. Yet she not only soaked up every ounce of energy sent her way, but her body remained thirsty for more.

Physically, emotionally, and magically connected to Gabriella as he was, he could feel the electric pulse of the Calbernans' selfless gift racing through her veins, igniting the magic in her blood. Her eyes, which had been open, fixed, and glassy, slid shut, her dark lashes curling against her wan cheeks. Hope surged through him. It was the first movement she'd made since he'd reached her.

"That's it, *moa kiri*. You can do it." She still wasn't breathing on her own, so he covered her mouth with his and blew air into her lungs, careful to keep the myriad broken blood vessels in her chest sealed as he did.

A few seconds later, he felt a slight flutter against his magic. A few seconds after that, the flutter became a more definite push against the seals he'd created to stop her internal bleeding. The sensation felt a bit like a hand impatiently nudging him aside. He pulled back, tentatively releasing a small portion of the blood vessels he was keeping in check. When blood didn't immediately start pouring from the ruptured vessels, he pulled back a little more. The torn flesh inside her began to knit together. The reparations were slow at first, but began happening with increasing speed as more and more of the damaged tissue began to heal.

Suddenly he wasn't pushing power into Gabriella anymore. She was pulling it *out* of him, and through him, out of every person connected to him. Beside him, Ari gasped and arched his back. So did the others whose hands lay upon Summer's skin. Like a ripple effect, everyone behind them gasped, too.

Dilys tried to move his hands and discovered he couldn't. They were glued to Gabriella's flesh. Just as the hands of those touching him were glued to him. Gabriella had seized control of their symbiotic network. Magic raced through them, roaring its way towards her, into her, into the flesh that was now healing and reshaping at a dizzying speed. Her back arched. Her hands clenched into fists. Her skin was so hot it was practically burning Dilys's palms, but still he couldn't pull away. His *ulumi* lit up, burning in his flesh like fire. The light beaming from his tattoos bent in visible arcs to flow like glowing rivers into her body.

Her mouth opened, as if on a soundless scream, and then came the noise he'd been waiting for, praying for. Deep, raspy, raw. A shuddering, painful breath as oxygen-starved lungs dragged air deep. A groan rattled in her throat as the newly formed gill slits along her ribs expelled the water trapped in her equally new sea lungs, then she jackknifed into a sitting position, coughing and gasping for breath. The network linking the Calbernans to Gabriella dissolved.

Tears spilled from Dilys's eyes, but he didn't even try to stop them. Instead, he gathered Gabriella close, holding her tight against his chest, muttering incoherent words of love, relief, and prayers of thanks as he pressed kisses into her hair, against her face, her lips, against the soft, fragrant brown skin that was once more so warm and full of life. "*Moa kiri. Moa liana. Myerial myerinas.* Thank Numahao. Thank Helos. Praise be to all the gods. I thought I had lost you, beloved."

"I think you almost did." Her voice was raspy, pitched much deeper than normal. She coughed a little more and hugged him back, her slender arms twining around his chest, her palms flattening against his shoulder blades, holding him tight. "I was dying. If you hadn't thought to bring me to the surface and into the sunlight, I don't think I would have made it. You saved me, Dilys."

He ducked his head. "I did, didn't I?"

"Yes. I could feel you inside me, when the sun was healing me. I could feel you with me."

"Yes." He drew back just enough to smooth back her soft black hair and drink in the sight of her sweet, lovely face with its full lips and thickly lashed eyes that had turned pure, bright gold. He could spend the rest of his life looking at her and never grow tired of the sight.

"I can still feel you there."

He blinked to clear the tears that were suddenly blurring his vision and nodded. "Yes."

"We're connected." She pressed one hand to her heart and laid her other palm over his. "Here. Inside us both. More than before."

"Yes." He caressed the side of her cheek.

"How?"

"I don't know. The gods, perhaps." What they shared now was deeper than their claiming bond. It was as if somehow her healing had not only transformed her body, but also their souls, melding the two of them together in a way that could never be undone. "Do you mind?"

She thumbed away the tears still leaking from his eyes and regarded him with a deep, solemn, steady gaze. He recognized that look. It told him Gabriella had discarded her many masks to give him complete, unvarnished honesty. "*Ono*," she said. "I don't mind at all."

She lifted her mouth to his, and he seized her lips in a passionate kiss, crushing her body against his, loving her so much he'd never known such feelings were possible. It was as if his heart had become a sun, filled with a love so limitless and strong it could light the whole world. He was hers, utterly and completely, body, heart, and soul.

"I adore you, Gabriella Aretta Rosadora Liliana Elaine Coruscate."

"Merimydion," she murmured, pulling his head back down for more kissing.

He obliged her—gladly—but when they pulled apart again to gasp for air, he shook his head and corrected her. "*Ono.* You are a Siren, the first of your House. I am Dilys Coruscate now, as is fitting for a mated and claimed male."

"Ah, but I am an *oulani,* wed to an *imlani* prince of a royal House. I am therefore a daughter of House Merimydion."

"But by the grace of Numahao, you are *oulani* no longer. For no *oulani* I know has ever developed these." He ran his fingers lightly over the almost imperceptible lines of the new, sealed gill slits along her ribs.

Gabriella glanced down in astonishment. "Are those . . . do I have . . . *gills*?"

"*Tey.* Do you mind?"

"I don't know. Do you think they work?"

"*Tey.* Now that the transformation is complete, I think they will work as well as any Calbernan's."

"Gills." She blinked and ran her fingers over them. "Biross . . . when he was dying after willing his lifeforce into me, he prayed for Numahao to save me. To save her daughter. Do you think . . . ?"

He smiled, ignoring the tears spilled from his eyes. "If anyone could grant a Siren sea lungs, it would be the goddess of all waters. Praise Numahao."

"Thanks be to all the gods, but especially Numahao and Helos." Then she suddenly went stiff in his arms. "Dilys," she said, her voice low but vibrating with urgency.

He bent closer, surrounding her body with his in an instinctive gesture of protection. The tone of her voice set him instantly alert. His battle claws unsheathed, sharp and ready to rend. "What is it?"

She hunched into him, moving deeper into the protection of his arms. Then in a move that couldn't have been comfortable, she craned her neck way back so that even hunched into him, she could glare up at him. The gold of her Siren's eyes had shifted back to pure, snapping Summer blue.

"How exactly did I end up sitting on the palace lawn, in full view of half your mother's court, *completely naked*?"

He couldn't help it. His lips spread wide in a besotted grin, and he laughed and laughed and laughed.

CHAPTER 31

The following morning, with Dilys at her side, Gabriella stood behind *Myerial* Alysaldria's pearl-encrusted throne. Gabriella's impervious mask of composure was firmly back in place, but this time every gentle emotion was battened down and hidden from view, leaving only the unyielding visage of a vengeful Siren staring down at Calivan Merimydion as he knelt in chains before his queen and the highest-ranking members of Calberna's court.

He'd been stripped of his *obah* and jewels, left to stand bare-chested and unadorned in a simple silk *shuma*. It was clear, however, that the chains and the divestiture of his outward signs of rank didn't bother him one infinitesimal fraction as much as the way his sister refused to even look at him. He stood before her, his eyes pleading for some tiny crumb of understanding or affection, but Alysaldria kept her gaze fixed firmly on the faces of her subjects.

For that clear loss of the only connection that he'd ever truly valued, Gabriella could almost pity him.

True, this man had tried to kill her, but the fact that he'd done it to save the dearest person in the world to him was something she understood. And if trying to kill her were all he had done, she might have been able to forgive him . . . at least enough to request that the death sentence he deserved be commuted to banishment, for Alysaldria's sake if no other. But Gabriella wasn't his only victim.

For his attempted murder of Dilys, and his part in the deaths of Spring and Autumn, Summer would accept nothing less than Calivan Merimydion's execution. The more immediate, the better. Because *those* were the people dearest in the world *to her*.

He also owed a blood debt for the lives of Biross and Tarrant and the goddess only knew how many other Calbernans slain either at his hands or because of him. Those men were all *someone's* dearest person in the world.

So no, Gabriella did not pity him, nor would she ask for mercy. Calivan Merimydion deserved none.

Alysaldria knew it, too.

The *Myerial* stood, held up a hand for silence, and pronounced, "We declare this Gathering open." Then taking her seat once more, she said, "The purpose for this Gathering is to hear the confession of and pass sentence on the traitor, Calivan Merimydion." Her voice was brittle, each word resonating with immeasurable pain. "He stands accused of conspiring to murder the *Sirena,* Gabriella Coruscate; of subverting through the use of magic a dozen sworn Royal Guards of Calberna to aid him in his plot; of the attempted murder of the *Myerielua* Dilys Merimydion; of conspiring with the traitor Nemuan, former son of House Merimynos, to kidnap the Seasons of Summerlea; and of conspiring to murder *Myerial* Siavaluana II and her daughter, *Myerialanna* Sianna."

The shocked gasps rippling through the gathered nobles grew notably louder at the last charge. The *Donima* of House Merimynos reached out to steady herself on the arm of her *akua.*

Alysaldria stood, descended the steps of the throne's dais, and walked with slow deliberation across the floor. The long train of the pure white gown she'd donned for the Gathering dragged behind her as she went, the color's symbolism not lost on anyone in the court. White was the color of death in the sea, the white of bleached bones and dead coral. Her hair hung freely down her back, the ends curling near her ankles. White sea stars, the symbol of House Merimydion, dotted the inky blackness of her hair. She'd dressed in mourning for the twin brother who was already dead to her.

Four warriors—each chosen from outside the palace guards and thoroughly checked for compulsion runes—guarded Calivan. They pressed the points of their tridents to his throat and chest as their queen approached.

"Alys, I—"

The *Myerial*'s hand shot up sharply, cutting off whatever her brother meant to say.

"The traitor will confess his crimes before this Gathering. Calivan of House Merimydion, *Confess. Your. Crimes.*" Her Voice throbbed with implacable Command.

With none of the arrogance that had been such an intrinsic part of him, Calivan did. The truth spilled out of him, all of it. From his plot to murder Gabriella, to his part in the kidnapping of the Seasons, to the mind-control runes he'd tattooed on Alys's guards, the same runes Nemuan had tattooed on Ari.

"You taught Nemuan this mind-control magic?"

"*Ono.* I suspect Nemuan and I both learned the ability from the same master of magic, the slaver known as Mur Balat."

"Why would Balat teach you or Nemuan this magic?"

"So we could help him acquire the magical artifacts he's been seeking his whole life. That's how we met, Balat and I. After you wed, when I went out in the world seeking knowledge about magic, Balat and I crossed paths several times. We became friends—or so I thought. It turns out he really just wanted to use me to help him acquire the artifacts he was seeking. That's how everything began."

"What about killing Siavaluana?" Alys asked coldly. "Was that Mur Balat's idea or yours?"

Calivan's chains rattled. "It was the only way I could

think of to keep you alive after Dillon died! Siavaluana's magic would give you enough strength to push back the Fade, and I knew your sense of duty would do the rest."

Alysaldria shuddered, as if the words were a physical blow. Still standing beside his mother's throne, Dilys shuddered, too, his gaze pinned on his mother's face. He clearly wanted to go to her, to stop her pain, but before the Gathering began, Alys had made him swear he would not interfere in any way.

Gabriella moved closer and took hold of his hand. They were behind the throne. The rest of the court couldn't see. Dilys didn't look at her, but the fingers curled around hers squeezed tightly in gratitude.

"And kidnapping the Seasons of Summerlea?"

"He approached me after the Ice King was defeated. I refused him at first, but he threatened to tell you about my involvement in the death of Siavaluana. I was still planning to refuse until you made that vow from the Sea Throne. I couldn't risk losing you, so I agreed. But he promised me they weren't to be hurt. I made him swear that much before I agreed!"

Alys arched a brow. "And yet you tried to kill Gabriella yourself."

Calivan's shoulders slumped. "You know why."

"Because, you would murder yet another rightful *Myerial* to keep me on the throne."

"Because I knew you meant to abdicate and then to Fade. I couldn't lose you. Don't you see, Alys? Everything I've ever done was to keep you alive, to keep you with me."

Alysaldria's lips compressed. "But, brother, I am not, nor ever have been, yours to keep. You had the privilege, as my beloved and most trusted twin, to contribute to my happiness and grant to me the selfless gift of your love and your strength, as I granted you the same. But these crimes you have committed, this blood on your hands, has made a foul perversion of what should only ever have been a loving and mutually beneficial bond. You have betrayed me and our House in a way no other in this world could have done. Do you have anything else to say in your defense before I pass judgment?"

Calivan's jaw trembled. Tears he could not withhold any longer trickled from his eyes. He shook his head.

Alys drew herself up, her spine rigid, shoulders squared, chin lifted. No hint of what had to be devastating grief showed on her face, only regal and unyielding authority. "Then as *Donima* of House Merimydion, I declare you, Calivan, son of Caldriana and Siavan Merimydion, to be *kado'ido,* outcast from the House of your birth, a son of Merimydion no more. And as *Myerial* of the Calbernan Isles, for the blood on your hands, for the regicide, murder, and attempted murder you committed or conspired to commit, I condemn you to a traitor's death. Before the sun sets on this day, you shall be chained to the traitor's rock at the edge of the Argon Abyssal and fed to the kracken."

His eyes went wide. His jaw dropped. "Alys!" Her name was a strangled cry.

Alys nodded sharply to the guards. "Take him from my sight." As the guards escorted Calivan away, she walked with slow, deliberation back to her throne, climbed the dais and seated herself with regal composure. "My people," she announced in a Voice of power, "it has been an honor and a privilege to serve as your *Myerial,* but in the face of all that has transpired, and with the gift of a true Siren returned to us, my time as your queen is over. As Our last act as *Myerial* Alysaldria I, We hereby abdicate the Sea Throne to Calberna's rightful ruler, the *Sirena,* Gabriella Coruscate." Alys stood, removed her crown, and turned to place it on Gabriella's head. "To the *Sirena, Myerial* Gabriella I. May Numahao bless her House, and may her reign be long and prosperous!"

Gabriella stood on the throne, stunned, as the gathered nobles of the Calbernan court shouted, "To *Myerial* Gabriella!" She'd been expecting Alysaldria to discuss stepping down as queen after her brother's crimes came to light, not just do it and hand Gabriella the crown! Now, Gabriella was the one clinging tight to Dilys's hand. He gave it a reassuring squeeze. What was she supposed to do now?

"You must take the throne," Alys whispered, "and declare this Gathering concluded."

Nervous, more than a little stunned by the abrupt turn of events, she did as Dilys's mother instructed, stepping forward and taking a seat in the pearl-encrusted throne. Taking her cue from the way Alys had opened the Gathering, she announced, "We declare this Gathering concluded."

An hour before sunset, Gabriella, Dilys, Alysaldria, and tens of thousands of Calbernans from the surrounding Isles sailed or swam out to the edge of the Argon Abyssal some seven miles south of Cali Va'Lua to witness the execution of the *kado'ido* Calivan, former prince and Lord Chancellor of Calberna.

Gabriella's new gills proved to work perfectly as she swam down to the submerged outcropping called Traitor's Rock, and gave the order to summon the kracken. Undersea Tongue was a new language to her, and one she would still have to learn, but Dilys had taken her to a private pool earlier and practiced the command with her until she'd been able to say the words clearly while underwater.

She did not flinch or look away as the man who had caused so much pain met his fate. Nor did Alys, but when it was over and they returned to the palace and exited the weightless environment of the sea, the strength of Calberna's former *Myerial* gave out. She collapsed beside the main palace's moon pool and was rushed to her chambers where the summoned doctors examined her and declared her to be Fading.

"There is nothing we can do," the senior physician quietly informed Dilys and Gabriella after concluding the examination. "Without the will to live, no magic or medicine can hold her to life." She patted Dilys's hand and bowed to Gabriella. "I'm sorry. This is a very sad day in a string of far too many very sad days. I will leave you to say your final good-byes."

They were standing in the receiving room just outside Alys's bedchamber. As the doctor bowed again and let herself out, Dilys put his arms around Gabriella and held her close. She could feel his body trembling, overcome with sorrow. "I am not ready to lose her," he said hoarsely.

"Neither am I." She'd known Alysaldria less than a week, but in that time, she'd come to both admire and love the woman who had given Dilys life. The depth of that love was probably owed at least in part to the deepening of the bond between herself and Dilys, but it had also been wonderful to have a mother again. Gabriella had never truly realized just how much she craved that maternal bond, or how much strength and happiness she derived from it.

The door to Alys's bedroom opened and her personal valet stepped out.

"She is asking for you, *moa Myerial*. She wishes to pass on her gifts before she goes."

Gabriella made a choked sound and grabbed Dilys's hand, squeezing tight. She knew his heart was breaking, too, but nonetheless, he wrapped her in his arms and offered her his unstinting love until they both felt strong enough to enter Alys's bedchamber and approach the frail, Fading woman on the bed.

Gabriella was shocked by the change that had come over Dilys's mother in the scant hour or two since Calivan's death. The former *Myerial* had quite literally begun to waste away. Her skin was sallow, her eyes and cheeks sunken. The flesh on her arms had gone paper thin, hanging on her bones. The vibrant gold of her eyes was fading to a pale, sickly yellow.

"*Nima!*" Dilys breathed, clearly appalled and horrified by her rapidly degenerating condition.

"No!" Gabriella rushed to Alys's bedside. She'd thought

Alys's Fade would take days . . . weeks . . . months, even! . . . but judging from her drastic physical decline, it would be a miracle if she lasted the night. "No!" Gabriella said again, and this time she Spoke in Voice of power. "You won't do this. You won't Fade tonight. I Command you not to Fade."

Alys lifted a shaking, skeletal hand to pat Gabriella's hand. "Some things, my dear, not even a Siren can Command."

"I've only just found you. I've only just begun to remember the joy of having a mother again. Please." Tears gathered, then spilled from her eyes. She stroked Alys's hand. "I know what you must be going through, without your *akua*. The fear of such a loss almost kept me from claiming your son as mine. So even though I know the pain you must feel each day without him, I'm still asking you to stay. Please. Dilys isn't ready to lose you, and neither am I."

"My child, you don't need me. Neither of you do. You have each other, and that is strength enough to last a lifetime."

"Call me greedy, then, but I need you, too. My mother died when I was very young. I've missed her terribly over the years. I had hoped, when Dilys told me about you, that I would find a new mother in you. And I have. Please, please, don't take my new mother away from me so soon. I couldn't bear it."

"Gabriella—"

"Please!" Gabriella interrupted. "If you won't stay for Dilys or me"—she dragged Alys's hand to her and placed it on her belly—"then stay for your grandchild."

For the first time since they'd entered the room, a spark of interested flared in Alys's eyes. "You are . . . with child?"

Dilys clasped Gabriella's shoulders, and said, "A granddaughter, *Nima*. A daughter of our blood. A Siren, like her mother."

Gabriella craned her head back to look at him in surprise. "How could you know that? I only just realized I was even pregnant!"

He bent to press a kiss on her forehead. "Yesterday, when I was trying to keep you alive, I took control of your blood and found her there, inside you, working as hard as I was to save you."

"You didn't say anything!"

"There hasn't been time."

Gabriella turned back to Alys, taking the thin, frail hand in hers once more. "There, you see? You're going to have a granddaughter. Don't you think she deserves to meet you, at least?" She stroked Alys's hand. "After all, you did vow from the Sea Throne that you would personally ensure she was born an *imlani* with gifts worthy of the throne. Would you want her growing up knowing her grandmother was an oathbreaker? And not just that but someone who would break a vow made from the Sea Throne?"

Alys arched a brow. "Are you not above holding a dying old woman to her vows?"

"I'm a lot more ruthless than most people think."

A wan smile curved Alys's lips. "So I see. That is a trait that will serve a queen well."

"Yes, but is it working? Will you stay? Will you fight your Fade . . . for us?"

Alys closed her eyes, took a deep breath, then nodded. "I will fight. Until the child is born and I can fulfill my vow. I will not have my granddaughter believing that vows made from the Sea Throne can be broken."

"Then may I share with you a little of what lives inside me, enough to push your Fade away for a while?"

Alys opened an eye. "Only if you call me *Nima, moa alanna.*"

Gabriella beamed. "*Nima,*" she said, flooding Alys with such a rush of love that the older woman gave a choked exclamation of surprise.

"Glory to Numahao," Alys gasped when Gabriella reined herself back in. "That is what you call a little?"

Gabriella blushed. "Sorry. I'm still not so good at controlling that."

"*Ono*." Alys reached out to pat her hand. "*Ono*, my daughter. Never be sorry for the magnificent blessings you possess. You are a gift from the goddess herself, an answer to the prayers we folk of the Isles have been making for over two thousand years."

EPILOGUE

"Honestly, Dilys, I cannot imagine how your *liana* managed all those years to fool everyone into thinking her such a mild-mannered, malleable young woman." Alysaldria stood beside her son as the two of them watched Gabriella subdue a roomful of blustering nobles with the crisp, unyielding authority that was rapidly becoming her hallmark. "Those qualities are the furthest from her true self as any could be."

Dilys's chest swelled. There was no mistaking his mother's admiration for his extraordinary, always-surprising wife. "She could have them eating from her hand if she wanted to, but I think she enjoys riling them up a little."

"And letting them know who's boss. Are you aware of all the Calbernan traditions she intends to change? Says she finds them disagreeable and won't abide them under her reign."

"Such as?"

"Such as the custom of sending young boys away from home for their warrior's training. She believes they can be trained just as well without separating them from their families."

Dilys arched a brow and glanced down at his mother. "You know you agree with that one, *Nima*."

"I can hardly deny it, can I? And, you didn't turn out too badly, even if I do say so myself."

He grinned. "Not too badly."

His mother laughed. More a soft chuckle than an out-right laugh, but still a sound that warmed his heart. Though she had accepted Gabriella's help in keeping her Fade at bay, Alys's sorrow in the wake of her twin's betrayal had become a heavy burden that rarely lifted. Gabriella and Dilys did everything in their power to ease that suffering and bring Alys joy, and though they never mentioned it to his mother, the two of them were hoping the birth of their daughter in the coming year would keep Alys's Fade at bay even longer. Decades longer, if Gabriella had her way about it. Dilys had high hopes. His beloved was very good at getting her way.

"And she refuses to be coronated as Gabriella Cor-uscate," Alys continued, "even though as a Siren-made *imlani* by the grace of the gods themselves, she is right-fully *Donima* of her own House."

"I have told her that many times. I did, however, get her to agree to a compromise last night."

"Oh?"

"*Tey.* Her biggest argument against becoming *Donima* of her own House was you. You are her mother now, and she won't give you up, not even in name."

His mother's eyes went soft. "She said that?"

"Mmm. I don't blame her. You're pretty wonderful, as mothers go." He bent down to kiss his mother's cheek. "Once I uncovered the root of her objections, I got her to agree to be coronated as Gabriella of House Merimydion-Coruscate. In personal and House matters, she will remain a daughter of House Merimydion, with you as *Donima,* but in matters of state she will act as *Myerial* and *Donima* of House Coruscate. Since Merimydion means sea stars and Coruscate means radiant, she liked that our children will all be named radiant stars of the sea."

"Merimydion-Coruscate. That does have rather a nice ring to it."

"I thought so."

A loud argument erupted from the gathered nobles. Gabriella silenced them with a few clipped words.

"What do you think that was about?"

Dilys smiled. "I think she just told them that she intends for the both of us to be coronated at the same time, that she has commissioned a throne for me to be installed beside hers, and that to the rest of Mystral, I shall be known as King Dilys Merimydion-Coruscate of Calberna."

"Ah," his mother said.

Within the Isles, the queen's mate was always called *Myerialakua,* the Calbernan word for king (well, actually it translated into something more like "mate of the queen" or "treasured mate"). But since the majority of the *oulani* world believed that a king ruled over everyone in his country, including his queen, the *Myerials* had always made it clear to the outside world that the true power in Calberna rested solely with her queens.

"I did tell her that men in my position are called Prince Consorts among the other peoples of Mystral, but she refused to hear of it."

"And why should I?" Having dismissed the nobles from her presence, Gabriella now came to join Dilys and Alys. "It's a load of sexist nonsense. If a king can marry a woman and make her his queen, then why should I—a queen—not be able to make you my king?"

To that, he had no answer, except to say, "My love, you can make me anything you like, as long as you always make me yours."

"Well, then, that settles that. Because you will always be mine, Dilys Merimydion-Coruscate." Smiling, she stood up on tiptoe and pulled his head down for a kiss. "My love. My husband. My very own Sea King."

SECOND EPILOGUE

Eastern coast of Ardul

The sun was shining in a blue, cloudless sky, turning the moist jungle air into a steaming soup. A sleek, three-masted ship lay at anchor in the crystal-clear waters of the small, tropical bay, hundreds of miles from any village or established port. A longboat from the ship was beached on the sparkling white sands, and the ship's captain and several of his crew busied themselves spearing fish in the shallow waters of the bay and harvesting coconuts, bananas, and papayas from the trees nearby.

High up in the fronds of a coconut tree, one of the crew gave a sharp whistle. His shipmates gathered together, readying weapons as the sounds of something approaching through the dense jungle brush grew louder.

A few moments later, the crew relaxed and sheathed their weapons. Four native guides hacked their way out of the jungle onto the beach, followed shortly by Mystral's most infamous slaver, Mur Balat, one peridot-eyed flesh-molder, an entourage of witches, guards, and servants, and two rumpled but very beautiful women being led by the collars at their throats.

"Ah, Captain Qurin," Mur Balat greeted, "good to see you. Have you been waiting long?"

"Less than a day," the captain replied. "You are right on schedule."

"I always am. You may begin loading my possessions." Balat remained on the beach as the most valuable articles of what had been his unsurpassed collection of magical artifacts, rare antiquities, and priceless jewels, were loaded onto the waiting ship. The loss of his magnificent fortress in Trinipor had been the highest cost of his current endeavor, but it had been necessary for the world to truly believe that Mur Balat and his influence had been wiped from the face of Mystral.

For thousands of years, the enchanters of the Balalatika bloodline, descendents of Ambris, Goddess of Order and Chaos, had sought to right a supreme wrong. Long, long ago, Ambris had tricked the other six primary gods of Mystral in order to raise to godhood the mortal hero Rorjak, beloved of Ambris's daughter Wyrn the White, goddess of Winter. For her crime, Ambris had been stripped of her divinity and sentenced to living lifetime after lifetime as a mortal. Her descendents of the Balalatika bloodline had been working ever since to restore Ambris to her rightful divinity. And now, at last, that moment was at hand.

Mur Balat had only to exchange the remaining two Seasons for the last two pieces of the divine Celestial Chalice, which he had located thanks to tireless efforts of generations of his forebears. Once he assembled all the pieces of the Chalice and retrieved another divine artifact called the Bloodstone, he would be able to follow the secret maps in the grimoire of the ancient witch-Seer Euphemia Nyxx to find the fabled Fount Æternis . . . and there, he, Murulandis Balalatika, would raise the mortal Ambris back to godhood and claim divinity for himself as his reward.

"Come, ladies," he said to Spring and Autumn. Such a shame that to fake their deaths, he'd had to sacrifice two of his three flesh-molders. Their sister had been far less productive and far less docile without them. But Dilys Merimydion and the Winter King would never have given up searching for the Seasons without convincing bodies. Giving a yank on Spring and Autumn's chains, he led the captive princesses towards the waiting ship. "Time to make history!"